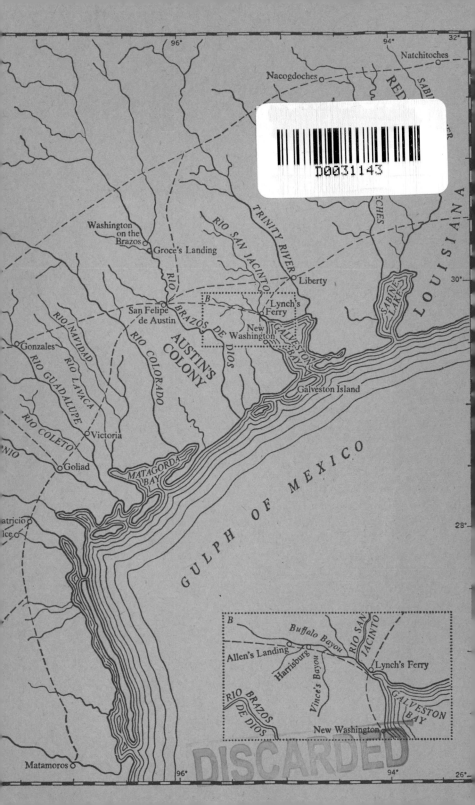

32°

96°   94°

Natchitoches

Nacogdoches

RED

SABI...

LOUISIANA

TRINITY RIVER

RIO SAN JACINTO

ECHES

Washington
on the
Brazos

Groce's Landing

Liberty   30°

RIO BRAZOS DE DIOS

San Felipe
de Austin

B

Lynch's
Ferry

SABINE
LAKE

New
Washington

GALVESTON BAY

RIO NAVIDAD

Gonzales

AUSTIN'S
COLONY

RIO LAVACA

RIO COLORADO

RIO GUADALUPE

Galveston Island

Victoria

RIO COLETO

MATAGORDA
BAY

GULPH   OF   MEXICO

Goliad

...NIO

...atricio
...lce

28°

Matamoros

B

Buffalo Bayou

RIO SAN JACINTO

Allen's Landing

Harrisburg

Vince's Bayou

Lynch's Ferry

RIO BRAZOS DE DIOS

GALVESTON BAY

New Washington

DISCARDED

96°   94°   26°

COME
TO THE BOWER

COME
TO THE BOWER

A Novel by

J. Y. BRYAN

New York : The Viking Press

FIRST PUBLISHED IN 1963
BY THE VIKING PRESS, INC.
625 MADISON AVENUE, NEW YORK 22, N.Y.

PUBLISHED SIMULTANEOUSLY IN CANADA BY
THE MACMILLAN COMPANY OF CANADA LIMITED

Second Printing May 1963

Library of Congress catalog card number: 63-10934

M B G
*Set in Weiss, Perpetua, and Times types and
printed in the U.S.A. by the Vail-Ballou Press*

With devotion

for *my* *devoted companion*

MARGARET

Author's Note and Acknowledgments

Come to the Bower assumes that every effort to extend the ground of liberty is also a campaign against the tyranny of death, and so is the search for love. The story begins in New Orleans, October 13, 1835, the day the Texan revolt against Mexico was announced in that city. It ends in Texas, May 8, 1836, two and a half weeks after destruction of the Mexican advance at San Jacinto. The war is less the subject, however, than a circumstance urging certain Americans to face interrelated problems of freedom, love, and death during their nation's youth.

The research and field investigation out of which the story grew entailed a heavy debt of gratitude to many people, and first of all to "Cousin Hally," the late Mrs. Hally Bryan Perry of Houston, Texas, grandniece of Stephen Austin. Still energetic, bright, and ebullient at eighty-two, she took me on my first and second visits to San Jacinto Battlefield and in memorable terms analyzed for me the events preliminary to the victory on that ground. Subsequently I received much help also from Miss Winnie Allen, archivist of the University of Texas, and from that Washington treasury of fact known as the Library of Congress. In draft, the story profited from critical analysis by my very discerning friend Gordon Graham, a Scot whom I met in Bombay.

J. Y. BRYAN
Karachi, Pakistan
August 1, 1962

Contents

COME
TO THE BOWER

CHAPTER I

I

An October foretaste of winter had the chimneys of New Orleans smoking under a moody overcast, and the smell of coal left in Perry's throat an acrid deposit. The Benevolent Loan Bank of Louisiana before him looked the worse because of the day, and the day worse because he had agreed this morning to visit the bank.

Its sign, done in large gilt letters, hung between pillars designed to claim for the place the dignity and sanctity of a Roman temple. The effect of similar pillars around the lobby within was spoiled by iron cages to right and left containing pale men expressionlessly busy over drawers of cash. At a desk between the cages a functionary with the loosening flesh of a gladiator long out of the arena looked up from a batch of papers as Perry approached.

"What's on your mind, young man?"

"Mr. Beaufait here, sir?"

"Yuh, he is." This fellow's eyes, lively and black, so abounded in cruel knowledge of human nature as to look almost kind. They measured Perry's unusual height, his hands too, and the quality of his riding boots, his linen, his cravat. "Got a engagement with him, have you?"

"At ten o'clock, sir."

"Hm." A gold chain with links as fat as kernels of corn hung between pockets on the man's vest, a silk affair florally embroidered. A twist of his finger around one end of the chain drew out a watch. "Aint but seven till."

"Thank you. That's not long to wait."

"Seat yonner, young man."

He tossed a hand toward chairs near oak doors to the rear. Perry nodded, but strolled instead toward a window in front, conscious of being watched all the way. Conscious, too, of men busy in the cages

I

he passed, he wondered how any rational being could bring himself to forgo all the enchantments of God's great world in order to spend six days a week locked up behind bars with somebody else's money. The gloom which that thought induced stayed with him as he stood at the window, hat down in one hand.

The overcast above buildings opposite had begun to loosen. A flight of pigeons ascended across a patch of hidden sunlight in exulting spirals, but the eloquence of their admonition to be of good cheer was broken by letters on the window:

LOANS ADVANCED
ON
REAL OR CHATTEL PROPERTY

The offer was repeated in French and so weighed doubly on Perry. Experience had converted his family into partisans of Andrew Jackson's war against the power banks exercised through money on loan, against the rule of paper over property, against servitude to collectors of high interest. For years interest had kept his parents in bondage: his home in Maryland, a fine old manor requiring spacious hospitality, frequent repair, and a leeching staff of servants, never had been free of encumbrance throughout his father's lifetime. Only at the cost of more borrowing could he be sent to the university for studies in law, and his parents had died more in debt than ever. The liege of the manor now was his older brother Rockford. The inheritance left to himself consisted of a racing stallion, his father's library, and a modest cash settlement. Their kin supposed he envied Rock's inheriting the land, whereas he considered himself better off not being bound by its debts.

A team of high-stepping Hackneys swung along the street, hitched to a coach after which ran two waifs trying to hook a ride on its rear axle. Not five yards behind them a team of bays on an express wagon began galloping to outrun the coach, so that if either boy fell he would have hooves and wheels upon him like hounds on a hare. A good deal of what Perry himself did these days seemed to him about as pointless as this race of theirs, and a conversation with Camilla Palmer earlier today came back to him of itself, the essence of it all present to him in that instant of watching the boys. . . .

He and Camilla at dawn had been riding matched sorrels of hers along a levee south of town, where spooky masses of fog altered familiar shapes, estranging everything. The mist at that hour was cold, surprisingly cold—as she herself attempted to be for no reason known to him.

"Today, Perry," she remarked, "we'd better not ride far."

Though she spoke placidly, her manner hinted that each word had been weighed. His effort to understand why brought to mind another conversation yesterday when she had observed that she must beg off going with him after dinner to the Discovery Day Ball (to celebrate the landing of Columbus) because a banker friend of hers, a *dear* friend of long standing, had just returned from outside the city, a friend she had said she would go with if he did get back in time. Perry braced himself to hear more in the same vein this morning.

"What's the hurry? This early, why not go wherever we like?"

"Your Uncle James wants you at the office sooner. He wants you to apply yourself more, and not just today, but every day."

"Hm! Who told you?"

"Little bird."

"That little cuss better watch out. The parrot's talking's what keeps her in a cage."

A feather of amusement tickled her lip. She removed it.

"He claims you've prepared only three briefs in the whole four weeks you've been here."

"Yes, but each one will produce a victory in court."

"Oh, that's what *he* says—*James:* you can do so well when you apply yourself. I'm very sure—we all are—that there's unusual substance in you, Perry, if only you'll apply it, quite unusual, but you—"

"But I prefer larking around."

"Just like me, yes." Glints of humor shone in her eyes. "That's it. James is *very* annoyed, and not just with you; with me almost as much, because it's me you've been wasting your time with."

"There's more behind it than that, Milla. Kin by marriage pretty often get along poorly because they're *obliged* to get along. We've reached the point where we both doubt that I belong in his office at all. We're restless over that and we're different every way there is, so a good many things seem right aggravating."

They had been holding their mares shoulder to shoulder in a cushioned, collected trot, Camilla riding her sidesaddle at an angle somewhat away from him. She now turned him a look of glowing conviction.

"Perry, able as you are to please people, you could certainly get along with James if you made a good strong effort."

"Maybe. Only around him I lose the wish to try."

"But *why*, Perry?"

She was not genuinely puzzled, he saw, merely of a mind to push him into fixing upon a course of life so that he would become a whole man. Equally he saw that there was some compliment in having such a person think him worth pushing. Why should anyone so fashionable and sought after as Camilla care to give it a thought? The bonnet and riding habit she wore this morning were pearl-gray trimmed with velvet, her scarf a crimson flourish thrown across one shoulder, her atmosphere just what to expect of a tirelessly courted widow of twenty-three whom nature and advantage allowed to be every bit as choosy as she liked. From her, any interest in what was wrong with him was something to welcome, not resent. Of course he in fact needed no pushing at all, since no one could be more troubled by his lack of a goal than he was himself; her concern about it was at one with his own.

"What it comes down to," he explained, "is that Uncle James and I don't suit each other in any particular. Around him I keep hankering to be someplace where he isn't. Aunt Sue, though—I sure do love Aunt Sue. For her sake I make out to get along with him most times, regardless."

A smile from Camilla conceded that what he failed to do for anyone like James Westbrook did count much less than what he took pains to do for someone he loved. She pondered it awhile in silence.

The morning mists were haunted by echoes without body, by shapes as elusive as joy. A heavy slap resounded upon the river, no doubt a large fish leaping, and from beyond a bush along the levee came a whimpery squealing, the cry of some tiny creature in the agony of lust or death. The union afterward of her glance with his so plainly acknowledged that for her, not less than for him, such a cry could speak of all lust, all death, all torment, whether hidden or gross, that he briefly experienced the sensation of being more than himself, of being double the person he generally was—an experience which four weeks in her company had made familiar.

The fog was dense in some places, thin or absent elsewhere. Discrete masses of it rode upon the Mississippi like fallen clouds. A gull tilted into one, trailed by a drawn scream. As that scream tapered away and left the mist silent, a ghostly finger stroked downward across his heart. Over Camilla's features also he saw a shadow pass.

And then there opened before them a stretch of water not fogged at all, and upon it a gray schooner manifestly familiar with the ends of the earth. Its sails hung slack as if stunned by exhausting adventure. There was about it a look of fulfilled purpose which sent through Perry an envying pleasure.

"Ulysses," he remarked.

"How so?"

"He must have come back like that after all those years at sea."

"Yes, *very* like that."

Her change of expression told him as distinctly as words that at first it had reminded her of another elderly man, Robert Palmer,— her father's friend, her rescuer from hardship, and then, for the two years she was married to him, her care, her patient, her grief. It was evident that she greatly preferred thinking of the schooner as Ulysses.

But even this did not divert her from her purpose long. "No doubt you and James would both tolerate each other better if you saw each other less."

"Most likely, yes."

"Being with him at home, and then all day at the office too—I suppose that's a lot to stand."

"Uhm. For him as well as me."

"Well, if doing something else would help any, I know of a position that ought to suit you fine."

"Oh-oh!"

"Now, Perry! How can you expect people to help you when you act like that?"

"You see, I *don't* expect it. But say on."

"Last night Edmond asked about you and said—"

"Edmond who?"

"Beaufait, of course."

"Oh, yes-yes-yes, the banker."

"He's more than a banker, Perry. He has some sort of interest in a great many enterprises."

"Hm! Every one of them perfectly legal, I trust."

"Hush, will you? I'm trying to tell you something you ought to be ever so glad to hear."

"Let's have it then, and I'll try to stand it."

"It's nothing to jest about, Perry. Mr. Beaufait is willing to consider you for a remarkable opportunity."

"Most flattering."

"Well, it is. Truly. He said how well you impressed him the time he met you before he left. He wanted to know all about you. Of course I gave you mighty high marks."

"Thank you kindly, mam. Only I've noticed that every misrepresentation has its price."

"See here now, Perry, are you turning your back on this without even knowing what it is?"

"No. What is it?"

"Why don't you ask him—Edmond? If you'll be at his bank punctually at ten today, he'll see you."

"*That's* white of him."

"Perry! He's an exceedingly busy man. When he grants an interview it's no small thing. Surely you won't just ignore it!"

Her eyes searched his as she adapted to her saddle—dark, perceptive eyes, unusually luminous and large. She had such a delectable mouth, too, that Perry had been slow to notice how firmly her features were boned. Her influence was all the stronger because, from such a source, strength came as such a surprise. Oddly, too, it was increased by her most obvious defect, a tendency of her eyes to drift apart if she let her mind wander, which she imagined made her look a fright. She had learned to prevent this by focusing intently upon anyone to whom she listened or spoke, a flattering habit which increased her ability to control others in pleasant ways because it so noticeably demonstrated self-control.

"Well," she persisted, "you're going, aren't you?"

Anyone of her subtlety, Perry thought, ought not let herself so openly desire the victory of his consent. But then why should he so stubbornly resist?

He looked away across the river. Around the becalmed schooner crept a bank of fog. As the ship ghosted away, he was reminded less of Ulysses than of his gaunt, gray father whose grave had not yet collapsed, a ruinously stubborn, harshly affectionate, brilliantly opinionated man whom he still revered and felt impoverished without. Once the fog had closed entirely around the ship he saw nothing more of it. A murmur of voices strayed from its decks, the creak of a pulley too, and the clack of some tool thrown down. What was all that, however, but a surrogate of memory among survivors when a life is gone?

The stir it aroused in him left him more oppressed than before by wonder whether, regardless of what he did, this friendship with Camilla would turn out to be no more than temporary.

"Yes, all right," he said. "And thank you for arranging it, Milla."

So here he was, waiting to meet Edmond Beaufait. The two boys had disappeared after the coach, still running at the risk of their lives, and he tried to stop himself from senselessly following that old prejudice of his against loans and banks and bankers.

"Cigar, son?"

The man with the ornamental vest was beside him, standing as tall as he could to bring himself a little nearer Perry's height. His nose was so crushed that the nostrils turned up like a mastiff's, but an indestructible liveliness shone in his eyes, and his grin hooked high on one side. His fingers balanced a fine Havana forward.

"Nosir." Perry nodded in gratitude. "Thank you all the same."

"You're what, twenty-four or five?"

"Twenty-two, sir."

"And still don't smoke?"

"No more. Not since I saw cigars made."

Mentioning it brought to mind a Baltimore cigar factory where chattery, quick-handed mulattoes rolled tobacco leaves together, softened them with saliva and licked them into shape as cigars. One as gaunt as starvation paused twice during the visit to hawk up lumps of phlegm. Thereafter it became easier for Perry to recognize that tobacco disagreed with him, depressed him. The world seemed more congenial when he kept his wits at their best.

"Wel-ll," his new friend philosophized, "you're young yet."

In time, his grin stated, all *real* men adopt all sins. A tug at the far end of his watch chain drew out a mother-of-pearl penknife and a dainty Chinese earspoon. Drawing back his coat for this purpose simultaneously exposed the butt of a pocket pistol holstered by his armpit, and a bowie knife in his left flank.

"New here, aint you?"

"Yessir—or was about a month back."

The man's penknife cut a wedge into one end of his cigar. On his right hand was a monstrous gold ring shaped like a dragon with diamond eyes.

"Come from Maryland, I reckon."

"Why, yes. How'd you know?"

"Chief's lookun for a new man here. That's why I'm in New Orleans—come down from the Baton Rouge bank to help a few days till he picks one." He let his cigar bobble unlit in the high corner of his grin while he talked. "Said this mornun a likely Maryland youngster was droppun by at ten, and I might get back to Baton Rouge shortly."

"I see. The chief's Mr. Beaufait?"

"Certainly Mr. Beaufait! Who the hell else but Mr. Beaufait?"

Perry felt his brow heat. Despite its being obvious who was meant, he had asked to be sociable, and to cover a wince at being called a likely youngster. Eyes astray through the window, he kept his voice cool. "Enjoy working for him?"

"Yuh, you bet. Anybody with drive and head is bound to. *There,* son, is one real heady gentleman."

"So I've heard."

"Always thinks two ways at once. Maybe three or four. Pays good too."

"That so?"

"Yuh, if you work to count, he does. Prove you're his man, prove you savvy when he says one thing and means different, prove you got drive, got fists, so he won't never have to hisself, and he'll pay you handsome."

Perry considered this through the window. A Negro out there was carrying on his head a gunny sack gorged with coal. His back was strenuously erect. As he passed, one white-rimmed eye rocked at Perry, who thought how well a straight back under such a load could speak for one man while praise for another could seem a defamation.

"You say to prove you got fists: is it that kind of work?"

"Looka here, son." He leveled one hand straight at Perry so that four fingers together thrust at his chest. Tattooed on the back of that hand was a burial wreath around the word MA. "People with interest due that don't pay what they owe, what's a bank to do? There's what banks lives on—interest."

"They can take it to court, and often do."

"Courts are teejus. The chief, for most cases, prefers a good strong reasoner willun and able to knock hell outa them that need it. Around his banks in Baton Rouge and Donaldsonville, that's me, his reasoner. That's what he needs here, a good stout reasoner."

"I see."

"You got the size. Question is if you know how to use it—and when."

Perry let that hang. He wondered what Camilla would say if told that the "remarkable opportunity" available here was to "reason" with debtors in arrears. Of course he might be offered something quite different, but his thoughts began running again with the waifs behind that smartly turned coach. What in the world would become of such as they in such a town? And of him?

From the oak doors to the rear, as they swung open, he heard gracious, hushed farewells in French. Beaufait's long face showed briefly beyond three gentlemen in clawhammer coats who came forward as the doors closed.

"State senators," whispered the man with the crushed nose. "They work for him too, them gents. Ever time he needs votes, they work for Mr. Beaufait." He blew out a snort. "Pimps, all three." A pause, and he jogged his cigar toward the rear. "Well, reckon you're next."

Perry shifted his hat around by the other thigh, uneasy. "Uhm."

"By the way, son, I didn't get the name. Mine's Cottier—Rex Cottier."

Perry accepted his handshake. It proved to be a trial of strength, so he let his grip outdo the power in Cottier's.

"Perry Allan, Mr. Cottier."

"Well, Allan, it seems you got some heft in you, skinny or not, but in there you got to look sharp. Here's his secretary, out to fetch you." He referred to a silvery little man who came tiptoeing toward them, a white mouse on two legs. "My advice to you is this: around the chief you got to remember every coin with a head on it likewise has a tail."

2

Edmond Beaufait's office proved to be rich but not ornate. His desk was clean of any decoration except a vase of carnations and what appeared to be a jeweled crucifix weighting papers on an open Morocco folder. He himself was rather like his surroundings—quietly and expensively furnished.

After he had seated Perry, he gestured at his papers. "These, Mr. Allan, include certain cases—some very meritorious indeed. To delay them . . ." Lifting one hand outward, he let it and a dedicated smile complete his thought without words. "You understand?"

"Yessir. Yes, of course."

"So will you forgive me if, while we talk . . . ?"

"Oh, do continue. Please!"

Beaufait brought a pen alert above his papers, first shifting forward the seeming crucifix, a fine worn relic on which rubies marked the stigmata with gruesome elegance. It was in fact a stiletto in a scabbard. The arms of the bleeding Christ lay along the hilt; the head was represented on the haft, and the thin, tortured figure continued down the scabbard, ever more emaciated, to the feet. As Beaufait penned a squiggle at the end of the topmost sheet and turned it to scan the next, Perry became conscious of a grandfather clock in a corner to his right sedately ticking off seconds.

Without any falter in his work Beaufait talked on. "How've you found Louisiana, Mr. Allan? Like it, do you?"

"Right well, sir. Though I *have* given thought to moving farther west."

"Oh?"

"Yessir."

"What brought you this far from home, all the way out here from Maryland?"

Perry took a breath. Beaufait unmistakably assumed that his travels proclaimed some well-calculated plan, whereas the truth ran just the opposite way: he had come west, not with any large purpose, but seeking one. Of course he could cite many "reasons" for coming—to visit his Aunt Sue (his dead mother's sister), to look for attractive opportunities, to get a better idea what this big, growing, half-known country he had been born in was really like, to taste adventure, to change his luck, to relish the meat of unfamiliar experience, the sauce of differing climates, the wine of fresh acquaintance, and so on. All such reasons, however, could not obliterate the shameful fact that, though already twenty-two, he still had little more purpose than some thirsty young horse wandering from one meadow to another through gates left ajar. All the prideful hope and draining expense and nagging debt that had brought him to manhood and into the legal profession had come to not one damn thing as yet, and gave no clear promise of doing anybody much good soon despite Camilla's professed faith in him. Five months ago, standing in tears by his mother's headstone while friends of the family lowered his father into the raw clay wound of a grave beside hers, he had resolved to achieve something to countervail death (theirs and his alike), to nullify its vacant finality by turning to real account the efforts spent upon equipping him to live well. Nevertheless he all this while had failed to think out any way to approximate such a result. Recalling a statement somewhere that man is three-fourths water, he in reference to himself mutely added, "At least! And the natural course of water is downhill."

His failure to speak moved Beaufait to speak for him. "Came looking for a good situation, did you?"

That was only a fraction of what he was looking for, a small fraction. But since Beaufait plainly wished to make agreement between them easy, Perry did agree. "Yessir, that and . . . and . . ."

"I understand. This brings us to why I sent for you—or did Mrs. Palmer maybe explain?"

"Some, yessir. Though honestly, Mr. Beaufait, I doubt if—"

"Yes, quite so." Beaufait looked up from his work, his manner confiding, his voice low, cottony and controlled. Even his breaks in mid-phrase had appeal because they gave his auditor credit for the intelligence to understand whatever intention he set afloat. "Behind my interest in you is this: banking, to be *sound* banking—how can it manage without capable men to look after it? It needs, it *requires,* close attention by such men wherever its work is done, isn't that so?"

"*Must,* yessir."

"Because sound banking—after all, doesn't it *express* itself in wide investment? Really, isn't wide investment just what makes it sound and keeps it sound?"

"Wellsir, I hadn't thought. But, yessir."

"The wider the better, Mr. Allan." Beaufait jogged his pen at his papers. "Banking investment—very essential to all other enterprise, whether farming or manufacture or transport or . . . or—it penetrates—that is, *supports* them all. Every blessed day we help our clients to—I believe you follow me."

His accent was not at all Creole. He must have brought it down from the North, very likely from New York or Philadelphia. His features were French, however, and almost handsome, except that his nose became too broad as it lengthened, whereas his mouth and chin were narrow. His attitude was disarmingly the opposite of what Perry expected. Instead of behaving like one rival receiving another solely because Camilla had requested it, he seemed to have arranged the interview himself out of generous esteem for the man before him.

"To be perfectly sincere and honest, Mr. Allan, I asked to see you because—well, we need a representative who's likable, who's courtly, who's knowledgeable enough so that, wherever our investments may be and whatever shape they take—you understand? We need to keep on excellent terms with our borrowers, *don't* we?"

"But, sir, is what you expect—is it the sort of work Mr. Cottier's doing?"

"Cottier?" Beaufait's gaze rose from his papers. A frown marred his brows. He reached for a bell-pull, after which he smiled. "You see, Mr. Cottier is our—you realize in banking we have to invoke law when law is ignored. Mr. Cottier's a sort of constable who sees to it that—"

At this point the silvery little secretary came tiptoeing through the door, smile in place. *"Oui, monsieur?"*

Beaufait, in softly emphatic French, observed that he had instructed Mr. Cottier an hour back to go out and inquire why payments on the Rambeau plantation were lagging. He was most surprised to learn that Mr. Cottier had not gone. All of this was tuned to the pitch of a viola offering melodies artfully low, and yet the secretary's hand, in reaching for the doorknob, trembled as if he had been ordered to hurl a thunderbolt. Beaufait then turned a dwelling gaze upon Perry.

"Vous comprenez bien français, n'est-ce pas?"

"Mais non. Mais un petit peu, m'sieur."

"Never mind. With your background—what can't a bright youth learn!"

"However—"

"And, *most* important, you know law."

"Not Louisiana law, sir. Not well. I'm just—"

"But you do know the principles of jurisprudence. Given that— after all, isn't Louisiana law simply a version of the Code Napoleon colored a bit by common law?"

Perry had to nod. There was in Beaufait's manner a requiring affability which assumed that any junior he chose to praise would jump at every chance to agree with him.

"Between you and Cottier, Mr. Allan, we would expect a considerable difference. What we need is a man of quality who knows law, and I think you're just the man." He smiled blandly. "To show my cards this way is—*not* showing them would be more clever, wouldn't it?"

"Maybe so, yessir."

Perry at this stage felt rather like a fatted sheep driven toward a gate through which floats the scent of slaughter. Beaufait shrugged up the hand holding his pen.

"*Much* more clever, no mistake. But there you have it as plain as I can say it: you do seem to be our man."

Perry did *not* think so, but what in Jesus' name would justify his saying so? Beaufait put his pen back to work. The pendulum of his clock stroked off bits of time. A sparrow chirped twice on a sill beyond the desk, then fluttered away to get at a sparrow's business, but Perry could think of no decent way to explain why he did not wish to work here.

At a loss and restless, he noticed off to his right a portrait which resembled Camilla. Shown in an Augustan robe, she contemplated the viewer from a Roman lounge between two fluted pillars, and not with any of the luminosity so characteristic of her, but with an icily regal stare, and the features had a patrician elongation alien to her.

Beaufait's pen scratched another paper. Like the ticking of his clock, this gave notice what a busy man he was. But Perry's mind was on that portrait. What did it signify? Nothing in it was exceptionable, certainly not lewd, and yet heat rose from his collar to his ears.

Beaufait, seeing him gape, rocked back in his chair. A connoisseur's delectation sloped his head sideward.

"Yes, superb, isn't it?"

Perry felt his ears burn hotter. He stood up. "Mr. Beaufait, I don't quite know how to—"

"Yes—yes, of course! You'll want a few days to consider. What I suggest is we try each other for, say, three months to begin with." Beaufait rose. Smiling, he clasped Perry's hand with his right and elbow with his left, using that intimacy to push him subtly toward the door. "More than that, I'll let you name your own salary. You're a fair-minded man, of that I'm sure. I'll leave the salary to you. That's eminently fair, don't you agree?"

What else could Perry do? He did agree that it was fair—and escaped under the impression that even his departure was the doing of a will much more adept than his own.

At a corner on the Rue Royale from which he first could see the wrought iron around balconies jutting from Camilla's town house, a paralysis of doubt stopped him. A long frown at the designs in that iron, and he stirred the coins in his pocket, fingering the worn currency of his faith in himself. At last he turned aside in the direction of the print shop where Camilla's father, Major Cedric Burleigh, edited his weekly, the *New Orleans Commentator*.

About halfway there a good firm hand gripped his arm from behind. "Hold on, boy! Where you bound?"

"Major! I was just coming to see you."

"What ails you, Perry?" Major Burleigh probed him with darkly vital eyes resembling Camilla's. "You don't look like yourself."

Actually, seeing this man made Perry feel better. Compact in frame and heedlessly handsome, Major Burleigh had about him an unthinking air of lineage. He still retained the buoyant ways of youth even though streaks of gray waved through his hair and salted his muttonchop whiskers. Erstwhile dandification showed upon him from hat to boots, never quite forgotten in his devotion to ideas. Years ago he had earned two citations for courage, one in fighting the Creeks, the other against the British during the War of 1812, and he still held the esteem of his wartime commander, President Andrew Jackson, who had offered him a post in the consular service. Instead of grabbing it, as anyone acquainted with his circumstances might have expected, he said he would stick by Camilla till she got herself married again. His valor and skill under arms seldom were recalled nowadays: brisk acquaintances considered him "weak," in part because he had failed at pretty nearly every undertaking since he left the army, in part because he lacked the sense to convert his *Commentator* into something better than a journalistic scorpion which stung and offended those people who could best afford to buy advertising, in part because he seemed to let his daughter's whims rule his life. Perry, during two demonstrations of mesmerism for which the major had volunteered, himself had seen a Viennese named Dr. Heinz Gebhard, a chinless sort of anteater in human shape, deprive him of any sign of will whatever, entrancing him into an utter puppet. Still, he knew of no other man in Louisiana he would rather talk with at this moment, or whose friendship seemed more complimentary.

"Heard the news, have you?" the major asked.

"News, sir?"

"About Texas, yes."

"Nosir—Texas?"

"Good God, where you been anyhow?"

"Over at the Benevolent Loan of Louisiana."

"Well, well!"

"Yessir. Beaufait tried to hire me."

"That so?"

"And at any salary I might name."

Irony glinted in the major's eyes. "Uh-oh!"

"That's my feeling too, sir. Ever run across anybody from Baton Rouge named Cottier?"

"No-o. Don't know as I have, no."

"Rex Cottier. You'd remember him if you ever saw him."

Perry described him: his tattoo, his chain, earspoon, pistol, knives and rings, his brutal face and fancy clothes.

Entertained, the major shook his head. "Damned bizarre; but he's a stranger to me."

"Well, he's working at the Benevolent Loan doing what I calculate Beaufait wants me to do—thug for him, though maybe in a nicer way. Cottier's a slicked-up thug who sees to it people pay what they owe or suffer if they don't."

"Hm!" Major Burleigh, after scanning the street both ways, pointed out a tavern. "There, Perry. Let's sip a little something and look into this."

At a table remote from the bar he listened over a chartreuse while Perry told about the interview.

"All along, sir, Beaufait implied he wanted me for grand services he never did exactly name, and he talked so good it seemed evil to doubt him. Then on the wall I saw something that made it all look twice as queer—a portrait of Camilla."

"Uhm, yes."

"Yessir, in a Roman gown and so on—very, very regal, and very false."

"Perry, that's the fad now."

"Trash all the same."

"Of course it's trash. One thing sure: all fads today are trash tomorrow."

"The damned thing riled me. You understand, major—a trophy in that bastard's den, *his.*"

"Hold on there, Perry. That's one thing she's not: she's not his."

"Then what's it mean?"

"Wel-ll, let's think a minute." He held a sip of liqueur in his mouth a spell, lips wetly, ardently red, the prototype of Camilla's. "Sometimes the more civilized we become, the plainer a streak of savage will show. Ever hear how a savage employs images? To bring critters in reach, uh? To evoke them, hex them, control them, voodoo them. Beaufait's as civilized as a sight draft, but that painting's a voodoo, nothing else."

"Maybe. I don't know."

"That's *all* it is. He invited us home one Sunday afternoon—Camilla, Yvonne Hanotaux, and me. A painter much in demand around town 'just by chance' so happened to be there, retouching a portrait of Beaufait's mother. So, while we talked, he painted Camilla and afterward surrounded her with that stylish Palatine background, which increases the impression that she sat for it for days and days and days, always available to do Beaufait's bidding. A voodoo, Perry."

"Looked more like a brag to me."

"That too, yes. He means to have her, no matter how long it takes, so he lets that portrait give out that he pretty near as good as does, though the way she's fancied you ever since you came here—that tells the truth plain enough."

"Nevertheless he wants to hire me. Why?"

"*Nevertheless?*" Tilting back, the major dug a pipe from his waistcoat and buried the bowl in a bladder of tobacco. "Maybe you ought to say *consequently.* Maybe he's in a lather to hire you *because* Milla's favored you too strong to suit him."

"Wellsir, that's too deep for me."

"It won't be when you know him. Beaufait's had to be devious, a pusher too. He's had a lot to bury, to cover up, to disguise. His first stake came from his mother, who earned it in New York, I'm told, as madam in a snooty French whorehouse."

"Go long!"

"Yup. Seeing my daughter involved, I wrote an editor up there, and that's what he wrote back. I reckon it's on the mark too."

"Hm! Has Camilla heard this?"

"Not from me, no, *sir!* She'd be wild." Vision of her at such a moment brought laughter to his eyes. "She'd tear my head off. She talks him up as a model gentleman, very feeling and cultured and considerate. Most ladies do. Anything men say against him is purely spite."

He fired a locofoco in a tube of acid, applied it to his pipe, and squinted through the smoke. "Pushers of that sort—ever notice how they buy their way to good opinion? They buy up finer, ever finer things to make *them* finer. Each new thing they value less for itself than for the new value it gives them. They climb on costly possessions to lift themselves above the common."

"I follow, yessir."

"Works of art, fancy teams, quiet but expensive clothes, grand mansions—they all help. But goods alone won't do. Why do you think he's so 'devoted' to Camilla?"

"Seems to me one look at her tells why."

"Gallantly said, Perry, but off the mark. *Others* admire her so much, therefore *he* does: any time he corners what so many prize he's that much better than they are. To keep himself welcome around her, he's never unpleasant, never the least bit demanding, and his interest in her furnishes a hemisemidemi-reassurance to her creditors. If he wants so bad to be seen with her, why shouldn't she enjoy the advantage of being seen with him?"

That advantage Perry understood. As his uncle James Westbrook was her attorney and executor of her dead husband's estate, he knew the facts about the supposed fortune she had inherited: her plantation up the river might look splendid, her town house too, but her credit was not. In fact the most impressive part of her inheritance was the size of the debts Robert Palmer had left behind him. Certain mortgage holders and a good many Louisiana tradesmen must feel easier in proportion as she spent more time with Banker Beaufait.

"She's acted offish and disappointed in me the last few days, sir." Perry shook his glass so that little golden waves washed its sides. "Now, when I have to tell her what I think of this 'remarkable opportunity,' things'll go from bad to worse."

"Nothing would be a bigger mistake, Perry, than to change your mind on that account. My word on that. Beaufait's game would permanently ruin you in her eyes. That's what it's intended to do, as I believe you'll see yourself directly. But you must—in any event, you've got to—expect her to become a little offish and cool. All this time with you, day and evening alike, has made people wonder. She knows that, and is bound to bridle it some. Anyway, how can a girl with expensive tastes like hers seriously consider partnering up with you when you haven't settled on anything yet, neither which way you're headed, nor how to make a living, nor where to try? You don't mind plain speaking, I hope?"

"Nosir. It's all true, sir."

"Same is true of her too. There was a time—after one of my own most awful failures—when she had to work in the fields just like a darkie, only harder, sweating around barefoot to keep hold of our home. She was fifteen then: it was seven or eight years back. Our friend and neighbor, Bob Palmer, helped her get back into school, after which she floated up on a balloon of storybook romance with a pomaded sport who wore lilac lace on his cuffs and sent her quantities of poetry and flowers and bonbons every day—until the police carried his razored corpse from the bedside of a Vieux Carré quadroon. Camilla never once had suspected him of any weakness for quadroons, and I've yet to see anyone else so stunned as she was, so ashamed of herself too, for letting herself be fooled.

"That's why she married old Bob: she thought she never would be able to trust romance again. That marriage to Bob turned into a pretty severe trial; through most of it she was a nurse, not a wife, and a good nurse too, one who seldom left his side and never said quit. Never. Then, after he died, she made up her mind to keep her independence awhile and enjoy life."

"Yessir. She makes no secret of that."

"None at all. She takes only a temporary interest in young bucks like you who want to squire her around. Seldom will you find any woman who wouldn't adore being always newly cherished if she could. Camilla can and does, but she would no sooner be seen with one of you to the exclusion of all others than wear one bonnet month in, month out."

"Nosir, reckon not."

"No. In her eyes each new courtship is rather like an evening at the opera: it may stir up all sorts of emotions but leaves them pretty much as they were underneath, ready for other drama elsewhere. Anyway that's how she has acted pretty much of the time since Bob died, at least till you came along. What most new acquaintances don't know is that she has another side to her of much longer standing— a remarkable loyalty, soundness, reliability, and insight; a remarkable capacity, too, for plain hard work. You'll discover that someday, Perry."

"Wellsir, I do believe it now. If you were in my boots, major, having this talk with Beaufait behind me, exactly what would you do next?"

"Nothing."

"Sir?"

"That is, I'd force her to make the next move. The one after that too."

His pipe bubbled as he sucked it. A grimace at its bitter juice, and he removed the stem to blow it clean. His deliberation in doing so invited Perry to deliberate.

"Jealousy implies a claim, doesn't it? Well, Camilla's not a mind to be claimed, not yet at any rate. I'd stay away from her, Perry. Let her miss you; let her worry about what keeps you away. She'll respect you most, and call you back soonest, if you let her go her way without a murmur while you go yours."

"That's easy enough to say, major. Doing it's another matter. Camilla has so much to her, much more than anyone else I've known. Everything around her turns better because she's there, not excepting me. To completely give her up . . ." Perry shook his head.

"Ho-ho! Don't let it trouble you so, boy. You're in love, that's all's the matter with you, and you know perfectly well you shouldn't be."

"*All!*" Perry, laughing without sound, slumped forward on his elbows to massage his temples against the heels of both hands. "Excuse me, sir. What if you told a doctor you felt mighty bad. Then suppose he said back, 'Now don't you worry any, major. You're dying, that's all's the matter with you.' What would you say to that?"

"Well put!" He clapped a hand on Perry's arm. "I'd shoot the damn rascal. No gun handy, I'd throw him down and gash his fool throat open with a sharp rock. Still and all, I've dealt with that girl a long while and, Perry . . ."

"Yessir?"

"One thing I'm sure of is this: the way to hold her is to let her go."

"Uhm." Perry thought it over. "That's sensible. In fact, it's so dang sensible I don't see how you could expect anyone to do it."

"No, but *you* will. I'd never waste the breath to say it if you didn't show signs of guessing it already. You've taken care, I've noticed, to act pretty lighthearted most of the time."

"That, sir, is just like whistling through the woods after dark."

"Of course, which aint a bad way to act in dark woods. She likes you the better for it, certain. When were you supposed to see her next?"

"She said I might come around right away—curious, maybe, about my talk with Beaufait."

"Might? To hell with her. It's not fixed?"

"Not exactly, nosir."

"Then to hell with her. Don't see her till you can't help it, till she knows you can't help it."

"That won't be till tomorrow evening. We're dining early with people from Texas, then going to the theater."

"Too soon, Perry."

"But it's at home, sir, and for her. Aunt Sue arranged it so Camilla could talk with the Texians, a Dr. Springfield and his daughter. Seems they live near some land out there that Mr. Palmer left her."

"Oh, yes-yes. Dr. Springfield used to practice here many years ago and knew Bob Palmer well. He'd been Bob's doctor. When Bob went to Texas, Dr. Springfield helped him pick out two Spanish leagues somewhere near his own, a regular principality in size, though all empty land of small value—pretty nearly nine thousand acres. Bob's aim was to retire there for his health, escape his debts back here, and make a new start toward a fortune. He built a house on it, a dandy place I understand. On the way back for Camilla, however, he came down sick and never again had the strength to get around. Now, as it's the only part of her inheritance not encumbered, she'll certainly want to see the Springfields. And, the dinner being at your home—no, that you can't avoid."

"Nosir, I can't."

"All right. But don't you let her catch you acting reproachful about Beaufait. Don't you mention that portrait or wonder what she's done with her time. Jealousy she resents, and never doubt it. It's possessive, and she's of no mind to be possessed."

"Can't say I ever liked it either, come to think of it."

"Take Beaufait: he knows how she abhors it and acts accordingly. Nobody's slick enough to catch him ever acting jealous when she might know. Now doesn't that bring us back to why he wants to hire you?"

"Let's see. Does it?"

"It does. Hiring you would declare that he's anything but jealous, though you've given him so much cause to be. As your chief, too, he'd become your superior, manifestly. He'd have you bought and paid for."

"That he would!"

"His offer to let you name your pay—that was just a handful of sugar to a young stud that he means to cut and break to harness. Finally—"

"By God!"

"Finally, any time he decides to get rid of you, he's still more superior."

"And to her more noble for trying to make me do!"

"*There* you are, Perry."

Absorption of too many staggering truths too fast left Perry a bit dazed. A hammer began banging against the front wall. He sat back to gaze sideward through a window in that wall. Clustered beyond it were heads of men staring at the point where the hammer struck.

"Major, what's afoot?"

"Drink up and let's have a look."

They strolled outdoors. A youth with a sheaf of placards across his arm was tacking one onto the wall while a semicircle of men spelled out its message. In shouty type it began:

WAR IN TEXAS

Lesser type declared that the Dictator of Mexico had sent troops against American settlements in that province. Over the signature of Major General Sam Houston was an appeal for volunteers:

*Liberal bounties of land will be given
to all who will join our ranks. . . .
Come with a good rifle, and come soon. . . .
Liberty or Death! . . . Down with the usurper!*

The placard concluded by inviting sympathizers to a meeting that night at Bank's Arcade.

"War!" Perry remarked, and exulting gooseflesh crept around his ribs.

"There, my boy, is what I was trying to tell you in the first place," said the major. "That meeting's one we'd both of us do well to see."

From Cedric Burleigh's Journal
October 13, 1835

What our thinking needs is a kick in the ass. Once a day is good. Oftener is better. An apple dropping on Newton's head suggested the law of gravitation, debt drove Scott to write novels which still enthrall us, scoldings at home kept Socrates out generating imperishable wisdom, and few of us get a fresh idea without some sort of comeuppance. Pretty nearly all of us have assumed in the last decade or two that American liberties no longer have any considerable enemies. Today the echoes of distant gunfire jarred that notion out of my head: Americans in Texas are up in arms. On maps and legal documents that territory may still belong to Mexico, but with guarantees of liberty on the American pattern under the Constitution of 1824. Now the dictator, Gen. Antonio López de Santa Anna, is out to abrogate those guarantees in Texas as he has elsewhere, and the excitement here exceeds anything I've witnessed in years. Americans are the world's foremost evangelizers for freedom; no evangelist could become more impassioned than we do when sacred Liberty is threatened. What Christianity amid the splendors of Rome was to the God-intoxicated who prayerfully fed the lions (and so converted thousands), Liberty is to America: not until we see the beasts of tyranny creeping forward to fatten upon it do our spirits come wholly alive.

At Bank's Arcade this evening a lusty crowd of us gathered to hear tell about the Texian Cause. We listened with utmost enchantment to Adolphus Sterne, a bright, eloquent, romantical Jew, the alcalde of Nacogdoches, whence he had just arrived to beseech our help against Santa Anna. The audience formed a Committee for Texas on the spot, with Col. Wm. Christy and Wm. Bryan as officers. The substantiality then signed pledges totaling $10,000, and opened rolls for two companies of volunteers to be known as the New Orleans Greys.

My young friend Perry stepped forward while others were writing down their names, but I persuaded him to hold back in preference for another possibility with more distinction to it. Mr. Bryan, a wealthy shipper, had begun the avalanche of gifts by pledging to dispatch to the scene of combat a gift of fifty rifles, plus as many shot pouches, pistols, and knives. Afterward I introduced Perry, with whom Mr.

Bryan was much taken and who was my nomination to deliver the weapons, on the argument that such responsibility is safest in the hands of one accountable man with a few aides of his own choosing. We three will lunch over the proposition tomorrow.

Perry had come to the Arcade in low spirits. He left there looking able to stay alive even if Camilla persists in being the same Camilla. The change in him, and the longing in me to assist the same cause, recalled a saying I heard in old Persia which might be rephrased thus:

> *If I be needed,*
> *and something is wished from me,*
> *then I have a place on earth.*
> *If I can answer that need,*
> *and fulfill that wish,*
> *then I have a place in heaven.*

CHAPTER II

I

At the run of parties Camilla preferred arriving late, not to assure
her entrances of a good audience
(as the spiteful liked to say), but
to avoid that introductory awk-
wardness when guests are most ceremonial, grinning, weatherwise,
and dull. Her long friendship with the Westbrooks, however, required
her to pay them the compliment of promptness. Her brougham wheeled
up their driveway just before six.

As she expected, Perry was waiting for her in the patio, reading
under an arbor of bougainvillea. He came forward at once, and the
peculiarity of his walk brought a fractional smile to her lips: he had
a long stride, light and limber in the knees, and given more thrust by
a slight forward twist. That he knew very well how to cover ground
was apparent.

His first effort was to help her coachman Esau quiet her team, a
sorrel beauty named Oriole and a three-year-old sister named Swallow, whom Perry had been breaking to saddle and harness. Both mares
were the color of fire, and Swallow often harder than blown fire to
control. Although Esau, in trying to stop her, leaned back on his
dickey seat so far that his reins sprung her jaws, she continued capering like a Spanish dancer until Perry took hold of her bit to steady
her. He met her eye as if courting her.

"You dang idiot, what ails you?"

"She got wings, sah," Esau declared. "I *mean* wings."

"You check her too snug, Esau." Perry forced her head up to release her checkrein. "Thing hurts her mouth."

"Yassah."

"Better not check her at all till her mouth toughens, and never
tight."

"Nawsah."

"You're driving the best team in this town, if not in this state, if not

24

in all Dixie, and there's no need to strap their heads up like nags with no spirit."

Camilla, motionless within the brougham, had to smile again even though still annoyed with him. Not one syllable had she heard from the scamp for the longest period in their acquaintance—not since yesterday morning. Edmond Beaufait last night had inquired what Perry had said about their interview, and lifted a brow in surprise when she could report nothing. Even so, she did find it pleasant this evening to relax in the plush embrace of her carriage, seemingly neglected in favor of her mares, knowing that Perry's tributes to them were addressed through them to her.

His clothes, too, reflected a desire to please her. A precipice of starched white collar stiffened his neck almost to his ears. From that a midnight blue cravat floated over foamy white ruffles which cascaded downward between his lapels. His coat, a black broadcloth, gripped him tight in the arms, exaggerating the size of his hands and curving in so drastically at the waist that, lean as he was, he now looked stricken by an unearthly gauntness. He also wore cream pantaloons as snug as paint. He must be hideously uncomfortable, all for her, and yet in opening her carriage door he quite apparently forgot all about it in pleasure at sight of her.

"Looka who's heah!" he began, mimicking the Dixie drawl.

He himself had an accent as peculiar to Maryland as terrapin soup, but he seemed to think that only people from elsewhere talked funny. He reached in to help her from the carriage. As she accepted his hand and met his glance a wayward throb jarred through her.

A Pennsylvania mother, a Virginia father, and two years of finishing in Philadelphia had left her speech little more Dixified than his, and yet she answered as if every breath her family ever drew had been sweetened by the scent of magnolia. "Evenun stranjah."

"How you feel an fine yoseff this evenun, Miz Milla?"

"Fit an passable, suh, thank you kinely."

He tilted his head sideward to admire her gown, a confection of lace, embroidery, gathers, and gauze as light as French pastry. "Oooo-wuh!"

"*Now* what?"

"If I wasun raised so strict, I'd pick off some frostun."

Her laughter fluttered out before she could stop it. Reflecting that she ought to be more severe with him, she cleansed her face of pleasure and brought her accent back to normal. "The Texians here yet?"

"Nome, aint showed so fuh."

She began drifting toward the arbor, petticoats gossiping among themselves while he put his saunter in step with hers.

"I particularly came early to have a little talk with you, Perry."

"Delighted, mam."

He crooked his arm for her because of late she had been in the habit of seizing it on happy impulse whenever they started off thus side by side. Tonight she ignored it to draw off a white lace glove.

"What in creation became of you anyway?"

"When?"

"All this time—yesterday, this morning, this afternoon. You know *when,* and don't imply you don't." Too late she recognized how unwise it was to begin so, but became still more annoyed at him for annoying her into exposing how annoyed she was. "You were to stop by, and you didn't."

"No, you simply said it might be nice to. However, you were also seeing Beaufait."

"Well, suppose I was! Whose business is that?"

"Three's a crowd."

"I didn't expect you both at once." She jerked the fingers of her glove straight one at a time. "Had you come right after you saw him, we could have arranged things fine."

"There are circumstances when—haven't you noticed?—when a presence lingers. Three's a crowd."

She compressed her lips.

In the arbor he nodded to suggest a bow as he swept a hand toward a bench for two along one side. She pointedly took the opposite bench, leaving the other for him alone. As he sat down he gazed away toward the west, where florid strokes of red and gold and pallid yellow sinuously intertwined across deepening blue. Those gray eyes of his turned dusky.

"Days are growing shorter."

"That's usual in October."

"Uhm. *So* usual." He let that balance awhile between them. "All these centuries, Milla, so many, many thousands like you and me have watched days die, watched them shorten this time of year, watched the approach of winter. Reckon that ever helped them forgive each other sooner?"

Her annoyance collapsed. Often simple prose spoken by this appealing lummox affected her more than verse. And he was right. A thought or two of the year's decline, of generations gone, of approaching night, ought to prevent these foolish spats. She reached for a book he had left in the arbor.

"What're you reading now?" She flipped back its cover. The title startled her: Napoleon's *Maxims of War.* "In heaven's name, Perry, why *this?*"

"Who knows soldiering any better?"

"But goodness me . . ." She tossed it aside. "Oh, well!" None of this was taking them one step nearer to what she wanted to discuss. A cleansing sigh, and she undertook to smile. "Edmond tells me he thinks you're just the man he's looking for. He thinks you'll do well."

He plucked a lavender bloom of bougainvillea from a spray by his elbow. "So?"

"First rate." It puzzled her to see him blankly watch his thumb and finger spin the flower. "Don't you?"

"No."

"Of *course* you will, Perry! He's certain you will, and—why not?"

"I can't work for him at all."

"But how silly! He'll pay whatever you ask."

"Doesn't matter." He kept the flower going in senseless gyrations. "I can't take it."

"Oh, why? In the name of gracious, why?"

"He's one sort." Perry threw the flower away. "I'm another."

"Yes, and how lucky. One of you is quite enough."

"Uhm."

"But it's such a remarkably generous offer. Who else would ever let you name your own salary?"

"Anyhow, he's the first who ever has."

"Tell me, Perry, what *is* wrong?"

"Prejudice, I reckon. I went there simply and solely because I'd like to do what you'd like me to do. From the hour I first met you, Milla, you've made the whole world seem better because it's got you in it, but there . . ."

Though he lost the ability to express what he meant, she already had gone tender inside. Her tone gently encouraged him. "Well?"

"Him, though, just the opposite. I don't like his cottony talk. I don't like what he does or what I think he expects me to do. I don't like *him,* truth to say." Though that had sufficiently shocked and angered her, he went straight on without a glance her way. "He has the look of a good man, but I don't think he is one."

"Perry, you realize Mr. Beaufait is one of my very closest friends."

"Uh-huh, I realize."

"I won't allow—I simply will not tolerate that kind of talk against him."

Perry sat back with each hand flat on the bench beside him to signify that she might have her view while he kept his.

A hack driver out beyond the driveway was shouting to a servant at a window on the second floor to ask if this was Westbrooks'.

"It's not one thing but spite," Camilla persisted. "He's very highly regarded here. At least by others he is."

"Uhm. Odd, isn't it?" He rose. One big hand, impelled loosely, awkwardly, from the wrist, fumbled into a pocket and came out empty. "I'd call him a weasel in rabbit's clothing, myself."

"Why, what a loathsome thing to say!"

"I've no doubt, of course, that he's as honest as the day is long— at the North Pole, on December twenty-first."

"Perry Allan!" More fiercely she added, "And I'll tell you this, sir: whoever wants to talk him down can just make tracks and stay away from me."

"Mean that, do you?"

"A good *stretch* away."

His lips had gone bloodless. A flush scalded his face. He rose to study the colors the brush of sunset had painted across the west. "Reckon I'll live?" He stepped outside the arbor.

Up the driveway came a graying, sunburned man beside a girl in a bonnet shaped like a prairie schooner. Her gown looked at least five years out of date.

"These must be the Texians," Perry remarked. "Shall we go out and say hello?"

2

When everyone looked comfortable in the drawing room, Susan Westbrook took leave to spur things along in the kitchen so that dinner would not interfere with Camilla's and Perry's plan to leave early for the theater. Meanwhile Perry let his lawyer-uncle, James West-

brook, monopolize Camilla while he devoted himself to the Springfields.

Camilla undertook to look gratified. With every ribbon, flounce, and
curl fetchingly in place, she assumed that serene quiescence everywhere expected of highbred ladies in the presence of voluble gentlemen. Most women in the congregation James served as an elder
vigorously admired him. He had a fine head of steel-gray hair, an
apostolic expression, and a storehouse of information on ever so
many subjects, much of it pretty nearly accurate. To talk with him was
effortless: he did next to all of it.

What exercised him tonight was conviction that America had been
going to the dogs ever since Andrew Jackson entered the White
House. Most persons of quality (except a few oddities like her father)
had been talking much the same way much too long; certainly James
had. Camilla soon could not help wishing him a Quaker instead of a
Presbyterian, so that he would put a higher value on silence. His discourse was deafening her to all but a fraction of what went on between
Perry and the Springfields.

Their chairs formed a cozy triangle off to her left. The doctor's suit
was loose and faded, his skin deeply weathered, his hair a rusty gray
so newly cut as to expose a border of white skin beside which his neck
looked a mummified brown. His daughter seemed a sweet girl but a
bit on the plain side, and two pimples on her left cheek advertised her
immaturity. Her hair, though a fetching fawn color, was brushed
straight back to a bun behind in a style outmoded several years ago.
Her gown, too, was one of those half-forgotten things with the waist-
line high under the bosom, hanging loose from there, and so lying
along her figure as to give notice of its contours, of eventual voluptu-
ousness, of unacknowledged inclination to arouse the beast in man—
and tame it.

Perry, the imbecile, acted utterly without armor against such adver-
tisement: he dwelt upon her as if she looked tastier than hot buttered
biscuits. To hear him bandy witticisms with her and her father, one
would think it just nothing at all to lose a truly caring friend, and quite
apparently the Springfields thought well of him.

At one point he so aptly quoted a couplet from Pope that Leticia's
giggles came rushing out like chickens thrown a handful of wheat. Dr.
Springfield then quoted another, which sent Perry's laugh crowing
after hers. Suffering from an impulse to kick him, Camilla required

her eyes to fix harder on James, but soon felt them wall disgustingly as her interest flagged; and when that worthy excused himself to fetch a paper which would prove what a natural-born jackass Jackson was, she let her attention steal back to the others.

"However," Perry was saying, "opinions differ so. To some Texas is 'just literally nowhere,' as the cant runs. To others it's the promised land."

"I wonder," said Dr. Springfield, and breathed two or three wondering breaths through a rusty mustache, "how many mortals from any city this size could like Texas. If you feel lost without people right outside every window, then Texas is not for you. No, stay here. On the other hand, if you can tolerate the room it takes to be one of the friendliest souls in this round world, she'll suit you down to the ground."

"I see. It's so big you value people instead of being sick of the sight of them."

"Exactly, sir! There's room there to develop a spacious view of life. If you're industrious as well, you're sure to prosper in time."

"However, I've also heard it called a lazy man's paradise."

"That too, yes. Game is so plentiful and the soil so easy, a man can scratch up a living for a cabin full of family without enough hard work to blister a schoolmarm. There's a saying, 'Tickle Texas with a hoe and it laughs with harvest.' "

Susan meanwhile returned and only awaited a pause from the doctor to announce, as if sharing a delightful secret, "Dinner is quite ready now. Do come, won't you?"

"Land, Papa!" Leticia smiled as they rose to follow. "It's not *that* fine! And gracious knows what the war will leave to anyone."

"It'll be so nice to hear more about Texas," Susan remarked hastily. "But can't we please keep away from that war? It so upsets Mr. Westbrook."

The shift of her eyes toward Perry hinted of wounds, not yet healed, from an earlier battle on that subject. Having summoned James from his study, she led the way into the dining room.

The dinner was not elaborate but well cooked—a *potage* followed by roast grouse and tasty accessories. Ordinarily Camilla would have been on guard against her appetite. Tonight, however, she had no difficulty finicking as fashion required: though the paper James sought had eluded him, he was by no means through with his discourse on "King Andy," and she still felt poisoned by Perry's sarcastic way of asking in the garden if she reckoned he'd live when she told him to stay away from her.

All these weeks she had known it was in her power to cut him open with a phrase or two and feed his heart to the crows. She had withheld that power, and what was the result? He had cut *her* open. Furthermore the rogue was enjoying the meal and that clucking little country chicken much too well to bother trading glances designed to patch things up.

What most disgusted her about Leticia was the senseless flattery of her attention to him. His brows were black and long, accentuating his eyes, which were the same light gray as his Aunt Sue's, only larger, more musing, and quicker to brighten in fun or darken in anger, obstinacy, or regret. That silly Leticia kept gazing into them as if he were some marvelous being, though he did not at all fit the present-day ideal, which was to appear raised under glass and to seem the descendant of ancestors whose chief concern time out of mind had been what to do with their leisure. Perry, instead, was manifestly an outdoor product, slicked up some and incongruously overexposed to libraries. Even his most careful grooming fell short of success, for his hair was dense and unruly, never parting quite straight or lying politely flat. Strong and large as his hands were, they were almost ludicrous: a blacksmith could do with such hands, or a carpenter—any leather-apron man—but how odd on a gentleman!

Still, it had surprised her how light and skillful they could be, how well they knew the language of touch, perhaps because he was so aware of elusive qualities in things which most people never felt. The emanations of his enjoyment of common fact had revived in her a sense of inexhaustible privilege in being alive.

Old New Orleans, stale, repetitious, and corrupt, had acquired a new fascination for her after she began showing him around, seeing everything in new ways because everything so keenly interested him. Whereas she previously had got so she avoided more than half the functions she was expected to attend, considering most a dreary, tiresome waste of time, and whereas a half-dozen days in town usually sufficed to send her upriver again to the realities of country life, going about with Perry had revealed new cause for wonder everywhere, for amusement too. Their rides at dawn had taken them places she never had seen before, and together they had enjoyed every sort of event, often three or four a day—horse shows, races, steamboat parties, turkey shoots, picnics, charivaris, balls, operatic performances, musicales, box suppers, and fish fries, as well as staider functions like soirees, levees, receptions, dinners, dedications, and military exercises. They had gone to church together each Sunday morning, usually again at vesper service. They had attended two utterly flabbergasting demonstrations of mesmerism by a Viennese physician and once had witnessed voodoo rites in woods beyond the city. When nothing else had to be done, they strolled at evening between the Rampart Promenade and the palmy Cathedral Plaza, where stern and deliberate bells warned this wicked city to prepare for night.

One of many traits they had in common was a disinclination to sleep. Often after a busy day and evening she played the piano for him before he went home. Instead of sitting by all the while, he was apt to stride back and forth across the drawing room. If the tune happened to be inexpressibly beautiful, as in "My Gentle Harp," a change in his walk indicated a degree of aesthetic suffering almost too strong to bear. She had come to feel, though he never said so, that he cherished his hours with her as if all were resonant with overtones of melodies he loved to hear.

Now, after all that, how was it possible for him so to relish the company of the first new girl thrown his way? The devil acted as if that pimpled child of seventeen were rare in judgment and looks alike.

At the moment he was saying, "If it's distance that limits your life so, then wouldn't railroads change things right much?"

"Why, I—I allow they would, yessir. The ships carry what little commerce we have, but we do need so many things more."

"Really? To hear your father talk, you'd think Texians want for nothing."

"Fudge! Stoves, for instance, are rare as rubies there, except along the coast, where ships bring them. Linens too, and books, furniture, china, pictures—all the finer things; besides necessities like plows, hoes, wagons, grinders, churns, kettles—whatever lightens the day or sweetens the evening."

Camilla discovered herself crediting the girl with honesty and good sense. No sooner had that concession voiced itself internally than she wrenched her attention back to James.

"If that scoundrel in the White House," he declared over a forkful of escalloped potatoes, "keeps on the way he is, we're going to have a panic. Mind what I say, Camilla—the worst panic in our history! Why, only the other day . . ."

Usually his talks to her took the form of intellectual courtship: without implying any expectation of a parenthesis in his attachment to Susan, he saved up ideas which he fancied would impress her and delivered them like costly presents. Not to act as if she valued them would be unkind, and she undertook to now—until her mind of itself drifted back to Perry and Leticia. Both were still eating with gusto and talking to match.

"Nosir, I haven't seen it," she overheard from Leticia. "I'd planned to go everywhere and buy so many lovely things. Truth is, I saved my pay for that the whole year long."

"Your pay?"

"Yessir. I teach school, the only one in thirty miles." Far from seeing any degradation in pinching pennies or working for wages, she acted proud of having done both. "I saved most every cent of it, but how you reckon I spent it?"

"New clothes maybe?"

"Oh, nosir! Sometimes I wish to gracious I had. But, nosir, on a stove—a wonderful Franklin cooking stove! And on books, ever so many books."

Camilla thought that fiendishly clever. His quotations must have told her how fond he was of reading, and Perry, the fool, did look impressed.

"What sort of books?"

"Every sort. Few of the neighbors have any, and taking plenty back will draw visitors often to our house. Books are good company, and they bring us company. Trouble is, I forgot about the imposts." She smiled woefully. "If the collectors stop us I'll have to depend on papa to get them into Texas."

"The imposts high?"

"Mortally high!"

Perry, having stripped the flesh off a grouse's drumstick, napkinned his lips. His glance shifted from his aunt to his uncle to make sure they were not listening. "And isn't that one cause of the war?"

"Yessir, people do resent it. But most wouldn't fight about it."

"You mean they aren't really going to fight?"

"Oh, yessir! It's started now, and people think we got to fight back, though we do so wish to settle it some other way."

"But isn't it true that Texians have been spoiling to fight for years?"

The care they used to keep their voices low had forced Camilla to listen more closely, leading James to wonder what robbed him of her attention.

"Only the hotheads," Leticia answered. "Now the Mexicans have attacked. Consequently more and more believe that war is our only recourse. How we'll ever crowd through it alive, though, I can't see. The Mexicans, you know, have seven million people, and we little over thirty thousand. So a war very likely will ruin us all."

"There!" James exclaimed. "That's what I've been trying to get into his fool head all afternoon!"

A distressing silence followed. Perry's brow reddened. Susan put down her fork and signaled to her husband in frantic appeal. The doctor examined a spoon. Leticia's frightened blue eyes concentrated on her plate.

In a tense effort to sound cool Perry observed, "Still, the way Mexico has been holding her down, Texas can't become much of a territory until she does win a liberating war. The French have a saying about circumstances like that: *'Il faut remuer la terre pour qu'elle produise.'* In other words, until iron tears the earth open there can be no harvest."

"As this applies to Texas," said James, "it's simply imbecilic, nothing more. A war would not be the making of Texas, but its ruination. Furthermore it would ruin New Orleans as well."

"Oh, hardly!" Camilla sniffed.

"No, certainly!" James had a name for winning arguments, in court or out; he would not let his regard for her restrain him in this one. "Only a few hours ago, do you know what I heard? The British consul told me that Britain, because of her interests in Mexico, can tolerate no interference from us with Mexican rule in Texas."

"Well, what's so new in that?" Perry asked and managed a grin. "Lord Palmerston can't sleep well when he thinks how fast we've grown. His unwavering policy is to stunt us. If he's so quick to take up the Mexican cause, doesn't that give notice how much good he thinks a victory for Texas will do us?"

"And Mexico herself," James cut him off. "Have you any notion what this port's yearly commerce with Mexico amounts to?" His fist banged the table three times to underline each of three words: *"Seventeen million dollars!* Does anyone imagine she'll give us this trade if we side with Texas?"

"Preservation of trade," said Perry acidly, "counts less with some Americans than preservation of liberty and justice."

"Bah!" James wagged a finger at him. "Show me a man who puts small value on trade and I'll show you an ignoramus—that, or an idler who has nothing himself, who never will have anything, and who'd as lief see the rest of us lose all *we* have."

"But, Uncle James, through all our history, a central current of idealism has always drawn us, always compelled us to assist the cause of liberty wherever—"

"Liberty and justice! Aren't *you* a fine one to talk about justice and liberty! What is justice to you but tedium? And what's liberty to you but a sanction for trifling your time away?"

Perry's jaw locked hard. One hand, knotting around his napkin, became ropy with swollen sinews.

"Perry!" his aunt pleaded softly. "Not a word, dear!"

In shaky haste she tinkled a silver bell. Two Negresses entered with trays, one to clear soiled dishes away, the other to replace them with lemon cream pie. Camilla, gazing down at a patch of embroidery on the tablecloth, struggled to think of some graceful digression. She was about to compliment the pie in the effusive way dear to ladies with nothing better to say when Dr. Springfield coughed and then spoke out.

"Justice *is* thwarted in Texas. Young Allan's entirely right about that. And liberty's in the gravest danger."

The others, except James, turned to him gratefully, glad to have him take off Perry the burden of defending Texas.

"What are the injustices?" The doctor scanned the faces around the table, then took a fork to his pie. "The Mexican authorities have outlawed immigration to keep us weak so they can deal with us as they like. They have levied imposts against all our imports, including the plain necessities, though they originally contracted not to. They invited us in to civilize a wilderness, to set up a barrier of fighting Americans between themselves and prairie savages who have raided them at will; and now that we are succeeding where the Spanish failed for two centuries, they deny us any right to govern ourselves. For two years they imprisoned Stephen F. Austin, our founder, the dearest friend to us all, never allowing him a trial, though he had gone to their capital on a mission of peace. There you have a few of their outrages to justice."

While his voice remained cool and mollifying, it hid an eloquence which, Camilla saw, was charming the rage out of Perry and the rancor from James. He had on his side the persuasive authority of knowledge at first hand.

"And what are the threats to liberty? We learned a lesson this spring from Santa Anna's campaign in Zacatecas. The Liberal party controlling that state had insisted upon the rights enshrined in the Constitution of 1824. His answer? He threw his armies upon them in a campaign of butchery, fire, pillage, and rapine unmatched in modern times.

"After the manner of tyrants, he rules less by law than by arbitrary decision, by decree, by caprice, by whim, and always with regard first for his own advantage, for his own enrichment. Now he orders the garrisons strengthened in Texas, each a little at a time, until he can bleed away the gains of our labor at will or, if we resist, shoot us down as he did the citizens of Zacatecas. He orders us to give up all arms, except one man in every five hundred. Our rifles not only keep us free, mind you; they also provide us meat and defend our cabins against the savages. They give us surety, too, that ill-paid garrisons will not plunder us as they do simple folk throughout the rest of Mexico. Thus no other deprivation could more utterly blight our lives. Those are a few of the threats to liberty.

"So now we are at war." His glance around the table became strangely serene, like a flame enclosed in glass. "Santa Anna is known as the Napoleon of the West. Certainly he is the cruelest commander now living, and one of the most successful. His troops are numerous; ours are few. But a scattered people like ours, few of them concentrated in towns and all of them fighters, will be hard to conquer. If a few thousand valiant kinsmen from the U.S.A. come to help us, I venture we'll turn him back."

Camilla felt an impetuous wish to respond with all her strength. In the doctor's account she suspected every bias a patriot could inject. She longed nevertheless to be a man so that she could volunteer.

"Well," said Perry thickly, "I'll help you for one."

A hush followed. Susan gazed at him, stupefied. Camilla blinked once, as if a jaggle of lightning had flashed beyond the windows, and then the inferences began rushing together within her: Perry going to *war!* A spasm tightened her back as if tardy thunder had come bellowing and bumping and thumping down around the house.

"In fact," he added, "I've already been measured for uniforms. I'll be ready shortly."

"If that's so," said the doctor, "why not come with us? We sail on the *Golden Eagle* three days hence. We'd be enormously pleased if you would, eh, Leticia? And we might be of use to you once we reach Texas."

"Wellsir, I think I can manage."

His aunt found her voice at last, a feeble, stricken voice. "What? Perry, you wouldn't! Surely you wouldn't!"

"Yes, aunt, I'm going. I meant to tell you today, anyhow tonight, but—"

"No, Perry," she wailed. "No!"

Going to her side, he patted her shoulder and attempted to reason her tears away. But she could not make him withdraw what he had said; therefore she would not be comforted.

"Gentlemen," said James, rising, "perhaps the study—shall we have coffee and cigars?"

After the men left, Camilla moved over beside Susan, who continued sobbing into her napkin. Leticia sat remorsefully where she was.

"Come, honey, you mustn't take on so," Camilla pleaded.

"But how can I ever bear it, him going?" Susan's eyes were red and wet and puffy, her nose too. "And to war, Camilla! To war!"

"Oh, that war's nothing but talk, Sue, I'll wager anything; a lot of penny firecrackers hurting nobody. Every now and then men have to talk like that to show they're men."

"But you saw yourself how determined he is. And with so few in Texas against so many it's so mortally foolish! Camilla, *you* make him stay."

"But I couldn't, Sue. He—"

"Of course you could! He adores you, don't you see?"

"Why, not in the least."

"Oh, but he does! He pretends it's all fun, but his heart aches for you. He'll do anything you ask."

"No, he won't. I've been fool enough to abuse him, and anyhow—"

"Milla, I'm sure he will, and so are you."

"No, I don't think so at all."

And she didn't, even though hearing the contrary did please her. With Susan so devastated, however, she had to offer something that might calm her.

"But we'll see, dearest. We'll see."

It surprised Perry how velvety and gracious Camilla had become when she called him from the study to leave for the theater. As they were starting early, she instructed Esau to drive around a bit. She rode beside Perry in calm and lacy loveliness, swaying a little to the motion of the brougham. Around her floated a Parisian scent rather like gardenia, but more musky, more insinuating, more beckoning, and her shoulder inclined his way.

She was softly melodic in saying, "Why so quiet, Perry?"

Through the glass on his side he watched pedestrians sauntering along under the street lamps of the Vieux Carré. A few turned in admiration as Oriole and Swallow flew by. Most simply drifted.

"Perry."

"Hm?"

"I asked you something: why so quiet?"

"Wel-ll, sometimes seeing things clear leaves a man speechless."

"O-o-oh?" The syllable lingered between her rounded lips until humor glistened over it like moonshine on a bubble. "Dear me! You do see everything clear now, do you?"

"Not everything, no."

"That's fine. I'd hate to find you that much like James." She smoothed one lacy white glove up her arm, and a splash of light from the carriage lamp by her window curved into the indentation her hands had left in her lap. "He was trying to be nice when we left. You must have patched things up."

"With caustic plasters, yes."

"I see." And after a pause: "Bright as you both are, you two ought to be able to get over this ouchiness."

"Yes, it's shameful, and I *am* ashamed of it. Somehow that hasn't helped much."

"He's so well meaning, James is."

"Uhm. Still, that too makes it very little easier to like him. We simply go from bad to worse. I'll be leaving none too soon."

Her gloved hands straightened her kerchief across her lap, implying a fidgety desire to straighten *him* out. Esau turned Swallow and Oriole onto the Esplanade, wider, darker than any other street they had come upon thus far, and more sedate too. Still, those hands of hers remained restive, and he wondered what tactic she would try next.

"The Springfields are pleasant company, aren't they?"

"Very," he agreed.

"The doctor—a fine person, so wise and kind."

"Yes. No bigger than a pint of cider, but a man it'll do to tie to."

"The girl's nice too."

"Uhm. She's that, and a great deal more."

Camilla's silence hinted that she thought his agreement a bit too hearty. However, he let it stand, watching three somber old trees approach and pass through the dark on his side.

"Susan calls her wholesome," Camilla proceeded on a note of silken condescension, "and she is."

"Wholesome?" He grimaced. "So's corn mush."

Camilla's head went back against the seat while soaring laughter shook her limp. She sobered, however, before she spoke again.

"Anyhow, you'll have to agree she's sweet, a very sweet and simple girl."

"Hm! Too much sweet sours a man's stomach."

Again her laugh was so gay that he began to feel guilty over being clever at the expense of someone he liked well. "I honestly think she deserves much better than *sweet* and *wholesome* and *simple,* don't you? This old world of ours would be a thundering sight better if it had in it thousands more like Leticia. Her being a Texian puts Texas in a right favorable light, even when she talks it down."

"Yes, she's a sensible thing. Attractive too—in a country way. She's developing what you fanciers of horseflesh would call 'a dern promissun conformation.' "

Perry conceded a chuckle, whereas Camilla kept her expression under as firm control as if all she had been saying had no more acid in it than a recipe for tarts.

"In fact, I imagine farm boys make quite a fuss over her."

"Uhm. Her features, I notice, resemble her daddy's."

"Yes. She'd have done better to take after her mother, a stunning beauty . . . though a Mexican."

Her hesitation expected him to be astonished. He was.

"Mexican?"

"Born and bred in Veracruz."

"And yet Leticia's so fair!"

"The mother equally so—a great rarity down there. Looked simply angelic." She drew her kerchief wide by the corners. "She came here with a troupe of players."

"No! Dr. Springfield's wife?"

"Before they were married, of course. In those days she was billed as 'the Angel of Veracruz,' though for no deeper reason, I gather, than because of her golden hair."

He pondered that awhile, and her strategy likewise. Angling a glance her way, he grinned in silence. She was so calmly urbane, so gracefully poisonous, so sure of her skill.

"But a little sage like him! Who'd ever suppose he'd take up with an actress—or interest one?"

"Well, her health, you know. Her lungs."

"Oh?"

"Yes, and his treatments did improve her greatly. In fact she seemed wonderfully well when Leticia was small. After a pair of twin boys came, however, she began to fail. So in twenty-nine or thirty, I believe it was, they packed off to Texas for better air and a fresh start. The climate *is* better, yet she evidently had sunk too far before she left: the poor thing died in spite of everything. That was four years ago, more or less."

Perry, during these casual and leisurely phrases, also heard the iron of her mares' hooves clattering over the stones of the Esplanade. The vitality of Camilla's presence gave the tragedy she delineated an unintended starkness. In his mind the death of that other beauty who had turned into a farm woman became analogous to the death of thousands, and pathetic in proportion.

The thought expanded as he observed a wall ahead of them, the end of the Esplanade, and in that wall a grilled iron gate which he recognized as the entrance to the Holy Field, the cemetery. Here Esau, having drawn the mares down to a prance, swerved over close to the gate, so that he could turn. Through the grille of iron Perry saw rows of tombs extending through the dark as far as darkness would let vision go. The damps of evening turned the tombs a lighter, more spectral gray, under which they seemed heaps of moist and moldering bones. A dread of ancient loneliness passed over him, of dark beyond the end of night, of oblivion where his father had gone, his mother too, and innumerable millions more.

"Four years ago!" As the brougham completed its turn and surged away, leaving the cemetery behind, he took off his hat and let it hang from one hand across his thigh. "That long ago I hardly knew what trouble was."

"Yes. Gracious heaven, how things can change in just four years!"

"Where you suppose we'll be four years from now, Milla?"

"Wel-ll, I haven't a notion. And you?"

"Depends on the war, I suppose."

"Perry, I've been itching to say to you: forget that silly war. You shouldn't even think of going, at any rate not now. You'd break poor Susan's heart if you went." She twisted around to face him, erect and intent. "Don't you realize, Perry? For years, with her own boy taken from her so young, she's been aching for a son to love. Whether you deserve it or not, she loves the air you breathe, the ground you walk on, and she'd pretty near die if you went frisking off to war."

"Well, I think the world of her too, but it's time I did something worth doing. What Uncle James says about me is pretty largely true: I haven't done anything yet that amounts to a tinker's damn."

"Except graduate *magna cum laude* in law, win gracious knows how many prizes for riding in shows, for running footraces too, besides others for debating, writing essays, and so on. You've also improved the land on Allan Manor. You think I don't know? Your family, your whole blood connection, is terribly proud of you, Perry, and has been a great many years."

"But for nothing of any value or interest to anybody else. In Texas, with American settlement growing so fast and promising so well and now needing help so bad, I might do something there of real account."

"Perry Allan, you stop thinking only about Texas! We need ability here too, here in New Orleans. Don't you understand yet what wonderful scope this town offers a bright young lawyer? It's the greatest American port south of Baltimore, and always will be. The key to the entire West is right here: this is the gateway between the West and the World. Every part of the West depends on it. And here—"

"Milla, you've told me this before. Your father's told me too. Uncle James's told me innumerable times. Who in thunder hasn't told me? The most eloquent politicians in Louisiana are always telling everybody. However—"

"Sh-h!" She reached over to press gloved fingers lightly against his mouth. "You don't have to raise your voice so. And please let me finish. What I meant to point out was that, here, you could put yourself in position to influence the growth of the whole West, not just this or that part. Here you can affect the entire forest, so to say, in which Texas is only one tree."

"Some tree! It's one I mean to have a look at directly."

"But, Perry, you don't have to be so precipitous about going. Nearly as long as I can remember we've heard alarums every few years about war in Texas—which always turned out to be words, words, words. Those Texians are terribly pugnacious talkers, and not much else."

"If the substantiality here didn't think this is the real showdown, however, they wouldn't be contributing any sum like ten thousand dollars. Anyhow, I'm convinced that I can't be just a lawyer and nothing else. Why did the Lord give me this hardy constitution unless to use it? Out in Texas I can develop a tract of land without any very large investment while also using law to help civilize that wild territory into a decent place where free institutions can thrive."

"Oh, fiddlesticks! What is there in any of that that you can't do right here? Free institutions aren't thriving any too well here yet, and Louisiana is far from being altogether decent. Certainly it isn't half civilized, not one-fourth. Pretty much of it, New Orleans not excepted, is barbaric, lazy, sinful, showy, and foolish. As for farming, most that's done here ought to be done ever so much better, and that's the truth.

"Say, Perry! That gives me a thought." She pressed a hand firmly on his forearm. "The Faucaults!" The enchantments of fresh vision enlarged her eyes. "Why hadn't I thought of the Faucaults before? They for months now have talked of taking their children to Paris for a year or two of schooling if only they can put their plantation under a manager who knows land well. You can handle it fine, Perry. They'll compensate you well, and as the crops allow, let you begin building a bit of legal practice too. I'm sure they will."

He took a breath to demur, whereupon she turned still more directly toward him and rushed on.

"It's a few miles this way from Palmer Hall, which I've been wanting to show you anyhow. We'd pretty nearly be neighbors!"

"You see, Milla, I've already—"

"Hush, will you? There's no good reason why other things can't wait at least long enough for a talk with the Faucaults." She drew his hand into both of hers.

"Tomorrow, Perry, we'll steamboat up to Palmer Hall, take the mares too, and ride from there to Faucaults'. Other days we'll ride through all the countryside, and you'll see that living here is better than you think."

The contrast between the energy of her purpose and the exquisite harmonies of her face, scent, and clothes became so marked that he had to smile.

"We'll take Pa too, naturally. Also Yvonne Hanotaux if he agrees. I'll get us invitations to all the hunts and balls and parties, and we'll just have the best time ever. Perry, what do you say?"

She tugged at his hand, still tight in both of hers. Her lips parted as she waited for his consent. A fan of light waved across them as the speeding carriage swayed, illuminating their ardent curve.

"I'd like so well to go, Milla, only the situation won't allow it. Last night a friend of your father's, a Mr. Bryan, pledged a big donation of weapons to the men actually fighting and wants them delivered the first day possible. I've said I'd—"

"But, Perry, you don't have to go yourself, for heaven's sake! Dear goodness knows this town is full of footloose adventurers who've got nothing better to do. Why should you sacrifice your whole future just for that?"

"What future do I have to sacrifice? That's so exactly what's wrong with me: I won't have any future worth the name till I make myself one."

"All right, do make yourself one, but make it *here*. Here you have kin and friends to help you, people who really care about you and what becomes of you."

"That's so, but it's time now to find out what I can do without any such help. The matter's settled, Milla. I have agreed to go, and now I've got to."

His finality visibly offended her. Her face went blank. Drawing firmly away, she sat back in her corner, arms together, as if the bland air had turned cold.

"In fact, I've been busy all day rounding up supplies, arranging things." By a fractional laugh he made light of it all. "On most any journey, getting started is the hardest part, so after a manner of speaking I'm halfway there."

"You mean you just . . . ?" Her voice broke. For one alarming moment, because of the way she blinked, he feared she was about to cry. Instead she fiercely cleared her throat. "So you just went ahead, did you, and bound yourself to go without the least concern what Susan or anybody else might think about it?"

"Now it wasn't like that, really. I meant to tell her right soon, but—"

"Perry, I don't think you really care *who* cares about you or what they think. Why else would you just be so brutally obstinate about it? Gracious me!"

"I'm not just being obstinate, or brutal either one. I'm merely—"

"And do lower your voice, please. Anyone would think I was on yonder side of some plowed field. If you can't talk in moderate and mannerly and sensible tones, don't talk at all."

"Gladly!" he barked, and in considerable volume.

He clapped on his hat, sat back in *his* corner, and gave undivided attention to the scene along that side.

At some point, unobserved by himself, they had turned off the Esplanade into a narrower, busier street which he was slow to recognize. She meanwhile rearranged her gloves, plucked and tugged her gown to give it the airy grace it had shown before, and aloofly adopted the air of a lady of fashion out riding alone.

4

Nearer the Opera House, Esau became trapped behind a slow queue of carriages. Swallow and Oriole, hot from their run, took this restraint at a head-tossing prance. The shouts of drivers, the cheery calls of pedestrians reverberating along the street, and the clatter of shod hooves aggravated the team's passion for speed. Their impatience infected Camilla, who leaned forward to survey the hurrying press of people.

"Wonderful attendance tonight," she observed, still without a glance at Perry.

"Late, aren't we?"

"Perhaps a little."

But the brougham had to stop. They then were by the Rue Toulouse, a cross street near the Opera House. All the vehicles forward were choked together, discharging passengers. Swallow began weaving between her traces, showing inclinations to rear. Oriole, with one anxious hoof, mauled the cobbles like a stonebreaker.

Perry opened the front glass. "Better turn on Toulouse, Esau. They're a little too frisky."

"I'n holdum, sah. I gottum good."

"No, make the turn. Pull up behind yonder coach-and-four. That'll do."

"Why, ye-es," Camilla musically agreed. "Notice the arms on the door? I believe it's Colonel d'Espinosa's." And as they drew nearer: "Yes, it *is* the colonel's. Beautiful conveyance, isn't it?"

"Uhm."

"Had it here last winter and must have left it. I hear he sailed in this morning on a brig from Tampico."

"Wonder why. What's he up to?"

"Pardon?"

"His coming seems right opportune, take it all in all."

"I don't understand."

"He's in mighty good time to spy on the work for Texas."

"Perry, how preposterous! I've no doubt he's here to buy supplies for their army, same as before."

"Maybe. He could also have come for darker reasons."

"Why, Colonel d'Espinosa's one of the Liberals who helped overthrow Bustamente. If the Texians are Liberals too, as they claim, he certainly won't be spying on them."

Perry was tempted to remark that, as Santa Anna himself had led the crusade against Bustamente under Liberal banners and since then had become more tyrannical than his enemy, ambitious followers would likely change their colors to suit his. Shy of any more fussing, however, he let the thought pass.

At the moment the colonel was assisting three aging ladies from a carriage blocking his coach, a self-serving courtesy because his team could not proceed until theirs did. He was not in uniform. Imperially slender and tall, with a spidery waist, he wore a black cutaway offset by white silk pantaloons, and lace bloomed from his cuffs like white lilac. To his rear was an aide who emphasized his elegance by antithesis, being short, thick, clay-faced, and indifferently dressed. He it was who noticed Camilla as Perry handed her down from her brougham. A whisper from him brought the colonel impetuously from the old ladies, leaving the last to toil from their carriage as best she might.

"So-o, la Señorita Palmer!" He brought his hat over his heart, and his teeth shone a smiling white under a hummingbird's wing of mustache. "What fortune! Char-r-ming!"

Seizing her gloved hand, he kissed it audibly. His hair showed thin on top when he bowed, and his face looked more time-worn than at a distance, a face echoing no more than the final refrain of lyric youth. For all that, he was exceptionally handsome. His lips in repose were a slack classic bow beneath his mustache, his nose a scimitar, his ears small and almost lost in curls obviously turned on heated irons.

Still clinging to Camilla's hand, he was saying, "Ah, señorita, this is such pleasure. I am so lucky, as you Americans say!"

The stress the fellow put upon *señorita* annoyed Perry like an elbow in the ribs. That she was a widow he certainly knew, yet acted as if he could not think of her otherwise than as an untouched maid. In return she became unnaturally arch, after the habit of ladies enchanted by foreign gallantries.

"We've missed you, colonel. You've been gone so long."

"Ah, and my ship she was so slow, my soul flew on before . . ." A sweeping flutter of a lace-fringed hand suggested a dove in passage. "To your window it soared, señorita, and brought to me such visions so beautiful."

To Perry's ears this sounded all the more asinine because he pronounced *such* as *sawch, visions* as *veesions, ship* as *sheep,* and so on. To hear the colonel talk of peeping into her window, one would think he expected her to consider that "char-r-ming"; and, incredibly, she did appear to.

Of course, like the colonel, she was "putting on." She was doing so, Perry understood, for his instruction as well as to please the colonel: she could do without Perry quite well, her coquetry was saying, whether he went or stayed. Boiling, he turned aside to help Esau maneuver the mares into the clear from behind D'Espinosa's coach, but she tugged at his arm to introduce him.

"Colonel d'Espinosa, may I present a friend from Maryland, Mr. Perry Allan."

The colonel, his smile going metallic, tolerated him enough to accept his hand. "So happy to . . ."

The phrase died in his throat as Perry's grip gathered force. The colonel's knuckles popped together, and a catch of breath hissed through his teeth.

"Polite report has already introduced you so well, colonel," Perry intoned in the high manner, "that I feel we have met before."

The colonel's hand, free at last, writhed feebly. He stuffed it inside his coat like a newly shot quail. "Never! If we had met, I could never forget *un hombre* so strong." Under the blades of his mustache, his disdain issued rapier sharp. "Strong as a neegar, *verdamente*. Around my haciendas I have no peon with hands so strong like yours."

Perry kept something resembling a smile decorating his face. "Well, colonel, that tells us right much about you, doesn't it?—since no true gentleman would test by hand the weakness of his servants."

The colonel stiffened as if a currycomb had grated down his spine. Without waiting for a reply, Perry turned back to help with the mares.

Both were fretting hotly. D'Espinosa's coach had started to back up, crowding them. Esau pulled their jaws asunder, until the brougham rocked against the team behind. At an outraged yell from that driver, Esau's eyeballs whitened. He snapped a rein on Swallow's rump to urge her forward again, after which he had to pull her back tighter. She reared, and Perry strode in to pull her down.

In the glow from a streetlight the foam dropping from her mouth showed red. "Esau, why'd you check this mare?"

"Yessah, I done loosed it one notch, sah."

"But you were to take it *off!*"

Camilla kept struggling through all this to maintain a sociable bonhomie. "Ever so good to see you, colonel." She waved a glove a little by way of urging him toward the Opera House. "Stop by at my box if you like."

"But most certainly, señorita."

"There'll be a chair for you, be sure."

"Ah, *muy bien! Muchas gracias, señorita.*"

What lacquered grimaces accompanied this Perry could picture. He could not look, however, because Swallow, further excited by his yells at Esau, had reared again. A forehoof slipped over her neckyoke, hung there, and threw her against Oriole as she floundered down. Both mares became as frantic as two cats in a gunny sack.

Perry, lunging in between their heads, had his hat knocked off, but ignored that to fasten a double grip on Swallow, half of it through her mouth in the toothless middle portion of the lower jaw, the other on the end of her upper lip, the one bit of flesh by which all the rest was easiest to subdue. That fist crushingly tightened. Her tendons began to loosen, and in a few moments she stood like a pointer.

"Señor," the colonel protested, "you hurt *esta yegua!*" The situation was attracting stares from other theatergoers hurrying along the banquette, and this encouraged his protective sentiments. "Señorita Palmer, this peon is cruel to your horse so beautiful!"

"No, he's gentling her, don't you see? Really," she continued anxiously, "there's no need waiting, colonel. We'll see you during the play."

Still wringing Swallow's upper lip in his right fist, Perry kneed up the neckyoke, unsnapped it to release her hoof, and reached around to unfasten the checkrein. He then removed it and the cruelly thin checkbit that cut her mouth.

The colonel pointed at her lips. "But her he does hurt, señorita! She bleeds. Her mouth bleeds, *no lo ve?*"

"No-no! It's only the bit. *Hasta luego, Señor Coronel! Hasta la vista!*"

"In short," Perry abbreviated in a flat, hard tone across a shoulder, "git!"

Swallow, with her mouth relieved, bobbed her nostrils at him, smearing pink slobbers on his shirt and coat. His hat was in the street, his hair rumpled, his cream pantaloons stained, and he in a mood to crack her fool skull. Instead, he gave her a rough pat.

Half a minute had been needed by the colonel to reach full anger over Perry's "git." He snapped his heels together, head lofty and lips ready for the duelist's honed retort—which he forgot as Perry squared around, looping the rein into a whip.

"Mrs. Palmer asked you to leave," he pointed out. "Why don't you?"

The colonel might bravely face pistols, rapiers, sabers, or bayonets, but a leather strap in such hands was less his style. He retreated in the wake of his aide, who had anticipated him by several lengths. A half-dozen strides, and he checked himself long enough to shake his hat aloft and shout a threat in Spanish.

Perry ignored this while throwing the rein, bit and all, onto the dickey. "Now you damned rascal," he barked at Esau, *"keep it off!"*

"Ye-yassah."

Perry recovered his hat. The crown was smashed and the brim torn by a calked horseshoe; he tossed it aside. His hands, coat, and ruffles were smeared with lathered sweat and bloody slobbers. After handkerchiefing off the worst, he still looked something less than ready for the theater.

"Milla, I've got to leave." He strained hard to keep his voice level. "These clothes won't do."

"But I can't go in alone!"

"Wouldn't that be better than—?"

"I simply can't, you know that. Why, it would be the jest of the town."

"If you'd rather come home—"

"And miss the performance? How *very* considerate!"

"Then call that infernal gelding back," he yelled, "and let *him* squire you in!"

Two couples tittered in passing. Perry, jabbing his handkerchief at himself here and there, made a decision. The D'Espinosa coach had pulled away. With a grip on her arm no struggle could break, he forced her into the brougham, climbed in behind her, and ordered Esau to drive home.

Esau held the team down to a skittish trot. Perry struggled to calm himself, frowning through his window at structures showing as massive black rectangles animated by squares of peaceable light. Camilla breathed hard over a study of similar geometry beyond her side. When they pulled into her drive she moved to fling out the door opposite him. He caught her arm.

"Milla—"

"Let go!" Quills of indignation bristled over her.

He kept his hold. "Just one last thing. I won't be seeing you, perhaps ever again, but I can't leave without telling you—"

"You needn't tell me anything . . . *peon!* Just leave. And don't come back."

He kept her arm, his voice achingly earnest. "Not once did I ever suppose we'd part like this. Throughout these last four weeks, Milla . . . *here,* for me, the world has had its center. Here with you. No matter how far away this war takes me, I'll not forget that truth. Here I felt blessed."

The rigidity slackened from her arm. He released it, noting how the glow from the carriage lamps delicately defined the quieting rise and fall of her breast.

"Perhaps in this war I can do something—think things out. Well, unless it puts me onto a better course, Milla, I'll—as you say—not come back. But if it does, and soon enough, nothing will stop me."

After another silence he climbed out. She accepted his hand in stepping down to the drive. The night was sulky and black, but parallels of curtained light extended across the courtyard from windows along one side. Palm fronds reached out of the dark to finger that light. A hush whispered from the house until the slaves determined who emerged from the carriage, whereupon a virtuously busy clatter revived in the kitchen.

He followed her to the vestibule. A whale-oil lamp near the door held aloft an immobile flame. A suit of armor beside it pointed its empty, visored stare at him as he stopped there, about to leave. A hush surrounded them, an emptiness as complete as that in the armor, a void before which both groped for something to say.

Camilla's lips parted, but her breath sighed away unused. Rank though the smell of horse was on himself, he could detect through it the gardenia quality of her perfume. He longed for some memorable and revealing phrase, some final honesty that ever after would hold a part of her for himself alone. She pulled off her gloves, eyes lambent in expectation of that phrase, but he could think of nothing. At last he drew up her hand tenderly and bowed to press his lips against it.

"So-o . . . farewell."

Her eyes searched his. One corner of her mouth trembled. Her hand locked on his with astonishing power. She kissed him hastily, awkwardly.

"Good-by," she whispered.

Breaking free, she hurried to the stairway. She never paused, never turned, never glanced back. Higher and higher up the stairs her hasty slippers flickered. The hem of her skirt disappeared, the slippers too. The armor beside Perry stared at him vacantly as he drifted outdoors.

He found the street quiet. Sulky drops of rain were darkening the banquettes. Hatless and reeking of horse, rain spitting on him unregarded, he stood gazing without armor of his own into the larger void of night until the habit of action began propelling him away.

From C. B.'s Journal
October 18, 1835

At the wharves this morning we made an affable party: we joshed as people do when seeing a soldier off and trying to disbelieve that they may see him no more. Susan and James were there, Yvonne too, but not that person everybody but me expected, not Camilla.

What ails her I think I know. Though she's a chaste girl ever (or, anyhow, gun-shy), she began pretty early to want Perry to want her more and more. Even so, instinct must have cautioned her that, until he discovers a course he can follow with enthusiasm, he will remain too restless to take her with him all the way to the end of life. Since nothing less would do for her, she slammed the door on him.

However, she neglected to turn the key. Any footstep or voice similar to his arrests her like a grip on the shoulder, and this morning she asked me to take along a package, a remembrance, a souvenir, which Leticia is to give him after they reach Texas. There is future in her thinking, that's plain.

It may not turn out to be the future she expects. That Leticia! One of these days she is going to become quite a woman, and lucky the man who helps her so become. The clothes she wears are not much more ornamental than snowy sheets on a featherbed, and the contours underneath as simply, purely guarantee sensual comfort. She is shaped for embraces, for bringing a strong man down and children up. That mouth of hers is more inviting than a chalice of claret, and her eyes, generous and feeling and considerate, are the blue of skies blown clean by western winds. Already they stray after Perry, weakly hankering. Watching her around him calls to mind how concordant things in nature sometimes are—how suited is the blossom for the assault of the bee, how adapted the throat of the doe to the fangs of the cougar, how inviting the voluptuous summer maple to the blast of lightning. Were I in his place, voyaging all that way with her—Jesus save me!

Accompanying him are seven volunteers he recruited, all captivated by the promise of "liberal bounties of land." Not one ever has been near a war, but all have agreed to drill with him a spell every living day on shipboard or off. They ought to do as a guard for Wm. Bryan's weapons.

How I envy them all! In Jefferson's phrase, "Opposition to tyranny is service to God," and men generally live better after they risk their lives in a worthy cause. War for freedom is adventure, *the* grand adventure. Travel and change are healers, *the* great healers of injured affections. Texas is promise, *the* bright promise of our time.

What Kentucky, Ohio, and Tennessee were to men presently advanced in life, Texas is to generations now rising. It guarantees a golden sunset. It's the poor man's dream, the rainbow's end. It offers a bountiful home to the disinherited, scope to the ambitious, opportunities without limit to the enterprising, compensation to the heretofore cheated, sanctuary to the pursued, a new stake to the debtor, fresh victims for the scoundrel. Whoever fights to free it stands to gain handsomely, and should.

Perry is likely to show well there in war and peace alike. Such descendants of the Cavaliers who settled Maryland, Virginia, and the Carolinas are taught during boyhood, as Herodotus says those Persians were who conquered the world, to ride well, shoot straight, and speak the truth. Perry, however, is equally the descendant of lowly Americans who train their young to work hard, apply tools cannily, and help their neighbors, a still more conquering formula. As he journeys into Texas, we in this household will await the consequences with the very liveliest interest.

CHAPTER III

I

Springfields' Homestead
Friday Afternoon
November 6, 1835

Through the kitchen door Leticia could hear faintly from a field behind the cabin the burr and catch of talk as the men raced to finish cutting corn before evening, her young brothers too. This was the volunteers' next to last day. Perry would spend tomorrow away, looking at land he might homestead, and all would leave for war the next morning.

"Dear me, Edna," she remarked to the housekeeper, who was tying a cloth over a pail of buttermilk for the harvesters, "how dull the place will be when they all go! I just hate to think about it."

"Nein, liebchen. Don't sink." As Mrs. Bauernschmidt's head wagged, a wobble of flesh beneath her chin underscored the weight of her views. "You got to be cholly. Who likes a rose ven it's vilting yet?"

Leticia conceded an unequal smile. "Though I'm no rose, gracious knows."

"Today ven you gif him puttermeelk, don't chuss stand looking at sa ground. Talk cholly."

Familiar though her accent was in this kitchen, the advice it so often expressed seemed to Leticia, since coming home from New Orleans, peculiarly vulgar. Edna and her husband Otto for years had been the mainstays of the household, with Edna in the role of substitute mother ever since the Springfield children lost theirs. Because nothing but further talk and hurt feelings ever came of disputing her bossy wisdom, Leticia detached herself from it by turning away to tie on a bonnet before a mirror over the washstand.

"He's easy enough to talk with when we're alone. But, others around, it's hard to think of one word, much less be gay about it."

"Anyhow, *look* at him cholly. Like so, you see?"

Edna put on a demure, humorless, absolutely awful grimace of joy. Under her Teutonic code woman's duty was to believe in God and

53

Martin Luther, hook a good hard-working man no matter how, work for him, obey him, bear him children if possible in proof of that obedience, and train all daughters and granddaughters in an identical sense of duty. The only flaw was that she never had managed to bear children of her own, so it was to Leticia that she willed her views.

"A man got no sense, *liebchen*. You vant him, you got to show it. Vishing," she concluded under sure brows, "don't fill no empty kettle yet."

Leticia winced at this way of talking, and forgave it too. "My conscience hurts me, there's one trouble." While staring at her own eyes in the mirror, she marveled how much more innocent she looked on the outside than she felt within. "It's not easy to be jolly on a bad conscience."

"A vut?"

Edna's shocked gape plainly asked if she meant she had "lost her virtue."

"No-no-no!" Leticia shook her head, not without amusement. "It's nothing dreadful, nothing I've done. Instead, it . . ." She heaved a woebegone sigh. "It's what I've left undone."

Not wanting to talk about it more, at least not just now, she took up three drinking gourds, a pot of cookies, and the pail of buttermilk, about to leave. Edna, however, stepped around before her, supposing she (like a watchful mother) must pry loose any dangerous secret.

"Undone?"

"Oh, dear me!"

"Liebchen, was gibt?"

Leticia looked away through the back door in desperation. To make Edna understand what was wrong would take ever so long, and never fully succeed. The morning she embarked from New Orleans, Mrs. Palmer's father had brought her a package with a note from Mrs. Palmer asking in the most winning words that she keep it for Perry until after they reached Texas. Not yet had she delivered it, afraid of it, afraid it would spoil the tender friendship their travels had nurtured, afraid it was given her for exactly that purpose. But how could she explain all this to Edna? She deplored her own weakness in mentioning it in the first place.

"It's only that I should have given him something and didn't." Having both hands anchored by vessels of cookies and buttermilk, she tipped her head sideward. "Now let me by, Edna."

"Gif him vut?"

"No, we might talk about it another time, not now. Those poor men, they should have refreshment now or it might spoil their supper."

She resolutely pushed by. All the way across the yard she was conscious that Edna kept watching her from the door. No doubt the good soul for weeks would be scanning her waist for signs of sin.

2

When the last of the corn was cut, suppertime was still an hour away, and so the volunteers set off for a dip in a brook hidden by woods below the cabin. Near where their path skirted the barn, Leticia was settling down beside a cow to milk.

"Oh-uh, Perry!" she called.

Her falter gave everyone to understand that he was to join her alone. Clubbing a folded towel against his thigh, he sauntered her way while the rest held to the path with no comment other than a communicative roll of the eyeballs.

She buried the crown of her bonnet in the cow's flank and kept it so even though he scuffed his boots through the grass as he approached her. By her milk stool lay a rectangular package as festive as Christmas. He wondered at seeing such an object there; but it was by her off side, evidently reserved for notice later.

"Gentle cow," he began and bent to examine the ground between his heels while sitting down.

"Very!" She turned him an overwrought smile. "You tired? *Tiene mucho consado, verdad?"*

Lessons in Spanish, her mother's tongue, had been a source of companionship to them, an excuse for being together awhile each day. Already he could manage simple conversation, but felt too slack this evening for much talk of any kind.

"Poco-poco, señorita."

He and his comrades, ever since arriving at this homestead, had worked hard daily for Dr. Springfield in return for a loan of mules to pack their gear on west to the army. Fodder had galled his palms, wrists, and neck, and a sweaty rankness nestled inside his shirt like a pet skunk. These discomforts, reminders of work well done, merely stimulated a sense of effective existence. Stretching out his legs toward the cow's head, he propped his weight on one elbow.

"This time of day, it's good to be tired if you've made a showing by it."

"Yes." And after milking a bit: "It's possible to be both tired and happy." A smile pulled at her lip. "At any rate, it's seldom work that makes us *un*happy."

The air, motionless for evening, was loaded with feminine scent. Emanations from the passive, bellied, uddery cow, from her warm milk too, and from Leticia's much laundered person blended into one female aroma welcome to his nose. This helped him to conclude that questions of happiness were, on the whole, a feminine preoccupation. He grunted in agreement, but was too comfortable, lounging there with an elbow deep in sweet grass, to go into that subject further.

Milk sudsed in her bucket under the force of her grip, and yet kept going nervously out of rhythm. He eyed her aslant. Her back looked unnaturally rigid, her arms tense, and he could detect not one clue to the reason.

Everything else was the reverse: the cow sleepily engrossed in her cud, the air tranquil, the sun a balloon of fire low in the west. Its glow burned across rolling reaches of prairie in the uplands, and peace had spread as widely as its light. A file of ducks from the brook waddled up a slope toward the chickenhouse, around which hens and cocks were converging. In a breeding pen by the barn the doctor's stud jack had ears the length of yucca leaves pointing in mute loneliness toward the tinkle of grazing bells on mares and mules at pasture far around the slope.

Leticia all this while seemed to Perry remarkably slow about revealing why she had called him. Still, he would do nothing to hurry her. Simply to be here near her was full of interest, silent or not. Unquiet contractions of her lips this evening added to his impression of them as hurtable, bitable lips. Under the poke of her bonnet her profile looked no more sophisticated than an oatmeal cookie, and yet it had become more attractive day on day because of some feminine appeal he had not been able to analyze, and because she herself was so unpretending, so anxious to please, so notably shaped to answer man's recurring wishes.

A whirl of thought spun him backward in time to a description he once had read about Marie Antoinette—about how, charmed by pastorales popular in her time, she played milkmaid around a tiny dairy of her own at Versailles, serving her courtiers milk in cups shaped on the mold of her own pretty breasts. He doubted, though, that the world ever would be so enriched by modish queens as by the likes of Leticia.

The prolongation of his scrutiny brought her glance toward him. Surprising on his face an intimate appreciation he was too absorbed to hide, she blinked rapidly, then returned to the topic he supposed was already out of their way. "Where under the sun did you learn to work so hard?"

"Home." Soundless laughter shook his chest. "At the limber end of my daddy's cane."

"No, it's *in* you to work. As Papa says, you work like steam. The others are mortally done in, trying to keep up."

"Oh, they worked very well."

"Deed they did, yes."

Agreement silenced them both. The jack, still flipping one ear toward the liquid tinkling of bells beyond the hill, began to pace the circumference of his pen, treading round and round as if to draw something near by a winch. In the process his sex became over evident, so Perry ceased watching him to observe a flight of blackbirds rise from the woods where his friends had disappeared. A shout down there was followed by another and another in random animality altered beyond recognition by a hill-borne vibrance of tone.

Summery evenings of his boyhood came to mind, evenings when he and his brother Rockford, lolling on an elm-grown sweep of lawn, watched twilight sow its mysteries over the bottomland below their home and listened in futile yearning to the shouts of roughnecks at play far below around the Allandale store. Up on the veranda, the cause of their being kept away from that rowdy chorus, sat their statuesque mother, firm in her opinions about how to turn her boys into gentlemen, and beside her their lanky, scowling, callused father, she gowned as lady of the manor, he in a white shirt topped by a black string tie, showing that he once had been a sport, but she had kept him under restraint year on year until he no longer seemed one bit more flighty than an oak.

Perry's breath hung a moment over thought that here in Texas, so far away, a tender girl so unlike his mother should be holding him away from "the boys" by some unmentioned need in herself fully as compelling as orders back home. How odd, too, that around Camilla, despite her inward force, he never once had felt tied—or could not remember that he had. Instead, she had endowed him with impressions of being freer than ever before, if only from ordinary views, ordinary restrictions, ordinary things. Restless, he pushed his weight up off his elbow to sit with fingers hooked around one knee.

"Prime weather to hunt land tomorrow."

"Fine, yes. But a change is overdue." With a wan smile fading to no expression at all: "A change for the worse."

"Well, after any change for the worse another's apt to follow—a change for the better."

"Pshaw, you wait a bit." She giggled in an unsteady alto. "First good stiff norther, and you'll wish to gracious heaven you were back in New Orleans!"

"Nome, not me. I know too well it can turn mighty cold in New Orleans, and in more than one sense."

"Speaking of New Orleans . . ." Her lips, though approximating a smile, went awry. "That reminds me!" She bent spastically for the package beside her. "Here, this is for you."

In handing it to him, she turned it topside up. He was startled to discover *Perry Knox Allan, Esq.,* inked across it in a strong, artful hand. Time and distance shriveled like burned paper; the ash blew away, and he was back in the moment and place where that hand had last pressed his.

"Remember at the wharf?" Leticia was saying in unnatural brightness. "Remember when her father came aboard to say good-by—Mrs. Palmer's father? He brought it."

"I see."

Perry tried to think of sociable noises that would ease them through these moments. But Leticia herself was the first to talk again.

"Her note to me said you were not to have it then, not until we reached Texas." She continued squeezing and stretching the cow's depleted teats, and so nervously that the cow walled one eye back her way. "Then you know how one forgets things somehow, and—but now you have it."

"Deeply obliged too, Leticia. Mighty good of you to trouble about it."

"Oh, no trouble whatsoever!"

"Of course it was." He put the package down on his off side, beyond her range of vision, where it might let him change the subject and escape. "Well, the day's about done. *Esta noche hace muy hermosa, verdad?*"

"But aren't you going to open it? How can you bear to have a present and not open it?"

Under his skin burned an embarrassment beyond his control. Which was worse he could not decide: for her to pry so or for him to neglect forestalling her curiosity before she bared it so nakedly. The queer thing, in her custody all this while, must have intrigued her as the box from Olympus did Pandora, and he could not be cruel enough to break away, leaving her unappeased. Bringing it around where everything would be under her eye in total candor, he broke the seal to pull off the wrapper.

Inside was a leather case surmounted by a letter to him, also in Camilla's hand. This he spirited into a hip pocket while fumbling at clasps on the case until it opened. There, in velvet compartments, lay a four-barreled pistol and its accessories—a bullet-mold, caps, patches, and a miniature ramrod.

Leticia commented feebly, "My, how nice."

Nice hardly fit it. Though beautifully turned, the pistol looked deadly as strychnine. By two hammers the top pair of barrels could be fired as quick as counting *one-two;* a twist of the muzzle then turned up the lower pair into position to fire equally fast. Here on the frontier, such a weapon would be a rarity with magical powers of protection and force. To the life, he could picture how luminous with thought Camilla must have become when she bought it.

"It's so nice," Leticia persisted. A tremor marred her voice. "But why didn't she have her father give it to *you?* After all, if you were to have it, why not straight off?"

Her suspicion of a stratagem poisonously concocted did not escape him. No matter how near accurate it might be, loyalty to Camilla required him to smile it away. His head dipped to suggest a complimentary bow. "No doubt she knew, being in such polite company all this while, I'd never need it till I leave here."

Leticia's shoulders drooped in pitying disgust at how little he understood women. Afterward her show of admiration revived. "A cunning thing, really. May I see?"

He passed it to her. She handled it as she might a locket with a treacherously scented curl concealed inside. Along the inner curve of the grip behind the triggers she discovered a line of engravure almost illegibly Gothicized.

"Oh—" she began in surprise but stifled further comment.

While her finger inched from word to word, and with him puckering across her elbow, she read in a whisper, " 'Guard Thy Heart Well.' "

Through a stunned silence, and with another flush burning his ears, he pried up his weight on one hand, then rocked to his feet. Sounds of life astir rode through the windless twilight, all abnormally clear —a gossipy twang of blackbirds at roost in the yard, a yelp from a hound dog kicked out of the kitchen, guffaws from bathers down in the woods, a silvery tinkling of mule bells, now frail with distance and, over, over, over again, the muted, yearning crunch of the jack's hooves as he paced his pen. Even the breath of the cow was audible as she grunted up another cheekful of cud.

Face averted, Leticia extended the pistol in Perry's direction. He returned it to its case without comment. She rose, pail in one hand, milk stool in the other. The portion of her cheek visible under her bonnet was spottily pale, her lips tortured, but not one consoling word occurred to him.

As their paralytic silence beside the cow prolonged, the jack shriveled his lips off his teeth to yawn in supreme boredom. A shake of the head, and he flung at the horizon a drawn, mournful honk, which changed into a cascade of sobs, gigantic and strangled. Multiplying from hill to hill, they pursued and rollicked with one another, these sobs, until they had more the sound of hilarity than grief. Perry could not help being amused and supposed Leticia would accept its medicine too.

Instead, she began climbing the slope toward the cabin, shoulder unnaturally weak to the pull of her milk bucket. One long, long breath of helpless sympathy mingled with relief, and he set off toward the woods.

3

No sooner was he out of sight among the trees than he snatched out Camilla's letter and turned from the path, unsociable as a cat with a sparrow. On the way he began tearing open the envelope. Where the fall of a decayed sycamore had left the ceiling of boughs open to a glow from the west, he stopped on quaking legs to read the pages within:

New Orleans
18 October, 1835

My dear Perry:
    Do you recall how we talked once of Bishop Berkeley's dogma that the Crash of a tree in a Forest, unless known to some Mind, to a Spiritule Being, has no Existance? Often since then I have felt Kindred to such a tree, relizing over and over how deep you were to surmize that We Ourselves may have only a poorish Reality in the absence of beings spirituly Receptive to us. Why else does Loss of a dear Friend so shrivel our lives? Surely the Quality of our existence, if not the fact, owes much to those who most freely and fully give us Afection.
    Yesterday I felt this most Keenly because I caught sight of you one last time while Esau was taking me to a collation near the Rampart. You were in Uniform, standing within the doorway to Proctor's Smithy. Despite the Ring of hammers and Stamp of hooves, you were urging some point upon three Idlers very corsely dressed, I suppose trying to Recruit them, though the Din must have deafened them to half of what you said. The blue and gold of your tunick were so brave and bonny, it drove an aching Pride through my breast to know you well. All the same, with sparks from the Anvills spraying around you, I noticed for the first time how Loudly uniforms invite the Fates to Scorch and Tear them, to Stain and Slacken them. Never before had I understood how Shallow women are to admire them, as nearly all of us Vehemently do. We ought to Deplore them, to turn whatever Cuning we have Against them—or discover some Magic to assist those who wear them.
    I told Esau to drive me, Not to the collation, but to a Gun Shop. Sending after you something from me particklarly useful to a Soldier, I reflected, might have an effect sustaining to us Both: in proportion as it is Useful to you, it will Remind you how vividly you live in my Thoughts—and so might keep Me alive in Yours.
    Let us not say Farewell again, but—

Au Revoir,
Camilla

N.B. Some 20 Miles from Springfields' is my Texas land. Whenever the Round of Pleasures in this Babylon confesses itself Empty, I dream of Removing there to live with more Purpose.
    How can I be Sure, though, what Actualy awaits me? Mr. Palmer left a family named Tipton in charge, and I do wonder what they have Done to it. Do Please visit it for me if you can, Perry, and write me a

*Speaking Likeness of what you see. Pray do not Flater it at all or
paint anything Gaudier than Life. In this, as in Everything else, I
henceforth shall regard Truth from you as the Ultimut Kindness.*

*For a Favorit Daydream in time becomes a Disease. One must
Act upon it or . . . or take Bitters against it. I trust your account
will Instruct me which to do with Mine.*

Ever,

C.

From C. B.'s Journal
November 14, 1835

Vile weather today: rain and gloom from dawn till dark—despite
which one ray of sunlight blessed us: mail from Texas! The message
of Pheidippides running in from Marathon stirred Athens less per
capita than Perry's letter did our home. I had brought it from the
Post Office at lunchtime, and tears in Camilla's eyes bespoke an in-
tolerable happiness because a silence she never wanted is broken at
last.

She read aloud certain portions describing country around her
Texas homestead. A fortune, Perry says, can be generated there as
surely as a goodly ship can be cut from a grove of oak—though it
may take nearly as much work.

That Eden, he conceded, does contain a snake or two, and suffers
much from its present Adam and Eve, Mr. and Mrs. Tipton. Though
what he calls "goodhearted and all," they are "no more fit to be care-
takers than so many goats." No harm intended, ever, but with no one
turning up to stop them, "it's in their nature to nibble things, to pull
things underfoot and spread a stink around."

Perry thought we ought to go ourselves soon and straighten them
out. An excursion could be managed inside of nine weeks—three for
a leisurely journey going, three for the visit itself, and as many for
coming back. Whether we may ever wish to emigrate there, and what
to bring if we do, we then would know. He felt sure, however, that
if we once "experience the seductions of this landscape, this delicious
climate, this marvelous amplitude of opportunity," we would want to
return for a longer time.

How much study he has given a visit by us is plain. He expects a

long spell of quiet in the Texas war after the present garrison at San
Antonio de Bexar is driven out. In time the Mexicans in great force
may come north for revenge, but cannot undertake that until next
spring at earliest because the deserts of Tamaulipas are too wide and
sere and forbidding in wintertime for any sizable army to cross. If
we give him one more month to help win the fall campaign, he will
accompany us from any port we name.

Camilla became jubilant over that suggestion. I expressed all sorts
of doubts, as a parent should. The lure of far places, beguilingly described, was what drew the lovely Helen off to Troy, I warned her,
and she was not the last runaway female to meet disaster. Camilla
received this comparison in hilarious gratitude.

She's too practical, of course, to stir far from Palmer Hall before all
her harvests are in and sold. Still, a sense of expanding opportunity
has turned her spirits out to pasture: they're kicking up their heels.

Mine too. Neither of us was capable of much more than three words
on any other matter all evening long.

CHAPTER IV

San Felipe de Austin
Sunday Morning
November 15, 1835

Such was Perry's opinion of the area around Camilla's homestead that his first act on reaching the capital, San Felipe de Austin, was to file a claim on a vacant league near hers. He then made a study of documents supporting her titles, copied them for her, and had the copies certified. That done, he was impatient to push on west the same afternoon.

Several of his companions felt otherwise. The weather had turned funereal as the year grew old. Moreover, incredibly few Texans were in motion toward the war. Most called it a great cause sure to draw thousands of volunteers from the States, as Dr. Springfield had, but they themselves were "stayn home awhile for the present" to finish their harvests, to round up livestock, to snug up their cabins for the winter, or, in the doctor's case, to deliver two babies due on neighboring homesteads "any day now."

Here in San Felipe every clapboard house, store, and barn, every shed, corncrib, smokehouse, lean-to, and loft housed Texans too busy talking to fight. Although part had come to frame a provisional government, most were loquacious idlers hanging around to see what favors or offices that new government would parcel out. A surprising number had been in the army and left it, tired of it, sick of it. So why should strangers from hundreds of miles east be in any lather about joining up? Perry's squad insisted, as a minimum, upon tenting overnight under a tree a few dozen staggers from the town's two groggeries.

All were tying packs on their mules next morning when a stranger rode their way. He was strongly tall, with long legs dangling loose around a flop-eared yellow pony too small to keep his feet above the stumps. His eyes, severely bloodshot, took in the men one at a time, at length settling on Perry, toward whom he swerved.

"Captain Allan, I believe."

"Perry Allan, yessir."

The stranger extended him a hand for some while unacquainted with soap. Though dressed in blackly soiled buckskins and a greasy bandanna, he maintained a grandeur of bearing which permitted no amusement.

"Sam Houston, sir."

Houston! So this was the celebrated Sam Houston! Perry had heard his story often: once the boy wonder of Congress and at thirty-four the governor of Tennessee, he had been known as a Man of Destiny, a favorite of Andrew Jackson, whom many thought he would follow into the White House. At thirty-six, however, he deserted a bride of two weeks, resigned his governorship, and turned his back upon civilization to live among the Cherokees, who saw reason to nickname him Big Drunk. Here in San Felipe he was politicking for the office of commander-in-chief of Texan forces on no stronger claim than that he had achieved the rank of first lieutenant in the U.S. Army after serving under Old Hickory, and later had himself appointed "major general" in the Tennessee state militia.

His face combined more opposites than Perry ever before had seen in one man—eyes inflamed by dissipation, yet large and judicious; jowls loose but jaw solid; features coarse but countenance handsome; bristle unshaved but expression courtly. It was a face both consecrated and damned, a parchment inscribed with hieroglyphs of countless possibilities.

As Perry began introducing others in the squad, Houston unforked his pony to stride from man to man, offering each his hand and speaking in a voice given timbre by an extraordinary, yet agreeable self-esteem. His manner took it for granted that everyone around him would look upon him as more a man than anyone else in sight, and all obliged—all.

The introductions done, he turned massively to let a hand grope over a pack on the nearest mule. One weedy eyebrow cocked at Perry. "These the rifles Mr. Bryan sent us?"

How did he know about those rifles? In any revolt, of course, weapons are a means to power through leadership over recruits who need them, and Perry saw them in danger of serving that purpose before they went much farther. "Yessir, he sent them." Then hastily: "He said to deliver them to the men engaged with the enemy, nowhere else. We're just now leaving."

"Hm!" Houston shifted over to probe the pack on another mule. "Pistols, captain?"

"Yessir. Knives too, and—"

"I understand." Houston constricted his brows. "Pistols and knives against cannon and bayonets!"

"Why, sir, they're all first rate. They're—"

"No doubt they are, captain. Hardly the best article, though, for a siege against a position fortified like San Antonio."

"But, sir, we also brought rifles, powder, lead—"

"So I hear." By an actory twirk, he pitied Perry's enthusiasm for these feeble aids. "The walls of the Alamo, of course, can turn rifle ball the way a duck does rain. Siege guns, sir—*there's* the article for San Antonio. Without them . . ." He wagged his head, and his bloodshot eyes appeared to brood over heaps of slain. "For bringing *any* weapons so far, of course, you boys deserve the gratitude of Texas." He conceded a benedictory nod. "You've served her handsomely, and I trust you'll see to it that these articles aren't wasted."

He strolled back to his nag, seemingly unaware how he had blighted the squad's interest in the fall campaign. Thomas Dunraven, a drifter from England with a clerical face, hands like a girl's, a Cambridge background, and a dreamy but inquiring mind, shifted toward him.

"You mean, sir, it's no good our going to San Antonio?"

"O-oh, I wouldn't say no good at all. At *this* stage it may be just as well to have boys like you camped there awhile—until we've the means to organize a regular army. No, if you don't lose patience and try to attack, that siege won't do any great harm."

"Except starve the Mexicans," Perry threw in. One of his duties as an officer, he thought, was to keep his squad's morale strong. At no other point in their travels had it looked so weak as right here. "If we maintan that siege long enough, hunger'll do more than cannon will."

"*Whose* hunger?"

"Sir?"

"Young man, have you any idea how big a circumference there is to guard beyond the range of San Antonio's batteries?"

"Nosir."

"So big that Stephen Austin, who commands there, would need five times his muster to keep his siege tight. Way things are, the Mexican garrison can slip out to forage any night they choose—until the whole countryside is stripped clean. After that, both armies go hungry."

This left the squad slack in the jaws. They pondered Houston's seamy, fascinating countenance. Plainly he thought Perry amusing, the rest a little pathetic.

"Are you saying, general," Dunraven asked for them, "that San Antonio can't be taken?"

"Oh, it can be taken, gentlemen." He nodded, lips pursed in thought. That this man, despite his dilapidated exterior, was capable of uncommon mental activity no one doubted at all. Indeed, his dilapidation added to their wonder at every assured and searching phrase. "Yes, it can be taken."

"Of course it can!" Perry seconded.

"San Antonio's not impregnable." Houston spoke at large, as if Perry had contributed nothing, and repetition gave his style a Biblical force. He straddled his pony, then continued from that eminence. "We can take it when we're equipped to take it. We can take it when we have enough cannon to take it—and enough men, enough training, enough supply, enough officers who understand military requisites."

He gathered up his reins. Before Perry could rally his routed wits, the general turned upon him in grave affability. "Pleasant journey, captain. My respects to Mr. Austin, please, the day you see him."

2

Camp of the Texan Army
Dawn, Saturday
November 21, 1835

Doubts originating in that interview were reinforced along the route westward by raw November winds and icy rains. Having to take shelter again and again, the squad did not reach the Texan camp above San Antonio until after dark on November 20.

Directly after breakfast next morning, Perry set out to find Stephen Austin's headquarters. Letters of introduction from Dr. Springfield and Mr. Bryan, the weapons and recruits he brought too, ought to assure a cordial reception. As the hour seemed a little early for a call upon a general, however, he used his eyes awhile.

The site of the camp was admirable. To besiege the town the army had crouched behind a great drawn bow in the San Antonio River half a mile north of the Alamo. Cottonwoods along that bow screened the Texans from Mexican lookouts, and its quiver was a redoubt for infantry supported by two cannon aimed at the fort.

But observation of the recruits bled away Perry's enthusiasm. Most had larked off to war in sunny October, equipped no better than for a buffalo hunt. None had tents, few uniforms, and many not even a coat. Though the day was sunless and rawly cold, scores were in summer clothes, hunching around their fires. Their munitions and sick were housed in shacks made of poles covered with hides or oilskins, but most men had no shelter except frosted cottonwoods largely denuded by autumn winds.

Those same winds, Perry thought, were likely to prove more fatal than Mexican musket balls. Nowhere did he see evidence of any firm arrangement to transform these clusters of wretches into one well-organized fighting force. Their effects and trash lay about in hideous disorder, calling to mind a dump on the outskirts of Baltimore. They looked no more military than billygoats, but much more unclean, for most had so few clothes that the price of washing them would be to shiver naked until they dried. He fidgeted over the realization that he could not possibly soldier among such men long without getting his clothes inhabited by all sorts of creatures they weren't cut to fit.

Often, as he passed one bivouac or another, the morning air repelled his nose. Mixed with smoke from the campfires was a stench of human waste carelessly released, and a reek of death glided in from a cornfield where blood and offal of beeves slaughtered daily were left as they fell. Vultures wheeled overhead in long drifting curves, while others at roost in the cottonwoods tilted patient eyes at the recruits below.

Perry felt cheated out of the energy and hardship he had invested in bringing his squad these many miles west. Where was the least sign that a mob this miserable ever would capture San Antonio? He could not see one.

Neither, apparently, could the town. Bells in the tower of a cathedral at its center tolled off a routine morning. Through the trees its many whitewashed walls looked serenely uncaring and secure, for anyone could see that each house built of stone and mortar was a potential fort. And what a stout old guardian the Alamo was! Once a mission, it consisted of half a dozen buildings joined by a high outer wall. Its massive shoulders, scarred by a century of resistance against Comanches and Lipans, could shrug off shot from the two small field guns

here in camp with nothing more than a puff of dust. Along its parapets, on the other hand, several cannon were so placed as to rake the
entire area around it.

Every colonist Perry questioned knew for a fact that within the
town and the Alamo were one thousand regulars, well equipped and
well drilled. But no one could tell him exactly what the muster here
in camp might be. When he asked at one fire, a ragged captain pruned
his mouth, scanned the treetops, and reckoned not half as many as
crows or buzzards. Most guessers claimed around six-seven hundred,
but every day or so men were arriving, others decamping whenever
the whim struck them, so who could say?

Often, en route from New Orleans, Perry had heard Austin described as "the truest gentleman in Texas." Now he did wonder if
this stock phrase hid a sarcasm he had missed. The fellow must be
another magnificent mountebank on the order of Sam Houston, or
why else would this siege be so sloppily prosecuted?

True, a good many of the ragpickers he passed did not look aware
of their own misery. It was common to see them pranking around their
breakfast fires like cur pups. One whole company was buckling and
bellowing in laughter over a recruit, bare from the rump down, who
raced this way and that to retrieve a pair of pants flying across their
fire from man to man, and then high into a hackberry tree above it.

Even so, Perry would not be mollified by their failure to feel as
bad about their lot as they ought to. The first duty of any officer, he
believed, was to take care of his men. Any commander who let recruits sink into the foul and shivering laxity characteristic of this
camp ought to be stripped of rank and sent home. Perry itched to
say something pretty nearly that strong to the general himself.

Or, no, perhaps not to the general.

On second thought, though, why not? No one in this hole had any
rights over him or his men. He could say what he liked to the general,
and for certain the damned rascal deserved it.

3

The general's headquarters proved to be a hut abandoned by peons
who once farmed there, an ancient *jacal* made of clay sunbaked onto

upright sticks. No guard was on duty. A circle of rocks out in front supported a coffeepot over a tulip of fire, and beyond that a Negro was washing shirts in a bucket while chanting a wistful, mournful, meaningless tune poignantly reminiscent of home. Perry stopped.

By sidelong action of the eyes the Negro had been measuring him and his uniform. He rose from the bucket of suds to dip forward in a plantation bow.

"Goodday, sah."

"General Austin here?"

"Yassah, deed so. You new from the States, capun?"

"Last night, yes."

"Step right inside, pleasah. General Austin be proud to see you, sutton."

The door was ajar. The jacal smelled of must and medicine and earthen floors but looked neat within. Two braziers improvised from *metates* gave it warmth, and all other furnishings were orderly: about eight kegs had been arranged as stools around a table of planks on which papers, an inkhorn, quills, pencils, a penknife, and three brown bottles of medicine were lined up before a smallish man—a neat, ascetic little bachelor, pallid, sickly, and worn.

But, after the first shock, Perry had no doubt that this was Austin. For this man, while stroking his nose in thought, was dictating a report to a youth at his elbow. In such an army, for sure, no one less than a general would have a secretary.

The latter was first to notice Perry. He had lively eyes which mutely, instantly, said to Perry's, "Just who the hell are you?" Without changing expression, he murmured sidelong to Austin, "Uncle, sir . . ."

"Hm?" Austin looked up. "Ah, yes!" He rose to offer Perry a fleshless hand. "You're Mr. Allan, I judge."

"Yessir. May I ask, sir, how you knew?"

"Wel-ll." Austin coughed into the thumb end of a loose fist. "In war, you know, we must be quick to discover who our friends are. Sir, my nephew, Austin Bryan."

Perry shook hands with Bryan, who could not have been more than sixteen or seventeen.

"Here, please." Austin waved hospitably toward a keg. "Make yourself comfortable."

"Sir, I only came to—I brought you letters from Dr. Springfield and Mr. William Bryan of New Orleans."

"Good. But sit awhile. Have a cup of coffee."

A sideward rock of his head asked his nephew to go out for some, which he proceeded to do. General Austin then had the manners to resist curiosity about the letters Perry gave him in order first to inquire about his trip westward. Sloppy though everything else in camp might be, his intelligence service was the reverse. Not only did he know the number and condition of men with Perry, but what extra arms they had brought, what ship they had taken, what route they had followed overland, the date they had left San Felipe, and something about Perry.

But what kept Perry most in wonder was to find an eminent frontier leader looking as this man did. He wore a military frock coat with stars on each lapel, yet no elaboration of costume could give him the look of a battlefield commander. His asceticism was accentuated by a long nose and pointed chin. His hair, wavily fine, had retreated under the wear of time and public care until his face had gone half to forehead. Curiously, he seemed without brilliance, merely educated and sensible. Nor had he any of Houston's engulfing charm; he was cordial, but without the power of drawing others swiftly into compliance with his views. His speech was hesitant to the point of stammering, in part because he coughed often, and every now and then his cheeks expanded around a genteelly soundless belch. He looked less fitted for conducting a siege than for a schoolmaster's desk—or a convalescent's bed.

Still, this frail little man—*this* was the first of Texas heroes. Here, where for two centuries frantically fierce savages had kept Spaniards fortified behind mortar walls, it was Austin who had the audacity and the vision and the faith to establish cabin living on widely separated farms. After winning agreement from the Mexican Government, he had induced thousands of his countrymen to follow him out here to till plains that never before had known any harvest except the savage hunter's. Other entrepreneurs brought out settlers after he had reduced the difficulties in doing so, but he remained far and away the most successful colonizer in Texas, and one of the ranking half-dozen in all American history.

But where no superlatives of personality were visible, none at all, there must be qualities underneath very instructive to identify. Perry dovetailed his fingers around one knee and opened himself from within to see more deeply. Any mortal whose outward show was so far from the heroic mold, who displayed little magnetism, stature, or force, and who yet could people Texas under circumstances requiring these, constituted a phenomenon not to be observed often.

Meanwhile Austin had turned to Dr. Springfield's letter. His nephew came in to leave two gourds of coffee before again going out. Although the aroma was inviting, Austin neglected his to read the letter through without pause. Moodily he sat stroking his long nose from bridge to fleshy tip.

"We need more physicians. Soon we'll need them bad. Dr. Springfield, instead of sending this, should have come with you. A man of his civic outlook—I'm most surprised he stayed home."

"You see, sir, his crops—"

"Yes, yes, the harvest! Though our population is above thirty thousand, we have hardly six hundred here under arms. Most are too busy harvesting to keep Texas free."

"He did tell me, though, that he intends to come later, sir."

"Hm. Others too. Later! The time we need help is not later. It's now."

Perry grinned but left further comment to Austin.

"In Mexico City I saw Dictator Santa Anna as we see each other here. Sir, he wears a pleasing appearance, but there's a cruel man. We are right as sunrise in resisting his decrees; and, now that war is upon us, we ought to prosecute it with conviction. If we lose our freedom, what do our harvests become? Tribute."

Perry saw nothing in that to gainsay. Austin paused to sip his coffee. One swallow, and a bubble of gas puffed his cheeks. He turned to the letter from William Bryan. When his eyes came up again, a dent showed between them.

"Both of these gentlemen advise me to commission you, sir, and no doubt with sufficient reason." Uncomfortable, he coughed into a fist. "Still, I don't know . . . You have only seven volunteers."

The remark sounded prefatory to a blow. Perry's impulse when he saw a blow coming was to hit back before it fell.

"Sir, those are disciplined boys. Traveling or not, they've drilled every day. They're worth twice their number of raw recruits in any army under heaven—most especially *this* army."

Embarrassed humor pulled Austin's lip sideward. His bony fingers turned his gourd of coffee half around.

"Yes, our men have little discipline—next to none." He roused himself and cleared his throat. "Of course, it's no use saying we're much better than we look, for that still isn't proved. But I hope you appreciate the difficulties, Mr. Allan. Until a week ago Texas had no government of its own, no legal instrument to create an army. Our militia was solely a congregation of farmers. We still have no source of revenue to supply and pay them. As an attorney, you surely grasp the implications of this weakness."

"Yessir, I do."

"To say it otherwise, the confusion here reflects our lack of civil authority to establish the necessary military authority. What powers a commander has, you know, must derive from government—unless he's a tyrant."

"But, sir—" Perry released his knee, rocked forward to his coffee, and drank a bit. "Why doesn't each troop hustle around and build themselves a shelter? Has anyone ordered them to?"

"Why, no!" A hint of pique lined Austin's forehead. "We have few tools of any kind, next to none for building shelters. I doubt if we've three hammers among us."

It might be well, Perry thought, to assemble all the tools there were and consider what could be improvised with them. He hesitated to say anything more in this vein, nor was it necessary. With surprising vigor, Austin drew the unspoken thought out into the open, and not unpleasantly.

"Believe me, Mr. Allan, our deficiencies could not be more evident to anyone than to me. Nor could my own lack of fitness to correct them." His manner gathered force as he talked, the gentle but irresistible force of completely plain dealing. "I have no military experience or inclination. My one desire is to make this wasteland flower with homes—freemen's homes. That has always been my goal: homes, not glory. My occupation, my whole study, my single hope, is to prepare the way for homes in great number, homes where free people may become as big in soul as God ever meant us to be. I have tried to see this accomplished, not through warfare, rather by civil means —which happen now to be insufficient.

"I never sought this command. I never wanted it. I would have preferred to avoid it. But"—humor and weariness tugged different ways across his lips—"I seem to have been the only senior officer not ready to pull a pistol on others in order to get it. All supposed that command here would assure them a name in history and a position of power in the state we mean to create. During the first weeks of war the rivalry for dominion almost destroyed this army. Their choice turned to me as a compromise, perhaps because I had no ambition for it.

"Since then further quarrels develop day and night. Any plan by one faction for taking San Antonio is resisted by another because each wants credit for measures that may bring us victory. Dissension, bickering, complaint, intrigue—these sap away our best strength."

The haggard amusement at play over his conclusion asked for no easing in judgment of his own shortcomings. He simply wanted to be understood.

"We need here the sort of leader—or even the sort of driver—who can make men forget their differences. Because nobody yet has shown he can, I must deputy for such a man. My own preference would greatly favor work in San Felipe: all my inclination is civil, not military in any particular."

His glance, voice, and manner kept an absolute honesty as clear as high noon. Perry wondered if this was not why he was so revered: because character has in it a surer captivation than any outward asset. Austin might be weak in appearance, yes, but the strength of his word was known over four thousand miles from Washington to Mexico City. Though not compelling in manner, he had one asset more rare: inward straightness, integrity. This in itself would explain why he had become accepted so widely as the first citizen of a territory invaded without end by self-seeking, disreputable, or ruthless men.

"It's not right, sir, for anyone as new as I to be critical," Perry conceded. "The only thing is—"

"The only thing is there *is* so awfully much to criticize," Austin said. "Often, walking among these slovenly troops, I do wish that, like the Old Woman in the Shoe, I could spank them all soundly and send them to bed—a *good* bed. But I can't even find fault without having men desert in a peeve. They're only citizens under arms, not an army, and can't be treated as more. Nothing whatever holds them here except the wish to be here."

"Nosir. Though there's a magic that bewitches men in the old army formula—in daily drill, in order, in discipline that molds men into a single force ready to strike as one."

Austin allowed that in time these would be established. The new government at San Felipe had voted a few days ago to develop a regular army under an experienced soldier, General Sam Houston, and would pay all ranks with land.

"Houston is a believer in that selfsame magic," Austin went on. "In a regular army, receiving pay, he can apply it."

"However"—Perry's face tightened between an impulse to grin and another to go wry—"isn't he equally a *dis*believer in this siege?"

"Oh, just a moderate detractor. To him it's an amateur campaign by amateur heroes under amateur leadership. But he leaves it to us. He's staying in San Felipe himself to work out the new organization.

"Now, regarding your present title . . ." Austin again took up William Bryan's letter. "Of course, you are the *de facto* officer of your own men, but . . ." He put the letter aside to massage one fleshless hand inside the other. "But, as there are only seven, I fear we can't rank you higher than lieutenant."

In secret Perry found Austin's discomfort pathetic. It reflected weeks of effort to quiet the claims of glory-seekers.

"To strengthen your hand a bit," Austin continued, "we'll add to your squad a few odds and ends of broken troops. I'll see to that today. We've very good reason now to improve our organization."

The army's strength would grow above eight hundred today, he said: a courier had brought word this morning that the New Orleans Greys, two companies strong, would arrive before nightfall. So would a siege gun, a big twelve-pounder.

"We've been delaying only for this," he said, rising, "and there's much to be done." He offered his hand. "Lieutenant Allan, my best wishes."

Perry went away curiously dizzied by the impact of their interview. As for greatness, no—Austin was no Great Man. But whatever this man who was not great might ask him to do, he would have to undertake.

4

He soon discovered other officers under no such compulsion, a clique known to their rivals as "them damn Houston stinkers."

Toward midafternoon the New Orleans Greys straggled across the valley with drums throbbing, baggage wagons wailing for grease, horses nickering, and officers thundering orders without any effect except to publicize who was theoretically who. A few of the Greys were mounted, some lolled on the wagons, most walked. For all that, they looked more martial than most in camp: they were in uniform; every man had a rifle, pistol, and knife; several had sabers or hatchets or bayonets. Tents were included in their gear as well, and the blooming of these in camp was considered auspicious.

The siege gun, a handsome brassy orator, likewise arrived as expected. Shortly afterward General Austin issued a written instruction: the army was to assault San Antonio by storm at three tomorrow morning. The rank and file hurrahed. Reorganizing for battle, the camp teemed like a colony of ants about to migrate.

Austin's reorganization added a Sergeant Herbert Molineau and four other colonists to Perry's squad, forming a platoon of twelve. Although talk of the attack enlivened everyone else, Molineau developed a silent, dubious pucker which Perry thought odd, for he was conspicuous for frontier toughness and had joined the Austin colony back in its first year when boldness was the definitive qualification. Instead of slicking up his weapons for battle, however, he propped a scrap of mirror in the fork of a mesquite and honed his razor.

At any time here, shaving was considered a little fastidious. It was amazing at a time like this. And no one in camp had less looks to pamper. The sergeant's nose hung like a parsnip from weedy eyebrows. His mouth wounded his face as if a tomahawk had chopped across it. The scars of volcanic pustules extinct with his youth pitted his cheeks under half-inch briars, and snaky black hair dangled over his collar to his shoulders. His one attraction was a canny, vital, humane look, which no act of vanity ever could improve. To have him beautifying cynically while the rest talked of battle damaged their spirit, but his brows double-dared Perry or anyone else to speak against it. Instead, Perry took him a bar of yellow soap.

"Here, sir. Lather up good."

The defiance waned from Molineau's glance. He turned the soap in hand. He sniffed it. "That should help considerable."

"They better watch out, uh, sergeant?"

"Who?"

"Not just the garrison. The señoritas too."

"Nosir." He stooped to lather the soap in a bucket. "Neither one."

"No?"

"Not if I know them damn Houston stinkers, no."

"Who're they?"

" 'Who're *they?*' " Molineau rose from the bucket. His gaze opened wide. "You been here ever sense las night and don't know that Houston bunch?"

"I mean which ones you talking about?"

"How many assault columns?"

"Two."

"Correct. And who's to leadum?"

"Colonel Burleson one, I hear, and Colonel Sublett the other."

"Correct again. And who's to lead the artillery?"

"Why, the commander of artillery, Colonel Neill."

"Son, you pass. Houston stinkers, ever damn one."

By reverting to his mirror he signified that enough had been said. His eye took in his own ugliness in matter of fact appraisal of the flaws he had to deal with.

"But they're patriots too," Perry observed. "They're here to fight the same as we are."

"Maybe they are and maybe they aint." Molineau massaged lather into the briars along his jaw. "Which is to say, maybe it aint the Mexicans they're here to fight."

"However, they helped elect Austin themselves. The choice *was* unanimous, wasn't it?"

"It was. When you can't lickum, joinum. That way, maybe what's done is only what you want done—in particular if you get yourself elected next in command. The real general in this camp aint Mr. Austin, young man; it's Mr. Politic."

Perry took that musingly. Molineau drew his cheek up tight against the pull of his razor, grotesquely cocking the wound of his mouth. Because his thumb pushed his parsnip nose sideward, his voice turned nasal.

"No, the Houston party don't want Mr. Austin winnun no battles. He's too high up in public thought the way it is. How'll *they* ever get the power whilst a plain dealer like him ranks so high?"

"Hm. Partial, aren't you?"

"That I am. It's the duty of ever thinkun man to see what's good and be partial towards it. Yessir, I'm partial. The reason is in broad daylight I stay wide awake."

Perry lifted a hand to grip a limb of the mesquite, waiting for

Molineau to explain the latest results of being wide awake. The only sound from him, however, was the rasp of a razor buried in suds. His silence required the question Perry had been sidling around.

"And why shave?"

"Young man, I been through camp and heard Mr. Politic sayun his say. Come tomorrow, men that's here to help Mr. Austin might just as well go home." He stroked suds off his razor onto the heel of his hand. "That's me, Mr. Allan. I'm shavun clean for that long trip home."

The fist Perry had hooked onto the mesquite stayed there. To lose a man like this would be a shame. In addition, it would likely mean losing others.

"Did you come here, sergeant, to help Mr. Austin or to stop the Dictator?" Molineau's gaze came at him wide. Perry met it without blinking. "To fight Houston's men or to lick Santa Anna's?"

Molineau's mouth closed in its bridle of lather. He frowned at the mirror in bringing his razor to bear.

Perry loosened himself from the mesquite. "Whether your partialities are right, sergeant, or whether they're wrong, I hope you stay. The righter you are, the more we need you." He sauntered off.

That evening Colonel Edward Burleson called a council of officers who were supposed to assault under Lieutenant Colonel James Neill, Lieutenant Colonel Phillip Sublett, and himself. The topic, however, was not how to carry out the order of the day, but whether to reject it.

Even so, Perry could not believe their motives solely political. The poisons of doubt by that time had killed the army's enthusiasm. Austin had offered no clever plan for men to follow, no saving, stunning tactic, no stratagem that hunters of the lynx, the wolf, and the cougar might admire. They were simply to storm into San Antonio de Bexar and take it, the most heavily manned and armored stronghold in Texas. From a handsome, gutty general an order to assault by storm might have fooled them into believing it could work. But coming from Austin, bloodless, ailing, and small—well, that was something else. Burleson looked like a good sensible merchant whose partner was jeopardizing every penny in the business.

All the same, one cocky young captain argued for the attack— Francis W. Fannin, the only West Pointer in camp. San Antonio and the Alamo had a perimeter much too extensive, according to Fannin, for a garrison of one thousand to defend well at all points. Therefore a surprise in strength at one or two points ought to break through.

Yes, Burleson agreed, they might break through. They maybe could. But could they get out alive? Common sense told him that few were apt to.

To prove it, he had Sublett, a vigorous and plausible speaker, review the facts gathered by their spies. The only part of the Mexican defense out on the perimeter was a few squads of lookouts. The bulk of the garrison was concentrated in two adjoining plazas at the heart of town and in the Alamo. Every street from the central plazas to the outskirts was blocked by barricades, and the enemy could easily turn heavy musket volleys and a picket fence of bayonets against any attack from behind those barricades. Few green recruits would ever reach any barricade, however, because each sheltered a battery of cannon kept loaded and ready to rake all streets to the outskirts. On whatever street you might choose, the Mexicans would have much greater advantage than the Spartans had when defending the narrows at Thermopylae; and this gang of farmers here in camp certainly was no Persian host. They had no men to waste, and there was no secret passage around behind those cannon.

As for surprise, wasn't it likely, and according to practice in war the world over, that the Mexicans too had spies here in camp to tell them what was going on? Most likely. An assault, instead of being a surprise, was pretty sure to be a slaughter. Common sense would not tolerate any other notion.

And common sense ruled. Burleson sent Austin a note refusing to assault on the ground that a majority of his officers opposed it. Austin, hurt and bewildered, had to countermand his order. On November 24, announcing that the convention in San Felipe had elected him an emissary to seek help for Texas in the United States, he resigned his command and set off eastward.

In the balloting for a replacement there was no prominent candidate to stand against Burleson, who received a winning margin of votes. But the opposing minority would not pledge to serve under him. They kept apart in camp. Some talked of going home, and dozens did, scores did. But around a great many the fascination of unfinished conquest had slipped its tether. They stayed.

So it was with Molineau. Quitting now, he said, ran against conscience. With two companies of New Orleans Greys and other units not so large, there were in camp nearly three hundred volunteers from the United States. If that many youngsters could come so far to help the Texas cause, the least the Texans could do was "stick by and help theirselves." Anyhow, Mr. Politic was still in camp, and mighty busy too. Somebody ought to be here who knew him when he saw him.

From C. B.'s Journal
November 24, 1835

Back late this afternoon from Palmer Hall in high spirits after supervising the last of Camilla's harvest. The hands had stored away enough loose cotton for upwards of three hundred bales, which she means to hold for a rise in price after the fall glut subsides. It's been a fair year, improved further by this shrewd dealing of hers. When all income is matched against all cost, she'll come out a few more jumps ahead of the hounds.

We returned today so that she could fulfill a promise to play the piano at a celebration of Edmond's birthday, his thirty-ninth. However, all concern about it vanished when she saw her mail, because it included another letter from Perry. Pointing out that a steamboat from New Orleans occasionally crosses the Gulph to ascend Texas rivers after cotton and corn, he asked why we couldn't put a coach and team aboard one of those, as we do on trips to Palmer Hall. That way we might start overland in comfort toward her homestead the hour we debark.

Camilla had coffee brought us in the drawing room, enthralled by this possibility. We were still discussing it when Obadiah tiptoed in to whisper, "Mahs Ehmon Beaufait awready come fuh you, Miz Milla." Her first conscience-stricken impulse was to race upstairs and dress, as she ought to have an hour earlier. Instead she had Edmond shown in and told him without a wince that mail from Texas had bewitched her out of noticing the time, then left him for me to entertain. Sample:

"Splendid weather lately, Edmond."

"Fine, major. Perfect harvest weather."

"Indeed so."

"Many a struggling family can bless the Lord for weather like this."

He said this in saintly compassion. I fidgeted with desire to throw some sort of harpoon at him. The struggling families he was thinking about, I felt, were those owing him a sizable part of their harvest for interest payments.

Some of us seek a place for ourselves in other people's minds by what we write, some by wit, some by complaining, some by style and show, some by gossip, by habitual lying, by forced laughter, by finding fault, by sarcasm or illness or jewels or anger or litigation or windy talk or quarrels or profanity or flirtation. Others depend upon drunkenness or martyrdom or collections of rarities or monstrous dogs or bizarre love affairs—or upon spreading a smell around, whether with perfume or a pipe, pomade or cigars. *His* chief means is by putting people under obligation to him, either through money lent them (at 10 or 12 per cent) or for favors done them. He gets himself known as a man of good deeds, and all the time who is he doing good to? Edmond Beaufait.

"Did, uh . . ." He arranged his smile carefully. "Mr. Allan stopped in the capital, did he?"

"Day or two, yes."

"I imagine he examined the records on Camilla's land."

"Of course, and just the man for that, knowing law as he does."

"That's true, certainly."

I thought it time to fork off onto another road.

"By the way, sir, felicitations on your birthday."

"Thank you, Major Cedric." He assumed a philosophic air. "We don't grow any younger, do we?"

"Well, but you could hardly be accused of wasting your youth."

"No, that's not my way. Those records—he find any flaw?"

"If so, no doubt he corrected it." Damned tired of his trying to slake on me a curiosity I knew he was too cunning to expose to her, I aimed a point at him where he's tender. "We're a good mind to see the place ourselves, whenever Allan's free to guide us."

"Oh?" His affability faded a bit. "You mean visit Texas?"

"Exactly."

"But can—please excuse this, major—can Camilla afford the journey?"

"If her cotton fetches the right price, yes. At least that will let her pretend she can."

His response was a half-sided smile. So, just to remind him that the harpoon was still in place, I took another pull on the line.

"Of course she won't seriously consider going till Allan can join us." I waited until his eyes showed that the barb had seated well before adding, "Which will be right after they capture San Antonio."

He was not slow to give that a twist he could muse upon with more composure. "San Antonio's very heavily fortified, isn't that so? There are those who say the Alamo's impregnable."

"The world is dotted with slattern forts once called impregnable. That one, like all the rest, will yield to resolute men."

"Though probably not without a very gruesome price." There was in his voice an overtone resembling what must have been in King David's when, enamored of Bathsheba, he gave orders that her warrior husband Uriah should be exposed to heavy fighting. But then Beaufait shrugged to make light of it all. "Still, I expect that town's safe enough. What have the Texanian victories amounted to that people used to talk about so? Not one's been much more than a skirmish."

"No-o, but—"

"Those rebels seem remarkably prudent men. Hasn't the grand sum of all their casualties been just two killed and six wounded?"

"Yes, while the enemy lost about one hundred and eighty. Twenty to one seems to me a respectable showing. And they did capture Fort Goliad."

"By catching it asleep, yes. A trivial place anyhow, and nothing to reassure us much." A sideward flip of hand dismissed the subject. "A boy's war, really. It's been a good while since any solid people in my acquaintance have reckoned it anything more."

Unhappily, he is right. For lack of any fresh success, enthusiasm for the Cause has languished: the sheep-skinned and silk-stockinged Quality now declare that any support to the rebellion is foolish, first because it won't come to much in any case, and second because it damages our trade with Mexico. Unless the Texians give us occasion for new faith in them soon, they will find further supplies and recruits from this quarter exceedingly rare.

CHAPTER V

I

Camp of the Texan Army
Friday Afternoon
December 4, 1835

Settlers who had finished their harvest were arriving daily, so that during one and a half weeks after Austin's departure the strength in camp, despite desertions, rose almost enough to equal that in town. Nevertheless Colonel Burleson circulated an order on December 4 adopting a course Sam Houston had suggested here more than a month earlier: the army was to lift the siege, fall back eastward upon Gonzales, and go into winter quarters. There they would train themselves as cadres for a regular army and avoid further action against San Antonio until massive help in men, ammunition, and artillery arrived from the United States.

The opposition provoked by Austin's order to storm the town was nothing to that set off by Burleson's order to abandon it without a showdown fight. A favorite phrase called it "fatal to Texas." As there was plenty of cannon and ammunition in the Alamo, why not capture that instead of waiting for some from the U.S.A.? No better way of winning help from Uncle Sam could be imagined than by winning victories, by showing the gumption to do for themselves.

Besides, the volunteers had sat by all these weeks, gazing distantly at San Antonio, aching for the comforts of its whitewashed dwellings, listening to the stroke of its bells and the lilt of its military band and the music of evening voices, until it had acquired a fictional beauty, a romantic fascination. It puzzled them, intrigued them, teased their minds. To think that within Texas, which always figured in American talk as a wholly new and vacant land, this town had existed more than a hundred years! An air of the Old World hung about it, of the Oriental too, the Moorish and exotic, the seductively drugging and ensnaring. The motto of the bright-eyed brunettes who lived there was said to be *siempre allegro*, ever lighthearted. Each sunny day brought out a contingent, doll-like with distance, to launder along the river and shuck off for a bath in waters warmed by hot springs. Who, watching them sport along those banks altogether innocent of clothes, could doubt that they would welcome lonesome and jovial visitors? Sacred tollings from the tower of San Fernando Cathedral shed upon their carnal promise an ethereal tone wonderfully enchanting to men far from home. Even those with families allowed that leaving such a pretty town "without no effort to free her whatsoever" did seem a damned shame.

A mounting number adopted Fannin's theory that one thousand regulars could not strongly defend all points around such a large area, that quick and clever blows at one or two points ought to succeed. What was needed was a resolute attack so planned that it would confuse and decoy away a part of the defense.

Such a plan had been worked out by a frontier fighter with long experience in Mexico, Colonel Ben Milam. He proposed to have one battalion feint at night against the Alamo on the near side of the river, drawing the garrison that way, while a much stouter force in two columns slipped around and into the town from its opposite side. There would be no attempt to storm the barricades, only to occupy strong mortar houses near them so that crackshots could clear cannoneers away from behind them and eventually go over the rooftops into the two central plazas at the heart of town.

Burleson and his aides argued that any attack under present conditions would only waste the blood of fine young men. Above a week before, scouts had reported a Mexican regiment under Colonel Domingo de Ugartachea hurrying northeast from the Rio Grande and already near enough to outflank an attack before the stronghold could be overpowered. More than that, bombardment of the Alamo with the big new siege gun during the past ten days, though responsible for a few breaks in its walls, had burned up a great deal of powder. There was not enough left to support any prolonged fight. By a little calculation anyone could see that thirty-three rounds fired from each gun of every description carried by all nine hundred men in camp would exhaust the supply. As no more was to arrive any time soon, the sensible course was to pack up today for a march toward Gonzales tomorrow.

When the president of the bank talks facts and figures, what solid citizen invests the opposite way?

Perry, however, did check the figures. Visiting a jacal and an old mill where the powder was stored, he found Burleson right, or pretty close. The supply *was* low. Nevertheless he remained restless with recollection of brave men throughout history who had successfully defied arithmetic. He thought of the handsome shepherd boy who had dared to fight Goliath, the citizens of devastated little Athens who had smitten all-conquering Persia at Salamis, the few English free-booters who had broken up King Philip's mighty Spanish Armada, the backwoodsmen under Andrew Jackson who had driven the pride of Britain back from New Orleans. The catalogue extended from the remotest times and places to the nearest. Here in Texas only six weeks ago ninety-two colonists under James Bowie, most of them now in camp, had been hemmed in by four hundred Mexicans near Mission Concepción: they had cut down more than one-fourth of the Mexicans and taken command of the field with a loss of but one man.

Moreover, optimism invited exactly the same arithmetic to support conclusions very different from Burleson's. If every gun in camp had thirty-three rounds, what more could an army of hunters ask? David, when equipping himself to meet the mighty giant of Gath, chose just five smooth pebbles from a brook—and used one.

Brightened by fresh conviction, Perry stopped at headquarters to venture a word with Burleson. But Colonel Neill was there, noisily arguing with Lieutenant Colonel Francis Johnson, a downright sup-porter of Milam's views and an equally downright detester of Hous-ton's. Burleson, who preferred affable companions, looked as upset as a bankrupt grocer hearing creditors quarrel over his till. Perry could see that a green lieutenant with more arguments to offer would scarcely be welcome.

He and his own men had improvised from poles and prairie grass a three-sided shelter open only toward the south and therefore good enough as winter quarters for any weather this part of Texas might bring them. He, nevertheless, on returning there, found them packing for retreat to Gonzales, saying that with most of the officers sure to follow Burleson, and therefore most of the men, it would be senseless to hang on. They called Perry's new analysis of the chances here mighty shrewd and dwelt on that awhile, until a baggage-wagon driver asked if they had their stuff ready or were they fixing to sit there till everyone else was gone so the Mexican cavalry could charge out and send them off to Glory? They resumed packing. Their lieutenant might be right, but it seemed better to be wrong than left behind.

While Perry was greasing his saddlebags before their camp shelter, a smart Mexican lieutenant came up along the river between two Texans, a deserter from town. About this fellow was an air of crisis and revelation. In answer to all questions he demanded safe conduct to "General" Burleson, and Perry, like the rest of his squad, followed along toward headquarters. So did a growing number of others as they passed through camp.

At Burleson's jacal the deserter declared that San Antonio had lost its will to fight, and its strength too. For more than a week the garrison had had no corn, their staple; they were living on the flesh of starving horses and mules. Many in secret were Liberals who sympathized with Texas, particularly educated, intelligent men like himself. Discipline was so lax among the sentinels that an attack by night would have a good chance to succeed. He would be happy to lead an assault himself.

In the discussion afterward Burleson said he wouldn't trust that cheeky rascal as far as he could spit on him. How could a traitor come over in broad daylight without being shot in the back unless he had been sent? Granted, the garrison was hungry and dissatisfied: three Texans had escaped from prison in town to report that much the night before. But wasn't the same true here in camp? In fact, couldn't anyone make the identical report to General Cos about this camp with just about as much truth?

Those Spaniards were trying, Burleson figured, to rig up an ambush; very likely they meant to place their cannon just so and have this smart little lead dog bring a flock of sheep in for slaughter. Other old-timers declared with emphasis that they smelled the same rat.

But that cautious view did not circulate far. Excitement was already spreading like fire through a canebrake. An officer would not desert, the average assumed, without a pretty good reason. Perry, seeing vitality quicken in their faces, felt his own heart stir inside his ribs. A fever glittered, too, in the eyes of two officers near him, Colonel Milam and Colonel Johnson.

"Ben," said Johnson, "why don't you call for volunteers? You're the man to do it, and now is the time!"

Milam—lank, seamy, brown as a boot—stared at him a moment. The web of creases on his face deepened in a smile. "Well, Frank, I believe you're right."

He sidled out through the crowd to climb on a log. Though he was by habit easy and loose-jointed, conviction stiffened him erect. His voice vibrated like a bugle. "Boys! Who will follow old Ben Milam into San Antonio?"

"Old" Ben, though but forty-seven, actually was old in experience as a brush-and-rock fighter. Born in the "Dark-and-Bloody Ground," he had grown up with three arms, the two God gave him and a Kentucky rifle. He had been cited for heroism in the War of 1812. Afterward he had traded among the Indians of the Great Plains, where astuteness and valor were essential to life. He had then assisted Mexico in her fight for freedom from Spain.

Later, among the Mexican Liberals who overthrew the tyrant Bustamente and installed Santa Anna, liberal at that time, Milam had risen to the rank of colonel. Because his convictions failed to change when Santa Anna turned tyrant, he had been rusting lately in a Mexican calaboose. His clothes, however, were comic proof of his durability and ingenuity under such hardship. Having escaped from jail by dark in nothing but his shirttail, he acquired a uniform by stripping a Mexican officer at the mighty fortress of Goliad, where six weeks ago he had helped a company of Texans slip in at midnight and force a surrender. His victim, plainly, had been a shorter man. His breeches extended barely halfway from his knees to his moccasins, exposing shins as free of socks as a whooping crane's. His call here in camp, however, had the more appeal because he was not by habit impetuous or declamatory, but reflective, humorous, and composed.

As the echoes of his call faded across the camp, Perry heard someone to his right drawl, "I will."

Molineau seconded, "I will."

"So'll I," said another.

A chorus took it up, and not hastily, but with a vitalized constraint, like a congregation saying amen to a timely and moving prayer.

"Then form a line," Milam suggested. "Over here, boys. Fall in line."

Strangled by a queer constriction in his throat, Perry sauntered over with Molineau and others in his platoon, outwardly sober and assured. They acted as if this were the one thing to do, but most avoided meeting other eyes. The line grew until a second had to be formed, then a third, a fourth.

Standing so, they made an odd collection. Only the New Orleans Greys and a scattered few like Perry were in uniform. The rest were in every sort of gear—some in homespun, more in linsey-woolsey or hickory cloth, many in store-bought jeans and roundabouts, a few in Mexican jackets and pantaloons. Others were in buckskins darkened by mud, rain, saddlewear, and grease. Next to a high "bee-gum" hat on one was a shako on a second, a bushy-tailed coonskin like Molineau's on a third, a wide-brimmed felt like Perry's on his neighbor. A pair of envied leather boots stood next to ankle-top brogues, these to moccasins, sack wrappings, or bare feet.

The men themselves were equally mixed. Among the predominating Anglo-Americans were several Englishmen and Germans, a score of Irishmen, a few Swedes, Poles, Swiss, and French. Two freed Negroes, three Indians, and a platoon of friendly Texas Mexicans added color to the ranks.

The Anglo-Americans, too, were men of every sort. Natural dandies rubbed elbows with men in rags, maturely bearded citizens with whiskerless boys. It was common to see a long cornstalk beside a ripely rounded pumpkin, or a big-barreled mastiff, like a Tennessean in Perry's squad named Mountain Bentley, towering over a bristling little terrier, like Mountain's sidekick, a Cockney called Elias Jones. But two characteristics were common to all—an energetic toughness and a will to act.

Now that Milam had a sizable unit at his command, he faced reality in his normally calm style. The time for action, he made clear, was many hours away; they might as well be at ease. Instead of bursting into oratory, as most commanders were likely to do when calling upon men to make history, he asked for a census.

A shuffling, tedious wait followed. Told there were four hundred and forty-six, Milam allowed that this, being nearly half the enemy strength, ought to be enough. On request, Burleson agreed that those who had not volunteered would not retreat to Gonzales after all, but stand by here in camp to provide a reserve, bring in supplies and take out the wounded. Tonight a battalion under Colonel Neill would help by feinting at the Alamo on the east while the volunteers for the real fight crept into town far around on the opposite side of the river.

There would be a rendezvous of volunteers three hours after midnight by the Old Mill, where they would begin their thrust at San Antonio de Bexar.

3

Saturday before Dawn
December 5, 1835

The clack of a hatchet in firewood startled through Perry a waking pang of guilt: he supposed he had overslept. Instead, he found his platoon's shelter still dark except where licked by glimmers from a senile campfire beyond the opening toward the south. Out there one of Molineau's squad, "Hushabye" Tuck, on watch since midnight, was chopping up branches. All the rest lay side by side within the shelter like a tribute of corpses some disaster had exacted.

Perry cocooned himself tighter inside his blanket. Till midnight he had stayed up writing to people he wanted to reach one time more before he risked his life: to Camilla of course, to his Aunt Sue as well, and to the Springfields, to his brother Rockford, then to Camilla again in a long postscript. Little though he had slept, conscience urged him to get up at once, but the air was cold, his blanket warm, and the opium of comfort gently held him down, until a male voice jarred his eyes open once more.

"All well here, Tuck?"

Reaching out to catch the fire's warmth across from Hushabye was Captain Alaric Welles, leader of another platoon, which Perry's was to join for the attack.

Hushabye kept his hatchet active. "Damn cold's all," he rasped. An arrow through his throat some years back had left him no voice much above a stage whisper. He generally sounded like an anxious father tiptoeing around a nursery; hence his nickname. "What's the time, capun?"

"Two or such a matter." Welles was a plain man with calm, observant eyes shadowed by a sloppy hat. "Yes, that wind's sharp." His arms squirmed together across his chest like a pair of hounds locked out on a stoop. "Got nip. Got bite."

"Damn if it aint."

"Puts me in mind of a timber wolf." His manner, far from complaining, took pleasure in his image of the wind as a wolf. Here in the army he had been honored with office because, before every sort of crisis, he maintained a composed and serviceable interest in others. There was a stanchness about him which Perry thought appropriate in a soldier named Alaric. From under the time-softened brim of his hat he looked skyward. "You boys better eat good. Chances are you won't again till night."

"Just so, capun. I'm firun up for breakfast right now."

"When Mr. Allan's up, ask him to stop by."

Welles left. A rooster faraway sent a lonely crow across the dark. There was no reply, few of his kind having survived the hungers of two armies. As Hushabye piled more wood on the fire, its smoke thickened to a gilded plume. A horse nickered from the shadows beyond it, after which Perry broke his cocoon to stretch.

"Any coffee, Hushabye?"

"Oh, mornun, lieutenit. Pot'll be hot dereckly."

Perry sauntered around behind the shelter. An icy wind quickened his blood. Here away from the fire the night looked less somber. Clouds as ponderous and crowding as buffalo charged across the range of heaven, but the dust of their stampede was silvered from behind by an invisible moon.

The camp lay quiet. Most fires in the direction of the Old Mill had died away to mere wraiths of smoke haunting the charred bones of last night's heat. A few, however, illuminated figures newly risen to start the day. Over to his left a sentinel whistled an old-time tune of love and longing. A gust tore it away, and a shiver coursed through Perry, a tingling compounded of anxiety and exhilaration. He circled back to the campfire.

"Better wake everybody, Hushabye. I'll be over with Al Welles."

"Yessir, he wants to chin he says."

By the time Perry left Captain Welles' bivouac, men everywhere were shuddering from their blankets, coughing at the cold, spitting out the dregs of sleep. A few pranked, some joked, but most prepared for battle with caution and reserve. There was no bugling, no drummer's reveille. Colonels spoke to captains or lieutenants, these to sergeants or sentinels, these to recruits. So the volunteering portion aroused.

On their way to the rendezvous Perry and his comrades passed a battalion under Colonel Neill preparing to steal downriver for a feint against the Alamo. They themselves hurried oppositely toward a lightless field beyond the Old Mill, where two columns were forming, one under Colonel Milam, the other under Lieutenant Colonel Johnson. Welles and Perry were assigned to Milam's.

Perry's closest comrades looked unfamiliar in the dark. Shoulder packs made of blankets and supplies had changed their shape, buried their individuality, turned all into hunchbacks indistinguishable from others before and behind them. They flapped their arms to beat off the cold, stamped to warm their feet, chuckled and whispered and grumbled; as their number grew, all took on this single anonymous character. The column acquired a presentment more animal than human. Grass whispered under the shift of restless feet, a reptilian creep of hushed motion. Appetite for action kept the line sinuously writhing from end to end, and an equally vital stir hissed from Johnson's battalion off to the left. The two columns became mated creatures strange to daylight, a pair of monsters waking at night to slake themselves upon a town asleep—or so Perry chose to picture them.

A tall, spare man in Mexican uniform came up to dip his head near. It was Old Ben.

"You, Allan?"

"Yessir."

"How many, lieutenit?"

"Eleven, aside from me." Calvin MacIntosh, a Yankee clerk, at the last minute had decided he ought to sacrifice the privilege of glory and stay behind to guard the shelter. "Dammit, we're short one man."

"Only one? Wish to God we all could say the same."

"What's the delay, colonel?"

"Not three hundred here yet. Waitun for them cannon too."

Milam went on. The restlessness grew. Dozens of clever fellows had decided not to horn in on the honors of battle—in fact, several entire units. It was another quarter-hour or so before the artillerymen came up from camp, pulling two cannon on grease-muted wheels, the new twelve-pounder and only one six, the other being left to protect the camp after service in Neill's feint at the Alamo. A few last stragglers also came along. Milam's and Johnson's tallies showed that only three hundred and one had kept the rendezvous.

But that, Perry felt, might still be enough: the creature of which his platoon had become a segment might be smaller than darkness made it seem, but its power was real. A groan was writhing from it like a hungering growl. It was ready for anything—or pretty nearly anything.

At last Milam came back. "Ready, boys?"

"*Been* ready."

"Hell yes."

"*Christ* yes."

There were no speeches, no harangues to valor, no calls to splendid endeavor.

On reaching the head of his column, Milam lifted his voice. "All right, Frank?"

From the other column: "All right, Ben."

In a hush once more, Milam tossed a command to the officer next along the line, "For-r-ward, *march!*"

The command came down to Alaric Welles, who passed it on to Perry: "Forward, *march!*"

It continued behind him through the dark: "Forward march . . . forward march . . . forward . . ."

5

They pushed west through cornfields, through open prairie, through patches of mesquite and cactus and chaparral, circling toward roads which led southward into town. Their efforts at stealth failed at first. Anxiety and shivers turned them awkward. Because they had no light except clouded siftings from a moon in decline, they stumbled often, knocked against each other, swore too energetically, laughed too openly, and even the warnings against doing so came out too loud.

But exercise gradually tempered them. Coiling over a rise, they caught sight of a fire tiny, glittering, and astral in the distance. A

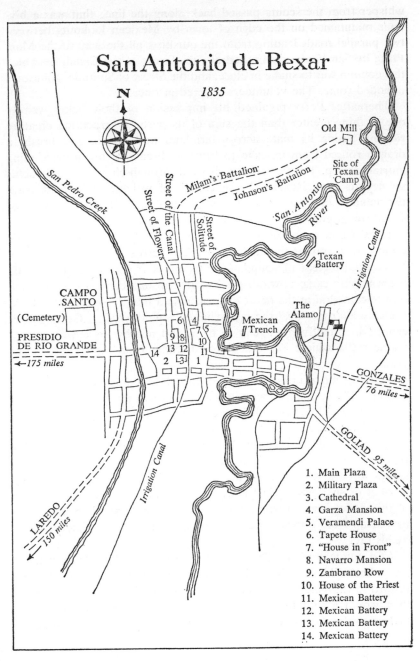

San Antonio de Bexar

1835

N

Old Mill

Milam's Battalion

Johnson's Battalion

San Antonio River

Site of Texan Camp

San Pedro Creek

Street of the Canal

Street of the Canal

Street of Flowers

Street of Solitude

Texan Battery

Irrigation Canal

CAMPO SANTO

(Cemetery)

PRESIDIO DE RIO GRANDE

←175 miles

6 4
9 8 7 5
13 12 10
14 2 3 1 11

Mexican Trench

The Alamo

GONZALES
76 miles →

Irrigation Canal

GOLIAD 95 miles

LAREDO
150 miles

1. Main Plaza
2. Military Plaza
3. Cathedral
4. Garza Mansion
5. Veramendi Palace
6. Tapete House
7. "House in Front"
8. Navarro Mansion
9. Zambrano Row
10. House of the Priest
11. Mexican Battery
12. Mexican Battery
13. Mexican Battery
14. Mexican Battery

whisper from the scouts passed back along the line: that was a bivouac maintained on the edge of town by Mexican lookouts between two parallel roads leading from the outskirts all the way to the Main Plaza by San Fernando Cathedral—the Street of the Canal, by which this column was to snake in close, and the Street of Solitude, Johnson's intended route. The volunteers sobered at once.

Thereafter Perry regained his impression of their being weirdly one, a thing greater than the sum of its parts, a serpentine creature rustling beside its mate across farmland and prairie and brush, a dragon roused from its cave to bring its breath of fire upon sinning mortals asleep. The fanged hiss of wind through chaparral and cactus seemed its own. Rearward, the crunch of weighted wheels beneath two cannon gave notice of its length and force, and the scuffle of feet through grass was a continuous reptilian friction.

Forward, however, all the sounds were pacific. That lone rooster's crow, blown frail at this distance, arched across the vault of night, a brave little meteor of sound. Monosyllables from an ax at work by the watchfire came upwind, prosaic and unsuspecting. From a watch on the cathedral in the heart of town rose a bored, routine cry, "Senti-*nail*ay a*lair*-ta-a-ay," the last syllable languidly dying. Other guards echoed it distantly from man to man, and nearby there was a spasmodic rattle which, Perry discovered, came from his own shivering jaws.

When within a furlong of the watchfire both columns crouched low. The only Mexican ahead who looked awake was the one cutting wood. Others huddled around their fire in unmilitary serapes, dozing or dead asleep.

A unit of Texan scouts under an acute frontiersman, Deaf Smith, tiptoed forward, part to one side, part to the other, their hunting knives loose and rifles cocked. In the firelight the woodcutter threw a ballet of shadows against a wall behind him. He seemed a captive of this ballet, enchanted by the rhythms of his ax, while the scouts moved up from opposite sides, so close up that all became yellowed by his fire.

At a command from Deaf Smith to surrender, the Mexican froze. After one wild stare he suddenly dropped his ax and ran, but not toward town, merely away into the dark where he could do less harm than would a shot to bring him down. His companions the scouts kicked awake. Dumfounded, they rocked to their knees and, babbling prayers in Spanish, thrust up their hands. Shackling them was simpler than tying the hooves of lassoed calves.

The two columns then proceeded along their parallel routes into the outskirts of town, which lay quiet as a graveyard. Entire blocks of dwellings in this quarter were rusting at hinge and lock. For, although San Antonio covered an extensive acreage, recalling its days as an outpost of imperial Spanish rule, prosperity had been absent a long while, driven out by a gay and leisurely people's weakness against raids by mounted Indians. Many of the farsighted in recent years had moved back below the Rio Grande. Behind windows Perry crept by he could see only desolated darkness, hear only the moan of wind-blown shutters and the squeal of hungering rats.

Milam's column avoided marching directly down the Street of the Canal, Deaf Smith having reported that a well-armed earthwork crossed it where it debouched into the Main Plaza. That barricade sheltered a battery of cannon so aimed that it could strip the street all the way to the edge of the town. Accordingly the advance had to be a crouching, coiling creep from one jacal or adobe or walled garden to the next, then thinly around that to the next and next.

After passing several, Perry began to detect signs of life. One corner reeked of recent urine. Faintly, beyond a wall which his shoulder brushed, an uneasy cat mewed. Canal water gurgled into a garden snugly wattled. A shed beside it exuded the sweet grassy odor of bedded cows. Through a shutter in good repair a snore bubbled like a hookah, and he heard a parrot squawk in drowsy alarm. He and his companions tried harder to mute every sound.

Still, absolute quiet was not possible. Boots gritted over gravel even on tiptoe. Packs on bowed shoulders joggled garlands of chili and seed corn hanging by doorways to cure. Rifles, sabers, and shotguns clicked against gates and posts, against pistols or knives or powder horns. This alien stir, however, was blurred by ghostly moans in the treetops and by grieving complaint of the wind in fences, shutters, and doorways. Moment on moment the houses remained dark. Each one the volunteers passed was another graduation along the measure of their luck. Each also brought them closer to those cannon loaded for just such an hour.

And yet Perry's anxiety was matched by exhilaration. Never before had he felt more alive, and precisely because the chance of death was just around the corner—every corner he crept by. Again and again he peered over the snaky column of friends ahead, alert for the flare of torches to fire cannon. Again and again he saw nothing toward the plaza but lightless dwellings silent in the dark.

When his platoon was about halfway to the plaza an explosion far leftward threw them frantically against a fence, a vibrant hoo-WOOM. No flash was visible, however, and so they understood that the shot was across the river, the first cannon fire in Colonel Neill's feint. Afterward distant rifle volleys rattled like stones rolling in a can— also part of that maneuver.

At the same time weakly remote cries in Spanish began rising from the Alamo, and more from the two plazas in town. A frantic bugling and drumming followed, a clinking of steel, a rattling of muskets, flaring of torches, barking of dogs. Out of the fort a series of rockets streaked up beyond the river, signaling for reinforcements from town to help stand off Neill. Their repeated bursting above the treetops in showers of fire heightened the frenzy in town. Wrathful officers could be heard bawling at sleep-drugged musketeers, hurrying them off across the river, and the Texans smothered a laugh at how thoroughly Cos had been tricked into reducing his strength where he would need strength most.

The objective of Milam's column was a vacated mansion belonging to a banker named De la Garza, which faced a cross-street within rifle range of the Main Plaza. Johnson's men were to take a mansion about ninety yards farther east, the palacio of James Bowie's father-in-law, Ex-Governor Veramendi; it faced the Street of Solitude at a point where no other buildings stood between it and the Garza place. Already the black mass of the Garza house was visible ahead of Milam's vanguard.

But their luck was wearing thin. Neill's six-pounder had shaken every feist awake. At first simply noisy about the general racket, the boldest came yapping along the Street of the Canal, making the night hideous with news about the myriad-footed creature they found there. A picket over in the Street of Solitude called a *quien vive* at Johnson's men. A rifle answered, and a shriek spiraled high on the wind.

At that ill-advised shot Milam's column became a human torrent racing down the Street of the Canal. Its gathering flow washed a final shore of houses along that street, then straight to the Garza walls. Shoulders, heels, and rifle butts knocked doors and shutters open, and the torrent flooded through tomb-black rooms. Perry floundered over a chair, tripped again in a tangle of legs, sprawled across a table, then plunged on with others who were grunting, stumbling, thrusting, swearing, but quick with little courtesies too, and with taut, coughing laughs.

When he reached a window on the side toward the plaza he was astonished to see no flash along the batteries mounted there. Every man of the column squeezed safely into the mansion or its outbuildings, while over in the Street of Solitude the last of Johnson's men were leaping into the walled grounds around the Veramendi palace. The Mexicans were still confused by the feint against the Alamo: it took them awhile to determine what section of darkness concealed the real attack and where to aim their cannon. They then spewed fire at the palace in amazing volume on the assumption that most of the enemy must be there. That gave the captors of the Garza place time to barricade its windows and open gunloops through its walls.

6

To gain some command over the Canal Street battery Milam, as day first spread a frail, smoky light across the town, sent the platoon under Perry up to the roof, where they cut rifle grooves across a parapet crowning the front wall, a tormenting job because they had no tools but sabers, hatchets, and knives, and waspish musket balls kept them down on their elbows. They cut only enough for six pairs of riflemen so that one in each pair could aim and fire while the other loaded for his turn.

Milam's artillerymen meanwhile projected breastworks of furniture and earth from the corners of the Garza mansion and wheeled their two guns into pits behind these. Once the twelve-pounder and six-pounder began bombarding the plaza, the Mexicans redirected most of their own cannon and muskets that way on a new assumption that the Texan force centered there. The cannonade rolled like gigantic boulders down a precipice, the musketry like a burying slide of lesser stone bouncing along behind.

But the bulk of this fire went wild, showering bark and twigs from the surrounding trees like a whirlwind blowing through trash. The ranks among the Mexicans were largely descended from dark, cheated, enduring Indians whom pagan rulers had tyrannized, whom the Spanish, too, had abused, and who still were kept in peonage under hidalgos, as if servitude to someone were in the nature of things. As civilians few had ever been trusted with firearms because too continually tempted to revolt. Since entering the army they had learned the niceties of drill, the pomp of parade, but not initiative and certainly not marksmanship. Their general, Martín Perfecto de Cos, was not a man to regret that defect, being a believer in massive, singly directed power. He put his trust in the "law" of war propounded by Napoleon: that God is on the side with the most cannon.

Milam, however, had picked his position well. The Garza mansion (and the Veramendi too) stood off line from batteries in the plaza, which were set in embrasures too deep to allow turning any cannon much either way. Even the best shots usually grazed the walls at angles damaging only the surface. Much infantry fire, too, was deflected by nearer buildings, trees, fences, and brush. The platoon on the Garza roof survived the sweep of that bombardment without one casualty.

On the other hand, at the outset they could not harm the enemy much either. The spatter of bullets against the parapet they hid behind reminded Perry of gravel thrown against a dashboard from the hooves of a runaway horse. The strain of working down on his elbows to gouge a slit through the parapet had left his arms quivering; and, whenever he rose to aim a shot through, musket balls spoke near his hat in unpleasant voices, one a yip, another a buzz, another sighing, humming, whining, hissing, whirring, or wailing away lopsided after deflection off the wall. Though aware that a bullet, like lightning, is heard only by those it does not kill, he could not help flinching when a close one shrieked by.

At the same time he was conscious less of fear than of fevered enhancement of life. Even the smell of battle was intoxicating, a sulphurous reek reminiscent of celebrations on July Fourth, and so was the shock of acquiring suddenly and legitimately this godly right over other human beings, the right of execution without inquiry or acquaintance. To exercise that right without compunction, however, took an amazing amount of practice.

After somewhat over an hour of growing daylight, a lull developed. Smoke hiding the barricade across Canal Street blew aside. Troops beyond it could be seen hurrying more munitions forward, and Mexican artillerymen were striving to improve the angle of each cannon by widening the pit it rested in and the embrasure it fired through. The twelve on the Garza roof were then able to justify their advantage in being up that high.

Three were among the best shots in the army—Sergeant Molineau, Hushabye Tuck, and a long, blond Kentuckian sixteen years old named Hugh Llewelyn, who had joined Perry in New Orleans. Others almost their equal were an Arkansas woodsy called "Butternut" Brown and the giant Tennessean, Mountain Bentley. Such country products had been nourished to manhood on meat they had hunted, and Perry himself had hunted since he was nine. Firearms to them were family tools about as familiar as hammers or saws.

Often more than one fired at the same enemy, not by arrangement but because trained hunters could detect a good shot about equally fast. Again and again cannoneers distantly before them would stumble by their guns or flounder away, crying for a priest or surgeon. Musketeers crossing the plaza wall beyond the debouchment of the street would suddenly waver on failing legs or constrict in the grip of death.

Their officers sent a detachment onto roofs bordering the plaza to respond from the same level. Those who survived this tactic did so by being quick and clever, not trying to aim much, exposing their heads only at the instant they meant to fire. Repeatedly a head visible along Perry's sights was gone by the time he climaxed a squeeze on his trigger. After wasting several rounds, he leveled his rifle at the groin of a break in a parapet where a musket lay ready to shoot. Before long the plume of a shako showed above the musket. Still Perry did not bring his trigger over its last hump of resistance because the shako had an empty jiggle: someone there must be offering it on a ramrod to draw off any waiting bullets before firing himself. After a ball from Butternut's rifle knocked the shako away, a sweep of raven hair rose behind the musket to shoot.

Perry's rifle bucked. The capless Mexican, wild in the eyes, lurched up clutching his throat, the other hand before him on the parapet like a zealot about to exhort a multitude. Three shots near Perry crackled with the unity of timbers under a collapsing platform. The musketeer dropped against the parapet, his skull vomiting brains and blood down the wall.

A stricken pause followed. Perry heard a moan. Thomas Dunraven, at the groove next to his, slumped down, rifle still faintly smoking.

Perry scrambled over to his side. "Tom, you hit?" He rolled him to his back. His body lay limp, lips gray. *"Where,* Tom?"

No blood showed. Feeling for a pulse, his hand shook too anxiously to tell him anything. Curly Callahan, a good-looking banjo player who had been sharing the same groove with Dunraven, gazed at him with doll-like blue eyes going moist.

"Jesus! Dead, aint he?"

Sergeant Molineau from the next groove, after studying the situation, sloshed water from his bottle gourd over Dunraven's forehead. The eyes fluttered open.

"Oof!" Dunraven gasped. His hand squirmed feebly to his stomach. "Poor chap! God forgive me."

The whole platoon together strangled with laughter. Of all the bullets fired at that musketeer, Dunraven's had been the least likely to hurt him, he having grown up the son of an English divine who had kept him as innocent about guns as a girl.

"Fainted, for Crise sake," Curly snorted. "No guts."

To leave no doubt about his own he aimed directly across the parapet, not waiting for Dunraven to roll aside so that he could use their groove. With his blond curls hidden by a big manly felt and his muscular shoulders straining their seams, he managed a cool shot, after which he as coolly watched for results around its smoke.

Suddenly his head jerked sideward, hat flopping off. He floundered back upon the roof, hatless, and clapped a hand over his ear. A freshet of blood flooded down his neck. "Th-they got me!" he quavered.

Perry could see that a bullet had merely cut the helix of his ear; but, striking just there, it must have sounded as if it had torn the side of his head off, which his eyes showed he believed it had.

"Disasterse," Molineau commented and emptied the rest of his gourd upon it. "Aint right to spoil such a perty ear. Sunzabitches should of hit you in the brainbox, where there aint a thing to damage."

Meanwhile the enemy hoisted a light swivel cannon into the belfry above San Fernando Cathedral, where it was beyond sure range from their rifles, yet high enough to shoot down over their parapets. It began by firing sprays of grape at marksmen on the roof of the palace. After some waste in finding the target, a single charge severely wounded two men, whose companions hastily lowered them over the back wall, then jumped down themselves.

The cannon next turned upon the Garza mansion. Its first shot splattered grape through trees to one side, but what a single hit could do had already been sufficiently demonstrated. Perry and Molineau hurried their platoon off the roof, tossed down the last supplies, and showed discreet precipitation in scrambling down themselves.

From C. B.'s Journal
December 5, 1835

Bilious today, and gloomy as hell—all the gloomier because the *Commentator* was off the press and delivered: nothing *had* to be done. As for writing new copy, I could not look at naked paper without loathing. The viands I generally relish were nauseating, my favorite tunes inane, and the sounds of daily life beyond my window (usually so vital and beguiling) meant no more to me than wind moaning through the shutters of a haunted house. Among people passing by, all but a few seemed to me deformed and miserable and foolish, most of them so homely, such monstrosities really, that I marveled how the human race gets reproduced . . . or why.

To walk, I knew, would only show me still more of the filth and ugliness and despair mortared together as a city, but I set off toward the Rampart. A stroll there along the willow-grown promenade above the Mississippi, I supposed, might put me in better spirits.

Under one willow three boys were operating a mechanical toy such as the Germans make, a tin hussar. Wound up, he would salute, and salute again, again, again.

When I returned from walking the length of the promenade, only one lad still took enough notice of him to rewind him. The other boys had their jackknives out, whittling. The next time I returned, their knives were prying the hussar open to see what made him salute, a fate any creature that tiresome had coming to him. In the end his two halves were abandoned there under the willow, his guts also—the spring and few gears which gave him life.

Something like this is what the gods do to us, and perhaps on similar grounds. For how tedious they must consider us mortals, seeing us go through our standard everyday follies and pretenses month after month, year after year, age after age!

Often tyrants as well must destroy people less in simple cruelty than out of disgust with life. Phalaris of Sicily, when trying out his new machine of torture by stuffing inside it the engineer who invented it, must have been sick of watching that clever rascal act clever. The minarets Tameurlane built of skulls by the thousand may well have expressed, not revenge alone, but a monumental revulsion against cheeky and repetitious man. When the Mogul conqueror Alau imprisoned the miserly Caliph of Baghdad in the \ower containing his riches, with nothing but his gold to comfort him or keep him alive, he was decreeing starvation to punish the greed of trivial little men in all lands throughout all time.

Everything considered, it's no wonder that so many of us help matters along by destroying ourselves, whether through drunkenness or addiction to drugs, or by taking senseless risks or neglecting our health, or putting a pistol to our heads. Destruction is just what most of us deserve, and we know it.

There is a kind of medicine in thinking the worst about ourselves. A little better already, I went home to discuss it with Camilla, for saying the worst is still more refreshing than thinking it. She, however, was about to leave. A note from Edmond had told her he was "unwell"; would she please come and read to him? Not one word did I utter against this. I simply rolled up my eyes toward heaven in wonder at what makes her give a cuss whether that fraud lives or dies.

She understood, and what an explosion! She quite overlooked the fact that her father was sick too. She simply ripped me open: I had no feeling in me whatsoever, and she was mortally tired of my disparaging the one person in New Orleans whom everyone else thought so well of, etc., etc. In short, she treated me as the boys did the hussar: she left me there with my spring unsprung and my gears ungeared.

Now, writing this, I find it comic. In articulation there is health. That is what started me keeping this journal in the first place: a belief, with the Greeks, that life is the better for being judiciously reviewed.

CHAPTER VI

I

San Antonio de Bexar
Sunday
December 6, 1835

Throughout Saturday night they toiled without light in an ant row of men, projecting from the Garza place toward the Veramendi palace a low breastwork of sandbags made by filling dresses, petticoats, and pantaloons from the mansion with earth and gravel. Behind these they dug a shallow trench, while another row of diggers from the palace did the same. Dawn showed a shallow communication open all the way from mansion to palace and manned with riflemen to prevent the enemy from driving a wedge between them.

Most of that day Perry's command fought from that trench, until squatting within it had them achingly out of shape. Relieved in mid-afternoon, they crept back into the garden behind the Garza house for a stretch, a gourd of water, a snack of pone and jerky beef, a few words of comfort to wounded comrades, a brief nap.

Captain Welles became absorbed with Colonel Milam and two scouts in a discussion of strategy which Perry was about to join when he detected a stir at a window in the first house west beyond Canal Street. A squat adobe less than half the size of the Garza place but strongly made, it stood a little farther from the plaza—just enough farther so that, if Mexicans took possession there in force, they could shoot along the rear of the Texan line. All its windows were shuttered except one covered by a hanging steer hide. What arrested Perry's eye was a twitch in that hide. He saw no other sign of life. That one movement, however, had in it a lingering stealth unlike anything the wind might cause. Steadying his rifle against a tree behind which he kept himself hidden, he leveled at the edge of the hide and waited for it to stir again.

"You, Allan!" Milam flapped a hand downward. "Hold you fire, sir."

"But there's someone there."

"That there is, sir." Milam strolled toward him. "We want you over there too, you'n your boys."

Perry's jaw dropped in disbelief. Between the Garza place and that adobe was open ground lying right across the path of cannon in the barricade at the plaza end of Canal Street, across the path, too, of all the muskets in that side of town.

"By God, colonel, *that's* news."

"You aint heard the best of it, Allan." Amusement deepened the web of lines in Milam's face. "What's in there is couple women and a pussycat. That's what's there." He let this have its effect on others who had edged up to hear what was going on. "While ago a arm reached out to grab the cat. From that arm, its looks and shape, I'd say you might find in there something uncommon delicate."

One of the scouts spoke up—Deaf Smith. "Place belongs to a lawyer named Tapete. He's old, but Señora Tapete—son, there's a looker!"

"Well then, to hell with the war, gentlemen," said Perry. "Let's trot right over and"—he swept off his hat to bow—"present our cards."

"So then you *do* volunteer?"

A snigger tiptoed around Perry. He had to smile. "What's the plan, colonel?"

"We'd like a couple dozen good shots over there to whittle away at that barricade." His head slanted toward the plaza. "We got to kill off any notion Cos might entertain about a drive around that side. A charge up that street after dark could turn our flank, then carry our works on the bayonet, or try to."

"Yessir. But how we supposed to get over there?"

"You're young, you and all your boys. You got vim, and what in Christ's name did God give you legs for?"

"That's true, yessir."

Dunraven had been standing by, weighing it all. "But *now,* colonel?" The amazement in his mild, rational gaze summarized what others were thinking: that at least two hundred muskets must be hiding in range of the area to be crossed; that those cannon in the Canal Street barricade could sweep it point-blank; that one volley well directed could chew up the whole troop. "In broad daylight?"

"In a stalemate *some*body's got to move. If *we* do, if our move has cheek enough, we'll scare them into stayn put."

"But just what chance do you suppose we have to live till we get there?"

"Nobody, sir, ever knows how much chance he's got till he takes it. If we mean to move, we ought to while there's still enough daylight to kill off some cannoneers at their end of the street. We need every minute from now till dark to convince that bunch that they better stay inside where they got cover. Now we talked enough. I say it's time to move. We'll scald their works with continuous fire so's to keep their heads down and their arms wabbly while you run for it. If you boys don't *want* to—"

Captain Welles broke in. "I aready told you, Ben, we got just the outfit to do er. Uh, Allan?"

"Oh, we'll 'do er.' Yessir. We *want* to, don't we, boys?"

"Yup," Sergeant Molineau agreed with a sigh, "we caint hardly wait."

Twenty volunteers lined up behind the east corner of the Garza place, facing Canal Street, facing the canal itself, facing the home of *Abogado* Tapete beyond it. Simultaneously the entire Texan line from mansion to palace loaded rifles, shotguns, pistols, cannon—everything that would help sustain a heavy fire to keep the garrison down out of sight and encourage a disposition they had shown to lift their muskets overhead and fire without aiming, without even looking.

While the twenty waited for their signal to run, which was to be a shot from the big twelve-pounder, Perry found his legs trembling. "First one there," he said for a little relief, "gets first pick."

Curly Callahan, with a bandage entirely around his head in honor of his wounded ear, croaked out bravely, "Aint fair. Let the perty one pick her *own* pick."

"Pick as you like, boys," Captain Welles drawled, "but don't forget: the pussy's mine."

Hilarity knocked them all limber. Suddenly they were mute again, waiting for that infernal cannon. The faces of several beside Perry were distorted by grins, gawks, and grimaces. Mountain Bentley puckered and flinched as if his feet hurt, and Butternut Brown munched his tobacco like so much hot taffy.

Such behavior was so understandable, however, that those who did not let themselves look nervous were the most conspicuous. Dunraven had about him the abstracted expectancy of a vicar awaiting a call from his bishop. Molineau, with his big nose forward, looked still and solemn as an old pointer on the scent of prairie chicken. Captain Welles, crouching for a fast start, could not have looked calmer if stooping for a coal to light his pipe.

The rattling fire of small arms was rising to crescendo when Milam spoke out. "Heads up, boys!"

The twelve-pounder thundered like a bombed arsenal. The twenty lurched away as if kicked.

All his life Perry had known the happiness of being swift and limber, of loving to run. With his shot pouch bobbing on his hip and his rifle jabbing forward like a toy lance in one hand, he settled into the balanced, driving sprint that so often in boyhood had won him pies at picnics, jackknives at fairs, kisses at clambakes, and medals at school. He pulled away from the others at once, from all but leggy Hugh Llewelyn, who somehow had known when that cannon *meant* to fire, who had started first, wore moccasins, and ran like an Osage. Perry's effort was to think of not one thing but overtaking that human antelope ahead of him.

Not until Hugh was crossing Canal Street did a cry of dismay rise from the Mexican outposts. Their muskets began popping, and quickly more, more, more, until bullets hissed through the air like blackbirds to roost. One snatched at the collar of Perry's tunic, so close that the concussion stirred his hair. A spasm of terror drove his legs harder, and yet Hugh, urged just as persuasively, remained ahead.

With one lengthened stride Hugh cleared the irrigation ditch from which Canal Street took its name. Perry jumped it extravagantly, pushing himself closer, so that he was on Hugh's heels when Hugh dropped a shoulder to slam against the door ahead. His drive shook the hinges, and when Perry's propelled weight struck beside him, both exploded through.

A gray cat darted across the room, fur on end, toward a door to the rear. Down beside a case of law books against the far wall two women cringed together in panic. Darkened as the windows were by shutters and hides, little was distinct about either except that one who was fat had her hands up in prayer while the other, eyes greatly enlarged, had both arms tight around the fat one.

Perry shouted, "Friends! We're *friends!*" Instead of reassuring them, his roar made them wince. He waved his rifle at a rearward passage where the cat had disappeared. "Go out! *Andales!* Bullets coming!"

He flagged his rifle at them again, driving them off, then swooped to break a hole through the shutter on a window toward the plaza. Hugh already had knocked his rifle butt through another facing the same way nearer the street, and several comrades were swarming in behind them.

From the windows they could see a knot of Mexican gunners with a torch at the Canal Street barricade, trying to force fire down the touch-hole of a cannon in which the fuse had been allowed to absorb humidity too long, those guns not having been used since yesterday noon. Hugh's rifle bucked his shoulder, and one gunner fell across the torch. It began burning his tunic and hair. The others ducked away, except their officer, who wrenched the corpse aside and again crowded fire against the breech of the cannon. Perry's shot knocked him into an irregular, wilting stagger.

In the meantime men from Welles' unit were skirting the house to deploy along a garden wall behind it, and the last of Perry's unit, little Elias Jones, who had fallen over a stone, came toward the door, flinching away from passing bullets as if each burned his skin. As he hopped through, an exultant yell went up from the Texan redoubts. Somehow all twenty volunteers had crossed unhurt.

2

Searing that end of the enemy works kept them too busy for thought about the women. Shouts and shiftings deep inside the plaza indicated that a large force was being assembled to bombard the adobe after dusk reduced the marksmen's advantage. Toward twilight Perry therefore ordered that furniture be used to barricade the doors and windows. He then went out to the garden for a word with Captain Welles.

Coming back past a lean-to beside the kitchen, he heard a drawn mew. He pulled the door open a bit to listen more closely; not another sound followed, but the feeling of life within was strong. From the kitchen he secured a candle, lit it at a brazier smoldering in a corner, and sidled into the lean-to, his four-barreled pistol ready to fire.

Beyond a cluster of big ollas containing onions, shelled corn, beans, chilis, wheat, and yams were some pensioned household relics, and beyond these a mound of what seemed to be prairie hay covered with an old counterpane. Holding his candle high, he poked that with his pistol.

A muffled screech underneath, and the mound erupted. Out of it sprang the fat woman, the gray cat in her arms, anger gashing her brows like a hatchet. She began swearing at him in a dialect of Spanish too impetuous to be anything to him but a family quarrel between consonants and vowels.

"Excuse me," he pleaded. "I didn't know . . . *dispenseme Usted!*" But she would not be mollified. As she ranted and gesticulated, the cat bolted out of her arms, out of the lean-to, out of sight. In the meantime the younger woman pushed up from under the counterpane.

The colors on her were as emphatic under the light of his candle as fields in flag: her bodice was yellow, jacket red, and skirt dark blue, embraced by a belt of hammered silver rosettes. The skirt, instead of covering her all the way to the feet, as custom back home imperiously required, extended little farther than her knees; her legs were bare, and they were something to see. While Perry wondered at her, she studied him without expression, eyes large and black in a face framed by luxuriant black hair. Seeing her brought Camilla to mind for no apparent reason—perhaps only because she was so good to look at or because his conscience was just then ready to smart over realization of how little he had thought about New Orleans since this battle began, and that did seem far, far longer ago than yesterday morning.

"Señora, I was only . . ." He faltered, knowing he ought to talk in Spanish but unable to remember any. "Suppose there had been enemies hiding in here—this I had to know."

She answered in fair English, *"We* never enemies to Americanos."

A splintering crash from inside the house mingled with the irregular explosion of rifles and the gabble of fevered, hasty men. There were other crashes spaced apart, as of something wooden being slammed on the floor. The fat duenna thrust Perry aside to charge that way, obviously convinced that he was a harmless booby, that there were others in the house who deserved her temper more. It was difficult to recognize in her the cringing lump who had prayed for mercy when she first saw him.

When he reached the front room in her wake, she already had taken a stick to Mountain Bentley, whom she had found on the floor, breaking the legs off a table to use the top as a barricade. He was writhing away from her blows, yelping in a plaintive falsetto.

His closest friend, the raggedly bearded little Cockney, Elias Jones, rushed in to his rescue. "Ha-*vast* there, woman! What the bloody ell!"

His clutch at her shoulder brought her around, and her stick too. He sprang away unhit, but she took after him in fierce resolution. His squawking leaps shot him around the room like a rag on a string. Equally energetic strings animated her: she was Judy to his Punch, cat to his mouse, hound to his hare, hawk to his dove, sparrow to his grasshopper, until the rest were hilariously collapsing. Molineau grabbed him as he bolted that way, twisted his shabby rear around to receive the stick (which it did half a dozen times without the least grace), and then himself got a wallop on the skull.

Their laughter weakened away to foolish silence as they noticed that the younger woman, having slipped in under the candle Perry held by the door, stood with one bare leg forward of the other, gazing tragically at the wreckage of her house. There floated around her a faint, musky scent of woman, which sent through him a skewering pang of desire, brown though she was. Except for some exaggeration in the lips and cheekbones, her features were precise and Caucasian; the effect was of good Aztec clay poured in a mold intended for Spanish porcelain, and a hushed reverence around the room conceded that men who caused anyone so appealing to look so grieved ought to be ashamed of themselves. Three bullets hit hammerblows around a window, emphasizing the silence. A trickle of dust loosened from the ceiling to sift through the bell of light around the candle.

Perry cleared his throat. "War, señora, it's not very considerate, is it?"

Her lips trembled as she reviewed the clutter on the floor. "*Pues,* how you make war with books and tables, with dresses, pillows, chairs?"

"The pillows become sandbags, the clothes also. Your husband's law books"—he nodded at the windows, where books had been stacked like cut stone, with rifle grooves between—"they help stop bullets. Your bookcase, tables, beds . . ." He revolved his candle toward a barricade across the front door. "We're shoring up for a cannonade."

"For what?"

"A bombardment. Pretty soon, with darkness coming down, they'll train their artillery on us if they can."

Bad as the place looked, he implied, it was bound to become much worse. A bullet splintered the edge of a shutter, bounced off the opposite wall to the floor, and rolled across it unevenly, like a battered marble.

Sergeant Molineau commented, "Better get the ladies outa here, lieutenit."

"Yes, you better leave right away. Here, I'll see you back to one of those empty houses out of range."

The girl's explanation in Spanish aroused the duenna to a furious, greedy concentration upon making up bundles of things to take with them, until their candle drew so many bullets that Perry had to blow it out.

3

They left through the garden. It was not Perry, after all, who led the way, but the brisk duenna, a bundle hanging from each fist. Next came her young companion, hooded under a shawl, which she gripped tight under her chin with an ostrich reliance upon it to keep her more safe. Perry came last, her bundles in one hand, his rifle in the other.

They stooped around a walled garden, skittered along a hedge to another garden, and from there to a road westward. As she crouched around difficult corners, he observed through her skirt that her hips and thighs were formed to provoke desire, and to allay it. Again, without his having noticed just this about Camilla, she came back to mind.

Sounds of battle declined and mellowed behind him. With this cowled, agreeably deferential thing so close before him, he developed an impression that she was leading him back to quiet excitements more adventurous than war, and more genuine. It might be, he thought, that this was why she kept evoking Camilla, this sense of matchless adventure which her nearness generated.

Exactly where she might be headed did not trouble him much: it was enough to believe that in her company he was returning to real life. The finger of a branch hanging from a tree which they stooped under flicked at his collar the way a bullet had when he was charging at her house, and he marveled to think how little ahead of death he had been at that instant, whereas being in her custody had put it so far behind.

Beyond a row of cottonwoods which marked the boundary of town something in the grass hooked over Perry's boot and almost threw him down—a wooden cross, once whitewashed, now bone gray in the dusk: they were in the cemetery, El Campo Santo. She continued over to a tomb of chiseled stone, where she stopped to face him.

"No farther, *teniente.*"

Along the darkening skyline ahead no house was visible, no work of man's other than tombs and crypts and wooden crosses more or less out of kilter. The graves had gone to weeds.

"Here?" He stood her bundles on the tomb, hand at rest upon them. "Why?"

"You stop. I not." Regret softened her voice. Her hand, in groping for the bundles, discovered his and rested a moment upon it. Her chin nudged southward at a parade of trees, black as paper cutouts against the horizon, where the main road from the Rio Grande passed toward town. "Not far now more *soldados.*"

"But if you come there, won't they—?"

"No, when woman asks *soldado Mejicano* can she pass, she can." Two musical notes of laughter escaped her. "In his heart he say, if he give pairmeesion, maybe one day he receive. So he let us pass."

Gaiety glinted in her eyes. The next moment a saddening in them, shadowed by the cowl of her shawl, reminded him of a painting he had seen somewhere, an Italian interpretation of Mary Magdalene re-formed. He sucked in a long breath and let it go.

"Where will you stay?"

"I sleep tonight *a la casa de mi hermano. Comprende Usted?*"

"Your brother's house?"

"Onofre's." Pride energized her voice. "I Corazon Gamboa-Tapete, sister of patriot Onofre Gamboa."

Perry never had heard of Onofre. The grandeur in Corazon's announcement, however, obliged him to give out that he had. "Ah, Gamboa the Liberal?"

"*El mismo, si.*"

"But why would a Liberal be there now?"

"*En el calabozo, amigito.* In jail." By a suction through her teeth while thrusting her hand sideward, she represented a rusty bolt sliding home. "Onofre weeps in jail. They would shoot him, but you Americanos come, so they too busy."

They still were busy. The musketry around the plaza persisted in querulous bursts. At this distance, however, and through the cottonwoods, through the windless dusk, through the scent of woman, it seemed to Perry less than real. Her companion, in wait some way forward, hissed impatiently.

"Who is she?" he asked.

"Doña Pomposa, sister of my husband, who far away in Coahuila."

"Ah!"

"She ver angry."

"Yes, and I must get back. *Ya es hora.*"

"But better away, *amigito,* not back! You not understand red flag?" Her chin lifted in the direction of San Fernando Cathedral, where such a flag had been afloat all day to signify that no quarter would be given, that every Texan taken in battle would be slain. "Many more *soldados* come soon from Tamaulipas. Therefore these flag of blood saying you must die."

"On the other hand . . ."

A quaking hoo-WOOM from the battery commanding the Street of the Canal, followed by arrogant shouts in Spanish, indicated that General Cos was mounting the big action of the night. Doña Pomposa rushed to Corazon, snatched up her bundles, and, gabbling crossly, hurried off.

After a hasty, "Adiós, teniente! I pray for you," Corazon followed the same path through the cemetery. She looked back, her hooded figure black against the skyline, a dense, widowed black between two time-battered tombs. He tossed up an arm. She waved in impulsive freedom, caught the side of her skirt, and, suddenly as lightfooted as a schoolgirl, ran to overtake her companion.

4

The thunder and lightning of the bombardment that evening were contradicted by the weather, which greatly improved. A palmy wind from the Gulf of Mexico swayed the treetops and broke apart an overcast already three days old. As clouds loosened away toward the north, surfs of limpid moonlight washed across the town; darkness flowed in behind these, then again the moon.

It seemed to Perry not a night for rifles or muskets or cannon, rather for guitars and castanets and the yearning howl of dogs. Bemused as he was by that feeling of resurrection which he had brought back from his walk to the Holy Field, the bombardment's squirts of noisy fire, seen through alternations of moonlight and darkness, looked stagily unreal, a theatrical imitation of war. Whenever the moon shone clear, marksmen assumed they could shoot almost as true as in daylight, with the result that every wave of light brought the racket of battle to a turbulent crest, which sank away in flowing dark until that surf returned.

During these rhythms the volunteers kept enough shots pecking at the plaza to kill off any immediate attempt to flank their line. Mexican cannon in return succeeded in hammering a few breaks in the Tapete house, but the bombardment died away not long after ten. About an hour later Milam sent over relief so that the twenty could return to the Garza place where their bedrolls were.

They groaned in gratitude. Except for exhausted catnaps which a few had snatched, they had not slept since the night before last. They were stretching out on hay behind the mansion when Colonel Milam strode over from a back door.

"You there, Allan?"

"Yessir."

After a few questions and congratulations about the Tapete action: "Friend of yours come in tonight, Dr. Springfield."

"No!" The load of weariness began sliding off Perry's back. All his earliest letters to New Orleans had given Springfields' as his address for lack of anything surer, and he had been inquiring for word of the doctor's arrival every day in the last ten. "He here, sir?"

"Not now. All that fire, I wouldn't tolerate him going over where you was; then him and Dr. Grant took away the wounded fit to move —moved them back to Burleson's camp."

"Bring me any mail?"

"He did, sir. Look yonner." Milam flapped at an adobe used as a temporary hospital a stone's throw behind the Garza mansion, which sheltered it from the plaza. "Had couple-three letters, which he likely left back there with Billy Bartlett, seeing that's the only place there's any light to read by."

In the hut with Billy, a casualty from Captain Welles' platoon, were two recruits who had established a watch to help him whenever he strangled. A candle in a glass chimney stood on a chair by his bed, its flame torn by wind seeping through a shuttered window, its glow illuminating a basin into which he had hemorrhaged a little now and then. A pitcher of water waited there too, and a rag stained red.

Both recruits, on chairs by a table showing lay-downs for rummy, had sunk lopsided into sleep. Not Billy. Eyes ajar, mouth also, he lay propped up enough to ease his breathing. Immeasurable pain constricted his brows, and bewilderment no less immeasurable. Dozens of men had taken extravagant chances in broad daylight, and usually got by unhurt, whereas Billy, simply walking off in the dark to relieve himself while helping to dig that trench the previous night, had been hit where his ribs were small. The bullet had ripped through the base of his lung and punctured his liver. With blood loose through the cask of his body, his breath labored in quick, moaning grunts. The surgeons had decided that carting him off tonight to Burleson's camp would kill him. All they could do for the present was bandage him, dose him with laudanum, and leave him here.

No one knew very much about Billy. Two days before Milam's call for volunteers he had reached camp, another runaway boy of seventeen hunting a new hold on life. The recruits with him tonight were not close friends: he had none. They were merely two acquaintances who understood how it would be to lie alone after dark during this time of final agony.

On the table with their cards were three pocket-worn letters tied in a cord. The handwriting across the top one Perry recognized as his Aunt Sue's, but manners compelled him to resist his impulse to swoop upon them. Instead he strode over to the bedside.

"Better, Billy?"

"Nosir. Not yet."

Wind sighed through the shutter, assailing the candlelight, bringing in the rattle of gunfire and the voices of men trying to save their own lives by taking others. A fugitive guilt made Perry shift his weight: not one of the deaths he had helped to inflict over there along the plaza had seemed to vitiate Christian vows any more than if those dying had been so many mice. Now, meeting this boy's anxious glance, hearing his gasps for breath, feeling twinges in himself of the torment which warped Billy's forehead, he felt his mind grazed by a thought that the salvation of every fellow creature ought to be of momentous concern to someone somewhere.

"Takes time," he said lamely.

"Reckon I will make out, lieutenit?"

Perry's mouth loosened for easy optimism. He held that back to observe, "Generally God favors the brave."

Billy's brows, after a moment of labor, unknotted in partial agreement. "Yessir."

There was in his voice an expectation of more. His skull was boned well, and no doubt crowded with brains—enough to realize that an immense amount more ought to be thought and said on this subject, and that he was not the man to think it or say it. His looks were those of good solid stock equipped to win mates easily generation after generation until, by the Grace of God and under the stimulus of freedom, some of their descendants somewhere sometime would do great deeds.

Standing over him, Perry became stricken by a sense of endless, wasteful failure of human potential to achieve its promise. These brains of Billy's never had been trained much. He never had acquired vision for many things beyond what his eyes could see. At no time till now had he struggled to reconcile the daily triumphs of his own vitality with the certitude of his eventual extinction. Perry was startled by the thought that he himself, despite more generous advantages, had not gone any great way farther, had not done much better at so applying what was in him as to make it count large, nor did he understand what his own potential in fact might be. Certainly he had done little with the problem of death. How then could he offer Billy any valid help at such a time as this?

Nor was death the sort of problem, gigantic and commanding as it was, that he wanted to put his mind on while those letters lay unread. He hung there by the bed, unhelpful, helpless, itching to get at them; he was ashamed at how badly he wanted to forget Billy and read them. His desire and his shame together stifled what little ability he had to think up words of comfort.

"Good man, Dr. Springfield."

"Mighty good, yessir. Done what he could anyhow. He . . ." His throat gurgled. He coughed to clear it. Jagged lightnings of pain showed on his face as his chest heaved, and yet he used his first clean breaths to pant out what he meant to say. "He spoke your name."

"That so?"

"Yessir. Brung you them letters yonner."

"Thank you, Billy."

Trying not to let his hunger show, he sauntered over to the table. His hand shook as, bringing the packet back to hunker down with it near Billy's candle, he saw that it contained one envelope from Camilla. He tore the goddamned cord off, gouged open Camilla's letter, and read it all through in ravenous sweeps.

The Troubel is [*she wrote after describing a soiree where she had played the piano*] *that so Much of what we do here has little Meaning to anybody. It promotes nothing Good, prevents nothing Bad, reveals nothing to us. The more we go to Other people's homes, the more we see the Same people. The more we hurry to Diferent functions, the more Alike they turn out to be. This social round is actualy a Tredmill. It has its Jolly side, but a Tredmill is still a Tredmill, whether caged Squirels turn it or Ladies and Gentlemen.*

But to Boldly step out of it, as you did, is less easy for a lady, if only because of the Misunderstanding it would provoke. You longed for Far Places, for Opportunity to do that which surely would benefit Others as well as you. Very good: what you Longed to do, you did set about Doing. Now I long for all this as well. I mortaly Worry Pa because I talk pretty near ready to Start. However, I keep thinking what Hard thoughts acquaintances will entertain about me in relation to thee if I follow thee—what Scandal they will make of it. I shrink too before thought of Storms and Depervation and bitter Cold. I fidget over the likelihood of Lice and Fleas and Bedbugs. Yes, I do so even though I know that None of these would in truth detract much from the Interst of a Texas excursion or seriously mar its Benefits.

You declared when we parted that you Never would come back unless you hit upon fine new Prospecks or did something ever so Worthy, etc., etc. But pray, dear friend, do not Wait for that. I doubt that I ever Can act so wisely Alone as with the support of great Affection, so do come back as soon as that depriving War will let you, and Then let us see whether I can be decisive too.

Au revoir,
Camilla

Joy flowed through him like moonlight through the town. That closing paragraph, did it not imply a readiness at last to travel life's road with him? No, perhaps not, but very near it. He floated on a warm and foaming wave of exaltation.

"Lieutenit?"

Billy, he discovered, had been watching him sidelong. Somehow he had forgotten altogether that a boy lay dying here by this same candle whose wavering light had transported him back to New Orleans.

"Yes, Billy?"

"From your sweetheart?"

Normally Perry's view was that his letters were his own business;

he kept them to himself. Hell, though, this youngster had cause enough to be clutching at every last shred of life, no matter whose.

"Uhm. Wonderful girl too."

"There's one thing I never had."

"No sweetheart?"

"Yes, but none that ever writ me none." His hand restlessly gripped and stroked the pallet he lay on. "Had me one a year back. Damn perty gal, and smart around a kitchen." He panted to store up air for more. "Then her fokes rid off to Texas. Said she'd write me sure, but never did."

"So you came."

"Yessir. Aint found her yet, though."

Perry slowly folded Camilla's letter away, watching the candle cast a wabbly shadow of it before him. That shadow capriciously resurrected an image of the first wild dove he had winged as a boy, debauching the rhythmic grace of its flight. A whole year of silence could be almost as maiming to hopes of love at seventeen, he thought, as a spray of shot that did not hit a dove true. Now close by this bed lay the edge of a silence without end, a solitude beyond the last echo of any voice, a darkness as immeasurable as the universe.

Shrinking from thought about it, he opened a note from Leticia. It was sweet. It was grateful that he had written once and, in being so, mutely reproached him for not writing many times. It trusted in Spanish and English alike that he would be back that way someday soon. As he refolded it, Billy snatched a new breath.

"Jesus, *two* sweethearts!"

"Well, this one's—she's just a very good friend."

"Damn if some men aint lucky."

Perry did not deny it. An elusive idea had been tagging his mind, then dodging away, ever since he first swept through Camilla's paragraphs. Why had he come to think of this war as only a sort of fiction when any sane man could see it was fatal fact? Why had he needed the scent of woman and a return of desire and the silent message of headstones to restore a feeling of motion along the currents of real life? An answer tagged his mind, and jumped away again, but not so far away.

For didn't Camilla's letter show a feeling of unreality fully as strong as his? It did. And the reason must be that, to the mateless and lonely anywhere, nothing is whole. Leticia's wistful message implied the same, and so did Billy's talk of luck.

Put another way, did this not mean (as Camilla had implied) that when two people join hands in great affection—that *that* is the way to be whole? He thought so. This was what they lacked to fit them for living well. Without it the world would never be right for such as they. He wanted to write as much to Camilla at once, and so become clearer about it himself, and not forget it. For here was one of those simple realizations which could act as a pocket compass for the trackless years of youth.

He stood up. At once Billy's following eyes, Billy's restless hands, Billy's panted breath, revived his guilt at the joy his own luck brought him.

"What about your folks, Billy: you like to write them?"

"Oh, they maddern hell at me, sir!" Gasping, gripping his pallet hard, he turned Perry a tortured smile. "I run away, and you bet your lass nickel Papa's itchun till *yet* to beat me blackunblue."

"Of course not! He—"

"Nosir, I know Papa. Mose times he's the bess damn pa, but *temper*? He's got it!" That twisted grin came back. "Don't never seem to realize how big I growed."

Before Perry floated an image of his own grainy, hawk-browed father. He understood completely why it should be, with Billy, that thought of a beating at home, and knowledge of the frantic, outraged affection behind it, could rekindle his flame of life.

"Billy, you know good and well they'll want to hear."

"Yessir. Only I caint write good."

"Oh, I'll write for you."

"*Would* you, sir?"

"Certainly I would."

"Say, I preciate—"

"Never mind. Quick as I get some paper."

5

Outdoors again in a rush of warm wind, a wash of limpid moonlight, Perry had to wrench his mind hard to make it interpret changes then in motion along the battlefront. That entire area had turned active as an anthill gouged by a hoof. Fire not from guns glimmered between the Garza mansion and the plaza. Night-blackened figures of volunteers visible against it had about them a thrusting resolution which indicated that startling, requiring news must have arrived while he was with Billy.

It had. A quarter-hour ago a unit of scouts had galloped in from the west to report seeing the campfires of Ugartachea's reinforcements not three days away by forced march. The fight now was in part against time: San Antonio must be taken in less than three days, or not at all.

So most of the rebels were digging their trench deeper and strengthening the embankment before it. In the meantime a couple of daredevils had belly-crawled forward to set fire to any cover that would burn—the nearest jacals, the sheds, the brush, the fallen logs from which Mexicans had been shooting at them ever since last night. Whipped by the wind, the fires were growing fast, lifting across the battlefield a screen of flame behind which a few Mexicans at a time leaped out of this building and that, dodging frantically in smoky moonlight with rifle balls hissing around them.

While Perry stood discussing all this with three recruits at one corner of the mansion, Milam came back from supervising work along the line. He passed the talkers, then stepped behind the mansion to ponder the men at work.

"Any you boys aint busy you better lend a hand in that trench."

"Yessir."

"Allan, it's time you woke your troop. They been asleep a good hour."

Just think, an hour! But, "Yessir."

"Time they relieved some that aint slept at all."

"Right away, sir."

And what about Billy? Who would help him with that letter? The truth was, of course, that the only help which would count much for anybody would come from rushing the battle to a decision. Any of the lucky who were going to stay lucky would have to renew their luck themselves every hour till victory was theirs. Still, after slipping away on the excuse of preparing to write for him, he could not simply forget him.

First, to rouse his platoon without yelling himself hoarse and shaking their teeth loose, he sloshed cold water over one face after another. They came up sputtering and profane: nobody in all Texas deserved tar and feathers more than a certain lieutenant. Nevertheless, he went

right on from man to man, impersonally giving reason for that opinion. The five or ten minutes it then would take them to adjust themselves to the awful fact of having to work at such an hour he planned
to use for one more quick visit to that adobe behind the garden.

On his way there he heard a horrible, strangled gagging. He charged
at the door. Both recruits were still on their chairs in a rumpled, ob-
livious tilt even though Billy, with his face sideward over the basin by
his candle, was belching, retching, coughing, about to drown in his
own blood. The veins on his temples were ropily swollen, on his neck
and arms also.

Perry lifted him from behind until his breath came freer. He then
propped him on a pillow, sponged his face with cold water, and
cleaned him up.

"Now, young fella, you better get some rest. No talk at all, and just
lie quiet. We'll write that letter tomorrow."

The word *tomorrow* brought a momentary stillness into Billy's
bloodshot eyes. Perry, reluctant to leave without making it clear why
he had to, talked of what Milam had ordered him to do, and the reasons for it. The battle would be over in another day or two, would
have to be. Then the surgeons would come in here and operate or do
whatever else had to be done.

Billy lay wordless, gasping. His eyes were no longer on Perry's. A
little ajar, they dwelt upon a crack in the wall. Meanwhile a gust swelling into the window tore at that precarious flame on the bedside candle until Perry shifted a hand over the chimney and held the wind
away. It then wobbled upright.

"Lieutenit?"

"Yes, Billy?"

"You been to church much?"

"Some, yes. Now and then."

"Fore you go would you maybe line me out one little prayer?"

Perry shifted his weight, suddenly aware how poorly prepared he
himself would be if tripped like this on the brink of eternity. Though
shy of orthodoxy like his father, he believed in deity expressing itself
through spirit, believed that spirit creates in men possibilities which
may approach the divine, believed the sum of those possibilities immeasurable. But how such belief could be adapted to the needs of
anyone facing the lightless silence Billy faced—this he never had
worked out. Still and all . . .

"Uh, sure. All right. Sure."

He knelt down by the bed, slow about it in order to gain time, to force upon himself the attitude essential to prayer. He knotted his fingers together, but what in the world to say?

Back in New Orleans he had attended church every Sunday morning with Camilla, and usually a second time at vespers. Bowed beside her, he had experienced in himself something akin to that trustful elevation of spirit which showed in her with unexpected conviction. Prayer was never difficult there, a beautiful act so in harmony with his cherishing regard for her that at times the poetry in prescribed lines gripped his throat like a carpenter's fist.

Here, though, *what* prayer? That remark of his, when he first came in, about God favoring the brave was too facile altogether. What did *he* know about God's ways? All he could see here was the crushing futility of this boy's life, especially of the extinction of that life, with not one deed to show for it or any achievement to be remembered. Nor was there in his dying so early anything unique except in its burden of pain: it differed little, except in its severity, from millions of cheating, futile deaths sweeping youngsters away like trash time out of mind.

Perry did have the reading to recognize, however, that incomprehensibles of such magnitude give greater reason to pray, not less. And, anyhow, Billy was a soldier, a volunteer, a man who had risked the end he faced here for the Lord alone knew what reasons, but one of them was to guarantee for this part of the world a better sort of life. The least a comrade could do was pray for him.

"Our Father in heaven . . ." He faltered, then simply let go what would say itself. "Be gentle, pray, with our brother Billy. Extend Thy hand above him. Ease his way wheresoever he must journey, and let that day come when he may sit among his kin." He knelt there second on second with his brow against his fists, but that was all. "Amen."

Billy whispered after him, "Amen."

Perry rose. He pressed Billy's arm fraternally once, then went over to jerk the nearest recruit upright. The boy hung as limp in his arms as if blind drunk. A slosh of water from the pitcher, however, plus a slap on the jaws, did put more strength in his legs.

"Keep on your feet," said Perry. "I got to leave, and Billy needs somebody awake."

"Yessir."

"You better wake your mate too, then one of you come up to help at the trench."

Feeling Billy's gaze follow him to the door, he paused there to meet it. He smiled as best he could, and Billy tortured his own expression much the same way.

"Good night, Billy."

"Night, sir."

That was the last Perry saw of him alive.

From C. B.'s Journal
December 6, 1835

Evil at its worst wears no grimace: it keeps a still face and shows nothing but results.

This morning Camilla went to Beaufaits' with a new book to amuse Edmond during his illness. Back home later she found a message waiting for her, sent down from Palmer Hall by steamboat.

"Dry lightning," it said, had struck one of her barns late last night. The whole building had turned into one enormous forge before the crackle of timbers, the screams of tortured plow mules, and the bawling of heated cattle woke anybody up to see it. Meanwhile a stout wind had carried sparks over onto the next barn, which was sheeted with fire on the windward side. That too went down even though every hand on the premises turned out to save it.

Together we steamed upriver by the first boat we could catch. At an astounding distance downstream we found the wind still polluted by the stink of burned flesh and cotton afire. The plantation looked utterly blighted. Where the barns had been were two blackened mounds of smoldering cotton from which charred ends of timbers protruded, and everywhere a veil of hideously revolting smoke.

Camilla investigated the particulars without one tear. Though deathly pale, she kept her balance. Her whole mind fixed on learning just what had happened, so far as anyone knew.

A Christian conscience leads her to assume the fire was an act of Heaven, a punishment leveled at her for some wickedness or other. That seems to me a pathetic misreading of such facts as we know. Not once in my forty-six years have I seen dry lightning. Therefore I believe in it less than in the destructiveness of man, which all of us do see much too often.

Now, supposing this fire *was* man-made, it had to be the result of cunning, not of some fool darky's carelessness, for it evidently took hold at several different places within the first barn. By the time the hands saw it, all four sides were blazing hot: someone must have lit it all around to assure that it would move too fast to fight. Further, I suspect the same agent, not the wind alone, of starting the second barn.

Camilla, however, cannot let herself accept any such possibility. Who on earth would hate her so? I had to confess myself that I could think of no one.

Curiously, believing it a punishment she must have deserved eases her mind a little. It gives her a courage I cannot share, an ability to look ahead with less disquiet. The act is done, and she has paid: now, she thinks, nothing worse will happen to her. And indeed it is difficult to imagine anything worse.

Me, though—a feeling of expressionless evil near us haunts me. Unless we discover who its agent is, and outwit him or overpower him, isn't he liable to strike again?

But at what? He has wiped away a pair of barns (crowded with harvest and livestock) worth a small fortune. Within Louisiana neither Camilla nor I now have anything much, in fact or in prospect, except debts, debts, debts, debts.

Tonight a tropical breeze has relaxed Louisiana, but we feel chilled. Tonight the moon is mature and gracious, but for us the sky is black from east to west, black from north to south. Tonight the blown live oaks speak in languidly poetic whispers, but what I hear is a hiss of serpents.

CHAPTER VII

I

San Antonio de Bexar
Monday Afternoon
December 7, 1835

Halfway through the third afternoon the volunteers suffered their most costly loss, a prelude to the concluding stage of the battle.

The Mexicans at dawn had begun sleeting lead over the Veramendi palacio from three new positions: from a brace of field cannon mounted overnight on the roof of the cathedral; from a battery established close to the river, under cover of darkness; and from a breast-deep trench freshly opened across the river where it could enfilade the palace gardens. Theoretically that end of the Texan line ought to have shriveled under this concentration of fire like a worm under a pine torch.

But the countermoves were swift and deadly. An early shot from the Texan twelve-pounder hit the cathedral's ridgepole, which broke as if a Samson had jerked away its supports, dropping the roof, the cannon and their wildly clawing gunners down among the pews. A group of marksmen then silenced the new battery near the river in their usual manner. As for the trench across the river, it was more useful to the Texans than to their enemies because it held the latter within range of sharpshooters able to pick off anyone who tried to fire or to escape: by 11:00 A.M. it was silent except for the wailing of men lying wounded among tumbled dead within it.

At noon, during enthusiasm over these gains, one troop of volunteers under Henry Karnes, a big fellow with hair which Milam called "red enough to light a cigar," began a daredevil drive from the Garza mansion to capture a long adobe building near the plaza, a stout survivor of fires lit the previous night. First Karnes ran forward alone with a crowbar and stove in the adobe's nearest door. His troop then rushed after him to plunge through and drive the Mexican defenders from room to room toward the plaza. Their shout of victory from the last room set off exultant yells in all the Texan works.

This first move forward from their base was completed by midafternoon. In order to discuss a much more roundabout and less risky method of penetrating the heart of town, Colonel Milam left the Garza mansion by way of the trench toward the palacio, accompanied by five of his officers, Perry among them. The jubilation around Milam worried him: he stopped often for calming talk with recruits along the way but sent his fellow officers onward to the shelter of the Veramendi garden. Waiting for him there, Perry helped a squad roll a log across a breach in the wall, and still Milam loitered in talk with the men he passed.

Most of them, warped opposite ways by the brandy of success and a drugging need for sleep, looked lately escaped from a madhouse. Billows of smoke around them eerily mottled the December sunlight. Across the area toward the plaza the earth was torn by gunnery as if by the hooves of pawing bulls, and flights of lead had ripped bark and branches off the trees to an incredible altitude. The smoke and bustle everywhere, the cries of the bleeding, the yells of fevered men, the firecracker report of rifles and muskets, the smokily flaming vomit of cannon—all to Perry's eye had the spectral insanity of a Fourth of July in hell.

Milam, though by habit reserved, had a talent for protective friendship simply expressed. His concern now was that his men should stop taking needless risks. Despite the quantities of lead the enemy had fired at them, their own loss in killed after three days of battle could be counted on two hands, those wounded badly on three. All so often had been missed so narrowly by so many bullets that they felt protected by a magical immunity, armored by the intangibility of goblins; but Milam insisted that, with the approach of a showdown, it was time to be more careful, not less. Everyone in the trench should lie low, not exposing an eyelash more than necessary to shoot well. As caution, however, was one virtue a Texan officer could preach only if not conspicuous for it himself, he did not himself crouch as low as he should have.

His worn, cornstalk figure, his colonel's stars and incisive profile began to attract more notice from the enemy as he advanced. A shot twanged off a rock beside him. Two more puffed through the trench's protective earthwork by his shoulder. Others ricocheted off the wall of the palace as he approached it. He ignored them. By the gate to the garden he paused erect to cast a tired, leisurely glance at the plaza.

The hum of a bullet ended with a splat, like an arrow puncturing cardboard. His head jerked backward; his hat fell off. He went slack as an empty coat.

For an instant most who saw him were too stunned to move; then several together rushed out and carried him into the garden. Captain Welles, face white and twitching, groped for the beat of his heart.

"Ben! You hear, Ben?"

Milam's cheek drooped against a stone. His eyes, a little open, stared at the gate. From a hole in his forehead a bright hurry of blood trickled across one motionless eye and into the earth.

2

*Onofre Gamboa's
Apartment
Midnight, Tuesday
December 8, 1835*

A line of adjoined dwellings known as Zambrano Row was situated along the Street of Flowers, parallel to Canal Street. The first apartment along the Row stood close to San Antonio's twin plazas near their conjunction beside the cathedral. The last, the farthest from the plazas, was the home of Corazon's brother, Onofre Gamboa. A single room, Onofre's place contained one table, a lighted candle, a brazier, a few cooking pots, and four pallets of hides along the walls. Now, through a noisy midnight, Corazon sat alone by the candle, sewing a dress. Onofre's wife Nita and her two children were asleep on their pallets, wearing all their clothes, because who could say when they might have to run for their lives?

A flurry of shouts in Spanish over toward the cathedral stopped Corazon's needle. She listened, breathless, eyes aslant at the wall in that direction. Muskets were barking in packs, whereas those fierce American rifles answered singly. Twice her light shivered as volcanic eruptions of cannon shook the town. Under all this she could hear running boots splatter into the Street of Flowers, and a furtive rousing of life at doorways along Zambrano Row. A gritty scramble of footfalls came all the way along to her front door. A hand tried the latch.

"Friends—open!" a man stage-whispered in Castilian at the crack.

Corazon merely stared at the door. A fist struck it hard. Something metallic then banged against it three times.

"Open! It is ordered: open quickly."

Nita sat up on her pallet, her baby boy tight in her arms. He remained limp as a rag doll, but her daughter Raquel, who was three, began to cry. As the door shook under new blows, Corazon abandoned her sewing to swoop across the room for Raquel, less to comfort her than for the moral shield of a child against the breast. She then hurried over to unbar the door.

A paunchy captain stepped inside, saber in hand. He was followed by eight musketeers. Their blue uniforms were ragged, shakos askew, faces gaunt. Most let their muskets drag by their heels like broken popguns. Only their captain came more alive in measuring Corazon.

"Much thanks, señora. And good evening."

Corazon's answer was to make the sign of the cross before herself and another over Raquel, who stopped crying to gaze at the soldiers. The captain concurred by a nod.

"We *are* from hell, señora, and how miraculous to find an angel here."

Words so romantic from such a man sounded like thrush notes from a duck. There were puffy sacks under his eyes. His cheeks were thick and pitted, his nose fleshy, his mouth also, and it seemed the more gross because he wore a neat little mustache expertly trimmed. He executed a paunchy bow.

"Señora, Captain Porfiro Martínez de Sangrepalo, for to serve you."

"We must leave, captain?"

"Leave? Señora, there are less mosquitoes in June than bullets in that street. No, these walls will protect us all, if you give permission that we stay."

Already his men, ignoring this appeal for hospitality, which they knew meant nothing, had barred the door. A corporal whom murmurs from the others identified as Chombo, a bony, expressionless Nahuatlan, blackly brown, circled the room with his musket alert, estimating everything. The rest merely squatted in slack exhaustion along the walls. The hang of Nita's baby in her arms had pulled her blouse off one copious breast so that its swollen nipple showed. A few considered it, but only in flaccid esteem before their eyes closed.

Corazon turned back to their captain. "But, sir, what brings you?"

He waved his saber toward windows in the back wall. "We will fight here."

"However, the fighting is not here. It is in the Main Plaza."

He drew a breath laden with unspoken judgment that she might look well fitted for certain activities but obviously not for thought.

"The back doors of the Navarro house—not far, true?"

"True, Captain. But gringos hide there now."

"Exactly!"

Corazon failed to understand his satisfaction: he ought to look mortified. Yesterday evening, amid *vivas* and exuberant music from the military bands, General Cos had issued his men extra rations to celebrate the death of Colonel Milam, sure that without such cunning leadership those untrained Texas farmers would be easy game. His best battalions he sent down by the river to prepare for carrying the Veramendi palacio on the bayonet. A swarm of Texans meanwhile spoiled his plan by tiptoeing around here to this end of the Main Plaza and capturing the Navarro mansion adjoining one end of Zembrano Row. They stampeded the general's men by firing straight across the plaza into their left flank. A steady, soaking rain shortly afterward had quieted the outdoor guns and kept them quiet until a drying interval tonight let them revive.

"You have no fear to come so near, captain?" Corazon asked. "They shoot very well, these gringos."

In limitless pain he closed his eyes, then opened them drearily. Still he would not give up trying to help her understand.

"How do they bring in their supplies?" The arching motion of his saber required his pupil's mind to picture the rebels carrying supplies across the garden in back. "Past these windows, true?"

"True, sir."

"Very well. Whoever comes to the home of Navarro, and whoever leaves, he dies."

"However, there has been much talk of killing them that has not killed them." She began pacing the floor; her niece, swaying in her arms, began to doze. "Perhaps they may live after all."

He whirled at his men. "Up, you pigs! Must you always sleep?" He whacked the flat of his saber across the nearest hams. "To the windows, peons! The shutters—break holes and shoot whatever moves. You, Corporal Chombo!"

"Yes, captain-sir?"

"Extinguish that candle. We will show them nothing and shoot them all."

In the dark Corazon and Nita returned to their pallets with the two children. Not long afterward another passing gust of rain dampened

the Mexican and Texan fire to a bickering sputter. Sangrepalo then
allowed his men to sink down in sleep, keeping but two at a time on
watch.

3

Corazon did not wake till dawn was an hour old. How deeply she
had slept was indicated by a long hole in the roof where a mortar
ball had smashed in after ricocheting off some building or other during the night, perhaps off the Navarro house. The ball lay below a
dent in the far wall.

A drizzle was slanting through that hole in the roof. This new rain
had silenced the cannon once more. The yip of rifles and yap of
muskets, unsupported by these, had a shrill triviality, a feisty insignifi-
cance. What had jarred her awake was an undertone of remote,
rhythmic thuds accompanied by faint screams.

She sat upright. "What is that?"

The musketeers on watch at the windows stared at her a moment,
then looked gloomily outdoors again. Nita, wearing a self-protective
indifference to everything, was grinding meal for breakfast, her
shawled baby beside her. Captain Sangrepalo rolled a cornshuck
around crumbs of tobacco. Weariness, dejection, and disgust had
grayed his face to the hue of the sky outdoors.

After Corazon's question he nodded. "Señora, good day."

"But what is it, that noise?"

"Precisely what it was: noise is the oratory of war." His tongue
sealed his cigarette. "The least dangerous part of war—as poetry is
of love."

Permitting herself no change of expression, she tucked her blanket
around her sleeping niece, combed her hair, and went by him to help
Nita prepare breakfast. The ominous thuds ceased awhile. When they
resumed, and louder, nearer, heavier, the captain joined everyone else
in staring at the wall toward the plaza. More clearly than before,
Corazon heard the screams of women and children. Some of those
screams emerged into the street. Footsteps at a run approached as
far as the Gamboa apartment, where someone began slapping the
door.

"Corita! Nita! Open, for favor! Open!"

With saber ready, Captain Sangrepalo, cigarette lifting its smoke past one squinted eye, pulled the door inward just enough to peer out. The foremost of those outside was Doña Pomposa. She drove her compact weight against the door, flattening his cigarette against his mustache and elbowing him aside. A younger woman followed her with two weepy worms of boys, a sister of hers, in whose room Doña Pomposa had taken shelter after Corazon had cuffed her thoroughly for saying she had acted like a cat in heat when that big American had prowled along behind her to the Holy Field. Nevertheless she now rushed to Corazon, clutched at her blouse.

"Through God, Corita, hide us. *You* know them, these goddamns. For favor, help us."

Sangrepalo had been rubbing the burned spot on his mustache, which looked as if a mouse had gnawed it. One eye continued watering in sympathy for it. "What brings you, woman? What happens?"

"They are spirits, the gringos. Nothing stops them, neither the *escopeta,* the bayonet, the hand of God, nor the walls of our homes. They come *through* the walls."

Her sister, badly stained by tears, whirled upon Corazon. "You have said they come to help us. But you lie! They are devils!"

"I do not lie. Doña Pomposa, when they broke into my house, did they hurt you? Did any even pinch you?"

"Ah, but those were not soldiers, only big children, clumsy boys."

"Among the Americans, *none* are soldiers, I tell you. They are patriots like Onofre. They come to make us free. If you think I lie, what brings you?"

Actually Corazon herself knew what brought them. Having spent three years before her marriage on the hacienda of an American family near Gonzales, where her mother worked as cook, she spoke the rough magic of English well. She could read too, and write and cipher.

Moreover, for a lover she had a gaudy, jolly, free-spending American who operated trains of oxcarts between San Antonio and the Rio Grande. The sneers this affair provoked were altogether hypocritical: a little straying was expected of every San Antonio girl once safely brought to the wedding service; and most of those who sneered too evidently wanted for themselves that sparkling visitor, so free with jests and bright presents, his one fault being that he was too seldom in town. Through him, through the family her mother worked for, through the great learning by which she could spell out scarcely believable things from books, she knew far more about Americans and their country than any other woman in their acquaintance.

"Very well, we believe you, dear one," Doña Pomposa conceded. "But if they break through *these* walls?"

"However, where else will you go?" Corazon shrugged. "In that street, the bullets! It's better to wait here and trust the Americans."

"So!" The captain grunted, his mustache wry. "You count yourself a friend of these rebels, these pirates, these traitors to Mexico?"

"I am a friend of the Constitution, and of others who are the same."

"Ah!" His eye gentled. "I too honor our Constitution." He nodded. "In my heart, señora, there is sympathy for the Liberals, though I must fight them. On my honor as a hidalgo, there is great sympathy. Truly, this is why I no longer am a colonel, only a captain." Sighing, he rocked his head from side to side. "But the gringos, señora, they will not bring Mexico freedom. The Americans I know little, but their brothers, the English, them I know well, and speak their language. I lived among them, it made five years, as aide to our consul in Liverpool. They are everywhere the same, these gringos—hungry for money. They talk much about freedom, but the freedom they mean is freedom to cheat the simple. Someday we will have freedom in Mexico, but it will not be the gringos who bring it."

"Nor you hidalgos, Captain Sangrepalo. Certainly not you hidalgos."

Corazon turned aside to prepare coffee for the newcomers. As the minutes wore away, the rhythmic thuds and shrieks revived, each time nearer. At last guns were banging only one room away, English voices bawled commands and women and children screeched as if being carved up alive. Nita, Doña Pomposa, and her sister snatched up the children to run outdoors, but Sangrepalo and Corazon forced them, with the children, to huddle down in the corners below the level of gunfire, then covered them with hides off the pallets.

Soon afterward gigantic blows began to boom against the partition nearest the plaza. This wall consisted of mesquite poles overlaid with adobe, which now shot off like clay from kicking hooves. Dust shook in spasms from the ceiling. Droplets of rain jarred through the wound broken open by the stray mortar ball, and at each blow stifled screams issued from under the hides sheltering the women.

Corazon, for lack of any way to use her assurance on behalf of others, now lost it. She upset the table against the far wall, ducked behind it and pulled a serape over the top, watching under the edge.

Meanwhile Captain Sangrepalo arranged his men in a semicircle near the partition, ready to shoot or jab with their bayonets. As the corner of a battering ram poked through, several fired.

"No-no, you dogs! You only help them break the wall. Reload and wait! Reload!"

But their hands were shaking. Only Chombo succeeded in fitting both a cartridge of powder and a wrapped ball into his musket. The bruised end of a log burst in around a yielding wreckage of mesquite and adobe, frightening the rest back.

As two of them dropped their guns to run for the door, the captain whirled to flog them with his saber. "Peons! Cowards! Only stand and they cannot pass the bayonets!" Pistol in one hand, saber in the other, he rallied them close to the breach. "First we shoot, then stick them like pigs."

As the ram butted the hole wider he shot into a ferment of legs dimly visible beyond it. In response a hand poked a four-barreled pistol through the breach and fired two amazingly rapid shots. A musketeer beside the captain doubled to the floor, adding his screams to those of the women. The captain himself was knocked in a wincing circle, hit in the armpit. Before the pistol could fire a third time, Chombo's bayonet jabbed at the hand behind it. Others caught his spirit as they never had the captain's, and began stabbing into the empty hole, sticking the end of the ram, which began battering the hole wider.

Unseen by any except Corazon, an unbelievably ugly Texan (whom she vaguely recognized) dipped his head through the hole in the roof. Snaky lengths of black hair hung along his cheeks, and his eyes resembled a crouching puma's. A lath-thin partner wearing a coonskin cap and buckskin moccasins, also not completely strange to her, lowered him through by hand and dropped in after him, both still unnoticed because of the racket around that expanding hole in the wall. Each carried a pistol and a butcher knife. Nodding, signaling, and grinning, they tiptoed toward the bayoneting musketeers, their bodies in a crouch so bloodthirsty that Corazon shrank lower under her serape, shut her eyes and pressed them against her knuckles. A weird Indian yell from the Americans was followed by a blend of agonized screams, accompanied by a chorus of squalls from the women; she jammed her fingers into both ears and began muttering whatever prayers she could remember.

Some moments later, still praying, she became aware that the feminine cries in the room had changed to hilarity. The serape over her was lifted on the end of a rifle. A giant as thick as a butcher block peered at her under its edge, a hideous animal in human shape: around a face brutishly disfigured by dirt, sweat, and whiskers hung strings of greasy hair astray from under his hat. Her little niece Raquel nevertheless sat quietly on his arm, peering through wet lashes at bristles in his ear.

Captain Sangrepalo sat on a pallet, eyes desolately on the floor, a hand against his wounded armpit. Five of his squad stood along the wall, hands up; three lay gruesomely slack before them. Nita and the other women, however, were trading hugs with the Texans, giggling in hysterical relief, and every child had been adopted by fathers lonesome for children miles away. Regardless of the corpses on the floor, the room had the vivacity of a fiesta.

The giant during his stare at Corazon let go a shout: "Lieutenit, looka here! What's the matter, miss? You plumb forgot ole Mountain?"

She pushed up slowly. She did remember him, yes, but the brutalization of battle estranged him. A tall, lithe officer came over beside him. Even though likewise whiskered, worn, and dirt-strained, he was instantly identifiable as the lieutenant who had been so gentle toward her when the battle drove her from her house. He unhatted to bow.

"Señora Tapete, *buenos días!*"

"*Buenos días, teniente.*"

"*Encantado de volver a verla.*"

A smile tugged at her mouth. Obviously, to be capable of this much Spanish, he must have thought in advance about what he would say if they met again, and memorized it.

"*Igualmente, amigo.* I have happiness to see *you*."

He extended a hand swathed in a bloodied handkerchief which he must have forgotten.

Instead of shaking it, she took it tenderly in both of hers. "Ah, you have hurt, *amigito?*"

"A bayonet hit me, but it's nothing."

"No, no, no! You must show me."

Others, however, were crowding in close to be noticed. As he presented each by name, she shook hands in growing pleasure, seeing under the grime on their faces a shy, respectful, happy hope that she had forgiven them for wrecking her husband's house, and now her brother's too.

4

While such amenities were in progress, Perry observed the Mexican captain push to his feet. After a few staggers he straightened his uniform and compelled himself, despite his wound, to assume something like a military attitude, then strode over to Eli Jones, who had picked up his saber. Tapping Eli's shoulder, he barked in curt British, "Here, man, my saber."

Eli, still beaming over the beautiful graciousness of Corazon, was so astonished by such lordly English from a Mexican that he let the saber go.

Turning the hilt to Perry, Sangrepalo clicked his heels. "Leftenant, to you, sir, Captain Porfirio Martínez de Sangrepalo respectfully surrenders."

This pomp seemed to Perry more than amusing: it was sad. It had the pathos of old armor rusting on a nail. Sangrepalo's pitted cheeks, his wisp of mustache, his wrinkles, his paunch, his tortured effort to act unconcerned about the blood darkening his tunic and sleeve —all made him look so old-fashioned and foolish that Perry suddenly liked him.

"No, captain. Keep it. Wear it."

"But leftenant—"

"Yes, I'm sorry I hit you. Who likes to hurt a brave man?"

The captain's high manner fell away. His shoulders drooped. Tears rushed over the puffy flesh below his eyes. "A thousand thanks, leftenant. You are *muy simpático.*" He drew a stabilizing breath. "It is only a question of time till I repay you."

"Thank you, but now—"

"Oh, the battle favors you now, yes. But every pendulum swings two ways, no? There is night, then day follows. Where tides ebb, they also flow. Soon we shall be reinforced, and after *you* surrender, leftenant, I shall beg my general to spare you."

Molineau coughed out a laugh at this. Perry, though, took it soberly: if not stopped in time, pendulums do swing. Every moment must be used to win the town before Ugartachea arrived. Further, this drive through the cells of the Zambrano Row had been expensive. A bullet through that break in the wall had hit Dunraven in the thigh, and a throbbing in his own bayoneted hand warned him not to neglect it.

"However, your wound, sir. Here . . ." A nod sideward, and he took Sangrepalo's arm. "Suppose we go and have it treated."

5

The Navarro House
Wednesday Night
December 9, 1835

Marksmen in the Navarro house and Zambrano Row were able before evening to clear the enemy from more than half of the Main Plaza and nearly as much of the Military Plaza. As the night grew, a force of Colonel Johnson's men captured the house of the priest, which commanded all the farther end of the Main Plaza. Tomorrow, it was jubilantly concluded, the enemy would have to abandon the town unless he managed by some unimaginable effort to loosen their grip. He might hole up in the Alamo, but not for long, since every prisoner confirmed that it contained very little food and was crowded with refugees already wailing with hunger. Of course, even though less than three hundred Texans were fighting now, they were running low on ammunition: they had enough for only two more days of battle—which ought to do.

Before the night was half gone the outlook changed: one group of newly captured Mexicans declared that Colonel Ugartachea had slipped into town from the west with six hundred men before moonrise and had crossed into the Alamo. The same was stated by other prisoners captured elsewhere. As conviction of its truth flowed from man to man, their hopes sank like wet paper. With their munitions low and themselves exhausted, they could not expect to hold out long against the added pressure of reinforcements amounting to more than twice their surviving muster. A fast courier, they decided, should be sent to San Felipe for help. Meanwhile they must conserve their ammunition and sell each life as dearly as possible.

So all need for haste vanished. With the spur of impending victory gone, with disappointment leaving them depleted and poisonously tired, the majority became incapable of anything but sleep. All but a holding force of one in every half-dozen or so lay down beside their rifles, ready for action if Ugartachea should come over to help Cos mount an assault before morning.

Perry's unit resignedly collapsed in a room of the Navarro house overlooking the Main Plaza. Only he and Molineau remained awake, each at a window, and Perry doubted his own ability to manage it long. His hand throbbed like a bad tooth, and a sickly exhaustion invaded him in growing waves. During boyhood he had read wide-eyed about Tartars under Genghis Khan staying on their horses two full days and nights without lying down, sleeping only in their saddles while their horses grazed. Tonight that seemed nothing. In five days he had not slept five hours, refreshed only by excitement and coffee, by conscience and responsibility. Now his head felt like a bucket of rocks, his eyes like rough glass, his stomach puky. But who else could stay awake? Somehow he had to manage it a little while at least.

The night was unlike any he could remember, a falsely beautiful night. No more than a dewy afterglaze of the day's rain lay upon the town, glowing under the moon. She was an aging but showy wanton, that moon, flirting with virile clouds which put on a shine as they swaggered up to her, then threw a heavier dark across the plazas while they had their way with her. Soon she was left naked in the path of still another cloud, and the town again reflected her wanton glow.

At about two-thirty, when Molineau had wilted down in sleep, Perry detected a commotion far over near the river where the Mexicans were beyond his range. He could see nothing well—only a rush of men through moonlight around and beyond the cathedral. Soldiers were slipping off roofs, sidling out of doorways, gliding through shadows, dashing across patches of moonlight, and trading hoarsely guarded calls. But as their direction was away from him, not toward him, why worry? He need only hurry them along with a few shots to convince them that the Navarro house was still full of alert riflemen.

Two ran from a house on the corner of the Street of the Canal to circle toward the river. The last wore no tunic. With his undergarment white in the moonlight, he made a good target. During a held breath, Perry swung his rifle, hazily wondering what ailed the fellow to run out coatless in December. Mechanically he increased the pressure on the trigger finger of his bandaged hand, and a shock of relief ran through him as an explosion kicked his shoulder.

Through smoke thinning away beyond his rifle he saw the Mexican go loose in the legs, still trying to run. He watched him stumble to the gravel, wabble up, fall again, and then proceed in a clawing crawl like a lizard run over by a wheel. Why didn't the poor bastard lie down and rest until he died? It would be so eternally wise and proper to let go and rest. That slow, agonized crawl was a torture to see, and why should he go on making others suffer by his failure to die? In his struggles he rolled to his back, writhing still. When at last his arms slackened, his body too, Perry released a long sigh, eased a shoulder down against the wall and let his head sag against his rifle. Instantly he was dead asleep.

6

The Main Plaza
Thursday Morning
December 10, 1835

He woke to find dawn around him and Mountain shaking him like a duster.

"Look out yonder, lieutenit! Goddamnit, wake up!"

"Hunh?"

As soon as Perry spoke, Mountain dropped him, satisfied to have him give up the irreverence of sleep at such a time, himself plunging after someone who passed with a jug of whisky. Perry sat up. His head was still throbbing heavily, his body torpid and ill. Men were dashing from room to room, peering through the barricaded windows, and bawling at each other in whooping, capering, teary-eyed joy.

With a drugged, hating effort, he forced himself up to the window. Corpses of dragoons and musketeers were scattered thinly across the two plazas. Texans were swarming among them, freely investigating buildings which had been spitting musket fire last night. He was sick as hell, but, drawn by the current of excitement, he drifted outdoors.

And then he saw what had turned everyone so wild. Against the brightening sky eastward, on the staff above the Alamo, a beseeching white cloth waved in place of the blood-red flag that had flown there yesterday. A plea for a truce! The timid loveliness of that banner sent through him such a thunderbolt of joy that tears turned him blind. He staggered out across the plaza, crying in pure pleasure, crying as he never had since his father, far back in his boyhood, had brought him a handsome black pony. He wabbled over to a watering trough by the cathedral, doused his head all the way to the collar, combed out the untamable weed patch he had for hair, and handkerchiefed his face until his vision cleared.

Wherever volunteers converged they formed snake dances, looped arms around one another, shook hands, played leapfrog, or paused to doubt and ask and speculate. Groups of women, children, and old men emerged from the back streets. Whatever allegiance to the garrison they previously had shown they cast aside and rushed in to join the victors, who, knowing little Spanish, gesticulated like exuberant deaf-mutes, frolicked with the children, and kissed the women no matter what their age or appearance. At the vortex of one group a drummer and fiddler accompanied Curly Callahan's banjo in knocking out quicksteps, waltzes, polkas, and reels, while another impromptu band by the cathedral played fandangos, hornpipes, and jigs.

When Perry crossed the path of a covey of women garlanded with strings of red chili peppers, they swerved as if around an unclaimed goose. *"Libertad, amigo! Victoria!"*

They smelled of onions and armpits and bad digestion. Even so he exchanged laughing embraces with old and young, fat and thin. In his unselective blindness he neglected a tiny young woman crowded aside by her bulkier friends. Feeling her grip his sleeve, he picked her up for a kiss thorough enough to compensate for his oversight.

She stood gazing up at him in expressionless quiet, her black eyes large with an unblinking, childlike innocence, while her pelvis covertly pressed his thigh twice. "Ah, *que hombre!"*

At this a grandmother jabbered something gross about mating a dog so large with a bitch so small. Screams of laughter from the others shook their garlands of red peppers like farcical imitations of blood flowing from sabered throats.

Wandering away with the message of that rhythmic pressure speaking through his flesh, he was amazed at the ways of woman—and of man. He had supposed he no longer could care much for any girl alive except Camilla, and yet here was his swelling desire for a little thing he never had seen before, and only a few days ago he was hankering after Corazon.

He ought to be ashamed of himself, certainly. Instead, laughing within, he recollected hearing the sport emeritus who was his father say (in response to his mother's complaint that their sons seemed to like fast girls): "What's a young fella dying for a drink to do, Mother, forget his thirst till he digs a well?"

Aimless and amused, wondering where Corazon might be, he almost tripped over a corpse, one in nothing but an undershirt and pantaloons, an Aztec as dark as volcanic stone. His arms lay back flat on the ground, palms up. His eyes, a dull black, had fixed on the dawn-bleached sky. A bullet, after hitting him in the side, had ripped out through his belly to erupt lava over his undershirt.

Perry sighted along a line to the Navarro house: the angle was right. Inured though he was to death, there was something so everlastingly forlorn about this man he had killed, so beseeching, so futile, so accusing, that he flinched a step away.

That Aztec stare at the heavens—how pallid and pure the sky was today! But how remote, how empty, how limitlessly empty, except where early vultures dotted it with mortuary black. Heretofore kept away by gunfire, they now were circling and weaving like diligent spiders across a window.

Watching them, thinking the bird of death remarkably graceful in flight, however repellent when close, he recalled standing by Billy Bartlett as uneasy and perplexed as now. Already that seemed half a lifetime ago, and what was the thought he had meant to keep in mind, a compass to guide him when this battle ended? His effort to reconstruct it evoked instead an image of Camilla beside him in her carriage at night in New Orleans, turning away from a gate in the cemetery at the end of the Esplanade, incapable of words for all they felt. And at once another scene revived in which Corazon, shawled and black against an evening horizon in El Campo Santo, waved to him from between paired tombs before running on toward San Antonio.

None of this helped at all, however, to release him from the stare of the Aztec his bullet had pulled down. Those glazed eyes urged him, required him, warned him, to reflect how little he understood this hovering fact of death, how little he had done as yet to release the limitless possibilities inherent in man, or to counter their perpetual defeat. He was sure only that, alone, he himself never would achieve more than a fraction of those possibilities or escape that defeat.

"Teniente! Oye, amigito!"

Corazon, he saw, was dodging from Mountain and Eli, running toward him. He hurried to catch her up in his arms, lips hungering for hers as if the sole beauty, the one salvation, the single refuge open in this life, was the joining of man and woman. His vehemence startled her; but, as he held her so, she began rubbing her cheeks and lips on his in a convulsively hysterical itch for the sting of his whiskers.

Presently Doña Pomposa was tugging at Corazon's blouse, saying in her rapid Spanish that chickens should run for cover when hawks are on the wing—this with a scowl at Perry. Corazon first made Perry agree to feast with them that evening, then accompanied Doña Pomposa toward Zambrano Row.

Most everyone else nearby had crowded around the two bands, one singing and dancing to "Old Zip Coon," the other bellowing out a lyric recently new back home which began, "Will you come to the bower I have shaded for you?" Very soon, however, the gaiety began to dissipate. More and more men drifted toward quieter groups, sobering.

Perry, at sight of Captain Alaric Welles nearby, asked why in the world the enemy should be flying that white flag so soon after being reinforced six hundred strong. Because, said Welles, the arrival of Ugartachea, instead of rescuing the garrison, was an absolute calamity. The reinforcements did total six hundred; but only one hundred were soldiers, the rest convicts brought in chains to earn amnesty by service in battle. Herding them across the barren reaches of Tamaulipas, then over torturing wastelands this side of the Rio Grande, had been such an ordeal that their guards had been able to transport no more supplies than just enough to bring them here alive. The whole column, on entering the Alamo, was too famished and exhausted to attack anything but its already gutted warehouse. The garrison, because they brought neither provisions nor pay, began to mutiny.

When General Cos, brilliantly handsome and despising, rode from town to silence the clamor in the Alamo, men unidentifiable in the dark pulled him off his horse, slapped him, kicked him, spat on him, and demanded that he stop the battle. He escaped only by crawling away through a canebrake of legs after he had fallen.

That was the story, but why couldn't it be part of a trick? Think how easy it would be, said Welles, for a troop of cavalry to charge this crowd of celebrating fools and cut them down before they could reach their guns. "So you better round up your boys, Allan. Gettum all inside and ready to fight again till we see what Cos aims to do."

"These . . ." Haunted by the lonesome quiet of the Aztec behind him, Perry nodded that way. "Maybe we ought to bury these first."

"Oh, no hurry about them. No, when they're that dead they aint in no hurry."

"However, nothing else waits." By a turn of the thumb Perry referred to a fleshless dog sidling near, flanks quickened by the scent of blood. Noting, too, that the vultures were larger, swifter, more numerous above the treetops, he turned without further talk, gripped the rigid, resistant corpse under the shoulders and pulled it to a battery guarding the Street of Flowers. There, not ungently, he laid it in the trench behind the barricade and shoved, kicked, clawed, a blanket of earth across it.

From C. B.'s Journal
December 13, 1835

Camilla at breakfast informed me she agreed last night to marry her savior—perhaps next June.

The announcement struck me dumb. A good thing too. Who knows? —had I always avoided saying anything to her against Edmond, her own predominating good sense might have steered her away from him long ago. Anyhow, my silence and loss of appetite did produce some effect: before long she too was sitting there motionless, staring at the silverware.

When I rose to leave early, still without a word, I went around the table to kiss her forehead by way of confessing that, no matter what damned fool thing she does, I love her because she is who she is. At that she jumped up to hug me hard, and wept like a little girl (something I've rarely seen her do), saying, "I had to, Pa. He's been so good." And that's how I left it.

What she implied is a fact: she is taking this step less in calculation than out of gratitude, out of an overpowering wish to recompense the generosity he has shown her. With her barns gone, her harvest too, and no wherewithal to plant new crops, what could she do at Palmer Hall? Borrow more and try again? But where? In most quarters she has less credit than a pickpocket. Under these circumstances Beaufait could not help perceiving how moved she would be by complete rescue. He bought up (at a discount) the mortgages on Palmer Hall and her town house. Against new paper on her prospective crops, her furniture, her personal effects, etc., he has paid off her current debts and established for her a substantial cash account at his bank. No matter what she may do he cannot in fact come out the loser, having in hand the legal instruments she has signed, but the boundlessness of her relief does not let her consider his self-protective papers any blemish on his benevolence, which she speaks of as "altogether wonderful." She naïvely supposes that it leaves no other course open to her but to accede to a marriage which I am certain she does not really want.

But who else will conclude that her acceptance of such arrangements was a generous response to generosity? It looks entirely too prudential. Already I can picture our more refined acquaintances referring to her as "remarkably dear merchandise."

Milla does not let herself see this aspect of it, not at all. Nor is she apt to any time soon. But that will not sweeten its odor.

Obviously I must not intermeddle. Every day every time I see her I must remind myself not to give the least sign of how I deplore what she is doing. And yet, feeling so sick about it, so crushingly ashamed, how can I help showing it?

CHAPTER VIII

I

New Orleans
Wednesday Afternoon
January 6, 1836

Not quite one month later Perry sauntered into the office of the *New Orleans Commentator*. A printer at a bench among the presses was tapping a make-ready while his devil fingered type from a font. Major Burleigh, at a desk near a counter across the front, was proofing copy, an eyeshade low on his brows, hair scratched alert and shoulders hunched.

"Afternoon, major."

A moment of consternation, and the major bounced from his chair. "Perry! Great God!" Seizing Perry's hand, he pulled him to a gate through the counter. "You sneaking horsethief, how'd you get here? Come in, sir! Come *in!*" He looped a hand over Perry's shoulder to lead him toward a chair near his own. "What are you, boy, a spirit? The despatches from San Antonio—you're cited, so we knew—here they are, sir." He pulled a paper from a pile on his desk. "How under Glory did you get here so fast?"

Perry began to answer, but a high crow cut him off as the major's eyes expanded over the braid on his uniform.

"A captain! Good for you, boy! That didn't take long!"

"Literally didn't, nosir. When I stopped in San Felipe, General Houston promoted me one minute, furloughed me the next."

"Furloughed? How long you staying?"

"I came to see Camilla, to surprise the truth out of her. After that, who knows?"

"Uhm." A constriction in the major's brows acknowledged that it was no wonder. "Yes. Heard she's betrothed?"

"She wrote me she was, yessir. I decided to come and see whether anything . . . how final it might be."

"Uh-huh, yes. Here, Perry, let's think a minute."

One hand flourished limply at a chair. Sagging onto one himself, he frowned at the clutter on his desk, then extended a box of cigars.

At Perry's negative wag, he augured one into pursed lips, fired a locofoco on a pad of acid, and worked up a protective screen of smoke. He seemed on the verge of plunging into the problem, but, shying away at the last moment, he snatched up a proof and forced his brow to clear.

"First, while I've got you here, sir, read that and give me your opinion."

Under a heading, "Intelligence from Texas," it called the victory at San Antonio de Bexar even more remarkable than was thought during the first enthusiasm for it. "With but 30 severe casualties, 12 of them fatal," it reported, "the Texians imposed a loss of more than 1400, with above 300 killed or wounded and 1105 captured. Only about 200 Mexicans, having decamped by dark during the last hours of battle, managed to escape. Thus a band of 301 men, most without any military experience, have destroyed a fortified army five times larger and captured a fortune in sidearms, cannon, and ammunition. Although General Cos swore to exterminate every man taken in battle, and flew a blood-red flag to publish that intention, the Texians magnanimously gave their prisoners weapons and paroled them to return in peace across the Rio Grande under oath never to fight again on Texas soil." The final paragraph was a jeweled peroration about "the unexampled chivalry, the liberality, the nobility of plain freemen in so responding to the tyrant's flag of death."

Reading all this, reflecting how astonished the amiable roughnecks who had shared in the victory would be to hear themselves so described, Perry suffered an attack of internal laughter, which manners would not let him release.

"Speak out, sir," Major Burleigh demanded. "What's so damned diverting?"

"Why, to see paroling those Mexicans called noble."

"But it *was*—in the circumstances, one of the noblest acts in the annals of war."

"Nosir, not . . . wellsir, there wasn't enough food for ourselves, much less eleven hundred half-starved prisoners. Further, we were too eternal tired to stand guard over that number. What we wanted to do was sleep, feast, and frolic, but how could we with them to control? Well and good, we sent the beggars home. To make them move, to get the worthless cusses off our hands, we staked them to a few rations and allowed them sidearms to keep them alive during their long journey through wild country. What we did was sensible, not noble. It was convenient."

"Mere details, Perry! The important thing is this: you licked them, and yet you treated them well. You gave them one of the grandest lickings known to history."

"Maybe, but not alone. Not by a long way."

"No?"

"Nosir. The deserts between them and their supplies helped us. Starvation among them helped too. Santa Anna and Cos and hidalgos like them—their low estimate of plain ordinary men, their scorn and distrust of such men—that helped more. *That,* sir, fought against Mexico harder than our own cannon."

He pointed out that the men in the garrison never had been trusted enough with firearms to learn their use. He related how wretched they became during the siege under officers who plainly cared nothing about them, how at last they began to mutiny, how they slapped and spat on Cos in the dark the last night of battle, and how the starveling exhaustion of Ugartachea's reinforcements on arrival compelled surrender.

"God above, Perry, how you do shame me!" The major pushed out of his chair to pace along his counter, the light of enthusiasm in his eyes. "Unmerciful! And justified, wholly justified. This war is a fight between two ways of dealing with men: between the way of the tyrant and the way of voted law. There, *right there,* lies its significance to us, to the world, to mankind. The antithesis between these two attitudes toward human beings, between the overlord's and the republican's, the irreconcilabilty between them, is what started this war in the first place.

"Anyhow, sir, I thank the powers you're here." He sat down, jerked his eyeshade lower, pursed his red lips, and slashed his pencil across the galley proof. "Come now, let's do this over and make it true."

"Yessir, but . . . you mean *later,* sir?"

"Oh." Major Burleigh, wrenching around in his chair, tilted back his eyeshade to focus on Perry. "Of course. You didn't come all this way to write about what you had the backbone to fight about, no. Let's see, when did you leave?"

"Left San Felipe nine days ago."

The major's brows jumped. "Phenomenal! Why, boy, you traveled like steam. Lord God, I'll venture your Aunt Susan pretty near fainted when you walked in."

"Haven't seen her."

"You what?"

"No, haven't been home. I came here direct from the wharves." Perry leaned forward. "If I'd gone there first, major, her darkies would relay the word over to your house right away. You see? That wouldn't do. If I can take Camilla by surprise, catch her unawares, isn't she more apt to show what she really feels? Then I'll know better what to do, and she the same."

"Well put, yes." The major handkerchiefed his brow. Valiant though he might be in print, he flinched at any prospect of a domestic convulsion. "But . . . uh, yes, well put."

"You see, I couldn't even risk being announced at your door. Only by confronting her face to face, wholly unexpected—"

"Of course, Perry. I do see the point." He flicked an eye at the printer and his devil, both of whom showed a mute devotion to duty indicative of oblique listening. "Anyhow, let's go for a little walk, uh?" He pried himself from his chair. Out of habitual nattiness he fussed at his cravat, leaving it less than orderly, yet rakish. He crowded on his hat, fingered the brim, and it too became carelessly dapper. "A walk will do us good. A man's most a man when he's on his hind legs."

He along the way linked arms with Perry, straightened himself a bit more than usual to seem nearer his height, and matched him stride for stride as one soldier companioning another. Between tips of his hat at everything under parasols, he reviewed the facts about the burning of Camilla's barns, most of which her letter to Perry had summarized.

"But as usual she had a knight at hand to help her—Edmond Beaufait. A fascinating study, that fellow. He's publicly so damned pure, a teetotaler, never touches quadroons far as anyone knows, an usher in church too, and contributes to enough good causes to make *Beaufait* and *charity* pretty nearly synonymous.

"Above and beyond that, he has enough power to keep people anxious to think well of him—controls three banks and holds the paper on the Lord God alone knows how many plantations, stores, sugar mills, gins, and steamboats. Understand, he doesn't own them —only the paper on them, only the right to skim off the profit in the form of ten or twelve per-cent interest. I tell you, sir, it nearly does me in sometimes, figuring what buckets and tubs and rivers of sweat are perspired each year in order to pay interest to the estimable Edmond Beaufait. What with all the whorehouses, gambling dives, and saloons he also has a lien on, it's got so a man can't even go to hell without paying Beaufait his tithe."

"But the ladies . . . to hear Aunt Sue praise him—"

"Yes, of course. And that's easy to understand. Suppose the interest is overdue on a farm held by a widow with a family the size of an orphanage. He won't foreclose if he can possibly help it. Not Edmond. He's not greedy for property, just for the interest, the annual profit which nothing but sweat can wash out of property.

"You see the trick? He gives her 'another chance' to pay his twelve per cent by such and such a date. The word circulates; he sees that it does. Soon the whole parish is scraping pennies together and helping her make a crop to 'save' her farm—that is, to provide him that twelve per cent." He tugged Perry's arm. "You follow, sir? Long as he can pocket just about all the profit her farm is worth, he is her protector, making the bank be easy on her. Every step of the way simple people talk him up as a man of benefaction, and the ladies think he's pretty near a saint."

"But, major, clever as Milla is, how can she help seeing through him?"

"She has the ability to, of course, but . . ."

Here the flutter of a glove from a coach wheeling by brought into Major Burleigh's eyes a sudden brilliance. He lifted his hat straight up to the highest reach of his arm. His expression openly said back to the smile a moment visible in that coach, *"Aren't* you nice, now!" Perry grinned over this reminder that he was the beneficiary of considerable experience with feminine impulse.

"The ability, yes," the major resumed, "but not the wish to use it. She's ever so grateful for his help, and she did cost him a pretty penny. He has apparently determined to beautify his lair with her and no other, regardless of how long he must wait, how much he must invest, or what humiliations he must undergo." He shrugged. "More than that, who else would help her enough?"

"Why, Uncle James would—a score of friends together if necessary."

"Her friends, my dear boy, would be idiots to consider her a safe investment. Certainly James Westbrook doesn't. Between her and liquidation, her one resource is Edmond. So-o he supplied what she

needed, for liens against everything she owns here and at Palmer
Hall, including all its harvests, until the debt is paid."

"In other words, with her crops really his for years to come. . . ."

"Perry, you've hit it: he owns her." The major blew away a sigh.
"She hasn't a show to be happy with that snake; but then, perhaps
as little with anyone else. After all, too, happiness is emphatically
not the goal of man: there is nothing which so many people so obstinately bar from their lives.

"And who am I to say what's best for her?" He stopped to face
Perry. "Why should I be bringing you home?" He again took Perry's
arm and walked on. "Because I like you and love her, I suppose.
Because you're ten times the better man, a hundred times better."

"Honestly, major, I wouldn't have involved you if—"

"No, but you negotiated God knows what arrangements and breezed
across six hundred miles like a western gale to see her. So why
shouldn't I help you do the thing right? Why shouldn't you find out
what you're here to learn by the quickest shortcut?"

He had chosen anything but a shortcut, Perry noted, favoring lesser
streets toward the river. He might be on the way home, but by
the most talkative way around.

"Anyway, it was right to come, dead right. It expressed one of
those instincts which father what little wisdom we have: as the guid-
ing impulse in war is to destroy, so the first in peace is generation.
The end of battle, as of winter, naturally begets song and frolic and
mating. There is a perpetual liaison between Mars and Venus. My one
regret, Perry, is that I'm not in boots like yours myself, a soldier
newly back from battle in the name of freedom."

Here he told about marching in along these streets twenty-one
years ago after he and his comrades under Old Hickory, during thirty
minutes of glory, strewed a king's invaders over the fields of Chal-
mette. His talk of the past confirmed that his vacillation about the
present was over. At the next corner he swung toward home.

2

Camilla's town house, like most in the Vieux Carré, turned a cold
shoulder on the street, looking instead into a palmy, blooming court-

yard walled from the public gaze. A porte-cochere on the side roofed a drive to the courtyard behind and sheltered the entrance. Thus Perry and the major could slip into the anteroom unobserved. They were also unlikely to be heard because, from beyond an archway to the drawing room, the vivacity of a piano duet exuberated through the house, while above stairs feminine talk competed with it in holiday effusion.

Major Burleigh nevertheless went tiptoe. He stabbed a finger toward the archway. "Camilla and her Aunt Marietta." And pointing upward: "Three dainty cousins. Just girls, you know, all mouth and ribbons and flutter."

Toward the patio was an alcove where a gardenia bush in an urn waxily reflected the January sun. He thrust Perry in there so that he would not be noticed at once by anyone looking through the archway. The major then tiptoed to a reception table guarded over by a suit of armor near the front door. There he scribbled out a note which he brought across to Perry.

It said: "The pity is that people see in only one direction at a time, and scarcely a tenth of what is there. How startled we would be if we looked around and saw everything!"

He winked at Perry over this, folded it, scribbled Camilla's name across it, and took it back to the table. Sauntering over to look into the drawing room, he rocked on his toes and clawed his muttonchops. The duet was by this time racing into a cadenza. As the last chords died, giving place to shared laughter, he waved his hat. "Bravo!"

"What, *you* home?" The voice drove a dulcet blade through Perry's ribs. "Come in, Pa."

"No, got to hurry back, honey." He began edging away. "Just brought you some 'male.'"

"But, gracious me, bring it here."

"No, got to gallop right away." He crossed the anteroom, calling as he went, "It's out here." And from the front door: "Looks like Texas male, honey."

Crossing his fingers at Perry, he clapped on his hat. As he hurried off, a rustle of skirts and whisper of footsteps approached the archway. So vivid were the memories which the subdued vigor of that walk awakened that Perry, through the alchemy of hallucination, smelled the fragrance he had always associated with it. Equally, the swing of her arm and the liquid motion of her gown were present to him before she appeared. While he measured by ear how near she was, one of his kneecaps began to tremble as it never had in battle, and his leg with it.

Her emergence through the archway startled him, not because her appearance had changed, but because she so fully confirmed every best remembrance. In transit from San Antonio he had pictured her as a more wistful, more subdued, more tragic person. Instead, there was about her a freshness as lively as ever. Her hair was dressed more simply, being merely brushed back from the part to a cluster of curls behind; her gown, too, was more simple, a creamy afternoon affair with a yoke, a tight waist, and a skirt less excessive around the slippers than any he previously had seen her wear. Every difference was external, however, and seemed to reflect no difference within.

At the table she sorted eagerly through the opened and aging mail beneath the paper her father had left. Only in the absence of anything else that was new did she begin scanning the lines scribbled across it. Intrigued, she read it again, brows tensing, and then did follow its recommendation to look around.

As her glance reached the alcove, her lips parted for a catch of breath, her eyes dilated. She drifted toward Perry like a somnambulist, hands limply forward from the elbow. Taking her hands in his, he merely stood blinking at her, too choked to speak. Her dilated gaze remained unchanged until, suddenly waking, she gripped his shoulders, kissed him, checked herself to read again the agonizing happiness in his face, and, as his hug engulfed her, hugged him with a power to match his own.

Meanwhile one delayed effect of the major's call was to bring the Negro butler, Obadiah, forward from the kitchen. Bowed by years of diffident ingratiation, and twirling a gold key chain received in reward for the same, he hurried into the anteroom. Sight of Camilla, embraced and embracing, stupefied him even more than discovering Perry had her. With his bent frame a question mark, his brows apostrophes, the line between them an exclamation point, his mouth an *O,* he looked the mummified personification of amazement. A moment so, and he hobbled rheumatically away, after which she and Perry staggered in sudden laughter. Dabbing her eyes, she turned Perry more to the light where she could examine him better, and fell to laughing again as her glance rejoined his.

At the piano her aunt had been fingering out a musical reverie, but the impetuosity of Obadiah's retreat, followed by the hilarity in the anteroom, brought that to an end. Her skirts rustled up as far as the archway, where, after one glance through, she delicately turned away until Camilla called to her and brought Perry over to meet her.

"Aunt Marietta—Lieutenant Allan from Texas. Perry, *voilà!*—one of the very nicest aunties alive, Mrs. Arthur Hamilton Yates of Mobile."

In the condition Perry then was, he could not help looking upon Mrs. Yates as next to the most adorable woman on earth. Much about her did deserve to be admired, or showed evidence of having sometime deserved it. Her figure may have become a bit plentiful here and there, but whalebone valiantly assisted her with that problem, and a wonderful concoction of some kind had reduced the gray in her hair to a remainder not worth noticing near the root. Besides, Perry was still boyish enough to consider maturity appropriate for an aunt, and in its own way captivating. So deferential was his bow and so genuine his look of pleasure in meeting her that she brightened as over a sip of champagne.

"Meeting this young man, Milla dear, helps me understand *you* better."

Even to Perry there was palpable in this a slyly amused implication that Camilla had been unenthusiatic about her betrothal.

Camilla hastened to obscure the point with a generalization. "Why, of course! The Creoles have a saying, 'Tell me of your friends and that will tell me who you are.'"

"It *tells*, Milla-sweet." By a wise, wise smile, Mrs. Yates invited notice of how deeply she fathomed the human heart. "Incidentally, isn't it *Captain* Allan?"

Camilla's eyes rounded at his braid. "How stupid of me! And, Perry, how splendid!"

"Not at all!" He laughed. "Captains in Texas are common as cockerels in a barnyard, and as obliged to scratch for themselves."

"Fudge! It's fine, and I couldn't be more proud of you if you were my own brother."

Thereafter her conversation strained to advertise that her feeling for him was solely that of an enthusiastic sister. He was in excellent time for tea, she said, and at once sent upstairs for her cousins; he was the very person to help her improve their visit.

"We're going to the opera this evening, everyone is." Though tension hurried her words, she preserved her look of bright-eyed sisterhood while sweeping a hand his way. "And, Aunt Marietta, what could be luckier? A squire for Irma!"

The youth previously assigned to Irma, she explained, had taken sick and only this noon sent his regrets. She had rushed off a note to Edmond to find someone else, but his mother was ill and he was hurrying so to conclude some business connected with this that he had not been able to help. Everything considered, it was providential beyond words to have Perry on hand tonight for Irma.

After her cousins descended from upstairs, Camilla became still brighter, chattier, and more sororal. Not one of them appeared altogether blind to the strain behind this pose. There was Dorothy, a sharp, attentive, weedy fifteen not easily fooled by anyone. There was Georgia, a self-absorbed beauty whom three additional years had equipped with opinions none too flattering to the rest of mankind. There was Irma, the eldest, most "finished," best read, and therefore most inclined to vivisect other people's emotions with phraseological cutlery borrowed from lady novelists. Over their stirrings and sippings Camilla, too wound up to act sensible, quizzed Perry about Texas, the battle for San Antonio, the trip back, and always as if chiefly to provide her guests with exclamatory moments. Meanwhile he noticed a sly wink from Georgia to Irma, whose lips twirked sideward.

A lacing of fine perfumes floated on the air, of tea and lemon and exquisite pastry, all making him feel tainted still by the horsy, smoky, excremental stinks of camp life. Wherever his eyes turned, the gleam of abundant silver, the sparkle of crystalline glassware, the colors of oriental rugs, the waxy polish of exposed floors, the bright and airy delicacy of afternoon gowns created a restless impression of estrangement.

In the institution of tea, however, he could see merits he had not noticed before: keeping his mouth, hands, and eyes busy, for instance, helped him hide the sympathetic torment Camilla's overwrought manner provoked. When she asked him if, frankly, he didn't think she had wonderful cousins, he could observe while munching a macaroon that to anyone so new from the frontier the sweets of civilization seemed delicious beyond belief. When she informed Irma that he was taking her to the opera, an oversized bite of fruitcake helped him look gratified. On learning for the first time that he would come with them to her plantation tomorrow, handy for any of them whenever an escort was needed, he could mask his astonishment by muzzling himself in his cup. But the culminating advantage of tea, he found, appeared only when it was finished, since that produced a so natural time for taking leave.

Camilla accompanied him from the drawing room. On the way, gaily audible, she pleaded with him to let Esau drive him home, while he defended the merits of walking. No sooner were they out of sight in the anteroom, however, than his voice dropped to a murmur charged with feelings previously disallowed.

"It's been such a long while, Milla, and . . . and it's you I came to see. When do you suppose we . . . when can I see *you?*"

"Did you notice my gardenia?" Her glance invited his toward the alcove. "Just before Christmas it was beautiful, perfectly beautiful, but during the last frost"—her lips gathered sadly, prettily, as if over the symptoms of a delicate child—"it seems to have caught a cold."

Perry ignored the goddamned thing. In passing the visored suit of armor by the front door, he tried to keep his expression equally armored, hopeful that when they were well beyond the hearing of anyone else she would drop the implication that her welcome when he first surprised her meant nothing capable of altering their lives. Instead, she used the privacy of the driveway to gaze up at a sunlit cloud above the patio and say brightly that she hoped the fine days would hold during their visit to Palmer Hall.

"There'll be parties every afternoon or evening or both," she chatted on, "and everyone will want to hear about Texas. You'll adore it all."

His jaw muscles knotted in awkward anger all the more troublesome because he knew it was not fair. His boot toed aside a wilted leaf, one spur muttering a brassy statement of his impulse to be gone.

"You *will* be coming with us, won't you, Perry?"

"That might be difficult, Milla. I've passage to sail back next Wednesday. Between now and then I'll need to buy many things—all it takes to start a farm."

"Oh, you can do that in a few days—*busy* days. There'd be ample time Monday and Tuesday."

"Possibly."

She waited, clearly expecting him to say something more. Instead he examined the sweat band inside his hat. Her head sloped to one side, watchful of him, thoughtful too.

"But, Perry . . ."

"Hm?"

The bright glitter in her eyes had changed to a darkly soft glow, extraordinarily appealing to see. "You mustn't be impatient with me."

"No, only . . . no, I've no right to."

"Much has happened since you left here, much that I've had to reckon with, and still do."

"Yes, I know."

"You'll see it all much better at Palmer Hall."

He turned his hat pointlessly and concluded by smoothing the brim. "Will Beaufait be there?"

"Oh-h, that seems unlikely now." Her hands with light grace fluffed some of the ivy leaves on the pillar of the porte-cochere as if they stood in a vase. "At least not for three or four days."

Edmond's mother, presently out in the country for her health, had taken a bad turn, she explained, and sent word today for him to come there soon. To reach her plantation he must negotiate five miles by carriage to Lake Pontchartrain, then twenty-five by boat to the farther shore, an awkward trip; but duty and his mother spoke to Edmond in the same voice. He had chartered a tug to carry him across the lake first thing tomorrow morning.

"So-o," she concluded, a confessional glint of fun and guilt in her eyes, "when I said inside there how nice it would be to have someone handy as an escort, I was thinking first of number one."

He flushed to think how blockheaded he must have seemed, sulking so on the way out.

"You'll recall how much I wanted last fall," she added, "to have you visit there and ride around the place, and through the loveliest, wildest woods you ever saw. I wanted to show it off to you, knowing how you'd appreciate it all, and now I'd like to show *you* off too. It's not everyone who knows a hero from Texas."

"All right, I'll behave. As for Irma, what time tonight should I call?"

From C. B.'s Journal
January 6, 1836

The devil's mission on earth, as I understand it, is to put us on trial, to test our strength of soul. For that purpose he carries a writ from Heaven to enlist angels as his agents—serpents, prophets, and scoundrels too. The agent newly accredited today to wrack my darling daughter is a brave and durable young veteran who has the smoke of battle still about him—Captain Perry Allan.

Soul I understand to be an essence in us akin to the divine. The surest proofs of it I have witnessed anywhere always have shown themselves in either of two ways—in creative endeavor or in action according to moral choice, and they are not so different as they seem. Soul never is more evident than when we become creators, or when we accept a hard but fruitful choice in preference to easy but sterile alternatives.

Camilla's trial began the instant she saw Perry. She is too "happy" to be aware as yet that it is a trial. Her problem is all the more bewildering because her father is helping him, a witting agent of an agent.

Indeed, my own guilt may be what persuades me that foretastes of hell are ordained solely to let God's children demonstrate which are worthy of heaven, whether on earth or elsewhere.

CHAPTER IX

I

Palmer Hall
Thursday Afternoon
January 7, 1836

Perry expected Palmer Hall to be another variation of the coolly pillared arrogance assumed to denote gentility from Maryland to the Gulf. Instead it startled him by the grace with which it put such undistinguishing distinction to shame.

It overlooked the river from an oak-grown rise, a *château de plaisance* built thirty-two years earlier, the last work of a Parisian refugee, Jean de Rebecque. Whereas most housing is a defiance of nature, a defense against it, a withdrawal from it, the mad Rebecque had stressed access to it. Full-length front windows upstairs invited anyone within to step out for a stroll among the treetops by way of a balustraded walkway which issued onto terraces roofing each of two wings. One could proceed forward over these to an arcade joining both wings across the front, thence descend twin stairs into a patio where a fountain danced in dappled shade. It was equally possible to ascend from either wing to a still higher terrace across the center, allowing a complete circuit of the mansion by way of its roofs. Arching over the arcade and terraces were live oaks ethereally veiled with Spanish moss, so that a stroll over the mansion seemed a departure from the earth into an evergreen retreat above it.

While Perry found the place exhilarating, he was perturbed as well, and increasingly as he saw more of it. Camilla had teatime refreshments served on the arcade. The appointments included furniture from London, silver from Paris, linens from Ghent, porcelain from Dresden, rugs from Isfahan, an urn from Venice, a brazier from Madrid. Even the plants blooming around the borders were exotic importations. Each item proclaimed Camilla's ability to command every sort of rarity wind-blown across the seas to velure the lives of the well-to-do. Each also mocked at the assumption that she might prefer life in Texas. Never before had he understood how she could have driven herself to marry a sickly old widower, presumably for no better reason than to share what he possessed.

Aside from the Westbrooks, the Yateses, the major, and Mme. Hanotaux, the guests included Wentworth Tuttenham, there for Irma, and Maurice and Eugene Chatillon for Georgia and Dorothy. Maurice, the reigning fascinator of the parish, had exquisitely hand-curled hair, a taste for duels, cockfights, and dice, and regarded all things (except pretty servant wenches) with the languorous dissatisfaction much approved these days by Louisiana's *haute monde*. After dark (and two or three drinks) he was apt to turn gay, whereas in daylight, when not looking simply bored, he put on a mantle of melancholy held together by inaccurate quotations from Chateaubriand, Byron, and Goethe.

Over the teacups he enslaved the attention of the younger guests by telling in elegant Creole English about a setter bitch who had died last week of worms. Her prowess in the hunt, it seemed, had been matched by deathless loyalty to him, which shone in her eyes even as he watched her "fail." So gracefully did he handkerchief his eyes during the denouement that both sexes dabbed theirs also, it being the fashion to display capacity for tender woe.

Entertaining though Perry found this, it provided one more proof, he imagined, that everything Camilla accepted as normal was alien to the frontier. He sauntered off to a divan at the far end of the terrace, where he poked into a book on a table beside it.

Camilla had enough skill as a hostess to make no point of being one. Having put Mme. Hanotaux in charge of the tea urn, she let Major Burleigh look after the gentlemen while Obadiah bowed here and there over a tray of edibles, herself not appearing to note whether they managed well or not. She came over to sit beside Perry.

From above the brim of her teacup her lashes flicked toward the circle around Maurice. "Ze Texas eagle does not understand ze Mississippi crocodile, *n'est-ce pas?*"

Perry jiggled his glass. It contained a cobbler in which ice off a Cincinnati steamboat floated amid bits of Havana limes in wine from Rouen. He tipped his glass to gulp one flooding, ambrosial mouthful, but the ice and lime convulsed against his lip, releasing only a dribble.

"*Non, madame.* But one thing about ze female eagle he *does* understand."

"So? What thing?"

"That if she flew the world around she'd be most unlikely, anywhere, to find a better aerie."

Her glance joined his, darkly intent. As it remained so moment on moment, the talk among the others faltered. Detecting their interest, she transferred her gaze from him to a cut of lemon afloat in her tea and kept her voice low. "Perry, you're . . . really, you're wrong."

"But I've never seen a more beautiful place, and I've seen a few."

"Beautiful? Yes . . ." The drift of her glance took in the moss-veiled trees, the luxury of grass beneath them, the continual river aglitter beyond them, the azure sky and swansdown clouds above them, the songs of mating and appetite perennially sung along their boughs. "But is beauty in a home enough? 'Moonshine dries no mittens.' And, after all, what *is* most beautiful here? Nature, which is surely more abundant in Texas. As for the rest . . ." A barely audible exhalation hinted that what seems everything to the eye may be little or nothing to the heart. Her fan tapped his sleeve. "Wait. You'll see directly. Dear Yvonne is stranded at the tea urn." Two of her fingers walked her thigh in that direction. "Shall we?"

2

After tea, while the rest talked on the arcade, she took his arm and treated him to a view of the mansion ordinarily concealed from guests. She said little, for whatever she showed him spoke for itself. Brushing back sections of ivy in the patio, she revealed stucco crumbling away underneath, in some places baring the laths. They went next into the library. Though handsome and spacious, occupying one entire wing beside the patio, it was dimmed by the density of foliage overhead. Her gesture at a water-stained break across the ceiling invited a poor opinion of roofs flat enough to serve as terraces under eighty inches of rain a year. The flexing of her nostrils drew attention also to a smell of mold, of rotting damp.

"This is the dry season, if you please."

Fine vellum editions crowded all the shelves. They offered an impressive quantity of the most improving literature in the very best bindings, but the pages of every book she drew out before him were crinkled, browned, and mildewed. The furniture, though fine Sheraton, was repellent to the touch because of a thinly sticky perspiration. The library had cost enough to provide for a poor family from birth till death, and yet no longer was a retreat to use in pleasure.

The grandeurs of the drawing room were preserved better—had seemed faultless to Perry when he arrived. Now, sensitized to the dankness so pronounced in the library, he found everything afflicted by a tinge of decline, a hint of must, an odor of age and chronic ailment. The floors, though newly planed and varnished, were uneven underfoot. Here and there they felt weak, debauched by rot or white ants. The walls bore the scars of numerous battles with cracks; the upholstery exhaled a mildewed sigh when sat upon; the drawers of the sideboards had swollen tenaciously shut or invincibly ajar. Camilla paused at the piano, a glossy Broadwood grand: in one flutter of the fingers she picked out three keys which stuck enough to take the joy out of any attempt to use it.

At the window nearest the piano she thrust the drapes more open. Even so the light this admitted, filtering through moss-laden boughs around the eaves, remained greenly wan. Perry at first had thought the pallor here in the drawing room restful; but, considering how uncommon brilliant days were in a climate so given to rain, he concluded that Palmer Hall must seem less a home than a mausoleum to anyone alone in it long.

"In short," she summarized for him, "what most beautifies it outside is what cheats and diseases the rest. Yes, and hastens its age." As she gazed out among the trees her expression reflected the disillusionment of the seasons which had slipped away since she first came to this moldering show of abundance. "It's old, old, old—though built not so long ago. One must always nurse it, and medicine the decay of age. It's too fine to neglect, too far gone to mend, but too valuable to tear down. It's like a senile relation, once very dear, who's turned into a care for everybody, and day after day such a bore, but one simply hasn't the heart to shoot him."

They laughed a little, then leaned against opposite sides of the casement.

"Perhaps I'm ungrateful," she resumed. "I *have* treasured it—this home, this site, that river circling by it. No doubt I'd miss it, supposing I left it, and would fret over things others might neglect." After a stare at pale green grass beyond the window: "But then it's far beyond my help, really. It already was before the fire last fall. High interest devours so much of the income, and the fields suffer so every time the river floods, that it needs a much better pocketbook than mine to keep it up. Already it's cost me nearly everything I possessed except that patch of wilderness beyond the Sabine."

"Milla, what you have in Texas is more than a wilderness." Thought of it brought sunlit pleasure glowing through him. "Nobody living there would need to hunt for Eden any longer: all you'd have to do is make it."

Her eyes contemplated this image, and continued to until they drifted wide from the line of focus. "But, Perry . . ."

"Yes?"

"Aside from the chance to make an honest living . . ." She leaned out the window to pull loose a tendril of bougainvillea. "Why would farming out there be any better than farming here?"

Her manner asked him to put aside any prejudice, to tell her the cold truth.

"Wel-ll, on that place of yours there is no real limit to what you might make of it if you try, and all that resulted would be your own. Still, I guess maybe most city ladies would call it a poor place to live. There's not much comfort around a new homestead, nor entertainment either, and little society. Here, Milla, you already have about everything, whereas—"

"No, please! Surely you're aware by this time how inaccurate *that* is."

"The comforts here, I mean, seem close to perfection. That they do."

"But haven't you just seen how imperfect this seeming perfection is?"

"Yes, only out there I'm afraid you'd miss it severely. To some of us, mostly to men, those endless unused savannas are the most beautiful landscape this side of paradise. They offer us more convincing opportunity than I ever saw anywhere else—an opportunity to make a new life, and make it much better. But to plenty of people, especially to ladies, most of Texas looks just like the far end of Nowhere. All that enormous empty space—to some it's more depressing than the bars of a jailhouse would be to me. As for making a better life—well, it's easy out there to keep body and soul together, perhaps too easy, but not one thing of any importance can be got there without hard work."

"Can it anywhere?"

"O-oh, maybe not. But unless a person really enjoys work, the sort of work that blisters your hands and aches your back but delights your eyes—"

"See here, Perry. You seem to be saying that I'm not one who ever could stand that. Not so. I've lived through some pretty trying years creditably, and you should know it."

He did know it. From his aunt and Major Cedric, as well as from her, he had heard much about those hardest years.

When she was fifteen her father, no longer in the army and impatient of making do on a small plantation, had ventured one bold leap at a fortune—invested all the cash he could raise to outfit a ship for trade in the Orient, going along himself to establish connections. Mail from him was full of hope at first, then silence month on month until a schooner reported him lost in the Arabian Sea during a monsoon.

At home meanwhile yellow fever burned through their neighborhood. The rich ran before it, the footloose also, but Mrs. Burleigh was neither. It wilted her down, then her three boys, and flamed up in the quarters. Eight slaves sickened too, whereupon the rest ran away, all except one pensioned old granny more a care than a help. Camilla nursed the sick, watched the fever consume her mother, her brothers, and slave after slave. She herself dug their graves. Out of all the stricken, just three managed a tedious and ailing recovery: two half-grown Negroes and one girl called Roberta, her shadow since childhood.

To keep them and herself alive, Camilla gardened and farmed, cooked and cleaned, milked and churned and traded in town. One day after cool weather drove the fever away and began bringing the rich back home, one of the neighbors, Robert Palmer, a friend of her father's, came over to inquire what he could do to help. He found her and Roberta loading cotton into a wagon, Camilla a woman of sixteen then, a sure hand with her mules, but barefoot, brown, and wordless. He arranged through her maternal grandmother in Philadelphia to have her entered there in a finishing school. She was still there a year and a half later when Major Cedric dragged home penniless from straying around the East, a derelict with a conscience maimed for life by the desolation he discovered on his farm.

"Tomorrow we'll ride the sorrels over to my old home, and you'll see," Camilla told Perry. Twirling the bloom of bougainvillea, she watched it solely as a point of focus. "The longer I live here, the nicer that old six-gabled clapboard place looks to me. The most beautiful homes, I recognize now, are not grand mansions like Palmer Hall, which the owner doesn't occupy half the time and, more often than not, doesn't half own. No, the old place had a more honest beauty than this, modest though it was. It's not architecture or expense that gives a home beauty, but the affection inside it. My mother dearly, dearly loved my father, and that made all the difference." She smiled, and her voice altered. "From him, too, there was always plenty of love for all of us: he put imagination into proving it. You know how he is."

"Uhm. Not only affectionate, but talented about it."

"Yes. And even after those crushing days when so many died— well, life at the old place, however mean and skimpy, had been more my own life than this. I liked working outdoors. I took pride in managing the farm myself. All the four seasons—to work in harmony with each when it comes seems almost holy: it fulfills the will of God."

"Exactly. It does."

"But to be poor—*poor!* Oh, how I did detest being poor! I quailed over the store bills, the tax notice, the warnings of interest due at the bank. My clothes—whatever I didn't wear out became too small; and yet, with so much owing everywhere, I thought anything new would look wicked. At last I had not one Sunday dress, and no shoes big enough to wear an hour. The shame of being seen then! You understand that?"

"Certainly, yes."

"I resolved then to get rich someday if I could, and just enjoy life. Afterward at school I had everything a sensible girl could ask for, and more. Mr. Palmer attended to that. But there, too, I felt poor, in secret poor. As every costly thing came to me from outside my own family, how could I rightly consider it mine? Furthermore I was far behind girls who never had been field hands.

"That all tells you why, at first, I prized Palmer Hall so. The luxury of it seemed such a joy at first, but I discovered pretty soon what a sham it all is. Now those years when I had to strive my best to overtake girls of my age, and then pass them—those were better for me than any since."

Sounds gliding in from the arcade in front announced that her guests were dispersing, the gentlemen to examine new barns replacing those which that untimely and inexplicable "dry lightning" had burned last fall, the ladies to drift indoors for two or three hours of beautifying for the party.

"As for Texas—no, Perry, a spell of hardship there would not seem bad if it came to something good. But just what you think it *would* come to, that's what I want to know. What do you plan to do that's unlike what duller people do?"

"Uh . . . well . . ." He felt like a pupil called upon to recite without his lessons done. "Milla, this may seem backward, but I still haven't thought it through. All I know is *who* I want to work it out with. If that choice is right, everything else . . ." He lifted one hand dumbly. "You see?"

Head a little sideward, she assessed this and him with it. He wished at once that he could withdraw it to say it better some other time. Here was his whole case, awkwardly blurted out, and how could he have picked a poorer moment? Out in the front hall the girls were speculating in high bright tones about whatever in the world might have become of Cousin Milla. Shouldn't everybody get upstairs and dress? Anxiety to be understood before she broke away compelled him to restate what he already had said before.

"That's why I came back—because you're the person I want to work things out with."

"Trouble is, I haven't thought enough either." Sighing, she pondered the delicate and doomed tendril of bougainvillea one last time, then crushed it in both hands as in a closed book. "Well, I must go." She pressed his arm quickly as she turned to leave. "It's *so* good you did come back, Perry."

3

"Cousin Milla," said Dorothy, who had sprawled across the foot of the bed, loosely, leggily comfortable, "you can't marry two, so why don't you give that soldier his walking papers? I'm just the party to catch him on the rebound."

"Unless," Georgia called from behind a screen in the corner, "I happen to myself."

"You better not, either one of you," Irma threw in. "Next to Cousin Milla, he likes me best, you know perfectly well."

"Next to Cousin Milla, pet, he doesn't even see you, much less like you." Dorothy lay with her cheek on a palm, watching Camilla in mischievous affection. "Honest to gracious, if that rogue ever turned those big gray eyes on me the way he does on her, I'd holler, 'Get ready fuh me, Satan: I'm on the way!' "

Throughout the giggles this excited, Camilla kept three pins tight between her lips while she and Susan Westbrook, kneeling around Irma, basted her gown a half inch above the carpet. She liked these mass preparations where a houseful of ladies unbuttoned and enjoyed freedoms they denied themselves below stairs. In one sense, of course, the other sex remained present; for, just as every art of the dressing room was dedicated to veiled thought of men, much of the talk was also: ladies could recite to each other freely here the candors or compliments they aspired to hear in masculine phrase. Even the smell of the room provoked a feeling of intimacy commingled with romance— a melange of scorched curls, bath soap, powder, active pores, aphrodisiacs, and pomade.

As for herself, there was alive in her still that quickened heartbeat with which she had moved closer, closer, to risking all the years she yet had to live. It was as if she and Perry, after canoeing around lily-grown backwaters, had entered a deep current and gone rushing toward a bend where misting rapids rumbled and birds soared on still wings above the treetops, in wait for whatever creatures failed to shoot through with skill. Her feelings about him, however, were not of a kind she wanted discussed here. She put her pins aside to create a diversion.

"By the way, Dorothy, I've a necklace you might like to try. Just one moment."

She slipped away to her own room. The necklace she brought back was her best.

"Pearls!" Dorothy cried. "How lovely!"

While Camilla resumed work on Irma's fitting, Dorothy sidled around her to the mirror. Eyes aglow, she fastened the necklace in place and tilted her head from side to side. Her glow faded, mouth drooped, arms went limp. "Oh glory! Pearls are so voluptuous, I'm just not up to them. They don't look right on *bones*." Without mercy she appraised herself, then stuck out her tongue to dismiss prettiness above the neck as all but worthless.

"Well, smarty-party!" Irma reached over to push her away. "How in patience do you expect me to see?"

"You aint the one who's doing anything; you don't have to see."

Dorothy nevertheless did move aside, at the same time expanding her chest to make the most of the little she had. "Cousin Milla, you've been such a darling and so generous in everything, but mercy knows it would be awfully nice if you'd do me just one favor more."

"That's difficult, of course, without knowing what you mean."

"Oh, if just for this one night you'd lend me that sweet, tender, delicious-looking bosom!"

"You imp!" her mother snapped from under the hands of a Negress smearing cream on her face.

"But it's so awful to feel like a woman and not *look* like one."

Georgia, quite expressionless, emerged from her bath behind the screen wearing pantalettes, yes, but no underwaist, exposing how bountiful she was where Dorothy was not. Actually, in that respect she was too precocious; already at only eighteen she was beginning to droop.

"Yes-yes, dearie," said Dorothy. "We've seen. However, it's quality I want, not quantity; apples or pomegranates, not mushmelons. But honestly, Cousin Milla, you reckon I'll *ever* have a bosom?"

"At fifteen, honey, I was thinner than you. Patience. Just wait."

"I've *been* waiting all this time."

"Common everyday muscle helps. The spring when I was fifteen was when times turned so hard. I hoed garden, chopped cotton, scrubbed floors, plowed corn, curried the mules, cut wood, and all the rest. Pretty soon, lo and behold, I had a bosom. The toiling of the poor does bring rewards."

"Mama," Dorothy ordered sternly, "you tell Papa to throw all that fool money away. I mean *tonight.*"

"Well, there's one thing we might do," Georgia spoke up. "Mama could sell off Lilla Belle. Then we'll kink your hair up small, tar you all over, and put you in the kitchen. If work's what you want, work you'll have."

"Lovely. Only don't make me black, just a nice light coffee. Then so very many ex-*treme*-ly high-toned gentlemen will court me."

Although this could have been counted upon to produce wry amusement among ladies elsewhere, it here drew scowls to remind Dorothy how hateful the subject was to Camilla, whose first romance, a thing constructed out of moonbeams, verse, and bouquets, had collapsed when her true love died by razor stroke at a quadroon's bedside.

Dorothy hastened to imply that her shot was aimed, not at her heartsore cousin, but solely at thick-skinned Georgia. "That, my pet, would be the perfect bait for your pretty Maurice. I've watched that creature, and I say no more than anyone can see."

"Well," Mrs. Yates put in, "what you say is too dreadful to mention. I in-*sist* that you stop it at once."

"Anyway," Georgia threw back, "why pick on Maurice? The whole litter runs to the same trough: if you don't know that, you simply don't know men." Here she carried the talk straight to Camilla to appear kindred with her in worldly disenchantment. "Isn't that the truth, Cousin Milla?"

"No!" Camilla's vehemence brought all eyes upon her. She compelled herself to proceed more temperately. "No, it's not true. Just because it's true of some, it's not therefore true of all."

"Well, perhaps not Mr. Beaufait, seeing he's so very, very nice. But *most* all. In fact, any average real live man, if you can trust him as far as from here to the quarters, I have never yet—"

Georgia's sentence broke as Dorothy, in walking past her toward the screen hiding the bath, shied a backhanded swat at her rump.

Camilla tilted her head, seemingly heedless of anything but Irma's gown. "A bit of lace," she observed, "would just suit that yoke. Don't you agree, Susan?"

"Why, yes, I believe it might."

In retreat toward the door Camilla remarked, "I've just the thing. Exactly."

As she pulled the hall door shut behind her, she saw her aunt flash a scowl at the two girls who had brought that vile topic forward.

4

It was the hour of reddened light and long shadows and expiring breezes, the hour when voices at a distance softly echo. Perry, downstairs alone before anyone else, loitered at a door to the patio, where the fountain sang in monotonous syllables like the tinkling of sheep bells along a hillside. Saturated with that music, he wandered through the mansion to another doorway toward the barns.

A handle clanged on a bucket behind the creamery, and some Negro beyond the barns wailed a call to the cows. Back beside the woodshed a crosscut saw was busy: its rhythmic grating, fuzzed over by Negro talk and laughter, sent a big amiable caterpillar of sound wavering around the house. Though no one at work was visible to Perry, he could picture chore time in progress throughout the countryside, throughout the whole imperial basin drained by the Mississippi. Imprisoned in his cutaway, he felt of no use at all to man or beast and, in a restless desire to do something, walked out to watch the sun go down.

As he followed a path around the end of the house a whistle floated down to him, light as a bubble. Camilla, dressed for the evening in pearl gray, leaned from a window overhead with both hands on the sill, her expression confessing an interest in the west to match his own.

"Glorious, isn't it?"

A sunburst fanned high above the horizon, a fan of ruddy gold and misted blue. Along its perimeter were puffs of cloud aflame.

"It'll do." He fingered a pocket pointlessly before adding, "It gives warning too. It says, 'Y'all take care now: night's a-comun.' "

Two birds fluttered by him, small, gray, anonymous. Swooping past ghostly moss on a live oak beyond him, they turned ghostly too, and his vision brought before him the litter of dead in San Antonio one month ago. Near his boot was the ruin of a bush now brittle and naked except for a single brown leaf. The leaf did not stir, but in himself a queer uneasiness did. He was here to accomplish something. He hadn't. He should be at it.

Rocking his head toward the sunset, he said, "Come along."

"Forgive me, no. I'd like to so well, only there's no one else to arrange for getting us off to Chatillons'. The boat'll soon be here. So . . ."

"Uhm." He spent a breath despondently. "Duties! Obligations! You do have them, don't you!"

" 'Deed I do, but none so everlasting as you make them sound."

While each watched this thought alter the eyes of the other, that caterpillar of crosscut sawing wabbled around them. A hungry horse nickered in the paddock. Mellowly remote, a steamboat mooed at a bend in the Mississippi.

"You tempt me terribly," she added, "I'll confess to that."

The air was scented by fishy waters, by oak and moss and manured grass. Three more gray birds flew by him, indistinguishable from the pair which had ghosted away earlier, and this reiteration of flight at dusk drove a lancing pang deep through him. It cut open the membrane of confusion which had been hiding from himself the essence of what, in the drawing room this afternoon, he had been trying to tell her.

"Milla . . ."

"Hm?"

"About why I came here. Over in San Antonio, where so many fell, there's one thing I learned: that what stands most steadfast against death, what fights it forever, is not just life, as so many people think. It's love. *That's* why I came back."

She remained totally still in the window. Her gaze became stricken by her effort to cope with such an assertion just here, themselves so separated and darkness encroaching around them. Behind her a door creaked; a voice spoke. She turned to answer, then again the door. About to withdraw from the window, she hesitated, lips warping with effort to speak well, but she ended by simply pressing a fingertip against them before pointing the finger at him.

5

Chatillons', she explained in starting for there, was most comfortably reached by the river. The trip by road was more direct but rougher. He himself had no doubt that it was also less enjoyable, for the steamboat embarked guests at this and that plantation en route, their gaiety gathering like taffy on a spoon as it paddled upstream. Its calliope whistled waltzes, polkas, jigs, and reels, and its lanterns from bow to stern threw a dance of light across the silken black of the Mississippi. Deep within it, too, he could feel the throb of hidden engines, the working of directed will. Its sure, cheerful mastery over the king of rivers was for him a sign that man is free to set himself a course and maintain it against currents pulling unwanted ways.

Nevertheless, immediately after arrival at Chatillons', he was needing to fight off a sense of subjugation to wills hostile to his.

The place fit the Dixie stereotype of colonnaded splendor but was more grandiose than any neighbor's. In chatting with him, Major Burleigh attributed its superiority to Senator Raoul Chatillon's thefts of public funds by means so intricate and on a scale so prodigious that few citizens recognized them as anything more than "politics."

The senator blanched at finding Camilla accompanied, not by Banker Beaufait, but by a nobody from Texas. A spare, monocled bird of prey with a sleekly groomed skull, he affected magnificent gallantry toward all pretty women (except his wife), yet failed to conceal his vexation at Camilla for her unprofitable substitution of escorts. He accepted Perry's hand as if picking up a clod to put it out of his way. For, her father whispered afterward, he no doubt had thought of this party as a fine occasion to remind Edmond just who should be rewarded for killing in the Senate a recent bill against high rates of interest. To him a vote without a price was unthinkable.

Mme. Chatillon either ignored or failed to note her husband's wish to have Perry slighted. In the dining hall she motioned him toward the place intended for Edmond, that on her right. At this lapse the senator violently gathered his brows. But she would not relieve Perry of the honor she had bestowed. She settled down to the luxury of indubitable martyrdom, and he to the guilt of being one cause.

He tried to make amends to her by manufacturing polite conversation. There was much around them to compliment, a glut of luxuries ranging from a silver fernery inherited from an acquisitive grandfather of hers to candelabra pawned away by a decaying duke. On the wall opposite him hung rosettes of swords, daggers, and dueling pistols, all very impressively out of date. But it took little acumen to discern that, for her, the luster of such possessions had dimmed long ago. She had been slighted, abused, and cheated throughout her married life, her eyes declared, and how could a guest of such fine sensibility so heartily admire a home where the wife was so unhappy?

Tonight's dinner and ball pretended to celebrate the twenty-fifth anniversary of her union with Senator Raoul. Her glance, however, in drifting toward her husband, was clouded by incurable hurt. Nothing about the party gave her much satisfaction except the food. Once long ago she must have been a belle, but the evidence of her sometime beauty had been vandalized by masses of fat. She now looked to eating as the one pleasure to be trusted in this life, taking massive consolation from a succession of dishes which four wenches and an elegant yellow butler ushered from the kitchen. Her answers to Perry were flaccid at best, and yet those martyred eyes of hers cherished his efforts to befriend her and invited him to struggle on.

He could not remember any day on campaign that taxed him more. His starched and ruffled shirt smothered him to the chin. His imprisoning cutaway dampened his armpits and stiffened him like a tailor's dummy. His hands, accustomed lately to forkless informality beside a campfire, fumbled over the niceties enforced by excessive silverware. His search for phrases in French, any at all, brought sweaty puckers to his brow.

At a moment when he was tempted to give up, he discovered Camilla at the senator's end of the table watching him sidelong. The half-amused anxiety in her eyes contained a hope that he would remain lighthearted and helpful and so keep open the possibility of turning this night into one of the best they ever had lived. To confess what a task that was, his eyes rolled up one droll appeal to heaven—after which he went back to his labors.

"Madame, you have very handsome children, a fine-looking family."

Mme. Chatillon loosened a tortured smile. Five of her six children, from Maurice and Eugene on downward, had the senator's predatory good looks, and yet their mother's expression acknowledged that they were something less than lovely to live with. Their talk and grimaces and laughter were soured by the acids of hearthside hate. In return for Perry's praise, she delicately intermingled modesty with refutation.

"They resemble their father, captain."

"Ye-es, to a degree they do."

"No, to such a degree—my friend, you see yourself how little they resemble me. Wild geese hatched in a chickenhouse could not be less like the hen. Often, trying to correct them, I feel just like a biddie scolding on shore while my goslings swim off too far to hear me." She looked conscious of some nobility in making light of her disappointment. "No, they are much more their father's than mine."

Perry undertook to give the topic a less personal context. "Among other creatures too, madame, sometimes a whole strain resembles just one parent. Among horses it's queer—Morgans, for example: generation after generation, they nearly all take after the first sire, Justin Morgan."

During the last sentence, masticating a bite of roast duck, he faltered over the impropriety of likening her husband to a horse at stud. But she was consoling herself quietly on a cut of breast. Its fat salved her lips, also the pain habitual in her expression.

"But Francine, madame," he said of her youngest, a plump little girl of eight, "is more like you. Especially her eyes. They duplicate yours."

"Yes, captain, Spanish eyes—windows of the soul."

To illustrate she opened her own wide. They brought to mind the eyes of a milk cow at home named Opal, now long dead. He tried to blink away the memory of poor dead Opal.

"Spanish? Then you are not French?"

"Not I, no." Her hand opened to offer him a fact she treasured. "I am from a family, captain, who came to the New World long before these French. The first of our line in America governed Cuba in the name of Philip."

Her expectation that he would be awed was too pathetic to disappoint. He nodded gravely. "Hm! Philip the Second?"

"Indeed so."

"Remarkable men, those early Spaniards. Where Coronado passed, Americans now, after three centuries, seldom dare to. We could learn much from such men."

"This is true, yes." Before conclusions so grand, however, she became uneasy. She returned from the windy sweeps of history to the snug present. "In Texas you learned Spanish?"

"I began to, señora." And brightening: "The fandango too."

"The fandango!" She abandoned knife and fork to clasp her hands above her bosom, plump as two buns. "Captain, you must dance with Monique." Her reference was to a daughter halfway up the table, a lithesome vixen of seventeen who picked at the feast in movements arranged to display her serpentine hands and wrists. Hearing her name, she took tactical advantage from her crystal of wine by peering like a hunter at Perry across its lip. "In this she is as I once was: she fandangoes beautifully, captain, beautifully, beautifully! Yes, we must see you fandango with Monique."

"Uh . . . señora, I could be no match—"

"No, captain. Enough! To fandango at all—ah, that is the queen of dances. During the ball—yes, I shall arrange it. You must please favor us this one time."

Harried and straying, his glance aligned again with Camilla's. Sympathy had sweetened her lip, and she flicked him a just detectable wink. Joy washed through him like fine whisky, and of course he would fandango or jig or stand on his head—anything to confound whatever opposed their happiness.

6

The senator led the opening waltz, not with his mate of a quarter century but with Camilla. Thus the privilege of partnership with Mme. Chatillon was thrust upon Perry. Camilla noted how amiably he covered his chagrin and with how much care he kindled in Mme. Chatillon a sense of courted charm. He whirled her round and round the ballroom, a carousel fringed by lacy petticoats and the flicking of his own black boots. When he had wound her giddily in one direction, he spun her breathless in the other.

On one of these revolutions he crashed backward into his host. It knocked the monocle from Senator Raoul's disdaining eye.

"Musyuh copitawn," he huffed, "I *bag* your pardawn."

With a look of witless amiability Perry lifted both hands to shake them sideward, and his head too. "No-no, sir. I owe every imaginable apology to *you*—I mean for usurping the first dance at your anniversary ball, with your very gracious wife." He bowed to Camilla. "Mrs. Palmer, shall we leave the honors to them?"

To the arm he extended, her waist yielded like a sheaf to its harvester. Away they whirled, and not a syllable from either, nothing audible except a cluck of her tongue to scold him for being so wickedly considerate, so aptly awkward, so politely and successfully rude.

For her, to dance with him was levitating: she floated without effort in the bell of her gown, and her spirit turned light as music windblown at twilight. All through dinner she had been longing to talk with him, no one else, and had seen him yearning toward her. Now that they could, however, they spoke much less through words than through movement, through touch and glance and patterned rhythm.

She had to shift to other partners, of course, many others. He too did such duty dancing as appearances required. At Mme. Chatillon's insistence, he risked making a fool of himself in a fandango with Monique. He danced also with medicined grandmas and diverse aunts, with all of Camilla's cousins as well.

Midway through the evening, while Camilla was minueting with her father and Perry with Yvonne Hanotaux, the music stopped and half a dozen servants hurried trays of cakes and wine and cordial around among the guests. The time had come for a long intermission, for visits to the billiard room, or library, or balconies, and for saunters (by those bold enough) into shadowy recesses around the grounds.

To Camilla's astonishment, Perry, instead of seeking her out, went through a door to the front garden, evidently propelled that way by Yvonne, whose wrist chummily curved around his elbow. Major Burleigh turned his back upon them, swelling his chest to force the cigars in his waistcoat more fulsomely against a patting hand.

"Now for a smoke and a little fresh air." He nodded toward a side door. "Come along, sweetheart. Nobody can take exception if you walk out with your own pa."

The devilment in his eyes alerted her that he and Yvonne had plotted a game she ought to like. She took his arm. They strolled out into moist herbaceous darkness.

"Whu . . . where we bound?"

"Where you think?" Humor jogged his breath. "To rob a bank."

Her question *was* foolish, of course. He being the sort he was, where they were going was sure to be a good place to go.

"Sometimes, Pa, if you weren't my pa I'd wish you were. Only now and then, mind you."

"Take care, Milla-honey. I couldn't stand such confidence often."

Not many other guests had ventured out as yet. Behind her among those held by refreshments, some youth with a high, clear, lilting voice expressed the general temptation by singing a new ballad very popular this season throughout every part of America:

> *"Will you come to the bower*
> *I have shaded for you?*
> *Your bed shall be roses*
> *All spangled with dew."*

Other voices had joined his before he finished the first stanza, and then many more over the chorus:

> *"Will you, will you, will you,*
> *Will you come to the bower?*
> *Will you, will you, will you,*
> *Will you come to the bower?"*

Her father softly whistled it with them, amusement warping his notes. She let him steer her along a rectangular pool extending toward the river. Among its lily pads the glowing stars trembled, and shadows of moss-veiled live oaks mutely embraced.

One of the strollers detectable through the dark to her right was Yvonne, with Perry still in hand, advancing at a mated pace away from the mansion. For Camilla the fascination of this game became crossed by spasms of undefined fright. The air smelled heavily of riverine life and lusty grass and fructive damps. Dewdrops fell like ripe acorns through the boughs overhead, starting circular ripples in the pool, and within a liquid swish of petticoats Camilla felt her legs waver like reflections of sticks in water. Although the month was January, frogs were singing by the river in precocious ecstasy, and the guests still indoors had again reached the chorus:

> *"Will you, will you, will you,*
> *Will you come to the bower?"*

Thus onward toward the end of the pool, where massively black japonica bushes crowned a steep drop to the river. A path skirted the pool inside them, but her father at that point elbowed her away from himself around them. Dimly she made out that Perry too was being shunted around them from the opposite direction, while Yvonne continued by the pool to join the major.

A flash of fire behind Camilla told her that her father was lighting a cigar. He and Yvonne, the dear fools, were children building sand castles out of gunpowder, only they were not the ones who might be blown to bits. Her pulse raced along its lightless corridors, and faltered, and raced on. There was no way to turn aside. Close on her right were the japonicas, fencing her there, and on her left the fluent Mississippi, more felt than heard, more scented than seen, except as a quivery version of the star-dappled heavens upside down. She *could* stop, of course, and go back . . . but, no, she could not.

For there, in the dark ahead, was Perry already approaching. His cutaway being midnight blue, she could see little more than the motion of his cream pantaloons, and their rhythm somehow made her acutely aware of her own thighs stroking the silk of her gown as she advanced.

Innumerable frogs close to them twanged their elfin banjos: the chaos of their ecstatic notes was a continual shimmer in the air, and the singers back in the mansion sounded as tireless as the frogs. A sea bird astray in the dark above the river emitted one drawn scream. As another dewdrop fell stonily into a bush beside her, a stone of fright dropped against her heart, and yet her slippers carried her on.

Perry came straight to her. He slipped both palms along her cheeks and brought her lips to his. Under the calloused strength of his hands she felt him tremble, and happiness shocked through her, deep through. Again and again his lips sought hers in hungering tenderness until her uncertainty and weakness gave way to electrifying quivers. Of itself her mouth sought his until their teeth clashed. She writhed against him, zealous to merge with him, to include him, to be him and herself together—that one moment, and suddenly she wrenched away, astonished at herself, and breathless.

A pause to banish those ecstatic quivers by the act of arranging her gown, and she took his arm. They walked on around the japonicas, away from the place where her father and Yvonne murmured together. Not until they were near the mansion again did either speak. She, however, took with her the knowledge that, in their wordless meeting there by the river, she had confessed more unguarded truth about herself than to anyone else throughout her life.

From C. B.'s Journal
Thursday, January 7, 1836

Flowery as roads to hell usually appear at first, few people who take them recognize that they lead to a place of torment. I myself, in helping Perry to hasten my daughter along what looks like one, wish to God I could go the same way.

Any wise and worrying father might better wag his head and mutter, "Poor Milla!" My conviction is, however, that she in fact took the widest turnpike toward perdition four years back (when she did her nature violence by marrying old Bob), that her compact with Beaufait put her into an express coach along the same road, and that the fragrant, seemingly downward digression she is skipping along with Perry will lead her instead to some thorny uphill path of escape.

CHAPTER X

I

Palmer Hall
Friday Morning
January 8, 1836

Camilla, dressed in a maroon riding habit trimmed with black, was drifting around downstairs next morning, a freshly steaming cup of coffee in hand, to see what last instructions she ought to leave with the servants before her ride with Perry. Beyond the windows the day abounded in wind-swept blue crossed by gliding swansdown white, and sunshine glittered over the greens of blown trees and moss and flowering shrubs. Elation at the thought of hours past and hours to be kept her humming snatches of music played at Chatillons' the night before. Cup breast-high in one hand and saucer in the other, she let her boots, under the flare of her skirt, tap out the beat of a roguish quickstep Perry had danced with her. In the drawing room she paused to straighten the coverlet on a lowboy, also a portrait of Robert Palmer above it, but the widowed solemnity with which she habitually regarded that image of benevolence deserted her because another tune, urgent and teasing, began repeating itself within her:

> *Will you, will you, will you,*
> *Will you come to the bower?*
> *Will you, will you, will you,*
> *Will you come to the bower?*

On impulse to play it through, she turned toward the piano. This brought her near open French doors through which she heard Perry's name float down from Dorothy's window overhead. Simultaneously she noticed the white linen of his shirt flash in rippling speed around a lot beyond the lawn, where he was testing Swallow at paces he had taught her last fall. Swallow, cantering through figure eights with sunlight pouring over her coppery coat and yellow mane, gleamed and blazed as if she were afire, while Perry's motion adapted to hers as naturally as smoke to flame.

"What lovely, lovely riding!" Dorothy exclaimed. "Notice that, Georgia?"

"Yes-yes, I see."

"The sooner Cousin Milla brings *him* into the family the better."

"She never will, though, mind what I tell you."

Between Perry and Camilla scraps of paper spun downward onto the lawn, where a thin little snow of them was beginning to show, and the snip of scissors punctuated the remarks between Dorothy and Georgia. On the theory that listening to talk not intended for one's ears is low practice, Camilla was disposed to move on, but did wonder over a musing sip of coffee just what had made Georgia so positive she would not have him.

"First, she's too sensible. She—"

"*Stop* that," Dorothy interrupted. "Will you put those scissors down, idiot?"

"But why?"

"You're littering up the lawn, can't you see that?"

"*You* don't have to clean it up, and Cousin Milla don't either."

"But it's so absolutely silly, Georgia."

"If I wasn't silly now and then, nobody'd know I'm your sister."

"Personally, I'd be delighted if they didn't, myself."

Camilla meanwhile began reliving a day fourteen years back (she being nine then) when she hiked alone into the woods she meant to show Perry this morning, a place of queerly shapen trees, of secretive blossoms, of dubious and vocal shadows, which made her heart constrict and thud and falter. That day she had idled beside a stream running through a patch of sunlight, had launched a succession of tiny boats upon it (twigs, leaves, and scraps of bark), fascinated by their passage over sunlit ripples and onward among shadows lower down. She had pulled off her shoes and waded along it, watching its crystalline water muddy until, on senseless impulse, she had urinated in it, then gone home. A wince of shame over that conclusion sprang through her whenever she recalled it, even though she now knew how common such acts were: always somebody or other could be counted upon to pollute the beautiful, just as Georgia was at this moment.

"Anyhow, mind what I tell you, Perry aint the man she'll tie to."

"And why not?"

"First and foremost, she knows too well when she's well off. See here what a gorgeous place she has."

"So gawjus it baws me," Dorothy announced. "Offer me a cabin with a big warm heart beating inside it, and I'd trade."

"Land alive, Dorto, it's not simply this place I'm talking about, but her *station*. Maybe she does love him bettern Mr. Beaufait (which aint the most flabbergasting preference I ever heard of), but anybody with *her* brains won't turn her back on a fortune she can get so easy, rely on that."

"Georgia Yates! You realize you're as good as saying she'd sell herself for money?"

"No, that she'd *marry* for money. That's different."

"Not a bit. You're as good as calling her a five-letter word—no better than a whore, to put it plain."

"No such thing. I'm only saying she's too clever to be a fool. She won't be no more of a whore now than when she married Mr. Palmer, which was *obliged* to be for his money. Anyhow, it's spoiled her for farming, these years of plenty. With that grand air of hers, imagine, just *imagine,* her toiling around some little rat's nest of a cabin doing *well* to contain a cradle, a spinning wheel, and a couple black cooking pots."

"Why, it wouldn't be like that at all. She'd take furnishings from here. She'd be clever there too, and her home would show it."

Dorothy put together a picture of frontier life at its best, which Georgia cut to pieces as heartlessly as the paper between her scissors. Camilla, all the while, continued suffering from the dagger thrust of that five-letter word. Her own acts of pollution, she recognized, had not stopped when she left that lovely nook in the woods: they included self-pollution too.

"Anyhow," Dorothy was saying, "she wouldn't have to drudge much herself. She'd take darkies to help her and do for her same as here."

"She'd take darkies, yes. And so much the worse, considering how *she* is. That's what I'm trying to tell you if you'd shut up and stop interrupting."

"Well, what?"

"If there's any woman, simpleton, who never will overlook what pretty nearly every girl in Dixie has *got* to overlook, it's Cousin Milla. And out there where there's no other distraction around—well, I'm sure women of color will see he's susceptible."

"That's a lie! He's not. I'm sure, because—"

"Oh yes he is. Last night, a while after he'd fandangoed with

Monique—which did open *my* eyes—I asked if any real Spanish families live in San Antonio, pure white Spanish. He said he'd heard so, but all of those left before the siege. The only ones that stayed are a mixed people.

" 'Dark?' I said, and he said, 'Mostly.'

"Later I asked was it San Antonio where he'd learned to fandango so well, and he says it was. Now, any dance that ornery to learn, you *know* he didn't learn it without consorting considerable with some pretty half-caste who's very likely darker than most quadroons."

"*Consorting* with her? All you've got any right to conclude is that he danced with somebody, not—"

"Oh, I don't conclude anything—only that he's susceptible to women of color. You said he wasn't, but I say he is. Just susceptible, that's all I'm saying."

"If just being susceptible's such a crime, why aren't we all in jail? For example, I'm mighty susceptible to him, but—"

"Now keep yourself out of it, stupid. Think how things are on a solitary plantation. Any wench can see the way to live easy is put massa under obligation. If he's susceptible, why, come what may, the pretty ones'll find a way to put him under."

Camilla tried another sip of coffee. Cold, it too now seemed polluted. Though Perry spun that burningly spirited mare of hers in a full double turn to the left, then started another to the right, her eyes wrenched away from him, refusing to watch the maneuver through. There was a murmur behind her.

"Miz Milla . . ."

A start, and Camilla, in order to appear cool, adjusted her cup in its saucer before looking around. Her personal maid Roberta was there, a bottle of medicine in hand.

"You leff this, Miz Milla."

To avoid being cross was a trial. "Of course."

"If you ridun past the fiel, maybe you carry it long for Naomi. Mizza Fontineau's fish fry won't leave you no better time."

Camilla's irritation subsided. Roberta, her lifetime shadow, the child of her father's wastrel brother, had a finely perceiving and prudent mind, as much a product of Burleigh family influences as her own. What she was saying existed around her words rather than in them. By exaggerating her darkie accent, which considerable reading and observation had equipped her to be rid of, she conveyed that she was breaking in upon Camilla's reverie only because duty seemed to

require it. In addition the medicine was a reminder, not simply of
another darky's illness, but of an opportunity through it to fulfill the
brag of the Palmer slaves that their mistress took their troubles to
heart and did what she could for them. Finally the reference to the
fish fry, which would empty the house, delicately pointed out that,
if she meant to ride far, she had better start, for the rest of the day was
committed.

"Very well, Roberta. You did well to bring it."

2

Perry, from her avoidance of his glance as she approached, and
equally from her grip on her riding crop, detected at once that she was
on edge about something. Nevertheless he called out sunnily, "Heah
them blood houns bayun, Miz Milla?"

No answer. Though supposed to say, "No, wheah's any houns," she
strode toward Oriole as if he were not there.

"Sent a pack out trailun you," he carried on, "thinkun you was
lost."

She commented icily, "I had some things to look into," and ignored the hand he extended to help her as she mounted.

Yet no one at breakfast had been gayer than she, every glance enlivened by the challenge of another day in his company. The change
in her now, he supposed, must reflect some trifle or other that ladies
allow to upset them. Cheerfully certain that she would change back
soon, he kept his mare equal with hers while they took a road through
the plantation.

The air was brisk, the trees softly vocal, and the sky a clean, clean
blue. Along the Mississippi a steamboat strained against the current
like an eager horse on a hill, shaking back a mane of smoke. He
flipped the loop of his reins in that direction. "Big one, uh?"

"Not very."

"Perhaps it only seems so because the air's so clear."

This brought no sound from her other than the squeak of leather
as she readjusted herself on her sidesaddle. The sorrels, held parallel
at a prance little faster than a walk, blew their nostrils clean, tossed
their manes, and fought their bits in hunger for an exhilarating run.

The scent of horse and heated leaves was crossed by the floral scent she wore, and her scarf furled gaily behind one shoulder, bright yellow against the maroon of her riding habit. These externals, however, only gave accent to the rigidity of her expression.

"Something wrong, Milla?"

"O-oh, not precisely."

"Rather not ride this morning?"

"No-no, maybe this'll straighten me out."

Attempting a smile, she relented sufficiently to tell about a scheme of hers for increasing her income by planting one field to onions, which could stand a little frost and with luck would grow fast enough to be harvested in time to plant the same field in cotton before summer. That field, the third beyond the barns, sloped down from the road into the flats along the river. Across it, liberally splashing it with color, were Negroes in gingham, calico, linsey-woolsey, and hickory cloth. A phalanx of men driving single-mule plows opened rows into which boys, girls, and old women dropped onion sets while the bigger boys, the more mature girls, the stronger women, followed along behind to hoe the furrows shut.

That is to say, their arrangement in the field suggested these activities, though at the moment not a plow moved, not an onion dropped, not a hoe stirred. Of all the excuses for stopping work to gawk and joke and speculate, one of the commonest was now in range: the steamboat. Even the overseer flaccidly accepted idleness as inevitable while they could see that boat paddling northward toward the land of freedom from which the river flowed.

"Jupiter," Perry observed, "they sure don't strain, do they?"

"Aren't they a torment? One-third as many, with application, could do twice as much."

Two of the women were not in the field but under a live oak beside it. The older, whom Camilla called Naomi, was minding a dozen or so children too small or weak to follow their mothers along the furrows. Rheumatism had twisted her into a shrunken knot of pain, despite which she rose to hobble forward as Camilla rode near.

"Mawnun, mistis. My, *ain* you lookun fine today! This gemmun too."

Her self-abasing smile, painfully ingratiating, exposed a set of broken teeth. Her companion, however, a shiny licorice girl known as Tongoo, the daughter of a jungle woman by the first mate on a slaver, remained slouched against the tree with both breasts naked, one at the mouth of a luxuriously drowsing boy well over a year old. Despite being so black, she had Caucasic features and hair neither fuzzy nor subdued by a bandanna, like Naomi's, but combed in coarse, loose curls tied together behind by a new red ribbon. The baby was a pale acorn—so light against her black breast that the difference struck Perry as obscene. Her eyes, prominent and round as grapeshot, scanned the two riders—not their faces, their bodies rather, from which she appeared confident of reading everything worth knowing about both. She offered no greeting, did not rise or nod or stir, merely continued her bold examination.

Camilla acted unaware of her, though Perry thought her irritation sufficiently clear. She gave Naomi a bottle of "bitters" containing laudanum to ease her pain, instructed her minutely in its use, then inquired after the health of children gaping at her from beyond the tree.

"Mose ud um sazfaction last few days, mistis. All sazfaction excusun Madlun's Hubut en Ezabelle's Tom."

"What ails Tom and Herbert?"

"Doon pully, mistis. Jus ain come up none."

The wet northers before Christmas, Camilla explained to Perry, had brought an epidemic of grippe, carrying off one mother, one prime hand, and two children. So easily did pestilence invade the crowded little cabins in the quarters that she wondered sometimes how any became so ancient as Naomi (who, despite looking eighty, was but fifty-seven). While the latter gave an account of this child and that, a boy palleted on gunnies beyond the tree began to cough.

"Thas little Tom coughun so, mistis."

"I see it is."

His cough, thick, pulpy, and strangulating, left him too exhausted to be curious any longer about the horses or the people upon them. He rested a cheek on one extended arm, eyes listlessly watching his wrist twitch the hand beyond it.

Anticipating that Camilla would want to examine Tom, Perry rocked from his saddle to take Oriole's rein and offer his hand. In dismounting with its help, she widened her eyes at his wrist.

"Perry! A wound! *Was* that a wound?"

"Yes, but—"

"Why didn't you tell me?" She pushed the sleeve back, keeping his hand gripped in hers. "To think, all this time together and I never noticed!"

"Wasn't serious, really. Bayonet tickled me some."

"Then why should it look so sore?"

It did look wicked, a puffy welt darkened by the strain of checking back Swallow's passion to run.

"Because it turned septic, though it was nursed well."

"Oh, it was!"

"Pretty well, yes."

"I dare say!" She released it as if it smelled. "And who nursed it? That half-caste you danced with?"

He gaped at her in stupefaction. Her knowledge of Corazon was bewildering enough, and her stress on half-caste even more so. Of course any woman not stone blind must know that plenty of men in Dixie now and then "crossed the color line." All the same, ladies were expected never, simply never, to imply before gentlemen that they were aware of such failings—*never*. Just why should Camilla deliberately open the snakepit of ugly feeling which silence on the subject was supposed to keep covered?

"What you mean?"

"I think you know."

Naomi, to seem unaware of their quarrel, bent delicately aside, applying a corner of her apron to the nose of a gawking girl-child. But Tongoo let her bullet-round eyes watch them as openly as a stockbreeder observing a mare and stallion. Meanwhile she scratched her lower belly, unconcerned that in the presence of Quality such itches were supposed to be allowed to itch.

"Triflun heathen haw, whuh's yuh mannuhs?" Naomi growled at her.

In French, Camilla asked Tongoo, "Why aren't you working?"

Tongoo's sole response was to draw the mouth of her baby, who had fallen asleep, back to her nipple. However, as the overseer, Wyatt Bowen, was advancing from the lower end of the field and would soon be at hand to discipline her, Camilla circled the tree to examine each of the children and instruct Naomi about what to do for them.

Perry, restless from the poison in her remarks, dug out his pocketknife to lengthen one of his stirrups by drilling an additional hole in the strap, then laid the knife on the saddle while moving the buckle. Swallow began pawing the grass, impatient to be gone, thus jarring the knife off in the direction away from himself. Tongoo swooped forward from her slouch against the tree to recover it, her baby still asleep in one arm. Instead of returning it to the saddle, she brought it around Swallow and presented it to Perry, her red-haw nipples pointing at him from licorice breasts, her face lit by anticipation that he would be pleased.

The coolest procedure would have been to order her by a thrust of the chin to put it back on the saddle. Instead, surprised as he was, he accepted it from her hand and, rigid though the code was against thanks to slaves, nodded in appreciation. Her smile revealed her triumph in being treated, not as a slave, but as a woman, and her hip-sway in returning to the tree indicated confidence that, if he was going to be the next master of this plantation, she would rise in the world a rung or two. Though Camilla acted too intent upon the children to observe this, he noticed a flush stain her cheek.

Meanwhile the overseer, stopping a deferential distance from Camilla, rested the back of his right hand on his hip, fingers protruding behind. Below those fingers a holstered pistol hung from his belt. His eyes, pale, attentive, and sad, gazed from a face creased and loosened like a bloodhound's. Perry noticed with a start that little Tom's features strikingly resembled his.

When Camilla rose to face Mr. Bowen, it was to ask how soon the field would be in seed.

"Tuesday evenun, mam."

"Not till Tuesday? Gracious land, we have to be quick with this crop or it won't mature in time. And so much else to do besides."

"Doon the bes I kin, mam." His manner contained no resentment over the impatience in hers, nothing but the imperturbable assurance of one who knew that the pace here was subject to his will, not hers. "It's a big fiel, an four-five hans still half sick. Work goes slow with things in this kine of a condition."

"Not if you kept them busy, it wouldn't." She looked away toward the Negroes in the direction of the river. With few exceptions they were hardly moving, so intent were they upon trying from afar to decipher what was occurring under the live oak. Her lips thinned, then relaxed. She spoke deliberately so that Naomi, when among them, could quote exactly what followed: "If by night tomorrow you've finished here, I'll reward all hands with two pounds of extra pork for every cabin."

He brightened, but not much. "Yessum."

"And if by dusk Tuesday you've also cleared away the driftwood that that last flood scattered over yonder canefield, I'll add five of yams."

Still without a spark: "Yessum."

"And for you, a cash gratuity of five dollars."

His weight lifted away from his extended thigh. "Reckon they'll liven up considerable, mam. They'll finish."

She came to the near side of the tree, her eyes glittering. She turned her back fully on Tongoo, who was still lazing against the tree.

"Mr. Bowen!"

"Yessum?"

"Why hasn't this wench weaned that boy?"

The charged quality of her voice made Perry look more sharply at the child's face. It resembled Wyatt Bowen's nearly as much as Tom's in quite a different way. Bowen, however, replied as if they were discussing a calf.

"Curious sort of boy, mam: won't wean. She don't let him have the tit, he cries an hollas an won't take nothin diffunt. Just *won't* wean."

Tongoo meanwhile squeezed a nipple over her baby's slack mouth, forcing out a jet of milk as proof that she was still capable of what she was there for.

"She'll wean him, or both go to market!"

Mr. Bowen sighed but did not answer.

"I've told you before: she *must* be treated the same as the rest. I tell you so now for the last time. Any more favoritism and I sell her."

The overseer again rested a hand above that pistol. His pale eyes temperately surveyed the horizon. As Camilla waited for an answer which did not come, Perry noticed a vein on her temple swell. A fidget came into the hand gripping her quirt, which trembled at the tip. He was surprised by the dread in himself that she might use it. Mr. Bowen, despite the weapon he carried, gave the appearance of being the kind of overseer who seldom used a whip himself, who assigned whatever whipping he thought necessary to some buck who considered that chore a joy. Hitting him before her slaves would be almost as unthinkable as murder. Perry's breath altered in relief as Camilla flipped the quirt up under her elbow, where its lash continued to quiver.

"Tell her to make herself decent and go to work."

Mr. Bowen appeared grateful that she at last had given him an order specific enough to act upon. He spoke to Tongoo in Creole which needed no translation to be understood by anyone: as he talked, he flipped four joined fingers in the direction of her breasts like a paint brush, lifted the same hand from the baby toward Naomi, and concluded with a gesture toward the field as gentle as a pat on the bottom. Without either haste or hesitation Tongoo drew her blouse across her breasts, gave her baby to Naomi, and sauntered into the field, her feet blacker than the furrows, but soles showing light as her walk exposed them behind.

Camilla turned from Bowen to remind Naomi what was to be done for Tom and Herbert. She then mounted her sidesaddle, careful to overlook Perry's existence altogether, and cantered off along the road.

3

Her abruptness carried her a good way ahead of Perry and quickly into the timberland along a trail for hauling out wood. Undergrowth, vines, fallen branches, rotting leaves, and weirdly distorted trees made much of the area wild and ragged, but it also contained intervals as orderly as a park. That her own extremes were matched here by outward equivalents on a vast and timeless scale ordinarily made it agreeable to her, and often she had thought how much more so it would seem with a companion able to enjoy it equally well—in fact, with Perry himself. She did not really have anything to be cross with him about except a piece of gossip which she had no business listening to and which came from a nitwit no sensible person should take seriously one moment. She reined Oriole in to an easy foxtrot, and presently Swallow was close behind.

For a while they rode so, she coolly ahead, he following. Where the road dipped through a glittering, musical little creek, the same one she had fouled at another place fourteen years ago, she saw a chance to break the stalemate by watering Oriole, and sufficiently on one side to let Swallow crowd up for a drink also. Not yet ready to risk meeting his eyes, she looked away across the creek into a cloister of live oaks steeply overarched by moss-laden boughs.

"Like my woods?"

He slumped forward, one elbow across Swallow's withers. His relaxation was offset by a kindling in his glance. The pleasurable way he sniffed the air alerted her to the fragrance of oaks and mold and covert blossoms, a tangy, vegetarian musk.

"Uhm. They're fine."

Waiting for him to say more, she heard instead the sipping of the mares, the perpetual tune of the creek, the sibilance of the wind through leaves and moss. Speckles of green-gold sunlight illuminated the cloister before them as through stained windows, and its serenity was accentuated by the wild disorder around it.

"Just what you need here too." His grin tilted sideward as he added, "With a man like Wyatt Bowen around, you need someplace like this to give you peace of mind."

"Oh, that *animal!*"

"But, Milla . . ."

"Yes?"

"Why tolerate anybody that bothers you so?"

"Yes, I loathe him. However, the main reason I loathe him is mortally difficult to talk about, at least to a man." An abrupt containment in Perry's expression told her that there was no need to explain what she meant, also that she was again on dangerous ground. "And the truth is, he *is* a useful overseer. He's been here much longer than I have. Mr. Palmer hired him years ago. He knows every acre on this place. He knows every peculiarity in every darkie here, and they know him. Under no circumstances will any of them cross him: he's mild and sympathetic most times, but *such* a terror when he's mad. They look up to him somewhat the way they look up to Da Lawd: any kindly being who can turn so ferocious is very good to have on their side, in trouble or out."

"Hm, yes." Perry mused about it. "Any man who can scare *them* so much can scare Evil away too."

"That's it. Satan himself better take care around Massa Bone, and certainly there's less devilment here when he's on the place. Once I did dismiss him, and all sorts of trouble started very shortly. The new overseer hadn't been here a week when two hands got into a cutting scrape that left one dead, and the other ran away. At that rate, *not* having Mr. Bowen would bankrupt me. The sheriff brought hounds to start a hunt, but the runaway came peaceably home in a wagon with Massa Bone. He'd run to him for help in his trouble!"

"So-o you gave Massa Bone another chance."

"Yes, because I couldn't afford not to."

As the mares had finished drinking, she let Oriole proceed along the road, but held her at a walk well on one side so that Swallow could remain parallel.

"Still," said Perry, "if he's so hard to get along with, so disagree-able—"

"No-no! He's not; he simply makes *me* disagreeable. Or, no, it's slavery that makes me disagreeable, not him." Having ventured that far, she rushed on more boldly. "Oh, dear heaven, what a wicked sickness it is—a black plague blighting us more than any pestilence ever has. Often, often, often, it does seem to harm the owners more than the slaves."

Sidelong she measured the effect on Perry. He was blankly exam-ining the woods around them.

"Of course, *some* people would think that's fearfully wrong to say. Are you offended?"

"No-o, just surprised is all."

"Why surprised?"

"Conditions being what they are."

"What conditions?"

"Without slavery, how would you manage?"

"But how *too* precisely the point, Perry! Gracious land, if I did know how to manage without them, is it likely I'd go on putting up *with* them?"

He said nothing. A cluster of redwing blackbirds twanging in a tree they were approaching seemed to have all his attention. Answer-ing her punitive tone by ignoring her altogether seemed to her as skillful as it was vexing. It required her to sound more reasonable.

"In Texas, Perry, where there's so much opportunity, so much room, surely it's possible to begin over in some totally different way. Can't one do without them?"

"Without slaves?" (This sounded to her like, "Great God, are you still harping on that?")

"Certainly! We're not speaking of silver plate or pianos, are we?"

He kept silent awhile. When he did speak, though, he somehow managed to sound calm and reflective. "The situation out there's peculiar. It's hard to do without them *because* there's so much room. 'The harvest truly is plenteous, but the laborers are few.' And the old rule applies: many acres, many slaves. Of course some farmers do without them, but those who do stay poor."

"All?"

"Pretty near all. How many plows can one man work alone? One! Just one. And one-plow farmers generally die in one-room cabins. I like handsome living, and I mean to develop it in Texas, but without debts. I hate debts. They bind a man and worry him and gall him till they spoil the sight of everything they helped him pay for. They can turn a handsome manor house into a sort of penitentiary, as they did with my own father. How to make big land pay big without plenty of help I don't know, and I'd be glad if somebody'd tell me."

"Well, you can't possibly hate debt any worse than I. But can't you hire help?"

"For a while, maybe so."

"What do you mean, *a while?*"

"There's so much cheap land, few men hire out long—just long enough to buy their own land."

"But not *all* men. Say what you will, Mr. Palmer hired the Tiptons, and they've stayed faithfully by, haven't they?"

"Uhm. They're there, yes."

A twirk of his lips brought to mind a letter from him hinting how near worthless the Tiptons seemed when he visited her place last fall. She hastened in growing irritation to cite a better example. "And the Springfields—your letters told of a German family who've served them all these years."

"The Bauernschmidts, true. They've been steadfast because Dr. Springfield took them in when they came off an immigrant ship near dead of sickness—and because he's deeding them one-third of his land, an eventual fortune, very likely."

"But isn't it cheaper to pay in land for help than lose one's soul to slaves?"

"Hold on now! Has everyone who keeps slaves given their souls away?"

To turn her words back upon her in this fashion seemed to her a piece of courtroom impudence. "That's *not* what I meant, as you know very well." She struggled to regain her self-control. "I'm only . . . for example, natives—can't one hire natives?"

"Indians? They won't work, and no Mexicans in fifty miles."

"But you sound so set about the whole question, Perry! To you it's all a closed book. Isn't it possible to manage some way?"

"If you can't manage without slaves here, how can you expect to in Texas? Out there we've several times the land. If we didn't have slavery we'd have to invent something like it, as they have in the rest of Mexico. What is peonage but slavery with a different name? Their pious talk about having abolished it is hypocritical foolishness, like a good deal of talk right here in the U.S.A."

"Well, I see no cause to act so ouchy. I'm merely—"

"I'm *not* acting ouchy. I'm just saying to manage right a planter needs slaves there the same as here. They're the only help he can count on. Actually that's one reason I came back, to buy a few good hands who can help me start a crop."

She thought she detected an implication that if she supposed love alone had brought him so far she might as well change her mind.

"I see no reliable way to get along without them and still prosper, none. The Mexicans seldom hire out singly. They like to stay near their own kind of people. They're sociable as beans in a bag. Of course some planters do use them, although—"

"I dare say!"

"Beg pardon?"

"Never mind."

"Some planters hire several families and let them village together right there on the plantation. I talked that possibility over myself with some Mexicans in San Antonio before I left, but—"

"Oh, you did!"

"Yes, I like them, the peaceable kind, and some farm well too."

"Merely like them?"

That brought a sharp look from him. "No *merely* about it. Plain like them, that's all. The only thing is—"

"And aren't the women pretty, though!"

"Some are. But I was going to say—"

"Cook and mend well?"

"Some, of course. But—"

"As well as they fandango?"

"See here now—!"

"Much better than they nurse a wound, I trust."

"Milla, what makes you say any such a thing as that?"

"Me? Why, it's only that I see so well what's the matter with you."

"*Stop* this infernal insinuating," he bawled, and so loudly the mares began to bounce in alarm. "Speak out and be done with it."

"I've discovered your weakness, that's all."

"*What* weakness?"

"Yes, of course, you do have several. The one I simply can't stand, though, is that you're so *color blind!*"

Having thrown that knife with all her might, she snapped her quirt at Oriole's flank, intending to gallop away. Perry's right hand lashed out, caught her rein, and jerked Oriole over against Swallow's neck.

"Damn you, what's back of this?"

The two mares reared together like wrestlers, but he held them so, glaring at her across the wild-eyed flinging and weaving of their heads. In a long overarm sweep she aimed her quirt at his scarred hand. She would have hit it a second time, but he caught the quirt as it came down, ripped it free, and whipped it away into the woods. Oriole, suddenly released, staggered back until her rump jolted against a tree. Camilla teetered giddily on her sidesaddle, clutching the mane before her in panic while Oriole spun away like a deer clawed by a cougar.

Perry, in the meantime, spurred up beside her to help her recover. In a passion to be independent, she wrenched herself upright and whirled aside.

"You get away from me! Don't you *dare* touch me again!"

He reined back. Once she had Oriole under control, she whirled past him, eyes ignoring him, and galloped off toward home.

But no thud of hooves pursued her—all through the woods, none at all. On reaching the first field she drew up to listen, motionless. Oriole lifted her head to throw a lonesome, puzzled whicker backward among the trees. The only response was a fricative murmur of boughs and a far, frail, trailing song from slaves who were seeding a crop for her nearer home. Hit again by a flash of anger, Camilla kicked her mare's ribs and galloped the rest of the way home alone.

From C. B.'s Journal
Friday, January 8, 1836

Warm, gusty, beautiful weather tonight, but it lacks any counterpart here within Palmer Hall, where the atmosphere has turned murky and cold.

Events earlier today remind me of a tale about an oriental princess, daughter of a doting potentate, who tortured her lover because he let a pretty serving maid stay too long with his tea: she had him publicly stripped and flung naked from a movable battle tower into an enormous tangle of wild rose bushes. Somehow he did struggle out, but more or less a eunuch and wearing a slippery red suit which so colored her thoughts that she sickened with a bloody issue, took to her bed, and never left it alive.

When I heard this told on my travels years ago, the originality of its barbarism astonished me, and still does a bit, though I'm aware now that tamer manifestations of it occur every day throughout every corner of the earth. The world around, too, such vengeance generally brings down at least two victims, the punishing with the punished. Certainly it did here today.

This morning Camilla returned alone from a ride with Perry. Later Swallow wandered in with reins and stirrups tied up across her saddle to prevent them from hooking on trees or gateposts: obviously Perry had released her to the horse instinct for home while he himself went elsewhere, presumably by steamboat back to town. Camilla withdrew to her room until evening, when she confided to Yvonne that she had tried to horsewhip him for some fling of his in San Antonio. The attempt hurt her worse than it did him, literally, for what she brought upon herself was a whip no eye can see. Her rupture with him spoiled all plans for entertaining her guests this evening and drove the West-brooks home, Susan being desperate to know what had become of him.

To escape the gloom seeping through the house, Ham Yates and I set off for Palmer Landing after supper for a little night fishing. As we walked down under wind-struck trees darkening the lawn, I was delighted to discover all the stars still in place above them. A "Dixie nightingale's" song came tumbling out of a live oak as black and bulky as smoke from an exploded magazine, every phrase of his melody speaking of timeless truths, as the voices of nature generally do for those who care to listen.

Then the river: though dark and subtle enough to prefigure death, it had a blown turbulence which teemed with life, as did the insistent current tugging at our lines and the pulse of waves below us and the smell of fish all about us. Though the air was summery, a bull alligator bellowing at a distance upstream sent through it a recurring shiver. Eventually a jerk came on my line almost too stout to hold: I pulled out a 28-pound catfish, the biggest landed near here in some while, a most admirable envoy of life unseen.

By that time I would have had to be very sick or very drunk not to acknowledge (as we must whenever we become wholly awake to what is around us) that the subtle and mysterious, the miraculous and lucky and terrible too, exist throughout all nature—wherever we have the wit and vision to discover them.

One of the miracles, however, is how seldom we do so discover.

Humanity can take shame in the multitude of nights such as this, which may complain like the children of the market place in Matthew:

> *"We have piped unto you,*
> *And ye have not danced;*
> *We have mourned unto you,*
> *And ye have not lamented."*

CHAPTER XI

I

New Orleans
Saturday
January 9, 1836

Perry's chief business the next morning was at the slave market. Situated near the Opera House, it received customers in a lobby dignified by plush drapery, hand-painted cuspidors, and statues of nymphs wearing wisps of marble drygoods strategically blown. A fashionable excess of servants anticipated each visitor's every wish. Doors leaped open as he approached them; cigars and locofocos were to be had at the flick of an eye; free wine, brandy, whisky, or mixed drinks further encouraged an attitude of reckless extravagance.

Perry accepted nothing, intent upon keeping his wits about him. His abstinence attracted a man easily identified as the prince of this palace: a brisk manner, jutting chin, bold nose, and bored, assured eyes announced him immeasurably elevated.

"Afternoon, sir! Mr. Archibald Hubbard at your service." The Dixie slurring of his *r*'s and *a*'s rendered his name as Mist Awchibold Hubbud, and not without elegance. He offered a hand lumpily fleshed and jeweled, meanwhile estimating the quality of Perry's clothes. "Your name, sir?"

"Allan, sir."

"Planter, Mr. Allan?"

"Becoming one. I'm opening some new land and—"

"So-ho! Making a fresh start, uh? Where's your place, Mr. Allan?"

"In the Otter Creek Country near one of the headwaters of the San Jacinto. It's not far from—"

"In Texas, sir?" The waning of Mr. Hubbard's interest announced small credit for anyone from "the penitentiary of America." "Buying for cash or paper, sir?"

"For the right sort of bargain, I'll arrange cash."

This prospect released in his host a suave cordiality. Propelling Perry toward a side door and not letting him get a word in edgewise,

194

he declared he could look at the plainer darkies whenever he liked, but first there was *one* bargain in the house, one of the likeliest he'd ever lay eyes on, which he must look over before he invested a single copper. This was a bargain even a stingy man would snatch at.

Such preliminaries brought them into a decently domestic sort of room furnished with five rocking chairs occupied by mulatto women busy over materials for crocheting, knitting, mending, or embroidery. Nearly all, though at pains to appear intent on their needles, took a quick, open-eyed interest in their visitor while making haste to tuck up straying hair or right a sleeve or draw a worn slipper out of sight beneath a skirt. Only one of them, glum and heavy-lipped, remained slackly listless.

"A smart lot of breeders here, Mr. Allan," Mr. Hubbard was saying. "Nara one without fifteen-twenty years of foaling in her, and all first-rate workers, first-rate. Beauties too, ever damn one. See that yourself."

Calling them beauties had some utility, Perry reflected, for otherwise the term would never have come to mind. Still, he would have been just as unlikely to consider them ugly. All except the glum one looked as freshly washed, starched, and kerchiefed as Sunday morning, but Mr. Hubbard's manner generated a sense of soiling association and impending vice.

He turned Perry toward a creamy caramel woman seated near a window by which she was highlighted like the central figure in a Dutch painting. *"Here,* Mr. Allan! Here's a wench I want you to look over fair-minded and free. Tell me straight, sir, aint that there the prettiest, smartest, likeliest-looking filly you seen in many's the day?"

Dimpling, she looked up from her embroidery, an arrangement on a pillowcase of five pink hearts inside a large one fringed in blue. Perry thought its sentimentalism funny, and yet her glance was so demure, so willing, so available for womanly acts, that he felt his ears turn red. Her clothes were the best in the room, the most neatly ironed, the most seductively arranged. At her throat hung a cross cut from mother-of-pearl, and she wore her blouse loose to reveal a plump caramel breast. In every detail her dress and manner showed care to look softly pretty, succulent, sweet, reminding Perry of a time in boyhood when he gorged himself sick on fudge.

"Stand up, Agnes." Archibald Hubbard tossed up one jeweled hand as if to flip a hotcake. "Let's have a look how you're made." His elbow jolted Perry's. "Can't judge a wench when the best of her's mashed on a rocker, uh, sir?"

Despite her dimpling over Mr. Hubbard's compliments, Perry had assumed that she must be a French-bred servant whose feelings needed no consideration because she understood no English. Beyond mistake, though, she understood every syllable and regarded it all as a normal, familiar, flattering part of any transfer from one master to another. Amiably coy, she began gathering together the materials in her lap.

"Come, come, Agnes. Stand up. Don't be bashful, girl."

"Yessir, sonnizun I fine them pesky scizzers."

Her smile exposed rot between her teeth. Around her floated scents of cheap toilet water and tainted breath, but every movement in gathering up her embroidery publicized the merits she did possess. Digging about in her lap for the scissors displayed the dimply grace of her hands—and the softly full outline of her thighs. In rising, she turned archly, but still demurely, thrusting out her prominences fore and aft. From Mr. Hubbard issued a hybrid between a sigh and a moan.

"Looka there, sir! Right fair condition, aint she now?" Answering himself, he added, "There, sir, is a human gem. Personally, I don't know when I ever run acrost a sweeter conformation, myself."

Perry shook his head. "You see, Mr. Hubbard, I want a useful hand who—"

"Utility *and* looks, Mr. Allan." Hubbard lifted the pillowslip cluttered with pink and blue hearts. "See there how clever she is. But she'd be a first-rate investment if she never done one licka work. Properly breed her, and every daughter she foals will fetch top money anywhere between Havana and St. Louis. In fact, carry them back here when they're thirteen-fourteen and I'll personally get you top money myself."

"But, sir—"

"How*ever*," Mr. Hubbard interrupted in loud authority, "before we go into this any further, Mr. Allan, I tell you what you do." He paused to draw from his waistcoat a silver case containing a thin, highly refined plug of tobacco. "Chew, Mr. Allan?"

"Thank you, nosir."

"Man's got every right to know just what he's buying." He masticated the chew he had offered Perry, spearing a finger toward a door to one side. "Yonder's a right nice little room. You just take Agnes in there and see for yourself if her price aint—"

"No-no!" Perry broke in. "Not at all! Her price and all that doesn't matter in the least. I just came to—"

"That's what I calculated, sir! On sight I says to myself, 'Here's a young blood that never lets price stand between him and a first-rate investment.' And thisun's guaranteed sound and healthy—never had pox or clap or chancres, ara one. Not hardly a scar or blemish on her anywhere, head to foot. Go in there and see for yourself."

"Workers!" Perry bawled desperately. *"Field* hands! That's all I want to see, Mr. Hubbard—*absolutely* all."

Hubbard paused to review Perry's expression thoroughly for the first time since taking him under control. He spat at a cuspidor. "Hands? Plain, common hands?"

"That's all, sir. Field hands."

"Why in thunder didn't you say so?"

"Why in thunder didn't you let me? You rattling on like a railroad engine, how you expect me to tell you anything?"

"Well, no call to give me any mouth about it." With an offended, scornful finality, Hubbard jabbed a thumb at a courtyard to the rear. "Out there, sir. Zachary Grey will show you the bucks."

Again the elevated commercial prince with no time to waste, he returned to the lobby. As Perry shifted toward the courtyard, the glum woman rose to speak.

"Won't you buy *me,* sah?" Her eyes, hitherto dull and defeated, acquired light. "If you want a fiel han, I be good to buy."

He stood with mouth loose, wondering at her. Her features, though heavy, were smoothly turned, and the change in her eyes generated a fugitive beauty, affecting him as an aching wish to help her. Could it be, he wondered, that all good women of whatever race or color turn beautiful whenever their goodness shows? He thought so.

"Will you, sah?" Having mistaken his hesitation for inclination, she continued with more spirit. "Wuk never yet hurt me none, sah. No hahm in wuk. But I dont like settun here waitun for some sinnun man to want me. You fixun buy me, sah?"

"No, auntie." Although his tone was firm, common decency required him to let her down gently. "No, where I live, you'd never be happy anyhow."

"Where, sah?"

"Texas. Some say Texas is heaven for men and horses, but hell for women and slaves."

"But ain Texas free?"

"Not Texas, no."

"Ain they fit a waw, sah, to make it free?"

"Free of Mexico, but . . . not free for darkies."

"Sah?" She directed at him an earnest, bewildered, loose-lipped pucker. "Ain darkies the onliest people ain free, sah?"

"Strictly speaking, I guess maybe nobody's free where there are slaves."

"Sah?"

"Never mind, auntie. Only a field hand, that's all I aim to buy."

"Yessah." Under the realization that he would not have her, she began to fade. Even so, she could not stop without one more effort. "You lookun for a fiel han, you'd fine me a *good* fiel han, massa. Texas or ennawhere, a Class A gennaman like you I wuk for you good."

"No-no. Very sorry, but I got to have a man."

Standing where she was, she looked, down at her needlework, none of which was expertly done. The hands holding it were knotted by far heavier toil and must be clumsy at anything less. She surveyed it in dull grief, as if every miscarriage of her hopes were summarized in its flaws. Her eyes showed no trace of tears, only dead black despair, so that, in leaving her, Perry took with him a sense of participation in a moral calamity almost too enormous to see.

2

Getting out into the courtyard did little to relieve that feeling. Half a dozen Negro men stood around the walls, each with a box, keg, or stool to mark his place. Although nothing but the presence of Mr. Zachary Grey prevented them from drifting about at will, they not only stayed put but were careful to solicit notice from every visitor. The one occupation permitted them was salesmanship of themselves, and there was self-interest in that because the higher their price the greater their prestige. On the far side two at once were crying up their merits to a customer beside Mr. Grey like vendors hawking watermelons, while those by the door, as Perry stepped through, addressed the same kind of chatter to him.

One among these spoke with an accent as native to Maryland

as beaten biscuits. Measuring him more sharply, Perry detected three additional distinctions: first, he kept his left arm behind him as if his backside hurt; second, his clothes were bleached with habitual cleanliness; third, he appeared aware that all the years he was to live hereafter might be affected by this meeting. His eyes, large and alert, took in every least clue as to whether he should try genuinely to be bought or subtly take pains not to be.

Perry stopped. "You from Maryland, are you?"

"Am that, sir! From about three miles above Prince Frederick."

Perry had to smile. Camilla used to tease him for (as she claimed) pronouncing *sir* as *sar, from* as *froom, about* as *aboot, miles* as *molls* and *above* as *aboov,* but hearing such usage here delighted him like a note from home.

The Negro ventured, "You from Maryland too, master?"

"Yes, though lately from Texas."

"*Texas,* master?" A rush of hope so overcame him that tears wet his eyes. "Oh, buy *me,* master! I could earn you more cash money than any two nigras here. That's the truth, sir, though taint easy to believe account of this."

The arm hitherto kept behind him came forward, amputated above the wrist. That would have turned most buyers away, especially as he looked too lank for the hardest work, having a long torso, a long neck, and a look about him more indicative of brains than brute strength. His face, wide above the temples, was narrowly extended from checkbones to chin, giving all its emphasis to his eyes and brow. Perry, however, detected in him a wiry toughness: his neck was sinewed well and his one good hand, half again as long as average, looked strong.

"I lost it young in a sawmill, but in here, sir," he declared, flexing his stub at the elbow, "I got more grip than you'd believe—holds a plow or mule, a hoe or adz or bucksaw too. However, my old master, he learnt me there aint no strength like knowing tools—knowing how to make a tool do what no hand can't do. I read some, write and cipher too, but there's what he said to count on most, sir: knowing how to make work light and fast with tools."

"Well, there's something to that."

"Yessir, and I do know tools. Give me something good to build, and I'll work by sun and moon and lanternlight. I was born to farming, but old master he was a miller, sir, and soon as he bought me he learnt me milling. You got a live creek, sir, I could build a mill to harness that water like a span of mules and make it bring you cash money every working day. That I could, sir."

"So? What's your name?"

"Hector, sir."

"What's your price, Hector?"

After a glance across the court at the busy Mr. Grey, and in a whisper: "Aint suppose to say, sir, but lowest price he come to yet was thirteen hundred."

"Hm! How long you been here?"

"Three weeks, coming four, sir."

"That long?"

"Yessir."

To Perry it seemed a wonder that such a man, regardless of his handicap, should remain for sale so long. "Then why haven't you been sold?"

"Didn't aim to be, sir—not after that third day. Only to somebody from Texas."

"Hm! You assume you might get free in Texas?"

"Oh, nosir! I hear that's why the Quality fought so fierce: them Mexicans don't like slaves. Aint that why, master: so nobody won't have to part with his slaves?"

While he was amused, Perry was also disturbed. For, although Hector provided a droll example of the self-aggrandizement by which men of whatever color see themselves the center and object of every major event, the slavery issue had in fact helped in some measure to send the "Army of Freedom" into battle. For the first time a certain fraudulence in its slogans became apparent to him. Might not purposely withholding any freedom from men of one kind weaken and debase whatever the rest won? He did not know, and a little resented being caught without any conclusion he himself could respect.

"Well, if you think that, what makes you want to go there?"

"My wife and baby, master. A Texas gennelman bought them. Course," he hastened to add, "I'd be mighty proud to have a Maryland master anyhow; twould seem like being home again. Only no place would be like going where they took my wife and little boy Byrd."

"Texas is a right large territory. Where in Texas?"

"Oh, at Mr. Gerard's, sir. He bought her. He lives in the Brazers Bottoms below San Flippy."

"That's a good stretch from my place, the Brazos Bottoms, and San Felipe too."

"Don't matter, sir. Long as I'm in Texas, you say to find her, I'll find her."

"Why should I want you to find her?"

"She's a hard worker and has sense, master, a natural-born good woman. The Lord never put on this earth any woman better."

"If so, her price will be high."

"You let me build you a mill after the crop's in, sir, and *that* would buy her. Take time, of course, but we'd get her, and Byrd with her."

Perry stiffened his face to avoid looking impressed. "What makes you so confident of that?"

"Done it once, sir. So I can again. First time I seen Hanna, I wanted her *bad*. And when old master seen her he said, 'Earn her price, Hector, and I'll buy her.' So he helped me put up a mill at a crossing above the Patuxent. I run it mostly alone, he putting aside half the profit to buy Hanna. Little moren two years and we had enough."

"At that rate he should have got rich. Why'd he sell you?"

"He didn't, no, master. He never would. But sickness carried him off, and none of his kin didn't want us darkies, just the cash. So a trader from down here bought us up and shipped us here to get the high money."

"I see."

Perry mused over the image of a mill on the land he had picked in Texas. The possibility had never occurred to him: it cautioned him that there must be still other possibilities which further thought would uncover. Not until Hector spoke again did he realize with what agonizingly anxious eyes his study was being studied.

"Might you buy me, master?"

"Wel-ll, if I meant to, it'd hardly pay for either of us to let that show, would it?"

Comprehension brightened Hector. "Nosir! Not hardly." During a struggle to suppress his delight, he added, "Suppose he asks too much, master, you could wait two-three days. He'd sell me cheaper then. I'll undertake he will."

"So? Well, we'll see."

As if putting thought of him aside, Perry sauntered on to quiz another slave. Though burly, he had nothing like Hector's vigor and clarity of mind. He talked up his merits chiefly because Mr. Grey, who had followed the other visitor out of the courtyard, might return at any instant. In the midst of chatter as standardized as the multiplication table, he began scratching after a flea inside his shirt. Perry had moved on to another man whose qualities were no more unusual when Mr. Grey, looking disappointed over the last customer but hopeful about the one still present, came bustling back to deliver routine half-truths about the Negro then under review, about his former owner, his talents, strength, health, disposition, etc. Perry cut him off to say it was a waste of time to tell him about darkies priced high. To a degree that amazed him, all were, the range being from sixteen hundred for a boy of seventeen to twenty-six hundred for a strapper who looked dull as a tired bullock. The average was nearly a thousand dollars higher than in Maryland. Plain arithmetic turned Camilla's sentiments about the evils of slavery one degree easier to share.

"To save words, Mr. Grey, show me the least costly first."

"Yonner, sir, is a buy nobody aint likely to beat." Mr. Grey flourished a chewed cigar toward Hector, who now sat on a box, bending toward his bare feet a depleted, sickly, hopeless gaze realistic enough to make buying him at any price seem a gamble. "Hector, what the livun hell you settun down for, uh? Get up there, boy, en let the gennelmun look you over."

Hector uncoupled himself from the box like a snake rising from a nap. "I'm a right fair worker, sir," he recited torpidly, eyes down. "Supposing you buy me, sir, I do most any work you say." He used his stub forearm to dab his brow, letting it sag back feebly to his side. "Sure am mighty tired, sir, not doing a lick in all this while."

"Many buyers passed you up, have they?"

"No, we aint had him long," Mr. Grey broke in, looking savage enough to skin him. "A few days—not so long. He's a Maryland nigra, sir—a sight better raised than canebrake blacks, and nigras from up there do twice the work. This one's a mechanic too, I hear. With all that, he's the lowest priced in the lot—lowest we had in weeks."

"*How* low?"

"Why, I might could let him go at, say, fifteen."

"What!"

"Why, sir, that's near givun him away! And him one of the hardest workers. They say he's got a world of ambition, a real go-ahead worker."

"Cripples generally can't work hard; sick men shouldn't."

"Oh, he aint a bit sickly, Mr. Allan. Except in that arm, he's sound as a boar hog. Never before seen him look so hangdog like he is right now." The last clause grated through teeth busy mashing the ruin of his cigar. As Hector failed to take the hint, he snatched the stub from his mouth to bawl, "Straighten up there, boy! Goddamn it all, what kind of ambition is that?"

Hector obeyed as if a dagger were gouging the small of his back. His exaggerated straightness made him look scarcely able to hold together long enough to be rejected.

"Well," said Perry, "you're asking too much."

"Too much? Why, a mechanic like him, the least you'd pay, the abso*lute* least, is three thousand—if he had that other hand."

"Which he hasn't."

"Well, Mr. Allan, maybe I'm too softhearted." After adjusting his features to reflect this shortcoming: "I'd like to see that nigra get a home—been too long without a good home. So I'll let you have him for thirteen."

"No-no, Mr. Grey." Perry began sauntering toward the door. "He might do, but not at that price."

"Twelve then."

"No, too much."

"Great God above, young man, where'd you ever hear of a better price?"

"Back home in Maryland. It looks like I'd better go back and—"

"Damn if that don't beat any price I ever offered in many's the day."

"Sir, if you'll take a lower figure, send me word at the office of Mr. James Westbrook, attorney."

"Why, Mr. Allan, I can't possibly—"

"But don't delay: I sail Wednesday morning. That address is Mr. Westbrook's on the Rue Royale."

He projected the last phrases over a shoulder during a pause on his way toward the lobby.

So "weak and poorly" did Hector appear thereafter, despite a curative of ten lashes the first day and twenty-five the next, that Mr. Grey wrote to Perry offering him at one thousand dollars. Perry bought him for nine hundred, and at once found his knowledge of tools, his quick will, and his enthusiasm for construction invaluable in assembling equipment enough to start a homestead. Tuesday night they had everything loaded aboard the *Gulph Breeze,* scheduled to sail at dawn.

Perry dined that evening with his aunt and uncle, staying late. Meanwhile a cold fog settled upon the city, motionlessly dense. On returning to the ship, he learned from the schooner's watch about an accident which set him pacing the decks, weighing its effect on tomorrow. At last he settled down over the sort of letter he had since Friday been wanting an excuse to write:

Ever dear Camilla:

I am scratching this off aboard ship by a lantern hung on a mast. Dawn should break in about three hours; but, with the night thickened by sooty fog, New Orleans is still as dark as ever I saw it, stiff dark. All the nearer streets are empty except for a solitary horse invisible here by the wharf. Along the city's walls his hoofbeats reverberate like stones dropped down a well. Listening to them, I hear again and again and again each bruising word we threw at each other that last hour. Listening to them, I want very much to speak to you once more with affection, if only through ink on paper.

We were booked to sail at daybreak, but that has become impossible: early tonight a tug raked and damaged our prow, delaying our departure a day or so. That is what heartens me to write: if this note goes aboard the first steamboat north after dawn for delivery to you at Palmer Hall we might yet arrange to meet and try to recover that harmony we enjoyed before our ride.

Since we parted I have done business at the Slave Market. There, in recollection of your bitter talk, I felt surrounded by, involved in, punishable for, a set of abominations almost universal in Dixie. I saw evidence of tragedies as numerous as sparrows, and hardly less shattering to our moral fiber than among the darkies up for sale.

In spite of that, however, I had to heed one unyielding fact: to tame more than the meagerest fraction of the land in my name without slaves would require a more ingenious scheme than any I have hit upon. So I bought one darkie priced very low. Should I discover any way to cut free of slavery anytime soon, I can manage it without an absolutely crushing loss.

The one hand I did buy is too literally one: he lost the other at work in a sawmill many years back. Nevertheless this poor crippled nigra, a mechanic and millwright, is so acute, so ready and helpful, that I feel greatly strengthened by him. Thus, while learning to deplore slavery, I am being taught to prize it more, and what can these opposite instructions lead to?

However, the more I think about our quarrel, the less I believe disagreement over slavery caused it. Dearly loved, may I be open with you? Certain of your remarks stick to my mind like burrs, tearing every thought that brushes near them: those about my liking Mexicans, about how my wound was nursed, about dancing with a half-caste. Such talk did contain much truth. Every American who survived the fight at San Antonio and who enjoyed dancing showed it more or less often with those the victory set free. That was as true of me as any, and I frolicked in other ways as well.

But a further, deeper truth is this: in such company I saw more clearly than ever before how vacant is life without love. I saw how much weaker before death is anyone who does not give and receive love without limit. My conclusion was that, as you are the one partner I have ever loved or am likely to hereafter, I should quit brooding over your consent to marry Beaufait and come back here to determine in person whether your heart, or only your head, inclined you toward him. In brief, the festivities there helped bring us together again. That, I believe, is the sole fact about them that should have any weight between you and me.

Have I touched upon anything you wish to discuss? If so, pray send me a note by the first boat downstream—this morning if possible; this afternoon at latest. Wherever you prefer a meeting, there I will be at the time you think best. If it requires giving up passage on this ship, if it requires missing the chance to seed a crop this spring, never mind; a delay which might repair the link between us would be time used as wisely as I know how.

On the other hand, should I not hear from you before we sail, I shall know how to go onward with no better reply than silence. Even that, however, will not discourage me altogether. It will leave me imagining that some day in Texas I may hear from you. For, though it may exaggerate things to say that where there is life there is hope, I am certain that where there is love, hope invariably stays alive. In fact I believe love to be the most preservative force in human experience.

Yours to the last,
Perry

From C. B.'s Journal
January 17, 1836

My father used to contend that hands lifted in prayer are less holy in the sight of Almighty God than those busy at productive labor. For sayings of that kind the faithful called him impious, though he never could gaze at the open firmament without a look of worship, and the Sermon on the Mount brought him seizures of exaltation unbearable without tears. Sectarianism repelled him, however; parochial dogma too; and the same is true of me. Because I do not hesitate to say so, even my own daughter considers me "lost" and tries stratagems now and then to draw me back to church.

At breakfast today she came in from the gardens of Palmer Hall, beautifully dressed for morning service and followed by little brown Rachel almost buried under newly cut flowers. While pulling these into shape, she began working on me with a suavity which should have put me on guard.

"Pretty, aren't they, Pa?"

"In the prime of life. But why cut only an armload? Why not a boatload?"

"No sarcasm now. They're for Mama's grave, hers and the boys'."

"Oh, I see. It's thoughtful of you, honey. Cut or not, they'd soon wilt, so might as well use them."

Having retreated so hastily, I failed to realize I had backed into a trap until she sprung it.

"Why don't you come along, Pa? I'm stopping there after church. How long since you set foot in that cemetery?"

"O-oh, a good while, I confess."

"Then do spruce up a bit and come along."

Her purpose was not merely to "save" me, of course, nor solely to honor our dead: it was also to avoid going out in public alone. Deserted by Perry, bereft of all her last week's guests, not to be joined by Beaufait and other friends until this afternoon, she wanted living proof that someone loves her enough to abandon his known convictions in order to stand by her. Always she can face the world most bravely with evidence close beside her that she is loved. I groaned a bit; but, yes, I went.

The congregation was small, a defiant little Switzerland of Calvinists glaring down in alpine superiority at Latin Louisiana. Their pastor made a virtue of their fewness through a sermon picturing all non-Presbyterians as like that madman with an unclean spirit who told Jesus, "My name is Legion: for we are many."

When we left (myself still of that legion), the sky looked like the ceiling of a coal cellar: a storm was approaching. Nevertheless we did take Camilla's flowers over where lies the dust of my darling wife, our three boys too. Though gusts snatched hard at her clothes, though trees mourned loud above us, throwing their boughs over before them like the hair of women out of their minds with grief, Camilla apportioned her flowers in unhurried reverence upon four grassy humps above which weathering stones declare the names I cannot utter without a breaking voice.

The futility of such rites seemed pitiable to me, the vanity of any rites at all over mold which every clue of spirit and loveliness so long ago deserted, being infinitely more detached from that residue than we ourselves are from last year's excrement. The wind at once began ripping her flowers apart, so accentuating their perishability that these too looked exactly wrong as symbols of Christian feeling toward kin taken from us, since our belief should be that the spirit of the worthy will never perish.

After distributing them, Camilla stood among them, head bowed and hands together tight, though the wind twisted her dress round her like a flag. She prayed in a low, firm voice, but without originality; her conclusion was the familiar graveyard phrase, "God rest their souls forever. Amen."

No, that too seemed wrong to me. In her mother dwelt a self-effacing diligence, an ever-helpful nature which God ought to be implored to keep active. Not eternal rest, but eternal life, was the legitimate prayer for a soul such as hers.

Somehow, though, such flaws detracted no more from our remembrance than did the rushing wind. They rather sharpened its poignancy. Standing there, a witness and critic of every act, I wept in shameless sorrow and wished with a sick and foolish heart that our dear ones could be alive again.

Camilla took me by the arm and led me back to the carriage. In it we rode through fusilades of flying leaves. Thunderclaps were dueling above us. One gust threatened to upset us, after which a downpour struck the brougham as if the clouds were bursted dikes, but we inside were both too removed in thought to be alarmed.

"Mama," Camilla observed, "always doted on you something terrible. She spoiled you, Pa—too openly adored you. Nobody thought you cared enough about her for that. Now she'd be very happy to know that, after all these years, you do care for her still."

The pity is, of course, that I didn't show it better then. If I had, if she had not been lonely and despairing when that epidemic cut her down, if she had known that so very long after her hand last clasped mine grief over her loss would strike through me still like a thrown spear, if she had been sure that I loved her enough to give my life for her, she might be with us today. It may well have made that much difference. I never should have left, and told Camilla why I thought so.

"Perry had the same thought," she remarked. "He once called love, not life, *the* great adversary of death. Whereas life and death require one another, perpetuate one another, love and death are everlasting opponents."

"Yes, very good. That *is* the same thought."

"Nevertheless *he* left too."

Her bitterness did not seem fair to me.

"But consider a minute, Milla. In his place, what would you do?"

For at least a quarter mile she jostled mutely beside me, watching sheets of rain slide down a glass in the door on her side.

"I'd sally off to Texas," she agreed at last, "and try to forget the fool I left behind me."

"Me too."

"I wouldn't stay single forever either."

"Wel-ll, no less an authority than St. Paul has said, 'It is better to marry than to burn.' "

"No doubt it is." A pause, and she added, "Anyhow, it would seem a blessing to love some man as strong as Mama did you—strong enough so you don't really mind whether he dresses you in silk or cotton so long as you're sure he cares for you." The swift jolting of the carriage did not alter her look of balanced judgment. "Besides, what's the good of having twenty silk gowns if, because of the way I came by them, I have to wear a hair shirt underneath?"

Startled by this clarity about herself, I merely sat watching the mares stride with enduring passion through the rain and mud. Much sooner in life than I was able to, she has discovered that possessions are worth little to the spirit except as proof of accomplishment in reshaping things of the earth to human use. The trouble with the possessions Robert Palmer left her is that they instead prove her dependency; they reproach her for remaining only what someone else has made of her instead of daring to find out what she can make of herself.

"What about Yvonne?" she asked, and that gave me a fresh surprise.

"Yes, Yvonne. Delightful person to talk with, don't you agree?"

"Pa!" For the first time in hours she laughed. "You're fiendishly clever sometimes, I do declare." And after sobering: "She deserves much better than that, you know."

"Infinitely better, yes."

"Afraid to love again?"

"Maybe. Like you, uh, Milla?"

"Like me, yes. However, I'm getting braver about it all the time." Suddenly she changed the subject. Or *was* it a change? "You afraid of death, Pa?"

"Who isn't?"

"Mama wasn't. When it came, she wasn't."

That left me mute again. Whoever lives in dread of death cannot half live, I know very well, and quite possibly an unconquered timidity about love may have similar consequences.

CHAPTER XII

Springfields' Homestead
Monday Afternoon
January 25, 1836

As Perry's note to Camilla brought no answer throughout his delay in New Orleans, none other than the rebuff of silence, he returned to Texas in low spirits. Texas itself was depressing: everywhere he heard reports of indifference to the possibility of new invasion from Mexico, of ruinous squabbling in the government, of equally ruinous insubordination, idleness, and vainglory among the men under arms. Frequent rains, too, confirmed the adverse outlook, until the afternoon of January 25, the day he was to reach Dr. Springfield's.

The prairies in that direction were wintry and wet, coldly wet, but with signs of improvement growing by the hour. When he and Hector rode over a hill from which they could first see the doctor's white-washed cabin, patches of sky beyond it were turning blue as seas on a map, and a late burst of sunlight over remainders of rain threw a misty halation over the grove, the crops, and pasturelands around it, a glow of refreshed life.

The wind had quieted for evening. Oval notes from a cowbell rolled across the hills. A boy shouted in fellowship with his own echoes, one of Leticia's young twin brothers, and Leticia herself was calling up her chickens, her voice a dreamy singsong. Every sound and quality of the day was so reminiscent of scenes familiar to Perry in childhood that he felt like a sailor returning from dissolute ports to the healing simplicities of home.

Followed by Hector on a mule, also by a pack train under mounds of supplies, he was riding a four-year-old stallion called Marquis, an alert steel gray, big across the chest, well tapered in the legs, and unusually fluid in motion. Marquis lifted a whicker toward the cabin, whereupon a trio of hounds commenced baying from the dooryard, and Leticia followed them foward to gaze into the distance at the visitors. Her outer clothes (a wilted bonnet and an old coat of her father's) were so unbecoming and so deceiving, so unlike the dear image which always came to mind whenever Perry thought of her, that he laughed in silence and at that instant wanted to hug her. He swung up his hat the length of his arm. Her hand rose in a jubilant flutter, after which she whirled to run inside the cabin.

By the time his train plodded up to the yard a committee of welcome was out to receive him: the hounds, the twins, Dr. Springfield, and his two aides, Otto and Edna Bauernschmidt. But Leticia was not there. Hector led Marquis and the mules to a feed rack by the barn while everyone else scuffed indoors with Perry, competing to show how delighted they were to see him. Still she did not appear.

Their cabin reassured him about frontier living fully as much as it had last fall. Using the products of the hills around their home, using little from town but books, the Springfields had combined ingenuity with taste to produce a cordial parlor. Limestone had been converted into ferneries, pelts into carpets, antlers into hat and gun racks, gourds into vases, bleached homespun into curtains, carved horn into lamps, hollow logs into flowering windowboxes, and lime into whitewash for the walls. The chairs, made of boughs and hides, were adapted to the facts of anatomy and kind to the guest. If only Camilla, he reflected, could see Texas as it was here, where comfort was so well established on scant capital, she would very likely . . . but no, it now looked most improbable that she ever would come to Texas, at least not before too late to matter greatly to him. And, actually, a good deal about this place did urge him to forget her, mutely stating that Texas could be an agreeable home without her.

To ask after Leticia was unnecessary: planks across the beams overhead murmured of light footfall. Noting his distraction, the twins shouted up a ladder in a passage through the cabin, saying she ought to hurry, her beau was here. She took her time, and all the more time because of that sort of urging.

When she did come down she tiptoed sidoward into the parlor as if tardy for a class long called to order. She managed just one word to Perry, and stammered over that. "Huh-hello!"

Excitement had darkened her eyes to the blue of twilight. Her dress now was one of her best. Her fawn hair, aglow with health and life, had been freshly brushed back, and a necklace of turquoise established how opposite to stone were her throat and breast. All this care to appear to advantage exaggerated her habitual look of hurtability, her air of anxiety to equal every expectation, to lighten every burden, to comply with every earnest wish. She blessed the room simply by being in it, or so he thought.

"Well, I missed you, Leticia."

"Oh, I wasn't fit to be seen, all mussed and dirty from doing chores." To divert attention away from herself she asked, "Where's your friend? The man I saw you with?"

"My boy Hector?"

Her glance showed tardy understanding that Hector must be a Negro. An alteration in her brows reminded him how vigorous were the convictions of the Springfields against slavery. Instead of speaking about that, however, she inquired if he'd had coffee and went out to fetch some for everyone.

2

After supper, after an evening of bonhomie around the fire, her father rose to observe that he had been young once himself. He saw to it that the parlor was left to her and Perry.

They accepted the gift in silence. The house resounded with diminishing voices, with receding footfalls. Though the night was windless, a frosty current seeped inward beneath the door. Three hounds, driven aside earlier by human competition, now crept nearer the hearth, sighs eloquent as they lay down bathed in firelight. Leticia too pulled her rocking chair closer.

"Those boys!" Refitting a thimble on her third finger, she arranged across her lap a pair of breeches out at the knee. "Never a time when they don't need patches. Seems like, anyhow."

A tilt in her lips added the judgment that the other sex in general was quite a trial. At the same time this emphasized how softly full those lips were. Becoming restless, Perry went over to kick chunks together on the andirons, then leaned on the mantel to watch her in silence. The fingers manipulating her needle were quick and competent, accustomed to bettering everything around her, whether at home or in the schoolroom. He took warning from the vigor of their application: no doubt she was considering how to improve him. The fault most evident in him at the moment, of course, lay in his owning a slave, so he prepared himself to be difficult about that in cheerful ways.

"What else do you expect of lively boys?"

"That's true, we do have to expect it." And after a pause: "How was New Orleans?"

"O-oh, as you saw it—an ornery place, most ways. Puts me in mind of a big zoo with rats in the feed bins, monkeys in the office, peacocks loose everywhere, and the lion's cage unlocked."

She enjoyed the image briefly. "Only that's *not* how I saw it, thanks to you." She hesitated in wistful reminiscence. "I've thought *so* often how kind you were, showing me the sights and all, while we were there."

Her eyes reflected the dance of flame in the hearth, then returned to her needlework. In the months since they parted, her outline had acquired a bit more promise of strong and comforting amplitude. In time she would have many healthy children of her own to sew for. Her domesticity in that rocking chair brought Agnes to mind, the enticingly symmetrical wanton at the slave market, but without any of the taint or pretense which had repelled him there. Instead she was the reverse of Agnes, an authentic prototype of what Agnes had feigned.

"And Mrs. Palmer? How is she?"

"Oh, very well." He shifted away from the hearth, but kept his voice light and chatty. "Charming, too, of course. And very busy. In short, much the same."

"Busy?"

"Uhm."

With each syllable being cautiously ventured, her diligence at mending gave her the advantage carrying a balance pole does when walking a board fence. To have something to do himself, to share in that advantage, he brought his saddle in from the passage, spread it before a chair in the firelight, and set to work dressing it with neat's-foot oil. Not until then did she carry her thought further.

"Strange! She has such an atmosphere of such perfect devotion to leisure."

He left this unanswered by way of resisting its bias.

"Though perhaps her plantation," she qualified, "does require attention."

"A good deal, or else she'd go bankrupt. And just now she's busier than usual."

"Oh? Planting time back there you mean?"

He was tempted to say dryly, "After a manner of speaking." Instead: "She'll be married soon."

"Married? Who to?"

Her breath waited for his reply, but he busied himself at wrestling his saddle into another position. Its stirrups scraped the floor like the hind legs of a dog with a broken back.

Leticia had to repeat herself. "Who's she to marry?"

"Someone she's known a good while."

"Oh?"

Just why, Perry wondered, should he make a game of dangling before her so cruelly a fact so painful to himself? "Yes. The 'estimable' Edmond Beaufait."

She released a long, slow exhalation, and he winced with pain at his pleasure in having tormented her. Her needle still remained inactive.

"Who's he?"

"Why, everyone knows Beaufait! A big banker, a regular nabob. Hundreds envy her, that's sure."

"Well, never mind. She *needs* wealth."

That shocked him. Never mind! What a motherly way to put it! Her voice was so comforting, so voluptuously maternal, and how extraordinary that anyone so young should be so prompt to see through him. One source of restraint around her heretofore had been his judgment that she was too young to know her own mind or be responsible for her impulses, whereas this consoling tone invited him to give up that protectiveness of his and recognize that, in certain matters, she might teach *him* a thing or two.

"She'd never care for this wild country," she persisted. "Not like you. All those expensive habits of hers, she'd hate the long struggle up."

"No-no," he protested, soberly loyal. "No, she's deep. She values many things money can't buy. She's convinced, I'm very sure, that well-being is never bought, that it has to be earned, then earned again, daily. She knows our struggles do us more good than our possessions do."

Leticia sat motionless second on second, eyes startled. "But how true that is, Perry! Whether she knows it or not, how good that *you* know it."

"Hm. No." He shook his head in disillusioned humor. "I want a

world of things very hard to get without money. That's why I came
to Texas—to make a fortune. What a banker can afford I'd like to
afford if I take the notion."

"Perry, I've never heard you *ever* say anything so misguided before."

"Not misguided at all. Nobody respects poverty. And why should
they? I mean to leave it behind me the quickest way I honestly can."

A jog of the breeches across her lap brought them back under her
needle. The hoot of an owl shivered around the cabin. One of the
sprawled hounds lifted his head in that direction, then toward his
mistress. As the click of thimble against needle continued unchanged,
he yawned cavernously, fangs bare in formless yearning, and returned
his ear to the place it had warmed on the floor.

There came into Leticia's voice a note of yearning too. "Well,
really, it's no wonder you're so bitter. She's truly fine, and so very,
very lovely, goodness me."

Attentive still to her patch, she seemed unaware how unprepared
he was for her praise of Camilla, or her conclusion that he was bitter.

She carried on in the same tone. "Most any man would want to be
rich if that's what she wants a man to be."

Through a pause afterward a mouse nibbled at a crack near the
door. Perry massaged oil into his saddle without a word. Again the
warmth of her sympathy permitted, indeed incited, desires toward her
as a grown woman—and this, strangely, when it was his love for
someone else they were discussing.

Suddenly she resumed, a bit impatient with him. "And I suppose
that's—yes, I see: that's your excuse for buying a slave."

"Oh, no. I meant to anyway."

His bluntness resisted that subject, but her eyes turned full upon
him, wide and troubled. "Perry, *why*? You did *not* come here simply
to make a fortune: it badly adulterates the truth to say you did. You
believe in freedom's power for good till you'd fight to the death for
it. Then why would you bring a slave after all?"

"I'd do without any if I had the imagination to see how. But I
haven't."

"Oh, fudge! Hundreds of people without one-tenth of your advantages and reading have managed. You could certainly manage if
you thought it through, and handsomely too."

She was so earnest, so concerned on his behalf, so evangelical, that
it seemed a shame not to agree. He on his own had given considerable

thought to "managing." For a start he had written from New Orleans to Hugh, Mountain, Elias, Butternut, and others who must be impatient with idleness in San Antonio, suggesting that, as there would be no more fighting for at least three or four months, they might come to the Otter Creek Country and help him put in a crop for eight dollars a month, payable after harvest. They should arrive within a week or two. But, if he did not have Hector, who would tend the crops and livestock after they were all called back to the Army for the summer campaign?

"I've been a slavery man all my life," he observed, tacitly reminding her that, as what he always had been had not stood between them before, she ought not to let it now. In fact he was certain it would not, because the domestic intimacy of her effort to improve him implied some impulse to succumb to him. Was it possible that good women attempt to make any man better by whom they are especially inclined to be made worse? Something like that. While he sat thinking so, surveying her, inwardly acknowledging how uncalculated and appealing her enticement was, a stone in her necklace throbbed over an artery along her throat and the mouse by the door gnawed in desperate impatience. "You knew last fall I intended to use slaves here. Why should that be so hard to forgive now?"

"Hard or not—yes, I do have to forgive it." She removed her thimble to roll it shakily on her palm. Her lips tortured sideward. Her throat constricted so hard that each phrase came out bruised. "There are friends, a few, we'd forgive most anything."

The torment of her confession turned her hand spastic. Her thimble escaped her, rolling along the vale of her lap. The hand plunging after it knocked it away beneath the spinning wheel. Though Perry stooped for it, she did too, bumping his shoulder, then rose to wait by him while he recovered it.

To give it back simply and be done with it was not possible. Her look of expecting some gallant act prevented that, and so did the feel of the thimble, a finely wrought matrix of silver, wifely, open, ready for use. The sensation of its excellence tempted him to try how easily it could be crushed, recalling a time in boyhood when, after marveling at four robin eggs arranged like rare blue pearls in the mud bowl of their nest, he pressed one until its shell collapsed around a naked squashy embryo, a loathsome little stain on his memory to this day. His hand turned more careful as it flexed around her thimble.

She waited, watching the thimble. In her eyes a need for love lay like a nude half awake. The fire hissed and snapped. Her sweet laundered female scent had become a little soured by nervous sweat in the armpits. Again the whittling of incisors by the door, and one of the hounds breathed a long breath. Her hand drifted up to fumble weakly at her necklace, whereupon he thrust the thimble at that hand.

"Chilly out tonight," he remarked thickly and turned to kick a burning chunk around parallel to the back of the hearth.

She said nothing. Neither did she move. Eyes down on the hand in which her thimble lay, she seemed in a trance. Her shadow and his shadow quivered together on the opposite wall. The night outside reverberated to a series of monstrous, shuddery hoots.

"Good to be in," he added, "not camping out."

As she still neither spoke nor moved, he carried his saddle back out into the passage. When he returned, she was putting her mending away on a table by the far wall. He held his hands near the fire.

"You folks get up early, as I recall."

"Yes, before dawn." She drifted over toward the passage. By the door she paused to nod at a divan of poles covered with a tick of prairie hay and buffalo robes where he had slept last fall. "That's for you again, Perry, your bed. I hope—will that do?"

"Thank you. It's fine."

"Good night then."

"Good night, Leticia."

She went out. While her footsteps grated on the ladder to the left, then crossed the rafters overhead, he remained standing where she had left him, his back to the hearth, his shadow quivering alone on the wall she had gone beyond. He was still there after her bed creaked, after the only sounds left were the nibble of the mouse, the hoot of the owl, the hiss of the fire.

3

By the time he and Hector had their mule train in line to push on-ward next morning, Leticia was absent from home and remained so through his leave-taking from the rest of her family. Above a little pole-cabin which housed her school on the upper side of the dooryard, agate smoke ascended from its chimney toward a frosty blue sky. The pupils would not be arriving for another half hour; therefore she must be there either to avoid a farewell altogether or to give him an opportunity to avoid it if he chose—though the school *was* near his route northeast. When about to pass, he signaled by a tilt of his hat for Hector to lead the mule train on. He himself pulled his gray around, dropped rein by a tree, and approached the cabin on foot.

The first Texas home of the Springfields, the veteran of a lean probationary struggle, it had tilted to an aging stoop. Props crutched it under the eaves on the lower side, and slab shingles on its roof had grayed and curled. As the area's first school, however, it was in his eyes more admirable now than it had been in the first place. Under the winter-stripped trees before it, he took off his hat.

Meanwhile Hector shouted at the mules by way of announcing that his master's wish to be left behind awhile was being fulfilled. A stir followed inside the school. Leticia came to the doorway, one finger in a book and her fair hair cowled in a shawl.

"Oh! You're leaving?"

"Not without thanks to you, no. Not without saying good-by."

"But any thanks should be from us, not to us; we like so well to have you, Perry. We'll see you often, won't we?"

"Well, my land is a good stretch away, so . . ."

Her eyes shifted from him to Marquis, tall, alert, and normally calm, but looking as if someone in secret had fed him on gunpowder.

"Not on *that* horse!"

"No. True."

"Next Saturday everyone's gathering at Bayards', the ladies to quilt, the men to raise a barn. Then they'll be dancing most all night. Won't you come?"

"That's only four days off." He turned his hat to stroke the brim. "We'd hardly have a shelter up by then."

"Your tent's been sufficient till now. Won't it do awhile more? Afterwards all us neighbors can help you put up a *good* cabin." Her lips in the effort to smile looked severely bruised. "I hoped you'd *want* to come."

"Of course I do. Certainly I do. It's only that—"

"If you—if Saturday you still do, why not come here first? We'll show you the way."

"That's very nice, Leticia. I'll be here, sure, and mighty glad you told me."

4

Highhorse Valley
Tuesday Afternoon
January 26, 1836

"What you reckon Marq smelling, master?"

Hector referred to Perry's gray. They were crossing a grassy flat toward a screen of post oaks between them and a ridge, a bluff, a limestone escarpment along which lay the league of land Perry had picked to homestead. Marquis, head aloft and ears quick, was striding more eagerly, belling his nostrils open to sniff breezes coming at him from beyond those screening oaks, and the pack mules behind him also began to look more alert.

"Acts like he's smelling horse."

"That he does, sir. And nearby where a horse is you genrully find a man."

Here, however, the nearest habitation was the big log house Robert Palmer had willed to Camilla three miles to the left. No house was visible, no road either, not even a trail. If any man ever had passed this way since Perry himself came last fall, there was no sign of it.

Nevertheless the area excited an impression of life unseen. From a distance that screen of post oaks deceived the eye into overlooking the fact that the ridge receded behind them to form a large grassy valley. Though narrow here at the entrance, that valley was spacious farther back and almost entirely enclosed by limestone cliffs. Who could say what a man might find there? Keyed up though Perry was by thought about it, he kept his reply to Hector matter-of-fact.

"Tru-ue, most everywhere back east man and horse do go together. But out here many a horse never so much as saw a man."

"Unless a few in skins and feathers!"

"Uhm, yes!"

"And most any minute, master, you stand to lose your blackboy Hector."

"How so?"

"We see one savage, and I'll turn white!"

Perry and Hector shared an interval of soundless mirth while riding straight upwind to assure that whatever Marq smelled would not smell them. Once they reached the oaks Hector reined up Mr. Jackson (a mule eared like a jackrabbit and almost as fleet, therefore a surpassing mule, therefore named after the President), to pull him farther back behind Marquis. He also tightened the lead lines on the pack train so that the other mules followed closer behind his own. Perry at intervals tapped his quirt on Marq's nostrils, a signal not to whicker. When deep among the oaks, deep enough to see beyond them, he stopped.

"Oh-oh! God above!"

Had the valley before him been empty it would still have been a sight to stop his breath. Although not much over one hundred yards across here where the oaks screened its mouth, it from there opened wide in the shape of a gigantic beet whose taproot, nearly a mile away, was a gorge cut through the cliffs from uplands eastward beyond it. Except for a fringe of woods which followed a spring-fed brook around the base of the enclosing bluffs, it was largely treeless, a harbor in which the wind played liquidly across winter-cured grass. To Perry (because all of it lay within his claim, and the overhanging uplands too) it was the most beautiful patch of earth he had seen since he came upon it the first time, a self-protected haven, an anchorage he thought would surely content him all his life.

But what electrified and stopped him now was a herd of wild mares grazing a furlong away under the seigniory of a chesty red stallion. Unlike most prairie herds, this one contained no showy pintos or buckskins or moldy roans, only sorrels and chestnuts, bays, grays, and blacks, a clean strain descended from Spanish Arabs. Beyond them half-a-dozen deer were feeding, a scatter of antelope too, all uncaring as goats. Two coyotes trotted past them, ignored and ignoring, their air of habitual truce suggesting that this valley lay in perpetuity under the spell of Eden.

Still within the shield of post oaks, Perry again tapped Marq's nose for silence. Stealthily he patted his neck to ask for stealth. Drawing him around half profile to the herd, he lightened him for speed by unshipping his rifle, bedroll, and saddlebags. He loosened his riata, dropped his hat, then brought his weight over to the left stirrup until his body was concealed and his head in position to watch the mares from around the pommel of his saddle.

Already Hector, not needing to be told what to do, had inched Mr. Jackson around like Marquis and tied to an oak the lead pack mule to which all the rest were tied. He then relieved Mr. Jackson of needless weight, dropped his hat, and unslung his riata. With that looped on his handless forearm and his good hand over the saddle, he sat on his ankle in one stirrup as Perry did and held himself tight against Mr. Jackson on the hidden side.

So prepared, they began a cautious advance. On the principle that a shot into an entire flock of partridge is likely to hit none, Perry ignored the herd to point Marquis sideward at a schooled half-right toward one filly nearer the oaks than most. A glowing mahogany bay, she seemed to him the finest creature there, short in the back, full in the quarters, light at the extremity of her legs, strong in the neck and chest.

Marq's advance sideward carried him toward her past tree after tree. His saddle faintly creaked. His hooves lashed through dryly vocal grass. Two prairie hens whirred up from underfoot, whereupon the filly lifted a trimly sculptured head to stare that way. A few concluding munches, and she stood in statuesque attention, mane and tail furled by the wind, wondering at the strange gray stallion. With his legs milling sideward, saddle creaking, neck arched, jaws split by the rigidity of his rein, he could not resemble any horse she had seen before.

Other mares were looking up now, but Marq's rein kept him angling toward her. She extended her muzzle to sort over currents of air which, gliding toward him rather than from him, could tell her nothing. Otherwise she simply marveled at him without motion, as step by step, like a cockerel toward a pullet, he sidled nearer, nearer, nearer. Despite the tap of Perry's quirt against his nostrils, he began to court her in moaning snorts.

Perry had his right arm hooked over the saddle to support his weight by a grip along the side nearest to her. He reset his grip so that, in another fifty feet or so, he could draw himself up for a sudden drive to swing a loop over her and trip her into becoming his. He tested the capacity of that hand to lift his weight, tested the freedom of his body lest any buckle or button might catch where it would check an upward swing. All was well. Nothing more was necessary than to contain and control his own fevers as well as Marq's until the last moment before she would catch the scent of man.

A neigh soared down the wind, a stallion's challenge. Galloping hooves drummed toward them across the prairie. An impulse to whirl in that direction brought Marquis rearing upward, fighting his bit. His snorts changed to a strangulated whicker.

The filly began to shy uneasily, to turn away. Perry ground his teeth. To have her heading, not forward, but the other way, was to lose one fraction of the time she would need to recover from surprise when he swooped toward her. Obviously about to bolt, she hesitated one moment more, flicking her ears from Marquis to the charging red stallion. Perry, although still many feet from being as close as he had hoped to get, saw that he could do no better. He lurched up into the saddle and let Marquis explode toward her like a puff of cannon smoke. The effect was much the same as if a cannon had fired. The entire herd stampeded, the red stallion and mares alike.

The drive of Marq's start halved his distance from the bay filly before her scramble to get away could open to a free run. As he always did in a chase, whether after a horse, steer, or buffalo, Marq ran with head forward in a savage, exulting, flat-eared thrust and balanced the rhythms of his hooves so exactly that the saddle ceased to rock; all his motion was forward, a dead-level gallop.

His speed lashed tears from Perry's eyes, and joy in it set him yelling to the beat of Marq's hooves. "Get er, boy! Get er, get er, get er!" He began to twirl his riata, supposing the range would soon be right, for he had discovered no horse not trained to race that could outrun Marquis long. Now that the filly had recovered from her flounder at the start, however, and with the snaky loop of the riata hissing behind her, she stretched out into a sprint which began carrying her away. Perry's yells weakened and died. Marq was already at the top of his speed, and yet she lengthened her distance forward. That his sprint could not match hers while he had a man on his back, at least not till she tired, was apparent to him as soon as to Perry; he relaxed into a striding gallop which he could sustain over amazing distances; he let her diminish before them.

Among other mares stampeding in the same direction Perry passed three so close that roping any would have been no feat. They were good runners, though heavily in foal; their reliability as breeders was proved; they could be turned into sound foundation stock for a herd of his own. By comparison with that splendid filly flying across the valley ahead, however, they seemed hardly worth a second thought. Head up without strain, she was running in a leggy, fluid, cadenced gait as smooth as an antelope's.

Her lead upon Marquis became more, not less, as the distance of their running grew. Despite his dismay, Perry realized she would not have been a fraction so well worth catching if easily caught. The rest of the herd was far behind, Mr. Jackson and Hector also, and yet his one concern was to keep her in sight and, since Marq's speed alone would not suffice, watch for any chance to take her by cunning.

Through the entire depth of the valley they ran her, almost a mile from where Hector had tied the mules. Although the chase thus far could not have taken two minutes, the liquid grace of her run created in Perry a feeling of timeless extension. His first preparations to capture her seemed much farther back in time than were the oaks in space.

Her lead now had lengthened to half a furlong. She was approaching a dense strip of woods bordering the creek beyond which limy precipices jutted above the treetops. A few seconds more, and she was plunging through those woods. There, to any rational mind, she must be considered beyond capture: a lariat would be useless where trees rose all about her. So much as to see her was possible now only in snatches, a wild creature flashing through sun-dotted shadows. The sensible thing would be to go back and team again with Hector to rope some of the gravid mares before all escaped.

But Perry kept Marq's gallop drumming behind her. In approaching a drop into the creek, she looped sideward, negotiating the turn with light-footed precision, then obliquely down the embankment toward the creek and out of sight. To gain time Perry did not follow the curve; he put Marq straight over the embankment on trust that sand instead of leg-breaking rocks lay below.

Actually the rocks were first, the sand farther out. Marquis, by stretching in midair like a steeplechaser over a blind ditch, managed to reach a patch of sand. He recovered just in time to show Perry the sun-glossed bay angling up the opposite bank fifty yards or so downstream and into a gorge leading toward open prairies above the ridge.

Here, surely, was the place to concede the rightness of hurrying back after a surer catch, but Perry clucked to encourage Marquis. That insane dive over the embankment had brought him closer, a good stretch closer. Dashing downstream over boulders and snarls of driftwood, he swerved toward a bank something less than sheer, scrambled up it in a series of jumps so steep that he seemed about to fall over backward, then burst straight through a growth of cane which she had curved around.

At next sight she was closer still, but well up the shadowy gorge all the same, and so no great way from the boundless prairies of the uplands. The assumption might have been that up there, fleet as she was, she could be wholly sure of her freedom. Already, however, with the walls of the gorge to prevent her from circling back, her ears began flicking uncertainly, her head shifting from side to side, her gait faltering. For the herd was now far, far behind. As Marquis had carried Perry upwind until all that end of the valley reeked of man, the herd had swerved downwind. To a sociable creature, what was the good of prairies ever so vast if they had to be faced alone?

Through knowledge of horses dating from his earliest memories, Perry divined her doubt. Marquis divined it as well. His gasps for breath were punctuated by grunts resembling groans; sweat had turned his steel-gray coat dark as a stormcloud; foam was sudsing along his bridle rein, froth around his bit. All the same, his ears were forward, his stride vital and clean, his eye eager, his nostrils alert to whatever the wind said about her. A big horse, he was all horse. The race, the carriage of his head declared, was still a race, and he in to win it.

But to take it pell-mell was no longer necessary. Since her wish was turning backward when she herself could not, the time had come to be patient, to conserve Marq's strength for the moment when her own need would begin snugging its hobble about her pasterns. He reined back to a panting, enduring lope sufficient only to keep her in sight.

How warranted was her sense of being cut off became clear as they drove her out the head of the gorge onto the treeless plateau to which it led. The view from there commanded all of Perry's valley and great distance-hazed reaches beyond the screen of oaks across its opposite end. The rest of the herd, tiny as crickets, bounded across the sea of grass toward the south—all the herd except herself and one mare Hector had lassoed about the neck but was not able, with only one hand, to trip in half-hitches that would tie her down.

The filly, circling along the cliffs which walled her away from the valley, lifted her head to throw high on the wind a desolate, pleading neigh. She called again, a third time too, and Marq whickered in return. But Perry did not let him follow. She was trying a tactic as old as the pursuit of horse by man or horse by horse—to decoy her pursuers away from the path of escape, then circle and race them back to its mouth. He checked Marq firmly, gambling that she, like himself, knew of no other nearby route to the lowlands; he rode back near the head of the gorge at an alert but restful trot.

At once he doubted his decision. She galloped up and up a gradual slope of prairie which drained from her direction into the gorge. In time she disappeared. Perry noted how low was the sun in the west.

He considered Hector, with the mare plunging at the end of his lariat in the harbor below; the poor fellow was almost as much her captive, for lack of help to hobble her, as she was his. Charity advised him to get down there, and plain sense insisted that the filly, after all, must know another route down or she would never have coursed so far off.

His one move, however, was to let Marq relax. Wind around them rustled the winter-cured grass like leaves of bleached corn. Marq's withers began to dry. The labors of his breath subsided. He dropped his head to graze, looking up at times toward the slope she had crossed, at times down toward Mr. Jackson and the captured mare which held Hector captive.

A quarter hour passed thus, a half hour, possibly more. Suddenly Marq's head arched up to nose the wind, not in the direction she had taken, but many degrees around to the right. He stood in marble attention, ribs and nostrils quick. A search above the compass of his head showed Perry nothing more than wind-blown grass. Farther around, however, he discovered the mahogany bay, warily bold, trotting over a slope far the other way from the one she had crossed in trying to beguile him out into the open. She had completed a tremendous arc, had given Marquis her scent in circling across the wind, then pressed farther on toward the cliffs before venturing back. Nevertheless there was plenty of run in her still, the alertness of her head announced. Perry saw again that he must have her somehow, anyhow.

He eased himself down out of sight on the stirrup away from her and, letting Marq graze in a show of pastoral unconcern, watched her around the end of his pommel. By degrees she ventured nearer. Marq pricked up to whicker congenially. She answered. She answered again, and not with reserve as at first, but from lungs inflated almost beyond endurance by lonely longing. Her cautious walk changed to a trot with bold force in the stride; nor did it slacken until, as Perry began to fear that she might try a dash straight at the gorge, he tapped Marquis toward it at the half-right, as he had earlier to approach her from the oaks.

She stopped a hundred yards away. Through a long pause she stood pondering the stallion, her lustrous, undefining equine eyes puzzling over him, measuring the ground between him and the gorge. Where she was, she dropped her muzzle out of sight in belly-deep grass to seek with quick, selective lip for the tenderest growth around the roots. Again, however, she brought her head high to reconsider Marq and the gorge.

Perry, with his weight knotted close above one foot in the stirrup away from her, began to wonder how he could bear the cramping, numbing strain until she chose to move toward the gorge—and how, when she moved, he could unkink his joints in time to use his riata. The sun lost its meager heat. Winter-pale, it side-slipped down upon the undulations of prairie west of his valley. From the opposite direction, from far out on the plateau, a flight of blackbirds dense as a plague of locusts emerged above a rise and passed overhead. Their chirping, twanging twitters in unreckonable thousands charged the twilight until the last of them glided over the cliffs toward the circlet of woods below. Along the wake of lonely silence they left behind them, a coyote threw out three yips and one drawn howl.

After its echoes died along the cliffs, died in all but recollection, the plaint of a dove moaned from trees nearby. It thinned away alone. The plateau became empty of sound except for the dry, cold, persistent rustle of grasses bereft of their life. The filly had her head up, her ears up, her mane and tail afloat on the wind, and Perry, watching her from one eye before the pommel, tried vehemently to be Spartan over cramps in his legs and arms so excruciating that, cold though the twilight blew, prickles of sweat itched beneath his shirt.

All the while Marquis grazed in seeming forgetfulness that she was near, though the tilt of his head and ears was continuously her way. As the wind-blown silence grew, she tried a tentative whicker. His answer was prompt, murmurous, gentle. One more dip of her nose toward the grass and, without a bite, she began to advance at a walk. That she did not trust him, however, and that her advance was toward him only of necessity she showed by carrying her head to the side away from him. Her pasterns were springy, ready to bound away or charge around him.

After a dozen steps she accelerated to a trot aimed toward the gap between Marq's rump and the cliffs barring her from the gorge, from the valley, from the herd. Holding Marq at a prancy half-profile until the instant to act should ripen, Perry struggled to loosen his numb legs for a lurch into the saddle. All his aching intensified, and as much from anxiety to select the right instant for action as from the agony of moving at all.

When she had closed about half the distance toward Marq, she broke into a sidling lope, then suddenly, resolutely, a gallop. Perry's lamed swing into the saddle did not stop her. She scrambled into a sprint so driving that her whole top-line was flat from nose to tail.

Marq did not wait for orders. While Perry was kicking a numbed foot at the stirrup so long left empty, he spun into the line of her drive. Instead of faltering, she managed somehow to accelerate. She appeared determined to bowl Marq away with her shoulder, and regardless of the humped shape which emerged on his back.

To rope her at such speed, Perry feared, would break some bones, perhaps her neck—if not his riata. Still, to let her slip free now was unthinkable. He had time to swing but once before whipping a wabbly loop out where her run should carry her into it.

Its reptilian strike stiffened her legs in terror. Her hooves gouged the sod, but the cliff was too near to let her whirl, and in the instant of her hesitation the riata snaked over her head. As it burned under Marq's backward snatch to draw out the slack, she sprang again down the slope toward the gorge. The jerk of the lariat hit her like a bullet in the brain. It flung her tail end around before her head, threw all four hooves out sideward together, and slammed her against the sod like a bag of oats pitched from a wagon.

Perry twisted off the saddle, snatching loose a set of hobbles and a rawhide thong hanging behind the cantle. Stunned, she squirmed so feebly that it seemed her back might be gone, but he sat on her head all the same and locked each feebly waving foreleg between his own legs while buckling on the hobbles. Next, with rapid twists of the thong around her muzzle and into the noose on her neck, he made a halter linked to his riata.

She was his—dead or alive, his.

Panting, sweating, shaking all over, he stepped back. A moment more of feeble struggle, and her head lifted. She rolled onto her knees. Trying in panic to bound up, she floundered in the hobbles on crazy legs until the rope on her halter, assisted by the hobbles, again threw her down. Her next attempt to rise was more circumspect, and more successful. She came to her feet a sound though shaken mare.

Laughing in relief, spent with excitement sustained too long, Perry sat by to let her learn better what it meant to be hobbled, to be his.

What was happening in the valley he could no longer see, nor did he care. His thought went back to Springfields'. That queer restraint last night now seemed to him lucky. Yes, he would accompany Leticia to Bayards'; he would be neighborly of course; but this evening without fail he would write again to Camilla.

His letter endeavored to show her Highhorse Valley (as he named his place) the way it looked to him. After relating how he captured the filly, he concluded:

Do you see what might be done here, Milla? Distance plagues every settler in Texas: no problem is more constant than distance, or more in opposition to civilizing these wild savannas. One solution is the horse, a good horse. Cobs, scrubs, mean-eyed mustangs, mules, almost anything on four legs must answer for most people, and their price is modest—as low as $15 or $20. But quality stock is rare, and very dear. Marquis cost me $210, and worth every penny. Still, he met his match in that superb bay filly. I intend to make her queen of the range here, the mother of a line which I believe will bring horsemen with deep pockets from many miles away. For, once the war is over, the tides of migrants sure to flow in across the Sabine will greatly augment our need for swift and reliable locomotion.

So my name for her is Vision. Heretofore all my calculations were chained to laborious arithmetic about how many acres I could plant with these two hands of mine, and what few others I might buy. But this valley is very easy to fence, since nature has nearly done that already. Therefore horses in quantity can be raised here with a few Mexican vaqueros, who will move great distances for work as herdsmen at six dollars a month, and much better for the purpose than the run of darkies who know horses best from behind a singletree. For the first time I now see how we might be free of slaves.

My goal will be to develop a strain of horses capable of a hundred miles in one day, swift and tough and handsome to see. I mean to make this place known as "The Home of the Hundred-Mile Horse." Vision and Marquis have in them that capability, and I believe your Swallow does, possibly Oriole as well. So does the racer my father left to me, a raven-black stallion named Mazeppa, eight times a winner before an accident stabled him, and I must bring him out from Maryland sometime after the first harvest to infuse the strain with Thoroughbred, unmatched for quality, stamina, and speed. Of other horses

*or mares only such will be the progenitors as can still go on after going
a hundred miles. How could we fail to prosper as we achieve that goal?
In the meantime, too, is it not believable that pioneering on such
terms will leave us a bit of liberty so that we can assist in converting
these wild lands into a new state?*

*To say we is presumptuous, considering how we parted and how
rapidly time is advancing toward your wedding day. But before that
day arrives, you should at least know of this possibility. You ride well;
you could do so only in fondness for horses. You have taken pains to
acquire fine ones, and not from vanity, as so many do, but to express
your own spirit through their merits. I believe as firmly as the Lord
equipped me to believe anything that you and I in partnership here
could found a life beyond measure more fascinating than most of our
acquaintances ever will approximate. Too, it would be a lastingly useful life: to give people any means of easier, surer travel is to increase
their liberty, to release them from the prison of empty distance, to
loose them a little more from our earthbound condition. I think it
certain that you would find nearly as much gratification in doing so as
I will myself.*

*To convince you of that in person would be difficult enough I know.
If undertaking it in such haste on paper merely provokes your smile, it
will accomplish all that a sensible man could expect. Let it bear witness for me, however, that I have tried my best to reshape each
thought of the future in a way that might excite in you some wish to
share it.*

*For I dearly love thee, Milla, and will continue to through all our
days on earth.*

Ever,
Perry

From C. B.'s Journal
February 3, 1836

Prodigious victories require a pugnacity so implacable that the victors themselves may fail to escape it.

Once the Israelites had put the Philistines to rout, they divided
under the banners of Saul and David to turn upon Israel the dripping
sword of Israel. After Greece humbled the last expedition from Per-

sia, Greeks became insatiably fatal to Greeks. French revolutionaries whose guillotine breakfasted and dined on the lords of France saw it sup on French revolutionaries.

A bloodless version of that old tale is being retold in Texas: the postscript to victory at San Antonio has been a row between Governor Henry Smith and ranting sachems in the General Council about which of them should control the troops, who are thereby encouraged to resist control by anybody. Some fiesta continually at San Antonio, fancying that they can stop any invasion there. General Sam Houston, on the other hand, has called lightly manned forts in open country nothing better than death traps for those who do man them; he has instructed the garrison to sink their cannon in the river, blow up the Alamo, and fall back upon Gonzales. That order is scoffingly ignored. Still another force under Colonel James Fannin, equally deaf to Houston, has put its trust in the fortress at Goliad. Houston himself is not present to discipline these whims: he left on the 14th or 15th last to quiet the northeasterly tribes of Indians, whom Mexican agents have been inciting to raid the settlements from that direction whenever Santa Anna strikes from the opposite way. Meanwhile still other volunteers have vowed to carry their banners down to the Halls of Montezuma: they are assembling now for an expedition into the heart of Mexico by way of Matamoros, a florid, wrongheaded enterprise by a few hundred braggarts who propose to overthrow a nation of seven million. The General Council is volubly for it, whereas Governor Smith is profanely against it.

Because of such differences the Council has deposed the Governor, which it has no authority to do. His retort has been to dissolve the Council, equally without authority. Thus at a time when no one can suppose that Santa Anna's passion to discipline the colonists has been extinguished, when he is reported instead to be snarling like a wounded jaguar, preparing to pounce upon Texas as soon as warm weather permits him to move a large army that far north, at a time therefore when Texas ought to be forging means to stop him, ought to be distributing arms and drilling troops and levying grains and assembling transport and winning external help, the whole territory is without any organized instrument of defense, without any genuine government, without any legal mechanism through which military preparations can be ordered and financed and controlled. Nor will there be any during these pregnant weeks of winter, none until March at earliest, when a convention meets at Washington-on-the-Brazos to form a new one.

What might save the Texians is that their enemies are notoriously dilatory. However energetic Santa Anna himself may be, he cannot possibly start a force of any magnitude across the wintry deserts lying both ways from the Rio Grande before April at earliest, if only because the dillydallying *mañana* spirit among his countrymen will not let them be either bribed or driven to move with dispatch. More than that, there will be no green forage along the way to sustain his livestock until after the spring rains fall. Thus a pretty safe calculation would be that he will not reach any of the American settlements before June or July, by which time perhaps the Texians will give up squabbling to arrange a sufficient resistance.

What concerns me is this: no other editor in the U.S.A. has beat the drum so hard for volunteers to join them or for donations to help their cause, so that their failure to trouble themselves (and at a time when that would serve the province best) reflects upon me. Lately I'm bruised with sarcasm on all sides. Even Perry, much as he knows, seems to take little thought of the matter. According to Camilla, at any rate, a letter from him which reached her this afternoon said nothing about the war, not a word.

One part which she did share with me told of a plan to develop a strain of Texas horses able to go a hundred miles in one day. She wanted to know what I thought of it.

"Totally brainless," I said.

"But why, Pa?"

"Not one dozen men in Texas have any notion which way they're headed. Why encourage them to proceed at any such rate as that?"

Despite her amusement, she paid me for my levity by keeping the rest of his letter to herself. I do feel deprived too: much as it has enlivened and brightened her, it must be a dandy.

CHAPTER XIII

I

New Orleans Because he was uneasy, and fight-
Thursday Afternoon ing a temptation toward anger, Ed-
February 4, 1836 mond Beaufait emphasized the
casualness and intended brevity
of his visit by stopping his car-
riage on the Rue Royale before Camilla's house and walking up the
driveway. He could hear her voice in the patio, busy, as yet unaware
of him; she was at work back near the greenhouse, helped by Abe, her
Negro gardener.

Abe noticed him first, acknowledging his approach with a wary bow
accompanied by a mumur to her. "Miz Milla, mam . . ."

Trowel in hand, she was mulching earth in a flowerbox, one in a
row of five. Her crouch over it shifted only enough to let her see who
was coming, after which she continued troweling as before. No one
would guess that she was expecting any visitor, certainly none of any
consequence: in addition to worn gloves condemned to end their days
in labor, she had on a rather spent housedress, attractive enough in
its way, but one which said nothing so much as that she had work to
do and cared more about that at the moment than anything else. Not
until he was close by, saying, "Good afternoon, dear," did she take
further notice of him, but then at once straightened up, flushed and
moist and bright. The back of one gloved hand thrust a straying wave
of hair off her forehead, and her glance met his, as open as his was
guarded.

"Aren't you early, Edmond? Your note said you'd be along at
four."

Pulling out his watch, he slicked its face with a thumb. "It's seven
till."

"Oh, so?"

"Yes, and I must be on the dock at five." The fact was he should
be in Baton Rouge right now, but he would say nothing to blame her.
"I can't afford to miss that last boat."

"While I'm about this, though," she said, "I'll keep on here till coffee's ready. It looks *so* like rain this evening, and, once it starts, there's no telling when I'll get at it again." She waved at the grass he stood on. "Do be seated, Edmond."

Anyone so well acquainted with him ought to know that he never sat on grass, simply never. The better it looked, the better it had been manured, and there were other reasons. First, his doctor had cautioned him that damps from bare ground were bad for piles. Second, it was likely to stain one's seat and mar the press in one's pantaloons. Third, he had noisy knees: if he tried to squat that far down they would crack like flintlocks, and he thought it impolitic to publicize the difference between his age and hers. Snapping his fingers while wagging at a chair over near a plashy fountain sufficed to send Abe hurrying to fetch it, after which Edmond dismissed him by a jog of the thumb toward the stables.

Camilla gave no sign of being conscious of this byplay. Having troweled the dirt fine in one box, she drew her glove off and, to his amazement, smoothed it with her hand, *her bare hand.*

"Tell me, Milla dear, what in the world is *that* for?"

"To start verbena, a lovely, lovely flower." She flicked the trowel toward each of the other boxes. "That one's for coleus, the next for begonia, yonder for cineraria, and this other for phlox."

"But why should *you* have to bother with it?"

"I don't have to, and it's no bother. I enjoy doing it. You know I do."

"But that's what we have slaves for. That's what you have Abe for."

"Somehow, though, they never quite understand. Abe never seems to grasp why the manure should be deep underneath. He likes it on top where I'll see he's used it, though the roots can't reach it there. Then, too, it's an everlasting mystery to him why seeds like I'm planting today can't be covered by more soil than the thickness of tissue paper, rather than inches of it, as on beans or corn."

"Well," Edmond observed on a droll note, "that's a mystery to me too."

"Because the seeds are so fine. They haven't the substance in them to reach through thicker soil. They smother if covered deep."

"Oh."

Her look at him deplored his dismissing it all with a mere *oh.*

"But it's simply prodigious, Edmond, an outright prodigy, what happens when you do start them correctly." She seized an envelope marked CINERARIA and opened it before him. "Look at this!"

What he saw brought on an impulse to sneeze. "Reminds me of ground pepper, really. That or snuff."

"Why, yes!" Her countenance glowed. "And to think that each tiny particle, bedded just so, can be converted into a plant so big, with large leaves and a huge bouquet of blossoms! When I have cineraria thriving in my garden—well, it lifts the spirit just to look at them."

He smiled. He had said *oh,* not so much to belittle her information as in wonder that any genuine lady should clutter her head with facts of that character. Gardening was much more than a pastime to her; she went at it as if the merit in doing it were to be gained solely through ardent application. Having smoothed one box, she troweled black earth from a wheelbarrow onto a layer of decayed manure in another and began mulching that as fine as she had its neighbor. Such activity did show her to advantage too, plainly dressed though she was: her body looked willowy, vigorous, and competent, all its lines flowing together in continual grace. For such work in warm weather she quite evidently omitted the superabundance of underclothes most ladies considered indispensable: the round of her buttocks showed when she stooped, and some intimation of the cleft. One of these days he would have to correct her on that score, but perhaps not until after they married.

"Many a lady," he observed, lenient and amused, "speaks of 'my garden' as you do, but you're the only one I know who actually dirties her hands at it."

"But, Edmond, it's not just what you call *dirty.*" She suspended the motion of her trowel to enlarge her eyes at his in adding, "Earth like this—after all, it has perfectly flabbergasting power to generate beautiful or useful things—whatever flower you like, and the most savory edibles too! Pa once said whenever people suppose God's place is only in the Heavens Above they ignore what their eyes tell them from the day they're born till the day they die: that He is forever and always at work in good rich earth also. And I agree. Hardly anything humbles me so, or gives me such a sense of true creation, as making things grow."

Edmond nodded, tolerating it all. Particular and cleanly as she was in her person, and in the management of her household, he did not think it hurt anything to let her be a mystic about dirt outdoors if she wanted to. What a well-ordered ménage she kept was being demonstrated even now, for her old butler Obadiah emerged from the kitchen with two mulatto maids, among them bringing forth a wash basin, towels and soap, napkins, coffee, cookies, fruit, and a side table on which to serve them, all this without any call from her, an automatic consequence of excellent instruction. In her, Edmond thought, he would be getting not simply an ornamental wife, but one with so much accomplishment always evident around her that he could well afford to let her see God in a clod if her fancy turned that way.

Obadiah set the table over by the fountain, a delightful place, musical, flowery, and moist. Having the servants there, of course, prevented Edmond from bending his talk toward the discovery which had brought him this afternoon, and there was relief in that prevention: it delayed what would surely prove a trying interval. He relaxed during the ritual of serving, until, at a signal from her, the servants withdrew to the house, when he perceived that he must seize the initiative at once or she would herself. His approach to their difficulty was from a direction she would least expect.

"Heard from Allan lately, Camilla dear?"

A start brought her eyes to his. She then shifted them back to her cup, which she tilted so recklessly to her lips that the coffee appeared to scald her. "Why, yes. He's fine. Arrived safely and all."

"See your property, did he?"

"Not yet, or evidently not, since he didn't say so." Her glance showed continuing amazement, and some alarm, at the shrewdness of his guess about what had chilled her toward him today.

Of course it was no guess at all: two of her servants were paid for supplying him such information, and liberally paid. Clever as she was, she had not the least notion with what care he informed himself about her.

She lifted him a direct gaze and pushed him closer to the issue in her own way. "You said you must go north at noon today. What stopped you?"

"Well, there was a business matter or two . . ." He fidgeted some crumbs of cookie off the tips of his fingers, intending to give his further comments a fine turn, but she pressed on.

"A certain annoyance in the note you sent me . . . to be plain, it made me suspect you were staying to see me because I emptied my account."

That was on the mark, painfully so. This morning she had come to the bank and, without waiting to consult him or explain herself, had withdrawn eight hundred and seventy-five dollars, leaving a token balance of eleven dollars. Perhaps she fancied that, as he was preparing to leave for Baton Rouge, he would be too busy to notice or to act upon it until he returned. But then, if she was trying to be secretive about it, why hadn't she waited instead until he was out of town? Her method had the color of defiance, not evasion.

"Were you?" she demanded.

Setting his cup aside, he toyed with his napkin. Suppressed anger made the fringes of the cloth tremble, so he put that aside too. This blunt thrust of hers was quite unfair, since, with her, he was scrupulous to avoid bluntness himself; if critical of her in any sense, he managed it in words so calm and oblique and finely chosen that most people would not suspect him of being critical at all. Another maddening thing just now was her implication (conveyed more by the flash of her glance than her spoken words) that she had a right to be annoyed, that *she* was the party wronged today, not he.

"Well?" she persisted.

"Camilla, my dear . . ." He recovered his napkin to scuff it across both palms, which had gone damp. He spoke at a pitch deliberately keyed so low that she would have to listen well to hear every word. "Perhaps you had forgotten that you have a large note falling due next Wednesday."

"No, certainly not. Every debt I owe I think about and worry about and wonder how in gracious I'll meet it when it's due."

He returned the napkin to the side table, then linked his fingers tight together and kept his voice bland. "With your account empty, it's difficult to see any preparation to meet this one."

"In the first place, it's too big for me to retire with what cash I have or can put my hands on any time soon. In the second, it's amply secured. You've seen to it that every debt I owe is *quite* amply secured, so I was going to ask you to renew it."

"And the interest? That's due too, you realize."

"Yes, the interest. I hadn't forgotten the interest, no. You never do, and so I take care not to. I was going to ask that you increase the note to cover the interest and principal both. Would that be asking too much?"

"Now let's not indulge in heat, please. You know very well, dear, that others have shares in my business. They expect me to run it *as* a business. I must account for every penny."

"Well, they need never trouble their heads about that. You will."

"Of course, it's understood that, after we're married, I'll simply assume the debts and—"

"Yes, but there's no fixed date for that yet, so let's please continue treating business as business." She relinquished her own cup and saucer to the table, then took up her work gloves from the grass beside the chair. These she gripped like a tool. "What do you propose to do about that note? Will you increase it and renew it or not?"

He gave his fingers a twist to lock in their impulse to fidget. The fool did not seem to understand that what she was asking for would gain nothing for him, only her, and therefore would not be business but charity. He already held liens against every last thing she owned in Louisiana except four slaves, two fine mares, one piano, and her jewelry—and he knew how to impound these also. The law—she had not learned as yet that he could manage the law about as easily as she could a good mount. By a little manipulation readily arranged, he could strip her of everything within reach of Louisiana courts—her plantation, her town house, her livestock, her implements, her furniture, and every slave without exception, every jewel, every book on her shelves, every pot and pan in her kitchens, every gown in her closets, everything. He could turn her out on the streets, penniless, without prospects, and pretty near naked. What would become of all this spirited defiance then? So complete was his unused control over her that in some measure he despised her. Their impending marriage would simply give a better color to her dependency upon him and add her property to his without the bother of going through the courts.

Still, he did not want to quarrel with her, regardless of the provocation. He merely wanted to know what new fancy had induced her to snatch out all that money. If he angered her enough, there would be no limit to the foolishness she might be capable of; and, while he himself would greatly prefer to see her his wife than a bankrupt, there were signs enough that her own preference was much less defined. The fact that her withdrawal of cash followed so close upon news from that good-looking ignoramus in Texas suggested an increasingly fickle state of mind.

"You see how it is, dear," he resumed in a hurt tone, very subdued, very wise. "In the light of all the candor between us before, I should have thought, being's I was right there in the office myself, you'd have let me know what your plans were before—"

"However, I couldn't do that without knowing myself, could I?"

"How's that?"

"I hadn't any clear plan requiring that money right away, and still don't. All I knew was that I wanted the freedom nothing but money allows a person in such a place as this. To be truthful, I did want to have hold of it before so much got gobbled up by that interest."

"But just as a whim? Or why?"

"Because of a sudden feeling of panic, if you must know. Often this tangle of debt feels like a noose. I wanted—"

"Though every debt on the books in your name is only temporary, of course. It'll all be canceled in due time."

"No, I'm beginning to fear that marriage to you, Edmond, wouldn't cancel it, merely renegotiate it, to use a phrase of yours."

"Camilla!" He put aching hurt into his voice. "What a way to talk!"

"Well, perhaps that isn't fair, no."

"I think not, no."

"I'm sorry I said it, Edmond."

She bent forward in her chair and turned a restless glance over toward her flowerboxes. "But I do have a plan for meeting that note. Among the nigras at Palmer Hall there's one that must be sold—two, if you count it right: a wench called Tongoo and her baby boy, a right black girl, strong but lazy."

"I recollect her, yes."

"The mortgage against my field hands isn't for half what they'd fetch today. Her, for instance—the loan value down for her is seven hundred, but I'll wager she'll fetch two thousand, very likely more with the baby. If you'll let me sell them, we can put our business affairs in order again."

"I see. A very complicated arrangement." He concealed a temptation to smile. Under that lovely exterior of hers lay a ruthless streak, one his own nature constrained him to admire. All her deploring of the evils of slavery did not prevent her from picking Tongoo to sell, a handsome wench sure to command a higher price because of qualities which appealed to man's baser nature. "Are you sure, though, you do want to sell her?"

"No, I don't. But I have to. She's a wicked thing, a bad influence. I have to sell her, and I know of no other way to see everything through and pay off all the interest I'll owe till I've crops to harvest."

"Well . . ." He drew a long sigh to let her know how heavily her difficulties weighed upon him. "It's a complicated matter."

"Still, it's the only solution I can see for the present."

He could easily see another. As he already had mentioned that twice, however, and without agreeable effect, he decided against doing so again. He fingered the watch from his vest. "Twenty till five," he remarked. "There isn't much time." No, and he still did not know what he had come here to learn. In his own subdued way he was a very determined man. "Camilla . . ."

While that hung between them he let the watch slide back and forth in one rocking hand, sensually aware of its smooth gold, its weighty, costly caress, and with the chain looped around his index finger. He fixed upon her an absolutely motionless stare. "You're thinking again about an excursion to Texas?"

That hit her so exactly where she was weakest that she stood up, eyes abnormally large, but again defiant. "Strictly, I've never stopped. I've never ceased to think of it."

"Oh." The one trouble with applying moral force to such a person was that what he forced was honesty, giving back to her a moral force superior to his. "I see."

"All I really own is there. Why shouldn't I think of it?"

"But what about your property here? That out there is worth a song, this a fortune."

"That out there don't amount to much yet, but it will. What I have here is just papier-mâché riches. All I'll ever have here is. It's all papier-mâché."

"But you can't just turn your back on it, dear. You can't just leave it till it suits you to look after it again."

"What I arranged for last fall will serve again: Susan Westbrook will look in here daily and see to things; at Palmer Hall, Mr. Bowen knows what must be done. And you, since it's all really yours now in all but name, I don't suppose you'd mind keeping an eye on it too, would you?"

That, he would neither affirm nor gainsay. He did not speak at all until he could assume a slackened, gloomy expression declaring that the brutality of her attitude left him absolutely gutted. "But, dear, I thought you felt so attached—thought your attachment here overrode all other considerations."

"Well, in a way. Maybe it's because I do feel so 'attached'—maybe that's what's the matter with me. It's got so I feel caught here."

The gold of his watch had grown damp from moisture on his palm.

By mutely caressing it as if left with only it to trust, he implied inexpressible shock over her fickle ways, and his lengthening silence affected her more than anything he had said.

On impulse she strode over beside him to press a hand on his shoulder. "It's very wicked of me, Edmond. I know it is, but then not to face what's true, might that not be more wicked still?"

He did not answer. By blinking a bit, he worked a trace of tears into the corners of his eyes.

Bending low, one arm across his back, she pressed her cheek against his temple and spoke as abjectly as a wronged man could ask. "Oh, gracious heaven, you're so good, and it's such a evil thing to hurt you. Come now . . ." Here she stood up straight by way of inviting him to show more spine. "I'll have ample time to think about it while you're gone."

He rose and pocketed his watch, still blinking. Taking her hand in both his, he pressed it.

His last words had little more strength than a whisper. "Very well, dear. Very well."

2

Sunday Afternoon
February 7, 1836

Because of rain on Sunday, a cold and nagging rain, Camilla dedicated the afternoon to making clothes with Yvonne Hanotaux for the orphan asylum, the Orphelinat des Soeurs, their favorite charity. Though they worked in Camilla's upstairs room, though Yvonne was so intimate to the family and so discreet that Camilla could tell her anything, she did not venture into the subject most on her mind until Yvonne herself brought it forward.

"I see nothing to indicate, *ma che'ie,* that you proceed with your trousseau. Perhaps I am mistaken."

"No, not a bit." After a shift of the sewing on her lap to proceed from a different angle, Camilla added, "Has it occurred to you that that trousseau might be a waste of time?"

"Mais non. A brilliant wedding deserves much preparation."

The twitch of a disallowed smile pulled Camilla's lips sideward. Yvonne, a plump and dimply brunette who was much more acute than any stranger would ever guess, exemplified what is meant by the French saying, "Men have intelligence, women antennae." No person of her awareness could fail to divine what Camilla implied by belittling the trousseau.

"M. Beaufait," Yvonne went on, "will expect that wedding to astonish everyone."

Hands relaxing in her lap, Camilla looked away. The fire in the grate sizzled languidly. Near it lay her cat, a fleecy Persian surgically converted into a perfect gentleman. Around and around in a glass sphere by the window a society of goldfish floated on veiny, swollen bellies, dragging capes and shawls and trains of excessive fin and lipping trifles without appetite. Raindrops spat on the windows behind them; and, warm though the room itself was, a contraction gripped Camilla's shoulders as if she were cold.

"No doubt he will."

"However"—Yvonne, her softly turned lips forward the French way, pronounced it *ow-evair*—"I see well how much you miss the pioneer."

"You do?" Camilla shook her head. "No, you can't."

Yvonne worked in silence. The tap of rain on glass and the sizzle of fire gave the measure of that silence, the humming of a Negro girl belowstairs as well. From beyond the windows a single row of hoof-beats reminded Camilla of the still and lonely night Perry had described in first writing from the *Gulph Breeze* so many days ago.

"Yvonne, do you consider me very foolish?"

"At times, certainly. Not yet do I know anyone especially good to know who is not sometimes foolish. But to marry M. Beaufait you are not foolish, not at all."

"No?"

"*Au contraire,* this match is as sensible as a Gascon grocer's. It is so sensible, so clever, so French, I wonder if you really are American."

Camilla felt herself color but was amused. Yvonne's temperate modulations, her pleasant misshaping of English through lips habitually pouted for Creole, did not entirely conceal a metallic sharpness in what she said. As the widow of a politician and sister-in-law of a notorious usurer, she considered no one else quite so mercenary as the French.

"What would you say, Yvonne, if I were to put the wedding off—if I were to leave soon? I mean *very* soon, next week."

Yvonne's glance came up to meet hers. "For Texas?"

"Yes." She found it necessary to clear her throat. "Just to see it. To visit."

"Ah, *oui*. To see the future."

"To see what is so, what is true."

"That will be difficult anywhere, to see what is true."

"You advise against going?"

"*Non*. Once my parents, when I was young and wished to travel where my heart had gone before me, shut me in a convent. There I stayed until they married me to Senator Vivien Hanotaux. How very fortunate too. For, though I quickly learned to hate him, he at last had the grace to bow from life and leave me independent. You see yourself how joyful this keeps me. However, as I am less wise than they, I have for you no fine advice." There had been on her lips a teeter of humor which now disappeared. She lifted gentle brown eyes to Camilla's. "I wish rather to understand you. Whoever one loves one tries to understand."

"But how like what *he* said!" Camilla turned to do what she had been wanting for some while to do: from a drawer of her dressing table she extracted Perry's two letters. Some revival of the anguished quickening they brought her when she first opened them shook the hand which thrust them forward. "Here, read!"

While Camilla resumed her sewing, Yvonne devoted herself wholly to reading. Again the rain and the fire dominated the silence, accompanied occasionally by the lisp of turned paper.

"Foolish, *oui*," Yvonne murmured. "How foolish you are!"

"In what way?"

"Two dozen ways."

"To have quarreled with him?"

"And for such a cause! Do you want a man to be less than a man? *Eh bien*, there is M. Beaufait."

"Is to be a good man to be less than a man?"

"*Mais non*. Neither does being thought a good man signify he is one."

"True. Nevertheless——"

"M. Beaufait finds profit in seeming a good man. He will also find profit in marriage to you. For a man who is already rich, having a beautiful wife contributes more to ambition, and gains more envy, than marrying for money."

"Should each not gain something in marriage?"

"That is sensible, *oui*. It is just. But one thing neither of you will gain if you marry him: that is happiness. The difference between happiness and gaiety you already know, and gaiety his wealth may sometimes afford you, but happiness never."

"Never?"

"How is it possible? Whoever is to gain happiness must give it; there is no other way. You cannot give happiness to M. Beaufait, not only because you do not love him enough, but because he does not value happiness for anyone, not even for himself. He values possessions. A lovely wife, widely desired and thought inaccessible, he would consider her a fine possession, like a magnificent home. As happiness in marriage is possible only with one to whom you can give it, you must forget it if he is to be your husband."

"So then you would not marry him under any circumstances?"

"I never said that, *non*. Your father's opinion is that happiness can *not* be the goal of life because, though nearly everyone talks about it, hardly anyone troubles himself to do what creates it. Myself, I rarely discover it in anyone, and no longer seek it."

"If one is not to seek happiness in marriage, why would you prefer someone with no fortune at all?"

"Not once have I said this, Camilla. However, if Captain Allan has no fortune he has something else. He is a sentient, courtly man; he has courage; his mind is large and growing; he loves you. What more do you ask?"

"Long as you have been my friend, Yvonne, you can't help knowing 'what more.' If he's susceptible to color in one form—"

"*Non-non-non!*" Yvonne interrupted through outthrust lips. "This is not what restrains you, or much less than you tell yourself it does. For you must have observed that, although we see very melancholy cases to the contrary, wives are most sure to hold their husbands if they love them without any reservation, and we learn how to forgive whatever men do so long as they love us. No, it is not this susceptibility you fear, but your own heart, which was too hasty once, and so you do not trust it. His susceptibilities, no. What he is most susceptible to is clear: in San Antonio, here, anywhere, he is susceptible to *you*. What does this woman of the celebration matter? With her he was only with you."

"Well, I suppose that may be partly true, queer as it sounds."

Yvonne held the two letters apart. "The second is proof that you ignored the first." And pinching down the corner showing the date of the first: "Why did you not answer him then?"

"That did not reach me then. The last came here before the first. The last came Wednesday evening, the first not till yesterday, because the steamboat captain failed to leave it at Palmer Hall on the way upriver. It stayed in his desk all the way to St. Louis, then on up to Freeport. He, though, when told at the plantation that I'd returned to town, took such pains to bring it here by hand and was so engagingly remorseful—altogether I freely forgave him, that is, until I learned how his tardiness cheated me."

"*Mais non.* That was not what cheated you. Let us be just: temper and misjudgment cheated you—your own." Yvonne's needle became brisk again.

Camilla studied her minutely. Her air of wondering how any sane girl *could* be so foolish made Camilla smile. "Is he *very* handsome, Yvonne? Oh, I know quite well he isn't, but why does he seem so?"

"Many are more handsome, *oui.* What of that? A woman who has beauty has no need for it in men."

"However, you do not answer me. Why does he seem more handsome than he is?"

"Perhaps because, like your father, he has a lively heart, an active brain, and a relish of life. In them we see more life than in other men, *non?*"

"True. Giving thought to all this, what would you do?"

"Ah! Beaufait has so very much! One must be young to throw all that away. Or, to say it otherwise, one must be brave to be free, *n'est-ce pas?*"

"Dear, deep Yvonne! You are most yourself when you talk two ways at once. What do you mean, 'to be free'?"

"Why, it means things as different as lives are different, is this not so? For example, to those who love, marriage is liberation; to those who do not, bondage."

"So? It might start as liberation and then change. However, you have not said what you would do. Suppose you were my age—"

"Nevertheless I fear I should marry the rich one." Yvonne shrugged. "What else is possible? We people who are not brave, we think first of the skin and stomach. Last, if ever, we think of the soul. I would eat wisely and dress well and do all things to remain lovely. When Captain Allan came back, as he could be encouraged to do sometimes, I would slip very cautiously into his arms, and my children would be his."

Camilla took that with a doubting smile. Yvonne, both because of such freedom in her talk and because of her dimply look of enjoying things of the flesh equally with those of the mind, had given gossips much to talk about. The knowing had long speculated that she must be Major Burleigh's mistress; but, whether because they were simply wrong or because she was too clever, too decorous, too discreet, no one could cite any proof. Camilla herself was not sure.

"You say that, Yvonne, because you know very well it's nothing I could ever do."

"And why not? 'One should not say, "Fountain, I will never drink of your water." ' It would be easier for you than for most who risk it. And why? First, though a coquette, you are known to be chaste, as the gentlemen,—who *never* tell such things—have so often reported in worshipful despair. Everyone would suppose you were only letting yourself be admired. Second, you could tell yourself M. Beaufait was being paid off according to his deserts since he must learn sometime that the love we buy is always counterfeit."

Without elevating an eyelash, without varying the rate of her needle, she continued in the same pleasantly subdued and modulated tone, taking it as a matter of course that Camilla would accept ironies as devastating to herself as to the man she had agreed to marry. "Third, when he found out—as in time he would, because once you succumb you will completely succumb—he would forgive it. He would forgive, not alone because he cares less for you than for the prestige he expects to gain through you, which he could never afford to sully by raising a scandal, but because he is French, at least on his mother's side, and knows that a womanly weakness for paramours is in the tradition of his home. Indeed, although his mother was of necessity his mother, his father was very likely so in merely an honorary fashion."

Camilla tightened her lips to counteract an impulse to laugh. There had been a time when innuendoes about how Mme. Beaufait had accumulated the funds to give Edmond his start in life had seemed too offensive and unfair to permit in her hearing, and she marveled at her tolerance of this one today.

"Of course," Yvonne continued, "such whispers about you would cost you some American friends, since Americans are simple people who believe the health, honor, and well-being of the home require chastity of the wife. Further, since you would secretly agree with them, you would see your immortal soul wither to a thing easily blown away. For what is the soul but the vision and the will and the strength to do yourself what you believe it best for others to do, uh? However, there are people enough who get along without any soul to speak of."

"It's curious, Yvonne, with what wicked words you manage to be so scathingly moral. You make it clear, too, that it is not only American friends I would lose."

"Not I, *non*. You are mistaken, *ma che'ie*. Certain of us would love you still. But we might alloy our love with condescension, for the weak are promoted by proofs that one who could be strong is as frail as they."

Camilla accepted that without comment. Her cat rolled to his back, fangs naked in yawning boredom, then lapsed back into dreams. Her fish continued their listless drift, the fireplace its sizzle, the rain its tap at the windows. From a clock deep in the house musical chimes announced the hour as if the flight of time were the prettiest, emptiest, idlest phenomenon in any given day. With the fading of the last tinkle, Camilla found herself shaken by a profound and quivering sigh.

As if that sigh were a statement, Yvonne remarked, "Yes, much time will pass, I fear, before you return."

"What makes you say so? Two or three months—such an excursion should not take more."

"However, what you need most is there."

"But Perry—"

"Not just Perry, Camilla. You are one of those who need trials from time to time. You need to prove your strength whenever others doubt it."

"What a surprising thought, Yvonne! But possibly true."

"And you need sometimes to suffer—I mean, to suffer in admirable ways. You are deeply Christian, *ma che'ie*. You think you have been shallow and wicked. *Eh bien!* You desire deliverance through the Cross—through hardship, through sacrifice, through admiration from good people. Therefore we cannot hope to see you back soon." She shook her head while sewing continually. "How very much we shall miss you—and your father too!"

From C. B.'s Journal
February 7, 1836

Tonight at dinner Camilla livened things considerably by asking what articles we ought to buy for a visit to Texas. After my first surprise, the scheme was much more welcome than I let her see. To act dubious is imperative, of course, first because that is proper in a parent regarding questions of risk and also because the way to keep her determination high is to oppose it, though without resolution. I spoke about the discomforts of such a journey, the perversities of February and March, the unsettled conditions out there, etc., whereas she takes the view that, though much could be said against going any time, most is in favor of it now, while the guns are quiet, the weather cool, herself restless, and her condition single.

Her refusal to let talk of hardships stop her I think admirable, and her readiness to be debonair about the difficulties. She needs to put aside sham problems and confront real ones. All healthy people do. What distinguishes us above every other creature is our talent for solving problems, and nature compels us to display it daily. Without sufficient exercise at mastering the genuine kind, we invent or borrow substitutes: we cudgel our brains over chess or whist or political argument, over today's scandal or how to match a lost button or the bloodlines of racehorses or some new theory about the campaigns of Napoleon. Vigorous men, during hours at liberty from work for pay, will take up gardening or build a boat or hunt bear or bowl or climb mountains or paint the house. Women without children to do for and worry over will adopt puppies or kittens or lovebirds or goldfish and worry about them. Not only is the call of the Frontier strong for Camilla in spite of the dangers and hardships, but I suspect these add to the attraction.

She talks of being able to go and return within two months. That may be, but I anticipate something very different: a glorious reconciliation with Perry, an abdication from this false regality here in Louisiana, a prompt wedding, and then my chaperonage will end. Henceforth I can use my life as suits me best, me personally.

What will suit me is change, and a good deal of it. In a Bombay garden once I saw a few carefully nurtured apple trees, poor, puny shrubs, all fruitless for lack of killing frosts or the stimulating hardship a winter brings. No amount of loving care would make them thrive: the sameness of tropical climate had sickened them, stunted them, and (as it were) castrated them. What killing frosts each autumn are to the orchard, I believe, change is to man—indispensable for keeping his growth vigorous, the fruits of his labor abundant and their taste tangy. We thrive on bearable change even when we grumble about it, even when it threatens (but leaves us) our lives. Man is *philometastatic,* to coin a word. At any rate this one is.

So I fidget with impatience to toboggan out of here. Once my daughter is safely wed I shall join the Texian Army until service in the war has earned me one of those "liberal bounties of land" so often promised to volunteers, knowing well that it will be worth a fortune in my old age whether or not I work it, and knowing equally well that every legitimate act to free Texas receives a special blessing from the White House. Thereafter I shall remind Andy Jackson of his offer of a post in the Consular Service. That will allow me to see something more of the world before this flame of life begins to fail, before this kettle of zest bubbling above it begins to cool.

CHAPTER XIV

I

Austin's Colony, Texas
Monday Evening
February 29, 1836

"Gracious Godalmighty, who'd have guessed it's so far?"

As the major restlessly changed position in his corner of the brougham, Camilla rubbed mist off the front glass on her side to peer forward. A wet overcast had so deepened the dusk that she could see only the straining backs of the mares, blackly dim against the sky, and beyond them a light beckoning as it had been for ever so long, but now more clearly.

"It's getting closer, Pa."

"So's the grave. So's Judgment Day."

Wind-driven rain assailed the brougham, and a sigh from Roberta, facing them in the dark on the seat before them, supported his weariness with their circumstances. They were damp and tired. Their bones ached from confinement in the brougham. They were chilled, hungry, worried, and cross.

Their misery was belittled, however, by stoic whistling from the coachman, Esau, who rode on the dickey seat in front, protected from the weather by nothing but an oilskin over his coat. His notes reminded Camilla of a standing intention of hers to take every difficulty in good part because this pilgrimage was her doing, hers alone, against quantities of advice from her father. Still, she could not at the moment think of one cheerful phrase.

Most of the way heretofore they had enjoyed a grand adventure. Unimaginably spacious and graceful savannas nearer the Brazos, where they landed, had refreshed their sense of the miraculous in nature, and the Texans had feted them like visiting royalty. Nothing seriously adverse had occurred until Saturday, when word flew across the countryside that more than six thousand Mexicans under the personal direction of Dictator Santa Anna were converging on San Antonio de Bexar three hundred miles west. No one to her knowledge, not even her father, had imagined that any Mexican lived who had the energy, resolution, and skill to push a force of such magnitude across Tamaulipas and West Texas for another two months at least. His advantage in surprise was enormous, for Texas still had no single military organization—only scattered bands of armed men under jealous and self-willed commanders. General alarm over being caught in a position so weak left the settlements too upset for much thought about how to entertain a "lookah from Nor Leans" who chanced to be passing through.

All the same, near as Camilla was to her own property, she did not intend to turn back until she had reached it and made a trial of living on it within visiting distance of Perry. But who knew tonight exactly where they were? Hours ago, while trying to short-cut, they had lost their way in the rain, straying since then across prairies as featureless as misted seas, and no sign of man anywhere until that one weak light showed on the horizon ahead.

"It's square," she declared brightly. "You can see that much now."

"Uhm," her father conceded.

"That means a window. It means a home."

"Of a sort, yes. A poky little hovel very likely crowded already."

"What makes you so sure?"

"Anything better would have windows taller than they are wide, and more than one to a wall; more than one lighted too, this early in the evening."

During their progress toward it Esau's whistling faded away. No sound came in from outside except the swish of wind-blown rain, the jolt of axles in greased hubs, the thrust of hooves through wet grass, and a laborious clink of bells on a train of pack mules slogging behind the brougham. The light before them kept the shape of a window, true, but without glass or shutters. There grew around it the night-blackened mass of a cabin hunching disreputably low, streaked by light through so many open cracks between its logs that the weather within must resemble that without. A moan gathering in Camilla's throat very nearly escaped her before she could stifle it. She had spent a night or two in dwellings no enormous amount better, but never in such a filthy norther as blew tonight. Even Roberta, seldom one to complain about anything, passed judgment by a deploring sniff.

"Miz Milla," Esau bent over from the dickey to bellow, "at ain no cabin. Ain nothin but the *ghose* of a cabin."

"Nothing but a sieve," her father qualified. "Keeps on raining, the place will sink. Man could throw a grown mastiff through any side of it."

Camilla reserved comment until the team stopped before a collection of slatternly planks on duty as a door.

"Dear-o-dear! Suppose we ought to drive on?"

"Drive *where*, honey?"

His *where* asked her for pity's sake to bear in mind how many hours they had not seen any other habitation whatever and how dark the night was. A queer little stir of dread came to life within her, and reason whispered to her that this trip might represent a mistake foolish enough to be fatal. The motives responsible for it, though, seemed to her far more nearly right than those which might have taken her straight into a rich marriage: in time it must turn out well because her intentions were good. Her sole answer to her father was to pat on fresh powder for the encounter within.

2

Meanwhile that overventilated door wavered open. A stringy, uncombed miss wearing sacklike homespun peered out at the carriage. She said nothing, nor did she move until a massive woman in a halo of bushy red hair pushed her aside.

"Who's at?"

"Cedric Burleigh at your service, madam, and my daughter, Mrs. Palmer."

"What in damnation you doon out there, evenun like this?"

"I do wonder, madam, truly I do. Where are we, please? What place is this?"

"Widow Frey's place. And I'm the Widow Frey—Amy Frey."

"Ah!" The major's syllable courteously, falsely, gave out that, of course, he had heard of her far back. "We were looking for Dr. Springfield's."

"Thunderation, you can't be."

"No?"

"Certainly not. That's twenty-thirty *horse* miles from here. Might as well be a hundred, weather the way it is."

"Yes, we lost the road this afternoon, and so—and here we are."

"Seen any trace of two young strappers ridun this way?"

"We've seen no one in hours, madam, not one human soul."

"Wel-ll, come in and stop makun me cold. It's one dollar a head here."

"We're four of us, madam—two darkies."

"Makes no difference, white or black, four or a dozen, you can't set out the whole long night, settun out in the wet and cold. Get indoors here."

The outside had fairly foretold the inside, a single room drenched to windward by rain blown through the walls. Its chief comfort was the hearth, where linguiform flames licked two steaming black kettles and a coffee pot. The drafts around Camilla blended aromas of turnips, onions, beef, and coffee with the reek of sweated leather, burned grease, mildew, and clothing rankly soured.

A middling male weed as red and freckled as Amy Frey huddled over a book on the nearer side of the fire. Beyond him another, in hand-me-down buckskins much too large, sailed a whittled schooner across a lake of ashes. Around them, along an arc yellowed by the fire, five men sat on chunks. They stared at Camilla's freshly powdered face and luxurious clothes as if hesitating to consider her real, and she did feel unreal in relation to the scene around her. Nevertheless, when her father introduced her to the Widow Frey, she compelled herself to speak and smile much the same as if being received on the Rue Royale.

In return the widow heartily shooed her in the direction of the hearth. "Step right in there, miss. Get in close and roast your ribs."

As they approached the circle of men a slim blond youth in buckskins sprang up to make way. By discreet kicks on both sides he brought the others floundering up also.

Camilla waved one removed glove. "Please don't trouble yourselves. Be comfortable, won't you?"

They remained reverently on foot. The little freckled sailorboy left his ship adrift among the ashes to gape at her. The redhead forgot his book. The girl who had opened the door circled up beside her to stare at close range. As all took in each detail of her features, her Parisian bonnet, her beaver cape and muff, her topaz earrings, her taffeta gown, satiny gloves, and kid boots, they acted as if their senses were not yet competent for such marvels as these.

The one person not awed long was the Widow Frey, who planted her hands flat against sturdily excessive hips. "Lord God, aint *you* a delicate piece!"

"Beg pardon?"

"How in damnation, travelun this kind of weather, can anybody make out to look so got up?"

Camilla surveyed her coldly. Her brow had been scarred by the blade of a coarse and corroded temper; her hair was a mass of tangled clocksprings, her hands chapped, freckled, and tipped by broken nails.

Not to be silenced by Camilla's silence, the widow belligerently spread a pair of feet encased in muddy moccasins and let fly again. "Where you from, miss?"

"*Mrs.* Palmer," Camilla revised for her.

"Well, I ast you where you from."

"Yes, I heard you." She let a long breath attenuate her annoyance before continuing. "From New Orleans, where people do take an interest in visitors, but without putting them on trial."

A snigger hopped from a raggedly whiskered little man among those standing by. The widow, obviously accustomed to finding women afraid of her, rounded her eyes over Camilla's demonstration that she was not.

"See here, we got no call to be hos-tile, have we, miss?" Her arms flung outward. "Come now, put off your things."

As she relieved Camilla of them, she tipped each to the firelight before handing them on to her daughter to inspect and put aside. When this eddy of hospitality subsided, however, Camilla recovered her cape: being without it sent icy tingles zigzagging between her shoulders.

"Perhaps I'd better keep this awhile, thank you."

The shift of her glance toward windy cracks in the walls set off a stifled cackle among the men. The fire this ignited in the widow's glance cauterized the grins off their faces; and Camilla, in the interests of peace, undertook to shift the blame outdoors.

"Coming in cold, one needs wraps awhile."

"It is a bit airish in here this evenun," Mrs. Frey conceded. "We been aimun to chink them cracks, but the weather's generally so easy hereabout—on fair days so handsome till you wisht there wasn't no walls in all Creation. Good weather, a little gunloop here and there don't seem to matter, and bad weather, which comes seldom, we got to leave it till better times."

As her pause for concurrence brought none, her challenging attitude revived. "Course, where *you* come from, maybe the air aint so healthy." And pointedly reassessing Camilla's jewels: "Nor Leans! What I hear, the wickedest habitation this side of hell. What brings you hustlun into Texas, miss?"

Camilla stepped over to extend her hands nearer the fire, too offended to remain still. Most Texans suspected men of being hurried that way by the baying of broken laws; but, as women were scarce, the custom was to honor them with assumptions beyond their due. After forcing her anger to subside she gave the simplest, straightest answer she could devise. "My husband bought a parcel of land here. When he passed away he left it to me. We're here to see it."

Her care to approximate a fine, above-the-battle calm was not an unqualified success.

Major Burleigh cleared his throat. "The luggage, madam." He jogged a hand toward Esau and Roberta, who had entered with effects from the coach. "Where would be convenient?"

"Don't matter a damn, sir. Please yourself." Her arm reaped a swath of air toward the center, where packs and rifles belonging to the five men leaned together. "Right there with that truck yonner. Good there as anywhere."

Camilla frowned at stalactitic trickles overhead. "But not where they'll be soaked, Pa."

"Practically no place where they won't, miss—unless, from pride and vanity, you'd want the beds moved where somebody'd sleep wet just to keep your finery dry."

"The oilskins, honey," Major Burleigh proposed, to maintain peace. "We'll cover everything so not a drop'll get through."

To withdraw from that subject, Camilla shifted toward her driver. "How're the mares, Esau?"

"Woe out, Miz Milla. Quality team like that, they ain meant fuh mud and trouble."

"Do get them under cover at once. Is the barn near, Mrs. Frey?"

"The barn?" Mrs. Frey's coppery brows arched high, then drew down. "Good kind Christ, a barn! Maybe everythin you got deserves betterun common, miss, your mares included, but you're in Texas now, and we treat all the same. They'll just have to weather through in that tember the Lord growed along the creek, same as the rest. All I can do to keep a roof for humans here, let alone beasts."

"And one must agree that that," said Camilla, veering away from a trickle, "has proved a bit beyond you."

A gagging cackle spluttered from the little man with whiskers, echoed by his friends, after which a guffaw burst from the red-headed student.

Mrs. Frey tried valiantly to smile. "Well, it's a mighty indifferent roof, I do allow. But we need a tight one so seldom, need so many other things ever livun hour, till it all-ways seems convenient to let the shinglun wait for a better time. And a barn, merciful God! Before the Lipans kilt my husbun, we talked of a barn, but nowadays, bean hard run ever way, bean woman *and* man here, mother *and* father, seamstress and butcher and cook and carpenter and planter all in one—it keeps me in such a devil of a hobble, how in Jupiter you expect me to build a barn?"

"It wasn't that I expected—you see, I simply thought—"

"No, the tember's the best we got, but feed aplenty." She about-faced now to avenge that guffaw from her red-headed son. "Russell-Robert, how come you loiter with at book when there's work to do? Git up from there!" Although she continued pretending to speak only to him, the flash of her eyes included the others who had laughed. "Anything I don't like it's loiterun when work's undone. How come you aint out there tendun them poor beasts? Git!"

Her flourish in his direction almost boxed the ears of a giant with a body like a rain barrel. He ducked away to bumble outdoors, followed by his companions. While some took care of the livestock, others brought in the mule packs and the mares' silver-mounted harness. Mrs. Frey assumed for herself the right to examine, feel, turn, poke, or squeeze each item until Camilla wanted to kick her.

Meanwhile certain men, after their return indoors, began contemplating a bit wistfully the kettles steaming on the hearth. Russell-Robert pointedly raked up the fire.

"God*amighty,* ma, aint we ever eatun?"

"What's at?"

"I'm hawngry, aint you?"

"Any sign of them two out there?"

"Nome. Too dark to see far noway. We caint wait the whole long night, waitun without one bite."

From the windward side of the cabin came a thin, wailing call. Mrs. Frey straightened up. Both her hands rose perpendicularly from the wrist. Everyone paused to listen while she listened. Dry wood crackled in the fangs of the fire. Negligible rain dribbled on the roof. Trickles through it splattered on the floor. The breath of the enduring wind sighed along the eaves, and again they heard that wind-thinned call.

"What ails you, ma? Aint nothun but a coyote. They aint commun till they get here, certain."

"Don't look like it, no. Well, Ellie-May, less get the sopper on. It's ready and moren ready—near ready to be rooned. Less get it on."

She and Ellie-May ladled stew out of one kettle onto each tin plate, hominy out of the second. After adding a slice of hot pone from an oven in the chimney, they poured coffee into each cup or gourd. Then they dipped out two more servings for Esau and Roberta seated at a workbench, and that was that. "Sopper" was on. The widow, with in-gathering revolutions of her hands, invited everyone to "come and relish it." Camilla at the time was toweling her own hands by the wash basin while Roberta changed the water.

"Mrs. Frey, I've some heavenly soap here. Wouldn't you ladies like to try it?"

Ellie-May's face came alive in a parenthesis of stringy hair. She started that way, but her mother jerked her back by the shoulder. "Oh, let me, ma! I sure would admire tryun some pretty-smellun soap."

"Stay here, Ellie-May. Sopper's ready and waitun, and we aint so dirty we're unfit to eat it."

Not from a trough perhaps, Camilla wanted to say. She made cool, cool use of a mirror from her luggage which Roberta held up before her, whereupon her hostess blew outward gustily.

"Less se-down boys, and wait settun."

They did. Having powdered afresh, Camilla expertly applied her comb. Her father meanwhile tried to apply to the widow's temper a poultice of baritone charm.

"Here's a puzzle, madam, that I'll wager you can't unriddle: we didn't sail to Texas or travel overland; how'd we get here?"

"Don't matter a hoot now, sir. For better or for worse, you're here."

"But you will agree it's odd to arrive in Texas without either sailing or crossing by land. Ever hear the like before?"

"Never heard the like of a lot you folks do before."

Camilla, still cool and ignoring, came to the table, beaver cape around her shoulders. The only place left was between the blond youth and Ellie-May, who had brought her neck alert somewhat as Camilla carried hers and was trying to twist the hair behind her ears into ringlets such as she had never seen before Camilla arrived. Her glance at the youth suggested a conspiracy to prevent anyone else from sitting there, and they had reserved for her, not a keg or sawed chunk or unoccupied part of a bench, but the family's only stool. Both of them, and nearly all the rest, were intensely anticipating her, whether or not they looked directly at her.

One exception was Russell-Robert. Brown eyes wide open under red brows, he was trying to read from the major's face the answer to his riddle. "Steamboat fetch you, sir?"

"Why, yes, son! How'd you guess?"

"Heard tell steamboats come sometimes."

"Yes, we steamed all the way to Texas in just three days."

"Then up the Brazos?"

"Right again, son. *There,* madam, is a right smart boy."

"I'll lick him right smart if he don't shutup. It's time to be cawn-trite; we got to ask the blessun."

Elbows on the table and hands up, she interlocked her fingers and leaned her dented brows against her knuckles, yet remained uneasily mute. Blown drizzle brushed the roof; the wind hissed and whined through the walls; it complained at the door like a hound wanting in.

"From many far places, O God," she began, "Thou has brought us this company."

Her voice altered. It became lyric and humble. Her face turned pacific, its harshness gone. With its planes unmarred, Camilla could see that it once had been comely, if only in a florid, overstated way.

"Thou hast gathered them together here to enjoy with us the fruits of our labors in this Thy Garden. Bless us all as we partake thereof; bless us ever one without no exception. Bless also them two strayun boys, wheresoever they may have got to. Keep Thy Hand close above them, likewise ever person here amongst us. Let these viands give us the strength to make ourselves more worthy in Thy Sight. Let the relishun thereof rid our minds of ever hateful thought, for Our Savior's sake, and hereafter hold us on the path that leads to the Dwellun of the Blessed. Ay-men."

All took it up: "Ay-men."

Camilla's astonishment lingered afterward. How odd to hear such prayer from a woman so profane, to hear a portion of the world so forsaken so gratefully called "this Thy Garden"! A few weeks ago the "fruits" before her would have turned her queasy, but her first dubious sample of the stew brought hunger alive in her like a startled dog. Not quite believing it, she tried a bit more, and more and more. Instead of being a listless union of meat and potatoes, which was standard on Texan tables, it also contained chili, salt, and onions, and the hominy beside it was sweetened with fresh butter. Camilla thought it deserved better praise than the troughy noises it was exciting around her.

"My, how good this is, Mrs. Frey! It's *very* good."

"Wonderful flavor," the major seconded. "Seasoned to perfection."

Mrs. Frey dismissed that quietly. "The best flavorun is appetite, sir. The meal is rare that don't taste good to the hawngry."

All this while the blond youth beside Camilla had remained decorously mute, but now ventured to say to her, "Never tasted the like."

She turned to him. "Every bite a joy, don't you agree?"

"Yessum." Having her eyes full upon him brought patches of red over his cheekbones. After swallowing two or three times, he forced himself to speak on. "Mrs. Palmer, I—the boys and I, we just wondered one thing."

His companions came alert. While they were tending the livestock, she gathered, he had been commissioned to speak for them.

She smiled encouragingly. "Yes?"

"Is your land twenty-odd mile northeast of Springfields'?"

"About that, yes."

"Family takes care of it name of Tipton?"

She nodded, searching his face. It appeared elusively familiar—a homely, asymmetric face, still fuzzy and immature, but given a look of reliability beyond his years by extraordinarily fine blue eyes. At her nod, pleasure deep within lighted those eyes.

"So we calculated. We heard Capun Allan speak your name to Mr. Tipton."

Her heart jumped so hard it knocked her breath out. "Y-you know Captain Allan?"

"Mam, he's *our* capun."

"Oh, I—*yes!* I know *you* too. That is, I never saw you before, but I wager you're Hugh Llewelyn!"

"Yessum. He wrote you something?"

"Of course. He thought so highly of you, and—but how strange to meet you here!"

Mrs. Frey had become wide-eyed and ruddily pleased. "Would *he* be why you come so far, miss?"

"Why, Captain Allan's a very good friend of mine, but—"

"Ah-h-h, how rosy you blush! See here, you needn't at all, such a fine big statute of a man ever way there is."

Before she had finished, the giant across the table remarked, "But seemed like he was sweet on Miss Leticia, though Hugh said—" His conclusion was a grunt violently elbowed out of him by the little Englishman next to him.

Camilla wagged a finger at him. "You—I'll venture you're Mountain Bentley."

Mountain recovered from the wound in his ribs enough for charmed agreement.

Her index stroked at the man who gouged him. "And you must be Elias Jones."

"Imsilf, miss." He bowed until his whiskers brushed the leavings of his stew. "Dependable Heli, hat your service."

The man the other way from Mountain she correctly identified as Butternut Brown. The fifth was a muscular, dark-browed youth named Burton Doty, from Sergeant Molineau's squad. And where was Thomas Dunraven? Curly Callahan? Calvin MacIntosh? Their friends put on a contest to be heard regarding them. Calvin was clerking in San Felipe, with plans to start a fortune by Yankee trading. Dunraven, hit in the thigh during their capture of Zambrano Row, was still in San Antonio, healing very slowly, and Curly had stayed with him out of pity for señoritas who he was sure would die without him.

They themselves, why had they left? Back in January, Captain Allan had written from New Orleans asking them, if they were tired of lazing in town, to come east and help him seed part of his new land. They had made the dirt fly and on wet days built some pole-and-brush fence to keep the livestock in. Yesterday morning they had left everything under the care of a darky lacking one hand while all headed west to rejoin forces assembling to turn Santa Anna back.

Camilla wanted desperately to ask where Perry was at this moment but felt too keyed up to risk it. Certainly he would not be far from his troop. Picturing the strangulating happiness that would follow his arrival transformed this miserable cabin into a haven to which Providence had guided her on exactly the right evening, a joyful lesson to recall whenever tempted again to question the wisdom of her journey.

"Let's see, we've accounted for nearly everyone. But what two were you waiting for, Mrs. Frey?"

"My biggest boys."

"Your sons you mean?"

"Yes, Raymond-McHenry and John-Paul. Both jewels, miss, but so damn own-minded till sometimes they turn me wrathy as a roped wilecat."

Camilla felt her brightness fade. A serpentine coil of dread writhed toward her heart. Of course it had no real cause to be there, of that she was positive: an officer like Perry would never abandon his men on the way to war; he must be joining them soon. Nevertheless a stammer tripped her tongue. "What became—where'd they go to?"

"Rid off with Capun Allan at dawn."

"*Dawn?* Dawn today?"

"Certainly today! God above, aint that long enough to have them gone, two boys hardly old enough to shave?"

Camilla turned to Hugh. "But you said you arrived this evening!"

"*We* did, yessum. Not Capun Allan. With the horse he's got he's most likely's again as far west by now."

"But why should he be so headlong?" She felt her face go chalky. "Why'd he leave you?"

"Sergeant Molineau and three of his boys farms near the Upper Brazos. The capun rid off to fetch them south whilst we head due west. That way they'll join us at San Felipe."

"The capun come *lass* night," Russell-Robert informed her tardily. "Had him a fine big stud horse and was choppun off miles!"

"That's it," said the widow. "Him and that stud looked so fine till when he talked about the war them fool boys begun slickun up their rifles. I give um hell *right,* and they cooled down considerable, or seemed like they did, but now I don't know."

"Then why'd you let them go?" Camilla asked.

"*Let* them? Let nothun. They said they'd show him where the flood wouldn't carry him down acrossun, then hunt on the way home. Triflun young varmints, if they *did* head back they could of hunted awhile and still been here hours ago."

"But, knowing your wishes, he'd scarcely let them go onward with him. Not Captain Allan. I do seriously doubt that he would."

"Doubt if you like, miss. I don't. *His* wish was to get help, get at the fightun, and get the war won. A man in that estate of mind, he don't care, he don't hardly realize, what a woman's wishun. They take no thought of whosoever loves um till they're down under foot, bleedun out their lives. No, he did *not* stop um, and they'll not be back this night. No, nor tamarra neither." She shook her glinting halo.

Worry had grayed her face. "No, gone! I dread to think so, but turnun your back on truth don't make it lies. Both gone!"

"But, even if they have, it'll soon be over. They'll be back in no time at all."

" 'No time atall'! Queer! That's near the last word I ever heard their daddy say. Smallish little man, and skinny like Ellie-May, he was oncet a printer, and so smart till you'd marvel how he'd read and cipher. Any trouble around, he was in it quick as a bank martin; so, when the militia set out to lesson some Lipans that raided above here, he says, 'Don't you fret, sweetheart. I'll be back in no time atall.' Where there's shootun, miss, no time atall can be forever."

The widow, having pushed back from the table, stared blankly at the fire. Her wrists lay slack across her thighs, hands slack in the hammock between them. A spark exploded from the hearth, but she did not blink. Camilla, listening outward, heard a sough of wind across immense and vacant prairies. Off in a corner a lumpy rustle told of rats impatient for human sleep to let them at the crumbs around the table. The sinewy coil under her breast constricted, and her heart fluttered within it like a bird newly caught.

"Well, Ellie-May"—the widow slapped both palms on her knees to push herself upright—"less do the deshes and get to bed. These folks traveled hard all day. The Lord brings night as a time to ress."

3

Camilla, in taking leave of her new friends next morning, privately gave Hugh a note for Perry, exacting a promise to care for it well until it was in Perry's hands. They parted in almost opposite directions, her route being northeast to Springfields'. There she and her retinue spent Tuesday night. As the skies cleared on Wednesday, and as she was impatient to reach her own land, she and her father pushed forward on horseback, leaving Roberta to follow with Esau, who had one pair of mules hitched to the brougham and the rest tied behind in a line, bearing the supplies.

A little before noon the road brought her and the major within sight of a ridge along which her land lay—part below the ridge, the rest beyond it. After passing into a belt of timberland along an exuberant

stream called Otter Creek, which they had to ford, they turned up
the side of a gorge cleaving the ridge, which the trail ascended in a
zigzag established long ago by buffalo, mustangs, deer, and migrat-
ing Indians. Their hopes mounted as they rode upward. A breeze
from the southwest gave the air the scent of spring. The trail along
its higher stages commanded ever more exhilarating views of prairie
land, which rose and fell in oceanic undulations below them. Across
it, tall winter-cured grass riffled under the wind like waters lazily
blown, and far out from the shore of timber along Otter Creek that
sea of grass was dotted with islands of trees as delightful as palmy
atolls in a story-tale Pacific. Camilla at last detected within a grove
above them a glitter reflected from a glazed window. That first proof
of civility so unlike anything at Widow Frey's drew from her a long,
long sigh equivalent to a prayer of thanks.

Where the trail crossed a grassy shoulder more of the house became
visible. Built of hewn logs set upright, it was two full stories high
and liberally wide, with double stone chimneys at each end, and a
deep log-pillared veranda across the front. This last of Robert Palmer's
attempts to anchor his life had profited from the same bent toward
magnificence which for years had won him more credit than he ever
developed the capacity to repay. Not since leaving the plantations
on the lower Brazos, where ships could unload products from ports
afar, had Camilla seen an equally generous home.

Her exclamations about it were interrupted by a flapping of vultures
which their approach startled away from animal bones in a ravine
below the entrance to the grove surrounding the house. The dooryard itself was littered with every sort of household trash, plus an
occasional skull, hoof, vertebra, or femur that kept the mares stepping
warily, rejecting the air through shuddering nostrils.

The house, seen at closer range, was no less distressing than the
yard. The windows had been glazed, yes, but several panes were
broken or gone. A limb blasted from an overhanging tree sprawled
over one end of the roof; the front door teetered askew; the ruins
of a wheelbarrow lay beside the veranda in a wind-blown drift of
leaves. A gutted antelope on a pillar at the end of the veranda hung
by the hocks, and beneath it pigs and dogs too busy to notice strangers
fought over the entrails.

Their arrival was observed minutely, however, by a man sitting far
over to the right against a gigantic pecan near the front of the grove
where the ridge dropped away to the lowlands. A rifle lay against

his chest, its barrel along his shoulder, and his forearms out beyond it, at rest upon his knees. His hands hung loose, his jaw too; he was loose all over. That, Camilla whispered, must be Evett Tipton. She and her father turned the mares his way.

The man remained exactly as he was. Hat low on his forehead and knees up, he kept his head back to let both eyes consider their approach. His expression was neutral. The fact that his rifle remained neutrally at rest against him gave it the innocence of personal furniture like a cane or umbrella. His ankles and wrists were slight, his neck also, and every part of him remarkably at rest. His attitude identified skinniness, not fat, as native to supreme ease.

Considering how vile everything else looked, he seemed oddly clean. His coat, long before he reached Texas, must have seen him through ever so many socials, weddings, christenings, funerals, applications for employment and requests for loans at this or that bank. Inside it was a collarless shirt, below it a pair of homemade doeskin breeches. Lye had bleached those doeskins to the hue of linen, and his shirt was white. Both announced him untainted by the pollution around him, as did his person, his skin being clear and oilless, though burned a deep brown.

Absorbed in these details, Camilla was startled by a free, voluminous yell: "Friends, there's a team!" He put into that considerably more energy than such a frame looked able to generate. Pushing back his hat, he let his admiration of the mares show in full. "All heart and ambition! Yessir, each one ever *inch* a horse!"

The major nodded. "Thank you, they are."

"That kind of a horse, it's good you don't pack no load." His way of saying so turned it into a politely roundabout expression of surprise that a man and a lass so well tailored should be riding overland without any gear. "How far you travelun, sir?"

"That depends."

"How come them mares is harness-marked?"

"Because they've been in harness."

"On a wagon or plow? *That* team?"

"On a brougham, sir."

"A brougham? I aint seen a brougham since I don't remember when. Where is it, capun?"

"Coming. We preferred riding ahead."

"Your gear in the brougham, is it?"

"There, and on some pack mules."

"Rid far?"

"From Springfields' this morning."

Tipton fingered his chin. He digressed to generalities.

"War news sounds bad, capun."

"It does indeed. We hear Santa Anna's attacking the Alamo in great force."

"Heard the same myself lass night. But Travis, Crockett, and Bowie—all them boys is brave lads. They got a world of cannon, so I hear, and they handle a rifle fine. Strong fort too. *Them* there, no force of Mexicans alive caint pass this way." His comfort in that thought relaxed one skinny leg full length along the ground. "Might of gone myself, only a man with a fine piece of property to look after, it don't pay to neglect it."

The major winked at Camilla. Perry and the Springfields had described Tipton as "a little shiftless." No one had called him a scoundrel, but it would seem that, while ruining the place, he might also be planning to claim it. Camilla, outraged by its condition, and as much again by this confusion of what was whose, could not trust her own voice as yet. She left the talk to her father.

"No," the major agreed, cocking a brow at the yard, "neglect never pays."

At once, and affably, Tipton adapted to this implication. "Oh, it aint that I strain none, no. That aint my way. And there's no need to strain, plenty as game is."

"Shooting good, is it?"

"Fair to fine, sir." His eyes, wide open all the time, declaring no wish to hide anything and thereby inviting equivalent candor in return, gazed at the major's rifle and saddle pistols. "That why you come, sir?"

"We might shoot a bit. Probably will."

"Reckon you come from the States."

"Who in Texas hasn't?"

"That's true, yessir. Come lately?"

"Rather."

"Hm." Tipton shifted his hat and gave the major a promotion. "Colonel, I hear a big syndicate's gamblun we'll win this war dreckly and make it a state—be annexed. Heard tell they sent out men to buy up land." His eyes became as wide as eyes could be. "Any connection, colonel?"

"None whatsoever."

"Mean you aint intrusted in land one bit whatsoever?"

"To the contrary, that's our chief interest."

"That so?"

"It is."

Tipton looked simultaneously enlivened by this admission and puzzled over the sternness of the tone. Using his rifle as a staff, he pushed to his feet. "Good gracious alive! Here we been talkun all this time and I never till yet thought to say you my name." He thrust at the major a hand as spare as a chicken's foot. "Colonel, I'm Evett Tipton."

"Burleigh, sir. Cedric Burleigh." No change in Tipton resulted: the name Burleigh lit no lamp in his memory. "And this . . ." Although the major's gesture contained the gallantry invariably his in reference to Camilla, he withheld her name. "Sir, my daughter."

"Please to make your acquaintance, miss." Evett touched his hat; but, now that she was placed with reference to the major, he reverted to larger concerns. "So you come to look at land. How much land?"

"Why-y, as much as there is here."

"You mean all you can get?"

"I wouldn't say that, no."

"Well, we got a nice little parcel here, colonel. Right fair piece."

The major's eyes met Camilla's sidelong. The contract between Tipton and Mr. Palmer (of which Camilla had a copy) agreed that, in return for keeping the homesite in condition and meeting the residence requirements under the land laws, he could put up a cabin for his family near the Palmer home and, after six years of fulfilling all conditions to the satisfaction of the owners, would receive title to two entire sections, 1280 acres. Thus he might eventually be an owner with a legitimate anxiety to find a buyer with deep pockets. He was in no position as yet, however, to assume proprietary airs. On the other hand, could he strictly be accused of assuming any? Thus far he had managed with remarkable nicety to stay just beyond reach of that accusation. Then what *was* his game?

Camilla leveled straight at him. "Are you offering this place for sale?"

Her tone was too charged. It brought Evett's wide eyes back upon her, busily adding this to all other knowns and unknowns about her and her father. She could detect his analysis yielding him a conclusion that there was something extraordinary about this visit, something that required more wary dealing.

"Coffee!" he bawled at a pitch that would have hurt her ears but for its purity of tone. "Land—we can talk about land any time. The mornun's done now; it's time for a bite and some coffee to rench it down."

4

In the house she deduced what purpose his yelling had served: the dust raised by a wild sweeping still hazed the air; Mrs. Tipton had got into a Sunday-go-to-meeting dress; three soiled, straw-headed boys had just been rushed out the back door; a fragrance of coffee, pone, and spitted venison was abroad, and the table set for four.

Camilla could not glance in any direction, however, without discovering reason to feel more outraged. A paneless section of the nearest window had been filled by a dreadfully weathered volume of Gibbon's *Decline and Fall*, part of a collection brought here with affectionate forethought by Robert Palmer. One of the embroidered doilies brought at the same time was on duty as a potholder, and a dish towel over Mrs. Tipton's shoulder bore a monogram identifying it as torn from one of Camilla's tablecloths. The table, highboy, and chairs, though excellent in design and sent out sound, were scratched, battered, pot-blistered, and loose in the joints. At each place around the table were more or less maimed veterans from a set of china Camilla herself had chosen for durability under rough conditions. The coffee server, a pewter wedding gift engraved with the Palmer crest, had been blackened over open flame and dented in three places on the side nearest to her.

Despite all that, Mrs. Tipton appeared nervously hopeful of a good opinion. She looked quite unused to exertion, a pale, frail, wet-lipped blonde indubitably born to female trouble and rocking-chair resignations. Her haste to make the best of things had brought her into a sweat and set her hair wispily adrift from its pins, but a sense of grandeur in playing hostess to Quality buoyed her through it all.

While sipping her coffee with her little finger elevated, she deplored the condition of "my china," the loss of "my bess lennun," and the way "them heedless, no-count boys" had jackknifed "my furniture." Her fittings, as she put it, was once pretty near the grandest in all Texas, leastways anywheres close. It was a mercy how things got tore up without no proper means of doing and fixing, but of course "things aint the same way out here like they was back home." There, if you had things right you could keep them right, but here, without no darkies to do for you, things sort of got out of kilter before you knew it, and stayed out.

Ev, as she called her husband, helped diligently to establish her as the product of high-toned origins. Her father never brought her up to work hard, he explained—never had the slightest notion she would ever have to. A piece ago he had been a mighty big man back in Scuppernong, South Carolina, was deputy sheriff for a spell ("That he was, for a fack!") and kept a right nice crossroads store. Time was when he had given her a wench to do for her hand and foot, but that dadblame worthless darky took off with a buck Indian before they'd been in Texas half a year, so was it any wonder if everything was a little tore up? A girl raised up to be Quality, you couldn't hardly expect her to keep a big house and raise three boys proper without no help, could you? Her daddy was mighty put out that she married a man without no means whatsoever, and never would of let her go west, "only hard times come along, and right now he aint in business no more for the present."

"Back there, times is still hard," Mrs. Tipton carried it along, her little finger still angular beside her cup even though the picture of home was deteriorating, and Camilla noted in some wonder how much more indolent and conspicuous her Georgia drawl was than Ev's: hers resounded with genteel slackness, with self-condoling languor. To her *hard* was *hawd; there, theyuh; more, maw; here, hyuh,* and so on. "I wish they'd come here. It'd be mighty gran, seen things is so lonely without no kin noplace near. My daddy would be plum comeover was he to see how Ev, who he all-ways said was no-count, has made out so good—has got him a fine big mansion house and one of the prettiest pieces of property—"

She flinched. Her colorless mouth warped sideward. In bewilderment her eyes went to her doting spouse, who evidently had kicked her shin. For her further instruction, he rolled his eyes at their visitors.

"Liz-honey, you know where these folks come from? Any idea?" In his haste to explain his kick he answered for her. "From Nor Leans, honey!" His wide eyes switched to Major Burleigh. "Aint that a fack, sir?"

"We are, sir. How'd you know?"

"Clothes for one thing. Another thing, them saddles. No small-town jake of a tanner makes leather that good. That's city leather."

"Shrewd deduction."

"Colonel, I been aimun to ask you: ever know anyone back there name of Pawlmer?"

"Certainly."

A calamitous pallor bleached Ev's face. "Mr. Robert Pawlmer?"

"Knew him very, very well."

"M-maybe his widda too?"

"Even better."

In a voice almost gone: "That so?"

"As well as I ever knew anyone."

Ev's lips hung apart. They were the color of dead minnows.

Amusing though Camilla found the change, sympathy for him compelled her to drop her glance, for his dismay did not seem to her that of a knave exposed, rather of a dreamer slapped awake. At no time, she now believed, had he worked out a scheme to beat her out of anything; he had simply hoped to acquire this property by the easiest downhill method—by her neglect.

Of course everything around her looked a fright, but were the Tiptons actually so much more to blame than she herself? Anyway, very little was wrong that a few weeks of brisk work (which she itched even now to start) would not improve enough to turn this into one of the most habitable sites within a hundred miles. Certainly his indolence was not unique; easy as the soil and climate were, Texas cast over nearly half her conquerors a spell that relaxed them under the shade trees to let the rainbow of immigration drop its pot of gold within their reach when it would. As for using the house, was he to crib up his family in something less while it weathered through season after season, emptily in wait for a childless widow who gave no sign of caring anything about it? He was a man disposed toward fair dealing, that much was clear. Even now, when he could not help wishing she were dead, he managed a polite concern.

"How is she, colonel? She keepun well?"

The major opened a hand toward her. "As you see."

Ev stared at her a long, long moment, next at the major, last at his wife. Mrs. Tipton, who had been slower than he to detect the more disquieting implications of everything said heretofore, was now catching up. Her pale eyes alternated between Camilla and the major. Four fingers of one hand came tremblingly upright against separated lips.

"You mean *she's* his widda—Mist Pawlmer's?"

The major nodded. "Yes, mam."

"But he was a *old* man!"

The major, gently: "True, he was."

"And I thought Ev says she's your daughter!"

"She's that also."

"Yall brought any things?"

"Not enough perhaps. But a fair amount."

"I didn't see no packs on them horses. How'n you stay long without no gear?"

"Our servants are bringing everything in the carriage. Should be here soon."

She studied the dregs of her coffee. Forcing a strengthless hand to the cup, she started to lift it, but merely fingered a nick on its side. At last her eyes came up to meet Ev's. As she appeared to know they would, his unblinkingly asked her to accept fact as fact: the place was no longer theirs to usurp; they could be driven off for unsatisfactory performance.

A sob quavered in her throat. She pushed back from the table, tears drenching her cheeks, and groped toward a rocking chair by the hearth. Across the back was the monogrammed portion of table linen lately in use as a towel. This she snatched to her eyes in sitting down and let go a cascade of moaning wails. Ev was already on the way to her side.

"Now-now, don't carry on, sweetheart. They're fine, fair-dealun people, caint you see that? They aint the kind to turn us out if we ack right. One way or other we'll make out . . ."

As quietly as possible Camilla and her father went outdoors. The major took the mares off to graze. Camilla, concluding that they would somehow have to fit themselves into this one house with the Tiptons, and do it amiably, strolled to the pecan at the edge of the bluff to watch for the approach of her carriage along the road from the west.

From C. B.'s Journal
March 2, 1836

Today we achieved Camilla's homestead, where problems and difficulties outnumber the rats in a garbage dump. Staying here, we saw at once, will be no frolic.

Of course Camilla thinks that what justifies the trip also cancels or compensates for every disappointment—her love for Perry, his for her. It's all done in the name of love, and so the price we've got to pay is none too high. Though romantics might agree, millions of sensible human beings in Asia today (if not in Europe too) would consider mere love a flimsy, brainless justification for any such adventure as this, and so would far the greater portion of mankind throughout history prior to our time. In that elder view sex has valid claims to respect, love none at all. In that view love is a silly disorder which a year or so of fulfillment generally converts into a burden or a joke. In that view love is therefore considered the least substantial basis for marriage man can choose, or for anything else except dalliance.

Most times I nevertheless side with love. What brings to mind the harsher attitude tonight is simple exhaustion. With the last mile of our journey behind us but still fraying our spiritual fabric, I recall the conclusion of an old sea captain I met in Naples:

> *The more I travel the world around,*
> *And the more of travelers I see,*
> *The more convinced I am that he was right who said,*
> *"Happy is the man*
> *Who never leaves his own garden."*

CHAPTER XV

I

San Felipe de Austin
Sunday Afternoon
March 6, 1836

Perry did reach San Felipe when he had told his comrades he would. With him were Sergeant Molineau, three of the sergeant's "boys," and the Widow Frey's two eldest. But the five he had left behind in his hurry were not there to meet him.

The proportions of the emergency would not allow him to wait long; after two idle days, he and the companions already with him pushed on as far as Gonzales, where militia were hastily gathering; for, as everyone had been informed, the defenders of the Alamo were holding back ten to fifteen times their number, with again as many more Mexicans approaching from the Rio Grande. Three despatches from the Alamo's commander, Colonel William Barrett Travis, had appealed for relief in phrases often read aloud.

"Our numbers are few," his third note concluded, "and the enemy still continues to approximate his works to ours. I apprehend an attack from his whole force very soon; but I shall hold out to the last extremity, hoping to secure reinforcements in a day or two. Do hasten on aid to me as rapidly as possible, as from the superior number of the enemy, it will be impossible for us to keep them out much longer. If they overpower us, we fall a sacrifice at the shrine of our country, and we hope posterity and our country will do our memory justice. Give me help, oh my Country! Victory or Death!"

Late on March 6 a rider brought to Gonzales still another appeal, this one dated March 3. With it the same horseman brought a packet of letters, one to Perry from Thomas Dunraven.

San Antonio de Bexar
3 March 1836

Dear Allan:

A few hours ago Colonel Travis informed us that John W. Smith, an acute scout, will steal out tonight to plead again for reinforcements, and will carry out our mail. Many of us ever since have been writing by our candles, doubting (though scrupulous not to mention it) that we ever again will communicate with those afar whom affection keeps near us.

For those of us presently here, victory is impossible, that we know. We number but 183. Smith's departure will weaken us to 182. So few can defend these long walls but thinly; therefore a great and determined army can overrun us by sudden thrusts at changing points. If the resolution of Santa Anna is as reputed, our eventual defeat is sure.

Nevertheless we cannot surrender: he demands we do so "at discretion," which a blood-red flag on the cathedral tower tells us means "for execution." The verdict of events elsewhere ratifies our conclusion that to yield would be to die more wretchedly than in battle; for reports Bonham has brought us say that a band of our old friends under Colonel Frank Johnson was annihilated at San Patricio on the 27th last, most of them after they capitulated. We prefer being shot as free men.

Never suppose, however, that we entertain gloomy habits of mind. Our spirits remain high, our luck incredible. In ten days of defense, we have not lost a man. Instead, we were augmented the day before yesterday by 32 sturdy lads from Gonzales who slipped in through the siege before dawn.

Though gallant Jim Bowie is down in bed, helplessly stricken with pneumonia complicated by injuries from a bad fall, we are fortunate in our other leaders, Col. Travis and Col. Davy Crockett. Travis is one-minded and persuasive in his determination to arrest the invasion here, and Crockett blends backwoods humor with pugnacity, competence, and will. Both have encouraged more heart than nature apportioned to the average of us. We could not secure wood for our fires, hay for our beeves, or corn for our pone unless groups of volunteers risked their lives often in sallies outside the fort. Always, whether in broad day or the dreariest hours of darkness, each sortie is carried off in the spirit of a coon hunt or charivari, and thus far without casualty—to the amazement of all observers.

Unhappily, my unhealed leg cheats me out of any part in such adventures. The same defect also keeps me idle while others dance. Yes, dance! Does that surprise you? At any rate I believe it does the enemy. We have fiddlers in Col. Crockett and "Popcorn" Phillips, a banjoist in Curly Callahan, a drummer in Travis's black boy Joe, and any amount of vocal support. The nimble have partners in Alsbury's and Dickinson's wives, also in several Mejicanas who have persevered in their attachment to us since we freed them last fall.

And now for a confession: after you departed, Corazon continued to nurse me because of your friendship toward me; she unburdened sweet and secret thoughts intended for you and brought me the viands you had relished most. No doubt she supposed doing so would conjure you, but at length it became a habit addressed to me through your default. My shell relaxed open. That shyness which began to fester in me so many years ago in my father's parsonage submitted to her matchless therapy. For the first time I found myself loving and able to show it, for the first time in some degree loved.

Thus my wound, which has held me here where I consider it a military mistake to remain, seems now the blessing of my life. Without it, what could ever have healed the defect that kept me a lonely and vagrant bachelor? Yes, I feel blessed, and despite realization that the compassion and generosity which bring her to me will submit her to someone else no less soon than when you left.

Yesterday evening, after moonlight began to silver these ancient rooftops, a crowd assembled near the chapel around our musicians. Corazon and I went over to watch the dancers frolic, whereupon a limber rake named Jefferson Dewitt, new from Gonzales, swept her into the dance. With Callahan's banjo cackling like a cockerel, the two fiddles squealing like shoats in heat, and Joe thumping on a tub like a giant buck rabbit, she whirled with Dewitt and others and Dewitt again, him again and again, until Travis asked them all to rest. At another time or with some very different lass, I suppose I might have been jealous, but all her lively, forthright ways came back with her, and if ever Dewitt should make her cry she will bring me her tears, as she did when you left.

Men time out of mind have known that one way to defeat the devil is to befriend an angel. That Corazon is no angel I do recognize, but to imagine a more delightful deputy exceeds my powers. If her nature would allow it, my choice would be to spend the rest of my life in her company. Forgive me for cringing just a bit at the reflection that indeed I may—as the boom of a cannon reminds me.

You must not conclude from the above that we of the garrison have been fiddling our hours away, trusting only in God and Houston to preserve us. Granted, we were ruinously slow to begin preparations, but we have kept our bombarded walls in repair except for one large breach in the northeast angle. Elsewhere we have proofed them against shot by throwing up dirt against them from interior trenches. Our own cannon, large and small, we have placed where they can inflict a fiendish slaughter upon any assault. Beside each, ready to load in them, is a heap of nails, bolts, chains, spent musket balls, horseshoes, or other scrap, as well as the more gentlemanly round shot, canister, and grape. Every man of us, too, is well equipped from the armory left here. Myself I have two pistols, a tomahawk, and a double-barreled shotgun— the last because our veteran Indian fighters declare that, although a rifle may do in skirmishes, a shotgun charged with "blue whistlers" is the article for stopping a proper assault.

Our first fear is that the enemy may surprise us by night and overwhelm us before we can receive him as designed. Often after dark he feints at us, especially during bad weather, perhaps to try our defenses, perhaps only to exhaust us by keeping many on the ramparts, shuddering in the rains and wintry winds. More than a score are sick now besides Colonel Bowie, but most of those remain active; for, as we recognize that our defense of the beautiful reaches to the east of us may be the culminating act of our lives, the impulse is strong to spare nothing in making it worth the price.

One reason for the little sally at dancing last evening was that the weather then was sharply clear after a moderate day. Simultaneously arrival of the lads from Gonzales had given us hope that many other Texians would bestir themselves in time. Now we no longer believe more will attempt it. One would suppose a great conflux would have rushed this way at our first appeal; but, apart from our reinforcing thirty-two, scarcely half a dozen here besides Travis and Bowie are authentic Texians, the rest of us having arrived since the war began.

While we have grown a little, our enemies have increased fearfully. They and the wagonloads of women they brought with them gorge the town. *They overflow into camps east of us, southward too, and off to the north near the Old Mill, where you and I were besieging* them *last fall. Their bugling, band practice, parading, and gunnery give the effect of a fair, though their cannonading reminds us that they offer but one article seldom welcomed.*

Santa Anna, in the speed of his winter march, in the care of his preparations, in the quantity, disposition, and vigor of troops around us, abundantly justifies his reputation for military prowess. No doubt the hurt our capture of this place last fall did to his pride can be assuaged only by cruelties which again will astound the world. He means to destroy everything Saxon in Texas.

For these reasons you would be gravely in error, excellent friend, to join any small *or* minor *movement through this siege. Do not, I entreat you, do* not *assist any further reinforcement unless it numbers well above a thousand, for nothing less would suffice. What better can we do with a few additional than without? The enemy will be no less able to overwhelm us, and we, just as we are, very little less able to give him, before we perish, a wound that will seep and corrupt and weaken him until, when at last he matches arms with the rest of you, his defeat will be sure and this lovely land free thereafter. My plea to you, Allan, is to prepare for that day.*

Presumably my service under arms will entitle me to about two thousand acres of this same land. As you are a barrister and have always shown affectionate interest in whatever concerns me most, I enclose a duly witnessed Will transmitting half to my dearest link with England, my young sister Maude Dunraven. The other half goes to my dearest link with Texas, Corazon Gamboa-Tapete.

May God grant that every restraint upon my hope will somehow be put aside, and that I shall feel again the strength of your hand.

Yours,

Dunraven

The Alamo
3:50 A.M., *Sunday*
March 6, 1836

"Tomaso!"

Dunraven, one shoulder against the doorjamb to a night-blackened room by the hospital, heard this from a cot behind him. Within the blanket he had wrapped around himself to the ears, Indian fashion, he tilted his head that way.

"Yes, my dear?"

"You not sleep?"

A sense of point prevented him from answering pointless questions, even from Corazon. He shifted in the doorway, however, so that his back was no longer toward her, only his side. Though the air was icy, the norther which had brought the temperature so far down was now almost spent. The sky was losing its wintry overcast; the yard and roofs before him were momentarily moonlit. Painted by that light, the scarred Moorish outline of the chapel to his left invoked visions of romantic living remote in time and place—of the Alhambra, of Old Morocco, of mounted Arabs carrying the banners of Islam east and west. Except for a plaint of wind through palisades and battlements, every quarter of the Alamo lay soundless, though he did know that along those battlements exhausted marksmen lay asleep, in position to unlimber their weapons if the enemy attempted any assault.

"Tomaso, you stand so long. Your leg hurts?"

"If I think about it."

"Then why you stand? It makes cold. Why you not sleep?"

"No bombardment. The quiet woke me."

"*Que tal!* If they sleep, why not you?"

"Too late now. I relieve Dewitt, who's tending the fires till four."

"But how cold! You make sick."

"The breeze *is* penetrating, but fragrant too." He inhaled it, savoring it. "A blind man would know that spring is on the prairies. Smell the grass?"

"*Que tal!* Smell it tomorrow. Sleep tonight and make the leg well."

"This *is* tomorrow. And there's Dewitt, poor chap, cold and tired."

Across the main courtyard of the Alamo he could see Jefferson Dewitt drowsily carrying an armload of kindling toward one of several little fires maintained near each battery for lighting fuses on the cannon; he was on his way now to an earthen tower in the middle of the court. Upon that tower stood a big-mouthed carronade where it could lob shots over any wall or mow down men who broke through.

"*Pues*," Dunraven grunted. "*Ya es hora.* I must let him rest a bit."

Twisting the blanket off his shoulders, he reached within the dark to a table on which his hand blindly found a belt weighted with pouches for powder, buckshot, and ball. He buckled it on. Its pliant, massive grip on his waist gave him a reckless sensation of strength. Under it at each flank he tucked a pistol the size of a blacksmith's hammer. Next he lifted out a double-barreled shotgun.

"You should dress, Corazon, and steal into town. You promised to go today. It's about two hours till dawn. This would be an excellent time, now, while there's no gunfire." As no answer came from her he added, "You should have gone with the other ladies."

"Not all go."

"The most sensible did."

"*Callete, chico!*" A quick stir in the dark and she came up to his side, a blanket around her. She shuddered in the luxury of defeating the cold by fitting her side to his. "Too much you say, 'Go away.' Is because you no want me?"

" 'Is because' I do want you. I want you as you are. I want you safe."

"Ah!" Her voice dropped to a whisper. Her breath was moist at his ear. "Then sleep a little longer, eh, Tomasito?" She brought up his hand and smoothed its light backing of hair under the stroke of her cheek. "Not yet you have to go."

"Quite wrong. Must be crowding four by now."

She overlooked that. In squirming for more comfort against his side she bumped one of his pistols. "Such big guns!"

"And doubly charged with blue whistlers, both of them."

Possession of cruel powers alien to anyone's expectation regarding him provoked his smile. It also provoked Corazon's, for very different reasons.

"Why you take pistols?"

She implied more than sufficient knowledge of his reputation as a poor shot. His sole answer was to contract an arm tight around her, to punish her with affection. She let her head subside against his shoulder and, like him, dreamily marveled at the moonlight beyond the door. A sweep of clouds rushed across it, blackening the fort, after which a few stars appeared far to the east.

"*Que bonita aquella estrella, eh, chico?*"

"Rather! I venture that's Venus. Must be Venus."

"Ah, Venus!" She sighed happily. "So clear, so beautiful. *Vistes?* She does not shake or change like others."

Under the influence of analogy her whole body for the time was remarkably still, at rest against his.

"Hm!"

"Why you laugh?"

"My dear, nothing in the heavens is more unstable than Venus— now the morning star, other times the evening; bright tonight, another time dim or absent. She's so inconstant that no astronomer can exactly predict this year what she'll do next."

Corazon weighed that awhile. "Tomasito, you still have jealous for Señor Dewitt?"

Dunraven's smile went one-sided. "*Should* I be jealous?"

"No. However, you should not laugh."

"I soberly agree."

He felt her deciding not to notice the dig implicit in his tone. She shook back her hair, still watching Venus, and again brought her head to rest on his shoulder. Her blanket had opened at the throat. From it he heard a smothered click-clack, click-clack, click-clack from his watch, which she wore hanging around her neck on its own chain, like a lavaliere, though it was a cumbersome antique inherited from his maternal grandfather.

He opened a palm before her. "*Ahora mi reloj, por favor.*"

She pretended not to hear him. She inordinately enjoyed possessing it. Perhaps she wanted by any jewelry whatever to publish the link between them, perhaps took assurance from its constant and sturdy voice, perhaps used it for evidence that what was his was hers. On the other hand she might value it only for the pleasant ritual of wheedling it from him whenever he came in, and of relinquishing it again with affectionate caveats about not staying away after such and such a time whenever he left.

He jogged his hand. "Come, my timepiece."

Her chin lifted so that he himself could unsnap the watchchain— and observe how close her lips were to his. They were sweetly full, modeled by the moon. He kissed them. He melted to them. Her response stole from his fingers their knowledge of the snap. Laughing softly, she let her blanket hang loose and released the watch herself.

"Ha! Almost you not go, eh, Tomasito?"

"Almost. However—"

"*Bastante,* I let you go." She pressed the crystal against her ear. Her tongue click-clacked to imitate its voice. Shifting it to his ear: "Like my heart it beats for you, eh, chico? When you hear it, think of me, eh? Then you come back pronto."

"It's not the watch that brings me." He tapped his breast. "*This* brings me."

"Ah! You talk so nice! *Entonces besame,* Tomasito."

She tilted up her cheek. He kissed her there, and on the other cheek too, but not as a lover might, rather as she preferred whenever they parted, with a husbandly calm assuming innumerable repetitions.

3

On a roof above officers' quarters forming the western wall only three men were awake half an hour later, Dunraven and two who, until he roused them, had been sleeping just here behind the battlements, Curly Callahan and an Indian fighter called "Spread" Rankin. Curly went over to hatchet mesquite for the brazier of coals kept handy for lighting fuses. It stood behind a massive cannon, an eighteen-pounder, a pet of Rankin's, who knew cannon well.

Rankin thrust a hand sideward. "Hush a minute, boy . . ."

The hatcheting stopped.

Rankin was called Spread because the width of his shoulders was emphasized by a habit of stooping around with arms out loose like a heated raptor's wings. Dunraven's reason for waking him had been that he saw moonlight flash on what he took to be many distant bits of steel, on the polished tips of bayonets, he thought, or on cavalry lances. Rankin was giving him the benefit of every doubt. Totally still, he waited, leaning forward across the parapet of the wall, hands taloned upon one of its battlements, elbows up, brows up, mouth open, and eyes so enlarged that the nearer one looked white. Far off to the east the funereal wail of a wolf spiraled across the heavens. Another echoed the same lament to the moon, and Dunraven could hear his watch in an upper pocket anounce the flight of time in sturdy accents. Curly grunted away a held breath; he resumed with his hatchet. Rankin flapped at him. "Hush, goddamn it! *Hush!*"

Curly stood up to listen also. For Dunraven there was only the click-clack of the watch in his pocket, and presently another elegiac howl from the hills. The fort seemed deserted, quiet as it was. The stillness brought alive in Dunraven a fear that so much sleep throughout the fort might tempt the enemy to assault, or that the silence of enemy cannon this one night was intended to induce slumber among the men besieged.

He pulled out his watch and bent its face close to the brazier. The small hand was on four, the big on seven. The authority of its statement recalled his grandfather's hope that he would read monitions from its reliability, from its adherence to duty, and he took silent pride in having been the one awake to discover something astir in the distance, though lately Corazon had seduced it into reminding him less of duty than of her.

Returning it to his pocket, he risked another explosion from Rankin. "What's their game, Spread?"

"Wish I knew." Rankin thumbed back his hat. "But don't look right."

Curly asked, "Whereabouts?"

"Seems like the ground aint steady way off there." Rankin flexed his elbows to loosen his arms for action. "Best we can do, I guess, is get ready—*good* and ready."

"Sweet Jesus!" Curly slammed his hatchet into the mesquite. "I reckon we aint been ready ever night, ever goddamn night, since who remembers when!"

"Plenty powder?"

Curly hoisted his chin toward a box beside the cannon. "Twenty-two bags."

"Water to swab her?"

Curly dipped into an olla and brought his hand out dripping.

"Rifles and shotguns loaded?"

"When aint they? It's bad enough when Tom wakes us because *he's* nervous, but you're suppose to be one of these cool heads and set a example—"

A bugle a quarter of a mile westward in San Antonio interrupted him—yes, a bugle. It had fragile clarity, a thread of golden sound shimmering through the moonlight. While its tune was still alive, another took it up northward along the river, then another to the south-east far beyond the chapel, and still another distantly eastward beyond the convent yard. Their notes overlapped; their echoes interlaced like the songs of mating birds.

Curly gaped at Rankin. "What they buglun about, such a hour as this?"

"Can't make it out. Boy, you run wake Colonel Travis, him and Colonel Crockett both. Go on, *git!*"

Curly dashed from their battery across the roof of the officers' quarters (which supported other cannon too), then down a ramp used for rolling up supplies. While the bugle notes were still at play a low unearthly stir began in the distance, a myriad-footed rumble. Rankin inspected a poker in the brazier to be sure it was red enough to fire fuses. He now bent over the parapet, staring forward across the prairie. A spasm drew him into a crouch.

"Christ Amighty, Tom! *Christ!* Look yonner!"

Looking, Dunraven felt his belly constrict. Out of a cloud's shadow to the northwest a dark mass of men emerged into the moonlight, running toward the fort, hundreds of infantry widely deployed.

In an avian swoop, Rankin jumped back to adjust the cannon. His voice was low and tight. "She's got grape in her. We'll learn um, uh, Tom?"

"That—yes, we will. Yes."

"Don't get nervous. Kick them others awake and yell to Curly to rouse the barracks."

As Dunraven returned from calling down across the court to Curly, he began priming his pistols. Rankin flapped a wing. "Save them for last, Tom. Grab a swab and help till Curly's back."

Rankin stepped clear of the eighteen-pounder to whirl the poker at its touch-hole. The carriage bucked away from an enormous smoky flash. The mallet of its roar crushed Dunraven's ears. Nevertheless he afterward heard a tangle of screams on the prairie, heard other gun crews around the fort readying cannon, heard shouts from half-dressed friends rushing from the barracks, the convent, the chapel, the hospital, and up toward battlemented roofs on all sides. Colonel Crockett began rallying his unit toward a palisade near the chapel, and Colonel Travis ran for a twelve-pounder above the weakest spot of all, a breach in the northern wall. "The Mexicans are upon us, men," he roared. "Give um *hell!*"

Far off a regimental band struck up a chilling, baleful march known as "El Deguello," "The Throat-Cutting," the colophon of all Santa Anna's preparations for slaughter. Above that line upon the prairie sabers caught the moon's silver. Shouts in Spanish exhorted the line forward, and cavalry rode up behind it to cut down any comrades who tried to run away.

All this Dunraven noted in helping Rankin swab the cannon, thrust home sacks of powder, jam in clusters of grapeshot, prime the touch-hole, roll the wheels forward, and jump clear as the red poker whipped to the touch-hole. Men newly arriving on the roof brought small arms to bear and swarmed around all the fort's cannon. Though most came with hair snarled by sleep and wore only undershirts and breeches, they were effective at once, for nothing else had been so discussed and practiced in recent days as what to do under attack. The bellows of the eighteen-pounder became part of a stupendous dialogue along linking walls, stockades, and palisades around the Alamo: the attack was from every direction at once. Flashes of fire before the batteries shimmered like lightning. Sulphurous clouds dimmed the moon, and explosions blended with their own echoes in continuous thunder.

To Dunraven's bludgeoned ears the bawls of frantic men sounded meager within that storm. The pain wrenched from his thigh by his stooping, lifting, turning, and thrusting to reload each time Rankin fired—that, too, seemed meager and remote. Still, he did moan in relief as Curly returned to help him.

At last Rankin let go a victorious whoop. "Breakun, boys. Look at them go!"

The enemy's lines had shredded into a scatter of runners diminishing away. Where they had been, the glisten of moonlight was speckled black with those whose running was done. A multiple cheer rose high along the wall.

Elsewhere around the fort, however, dooming reverberations of cannon were still linked tight by a ripping rattle of rifle fire and the rounder report of shotguns: the attack from those directions had not yet collapsed. Flights of lead high enough to clear the battlements swished above Dunraven with the dense, winged hiss of bats leaving a cave—so dense and close that many of the stricken Mexicans on the other side of the fort must be the victims of wild roundshot or musket balls fired across it by their comrades.

Shortly the thinning squadrons which had pressed the northern and southern walls, like those driven away here along the west, were reeling back over the bodies of screeching friends already trampled once in the fervor of assault. Perceptibly, however, the battle was not won. Some of the lucky, the unhit, had taken shelter close under the walls where the cannon could not reach them. From every direction, too, cavalry galloped forward along the battlefield's perimeter, sabers and lances flashing, to turn the deserters back. Meanwhile reinforcements marching forward absorbed shattered units for a new assault.

"Ready them weapons, Tom," Rankin directed. "Prime ever one." While helping Curly assemble more ammunition for the eighteen-pounder, he pushed Dunraven toward a fagot heap of shotguns and rifles.

As Dunraven poured powder into the primers and handed them to men nearby, he could see, through blown veils of smoke, hundreds of musketeers approaching at a run, beetle-black in their night-darkened blue, fire spurting here and there among them. During one of his glances that way, a stony blow hit him where his watch loosened his coat outward. A trickle coursed down from his armpit, but he realized it was only nervous sweat. His benumbed ears recorded the hum of musket balls flying past him, and the hammer-rap of others against the wall. Luckily the one that hit him had been spent, but it did caution him to stay low behind the battlements.

The enemy was still too far away for a shotgun to reach. Snatching up a rifle instead, he fired it offhand, then deplored his haste, for comrades on either side, no matter how feverish, took care when firing to be deliberate and precise. The succession of victories they had won last fall owed much to that deliberation of aim, that deadly precision. In bringing his rifle to bear again, he aimed at one spot in the lines, one black unit forward of the mass. Whether his squeeze on the trigger altered that unit he never knew, for the eighteen-pounder vomited its deafening flame as he fired, and his eyes flinched tight shut.

When the smoke again blew thin, the beetle-black lines were less dense in front, but coming on still, and near enough now to emerge as men. He put aside the rifle for his double-barreled shotgun. Thought of the deadly spray of buckshot ready to leap from each barrel brought a quieting assurance to his hands. Among the nearer Mexicans were several carrying ladders. His aim was at one by the foremost ladder, which was already protruding across an irrigation ditch, the fort's stale moat. Beyond the puff emitted as the stock kicked his shoulder, he saw the man whirl in a frantic convulsion, and was surprised to hear himself laugh. He fired the second barrel hastily at a musketeer struggling with the opposite side of the ladder—too hastily, for he could see no effect.

Dropping down to reload, he noticed Spread Rankin crowding a logchain into the eighteen-pounder. Thought of the flesh that chain would mangle revived Dunraven's sense of pain. As the ruby tip of the poker arched toward the cannon, as its bucking bellow followed, he winced so hard that a dagger-blade of agony from his thigh slashed upward through his belly.

When he looked back through the smoke the enemy battalions were veering raggedly, lamely, sideward. This time, however, no one cheered. This time, they knew, the falter of the enemy did not mean victory, only another reprieve.

Though a new sweep of clouds blotted out the moon, enough of dawn had risen to bring a frail, smoky light across the valley. Beyond all the Mexicans cut down near the fort, several times more were re-grouping in the distance, and there must be scores up close here be-tween the canal and the fort: many in the charge from the south had veered under this wall on the west, those from the west under the north wall, and so on, bringing their ladders with them. Over toward the south Colonel Crockett and his sharpshooters were stooping an-gularly over their parapet for quick shots at the huddles hiding be-low, and Travis by the twelve-pounder on the north yelled for every-one to ready all weapons for a new assault.

Then a fresh summons from the Mexican bugles, and a third wave of troops surged forward to join those under the walls. Their advance evidently was strongest against defenses along the north and east: during an interval of loading Dunraven noticed on a roof across the court behind him a tangle of cursing, howling men writhing together in dawnlit coils of smoke, and with queerly little fire. The third wave there was washing over the walls.

How that should affect action up here he had no time to decipher, for already ladders rose against the wall before him and shakoed heads appeared above the battlements. Two ladders flanked the eighteen-pounder. Spread wrestled one like the horns of a bull, twist-ing it off balance to heave it away. Dunraven enforced upon his quiv-ering hands the control needed to aim his shotgun at a head above the other. The shako flew off as he fired; the head jolted back, its face pulpy under the moon. Another head quickly replaced it. He fired his second barrel, but panic sent that shot wild. Curly then scooped the whole brazier of coals over the ladder. A fountain of screams rose with the sparks, but musketeers from other ladders were pressing up from left and right along the roof. Some fell before point-blank fire; some wilted under the crush of rifles clubbed by the muzzle; some were thrown bodily over the parapet; others staggered under the flash of bowie knives, the gash of hatchets, or the smash of fists. But more came on always, muskets forward, bayonets parrying, stabbing, gouging—and leaving fewer Texans to meet the many pouring up across their dead.

Curly, his face anguished, backed over near Rankin. He clubbed with his rifle while Rankin slashed and jabbed with the ruby-tipped poker. A Mexican to one side, bayoneted musket up like a javelin, let drive at Rankin. Dunraven threw his empty gun at him, but the Mexican, the musket, the bayonet, drove on until the bayonet disappeared in Rankin's chest; he went down by the eighteen-pounder. Dunraven rushed forward, bare hands like claws, just as Curly whirled his rifle to brain the man behind that bayonet, and Dunraven floundered down across the crumpling body.

"You hit, Tom?" Curly screamed at his shoulder.

"No—no!"

"Look—cuttun us off!" By a flash of eyes distended with terror Curly indicated an ant swarm of black figures flowing through the breach at the northeast corner into the main court of the Alamo. Travis lay dead across the cannon above them, his nearest comrades dead too, and snarls of men fighting hand to hand were tumbling inward from the remaining walls. "Below! Run down below, Tom!"

Curly bolted for a ramp down which other survivors were plunging to make a stand in rooms off the court. But Dunraven's flounder had knocked the pistols in his belt against his diaphragm, a reminder of Corazon's doubt that he could make them count. As he snatched one out, a spurt of fire from a musket before him exploded breath-stopping agonies through his flank, through the whole cask of his body, knocked him back on wobbling, failing legs. The musketeer rushed at him, bayonet high, teeth wolfish. Clutching the pistol, which wavered in his struggle for balance, Dunraven kept his legs propelling him back, back, back from that oncoming bayonet until they carried him over the edge of the roof.

In his somersault backward he saw the smoke-lashed moon swim pallidly between clouds lower in the west; saw muskets on the roofs and around the yard flash like meteorites displaced. The vision ended in a burst of fire as he struck the earth.

Through a ravel of nightmares he became aware of a slamming cannon shot followed by musketry and overlapping yells in Spanish, only in Spanish. His eyes opened. Wind-blown dust and smoke floated above him, and Venus too, fading alone. Below her, across the roof of the barracks, bodies lay tangled together like driftwood washed up by a tidal wave. A face with fixed eyes stared at him over the edge. Beside it lay a handless arm in the tatters of its sleeve, a shoeless foot too. The wall beneath these was pocked by bullets and streaked with blackening blood. Across the court around him lay more men than he ever had seen in the Alamo alive, most wearing Mexican blue stained blackly red. Hundreds lay there, comrades and enemies intertangled, blending their blood. In this tormented, dreamy moment of revival, he felt an equal pity for all, for himself with all the rest.

From the roof behind him off which he had fallen a snarl of Mexicans yelled crossly at each other while pushing the eighteen-pounder onto the ramp leading down into the court. Other yells spilled off the artillery tower to his right, where more Mexicans competed to reload the big-mouthed carronade, which must have been what jarred him from his coma. While he blinked at it, vision wavering, three rifles almost in unison fired from a window midway along the barracks: two of the Mexicans slumped off the tower as floppily as puppets when their master drops their strings.

Dunraven tried lifting his head to see better. A heavy pain below his ribs dizzied him; its weight suffocated him, forcing him to lie limp. Venus danced drunkenly in the rags of blown clouds, and he recalled the disenchanting truth that, however steadfast she might appear at times, her course is wanton, her name debased. Years no one could number seemed to have hurried by since he had said as much to Corazon.

Corazon! Close against his collarbone the sober click-clack-click of his watch, which his backward fall had thrown that high inside his coat, spoke its tireless rebukes about duty, mingled with reminders of love, but emphasizing duty, duty, duty, as the root and stem on which love flowers best. The one duty, the one intention most imperative just now, was that, so long as he had any life in him at all, he ought to be using it to kill those gunners who were preparing an Alamo cannon to slaughter the last few defenders hidden in buildings around the court. The smothering weight of pain inside him, however, held him still.

As the eighteen-pounder rolled down the ramp, a wheel wrenched screams from one of the fallen in its way. An officer silenced him with his saber, then ordered a pathway cleared through the bodies toward the barracks. One thrown aside so tumbled that a stiffening arm flopped across Dunraven like a bat. Instantly the weighted agony within him magnified beyond endurance. The sky went black.

When at last his eyes did reopen, he could see only as if through fumes wavering off an overflow of lava. Venus was gone. A scudding cloud where she had been was bleached by sunlight not yet quite high enough to shine across the barracks.

By this time the carronade on its tower had been wheeled around to bear upon the chapel, at which the eighteen-pounder too, now far over toward it, let go its massive bellow. The entire line of barracks had been gutted by cannon fire; each section had been punctured by jagged wounds bigger than a washtub, and fragments of timber protruded from each like splintered bones. Mexicans pushed in and out of battered doorways, most of them heedless of the shots around the chapel, which proved that the battle was not yet entirely over. Most were carrying out loot—blankets, shoes, hatchets, pistols, watches, anything salable.

A shriek near Dunraven drew his glance leftward. Not ten yards away four musketeers with sun-baked Nahuatlan faces were jabbing bayonets into a body clothed in Texas buckskins. One fired a ball into it, after which all bent to rifle the pockets. Other squads circled elsewhere among the fallen, seeking out Texans among the slain.

The turn of his eyes discovered the arm of that corpse in blood-splashed blue across his waist. His own right hand, still clutching one of his pistols, was half hidden beneath it. Those pistols: so cannily, cruelly loaded with a double charge of buckshot, and he had neglected to use them! The one still in his belt, when exposed by moving his arm, was slimy with blackening red, but the other was dry. Though the strain of drawing it clear set his diaphragm quivering in torment, he did get its muzzle up to rest on the arm which had concealed it.

Through a frenzied, feeble tapping of his pulse against his eardrums he again heard his watch declaim on duty, love and duty. How odd that only here, only at the end of life, he should discover the possibility of union between those two! Could the secret of good living be found in harmonizing love with worthy performance? Or was that the way to word it?

Never, he knew very well, would he have time to think it through. Never. A sober Christian, hearing his last moments tick away, would make haste to "prepare for the Hereafter," as the phrase ran, but not for years had Dunraven considered this a sensible exercise: all his reflection had convinced him that death is no less impervious to prayer or worry than the moon is to the baying of hounds chained outdoors. The surprise was to find himself impatient for it. Here, where his life had attained an unforeseen excellence, this reversal to agonies so boundless made further life unthinkable.

He could see its end move closer. The four musketeers were stepping over bodies to one in a hickory shirt, a volunteer he recognized as Myles Abbey, a graying veteran of 1812, a man of some polish who, like himself, had helped many wordless youngsters write letters home. Abbey's head stirred as the four approached. Their sergeant noted this, his weary, wary, adobe-brown face impassive even as he brought his bayonet around before him.

"Shoot! Don't stick me, señores!" Abbey pleaded. "Shoot! Just shoot!"

The sergeant and a private beside him together speared him. A third kicked his head, and again the group bent over to search. Watching them, Dunraven was sure they understood no English; they must have been ordered to kill all survivors, and any method would do. His hope was that he could manage his own last duty with equal finish.

Although within good pistol range, they were not yet an absolutely sure target. Soon they would come his way. They would find him ready.

5

Gonzales, Texas
Friday Night
March 11, 1836

Day after day Perry in Gonzales, drilling a half-formed troop not yet joined by the squad he had left behind near Highhorse Valley, learned nothing about the Alamo beyond what Dunraven had told in his letter of the 3rd. Scouts daily on patrol in that direction reported hearing the far, faint thunder of artillery until the 6th, and thereafter silence, only silence. As every family in Gonzales had relatives and close friends away in that elongating silence, there was someone at the western edge of town every daylight hour to watch for bearers of news. None came until after dark on the 11th, when two Mexican horsemen arrived to say that the Alamo had been overwhelmed at dawn on the 6th, that every defender in it had been massacred, that their bodies were piled up with logs and burned, that the garrison in dying slew a host nearly ten times their own number, so many that the San Antonio River still reeked with the stink of cadavers thrown into it because they were too numerous to bury.

Hysteria followed this report as it spread through town. From night-blackened hovels everywhere rose the most heartbroken female wailing and shrieking Perry ever had heard; and men meanwhile gathered in hushed clusters under the stars to wonder how in the world they could defend Texas now. With the Spartans of the Alamo dead, where would the unconquerable Santa Anna strike next? At Gonzales, of course. And who was there to stop him? Only three hundred and seventy-four unorganized volunteers with but two usable cannon and no fortifications whatever. Their commander, General Sam Houston, had not arrived from Washington-on-the-Brazos until four o'clock that afternoon. They had just two days' rations, trivial supplies of powder, and numerous opinions about the folly of lingering in the path of the Dictator instead of dashing eastward to help their loved ones escape. Many civilians and not a few recruits caught up horses and melted off through the dark.

To quiet the panic Houston denounced the Mexicans as spies sent out by Santa Anna to disorganize resistance by spreading false information. He had them jailed.

Curiously, even though Perry overheard many men call this a trick to hold the army together, it presently did reduce the desertions. Houston's way was difficult to resist. Whether in filthy buckskins, in uniform, or in some outlandish turban and serape, Big Sam had grandeur. About him floated enough mystery, enough atmosphere of undefined power, to keep plain men in awe of him. His ability had been tested alike in city and forest, in warfare and in Congress, among savages and among America's elect. That President Andrew Jackson, when he was in Washington, had treated him as a favorite was common knowledge, and who had ever heard of Old Hickory turning his back on a loyal friend? With Houston in command of Texan forces, might not eventual victory be guaranteed by the U.S. Army? That was how Perry found the talk drifting as men put aside temptations to decamp.

Next day the general kept them pantingly busy shifting eastward across the Guadalupe River to put that barrier between themselves and the enemy. Again on the 13th, Sabbath though it was, he drove them too hard for thought of much but soldiering: he started regular drill, perfected the hierarchy of command, parceled out responsibilities, and established penalties for breaches of discipline. Meanwhile he despatched one unit to the Gulf for powder and lead, another to Brazoria for cannon, still others into the countryside for supplies.

Meanwhile too, though a few men did steal away on the sly, scores of new recruits arrived. Among them, during the evening of the 13th, were the five companions Perry had missed in San Felipe. They had been delayed because wild mustangs drifting near their camp by night had bewitched their horses away and left them afoot. With them came the unhinging information that Camilla was in Texas, as proved by a note from her which Hugh delivered.

His impulse to gallop off and join her at once brought upon him a shaming sense of responsibility, a realization of how inextricably he was caught in the gathering net of disaster. The one rational response would be to warn her away before it caught her too, but he delayed writing to her in the hope that some other course might show itself in a day or two.

From C. B.'s Journal
Monday, March 21, 1836

All the sluices of the firmament reopened this morning to spill out a succession of downpours even heavier than yesterday and both days before. Such a glut of gloomy weather, after so much dire news from the west, threatened to overcome us, but Camilla kept everyone too busy to act "down" long. We plastered a viscid blend of mud and prairie hay between all logs around two rooms upstairs, brushed another coat of whitewash over those which two families of neighbors, the Timberlakes and Nuhns, helped us plaster tight the week before last, and then we repaired the kitchen floor.

In the flush of accomplishment Camilla remarked to me that the *right* to optimism has to be *earned,* and newly earned every day, that any little beginning toward inward peace and contentment is not a state to be found but an accomplishment to be achieved daily, then reachieved tomorrow. She may have arrived at this conclusion only by temperament, by feeling, without logic or definition, and yet it's profound. I do wish I'd thought it up myself.

Strictly, however, mortals in such surroundings as these have no right at all to feel down. Toward noon a pause between rains sent her and me together out along the bluff to estimate the weather. The view, however threatening, was stupendous. Everywhere the spendthrift bounty of spring, and Otter Creek ran jubilant and frothy through that new haze of green the woods now wear. One drifting sunbeam blazed across it, then coursed away upon swells of prairie which lope inexhaustibly toward the horizons, taking one's spirit along as if on a winged horse loping in effortless sweeps.

With such handiwork of the Lord inviting us to see wider than ever before, and to do better than before, feeling low seems a form of sacrilege. It's agnostic, a failure of vision and a denial of God, a dream of hell upon the ramparts of heaven. We have no call here to feel less than exalted.

Saying so to Camilla brought her glance alert in that searching way peculiar to her.

"Do *you* feel low, Pa?"

"Not every minute, anyhow."

"No," she said. "You always act so cheerful."

"You too," I said. "You act more cheerful than *anybody*—not excepting you."

She laughed a little, then gazed away to the west. I ventured to sigh on her behalf, as well as mine.

"It's harder than you reckoned on, this life in Eden, eh, honey? And less romantic."

"Not unbearable, no, but more lonesome. Dear heaven, I never, never imagined it could get this lonesome."

A pat on the shoulder, and I left her there with her yearnings. What troubled her most was easy to divine: no doubt it *is* the war that prevents Perry from dashing back to marry her and thereby vindicate her coming all this way at his instance, but why can't he at least write her?

For a day or two that forgiving letter she got from Edmond last week fortified her: by offering rescue again, even though she so flagrantly jilted him, he gave assurance that someone treasures her through thick and thin—which reminds her, however, that someone else does not, or fails to show that he does. Therefore, rain or shine, each and all of us (even the curious fools who come from so many miles away to see "that stunnah from Nor Leans"), we must work like mules and forget everything that's missing here while we make the best of what is not. If that boy had any idea how his neglect of her sweats the rest of us along with her, I'm sure he'd risk court-martial for neglect of duty in order to ease her aching heart—and our aching backs.

While commiserating with her, I envy her as I envy him. Impatient about the present they may well be, but their prospects are as good as energetic young people could ask. I like to farm (when it pays), just as they do. I like pioneering better, as they together have much better reason to do. Farming is continuously creative, pioneering more so. Creativity generates zest. It *is* zest, the paramount zest, next to love, which is creativity in a personal and poetic form. And Perry's scheme to develop a strain of hundred-mile horses able to free people from the prison of empty distance will help them shape out the most creative pioneering anywhere around here.

Camilla has the practicality to realize that they must have cash crops in the meantime, big ones, and that the war will give a good harvest two or three times the usual value; hence her determination to make the most of every blessed day, to let nothing deflect either ourselves or the Tiptons or Roberta and Esau from planting all the acreage the weather will let us till.

More broadly, what she is doing is only what all thoughtful people everywhere are doing when at their best—seeking salvation. However lonely and disappointed and tired at times, she experiences a peculiarly American kind of relief in working admirably, in being cleansed, not by the Blood of the Lamb, but by the sweat of her face, in thus expiating the unearned luxuries she reveled in heretofore. My own encumbered conscience requires me to do likewise beside her, to seek the daily medicine of callused hands, sweated brows, and weary joints.

And when I'm free to act for myself? No doubt more of the same, though in quite different ways. For after all:

> *Mere sense of sin is not*
> *what keeps us children of Adam*
> *straying through the earth.*
> *It's apprehension that all of us*
> *must rediscover Eden for ourselves . . .*
> *must delve for it daily as we go,*
> *delve with spade or plow*
> *or chisel or microscope,*
> *or with that best of tools, the pen,*
> *or its consequent, the book.*

CHAPTER XVI

I

Camilla's Homestead
Tuesday Noon
March 29, 1836

Listening, Camilla straightened her back, hoe upright under both gloves. The air was warm, thick, still—amazingly warm for March. A dove mourned in the dooryard grove to her left; voices identifiable as Liz Tipton's and Roberta's drifted from the kitchen; and woods behind and below the barn were vibrant with far cries from her father, Esau, Ev, the Tipton boys and the Tipton dogs, all down there since noonday dinner to round up straying brood sows. She held her breath to hear beyond all that because, from the family lookout on the bluff twenty or thirty minutes ago, she had seen a rider, pygmied by distance, approaching along that westerly trail which linked Hoping Hill (as she had named her place) with neighbors, roads, waterways, towns, and great events beyond the horizon. Hearing no click of hoofs on twigs or stones, she returned to work.

Tilling God's earth, she believed, ought to be conducted as sacred observance, and part of the time she worked in that spirit. With the handle of her hoe she marked out rows in parallels like staves for a hymn, then dropped nodular beet seeds along them with reverence for that mysterious potential in each which the ferment of moist and sunlit soil would enlarge within a few months to the size of a human heart.

Nevertheless the poke of her bonnet did lift often from these rites toward woods out of which the trail from the lowlands emerged. Not for almost a week had a single visitor ascended to Hoping Hill, all the neighbors preferring to go where they could pick up news and hear the latest oracles about whether to rush toward safety or risk staying awhile longer. Neither had she received any new mail. Her loneliness at times reminded her of an entirely flat prairie over beyond Widow Frey's, where there had been just one horizon—a featureless circle completely surrounding her.

When at last the strange horseman did appear on the trail, her hand fluttered high in welcome. He failed to wave back. Body slumped and forearms at rest on a rifle across the pommel before him, he merely stared at her while his gelding wearily climbed toward the garden.

She forced a smile. "Hadado, sir."

His gelding, though a well-made paint with a white clover on his face, was droopily exhausted, and bloody along the barrel from constant roweling. To stop him, the man simply relaxed his spurs.

"Lady name Palmer live here?"

Camilla's blood jumped. "I'm Mrs. Palmer, yes."

"Man name Cottier been here?"

"Cottier? No-o, I—"

"Rex Cottier."

"No. Is such a person supposed to be here?"

Insolently delaying to respond, he spat across his left elbow. His face, irregular and heavy, resembled a bent iron kettle long thrown around in domestic quarrels. Over a collarless shirt he wore a black coat of the knee-length type favored back in Dixie by preachers, undertakers, bankers, gamblers, and politicians. A matching black hat sat low upon his brow.

"Said he'd come west and meet me commun east. Thought he might of got this far by now."

"Well, not as I've heard at any rate."

He shifted lightless eyes toward the house, the poultry shed, the barn. Though his expression admired nothing, it should have. The transformation she already had forced upon everything was thought miraculous among the neighbors, and not less because, instead of attempting to do it all herself, she had taxed her ingenuity to the limit in winning help with it from others, dozens of them. Her tactic among visitors, who had come only to "set and visit awhile" (that is, to look her over), was to busy herself at projects they obviously might lend a hand with if only they had the gumption. So they did lend a hand. The yard now was free of bones and rubbish. Sprouts which would become flowers showed green in beds of black earth around the veranda. Snowy curtains floated behind the windows. All fissures between upright logs forming the walls were snugly sealed, and newly hewn slabs calicoed the roof wherever it had leaked.

Nevertheless this new stranger seemed to be reviewing the place solely to consider who else might be here. She spoke out boldly.

"Your name, please?"

"Huh?"

"May I know who you are, sir?"

His mouth retained a tight sideward droop. With thick, hairy wrists at rest over his pommel, he let his eyes probe her clothes. That in itself did not distress her; she was accustomed to it. However, he seemed to be doing so, not in simple male estimation, but to discomfit her, belittle her. Even so, she persisted in looking for at least the rudiments of manners.

"If you don't make yourself acquainted, how else am I to know who I'm dealing with?"

"Name's Reed. Most call me Blacky Reed."

She thought "Blacky" exactly right. His eyes, his hat and coat, his nails and the bent iron of his face accorded with that label. She tilted her head sideward. "You've been a long way west, have you?"

"To San Flippy. Come from there in little over two days, ridun steady."

"San Felipe! Did you—were any men there from close around here?"

"I aint the one to know. Had business of my own to mind."

"Yes, no doubt." Although tempted to ask if he had concluded it in jail, she recollected how often she herself had found the pertinacious curiosity of Texans annoying. She required her tone to sweeten. "Any late news of the war?"

"Heard about Colonel Fanning?"

"About his fortifying Goliad? Yes." Because Goliad was farther away than any remaining outpost, she had accounted to herself for Perry's queer silence on the supposition that he must be there with Colonel Fannin and unable to get letters sent this far off the direct route east. "I hear we have a lot of fine men there."

"Aint no more, lady. Fanning surrendered, and with him pretty near all the volunteers from the U.S.A."

Camilla's knees loosened as if hit from behind. *"What?"*

"Yup."

Camilla supported her weight on her hoe. In the sullen quiet she heard the sobs of mated doves, the lisp of newly leaved trees, the hum of a bee going by. Intrusion of a statement so calamitous upon harmonies so commonplace blurred her capacity to receive the news as real. Blackie himself seemed to detect the ghostliness it had for her. He talked on to give it more body.

"Means *another* slaughter."

"Bu-but *who?*"

"All that was there; that's all I know."

Instantly she chose to interpret this as meaning that the surrender had no connection with whatever errand had brought him. Her breath revived.

"Perhaps it's only hearsay."

"It's true, I reckon. The settlements west is all a-runnun for the States fast as they can git. The Guvmunt's run too—everbody has. Santa Anna's word is kill all the men, give *his* men the women and land: that's his vow."

"Well, *our* men, I fancy, will change his mind."

"None that already met him won't. Not one. Best thing you better do, lady, you better pack up and git."

"Goliad—how can you be sure, how do you *know* it fell?"

"Word come from Victoria, word I don't see no cause to doubt."

"Oh." She held the hoe handle upright before her, taking instruction from its hickory strength, and brought out what she most dreaded to ask. "Is there some reason in this, Mr. Reed, why you've inquired for me?"

"What you mean?"

"Why *have* you come? You've a message for me?"

"Just so. Moren one."

From his coat he extracted two envelopes. In doing so, he kept the writing upward so that she could not guess who might have sent them. Nevertheless, seeing them drove her heart so hard against her ribs that it beat itself weak. She stepped quakily forward, one hand extended.

"How good of you to bring them, Mr. Reed!" Excess of emotion brought tears to her eyes. "I hope it wasn't too much trouble."

"Trouble enough."

He returned them to his pocket. Her hand sagged away. The eyes in that iron face of his took satisfaction in her tears, her bewilderment, her weakness.

"First the fee."

"The fee? Oh, yes, of course! You've a right to a fee. How much, please?"

"What they worth to you?"

"But letters aren't something one bargains for. If they're addressed to me, they belong to me."

"Possession, lady, is nine-tenths of the law. Without you pay the fee, no letters."

"It's not that I object to *any* fee, Mr. Reed. But how can I pay it without knowing how much?"

"Way you act, they're worth a lot."

"They *may* be. How do I know? I just don't know."

"What the man said that give me the first, I allow that one is. He said whosoever sent it, he talked mighty strong on the importance for you to get it."

"*All* letters have *some* importance, of course. But you still haven't named your fee."

"Ten dollars plus found for—"

"*Ten?*"

"In solid coin, plus found for me and this paint."

"Why, you're welcome to what comfort we have, certainly, but ten dollars! I never heard the like!"

"Big bother to come here, lady."

"But weren't you passing east anyhow?"

"Come up that hill, lady. That aint like steppun over a sty."

"But ten dollars! Mr. Reed, that's plain banditry!"

"No such thing. I aint compellun you to pay. No banditry about it—just business. Ten dollars, plus lodgin for me, plus plenty corn for my horse. Take it or leave it."

With little of Mr. Tipton's small harvest from last year still left, and that little needed for seed and pone, corn was in some ways more valuable than cash. All the same, what was she to do?

"Wel-ll . . ." Weakening, she extended her hand. "The letters, please."

"Without no pay? Ho-ho! In *advance,* lady."

A shock of rage and shame jerked back her hand. "A moment, please."

On the way to the house she reflected how he might prolong this torture: he might insist on receiving a night's lodging before allowing her so much as another glance at her letters. A whole afternoon, a night, another morning of torment might be exacted before she could touch the pages she had a right to read now.

Roberta and Mrs. Tipton had been watching from the edge of a lazily blown curtain in the parlor. When she came in, their eyes reflected the distress they saw in hers. Even though she closed the door, Roberta rushed over to press it behind her.

"What happen, Miz Milla? What he done?"

"Only tore me wide open is all. Run fetch the men from the woods, Berta."

"Yessum."

Roberta began to back toward the rear door, hiking up her skirt to bare her feet for speed, her normally calm brown face vivified by anxiety to help.

"Tell them to come in through the back."

"Yessum."

"If they can get in without showing him how many they are, all the better. But they must *sound* like many. Hurry now, Berta."

2

While Camilla at a wash bench behind the kitchen scooped water against her face to cool it, the men and boys came up from below the barn. Her father's nearness reassured her. Texas had toughened him, rejuvenated him, in acknowledgment of which he had shaved off his muttonchops. Nothing calendared his years except lacerations of gray through sweat-darkened hair waving from his temples to his collar. Though in workshirt and trousers, though afield from dawn till noon following a one-mule plow, he had about him a zest recalling how he had looked when she was a child.

"What's the matter, honey? This guest won't work?"

"No, he—"

"*Where's* the trifler?" Cocking his double-barreled shotgun, he scowled ferociously. "Man won't work even *one* full day for cuppa coffee sweetened with pretty smiles aint fit to live!"

The laughter all around tickled her too, helping to calm her. As she toweled her face, hands, and arms, massaging them to relax them, her summary of Blacky Reed's demands put all three men in a fidget to negotiate for her letters over their flintlocks, but she forbade them to let him see them.

"It's enough to have you near—and him to know men are near," she explained. "He's the kind of beast who likes to make decent people crawl, and when they crawl he tramples their fingers. I'm not going to crawl any longer, and I want him to know this is no place to *try* making people crawl." Her father she asked to arrange the men according to what she once heard him describe as "tactics of hidden strength," letting Blacky be aware that armed men were around, but not how many or what their weapons were. He stationed them behind the curtained front windows while she, freshly combed and powdered and aproned, went through the front door onto the veranda.

Blacky Reed's paint, now unsaddled, stood by an oak a short way off. Blacky had bent over a saddlebag, meaty back tensing his coat. His rifle stood against the oak.

"Mr. Reed."

He continued his attention to the saddlebag, but she did not call again, sure that he had heard. After a bit he rose, turning with rude deliberation to fix upon her a shadowed stare. That was his response.

"Saddle up again, please."

"Huh?"

"Saddle your paint, sir." Although her intention had been to act icily grand, swollen pulsations in her throat made her hoarse. "You'll have to leave."

His brows gathered. He walked toward her, black hat level, hairy neck forward from its naked collar band, arms outward at the elbows. Camilla kept her face stony, one hand politely at rest within the other. To be a woman condemned to live in excessive drygoods had its advantages because her knees could shake like bell clappers in skirts and petticoats as voluminous as hers and no one but herself would know.

About halfway to the veranda, puzzled by her show of force, Blacky stopped. "What you say?"

"I said to saddle up and leave."

"What about them letters?"

"Never mind the letters. You're to leave."

He squirted tobacco juice to one side, then presented squarely toward her the sooted iron of his face. "You don't say."

"I do."

Coldly, despisingly she reviewed his neglected stubble, the droop in his mouth, his grayed and shriveled collar band, the soiled fakery of his coat. A twitch jerked one of his hands. He flexed it to make it quiet.

"Well, I declare!"

"You have *nothing* to declare, Mr. Reed. You have only to leave."

"But this aint right! Lotta trouble commun here, fetchun them letters. Man does you a favor, he deserves his fee."

"Any reasonable fee I would be glad to pay. What you demand is simply outrageous. You said take it or leave it. I leave it."

"Aint no call to be so uppity, lady. Aint no law to make me leave here neither."

"Quite wrong, sir. There is."

From an invisible depth behind a curtain on the kitchen side of the veranda Mrs. Tipton squalled, "Junior! Harold! Yall stay clear of that winda. You too, Buddy."

Evett's voice seconded her from much nearer. "Great Godamighty, boys, git back outen the way. Man caint have you pokun your nose right agin his rifle time like this. Git back outa range."

"You're trespassing on this property against the wish of the owner," Camilla proceeded without a flicker. "I tell you to leave, and you're violating the law if you don't."

"Right," Evett seconded. "Hear that, Esau? Dead right."

From the next window came the rumble of Esau's bass. "Daid right."

Blacky scanned the kitchen windows one at a time. Their curtains welled and relaxed in leisurely grace. From behind another on the parlor side the invisible major cleared his throat. Blacky's thyroid cartilage rose and subsided in a lumpy swallow.

"You say any *reasonable* fee, lady. What you consider a reasonable fee?"

"A quarter would be a reasonable fee, half a dollar an extravagant one."

"A quarter? Why, that aint hardly worth this talk about it."

"There's no *need* to talk about it. I haven't offered you anything; I've only expressed an opinion."

He studied her politely adjoined hands, her crisp apron. "Letters aint no damn good to me, lady. What *do* you offer?"

The shaking of her knees had quieted. Her tone was flat and final. "One dollar for both." Before he could accept or reject it, she added one more stipulation. *"Plus* your immediate departure."

"Give er here."

"On delivery, Mr. Reed."

"Mam?"

"You seem to trust no one. Why should you be trusted? The fee is for delivery of the letters. I'll pay when you've delivered them both, not before."

"Right and proper," Evett murmured. "Puffuckly right, puffuckly proper."

Blacky, drawing the envelopes from his pocket, tapped them against his palm, then shuffled forward. He passed them toward her. The handwriting upon the uppermost, strange to her, brought a flash of dismay through her, but she kept her hands tight together to prevent them from seizing it.

"You understand you're to leave at once?"

"Who wants to stay here? *Take* the damn trifles."

Still she let his extended arm tire. With fine leisure she delved into her apron pocket for two half-dollars which she transferred to him while accepting the letters, then stepped to the door.

About to enter, she nodded. "Good day, Mr. Reed."

He clicked the coins together like poker chips. His shadowed eyes drifted from her to the windows. A squirt of tobacco sideward, and he lumbered off toward his gelding. Camilla dipped inside the door, closed it, dropped its bar into place, and whirled to run upstairs, the letters against her heart.

3

Cedric Burleigh kept to his chair behind the parlor curtains, watching Blacky saddle the paint while also listening for motion in Camilla's room overhead. The silence above was entire. His inner ear retained the record of her footsteps running on the stairs a few moments ago, of their murmur across creaking boards to her room directly over the parlor, of her rocker receiving her. Since then no stir had followed.

Blacky's preparations to leave, though deliberate, showed the strain of realizing that eyes he could not see observed everything he did. He impressively examined his two horse pistols while assembling his gear, but for Cedric there was something much more noteworthy in the continuing failure of activity overhead. Out of soldierly fixation to duty he sat there watching while Blacky saddled up, mounted, and roweled his paint out of the yard. Evett and Esau over in the kitchen gustily enjoyed his going; but, as the ceiling boards remained mute, Cedric too kept quiet, listening.

The paint was diminishing over a rise of prairie northward when faint shuddery sobs brought him hastily up from his chair to tiptoe upstairs. The door to Camilla's room stood open. She sat in a rocker by the front window. A half-dozen unfolded sheets of foolscap lay upon the bed beside her. Another letter one page long lay on the floor. She had bowed her face into her apron, which both hands crushed against her eyes and mouth without quite muting her gasps for breath.

"Honey . . . ?" He stepped in, awkward in his anxiety, and pressed her shoulder. Its shudders jarred through his hand a shocking, wholly irrelevant remembrance of her mother in moments of ecstasy. "Bad news, uh?"

"No-no! I'm awful silly is all. Take it." Her elbow lifted sideward at the foolscap on the bed. "Read it."

Warily, as if handling chemicals which, put together, might very well explode, he picked up a sheet at a time until all were in order. They were from Perry.

Camp on the Colorado
March 20—Sunday

Ever dear Camilla:

The wonderful joy of learning that you have defied all dangers and come to Texas has been matched ever since the hour I read your letter by a realization that to leave the army now would be criminal. Not until the evening of the 13th did Hugh arrive with it. Shortly afterward Captain H. Karnes galloped into camp from the west with tidings which let Turmoil loose amongst us.

He was one of four scouts Genl. S. Houston had sent out to sift a report about disaster at the Alamo. That day they came upon Mrs. Almaron Dickinson, wife of an artillery officer, and her little daughter Angelina, who had hidden in the chapel of the Alamo with several other women and children, and thus survived.

In the onslaught upon the fortress proper every defender fell. There was no exception. All were piled up with logs and smeared with grease to make a bonfire, a beacon, a hideous signal declaring that the Dictator means to obliterate everyone foolish enough to take up arms against him. He was sending Mrs. Dickinson east with a nigra named

Joe, a servant of Colonel Travis's, to spread this warning. Karnes, having the best horse, hastened back ahead of the party to report that Santa Anna's advance, under orders to crush us with all dispatch, already had crossed the Cibolo, leaving no barrier betwixt them and us except the Guadalupe.

On receiving Karnes' report, Genl. H. required us to break camp that same night and burn whatever possessions we could not carry on our backs. There was no other means of conveying anything, for settlers flying off in the first stampede had stripped the region of wagons and carts. They also had appropriated most of the horses out grazing at the time. The few left us we lent to transport women, children, and the sick, my horse among them: we have become footsore infantry supported by only two baggage wagons. Even our two cannon, however precious to us, had to be sunk in the Guadalupe for lack of teams to draw them with us.

How sad and grim and anxious that procession was! Toiling through the dark over the long swells beyond the valley of the Guadalupe, we reached a high point from which Gonzales used to be visible by day. Where it had been, a forest of flames waved in the wind. The scouts, staying behind, had set fire to every house, cabin, store, barn, or shed. They were leaving there nothing to nourish or shelter the enemy.

Picture, if you can, how grieved were the families who had lost their men, leaving no one to defend them or till their land in a country where safety requires the rifle and bread derives from the plow. Now their homes were gone. Never in my life have I heard such wracking anguish. It was a dreadfully hard hour. We pushed onward during the night, but the somber red on the horizon behind us represented our thoughts.

Before day we heard a series of heavy explosions from that direction. Was it the cannon of the enemy? The question raced along our column, and with it a wave of panic. This ended in embittered laughter as veterans assured everyone that the cannonade was in the grogshops: the fire was exploding barrels of whisky!

At dawn we camped for breakfast and a brief rest just beyond Peach Creek, then onward to put between us and the invaders still another of the many streams running south across Texas. Through rain and cold and sunny heat we have pulled our whole force, with its escorted refugees, across the La Baca, the Navidad, and on the 17th the swollen Colorado—a very respectable distance for unencumbered infantry on any terms, and prodigious for us, as we have been gathering burdens hourly along the way.

For, while the bulk of the army moved forward, some of us scoured the country both ways from our course, emptying it utterly where it is not empty already. Most cabins are deserted because runaways ahead of us have spread terrifying exaggerations about the magnitude and speed of the host pursuing us. They have been declaring that, after the enormous loss the enemy suffered at the Alamo, he still has thirty thousand with him. This must be pretty close to five times the fact, and yet has been widely believed.

So panic runs everywhere the deserters do. Many colonists, in their passion to escape, leave dinner smoking on the hearth, wash blowing to shreds on the line, hens cackling unheard in the yard. Day after day we find evidence of hasty abandonments: calves bawl alone on their tethers; buckets stand half filled by the spring; doors hang ajar on squealing hinges; plows rust in furrows they were breaking open at the moment the stampede began. Other families, equally without sense, have tried to bring away all their movables—all their pets and household treasure heaped onto wagons, carts, sleds, drags, anything that will hold a burden. Thus to the manless women and children from Gonzales who came grieving along with the army, more, more, more are added, ever more daily—so many that one's pity is all used out by dark, and still there is help to give until we sink down totally spent.

What with the spring rains and haste everywhere, the trails are hideous wallows, the confusion along them so horrible that it turns funny. In every stretch of deep gumbo, muddy civilians of every age eddy around mired carts, floundering livestock, and scraps of discarded furniture. The scene at every ford, ferry, or camp is so bad that I myself could not stand it but for this perverse inclination to laugh over the human tangles we help unsnarl. My boys and I, loosening out wheels sunk to the axle (or babies, shoats, oxen, and grandmothers which have got stuck like flies in molasses), ourselves become caked with mud from head to foot.

Our purpose in such help is military as well as humanitarian. Houston promises to stop the invasion here at the Colorado. That may be feasible only if we leave the countryside westward an empty, grainless waste. We take away or devastate whatever might nourish the enemy. Even the prairies on which his cavalry and mule trains must feed are set afire. Thus along this rising river, where we already have constructed earthworks, we retain access to the granaries of the fruitful Austin Colony, receive reinforcements daily, and hold positions from which to challenge our Enemies at the few crossings, thereby confining them to the depleted west, far from their base, until our strength grows to match theirs.

Looking back over the follies of overconfidence which our victories last fall have inspired since then, we have agreed that our slaughtered friends are the victims of our foregoing success. We now intend to bide the time when we can turn the case around so that the same may be said of the invaders who slew them.

Through the interim, as far eastward as you are, you need not share at all in the pandemonium which has shaken the life out of settlements this other way. Seeding big crops will serve Texas well, and you will prosper from it too, since good harvests are as indispensable for war as cannon are, or squads of riflemen.

Once the situation turns less precarious I shall seize the first opportunity to join you, however briefly, and I hope you will agree that the day we are reunited should unite us for life—that it should be our wedding day. But do you comprehend, dearest person, why I cannot leave here while so few of us must hold back the Invader?

Thought of seeing you thereafter will be my lamp to read the future by. It will illuminate every darkest hour. It will keep before me the wisdom of ignoring my immediate wishes. It will teach me to employ whatever strength nature allows me and whatever lore my elders taught me to help preserve our freedom so that we may choose how we shall live thenceforth.

Meanwhile, please determine occasionally how Hector is keeping Highhorse Valley: consider the prospects there as much your concern as mine. And never become one with the many who are losing faith in Texas. So long as we have an army in position to shift, gather

*strength, and strike when the enemy least expects it, this blessed land
may be counted upon to destroy her ravishers.*

*Remember us in your prayers, dearly loved, but believe in our
victory.*

Until then, and ever after,
Yours,
Perry

Before Cedric had finished the first page Camilla was up to blow
her nose relievedly and freshen before her mirror, after which she
came back to review swiftly those sheets he put aside.

When he released the last to her he grunted. *"Well . . ."*

"I know, Pa. Not one thing to cry about, only every part is *so* like
Perry. After coming all this way because of him, after these lonely,
lonely days, these excruciating weeks without hearing one word, wondering what had become of him or what on earth could be the matter,
and he does say so well as much as reason can let me expect him to
say. Besides that, there was the strain of dealing with that beast who
brought it, so I reckon I just needed a real good bawl."

"Uhm. Wonderful letter, I agree." He nudged his chin toward the
one on the floor. "What's the other say?"

"Oh, nothing of any consequence. Just rubbish."

One sweep of her hand scooped it to him, after which she strode
across the room to a drape of calico behind which her thrusting hand
exposed a row of clothes on a pole. As she dipped her neck sideward
to unbutton her dress, preparing to change it, Cedric rose to leave,
but she flourished at the rocker.

"No, sit there, Pa. Just turn your back. I'd like to talk some more
when you're through."

Dutifully he turned the rocker to face the front window and settled
over the second letter, which came from Leticia Springfield. It was
in conscientious, rounded script as feminine as hooks-and-eyes.

Monday Morn—March 28

Dear Mrs. Palmer:

*Many days now Papa and I and Mrs. Bauernschmidt have talked
of calling on you again, but it's so far and everyone tells how remarkably you are managing and we have been much occupied on the land*

so that Papa can wrest away and join the army. For he calls it the saddest, surest truth of war that victors and vanquished alike require physicians.

This morning a courier declared that all the boys with Colonel F. Fannin have been captured—those not killed in battle. Everyone here is terribly stricken, and much alarmed, for under the shock of that loss Genl. Houston is retreating away from the Colorado Riv. That will permit the hordes of the Dictator to ravage still more of Texas, no one knows how much more. A wild rush of settlers are in motion toward the U. States, and some here too. Already today we counted sixteen wagonloads from upcountry passing below here on the southeast fork.

One reason is that we have confirmation of Mexican agents among the Savages northeast of here, exciting their will to slaughter, and the diverse calamities our armies have suffered will encourage them to think us weak enough so that they can dispose of us howsoever suits them. A still more immediate danger is from the bands of rascals riding out of the Redlands to raid farms where the men are gone. They have robbed and burned—and worse.

Most neighbors here have resolved to migrate to safety a few days hence, unless the alarm quiets before then, because the able men must leave as soon as possible to meet the Enemy. Our plan is to wagon overland southeastward to the road running from San Felipe through Liberty to the U. States.

As there is greatest safety in numbers, we shall move in a body. We all value you so, and would be glad if you will share the fortunes of our journey. The best course would be to hasten this far tomorrow, or the day after at latest, and shelter with us while a strong body assembles. Do speed word to us so that we shall know whether to expect you.

With assurances of our lasting esteem and good wishes,

Your obt. servant,
Leticia

Cedric kept these words in hand, weighing them while gazing away through the open window before him. Every tree in the dooryard grove stood motionless, leaves metallic under the Midas touch of sunlight. What had Camilla seen in this letter to call it rubbish? He wagged the unfolded page above one shoulder toward the fragrant rustle of drygoods behind him.

"Planning to ride over to Springfields' about this, honey?"

"No, certainly not."

"She's right, though: to leave with others—in that she's wise."

"Cunning rather. She wants me out of Texas, and what lengths wouldn't she go to to get me out!"

"Milla! Can't you see how unfair that is? Leticia's an uncommonly sweet, considerate, simple girl who—"

"Oh, hush. Under that sweet look beats a heart that fails to hate only because it's too small. It lacks the capacity."

He snorted a laugh. "Or the venom."

"Besides," she continued, ignoring the hook on his line, "if we ran away now, how would Perry find me? He said, 'Stay where you are. Wait for me there, and one of these days pretty soon I'll be there for the wedding.' Well and good, I'll stay."

"No, he merely said—"

"He the same as said it. All these dangers she's fretting about are miles from here, several days' ride from here."

"But *his* advice is nine days old, Milla, hers just one day. Where cavalry is sweeping around, and resistance collapsing, millions of acres can change hands in a week, and thousands suffer for it. You'd better thank her and heed her and join her, that's my opinion."

"Not mine, no. Last time Perry reached out his hand to me, I was fool enough to turn my back. I won't again. Under no circumstances will I leave Texas except hand in hand with him, mark my word." She by this time was in a riding habit and at the door, waiting for him. "Come along, Pa."

"Where you bound?"

"To Highhorse Valley, of course. My future husband said to look after it. Tonight when I write him I want him to know I take his word to heart."

From C. B.'s Journal
Wednesday, March 30, 1836

At breakfast Evett, whose patriotism has grown in proportion to his weariness with our rate of work, announced that "times like these us crackshots belongs in the army, not triflun round a farm." Regardless of a drenching storm from Mrs. Tipton, he slung his rifle on one arm and went off west in sacrificial grandeur, his hounds frisking along behind as if they knew this was only a lark. Watching him diminish in the distance, I wished I too could shift as lightly upon others the task of looking after my family in order to play the glorious game of patriotism.

Without Ev's amiable yelling around, and no baying of damnfool hounds either, this place seems deserted. Every long silence reminds us how swiftly people have drained away eastward. And the exodus, if not imperative, is at least understandable. For a dynasty of disasters rules over Texas. My calendar of those presently known here shows a round dozen in one month:

Feb. 27	Lt. Col. Frank Johnson's command destroyed at San Patricio.
Mar. 2	Dr. Grant's command massacred at Agua Dulce.
Mar. 6	Battalion under Cols. Bowie and Travis obliterated in the Alamo.
Mar. 11	Mexicans reached the Cibolo, extending invasion eastward.
Mar. 14	Gonzales abandoned and razed to foil Mexican advance.
Mar. 16	Captain King's company slain after surrender at Refugio.
Mar. 18	Texas Government fled from capital toward Harrisburg.
Mar. 19	Colonel Ward's battalion overwhelmed at Victoria.
Mar. 20	Column under Gen. Gaona reported advancing swiftly along Camino Real (and already at Bastrop) to flank Houston on north while devastating northerly settlements.
Mar. 22	Mexican invasion through center under Gen. Sesma reached Colorado River opposite Houston's camp.
Mar. 23	Col. Francis W. Fannin, commanding nearly 600 of our best troops, surrounded and captured near Goliad. This releases Santa Anna's southern column under Urrea to sweep across the lower settlements and flank Houston from the south.
Mar. 27	Houston withdrawing from the Colorado to avoid being surrounded.

What intensifies the general alarm over this succession of blows is the want of sufficient means to stop them. Very few people now suppose that Sam Houston will manage to. His reputation is declining fast, and yet all the cruelest losses could have been avoided by fulfillment of past orders from him.

Last winter he often argued that a frontier fort, while creating an illusion of strength, in fact tells everyone where you are and holds you there for disposal at the pleasure of aggressive and persistent enemies. He himself prefers freedom to move and replenish and move still further until he can strike where circumstances favor it. During January he sent Colonel James Bowie to San Antonio under orders to remove all cannon from the Alamo and blow the place up. Early this month he also ordered Colonel Fannin to dismantle Fort Defiance at Goliad, then fall back on Victoria in preparation to join him east of there. The spell of castled walls, however, falls bewitchingly upon chivalrous men. It enchanted Fannin. It mesmerized Bowie and his partner in command, Wm. Barrett Travis. None of the three could destroy the forts they held. This has made a name for all three—to the sorrow of thousands.

A glance backward through history suggests, however, that our prospects are not quite so bad as they appear. For Houston seems to know that instead of meeting a superior enemy head on, it is best to hop aside as from the path of a charging bull and cut at him as he tires. How was it the Romans nullified Hannibal's unequaled genius for attack? Through a policy of retreat and delay and evasion devised by Fabius Maximus. Employing similar tactics, Arthur Wellesley bled Napoleon's strength away in Spain during the Peninsular War, and Russia in like manner manured her fields with Frankish dead in 1812.

Those who despair of a Fabian Policy assume that only by a succession of victories can a campaign succeed. During our War for Independence the British in the South defeated Nathanael Greene every time they closed with him, but he regularly was able to draw them enough, divide them enough, gouge them enough, and bleed them enough so that at last they despaired of their southern campaign and, leaving Greene in control there, drew away northward toward eventual catastrophe at Yorktown. George Washington never won a battle of any real magnitude—except the last one. With the invader as with the flea, the bedbug, the tick, and the mosquito, the more he sucks our blood the easier he is to kill.

What we do not know for sure is whether Houston *is* a witting Fabian or simply indecisive. But he is no coward. When we were both youngsters in the Creek Wars, he seemed only an unfinished product of the forests, strong and tall, desperately ambitious, flamboyantly brave, and with a striking presentment, though I did not then think much lay behind his good looks, being three years older than he and a captain, whereas he was only an ensign. Here, whatever else is true of him, he has reason to be wary. With Bowie's force gone, and now Fannin's too, his men are left the sole hope of Texas. I take comfort in his reluctance to commit them rashly.

Meanwhile, itching to be with them for a shot or two at that pack of assassins myself, I wonder continually how to inveigle Camilla away toward safety eastward, and the other women with her. Yet I know trying to hurry her would only make her dig in tighter.

That has always been so. When she was nothing but a curly little doll less than three feet high, and adoringly petted, her mother one day let her play with her button box. Camilla took it to her heart like a chest of jewels. The next time it was needed the contumacious little rascal fought like a lynx to keep it. It had been given to her: it was hers. She would not give it up, not one button. The only way to use it was to wait until she fell asleep, then steal from it and replace it until a gradual emptying transferred most of its contents to another box.

The years have taught me subtlety in dealing with her. Still, I recognize that to move her from here while she is so determined to start an honest fortune by seeding large crops is beyond my powers—perhaps beyond the powers of heaven.

CHAPTER XVII

I

Hoping Hill
Good Friday
April 1, 1836

The first day of April Cedric was plowing open rows for corn in a clearing below the bluff while Roberta dropped kernels along the rows and Esau hoed them under. All now and then eyed a fissure westward through woods along Otter Creek, for Camilla had ridden that way after news and mail two hours earlier, and should be back.

The day was drowsily warm. A bulky gust of wind from time to time rolled its weight across the woods, and the heavy, sibilant friction of leaves brought to mind a giant turning over in his sleep. Directly after one of these wide stirrings, Cedric's mule stopped at that end of the field, both ears exclamatorily westward.

Cedric himself could hear nothing new. Otter Creek, fed on spring rains, exulted like a galloping colt. Doves mourned above it, killdeer shrieked in flight along it, and cowbirds in search of grubs conversed sociably as they walked the furrows he had plowed open last. Listening, he felt yawning open in himself a restless, lonesome, far-seeking hunger not unlike homesickness.

He loved the wild spaces around him. He hated city life and never hesitated to say he did. Souls consigned to hell no doubt were mortared into loud and reeking rectangles like those collectively known as New Orleans, and he was positive he never again would be content there long. All the same, listening for the dactyls of loping hooves, he wistfully recollected the clang of horseshoes on cobbles, the clack of revolving hubs, the bawl of hawkers, the music of hammer and forge, the tinkle of peddler's bells, and the intertangling of wit with obscenity, of news with opinions, of candor with humbug, of commerce with plain damned foolishness so characteristic of busy American towns. He had no trouble understanding why so many mortals who complain about city living cling to it all their lives. He missed its variety, good and bad alike. Privily he missed the opportunities for

313

dalliance too, and likewise for exchange of ideas, for enlivening friction of mind on mind—that most of all: the interplay of judgment between cultivated minds. Jupiter, he would rather have an evening's talk with a discerning companion like Yvonne than bed with any female he had met in Texas—excepting only one, and she was too young, too kind, too openhearted for anyone but a villain to despoil. Minds like Yvonne's, of course, were pretty nearly as rare in New Orleans as they were here; he knew few others there whom he would enjoy talking with as well as with Dr. Springfield or Sam Houston, for example—yes, or Perry Allan either.

Tilting his plow down on one side, he sat on it, filled his pipe, and then saw the gold of Oriole's coat flash within the green of the trees, also the maroon of Camilla's riding habit. She slowed to a walk before wading through the creek. As she came up the near bank she rocked into a canter homeward, merely fluttering one glove at him.

"Ay, Milla!" he rose from his plow to call.

"No mail for you, Pa."

"Lord God, *any* mail!" He waved his pipe. "Come here, can't you?"

Though she heeled Oriole his way she blankly resisted the probe of his glance. That she would take him into her confidence in due course he knew very well, and that he meanwhile should not pry, but he was too curious to wait.

"You heard something?"

Roberta and Esau stalled in their work, listening while pretending not to. Camilla drew from her blouse an envelope torn across one end. Recognizing on it Perry's angular script, Cedric pushed a hand upright to wag it sideward.

"Oh, no, I didn't realize . . . Nothing else come?"

"This is all. Here, Pa."

"No, that's *your* affair."

"Take it."

He turned it to examine it as something to be approached with caution. Across the back he discovered:

Mrs. pollmer this come for you las nit. Man brung it says a regular Hurrycane of Terrors blown acrost the hole terratory. Everbodys on the run the army not acsepted. Its time we run too. Weed of sent for you acsept you said so Positive day for yestiddy you dont aim to go. Goodby til better times.

Jake Timberlake

Cedric visualized the "Hurrycane of Terror" sweeping people away like shingles off an unfinished roof. He raised the envelope. "Where'd Jake leave this?"

"Tacked on his door."

With gloom darkening her eyes, she told how the Timberlake cabin had looked—its door nailed shut, its chimney smokeless, its fields as empty as the prairies round about.

"The Nuhn cabin is vacant too," she said, "the Wallace and Mc-Henry cabins the same. All must have gone day or two ago in one caravan." She nodded at the letter. "Read it."

He pulled it open. It was dated at the Brazos River, March 27.

Ever dear Camilla:

I write in very great haste to plead that you leave for Louisiana, and by the quickest means. The surrender of Col. Fannin has required us to retreat to avoid being flanked, and no one now can say how far east the scourge will penetrate.

Please be prompt to move beyond its reach. I know you are brave. I know you therefore will wish to outface what others fear. But the enemy has cavalry, which may elect to move fast, and you should do the same. You can leave any livestock you like at Highhorse Valley along with mine because the fences my soldier friends helped me build will hold them there, and I'm writing Hector to stay and mind both places, nigras being in no danger from either the savages or the Mexicans, as both hope to make them our enemies, not comprehending how loyal to us are hands like him.

The need to warn you away gravels me because there has been so much inspiration in thought of you near. But do at once assure your safety. I urge it strongly. I urge it selfishly too, because thought of you safe will strengthen and preserve me.

From now till we meet again—and ever after,

Yours,
Perry

As the major scanned again the page in his hand, that drowsy giant of wind stretched himself upon his couch in the treetops, a mourning dove grieved as before, and the shriek of another killdeer blew frail above the creek. Nevertheless a secret elation rode the beat of Cedric's pulse. Resisting it, he creased his brows as befit the national calamity. "Mighty unsettling, this new retreat. Good letter, though."

Camilla sat her mare without motion. "It's a wretched, pusillanimous letter."

"Milla! How can you be so unfair? It's *very* good."

"From anyone else it might serve as a letter. Not from him. Three or four times I've cut my heart out whole, wrapped it up in paper addressed to him, and how does he answer back? After all these days on days of silence he says to me, 'Leave me, woman. Go home.' "

"Why, honey, that's not his drift at all! And picture how difficult writing anything whatever must have been! The whole army in a lather, scrambling for a better position, and yet he, with forty-fifty men to look after, he stole the time to warn you away."

"Who *wants* to be warned? And Louisiana of all places! Is there anyone, is there one human soul back there you can name, who will not know I snapped my fingers at a fortune and crossed hundreds of miles of wilderness because Perry Allan is out here? How can I possibly go back there unmarried after that? And how could I ever manage to live there a week without crawling to Edmond again for still more help?"

"Possibly, but with the army outflanked and retreating, and no one around for miles, this is no place for ladies."

"What's more, you're glad of it. Isn't that so?"

"Glad?"

"Don't claim otherwise, Pa. You are. It shows. You're sick of it here? You miss that filthy city?"

Her enormous rightness and matchingly enormous wrongness alike dismayed him. "In some ways it's true, Milla: I *am* glad. But for none of those reasons."

"Then why?"

He hesitated. An awkward revolution of one arm arched his pipe upward. "When the old war horse hears a bugle he . . . he lifts his head." He knocked his pipe clean against a heel. Removing the stem, he blew out a dribble of bitter brown juice. There had developed inside him a gaunt and shaky sensation which he strove to conceal under these trivial rites of smoking.

"As you please, Pa. Go whenever you like."

"Oh, but not till you're safe, Milla! I'm with you till you're safe. After all, you don't have to go clear back to Louisiana, only to join the other families."

"I don't see any real cause to go at all. It's shameful how everyone's running away, and not a Mexican in a hundred miles. It's craven, and ruinous too, and I don't intend to do it. So go when you think you must, Pa. With Roberta and Esau to help, I'll *still* make a crop here."

As her glance swept their way, Roberta compliantly resumed seeding the land. Esau, however, instead of putting his hoe back to work, jogged it toward the bluff above them.

"Miz Milla, look yonna!"

High on a prominence before Hoping Hill, Liz Tipton was signaling with a towel toward slopes along which the trail hairpinned downward. As the major, Camilla, Esau, and Roberta all stared that way a horseman rode out along a curve in that trail, then disappeared where it tunneled into woods toward the bottoms. Another rider crossed the slope behind him. A third and fourth also followed. The outline of the second against the sky was instantly familiar.

Camilla murmured, "Blacky Reed!"

As the times required of every pioneer, Cedric and Esau had weapons handy: a pair of shotguns with which they retreated into thickets where sides of the field converged toward its far corner. While Roberta continued planting corn where she was out of range, Camilla maneuvered Oriole across a path leading back through the woods between the concealed guns, a means of retreat. Such positioning, if it accomplished nothing else, would again confront Blacky with the tactics of hidden strength and notify him that bullying here would always be risky.

From woods opposite to her the four riders emerged one at a time to wade their horses across plowed land. Blacky remained in second place. He rode the same paint gelding with a clover on its face as before, Cedric observed through his screen of brush, and rode in the same brutal slouch. Again he came heavily armed, as did the two behind him. All three were reduced to ciphers, however, by the bearing of the man in front, who carried one carbine in a saddle holster and nothing else, unless the bulges under his coat represented a pair of pocket pistols. This man put his horse straight toward Camilla.

"Hado, lady." His eyes, bold and black, were set far apart. Something long ago had crushed the bridge of his nose, turning the nostrils up like a bulldog's, and his mouth hooked high in a lopsided grin. "Mrs. Palmer, aint you?"

Camilla nodded. "Yes, I am."

He removed his hat, a fine soft felt grandly wide in the brim. In studied languor he tilted his head as knight to lady, exposing a dense, well-greased flourish of black hair. "Delighted, madam!"

She stonily failed to reciprocate. Cedric thought him vaguely familiar, perhaps only because of seeing him pass on a street, for he instantly offered the eye an image that stayed. Up there on horseback he seemed big, being long above the waist, heavy too, and his head was large. He had more jaw than he needed, more jowl, more hair, and more gold on his hands and waistcoat.

Camilla, erect on her sidesaddle, spoke coldly. *"Your* name, please?"

"Rex Cottier, madam." His wide-set eyes looked positive of disarming her. He put his hat back on at a rakish tilt. "I come from Memphis, so maybe the name aint familiar here."

For Cedric, actually, it did jar alive an echo from many months ago. Just where had he heard it first? Sometime or other, for sure, he had deciphered the bizarre combination of *Rex* with *Cottier.*

"Well," said Camilla, "Mr. Reed stopped here to ask after you a couple days back. That a little acquaints us with you, Mr. Cottier, and not to your advantage."

"Who, Blacky?" Rex laughingly waved that away, and the flash of a ring the size of a baby's fist embellished his gesture. "Why, Blacky —he aint what you'd call sweet to look at, no, but reliable in matters of business. I rely on Blacky considerable."

"So? In what business?"

"How?"

"What brings you so far off the road?"

"Yuh, I'm commun to that, lady. First, answer me this." He let his gaze drift in amused wonder. "The men—what's come of them?"

"If you're wanting my father to hear you, speak up. He'll hear you."

His eyes scored the woods. Across the embroidered silk of his waistcoat, from pocket to pocket, lay a gold chain with links as fat as kernels of corn. A tug at it fished out a dainty pearl-handled knife and a Chinese earspoon which squirmed before him like minnows baiting hooks for bass. His other hand negligently drew a Havana from high in his waistcoat, exposing the slicked handle of a knife in his belt and a pistol by his armpit. He ceased eying the woods to cut a wedge from one end of the cigar.

"Mean they're close by?"

"Shrewd of you to realize that, Mr. Cottier."

"Durn!" He ignited a locofoco by dipping it into a tube of acid, applied it to his cigar, then held the match upright and let the breeze worry the flame away. On his hand was a tattoo half hidden by a soiled but costly cuff, and in addition that ostentatious ring. What the tattoo might be Cedric was too far away to make out, but this combination of tattoo, ring, embroidered vest, and oddly evocative name —an impression of past acquaintance with them glided by like the scent of smoke blown invisibly thin. Meanwhile Cottier dropped another scorning look along the woods. "Seems queer—father run and hide, leavun a girl and her wench to meet strange men alone."

Down in his ambush Cedric did feel silly. His maneuver might serve well against Blacky and his like; but he thought Cottier less apt to overmeasure what he could not see. Nevertheless Camilla played it for all it was worth.

"My father was an Indian fighter. So was his father before him. He fought the Creeks with Andrew Jackson, and the British too. That taught him that every weapon out of sight is worth three in the open. Furthermore he's a prime shot, Mr. Cottier, a celebrated shot."

A thrill of pride in her lanced through Cedric's ribs. There on that superb golden mare she was a sight to behold, straight and able, as distant from the likes of Cottier as the moon is from a howling dog. She had stature, by God! She had more to her than any such father as he was could rightly hope his daughter would possess.

But Cottier guffawed around his cigar. His mare, a mincingly elegant black, trod the ground uneasily until he jerked up her rein to quiet her. "So you class me along with savages! By ginger, that's rare!" Lipping his Havana all the way over to the highest corner of his mouth, he waggled his head. "This aint—speakun perfuckly plain—this aint what you might call a very genteel or high-tone sort of hospitality."

"Now aren't you a little in advance of us, sir, criticizing our hospitality before any whatsoever is offered?"

His invincible grin slipped a bit, after which he hooked it back up around his cigar. Whatever retort he was concocting, however, she headed it off.

"Complete strangers, Mr. Cottier, would be received here as friends until proved otherwise. We think association with Mr. Reed does pretty well prove you otherwise."

"Now Blacky, mam, the sole and single reason Blacky come back this way is to show me the lay of the land and help a bit."

"Help with what?"

He expanded his widely separated eyes. "Journey like this, a man needs hands."

"That is to say, *guns.*"

"Yuh, puttun it frankly, guns. With Mexicans loose on the country, with savages paintun for war, and there's gangs of white rascals, too, scourun the land, fattnun on people like you and me that just want to go our own way and mind our own business."

"Whatever *that* is."

"How?"

"Whatever your business is, Mr. Cottier."

"Why, I'm buyun property."

"Oh?"

"That's right. Some one place, some another."

To land-poor Texans no subject was more enthralling than the market value of the acres around them. Cottier devoted the very nicest attention to his cigar in confidence that Camilla would swim to the bait. She did look tempted.

"For yourself or a syndicate?"

"A sort of a syndicate. But what's bought, I buy."

"However, you still haven't said what brings you *here.*"

"To be perfeckly honest and plain, Mrs. Palmer, I fancy *this* place."

"Why, you've hardly seen it. You've hardly ridden halfway across it. More than that, how do you know the title's sound?"

"Oh, I know, all right. I know. That's part of the scoutun Blacky done: first step I took was sent him ahead to copy titles in San Flippy."

Camilla, startled by his openness, sat her mare in silence, swaying adaptably while Oriole lifted hoof after hoof to strike at gadflies.

"Main question," Rex resumed, "is whether your price suits the times."

"No, we've no price. This place is not for sale, thank you all the same."

"Now don't say that, lady. Aint you heard the mournful tidings? Thunderbolts of disaster's struck the whole country so hard the government's run off, and the army too. Everbody's drainun away like water down a funnel. Times like these—why, in all Texas there's no such thing as land that aint for sale."

"*Here* is such land, sir. You're on it this minute, land not for sale."

"But don't you realize, my friend? Why, a few weeks from now any land around here is liable to fetch pretty near nothun."

"Yes, I realize well enough. But what I don't understand is why, thinking that, *you* should want it."

"Frankly, madam, I'm a gambler. I figure one of these days—"

"So do I! Sir, I figure too. I gamble on this land. Who is General Sam Houston? A Tennessean, a stanch old friend of the President's. I suspect Mr. Jackson keeps an eye on Sam Houston. Why else should he have General Gaines mustering troops near Natchitoches? Mr. Cottier, is that why your syndicate sends you?"

Jollity shook through Cottier. His eyes invited his companions to share in his amusement. Blacky remained humorless as a smoked pot, but the other two compliantly grinned.

"Wrong but shrewd. For a lady, that's real cute. But, no, I just come to pick out some choice places while a buyer with cash can be real choosy."

"As I've told you—"

"No-no, Mrs. Palmer!" He raised a hand against her saying more. Though thickly strong, that hand, it kept his Havana nipped between thumb and finger like a bonbon. "I don't want no answer today. Tell you what we better do." To emphasize that his conclusion was taking shape, he straightened his reins. "You give it your best thought a few days while I look around elsewhere. Then I'll stop by another time." He tipped his hat. Again the flaunting flourish of greased hair beautified his bow. "Until then, lady, good day."

He spurred away at a singlefoot. One of his black's rear hooves toed outward like a cow's, giving her quarters a mincing, stylized twitch. Cedric noted from cover how the iron of her shoes flashed above the black loam she crossed. To him it seemed curious how that union of style and earth and flashing iron summarized Rex.

"Mam," Blacky remarked as he yanked his paint's head up, "he give you good advice: sell."

The rider next to him, proportioned like a scarecrow, pursed his lips to spit. "Be smart to sell quick, mam."

"Hank, that's Gospel," said the fourth man, evidently Hank's brother. He turned her the vane of a chinless face beaked like a rooster's. "She don't sell, and the day'll dawn when she'll mourn the failure."

They turned to follow Rex. His singlefooter already had carried him to the fissure cut through the woods by the trail west. Another giant of wind, tilting the trees, turned their leaves until the silver underside flicked upward like the iron on his mare's hooves. Afterward both

together, that iron and that silver, flickered repeatedly within Cedric
where his fears were at home.

2

At bedtime he took a sentinel tour around the yard. A downpour
before supper had left the ground spongy. The air, warmer tonight,
was heavily damp. Along its current the weeping wail of a screech owl
quavered, and faint, spooky syllables of wild geese propelled northward by the rise of spring came down through the dark.

He smiled to think how portentously others might read these omens.
But there were favorable signs also. A concealed moon brightened the
clouds to the east, and his circuit through the grove brought against
that lighter sky the reassuring rectangle of the house. Its upright logs,
veranda, second story, and chimneys of stone gave it character.
Though most of it was dark, squares of decently curtained light still
marked Camilla's room above the parlor. Those windows of hers, as
he eyed them, went black, declaring the peace of sleep close by her,
and the silhouette of the house became more solid.

His walk carried him around to the family lookout above the bluff.
From there he discovered a glow on the horizon to the southwest.
Unlike hidden moonlight, it was not diffused through clouds. Instead,
it shimmered upon them, a yellowish red.

Something beyond a high undulation in the prairie must be on fire.
Wet as the night was, it could not be grass burning, not a canebrake
either. Then a cabin or barn? The Timberlake place was in about that
area. This morning, however, Camilla had reported the Timberlakes
gone at least one day. Cabins with cold hearths and damp walls do
not catch fire, not by accident, and neither do empty barns.

Out of today's experience floated an image of Rex Cottier holding
up a locofoco to let the wind blow off its flame, and of iron flicking
beneath his mare as she carried him off southwest. Without any pedes-
trian logic, Cedric took the glow to be a warning posted for everyone
here at Hoping Hill to see.

But why trouble Camilla or anyone else about it? Timberlakes' was
four and a half miles away. What good would come of riding there
tonight? Cedric had the aches of a day's hard work to sleep off. To-

morrow would be soon enough to investigate, and likewise to tell Camilla.

All the same he took the worry to bed with him. It hounded sleep away from him a wearingly long while.

3

Timberlakes'
Saturday Morning
April 2, 1836

They found the Timberlake home a skeleton eaten out from within. So much was left only because it had been too wet to burn well. Nowhere could Cedric find signs of much effort to make the burning seem accidental. Instead, several clues proclaimed that men weaponed with fire were in the neighborhood to have their way. The fire evidently had begun in ticking ripped from the mattresses, for the walls had burned most thoroughly above heaps of ash where the beds had stood. Across these heaps lay burned fractions of other furniture—stools, a table, a washstand, a loom, all presumably thrown on to assure a strong blaze.

He noted with surprise that Camilla resisted and disallowed such evidence, though it turned her pale. Back in Louisiana she always had deafened herself to any speculation that someone deliberately had burned her barns, and to interpret the ruin before her here as an evil intention aimed at her was still unthinkable.

"You see for yourself," she remarked, "how bad the roof burned. I venture a thunderbolt smashed right through the ridgepole."

"Think so?" Cedric let his eyes review the peculiarities of the ashes before them. "Curious how every stick in the place got piled together to help the fire along. Been a good while, honey, since I've seen lightning that mean."

The distress this generated in her carried her out to examine the yard.

"Pa, look here!" She was bending over tracks in a patch of naked ground. All were from unshod hooves. "Didn't their horses wear shoes?"

"Uhm. At any rate Cottier's did."

"Yes, Blacky's too, and the rest must have, though I didn't observe." She looked relieved. "You see, it was only Indians—a few braves riding through!"

Only! He pitied this preference for roving savages. "Horseshoes aren't hard to pull off, Camilla, and reset again later. Cunning men would leave room for doubt about just who's to blame."

She blinked. Her relief faded. During another circuit of the place her eyes rapidly reassessed every clue. Untended chickens followed after her from around a shacky little henhouse, alert for table scraps unserved since the Timberlakes left, and a cow grazing with a calf beside her lifted her head to low.

"Since when," he asked, "did savages have so little taste for chicken and beef that they'd leave all these behind?"

"Pa, you do annoy me sometimes. I suffer enough from *being* a fool without you exposing it so plain."

4

The sky after dark reddened again, as he had feared it would, this time nearer than the night before—above the vacated Nuhn homestead three miles west, the sole place between Timberlakes' and Hoping Hill. The flame at its height was visible from the home bluff.

Dawn of Easter Morning, April 3, brought across the prairies a pure golden light befitting the holiday, but its glory was spoiled by what he and Camilla discovered at Nuhns'—a duplication of the scene at Timberlakes' except that, besides tracks of unshod hooves, they discovered bootmarks which no one had bothered to rub out. The message coded in fire and footprint stalked their thoughts after they returned home. Hereafter, they agreed, someone must stand guard around the yard every hour every night.

Monday all hands planted potatoes on level acres near the garden. Liz Tipton dropped cuttings for Cedric while he hoed them under, Junior Tipton the same for Camilla, and Harold for Roberta. Meanwhile Esau, driving one mule on a plow, opened rows for all. The only person on the place not of much use was Buddy, the smallest Tipton, who rode on Esau's mule.

Liz stopped often to nurse her back in martyred recollection of a fall two weeks ago when helping Camilla whitewash the kitchen.

Every now and then she reckoned "this mizry that's on me" never would let her hold out till evening. That was her way of begging for another pill, and Cedric thought Camilla astute, though a little late, in neglecting to heed her. The pills given her at first to ease her back were laudanum, which he himself, out of a soldier's acquaintance with accident and dysentery, had included among the drugs brought from New Orleans, for he had seen recruits wracked with "runs" which nothing else would quiet, and others with broken bones or gouged flesh who pleaded with comrades to blow their brains out until eased by some form of opium: if calomel was king in the frontier medicine kit, opium in one disguise or another reigned as queen. Camilla, however, too often had indulged Liz's whines for more, until it became apparent that her back was hurting her much less than spiritless boredom and hunger for Ev's doting attention. So today her complaints brought her hardly a glance. She would drop potato cuttings before Cedric a spell, then unbend to scold Buddy or Junior or Harold for dawdling, after which she would rub her spine, willfully afflicted, her bonnet open toward this or that horizon. Suddenly she straightened high, forgetful of her back, to stare at a rise toward the northeast.

"Lan alive!"

Rex Cottier was singlefooting across that rise, with Blacky behind him, also the scarecrow called Hank, and the latter's brother. Rex spurred directly toward the potato patch, where he brought his mare mincingly around sideward near Camilla.

"Afternoon, folks. How yall today?"

Liz seemed to think anyone so awesome ought to be answered. She did so in shrinking gentility. "Afternoon, sir."

Cedric nodded and grunted a hado because his own sense of fitness would not let him ignore any visitor, no matter who.

Cottier's wide-set black eyes enlivened in return. "Hadado to *you*, sir." His mastiff nose sniffed while he pondered the sky, dulled today by clouds of many densities. "Smells like more cranky weather's commun."

"Maybe."

"Anything new hereabout, sir, since we seen you last?"

"Wel-ll, only that some pack of sneaky damn rascals put two cabins to the match."

"Tsk!" Cottier sketched an attitude of mournful fellowship. "We heard tell they did, yessir. Tragic thing."

"Where'd you hear it?"

Cottier rocked his big head northward. "Couple wayfarers told us they seen the burnt ruins." His eyes took pleasure in the advantage of having thought of everything. "Said it looked pitiful, all them ruins." His head tilted indolently toward the three men sitting their horses behind him. "Member how they told it, boys?"

The sooted iron of Blacky's face did not alter, but the scarecrow nodded, the man called Hank.

"Mighty sad."

"Heartbreakun," his brother agreed.

Cedric's hoe worked jerkily, drawing loam over Liz's potato cuttings. Watching the blade slice the earth, he recognized that a hoe *could* be used to kill a man.

"Anything I don't like, it's fire," Cottier added. "Awful hard to control, day *or* night—fire. All that work puttun a home together, and then a spark or two loose somewhere"—he snapped his fingers— "whole place goes up like that." His hand groped sensually along the chain crossing the embroidery on his waistcoat. "Nights in particular. Fire moves fast on windy nights. People asleep and fire gets started, who knows if they get out alive or not?"

His index finger looped around the chain to draw forth his penknife and earspoon. Toward the latter he tilted his head and applied it, his thick least finger hooking upward. Today Cedric was near enough to make out that the tattoo on that hand was a burial wreath crossed by the word *MA*. His heart kicked his breath out: for an instant he again heard Perry describe such a tattoo on a similar man after a visit to the Benevolent Loan Bank of Louisiana last October.

"Mr. Cottier," he put in, "where you say you're from?"

"Memphis, sir." Cottier withdrew his earspoon to thumb it clean. "There's my headquarters—Memphis."

"But worked a spell in New Orleans?"

"No, Memphis."

"Seems to me I heard tell of you in New Orleans."

"Well, I'm from Memphis." Through a high-sided grin he added, "Tickles me to hear I might of got celebrated far off as Nor Leans, but my town's Memphis." His glance withdrew from Cedric to fix upon Camilla. "Never seen a neighborhood lonesomer or godforsakernern this here, lady. Anytime trouble strikes in country this solitary, who can you look to? Aint the capability nowhere to stop such tricks. No help near; no law to back you either. Awful lonesome place."

"Since you find it so trying, sir"—Camilla straightened erect with

both hands high on her hoe, the poke of her bonnet toward him—
"why don't you travel on?"

"Yes, Cottier." Cedric, precisely because he was deeply, dangerously shaken, undertook to sound droll. "What keeps you?"

"Business first, friends. I come to make you my offer, and it's worth
your waitun awhile to hear. For this place, as is, I'll give you twenty
thousun dollars."

The major gaped. That figure came to more than two dollars an
acre, a respectable offer in normal times, and bewilderingly generous
now. But how could he make Camilla recognize that it had poison in it
merely by telling about a conversation with Perry six months ago? He
leaned on his hoe, hoping an instinctive wariness would restrain her.

"One thousun I'll put up right here and now, cash money." Cottier
began tending his other ear, grandly casual about it. "For the balance
I'll give you a draff payable in Nor Leans thirty days from date."

Again Cedric's breath hung in his throat. The terms sounded marvelous, and in a sense they were: for a mere thousand dollars she could
be drawn back into Louisiana, where Beaufait would enjoy the legal
right to apply the debts she owed him in retiring the balance on Hoping Hill. Thus he would get this property for just one thousand, and
likewise bring her last two slaves back within reach of his process
servers. It all fit together neatly; but Cedric, in fairness, had to discount
it on the ground that he was simply guessing.

"Come now, Mrs. Palmer." Cottier's eyes measured her, pleased
by her astonishment. "Aint that handsome? What you say?"

"No, thank you."

His grin teetered unequally. "Suppose I raise it to fifteen hundred,
cash in hand."

"No."

"Two thousand then."

"No. What I've said to you I'll always say to you: *no.*"

He dwelt upon the faded gingham of her bonnet, upon a patch in
her apron, also upon her shoes, once suitable for wear to fashionable
outings, but now a mud-caked ruin. "Things the way they look, *no*
don't seem like a very bright answer."

"All the same, that *is* my answer."

"Don't you realize that twenty thousun dollars—?"

"I realize it's a fine price, but I won't sell to you at any figure."

"Madam, that don't make no sense whatsoever. It aint a reasonable
way to talk."

"My reasons, though only a woman's, seem to me sufficient. First, I love this place and do not choose to leave it. Second, I suspect you of arson. Under no circumstances can I ever deal with you or make you welcome here. Trails lead away from here two ways." She tilted her hoe northeast and southwest. "Take your pick."

"Now, Mrs. Palmer—"

"No further talk, please. Just go."

"Excellent advice," Cedric observed.

Cottier's grin slipped. "That your final say?" His upturned nostrils and overdone jaw dominated his face.

"It is."

His eyes remained upon her, black and round and motionless. Suddenly his big head rocked toward his men. "Well, boys, you see what it's like when you try to be nice to people."

Blacky jerked his paint awake. "I seen before."

By a toe on one side, a tickle with his spur on the other, Rex twisted his mare around so that he could contemplate Hoping Hill. His eyes roved to the barn, then back over the house from end to end. Watching this, Cedric thought its fort-solid walls flimsy as paper. Although Cottier angled his next talk down at Camilla, he continued pondering the house.

"You're right clever, madam, a well-spoken lady, but not far-seen." He gathered up his reins. "We give you ample opportunity to profit, but you aint far-seen."

5

Hoping Hill
Friday Afternoon
April 8, 1836

Two adults at a time during the following nights maintained four-hour watches from bedtime till dawn, either Cedric or Esau patrolling the perimeter of the yard while Camilla or Roberta watched indoors from a circuit of lightless windows. Tubs of water they kept handy on each side of the house, and every shotgun, pistol, and rifle freshly primed. But nothing happened: possibly one or more of the four riders had scouted the place and concluded that a strike here would be too risky.

The rains returned often until Friday, which brought intervals of condoling sunlight. Cedric, out with his shotgun that afternoon to replenish the family meat supply, went prowling through timber shoring a high sea of prairie eastward from home. Intimacy with the woods refreshed him, recalling his boyhood: he experienced that resurgence of life which men gain from hunting, from taking life. Near the end of the day, however, where a deer trail crossed a brook, he discovered tracks of shod horses fresh that afternoon. Among them was one toeing outward like a cow's.

Consternation knocked him weak. The ghostly terror one footprint roused in Robinson Crusoe must have resembled this. The tendons in his legs went slack and sat him down on a log. He tried to convince himself that what bothered him was lack of sleep, but honesty would not let him give the wave of weakness washing through him any tamer name than fear.

To defy it, he considered following the tracks for better clues. With the sun already low, however, every shadow around him was long and black. Twilight would come soon. Tonight of all nights, he should hurry home to get everything ready before darkness fell.

Once there, he could think of little to do beyond what it was the family's habit to do each night—top off every tub and rain barrel with water from the spring; fill all vessels and place them handy near the doors; load fresh charges in the firearms; tie the mares at a rack behind the house and arrange the saddles close by for quick use. He also planned to post himself on patrol during the darkest watch before moonrise, which he thought would be crucial.

Meanwhile he took care that the wasting effect of worry should not spread beyond himself. The camouflage of gay and gabby case he wore at suppertime deceived everyone except Roberta. Of his brother's blood, she was uncannily aware of whatever troubled him. While she padded barefoot around the table, serving everyone, her clairvoyant brown eyes repeatedly probed him. She had the intelligence, however, not to question him until he went out to begin his watch. With a pan of table scraps for the pigs as excuse, she then followed him into the backyard.

"Mahs Ceedic, what you seen?"

"Never mind, Berta."

"Look to me like you mindun."

"Go finish your work and rest."

"Looks like you seen a evil sign."

"It's late, Berta."

"What you seen, Mahs Ceedic?"

Meek though her tone was, she remained stubbornly in his way, the pan of scraps before her in both hands. He was tempted to bark at her, but esteem and affection for her helped him relent.

"Tracks of shod hooves in those woods eastward. Fresh tracks."

She stood motionless there in the dark, eyes enlarged and rimmed with white. At last she shifted the pan of scraps around to rest on one hip. "Let me watch too, sir."

"Very well, Berta. You stand the first watch indoors while I'm out here. That's the time they'd favor, before moonrise, the darkest hours."

"Most likely, yessir."

"But not a word, mind. No use spoiling others' sleep. We'll let them refresh for the end of the night and for tomorrow."

"Deed so, yessir."

About to remind her to watch from different windows in succession around the house, he held back. She had brains. She knew how to watch as well as anyone.

"Anything you suspect at all, whether you're sure or not, give me the sign." This was to hang a towel over a window sill on each side of the house so that, no matter where he was on his circuit, he would see it. "I'll slip up the minute I can manage."

6

The others, in lying down, kept their clothes on as they had each night, but only in grudging prudence: they no longer believed that *this* night they might have to rush from a house on fire to fight that fire. When the last window went black Cedric was crouching by a rock above the family spring forty strides west of the barn, careful to project no silhouette of himself against the skyline.

Lack of sleep kicked rhythmic aches through his temples, but the night itself seemed free of evil. Stars on a wing of Pegasus glittered through an opening among boughs overhead like candles within a shrine. Tides of wind from the south brought around him a lulling, murmurous warmth. The scent of grass plump with juice enriched the air, of oak buds seductive to bees, of wild peach in the draws and bottoms. He could detect nothing to distrust except those surges of wind, which were growing as the night grew. Off above the house a swirl of boughs scoured the Great Dipper: they stirred up his fears as they did the leaves, for men could slip up unheard during the sough of trees so tossed around.

He too, though, could use the wind to cover his advance as he crept to the barn, an arrangement of poles overlaid with prairie hay. From there he scrambled across the backyard to the poultry shed, built like the barn of poles blanketed with dried grass.

Because hurrying that far bent double had made his head thump, he stood up by the shed to rest. The grass, exhaling its fragrance as it took his weight, revived memories of his youth when he had stolen naps in hay—and other delights. A goose inside the shed yammered once. Two hens quarreled as they shifted at roost. After that he could hear only the wind. Waiting for it to subside, when he would have to listen with every sense keen, he pulled off his hat, hung it on the double-barreled shotgun standing between his feet and let his head rock back against the shed. The upright and weighty feel of his gun reassured him: it carried a charge and a half of greased buckshot in each barrel, and experience as an Indian fighter had taught him that a double-barrel well loaded with blue whiskers is a firmer friend in any tight corner than the best rifle made. Besides, he was handy with it: whatever he leveled it at would need uncommon luck to escape unhit. Resting in that knowledge, he never did hear the wind die away.

Alarm without definition shocked him awake. At his start a bat squeaked an arm's length above him and flapped spectrally away. A choir of novice frogs sang below the bluff. One of the mares munching prairie hay near the house scraped a halter buckle against the rack where they were tied. Then nothing—until the ghostly laughter of a coyote shivered a thinning distance away toward Highhorse Valley.

When the last note tapered off, his ear anticipated some answer from coyotes nearer the Hill. There was none, and he realized that none of the big canny hunters had signaled from anywhere nearby since an hour or so past dark—no coyote, no lynx, no cougar, no lobo. Why not, unless lurking men kept them away?

How long had he slept? He could not tell, but the moon, which would be old tonight, was not yet up. Tiptoeing around the poultry shed to scan the yard, he made out against the black mass of the house a patch of white beneath a rear window. A towel!

God *damn!* All these nights he had kept alert, and not one signal.

Now, in the sole hour when his toughness failed, the moment to act had come.

To show he had seen the towel, to show also the direction of his approach to the house so that no one within would shoot him, he threw two pebbles. They clicked on the roof, then dribbled down over the slabs like rolled dice.

But he could not cross the yard to the house until another wave of wind rose from the valley. Just now the yard was so quiet that, although his pulse was hammering his eardrums, he could hear flabbily adenoidal snores from Mrs. Tipton inside an open window.

A nervous impulse to laugh tickled his belly, for Liz complained every dawn that that mizry in her back hadn't let her sleep a wink, though every night she snored like a ripsaw. The joke had its bitter side. This morning Camilla had discovered a depletion in the stock of laudanum: while everyone else had been working in the fields, leaving the cookery to Liz, those pills had been consoling her through her loneliness. Camilla lectured her severely, locked and hid the medicine chest, and put Roberta in the kitchen in her place, working Liz in the fields so relentlessly all day despite her whines about her back that tonight she had fallen asleep directly after the dishes were done.

At last wind again began flowing over the bluff. Once its swish had grown loud, he hurried at a crouch straight toward the back door. Dimly he could make out Roberta's apron. She bent toward him as he slipped inside. Her whisper was hasty and harsh.

"Mahs Ceedic, you cough?"

"Not me, no."

"I heard *some* man cough."

"Yes?"

"Deed so. A choky cough like through a hand."

Camilla appeared beside her in the dark: his pebbles on the roof had sufficed to wake her. Brushing sleep from her eyes and hair, straightening her dress, she stood silently, guessing what they had said before from their whispers now.

"Sure it was a man's cough, Berta? Not one of the mares?"

"Deed not, nosir. It come from out front."

"When?"

"A piece back. First, maybe ten minutes back, then again three-four minutes back."

"Exactly where?"

"Soun first like maybe from Miz Milla's garden. Second time, I don't know—soun tereckly out in front—"

"Pa," Camilla broke in, "shouldn't we wake Esau?"

"Sh-h!" He gripped her arm, but as much to sober and steady himself as her. "Wake him, yes. Wake everyone. But keep them all in here to help you at the windows. Leave scouting the yard to me. More than one outside, we'd be shooting each other first thing we know."

7

Out in back again, he tiptoed around the house to the front corner eastward. The wind fingered the logs beside him. His daughter liked to think Hoping Hill a frontier castle, a fort. It was. With the bluff as an outwork and these walls impervious to arrows or bullets, it permitted the daydreams of security forts induce. What apter reason is there for calling a fort a keep, he wondered, than because your enemies can contain you in it? Lurking beyond range, they can let it hold you until you are too exhausted, neglectful, or famished to withstand attack.

At a low crouch he pushed forward through the grove to a hackberry tree by the trail from the bottoms. Face near ground level to project everything against the skyline, he could see nothing but rocks, stumps, wind-stirred bushes, and uneasy trees. He fancied, however, that he smelled a trace of sweated horse. Or did he? After a few sniffs he could detect little except the must of leaves fallen seasons ago and the juice of grass crushed under his boots.

The wind ebbed. He could hear the trill of a cricket, the hungering whine of mosquitoes, and the creak of a stool behind a window in the parlor. From deep down a ravine before the yard he thought he heard a metallic click. It sounded like a snaffle chewed by a horse, though perhaps only because he thought he had smelled horse. Before he could be sure, it stopped.

What he heard next jarred through him a start deeper than if a panther had screamed—a grunted oath from over around the bluff. It was punctuated by a rock bumping through brush: someone must have slipped while climbing toward the yard.

At once he saw how to win an advantage. The bluff was composed of deep ledges of limestone one above the other, each wide enough to walk on back here by the ravine, but narrowing around toward the front of the yard, and he knew well where a man could climb from one to another. By stealing around that way on a lower ledge he would project anyone higher against the sky, a clean target.

As soon as the breeze revived he crept down to the second ledge below the rim. Well around the bluff a wind-warped oak rose from a battlement of stones and shrubs bordering the yard. A ladder of toe-holds ascended strata of limestone to that oak. His aim was to climb up there before the wind should die, but the footing narrowed until one boot could hardly pass the other. Then the wind relaxed. He had to freeze, holding to a shrub rooted in a crevice above his head. With the other hand he propped himself on his shotgun. Muting his gasps for breath, he grimaced at the fancy that Texas had revived his youth. The strain of haste and danger had his legs trembling, his lungs starved. His heart bumped around inside his chest like a stone in a shaken drum.

A twig on the bush supporting him crushed inside his grip. Oddly, that provoked no sound or movement above him. He also thought it odd not to have seen anyone up there against the sky along his way around the bluff, for he was about as far around now as any man could go. The silence everywhere suggested that whoever had grunted was already up beyond the rocks bordering the yard, perhaps advancing now to fire the house. During the next gust it would be imperative to get up there.

A wide, liquid swish welled up around him, abrupt and boisterous. He crept up the ladder of toeholds, his gun baffling his legs, until the boulders at the base of the oak were just above his hand. At that point the gust blew out as suddenly as it had begun. He had to stay where he was, leaning against the eroded top layer of limestone.

A storm decades ago had broken the oak, leaving it stooped and angular. Its contest against the right of time to destroy all things that live was almost done. Its boughs clutched at a thinning growth of leaves like the senile at memories of years long spent.

But might it not outlast him? During explorations hereabout he had found in the limestone seashells which recalled Aristotle's conclusion from a similar discovery: eons ago marine waters must have lapped here, heaping together enough detritus of extinguished life to form this cliff where now the only tides were of wind. The gouge of stone against his chest reminded him how vulnerable flesh is always. A little mistake or two now and he would sink under oceans of time to partake of the oblivion of those mollusks whose vacated armor composed Hoping Hill.

His reverie was interrupted by the crunch of a boot on leaves. Panic flashed through him: that footstep was not above but well below him. He had failed to foresee that his adversary, instead of remaining high, might climb down to target *him* against the stars—or that there might be two men, one above, one below.

A further possibility: the coughs Roberta reported might have been deliberate, also the oath he himself had heard, the loosened stone too, and even this footstep. Each sound might have been devised to decoy him away from other prowlers sent to fire the house.

Through the woods down near Otter Creek a fresh wind drifted toward him, urging him to be quick, to decide just where to move under its noise. When it reached full velocity he was still undecided, still motionless.

A shriek spiraled out of the house. Another and another followed, a few naked words thrown into the darkness and whirled by the wind. From where he lay against the cliff he could see nothing above him but the oak, with Orion the Hunter astride it, but he understood: fire! He *had* been tricked. Despite all he knew of fighting by stealth, he had let a feint draw him out of the way.

He thrust his weight up toward the oak, heedless of whoever was behind him. His boots slipped. He tore his jacket on a root, his shins on stone, his face on brush. None of that troubled him a fraction so much as the agony of discovering how thoroughly he had been duped.

What he saw beyond the oak knocked his breath back down his throat. The house stood forth dead black against shimmering, wind-whipped red, not afire itself, but bodied forth by fire behind it. A high balloon of light reached up among tree tops above where the poultry shed was—or had been. Mingled with shouts and cries from Camilla, Esau, Roberta, Liz and the Tipton boys was a hideous squawking and skirling of hens, geese, ducks, and roosters roasting alive as their shelter burned.

Much nearer, a tiny light, cupped in a pair of hands, flickered like a firefly where the veranda joined the front wall of the house. Trivial though it looked, he saw that as the real strike. Cottier's strategy at last could be deciphered: one man had been baiting him over the bluff, while another behind the house lit the poultry shed to draw the family out that way, and a third ran in to fire the house in front, leaving a fourth ready to bring horses up from the ravine for their escape. That hand-held flame by the veranda curved toward a heap of grass against the house, disappearing behind the angle of a shoulder. Briefly it illumined a familiar hat and profile—Blacky Reed's.

He whipped his gun up beside the oak and fired fast, trusting the load of buckshot to spray wide at that distance. A wrenching spasm whirled Blacky away, a howl grating in his throat.

Like an echo to his own shot, Cedric heard an explosion down behind him. A bruising blow hit him low in the back, kicking him forward so hard that he fell face down. A weight pressed through his back into his guts, a pain without sharp edges, but the worst, the most nauseating, the most terrifying pain his years of life had ever brought him.

Through the grieving of blown trees, through the ground his body pressed, he could hear feet stumbling at a run toward the groin of the ravine where he had smelled horse. Hooves began thudding up that ravine toward the side of the yard. The tortures in his back were leaping up to claw his brain, but having got off one good shot and spoiled the perfection of Cottier's scheme sustained him a little and helped him resist a faint.

The gun in his hands had a second charge unused. In veteran conviction that defeat is final only for those who stop fighting, he blinked his vision clear so that, lying there on his side, he could spray buckshot at whoever was scrambling out of the ravine. He aimed along a gap through the trees toward Camilla's garden, holding the aim at the skyline until the silhouette of a man riding one horse and leading another crossed it. He then closed his grip on the trigger.

The smoke of that shot, and the blinding convulsion it jarred through him, prevented him from making out anything more about its result than that the hoofbeats wildly altered. That seed of light by the veranda was growing, however: tendrils of fire had begun climbing the wall, a yellow, wind-blown ivy. Though still so small that he himself might finish it if only he could run there *now,* it was growing fast.

Somehow he *must* reach it. He strained to rise but could not: the attempt drove agony from his hip deep into his bowels. Nevertheless, digging at the fibrous, juicy sod of the lawn, he began clawing, writhing, forward. At each gasp for breath he shouted as loud as his stifled lungs would let him.

"Camilla! Ay, Camilla! Camilla!"

But the farther he tried to crawl, the heavier the gnawing weight on his back became; and the harder he tried to shout, the less he could see that blaze through mists dimming his eyes. He tried rolling to crawl on the other side. With the twist of his body a pouncing wolf of pain crushed the last shout from his lungs.

8

The wind, when next he became aware of it, seemed to have become water, the cooling sea, the deathless sea. Lapping over his face, it cut off his breath.

"No more, Berta," his daughter said. "He's choking."

The splashing of water stopped. Above him he could make out Roberta against the stars, a bucket in hand. Someone else was kneeling by his shoulder, feeling for the beat of his heart.

"Camilla?"

"Yes, dear one." Her lips came down to his forehead. They felt infinitely tender; they had in them the quiver of crying. "Lie still, Pa."

"They gone?"

"Driven off, yes."

"The fire, honey?"

"Out. The worst's all over."

"House burn?"

"No, safe. We heard the shots. We heard you call and got here in time."

"By God, safe!"

"Lie still, Pa. Don't strain at all. I'll get you to a doctor if it's the very last thing I ever do."

One hand stroked his brow to rub it dry. A turn of the head showed him the black silhouette of the house, still as solid as before. Safe! He could hear people running, hear thrown splashes, and he understood that Esau and the Tiptons were still rushing water to that spot by the veranda even though nothing was left of the fire but steam.

CHAPTER XVIII

I

En Route Southeast
Saturday Noon
April 9, 1836

"Camilla . . ."

"Yes, Pa?"

From behind the brougham, where she had been examining a line of three pack mules, Camilla trotted Swallow forward beside her father. They were hauling him on a litter mattressed with pillows and extending through both the brougham's doors, which had to be left open. Its jostle announcing the start of their journey had aroused him. Stupefied though he was by suffering and laudanum, he raised his head to ask about the lockable case for his journal.

"Bring my writing, did you?"

"Deed we did." She flung one end of a sunlit yellow scarf into the wind behind her shoulder, and her smile urged him to look less troubled. "It's in there beside you."

"Land map and compass?"

"Yes, of course."

"Uhm. Soon be lost without those." And after a difficult breath: "Locofocos?"

"All we possess."

"Utensils and food?"

"Packed on the mules."

"Good." His eyes weighed shut. He forced them open to focus on a rifle and pistol in her saddle holsters. "The other weapons, where're they?"

"Right inside there." She nodded at baggage crowding the carriage seats above the level of his waist and joining across him. "Where they'll stay dry. Medicine chest too. *And* the Bible."

"Well, can't say I'd thought of that myself."

"We also brought the evidence—that earspoon, penknife, and broken watch chain Roberta found down in the ravine. Most impor-

338

tant, though, we've got all we need to save you, Pa, and don't you imagine I'll let anything on this earth prevent it."

"No, honey. There comes a time when *nothing* will save us unless we have the means of salvation within us—and the wish to attain it."

Astonished, she met his gaze a moment, then pulled Swallow around toward the mules again as if only talk of material things had passed between them.

2

Sunday began in a sulk. The air was moody, hazy, still, hot. Liz Tipton, because of whimpers that her own back told her "what mortal torment yuh daddy suffers," was allowed to ride inside the brougham among stacks of effects which bad weather might spoil. With the exception of Esau on the dickey, driving a span of harnessed mules, everyone else rode a horse or mule—Camilla on Swallow, Roberta on Oriole, and the Tipton boys on three relief mules which also carried packs and bundles.

Toward noon, when they were crossing an utterly vacant prairie, a rowdy wind from the northwest brought a rainstorm upon them. Camilla caped everyone in oilskins and kept the caravan moving. But prior rains had already softened the road, which deteriorated fast. Greasy black gumbo fattened the wheels. It winded the mules. It baffled their hooves. It strained their silver-mounted carriage harness worse than plowing.

Their load, she saw, ought to be reduced. But how? Liz had in her effects such reminders of better times as a dented brass bedwarmer, a clock mute forever, a cracked mirror, a china coffee pot with half its spout gone, and a lockless horse pistol of Ev's. All trash, of course, and yet treating them as such would be too cruelly debasing to Liz, who owned not one thing in this world very much better. The slaves, too, had put aboard several weighty bundles without much value except as proof that they, the owned, also owned something. In the shipwreck of their pioneering, all had treated the brougham as a saving lifeboat, loading aboard it the treasures of each. What belonged to Camilla, however, amounted to far more than everything else combined. In simple justice she could not require others to cast off anything unless she gave up ever so much herself.

And what *could* she dispense with? A meeting with Perry must be only a matter of time, after which such changes of costume as she had saved would hardly be equal to events sure to follow. Her solution was to shift part of the load off the roof of the carriage onto the mules Junior, Harold, and Buddy rode, those bundles which rain would damage least.

Liz meanwhile guarded against being asked to ride outside by keeping up a drizzle of complaints about how "powful sore" her back was, how gloomy, lonesome and "mizzuble" the whole countryside was too, until Camilla wanted to wring that chickeny neck of hers. Instead, she pointed out cheerfully that, bad as things looked, they must change for the better soon because they never stay the same long and could hardly be worse.

She was wrong. They could.

As the afternoon began to wane she loped forward alone to hunt shelter for the night. The best she could find was a derelict cabin very little better, as she savagely concluded, than a three-hole backhouse. Dank, dim, and roughly knocked together, it had but one window. Its floor was packed earth on which half a dozen puddles had formed under leaks from the roof, and it smelled of tallow, rotting potatoes, mildew, and urine. Scores of refugees passing that way since it was abandoned must have made free with it, for it was littered with recent bones, parings, feathers, scraps of defunct clothing, and "sign" of rats. A menstrual rag lay unburned in the hearth. Loathsome as the place was, she would have to clean it up enough to make it do. Though the rain had declined to a cold drizzle, it required her to accept any sort of roof for the night.

Cantering back to the brougham, she found the front wheels down to the axle in a draw. A heated mist rose around the mules. Their ears hung loose. Their legs quivered wearily, trapped in waxy gumbo. A tug on the harness, once so fine, had pulled apart and must be replaced by rope.

To lighten the load, Esau and Roberta were carrying baggage forward to higher ground. Both at that moment were sinking in mud ankle deep. All three Tipton boys were off to one side poking sticks down a soggy gopher hole.

"Junior," Camilla asked, "where's your mother?"

"Mam?"

Blond, skinny, loose in the mouth like Liz, Junior looked vacantly surprised that anyone should wonder.

Roberta's eyes rolled toward the carriage. "Still in yonna, Miz Milla."

"Why don't she get out? It's loaded much too heavy as it is."

"She been at that box again. She *gone*."

Camilla dismounted to peer in over her father's head. Liz had sunk limply among boxes and bundles not yet removed from the back seat. Her underlip drooped to the tilt of her head, and cobwebs of ash hair strayed across her eyes. Half hidden under her elbow was a maple medicine chest.

"Mrs. Tipton!" Camilla shook her wrist. It yielded like a rag doll's, and again hung as loose. "You wretch, get up from there!"

But Liz's thick breathing never altered.

The major's eyes swam in an effort to smile. "Too late, honey. No use whipping a dead horse."

"Whipping's too good for that woman. She knows how bad you need those pills!"

"However, she has troubles too."

"Troubles! *I'll* give her troubles."

She yanked the chest out from under Liz, who merely settled into the corner; after a catch, her breath resumed its tranquil rasp.

"How *could* she be so selfish!"

Camilla took from the chest a gilded tin box. It felt light. A shake made its diminished contents rattle. About to open it, she decided that she must not here where her father could see, for how could he bear the thought of jolting along without any drug to ease the tortures in his back? In putting the box away, she covertly shook it again, confirming its lightness, its diminution, and a cold little monkey paw of fear gripped her throat.

3

That evening, with her father's litter before the hearth, lighted and warmed by a generous fire, she and Roberta dressed his wound. The bullet had gouged upward from behind, presumably lodging in the small of his back, where a puffy lump had risen. Though they chatted hopefully over it, the matter seeping from the orifice was uglier, and the lump larger, darker, hotter. Cleansing it and bandaging it made him shiver from the muscles of his jaws to the last joint in his thumbs. One word haunted Camilla's thoughts: worse. Each night, each morning, any honest reckoning forced the same conclusion: he was worse.

Still, she delayed giving him a pill to ease him through the silent hours while others slept; every last one must be stretched as far as possible. Only after everyone else was down for the night, and she in her nightdress, did she bring the tin of laudanum with her to sit on a stool by his litter, offhanded about it all, letting the box subside into a hammock of nightgown between her knees.

"Such a day, uh, Pa?"

"Uhm." He lay watching the fire. His swift loss of flesh was more conspicuous under its shadowy light. The silence of his musing became magnified by the rhythms of sleep behind them, by rain on the roof, by the snaky, steamy hiss of trickles down the chimney. "Remember Gebhard, Milla?"

"Who?"

"Heinz Gebhard."

"Ach, yah-yah! Herr Dawktor Gephart." The name conjured a mesmerist out of memory, a little blond creature with a face like an anteater, a head like a pot of smearcase, a lisp in his talk, and a phenomenal ability to make fools out of accommodating acquaintances like her father. Even now, recalling his demonstrations of mesmerism, she again felt amazement that such a complete cipher could so impose his will on others. *"Jawohl."*

"Recall how he pushed a nail into my shoulder?"

"Don't mention it. I cringe at any thought of it."

"I didn't hurt *me,* though. That's one thing about mesmerism: it can obliterate pain."

"Oh, rubbish. I've yet to meet any sensible people—you excepted —who don't consider it little more than witchcraft."

"All science seems like witchcraft until you understand it."

"Perhaps, only—"

"Whatever it is, I felt no pain."

"Well, no use to dwell on that. Dr. Gebhard's a long way off."

"You aren't, Milla. And you watched him work."

Her brows went high. "Pa, no!" Fright added vigor to the shake of her head. "I couldn't."

"You could." He forced a smile. "If anyone in this territory can bewitch a man, you're the one."

"My answer is *no,* and has to be."

"But why? If you're willing to rely on a pill, a clever substance designed to lull *our* substance, why not also trust a mental process which lulls the mind?"

"Because I'm afraid of it. I can't be a party to what I'm afraid of." An intention to leave the subject and go to bed straightened her back. "Like a pill now, would you?"

"Never seems too soon for that." After taking one, he followed it with a gourd of water which she held for him. "Not many left, uh?"

"Wel-ll—"

"How many?"

"Enough, I think."

His glance doubtingly searched hers, and the fact was that what was left could not possibly last even as far as the San Jacinto. There, at Sawmill Simpson's Landing, they would be able to secure enough logs to float south by raft, and so travel without jolting. She had hoped that he would improve sufficiently by then for reasonable comfort without any drugs: only, of course, he was not improving.

"If I can just keep *her* out of them." She scowled at a corner from which Liz's snoring rose. "How anyone can be so disgustingly weak and selfish, I don't understand."

"Well, weakness is common enough, God knows."

His eyes sloped away to the slicked barrels of the family weapons standing by the hearth: two shotguns and as many rifles and horse pistols. A dent between his brows visibly regretted weaknesses of his own which his wound augmented. But, she reflected, those traits of his which she herself had once thought weak were in fact corner supports to her: by habit he was so helpful, so easy to be around, so undemanding, so easy to get around, that he tricked self-willed, aggressive people into imagining he had little will of his own. She knew, however, that there was much thoughtful purpose in him, and he showed it now.

"Milla, what's the best *natural* healer most of us ever know? Sleep, uh? Natural sleep. Mesmerism can induce sleep, the deepest sleep. That alone should recommend it."

A trickle in a puddle close behind her played a little tune. Rain stealthily tapped the roof and spat in the fire.

"Mesmerism, as Gebhard explained it," he resumed, "requires no inborn faculty. None. It compels the mind to dwell upon one idea at a time without interference from wakeful doubts until the idea fulfills itself in action. The results then can appear miraculous."

She sat with the gilded tin in her lap, letting him talk. In the long look he twisted toward her there was recognition that that was all she was doing, letting him talk. However, he was not yet willing to give up.

"Of all the medicines known to man, opium has been most venerated through the total of human history. And why? Not simply because it quiets pain, but because it loosens the most secret rigidities of flesh and nerve, thus promoting their inclination to heal. And have we not seen that mesmerism can do the same much more profoundly? We have. So I say let's put it to work.

"In the Orient its use is at least as old as the oldest carved stone. That's why Gebhard could succeed with me so quickly: knowledge and belief were in me for him to work with. In Mangalore I watched a sadhu entrance a man who had five boils to lance, and—"

"Yes, so you've said before." Her tone was abrupt because she felt a growing temptation which she was in haste to disallow. "I'm no sadhu, dear, and no Gebhard either."

"No, but I'll wager anything, if you'd just put your mind to it—"

"*No,* Pa. I've told you as plain as I know how: *no."* She stood up. "Well, it's taxing you to talk so much. Time now to get to sleep."

She drew his sheet up to his chin, brusquely tender, and tucked the sides in too. He contemplated the fire without motion. His eyes wearied of it. They closed, reopened, and she saw him slant another look at the guns standing by the hearth, all so close to his bed because, after having them cleaned and oiled, he had ordered Esau to leave them there, presumably to dry in the firelight. But *was* that why? Fear again gripped her throat, and hard. After locking the tin of pills in the medicine chest and storing that under her bed where Liz would not dare tamper with it, she turned to pick up two guns at a time as if in afterthought.

"Somebody tending the fire in the dark," she observed, carrying them over to a dry corner, "might stumble over these."

He lay quite still, mouth ajar, cheeks gaunt, brow dented. His expression drove her to pretend that they never had stopped talking about Gebhard.

"It's true, though: what he did *was* remarkable." She bowed over him impulsively to kiss his forehead. It burned her lips, and anxiety turned her next words queer. "If it only . . . well, good night, dear thing."

"Night, sweetheart."

Once down in bed, though so tired that her legs twitched, she could not prevent her eyes from reopening to watch firelight wobble over the rafters. The Tipton snores were loud from their corner; stealthy rain persisted on the roof; spatters beat out tunes in puddles on the floor. Now and then she heard her father's arm stir or his litter creak or his breath catch, reminding her that he had been through hell to the far end and back, and what was there in Gebhard's demonstration so bad that she was too good to try it, if only to humor him a little? What else but her own obstinacy had got him shot to begin with?

Twenty minutes of thought about it, and she twisted her feet out onto the floor. She groped over to his litter.

"Pa . . ."

"Hm?"

"I'm ready if you are."

"Good girl, Milla."

"That pill you took should help some, and they're all asleep now. There'll never be a better time."

"Never mind them, honey. There's not one thing in it to upset them, or you."

"Except, of course, that women have been burned at the stake for less."

"Now, see here—"

"*Any*how," she cut him off, "let's try."

To approximate the arrangements she had seen Gebhard use, she stood a lighted candle on a chunk of firewood a few feet from him on the side toward which he faced. She asked him to gaze at it, to see nothing but its flame. Meanwhile she stroked his forehead from behind, all strokes equal. Her heart beat shakily, tilted forward over him as she was, and she quivered with dread lest these mystifying rites produce results beyond her control. To quiet herself, she brought a low stool close to the head of his litter where she could sit stroking him with less strain. Her body swayed equally right and left to the sweep of her hands across his forehead, and in time with this motion she recited a low-voiced chant.

"Watch the candle, Pa. Think only of rest. Be easy and rest.
"Go limp all over. Relax from head to foot. Relax and rest.
"Think always of rest, long healing rest, completely painless rest.
"Watch the candle flame, that restful candle flame. Think of healing
rest . . ."

In time with her incantation the stroke of her hands continually passed between his eyes and the candle, producing a rhythm of light and shadow in harmony with that of touch and voice. After a bit she spoke with more insistence, more command:

"Your eyes are growing heavy, growing very, very heavy.
"They want so much to close, and yet they do not close.
"Heavy, heavy, heavy, and still they do not close.
"Though they try to shut, they simply will not shut.
"They cannot cease to watch that restful candle flame . . ."

His lashes quivered in their attempt to close but could not. An electrifying confidence shocked through her, for his eyes were fixed, a vacant black except for the reflection in them of that poised and silent flame.

As a further test, she now told him that, in a few moments, he would be unable to keep his eyes open. They would shut of themselves. She would count to ten slowly; and at ten his eyes would shut despite any attempt to keep them open. She stroked and counted as evenly as the tolling of bells. At ten his eyes were shut, heavily shut, and so they stayed.

Next she made the arm on his upper side rise, lower again, then rise higher. Without any effort from him, she declared, the arm would become too strong for him or her or anyone else to push back down. This happened. Though the uplifted hand drooped at the wrist, the arm itself turned cataleptic, as firm in its position as the beam on a plow, and seemingly as disengaged from any will of his. A flushed yet waxen immobility in his features gave him a look of mummified calm.

Her success alarmed her while it also set her aglow. A moment of reflection told her, however, that it was his success more than hers. Without his bold belief in it, nothing would have come of it. What was she doing but carrying out *his* will to evoke powers ordinarily stored away beyond his reach?

Dr. Gebhard, having brought him to this stage, had shifted over to the spectacular, the bizarre. By soft commands alone he had stretched him out parallel to the floor, head on a chair, feet on a piano stool. Nothing, he said, would bend him. To prove it, he had a guest weighing upward of two hundred pounds sit on his stomach, demonstrating, he had said, that all of us have in us far more strength than we know, for that cataleptic body, without evidence of effort or distress, sustained this weight like a footbridge. Gebhard had also asked her father to tell what he had written for the first column of page two in the *Weekly Commentator* one month before. At once, in hollow tones, he had begun to recite the first installment of a satire about certain elegant wasps which, invading a beehive, corrupted and polluted its rational society as politicians (like Senator Chatillon) did that of Louisiana. He had kept up this feat of memory until ordered to stop.

And now, seeing open before her that same shadowy warehouse of unutilized human talent, what ought she to call forth? Her impulse was to try rousing him, as Gebhard had done, by saying that she would clap ten times and have him awake and wholly refreshed at the tenth clap. What was her purpose, though, but to give him sleep, peace, painless rest? Then why wake him? What could be truer than his own description of sleep as a sovereign tonic?

"You'll sleep well now, Pa.

"Without distress from anything, you'll sleep the whole night long.

"You'll sleep till coffee's ready, and breakfast on the fire."

Here she bent closer to watch his face. Her voice returned to normal. "You understand, dear? Nod if you understand."

He did not. Her chant resumed:

"Think of sleep alone, Pa, of not one thing but sleep, long healing sleep, deep painless sleep—

"Sleep to steal that pain away, sleep to give you peace again, Sleep to make you well . . ."

Presently, abandoning the incantatory style, she again bowed close to his ear. "I'm going to stroke you ten times, Pa. At the tenth stroke you'll sink into a sleep that nothing at all will disturb till morning. It will help your wound to heal. It will take your suffering away. All day tomorrow you'll feel very much better. Now . . ."

She began stroking his forehead, chanting the single word *sleep* at each stroke. She stopped on the tenth. His lips were apart. He had the look of a man in deep untroubled sleep.

And at dawn he was still heavily asleep. He remained so immobile through preparations for breakfast that she began to worry about whether she ought to wake him. She sat down by his litter to observe him closely, a gourd of coffee in hand. As its aroma floated around him, his eyes loosened open.

"*Well,* Pa!"

He considered her drowsily and without expression. For the first time since Friday night, no constriction of suffering marred his features. Gaunt as he had become, and with beard growing, he had acquired an other-worldly look, an air of fleshless detachment, a look of prophecy. In part for that reason, the simplicity of his first words was so unexpected that she laughed aloud.

"So-o," he murmured, "coffee's ready, is it?"

5

Van Diemens' Place
Midnight Monday
April 11, 1836

Halfway through the next night, which they spent many miles eastward in a very different cabin, a stealthy noise wakened her, a subdued bump, a click, a muffled scrape. Rabbity throbs jumped along her throat as she sat up to listen. The only unusual sounds she could hear then, however, were a liquid rumble no great way outdoors, the bellow of a distant alligator too, and the witless singing of peeper frogs by the thousand.

That rumble of water had been there when she lay down. Noting also that the room was large and snug, with an active hearth at each end, she recollected that this was Hanford Van Diemen's place on Loping Creek, a tributary of the San Jacinto River. Something of her joy at first blundering upon it during the afternoon came back to her there in the dark, quieting her alarm.

Several times that day the rain had been heavy, never really stopping until night, converting wide sections of lowland into marsh. Esau often had to swing the brougham away from the road and let alternating teams of weary mules pull it over soggy, trackless rises above the water line. By noon they had lost the road altogether. Thereafter they simply toiled east, east, east, until they came to a deep strip of woods loud with the boiling of a stream in spate—Loping Creek. Following that southward had brought them to Van Diemens' homestead. Far off the road and therefore not visited by other runaways, it was neat as a Dutch apron, and it still had an untouched note of welcome tacked on the door beside its latchstring:

You who wander here homeless while we wander onward, enter this door as you would the one this War closed behind you. Freely employ whatsoever will serve you whilst you rest here. Pray feed the Chickens, tidy the house for the next who come, and God go with you as you journey farther.

Martha Van Diemen

Arrangements within the house fully supported the generosity of that note. The cupboard was well stocked. Near it stood a row of pots, scoured and ready for use. There was a stack of cured firewood by each hearth, clean bedding on the cots, a bleached wooden tub for baths by the back door, and a pair of homemade candles on the table. Wherever Camilla looked, she felt herself gently, memorably rebuked as, by comparison, a selfish creature who too often forgot that the Christian way to deliverance is through acts which assist others, whether or not they deserve it.

Now, though the night was half gone, weak firelight still relieved the dark, and yet she could see no evidence that whatever had wakened her had disturbed anyone else. From her father's bed came a succession of low moans spaced like breathing, each a gutty grunt when he exhaled. These reassured her because, no matter how that wolfish wound of his might gnaw him, he never let on when awake: his moaning meant that he was asleep. It also meant that part of her evening duty had been left undone: her intention when giving him a pill at bedtime had been to mesmerize him again after pretending to drop off herself so that everyone else would sleep, but her pretense had turned into fact: she had not stayed awake five minutes.

Tired as she had been when she lay down, what *was* it that could have wakened her now? If anything, there was less noise than usual, because Liz, for once, was not snoring at all. Camilla looked over to the corner assigned to Liz and at once began to understand; for, now that her eyes were becoming accustomed to the flicker-lit dark, she could make out that Liz's bed was empty.

Thrusting a hand beneath her own bed to grope for the medicine chest, she found nothing. So that was what had caused the bump she had heard, the click and scrape too!

A faint stir drew her glance over toward a deal table to the right. Under it, licked by dim firelight, a nightgowned figure crouched on something like a cat on a stump. Camilla flung aside her covers and swooped over that way. But Liz, for a woman with an ailing back, was amazingly agile. She sprang from under the table on its opposite side, medicine chest clutched in both arms. Her hair hung loose for the night. Her eyes were dilated and moist behind wisps of hair cobwebbing her face. Reflections of firelight gave them a feline glitter. Her lips, ordinarily slack, grimaced around bared teeth.

"Lemme lone now. You lemme be."

"Put that down." Camilla speared a finger at the chest. "Put it on the table."

"Wone do it. I got to have one-two pills, and *aim* to."

At Camilla's enraged start around one end of the table, Liz essayed a witchy shuffle the opposite way, then whirled to grab up a poker from beside the hearth. Camilla sprang upon her, seized deep into the hair floating out behind her, and swung the other hand against her ear with all her might. It popped like a board on a bucket, knocking out a squally screech.

"Drop that, you wretch!"

Liz did drop the poker but crumbled down to claw the chest tight against her. Camilla began whacking her bottom, knocking screeches out of her until her own hand felt as if it had been run over by a galloping horse. Everyone except the major sat up in sleepy consternation to stare at them both. Liz, in squirming away from Camilla's blows, abandoned the chest to scramble over to her bed, Camilla still walloping her until she had plunged in and snatched the covers across her rear.

"Now will you learn?"

"Yessum! Oh, yessum, yessum! Mussiful God, don't hit me no more, mam! It was them torments was all."

"Torments my Aunt Fanny! I'm sick to death of hearing you complain, complain, complain, complain!"

"But, Miz Milla—"

"Now *hush.*" Camilla arched a battered hand above her. "One more complaint and I'll give you twice the beating you've had already."

"Oh, nome, ple-e-ease! I won't, mam."

"It's time you stopped acting like a spoiled child that everyone else has to help. It's time you acted like a grown woman and took thought of others."

Meekly: "Yessum."

"And don't you dare ever touch that chest again!"

"Nome."

"You do, you fail to brace up and help instead of hinder, and I'll turn you off to shift for yourself." She held up an inflamed and quivering finger. "Mind that now!"

Still more meekly: "Yessum."

Camilla glared around the room. "The rest of you get back to sleep."

In mousy quiet they pulled their covers up to their eyes. There was nothing else for her to be vexed with except the burning bruises in her hand—and her own un-Christian fury.

6

A quarter-hour later Cedric was lying on his side, watching Camilla through firelit dark, hoping she might propose that they follow last night's success with a fresh attempt. Too overwrought to sleep, she sat at the table with a coat over her nightgown and candles on either side of her Bible, through which she leafed restlessly. A spell of rage generally left her like this—at once on fire and penitential.

What she did not seem to realize was that there are people who get a world of good out of a damned smart thrashing. Evidently Liz Tipton was one. She had sinned, yes, but had paid in full: her account was in balance, her conscience purged. Slack, bubbly snores from her corner announced that, already, she slept with the abandon of the blessed.

Watching Camilla's self-driven quest through page after page, he pitied her. There by the candle, with her hair freshly brushed, with brows thoughtful, with passion still abnormally enlarging her eyes, she was as lovely as any woman has any right to be. Nevertheless he did pity her.

He could guess what she sought: divine guidance capable of subliming whatever is brutish or irrational in persons like herself and Liz. She wanted to be reconvinced of the possibility of regeneration, and the pity of it was that she still imagined herself likely to attain it through what she read rather than through acts on behalf of fellow mortals.

At about the same age, as a green captain brooding over campfires in the dismal forests of the Creeks, he too had devoted himself often to the compact verses of Scripture. That exercise reminded him of visits in boyhood to a hickory grove abounding in nuts with tiny kernels locked inside acrid partitions which any blow to break the shell usually mixed with them; but, if selected with extreme care, the meats were so delectable that he would hammer at the stubborn things by the hour, trying greedily to get his fill for once, and never succeeding. So it had been with his soldierly application to the Bible, until he could quote hundreds of passages verbatim.

She tonight picked through page after page, but with too much passion, too little patience. And that nutriment which she craved, could that be found there at all? *Was* her nature one to be appeased there?

Blessed are the meek, true. Blessed are the poor in spirit, the pure in heart and they that mourn, and well for them. But what of the able, the strong, the creative? What of the cheerfully vehement, the seekers? What of those to whom total submission to chance or to any externality is unthinkable, to whom so much in the world is flawed and in need of reshaping by vigorous hands and visionary minds and boldly hopeful hearts? Is there no beatitude for them?

Well, his own conviction was that blessedness is humanly created at least as often as divinely given. Shall the meek in fact inherit the earth? Well, perhaps; but then the proud shall take it away from them—as they did repeatedly in Mesopotamia, as they did millennium on millennium around the Mediterranean, as they did along the Indus, the Nile, the Hwang Ho, the Yangtze, the Ganges too. Is it not possible for energetic shapers to find their beatitude in proof that their acts bless daily life? Someday he must speak to her of all this, though he knew that, regardless of how well he might say it, she would obstinately prefer what Faith since childhood had taught her to accept as sure.

Her efforts with him last night, which she herself thought in some way sacrilegious, had been a blessing indeed, had muzzled the slavering wolf which that bullet had brought upon him. Since then the beast had lunged at him whenever he stirred, threatening him, but without any fanged bite all day.

Her success would not endure, of course, unless she repeated it and enlarged upon it. Discreetly, significantly, he cleared his throat. At once she tiptoed over to bend across his litter so that a fragrance of soap and health and secret female loveliness, recalling his wife's in their first year of sharing one bed, floated all about him.

"Pa," she whispered, "you wake?"

"Nome. You said get to sleep so I got."

Her smile came alive. "How you feel?"

"Skairt to death, of course."

"Need another pill?"

"How many left?"

"She didn't get a one. The chest was locked and—"

"So how many left?"

"You've used only three today, so they're stretching out."

"But how many *left?*"

"Wel-ll, four."

"Then don't tempt me."

"That infernal thief! I hate myself for walloping her so, but every time I think about it I want to light in on her some more."

"Well, whatever she's taken wouldn't last me all the way anyhow. Now, after last night, I don't think that matters. You've got more healing in you than those pills."

"You honestly think so?" Her breath caught to snatch the words back. "But, of course, you wouldn't say so if you didn't think so."

"It worked remarkably well, considering."

"Yes, I've thought about it ever so much today. I've thought of so many things I might have said and done if I hadn't felt so scared and wicked at the time." She straightened up to gaze around the room. "Well, Pa . . ."

She stood musing in silence, eyes straying vacantly toward the fire until they walled worse than he had seen them do in many months. So plainly did they tell how heavily last night's concentrated effort had taxed her that he reached over to press her hand in sympathy. That brought her alert at once.

"Yes, Pa. Right away."

As much to delay as out of caution, she tiptoed around to peer at each bed and pallet, making sure everyone else was asleep. On her return she blew out one candle and brought the other over to place it on a stool before his eyes as she had last night. She then sat behind him, bringing that fragrance so reminiscent of his wife's abundantly around him.

Gazing at the candle as he knew she was about to command him to do, he felt an anticipatory calm steal through him, and with it a pervasive sense of being about to commence a journey reaching farther and showing him more than any through space could ever do. The greatest journeys are within, he reflected. So are the direst combats, the most maiming defeats, the brightest victories, the richest buried treasures, the greatest deprivations, the most brilliant discoveries, the boldest adventures, the most galling subjugations, the least arguable freedoms. Rescue, he concluded, might yet be theirs through the simple discovery that they had in their own minds the means to effect it.

"*Now,* Pa." Her hands began stroking his forehead. "Look only at the candle now. Think only of painless rest, calm and easy rest, long healing rest . . ."

Beyond the rhythmic passage of her fingers before his eyes, that yellow flame stood serenely on its candle. As it lighted his way, as she set him afloat toward realms without pain, he had a momentary impression of drifting unseen through a loftily arched cathedral where one clear voice recited a litany.

From C. B.'s Journal
Tuesday, April 12, 1836

Were I a clergyman I henceforth would take my text often from that staggering declaration in Luke: "Behold, the Kingdom of God is within you." To this I would add, "And so is the Domain of Hell."

As I lie here writing, I suffer nothing worse than a throbbing pressure in the wounded area, an enfeebling stiffness, a disinclination of that flesh to stir. Camilla says it looks less inflamed, and it fevers me less. I was able this morning to bear letting her press out suppuration, and that has reduced its tumescence.

Of course, the bullet is still there. So is its ability to kill. Very probably a hardheaded doctor would discount every sign of improvement as "simply mental." Maybe so, but the effect within myself makes all the difference between a desperate impatience for death and a sense of luck in being alive: two days ago I was ready to blow my brains out; tonight I relish simple existence.

Meanwhile Camilla did Mrs. Tipton nearly as much good from the corporeal end as me from the mental—that is, by pretty nearly beating her rump off. She literally knocked the discontent out of her. Today her spirits appear greatly refreshed, and for once she has been useful, anxiously so. She did not so much as hint that she ought to ride inside the carriage. Instead she shared a mule with Buddy, and complained less than at any other time since Ev went off to war.

Actually, our journey was more difficult today, and much more dangerous. Loping Creek looked savage. Rain on rain on rain had turned it dark. Its ripples across the ford toward Sawmill Simpson's

Landing resembled knobs on the back of a charging bull alligator. It swam muscularly around protruding rocks. It bit at the legs of our mares in frothing lust. It lashed with fangs of foam at the carriage wheels, then rushed past them to squirm off the ford into swirling depths beyond.

Esau said of it as we prepared to cross, "This here's a evil crick, Miz Milla."

"Oh, nonsense."

"Looks evil to me, mam. Evil as a crick can be."

"Don't matter. This close to the San Jacinto, we can't just sit here till it behaves."

Amid geysers splashed up by Swallow's hooves, she rode before us to test the footing. About halfway across, where the water was up to her stirrup, the bloated carcass of a fawn came directly down across her course. In Swallow's loathing writhe away from it, she blundered over a concealed boulder and went down head first, throwing Camilla in before her, then whirled wildly back against the mules hitched to the brougham. Already the wrestling of that reptilian current had made them nervous. Despite Esau's best efforts, they shied downstream along the edge of the ford where the wheels lurched crazily over hidden rocks and the current leaped down into a swirling lake deep enough to swallow carriage and all.

Fortunately Camilla did not stop to deplore her own condition. With her bonnet, hair, and clothes plastered tight around her, she lurched over to seize a rein on the near mule, jerked him upstream hard enough to pull his mate with him, then grabbed the head end of my litter and waded beside me to steady it while they splattered on to the east bank.

Afterward, when everyone was safely ashore, she took her soaking as a topic to be hilarious about while others built a fire where she could change and dry her clothes. Thus she reminded me, as she has so often in recent days, of an ancient saying from the Orient which may be rephrased thus:

> *If the Bird of Fate should fly above me,*
> *I cannot prevent her*
> *from casting her shadow upon me.*
> *But I can undertake that she shall not*
> *nest upon my head*
> *and hatch her eggs there.*

CHAPTER XIX

I

Magruders' Homestead
Tuesday Night
April 12, 1836

Eleven greased buckshot were poisoning Rex Cottier's leg below the knee, each with a gathering around it and hurting fierce. He ought to find a doctor right away, and yet how could he until somebody rode back to Mrs. Palmer's to finish what he had been sent here to do? Blacky was in no condition for it, he being little more than a groaning cadaver. That left only Hank and Anson Weatherford, and those two trashy bastards could hardly think of one thing but how to conjure banknotes out of the moneybelt they knew was on him.

"Seen a few stars," he announced that night after a final trip outdoors. Hobbling out and in with a mattock handle for a cane had pulled sweat out on him like hammering at a forge, but he put on a prosperous, talky, cheerful front and gave nobody any need for an earhorn to hear him. "Looks like maybe the rain's over."

Hank, who sat on the floor dealing twenty-one into a splash of fire-light, looked up only at Anson, his sole opponent. "Time it was over."

"Past time," Rex agreed. "So everlastun ruinous, rained in like this."

Blacky rolled half sideward on his bunk in a corner by the hearth. "*Still* rainun?"

"No-no, it *aint*. It's relentun. It's forbearun."

"Jesus," Blacky moaned, subsiding, "without it lets up, where *are* we?"

Everything Rex knew about where they actually were was bad except that nobody else knew. Letters jackknifed across the door said their cabin was T. Magruder's. On his map from the Land Office, Magruder's looked about twenty-two miles west by north of Mrs. Palmer's, though the four of them must have covered nearer twice that in zigzagging all sorts of ways to leave no clear trail. In his present condition that forty-odd miles there and back—that, *plus* a long, long ride to find medical relief afterward—no, that would be more than his condition would tolerate. Besides, several buckshot had punctured his mare—enough to leave her hunched in the middle, coughing flecks of blood, and unfit for any gait faster than a graveyard walk.

"You two better get you a good sleep," he told the Weatherfords. "Tamarra, if it stays clear all endurun the night, you got to get your butts in them saddles and *ride*."

Anson slammed down a card. "You mighty right we'll ride." His beaked face swung around, waveringly yellowed by the fire. "And I'n tell you where to." For support he looked to Hank, who merely sat fluffing the cards he had not dealt. Anson had to shape out his whole thought alone. "Home to the Redlands, there's where to. *With* our pay. We done *our* work, what the goddamn hell."

"Not right you aint done it. And not one red cent till you do."

Anson, fidgety with sass, pruned his mouth to spit sideward, skinny neck loose in his collar and Adam's apple out like the craw on a molted rooster. Hank, a cooler customer by a long stretch, cuffed his knee in the act of dealing, a reminder that *they* now held the best cards, and patience, patience, patience.

Two swings of his mattock handle, Rex knew, would bust in their skulls right there where they sat before they could rise to their knees. The temptation to prove it took him back to a blacksmith he'd been apprenticed to until sixteen, when he'd issued the man a ticket to hell (a good stout lick behind the ear with a whippletree) over a difference about four bits in his pay. A hot race with the law, and after that a long spell at sea, had taught him to handle his strength better, and his temper too, and not bloody men up unless they were just too boneheaded to see reason, and never, never unthoughtedly kill without a good reliable plan for obliterating the evidence. Far-seeing headiness of that character was what had brought him along so high since then. It had converted him into a gent, a sport always very choice in his cigars and fastidious about his drinks and no end of style to him, a man of substance who could afford sumptuous feeding and ample gold ornament and every description of fanciful vests, a sort of aristocrat that all the toniest whores were happy to entertain, a somebody that common nobodies wanted to keep on the good side of.

However, as he stood there eying the Weatherfords, a sensation of watery weakness reminded him how difficult it would be to do without them, and his hatred of the ferrety, worthless cusses sharpened in proportion. He must keep his ways free and outspoken all the same: he had to convince them he was still boss in every way, so he squashed his first impulse to lie down on his bunk and went instead to the hearth to light up the butt of a Havana with a stick of kindling.

There on the mantel he had required all the rest to shelve their weapons, handy for him to control, his bunk being just to the right. As far as he could see, nobody had touched any while he was outdoors, so he looked down tolerantly upon their mangy cards and kept his tone as peaceable as any gang boss could afford to sound.

"What the Chief says was, 'Buy it or burn it down.' There was his orders. Well, that sassy looker wouldn't sell, and till yet it aint burnt down, and nobody here better not even *think* of nothun else till it is."

Hank Weatherford, by a wink at Anson, said almost as plain as speaking that he had no trouble whatever thinking of something else. Neither one ever had seen the Chief and had no idea what it was to fail him. Strictly, of course, the failure came from having to decoy Mrs. Palmer out of the house by firing the outbuildings first so she wouldn't get hurt. That was how Mr. Beaufait ordered it, but he'd never think to blame anybody but the man he gave the orders to.

"We *have* got a tolable excuse," Rex allowed. "Only the Chief— the sole thing *he'll* give for excuses is hell, and in ample supply. He pays cash solely for results, and then he's liberal as a king. Same with me. What I ask is: take advantage of this dryun, favorun weather while it lasts. *All* I ask is: get that place burnt down. Do that, and bring me some kind of a sign to prove beyond any cavil you done it, and I'll give you fifty dollars extra, cash money, *plus* full pay. On the spot too."

Anson, from under his brows, considered the effect on Hank, who kept the vane of his face pointed at his cards.

"But don't bungle no more," Rex went on. "The perceivun thing would be to so arrange and contrive that you can't bungle."

"Bungle, my ass!" Anson yelled. "You'n Blacky was who bungled, not me'n Hank. You'n Blacky is all."

"Huh?" Blacky grunted.

He stopped groaning to turn his good eye their way. This brought firelight across his face. Buckshot cutting at him from the side and rear had chewed him from the back of his neck to the bulge of his chin, also down his shoulder, where his coat had turned leathery from blood and pus. One shot, straying high, had clawed his nose open.

Another had torn open the near eyeball. Bloody, mattery tears seeped down his cheek as glimmers from the hearth played upon it.

To look straight at him turned Rex puky. The cabin being narrow, their bunks were only six or seven feet apart, with all the heated air between them worse than around a penned boar hog; when hit, Blacky had lost his urine, which had been souring in his drawers ever since, and that stench was aggravated by stale sweat and spoiling wounds.

Somebody ought to do him the benevolence of putting him out of his misery, as he had begged Rex to do several times the last few days, but still it was necessary to tolerate him because there was nobody else to help keep those two slinky Weatherfords in line. Blacky always had been ouchy around them, watching for reasons to snap at them or slam them in the face if they got too lippy, so that Rex, despite the fortune he carried around his waist, had no worries about what they might attempt behind his back as long as he had Blacky there to back him up. Four days the next thing to crazy had not improved Blacky's disposition any: he was liable anytime to swing a chunk at them, or a rock, a boot, a pot, anything handy, and tonight he was too near out of his head to hear well.

"You call me?" Because one shot had punctured the root of his tongue, the words came out slurred. "What you want?"

"Not you," said Anson. "Get to sleep, for God's sake."

"Then don't call me." His head sagged out of the light.

Anson gave him a moment to calm down before restating his case to Rex. "Aint right to lay the blame on them that done their job right."

Rex lipped his cigar over to the highest corner of his mouth. "Balls."

The brutal economy of his scorn brought their eyes upon him. He took advantage of that to slide a hand in around the bulge of his vest and let them have a look at his utensils of homicide, drawing out a bowie knife slicked with practice and applying it lightly to his nails. It might not be as thoroughbred as the pearl-handled penknife he'd lost down there around Mrs. Palmer's, but it had a sight more point to it.

"Who *was* it I hired was suppose to be such a sonofabitch with a rifle, uh?" His knife jabbed sidehand toward Anson. "*You* was, you whiny low-life. Why'd I so particklerly put a crackshot out in front of that house? Solely to insure that nobody wouldn't have no chance to shoot *us* down. If you'd done what you was there to do, I'd be a well man tonight, and Blacky too."

Blade first, he switched the knife over to the other hand with a twist perfected for quick throws. He wagged the hilt at Anson. "You bungled, goddamn your sorry soul, about as bad as a man could bungle." His glare dared either one to dispute that.

They let the opportunity pass.

"Your pay! What I owe *you* till now is eight inches of cold steel. Tamarra you better see to it I owe you something different. What I owe I pay."

Hank licked a thumb before using it to press one card off the stack in his hand. Anson simply gazed at Hank, mouth ajar in idiot doubt about what to do or say, and expecting his brother to show him.

Watching them, in a sweat over the awful throbbing in his leg, Rex wondered why in sense he didn't just take it for certain that, once they were out of sight, he would not be able to trust a thing they did or said they did. Anyhow, he would have to chance that because the growing fever in him told him that what he ought to do and would have to do was get them out of the way long enough so that he could slip off on a well horse to hunt himself a doctor where he was surest to find one and also least liable to meet anyone who had seen him before. He did not intend to go east at all, where they would be positive he'd gone, but west to the army, which would have doctors practiced in probing out lead.

The last he'd heard, the army was moving up the Brazos from San Felipe, which they had burned. They must be hardly eighty miles away any more, whereas Nacogdoches, the nearest place eastward where there might be a doctor left, was anyway three times that far, and not a safe place to ask, since he had stopped there a spell to hire the Weatherfords as he came out from Louisiana. Anyhow, the infernal snakes might possibly do the burning right, and he'd *still* have all the money. The thought that they also might not do it at all helped him to maintain an indignant, worthy, right-thinking wrath which kept their eyes jumpy. He sheathed his knife, stored his cigar on the edge of the mantel with fastidiously adjusted fingers, and again took up his mattock handle.

"Now you two been told to get to bed." As he began limping toward them with a double grip on his cane, both scrambled up. "So *get.*"

They did—in all their clothes, boots excepted. He did the same.

Because his right leg was the bad one, he lay on his left side, back to the room. His ear, though, kept alert to every move behind him. Both Weatherfords remained restless. Blacky, too, stirred on his bunk, mumbled and ground his teeth and kept up a piteous profane groaning. Rex under his breath heartily cussed him and yet thanked God he was too deep in the fires of hell to sleep and too dangerous for the Weatherfords to try sneaking any weapons off that mantel with him right there awake.

He himself eventually dozed a spell while undertaking not to. A heavy creak from Blacky's bunk roused him. Blacky at that moment sat propped up on one hand, eye bloodily weeping in a flicker of fire-light, spittle overflowing from the low side of his mouth, and breath laboring in hoarse, grunted moans. His good shoulder projected his free hand over to grip the end of the hearth as he pried himself upward.

"Blacky, what you doon?"

"Gotta go outen piss."

"Walk all right?"

"Get *up* I'n walk."

His hand groped to the mantel and clung there while he waited on wobbly legs for his head to clear. With the full glow of firelight rising up around him he looked so monstrous, so inhuman, so pitiful and sickening that Rex again turned to the wall. Over a spell of wonder at the enormous number of people in this world who really ought to be disposed of, he let his eyes drop shut and wished to Christmas he was free to sleep, by God, *sleep*.

During the passion of that wish he heard a click behind him which he failed to interpret until a blunted explosion jolted his ear. At the instant he looked around, Blacky's knees were loosening forward to sit him on the floor with his back against his bunk, shoulder to the wall, and head slackly dribbling blood over his shirt from a burned puncture in his temple. A horse pistol in one languishing hand so tilted over backward that it drew the trigger finger upright. His legs tilted sideways. Between them a wet stain spread into the firelight as his bladder relaxed.

Hank padded barefoot out of the darker end of the cabin to stand motionless in yellow light from the hearth. Anson followed him, beaked face forward on the gristles of his neck and eyes idiotically protruding.

Anson spoke in a high quaver. "They'll think *we* done it."

Rex spat at the floor. Knowing how unpredictable gutless men can be when terrified, he swung his puffy leg out before him, got the good one close under him where it could manage his weight if he had to act quick, and pulled both sides of his coat open so that either hand could dip inside smoothly.

"Who'll think it?"

"Huh?"

"Get ridda him, and nobody won't know."

"There's those in the Redlands knows he come with us. We get back there, won't nobody believe a man like him ever kilt hisself."

"And them we tell will wonder where he picked up so much buckshot it drove him outa his head."

"You dumb baboons, don't say he killed hisself. Say the Mexicans got him. Times like these, nobody's got any call to be surprised, no matter who don't come back, or how many."

Hank angled him a sharp look, so clearly picturing him somewhere a week or two from now maybe accounting for them the same way that even Anson saw it.

"I aint stayn no more," said Anson. His eyes considered the door, then the mantel, where lay the weapons they would need to ride across wild country. "I'm clearn out."

"Shut up and get to work, you chickenhead," Rex ordered. "Lay him out flat over there where it's cold. Dead man's easier to handle and easier to bury that stiffens flat."

"You mean take him over by *our* bunks?"

"Certainly. Here it's too warm: he wouldn't keep so good. And outside he'd draw the wolves. Let him lay there till mornun, then bury him deep in the canebrake, where greenery will overgrow the grave quick, and leave it unsuspected."

"I aint stayn."

"What he says is sense, though," Hank admitted.

Estimating the altered situation had kept Hank's eyes busy. Their first glitter of panic quieted to a shrewd glint in which Rex saw a realization that patience, simple patience, was much more on their side with Blacky gone than before, very much more. But Anson was still goggling.

Rex, always two or three thoughts ahead of such fools, by this time pictured both of them lying here peaceable with Blacky while the cabin took fire around them so that no one would ever be able to make out who they were or what struck them down. Without Blacky to check them, how could they be relied on for anything but trouble? So what good were they?

"Me, I aint stayn," Anson protested. "I aint sleepun here with no dead man."

"Shut your mouth, Anse," said Hank. "Les lay him out."

Hank cheekily presented his back to Rex in order to bend over Blacky's feet. However, he acted a little exquisite about polluting himself by touching them, filthy as they were. Instead he groped for a good hold on the britches above them. "Hump there, Anse. Grab them arms."

Anson shifted over that way, his steps jerky with impulse he wanted so much to hide that Rex made out what was to happen and lunged up off his bunk the instant Anson jumped to grab a gun off the mantel. Him Rex always had judged to be easier to handle in a showdown and therefore to be disposed of second, not first. His one stride forward was toward Hank, and with bowie knife aimed at his bent side, at the small ribs where the steel would start a flood in his lights and liver and belly, all three. Under the shock of that blow Hank opened his mouth to holler but brought out only a whimpery grunt, long drawn and faint at the end.

By the time Anson, after a fumble among the weapons, had snatched up a rifle, the knife was already out of his brother and coming up point first, again without the wasteful double movement needed to slash, but in one upward thrust aimed just below the ribs. Rex increased the certainty of burying it to the hilt by grabbing the rifle to snatch him forward; and he felt a peculiarly sickening exultation as the blade slid through all the soft organs inside until it jolted against the spine behind.

2

The Brazos Bottoms
Friday Afternoon
April 15, 1836

The first day and the second he rode clear of trails wherever he could. That way he avoided travelers, rarely seeing any, and giving them plenty of room when he did. Not until Magruder's burned cabin and the clinkers of those corpses among its ashes were two full days behind him did he take the chance of asking darkies at work about how to reach the army and what it was up to.

Three shoveling open a ditch to drain a flooded cornfield in the Brazos Bottoms told him Friday noon that General Houston was on the run again: he was withdrawing his troops across the Brazos to its east bank at Groce's Landing fifteen miles south. Thereafter Rex boldly put his pinto gelding (formerly Blacky's) onto the road in that direction.

Seldom today did he attempt any gait faster than a walk. He no longer could see well, his eyes burned so, and the pains shocking through him whenever he stirred his leg were matched by thudding aches inside his head. He had been sleepless too long. Often as he rocked along in the saddle he slumped into a doze, waking to find his fool pinto grazing or heading back northeast or drifting off toward some abandoned homestead with the smell of horse still afloat around it.

At the end of the afternoon he wakened from one of those spells to feel his mount shaking like an earthquake, whickering on the bank of a freshet within a belt of timber. What set off all the horse conversation was a droopy bay mare beyond the opposite shore. She was loaded with game: wild turkeys and grouse hung from her saddle by the feet, and also an antelope. Two men near her were gutting a deer, or had been. Just now their hunting knives hung idle in their hands while both gazed across the freshet, a slim blond youngster in buckskins and a man in a threadbare boughten coat. He was slighter than either of the Weatherfords, this older man, but had a clear, carrying voice too strong to seem his.

"What you doon there, mister?"

His knife was bloody, his hands too, and the boy's the same. The sledge of Rex's pulse began hammering hot iron inside his head.

"Huh?"

"Where you bound to?"

"Texas Army."

"That so? We're takun victuals to it, and glad to show you the way. You'n put that paint acrost?"

"Yuh, reckon so."

As Rex roweled his horse, the talky one dropped his voice, but not low enough. *"Where* of I seen that paint before? Seems like I seen the image of it somers."

The hammer in Rex's head hit ringing blows. He snatched his rein tight. He didn't have to cross, did he? On the other hand, how long could he hold up if he didn't? Those two woodsy bastards, knives and all, did not look uncommonly hard to handle. He might be damn sick of killing, but any such pair, if they crowded him close, would learn he was pretty cute at it when he had to be.

"I disremember where," the same man ran on. "Familiar to you, Hugh?"

"Nosir."

The way to avoid exciting doubt was not to act doubtful, Rex knew, so he spurred on across the brook. The mouthy man's eyes became still wider as Rex rode abreast.

"Mister, you look like *hell.*"

Rex knew he did. Aside from what buckshot and poor eating had done to him, he hadn't laid a razor to his face in days. His clothes, once so fine and full of ornament, had soaked up rain and mud and sweat till a self-respecting hog wouldn't wear such trash, and so many fleas and lice fidgeting around inside them till every waking hour was just one long misery.

"Mexican patrol give me a big blast of blue whistlers . . ." He laid a hand ouchily along his leg and let that complete the fiction for him.

"Patrol? *Where?*"

"North a piece."

"Hugh, what you make of that?"

The youngster did not speak or stir, merely let wondering blue eyes drift over Rex, so damned intelligent and honest that they provoked him in a way he could do nothing about.

"How'd you get away?" the older man asked.

"Oh, this pinto can run when he's got to. They give me a chase awhile till I crossed a crick and stood them off."

"Reckon that must of been one of Gaona's patrols. Heard tell they was scoutun north."

"Most likely." Rex's breath came easier. "Army got any good doctors?"

"They's three, one the best I ever seen, Dr. Springfield." The talker acted personally elevated in adding, "He's *our* doctor—lives only some twenty mile west of my place."

"Where's he at now?"

"With the sick down yonner below Groce's." A twist of his knife pointed beyond the woods and toward the south. "Three-four mile from here."

"Well." Rex pulled his paint's head up. "I got to see him, and quick as I can."

"Oh, we're headun there right away ourselves." The windbag looked as if anybody ought to consider it a treat to have him along to talk to—that is, listen to. "Be dark before you get there, and you'd likely stray, so I'll take you right to him, personal."

"Give me a hand here, Evett," said the boy. With knife rigid, he had turned to the slain deer. "This man aint in no estate to tarry."

They finished slicing the deer's guts out, washed the carcass by one quick dip in the brook, and hung it on their mare so as to balance off the weight of the antelope on the other side. Both then walked along between her and Rex's paint, each carrying a rifle in the loose, heedless, handy style of men who learned to shoot by the time they could whistle. The one called Evett was a walking military gazette, full of bad news and enthusiastic about getting it told.

Things was in terrible shape these days, he said, and there was the bedrock truth. Back when they made a stand on the Colorado the army reached a strength around a thousand, all hoped up and full of ginger, and spoiling to fight. Just when the time came to drive across the river and larrup a force of Mexicans threatening from there, Sam Houston took a notion to sneak away to the Brazos under cover of night, and no explanation to nobody. That killed the spirit off, because what sort of a apology for a army was it that the general of it he wouldn't let nobody fight?

From then on, all they ever heard about was disaster. Each new one outclassed the last "until disaster don't describe it no more: here in Texas we need a new word." A fine lot of boys from the States that soldiered with Colonel Frank Fannin about five-six hundred strong had been forced by lack of ammunition to quit fighting under articles of surrender near Goliad. That was bad enough, but after holding them three-four days under guard, the Mexicans lined them up, two ranks of unarmed Americans facing two ranks of Mexicans with bayonets, and butchered them where they stood. Twice as many fell in that massacre as in the Alamo, a case of cold slaughter unexampled along the whole frontier. For brute unmercifulness it never had been approached before, not even by the savages.

Now, if only the army had any least accomplishment to brag about, the outlook might have a streak of light in it somewhere, but no such thing. On the 29th day of March one battalion, left to hold San Felipe, went out of their minds when they saw what they took for Mexican cavalry approaching: they set the whole town afire without even delaying to save the food and supplies. Seemed like, while the town was all so gloriously blazing, they felt mighty splendid about so much sacrifice (of other people's property) until they discovered that the approaching cavalry was only a herd of cattle.

Next thing to happen, General Houston camped his main force right in a fork between the Brazos and Mill Creek, where they shortly had overflow from both streams racing around them. The camp turned into an island, the whole of it soft as a pot of paste. Things looked awful bad, but Old Sam called no councils. He asked no advice. He would only state and repeatedly state that drill was the single thing the army was fit for. The only way he knew of to turn it into a real army, ready for a showdown fight, was make everybody drill, and after the mud went ankle deep he still held the same. Bellyache or not, they had to drill, drill, drill, every dern day drill even though rain came at them like cats a-fighting. And all the time those Mexican butchers had the rest of Texas defenseless before them.

So more and more men began to wonder if helping their families wouldn't be better than just trifling around in the mud. A few at a time kept dwindling away until hardly seven hundred was all that stayed.

"Fact is," he confessed, "I took a notion moren once I ought to get back home myself. Got me a famly of my own I ought to see after, a real delicate lady for a wife, and three snotty, good-intentioned youngsters, ever one cute as speckled pups. There they are, left there defenseless, and disasters pilun up higher all the time. I ought to carry them off east."

Rex walloped his horse on the rump to make him step along better. "Then why in nation don't you?"

"Wellsir, I'll tell you about that. I would of only our capun aint the kind of feller it's easy to disappoint him. Last night when everbody looked asleep but the sentries, I *was* fixun to leave and had my personals bundled for it, but Capun Allan roused up and give me a look like Judgment Day. It shamed me till where I aint got the heart to try it no more for the present.

"Anyhow, my famly's no worse off than his lady friend, which they live with, along with her father. She's a high-up young widda woman, a mighty rare stunner and used to high livun, and if she can stand it —which I'm sure she can—so they'll have to too.

"They're livun comfortable in a out of the way place the Mexicans aint likely to find, or not quick. A right good place." He let his glance fix on Rex's a bit queerly, walking along close beside him in the twilight, seeming to expect to be asked just where they lived. When no such question came, he went on as if it had. "It's over above Otter Creek."

Again that hammer of aches clanged in Rex's head. Ev's eyes were wide open, stuck that way, and so innocent of the least cunning that Rex considered him full of it.

A change in the man's voice when he asked his next question showed that he was. "Ever been there?"

Rex let his rein drop onto his pommel, let the paint walk as he would, and drew out his knife to dig a thumbnail clean. "Never heard of it."

"Reason I asked, that horse, I could of swore I seen him there. Or else somers else."

"Well, one pinto sort of looks like another."

"Well, yes and no. Some is marked peculiar. I seen just one with a face marked the image of thatun's somers, a clover between the eyes like thatun, the same shape as the ace of clubs only white, and the other markuns just the same too."

"That's like I noticed myself. I seen two-three others he favors considerable."

With his heart pounding and the fool horse slogging through damp sod, his knife was none too steady against the quick under his nail. To eternally hush up this mouthy hayseed would be no trick at all if he had him alone; but that boy Hugh walking along, silent and watchful and apart, full of spring and purpose and active brains, tangled up the outlook more than he liked. Besides, the army was no great way off—too close to start any sort of ruckus that might get out of control. He pushed his knife back into its leather and gave thought to the future.

"What's Houston up to that he pulled you across the Brazos?"

"Mister, there aint a thing we'd liefer know. All he says is the Guvumunt run to Harrisburg and has got to be pertected, so I reckon we'll hustle thataway too. Whether it's them we're runnun to pertect, though, or old Sam Houston—that's disputed powerful fierce."

The day had worn out as they talked; the afternoon, dulled by sooty clouds, had changed to twilight. Stiff black dark was not far off, and neither was that doctor. From horseback Rex had been able for some while to make out a long row of redly glowing lights ahead upon the prairie, the fires of many bivouacs, and the moist air of evening distantly hummed with the voices of energetic men.

and bright, and all around them the wind-blown smokes and stinks

After a bit those voices were distinct beside them, the campfires big of an army camped for the night.

3

At the time, though the air was sulky, threatening still further rain, there was more cheer from fire to fire than Perry had seen in days. That afternoon all ranks had completed their crossing of the Brazos on a requisitioned steamboat, the *Yellowstone*, something of a lark in itself, and then toward evening they took part in a droll ruckus on the plantation of Charlie Donoho.

Donoho was a Tory who chose to stay on his land and denounce the rebellion, expecting favor from the victorious Santa Anna. He complained profusely and profanely to General Sam Houston because the "wuthless rowdies" under arms had begun cutting his timber for their campfires. The mannerly Houston guaranteed to stop that: marching them out of Donoho's woods, he deployed them along a fence of well-seasoned rails, handy to cook with, and issued a warning that whoever cut any more trees would be punished. Donoho's fence vanished, and with it his gratification in getting the troops moved.

Evett Tipton and Hugh Llewellyn brought in their load of game a little after nightfall. Perry at the moment was hunkering down close to his campfire to needle out a splinter which tearing the rail fence apart had buried in his palm. Beyond Evett and Hugh, out near the circumference of darkness, he noticed a stranger on a pinto horse, an unshaven rough in costly but polluted clothes. The fellow looked a fright—cheeks sunken, mouth angled over in desperate pain, and weariness had bruised the sockets of his eyes a bluish black. As their glances met, Perry felt he ought to know him, and the instantaneous arrest of those tired eyes implied at least equal recognition.

That, and then the stranger sent an empty stare forward into the dark. His attitude said, no, they had never known each other, and resisted any assumption that they had. Perry again applied the needle to his hand, wondering. A moment later, when he glanced back, the pinto was stepping along the line of fires and shortly disappeared.

Perry then went over to Evett, who was unloading game at the supply wagon.

"Ev, who's that who came with you?"

"Wellsir, the name he give me he said it was Buck Bancroft. Queer sort of fella—expensive clothes, and jeweled some too, but all dirty and stinkun and out of sorts. Say, where's he went to?"

"On up the line."

"Lookun for Doc Springfield, I reckon. Poor devil's crippled up awful bad. Mexican patrol run him a ways and give him a blast of blue whistlers."

"So? Where was that?"

"All up and down from knee to ankle."

"I mean where'd he meet with any patrol?"

"North apiece."

"But *where?* If patrols are working anywhere near we got to know where, and report it."

"Wellsir, we'n ask, though he aint in no estate to talk much. Leg's swole up right fierce. *There's* a sick man."

"Uhm. How long's he been like that?"

"Don't know, capun. He was hit right bad was all he tole us."

Perry went back to probe out his sliver. A sense of nagging unknowns grew upon him as he dug deeper into the injured quick of his palm. How could it be anything more than prejudice which, on sight, made his mind so firmly link that cuss with evil? After he brought the sliver swimming out in an ooze of blood he went back to Ev.

"That pinto—see any signs that buckshot hit him?"

"None that I took no notice of, nosir. You, Hugh?"

"Nosir. He was dog-tired but looked sound to me."

"Seems right odd a man would be off his horse with a Mexican patrol after him."

"Sir?" Ev's eyes widened in the firelight. *"Off* his horse?"

"If he'd been horseback a spray of buckshot on his leg would give his horse a bellyful too."

"That's certain, yessir. And you know, capun, I seen that pinto somers before. But not him. Reckon he stoled it?"

"Well, I don't see how we'd prove it if he did, times the way they are." Perry impatiently wrenched his thought away from the whole problem. There was too much else to attend to at present. More rain was on the way tonight, or he didn't know weather; and, even though the run of his men could hardly be forced to take measures against rain until they could feel it, or at least smell it, he meant to have them put together shelters covered with prairie grass before the first drop fell.

It was on them, however, before they could finish. That night, for many, was a sorry time.

4

The next day was worse, much worse.

The road churned into a wallow under the toiling feet, the trampling hooves, the laboring wheels of an army on the move. Houston kept it moving, moving, moving—its canvas-covered supply wagons, its two cannon, its ammunition carts, its baggage, its pack mules, its loads of sick, and the tag-along line of refugees behind—all of it. The lowest, gummiest stretches of trail so glued wheels down that ant rows of men had to carry everything liftable forward to high ground, then put their shoulders to mud-greased fellies and force each vehicle onward until the carried articles could be reloaded. Not even the general held himself exempt from these labors, dismounting to help push out any conveyance he saw stuck. By noon the entire army was plastered with gumbo, uniformed in it, tiled by it. Perry in weary humor saw some advantage in never catching an honest rest, reflecting that if men coated with that much gumbo ever let it dry they would stiffen into terra-cotta statues.

Meanwhile he learned that Dr. Springfield had stopped long enough to operate on the man called Buck Bancroft. During the afternoon he dropped back for a look, walking to let two recruits with measles ride Marquis. He found Buck in a cart for sick jostling along behind the winding serpent of wagons, men, mules, oxen, and nags which composed the army, and just ahead of another serpent of fleeing homesteaders. Buck was unconscious, reduced to slack flesh by opium and exhaustion. Perry for the first time had a look at him from close alongside.

At that range he could not be mistaken: he *had* seen him before. His crushed nose, his wide mouth, and the stained, embroidered waistcoat tightening and relaxing with the labors of his breath revived the sensation of standing beside him in the Benevolent Loan Bank of

Louisiana. Perry remembered him fastidiously knifing a wedge from one end of a Havana, the same man, and once more he felt the apprehension of waiting to be interviewed about an "opportunity" nobody but a thug would accept.

This, then, was the "reasoner" with the odd name which Major Burleigh later had said meant both *king* and *peasant*—Rex Cottier. Perry's head turned into a hive of speculations about why Banker Beaufait might have sent such an agent out here, and yet he could not cross-examine him any time soon: the fellow was nothing more for the present than limp flesh sacked up in filthy clothes.

No doubt, too, it would be better first to piece together all possible clues. So, near sundown, when the cavalcade halted to water and feed, he sought out Evett Tipton.

"That paint of Bancroft's, Ev—believe you said you saw him before."

"Yessir, and I finely studied out where: right in my own front yard! Meanun, of course, in Miz Pawmer's."

"Hm! You sure of that?"

"Certain sure. Been aimun to tell you, but—"

"When'd you see him there?"

"Not long before I took off. Let's see, just near the end of March. Been hardly three weeks back."

"You couldn't be mistaken?"

"Aint no doubt, capun. Never seen but one paint in my life had a clover on his face, and thatun's him. He was rid that day by a mean-lookun skunk name of Blacky Reed. I *mean* mean. Had a face on him like a sledgehammer."

"I see. What brought him?"

"Well, I don't rightly know. He brung couple letters for Miz Pawmer and asked after somebody else, but I disremember who—if she ever said. Bastard come there full of sass and bad news, and so uppity till where we lined him up on our gunsights and run him off the place."

"Did he mention anybody named Beaufait?"

"Not as I heard, capun."

"Anybody named Cottier—Rex Cottier?"

"If he did, I disremember. I don't recollect no ins and outs of what the man said. All I know is he come on that paint, and plumb full of brute evil, clean up to the eyes."

Increasingly restless over the matter, Perry intended to ask Dr. Springfield what he had been able to learn about his patient, but was called to a council of officers. A move was afoot to have General Houston impeached, and one of many who noisily favored it was Lieutenant Richard Garrick, Perry's top subordinate.

5

Perry rode away from the council alone, not lingering, as Garrick did, to hear more talk afterward from anti-Houston men. Night was fully established when he reached his own company's supply wagon.

Sergeant Molineau, who stood at its tailgate carving a haunch of yesterday's antelope under the light of a cypress torch, paused to watch him dismount. His big tuberous nose came up, scenting trouble. "Capun, you look right given to thought."

"Tonight's a good time for thought, unless it's already too late."

He pulled the saddle off Marquis, slipped a halter in place while easing his bridle free, buckled a pair of hobbles around his forward pasterns, and slapped his rump by way of blessing as he let him go to graze. Though Molineau and the rest waited in silence for him to explain himself, he merely picked up a slab of wood onto which Molineau served three steamy slices of antelope and a brace of roasted potatoes.

"You still aint said, capun," Mountain Bentley spoke up from across the campfire, "what they said at the council."

"Damn foolishness is all."

Taking his saddle along for a seat, he shifted over into a horseshoe of comrades looping both ways from the wagon around the fire, which had been raked to a wide bed of coals licked over by tongues of flame. Above these hung spitted chunks of venison and antelope, juicily sizzling beside a lidless black pot in which turnips and potatoes from a runaway settler's cabin bubbled together. Like most of the men, Perry had nothing to eat with except a hunting knife, which he speared into a cut of antelope, bit off the whole thing, and God how good!

"But what *kine* of foolishness?" Mountain persisted.

"Lieutenant Garrick will be here directly. Let him say." Perry chewed his meat a moment. "Word from another quarter concerns us more, word from General Houston. He's dissatisfied with our showing today. All this time on the march, and we're only seventeen miles from Donohos'."

"Christ on high, *only!*" Molineau rubbed the heel of his hand against his nose, sending his butcher knife straight up before him. "Standard for infantry is fifteen. In this gumbo, seventeen is prodigious."

"Not enough though. Tomorrow we march again before dawn."

Agonized yelps rose from several at once.

"Capun, you're teasun, surely," Mountain whimpered. "Tamarra's Sunday, the Sabbath, the Day of Rest. On the Seventh Day even God rested."

"Well, this aint a week when we've measured up to God." He let their laughter subside before adding, "Anyhow, what was all this talk I heard about yall pining so for action?"

"Such a march aint action," Molineau pointed out. "That's suffrun."

Lieutenant Garrick, leathery, tall, and so erect that his head was unnaturally reared back, meanwhile had ridden a tired roan up to the supply wagon, dismounted, and tied her to a wheel. In the stiff spraddle of a man who never went anywhere afoot if a horse was handy, he strode over to the fire, drew his saber, and speared it into the pot, bringing out a turnip, which he blew on and ate. Around the circle there was an effort not to watch him, largely unsuccessful because he did have a self-esteeming style to him.

"Well then," said Perry, "we start suffrun again before day. The scouts picked up word the Mexicans are at Harrisburg, or were yesterday."

A bruiser named John-Paul Frey, eldest son of Widow Frey, called out from his perch on a stack of firewood, "That mean we're marchun that way, capun, or runnun thother?"

"Now there, son"—Garrick used his saber like a schoolmaster's pointer—"there's one damn cute question. So happens tonight, though, I can tell you exactly which way."

"So can I," Perry inserted. "We'll go the way we're ordered to go."

"Depends on what's ordered, sir."

Because Garrick had a political itch to scratch, also because he was Perry's senior by eight years, he time and again had sent hints up the hierarchy of command that the captaincy of their unit should go to him, the lieutenancy to Perry. Houston's neglect of that opinion offended him. To avoid open collisions with Garrick, the kind which bedeviled so many other companies, had kept Perry's wits nimble. Tonight, however, he was too tired for anything more than plain words.

"Not at all, lieutenant. It depends solely on whether the order's issued by the commander of this army."

"You heard the council, captain."

"But *we* didn't," John-Paul threw out invitingly.

"What *did* they say?" a voice from the shadows demanded.

"Something, my friends," Garrick gladly supplied, "which, if you use your head about it, it may affect the whole future of this territory for all time to come." He began drawing on the ground with his saber. "Here's the way we go tomorrow, which I mean we start on before dawn. One mile east of here we come to a fork. One prong bends southeast to Harrisburg, where the enemy sits and enjoys theirselves out of Texas corncribs and stores and smokehouses. The other prong, it bends northeast—*which* some claim Sam Houston aims to take, though of course nobody knows for sure what Houston means to do because he's too perpetually *con*-trary to say, *and* too pusillanimous.

"Anyhow, all we can expect is some new abortion or other from Old Sam. So right many officers at the council, Captain Mosley Baker and Wiley Martin and fine, patriotic old Texanians such as that, we put the whole thing this way: if he orders us northeast, instead of down to Harrisburg, we should ignore him, impeach him, chain him up, shoot him, hang him, anything, only march on southeast and *fight*."

Grunts of approval came from some, chiefly from Garrick's platoon. Butternut Brown, however, spoke up in his Arkansas drawl. "Ef I been there I'd of said cut his balls out, because a general that his men can do whatever they taken a fancy to do he's got to have no balls."

Through the laughter which followed, Garrick remained heavily expressionless, waiting for silence before he resumed. "I admit there's some like Captain Allan that they didn't agree at all. Any fiddle-footed adventurers that's come larking out here late from way back East, they can't appreciate how us old Texanians feel who've borne the heat and burthen of the day since early times, us *real* Texanians. No, they can't. But *we* say let's fight *now*."

A planter from the Trinity River, Garrick rested his claim to being an "old Texanian" upon the fact that, though but thirty-one, he had arrived six years ago.

"And *why* are we spoiling so to fight? Just think how many kin and comrades those Mexicans cruelly slaughtered, *which,* if you picture how they piled them up like cordwood and burnt them pitiless, that was about the worst brutality to Christian men on this continent since Columbus landed. Think of our ladies running to escape pollution, of our children homeless and hungry, trailing through this mud, growing sickly and weak. Goddamn it to hell, just think about *that* a little, which if you do, you can't *help* but think like *real* Texanians."

At his summation he was almost in tears, a victim of his own eloquence, and not a few admired it almost as much as he did. Perry began to wonder in melancholy humor whether he had them all bewhiched.

Sergeant Molineau, however, let go a snort. "Lieutenant, sir . . ." Molineau ran his tongue across the ragged rent of his mouth, amiably amused. "I'm a old Texian too, been here twicet as long as you. But who's fit the big fights in this war? Last fall who *was* it snuck into San Antonio and smoked out four-five times their number, uh? Not old Texians, no. *Hell* no. Nosir, I'll tell you who: boys like them." He wagged his knife at Perry, Butternut, Mountain, Hugh, and Elias. "There's who done it—'fiddle-footed adventurers that come larkun out late from the States,' as you call them. They took San Antonio *and* the Alamo.

"The reason I know I just so happened to be there because that newcomer there, Capun Perry Allan, talked me into stayn by him. But us *real* Texians was right scarce—hardly one in ever half-dozen, if that. Where was the rest at when we took San Antonio? Them that wasn't home—like you was—elected to set aside on their butts a comfterble stretch out of town. They give us supplies after dark, when it was safe, and by day they set there sayn they'd pervide a reserve."

A sniggering repetition of "pervide a reserve" circled around the fire.

Molineau lifted his knife for quiet. "You told about comrades massackreed in the Alamo. Who was *they?* The great proportion and majority never set foot in Texas before last fall. And Goliad? Why, at Goliad, Fannin wrote not long before he surrendered that he could hardly name six in six hundred who'd been in Texas six months.

"Where was all the real Texians *that* time when they was needed so bad? *Talkun* somewhere, no doubt talkun big about the war, shootun off their mouths, not their rifles. Lieutenant Garrick, I *am* a real Texian, for sure, and the more I think about it, the more I smart with shame."

Whoops of laughter applauded him. Lieutenant Garrick flexed his saber between his two hands in detesting impatience until the circle quieted.

"Tomorrow morning," he resumed, "if Houston tries to lead us away from the enemy, are we obliged to follow? What did we take up arms for? To meet the enemy, of course. All *right,* I say *meet* him." He whipped the saber sideward. "I say *lick* him." He jabbed toward the west. "I say run him clear the hell out of Texas, and quick. If Houston orders us away from another chance to fight"—he threw his empty hand flatly to the left—"then I say that's *all.* He aint fit to command us. Obeying him would violate our patriotic duty. Gentlemen, tomorrow we got to *act.*"

His peroration was a little spoiled by one word from Perry: "Correct!" Striding to him past the fire, Perry brought a finger down before him like a pistol. "And be mighty damn careful *how* you act. Strictly speaking, a soldier has just one duty: to obey orders. In arguing otherwise, sir, you *seem* to be inviting these men to mutiny. That, sir, is sufficient reason for court-martial the world over."

"Captain, is that a threat?"

"It's a statement of fact. The custom is to shoot men for mutiny."

"Unless, of course—"

"No unless about it. That is recognized and accepted practice. You better recollect also that, on the Brazos, General Houston stated in writing he intended to follow that practice." He turned to the circle around them. "Anyone who's been with me long knows how I've disliked this or that about Houston's policy. We especially never liked his neglect to let us know just what his policy *is* so we can judge sensibly whether to like it or not. But he was duly elected commander-in-chief of all forces in Texas. The intent then was that *he* should give orders and *we* should obey them. We *must* do so, for an army which does not obey is no army: it's a mob. In the ranks we don't make decisions. We carry them out."

"See here, captain, are you trying to say—"

"Silence!" Perry bellowed. Because he was by habit considerate, humorous, and courtly, his roar at Garrick jarred a deeper hush through all the men in hearing. "I *am* trying to say. You were given your chance to speak, an ample chance, and what you say proves it's past time you pinned back those ears and *listened.*

"Boys, a crisis in this war is not far off. Can't be. The Mexican columns are widely separated. Each one is a long ways from help, whereas we are closer to our support every day. If there's anyone to thank for this advantage it's Old Sam, because the goose-chase he's led them is what scattered them and took them so far from their resources while bringing us nearer to ours. The time is at hand now to close ranks for the showdown and act like soldiers.

"Ever since the first day I joined this troop I have tried to help every man here through any difficulty known to me. I have tried to be your brother, your nurse, your servant. Still, that does not mean anybody whatever can disobey a direct order. Boys, when we come to that fork tomorrow, we will be guided, not by what any of the mutinous may do—tonight, tomorrow, and every day we soldier together, we are going to act *as ordered.*"

He scanned their faces. The majority looked compliant.

"However," said Garrick, "we're still free men in Texas. If some decide different, who's to stop us?"

"Me, for one." Perry thumped his chest. "Yours very truly." He cocked one big fist up before Garrick's eyes. *"That* will. Never once have I raised it against any man in this company, and I hope I never have to. But God made it a mallet, and by Christ I will personally knock the eternal daylights out of any man who makes one move toward mutiny. After that's done to satisfaction, I will institute a court-martial against him. *Now"*—he strode over to where he had the supply wagon close behind him and glared around the watching company—"is there *anybody* who doubts it?"

Silence. The firelight leaping against motionless faces around the fire heightened the impression of uncommon mental activity.

Molineau stuck his knife upright in the tailgate and shifted over beside Perry. "Anybody that does doubt it, he's got me to whup first." After giving that a moment to soak in: "I never thought high of Old Sam, but I don't aim to let *nobody* trouble Capun Allan to knockum on their ass before I accommodate you first myself."

"Far as that goes," said Mountain, rousing briskly, *"we* been on his side since times immemoral—me and Eli and Butternut, and still are." Hauling them over by the scruff, one in each hand, he gave both a shake. "Aint that so, boys?"

"Blimey, hi'd ite to deny it." Once free of Mountain, Elias backed up between him and Perry, looking half their size, and waved to the rest. "Well, boys, don't stagnite. Oo the bloody ell is too yellow-livered to jine us?"

During a chuckling, shoving rush to be one with the loyal, John-Paul Frey and his brother Raymond-McHenry crowded Garrick over with them whether he liked being there or not.

Perry clapped Garrick on the shoulder. "Boys, here's a sportsman, sure. Let's give a cheer for the lieutenant!"

They chorused with him, "Hooray for Lieutenant Garrick"—though a little raggedly.

As they dispersed, Molineau stirred up another guffaw with, "By gum, *that* was unanimous, and one over."

Not until afterward, not until he was cocooned in a buffalo robe for the night and about to sleep, did Perry give further thought to the puzzles centering on the man he knew to be Rex Cottier. All the unanswered questions connected with him would have to wait, obviously, until a less critical time.

From C. B.'s Journal
April 16, 1836

River travel proves neither as easy nor as swift as we expected. We must stay in sluggish waters near shore to control our two rafts with poles because the deeps of the San Jacinto are quite untrustworthy. Much too often we have not been on the water at all, but fleeing another rainstorm or drying around a fire or hunting shelter for the night or scouting after victuals. Inexperience hampers us also: one raft or the other was hung up seven times today, twice on sandbars, as often in snarls of reeds, afterward in the suck of an overflow, and so on.

Whatever the crisis, my wound keeps me merely sunning myself under the care of our ladies, a shameful thing, but I *am* getting better. This evening I walked a little on crutches whittled from forked saplings. What an extraordinary sense of triumph! It is like being reborn, this learning to walk again, particularly so because, despite the dragging weakness in my hip, I experienced today a tingle of renewing health, a secret exuberance such as used to flash through me when I was young.

There is incomparable advantage in overcoming fear of death. When this flesh of mine was hurting so, and threatening to rot away, I perceived that my body was about to become only another manure; that a corpse is the excrement of the soul, that death is the equal of birth, and as useful to the race, which it perpetually cleanses as elimination does ourselves. Nor is death any less useful to each individual person who has become so worn out or so tortured or so intolerably tyrannized that he sees his ladder upward all in ruin. My own prefigured corpse a week ago seemed nothing to regard with horror or pity any more: I saw it rather to be a product of the earth preparing itself for restoration to the earth where roots will draw vitality from its dissolution.

Now then, can any freedom whatever be prized above freedom from the dread of death? I soberly doubt it. For are not all other fears subsidiary to this one? I think most are. That being so, whoever rids himself of this primary fear is in a condition to live much better because he can apply more boldly to the problems of life whatever endowments hide within him.

Looking back over the past week, I do marvel at how much new life a man may gain by all but losing it. So keen is the feeling of resurrection and fresh revelation and vast advantage that I wonder whether, if I ever meet Rex or Blacky again, or those two birds they chummed with, I ought not to thank them—before I shoot them. At this hour I cannot picture myself wanting to hunt any of them down, as sound men will expect.

Of course I know even now that such relaxation will not do. Death must be resisted and evil stayed. Out of our efforts to do so grow our greatest accomplishments.

CHAPTER XX

I

San Jacinto River
Sunday Afternoon
April 17, 1836

"Sh-h, listen!" Camilla raised a thimbled hand from her sewing toward Roberta, who had been humming a work tune while poling their raft south. Ahead lay a bend toward which Camilla tilted her bonnet to catch every sound. "Voices . . . a crowd! Pa, you hear?"

"Can't say I do, no."

"Fudge! Do listen, and you'll hear."

He, tillering their raft from a couch of hay and pillows, listened dutifully. He heard water gurgle under the logs below him, that and a quail whistling beyond the shore westward. Also he heard Esau, on the livestock raft a furlong or so behind, speak to the young Tiptons, who venerated him and squabbled for the privilege of steering while he poled.

Cedric wagged his head without apology or regret. "Map doesn't show any town along this water, Milla. We must still be a good piece above Lynchburg."

To avoid being dazzled by the sun, Camilla moved deeper into the shade of the brougham, which dominated the raft like a pilot house, and bent again over renovation of a dress she had given to Liz.

"I do think I heard people, town or no town."

Roberta resumed her poling, her dreamy humming too, and he his wonder at the Rio de San Jacinto. The River of Saint Hyacinth—the name itself had a loveliness to match that given the eye. Nature did not look wanton here: everywhere he saw the artfulness of grandly conceived design. The river coiled between colonnades of cypress, tall, tapered, and stately. Newly green savannas as wide as the day lay beyond them except where overflow from the river had formed lakes dotted with islands of higher land. No trace of man, aside from the raft, marred the wild peace of these waters: not so much as one skiff had they seen all day. Across an azure sky, however, cruised a fleet of white clouds with the grace of sloops in full sail, and under-water duplicates of these floated between rows of cypress wavering upside down.

The tune Roberta set adrift along the river was the sort darkies at work sing to lighten hoes or brooms, mops or mallets, axes, buckets, churns, or flatirons. Barefoot, she carried her pole eight steps forward along the shoreward side of the raft, thrust it deep, and pushed it eight back. Her melody was in quavering minor, its rhythm strong, and her footsteps whispered with it. Over and over it repeated itself, each time with some variation, while over and over her footsteps wore the raft eight steps forward, eight steps back.

Here, Cedric thought, was an enactment in brief of all daily routines from which ordinary lives derive their substance throughout all time. Her work had about it the spell of the revolving wheel, the grinding stone, the pump at work, the scythe at harvest, the cradle rocking; and the tune she hummed so echoed the unappeasable longing of lowly, timeless people the world around that he could not follow it without a sense of concord with such people. It made him feel all the way into his bones the miraculous advantage of being back on the current of common life. He flexed the tiller, not to change their course, only to stir an eddy, only for the pleasure of feeling afresh that he was of some use in this long journey toward the Gulf.

"Pa, there!" Camilla's eyes sought his. "Hear that?"

Her trick of smiling without change of face, with nothing more than heightened illumination, flowered its best, reflecting the ardor of her wish to immerse herself awhile among people, people, people. She wanted also, he knew, to relinquish his care to someone competent to cure him, whereas he could not picture himself confronted by a surgeon without rising dread. Her application of mesmerism had been helping his flesh work out some sort of compromise with his bullet, an adaptation to it however temporary, so that he had no severe pain at any time, and no recurrence of fever. Surgery, of course, would put him in hell again, and his feeling was that he had been there long enough. He liked things pretty well the way they were.

"Can't you hear?" she insisted. "Or *won't* you?"

He did check his breath to listen. Roberta listened with him, Mrs. Tipton also. A breeze from around the bend stirred their bonnet ribbons. Faintly on its swell—yes, he could hear voices, many inter-tangled.

"Plain," Liz answered for him. "Souns like a fish fry, Miz Pawmer."

"Or a fair," Roberta ventured.

"Right like that, deed so."

For once Liz's vaguely drifting, wanting eyes turned bright. Her palms stroked wisps of hair back under the poke of her bonnet to pretty up. Not since coming to Texas had she been near a town or any crowd bigger than a quilting would draw—not in two long, long years.

"Ain it time to refresh ourselves, mam? We cain go on lookun thisaway."

"Lookun whataway?" Cedric demanded. "Yall look perfectly decent the way you are."

"Please now, Pa. Do put ashore."

"Most likely they're settlers running for their lives too, Milla. No use suffering so to look grand for them."

"They fokes," Liz shot back.

"Mahs Cedic," Roberta put in, "you *know* you want yuh daughter keepun up."

"Don't know as I ever saw her when she didn't."

"Come, Pa. Stop deviling us so and turn ashore."

"Bawn a lady, sah," Roberta carried on, "she got to *act* a lady."

Against doctrine so lofty, he perceived, no male contention could prevail. He so pulled the tiller as to ground the raft upon a prominence where, beyond the shore-line colonnade of cypresses, lay a sunless and secretive grove, a passable dressing room.

While the women were taking ashore what baggage they needed, Esau and the boys drifted near on the livestock raft. Along its center stood the chestnut mares and teams of mules, all paired off side by side and head to tail, peaceably switching flies. Cedric waved Esau onward to beach his raft farther around the bend. Esau, all his life acquainted with how ladies put on for company, poled a bit farther downstream in perfect understanding.

Alone, Cedric relaxed in the fellowship of his pipe to contemplate the lovely Rio de San Jacinto. Experience had taught him that, as the apple of contentment is a most perishable fruit, the wise will relish it while they may.

When the women emerged from the woods the sun was far down the sky behind them. Camilla was in a hurry to reach civilization before twilight, and too brimful of curiosity and happiness to sit idle. Regardless of her ribbony clothes, she took up a pole to help Roberta speed the raft along, as nothing useful could be expected of Mrs. Tipton, who was very nearly paralyzed with pride in one of Camilla's dresses from New Orleans, altered to fit her well. Yet she too was in an agony to reach the source of those thronging voices. All were—all except the major, who annoyed Camilla by looking entertained over their haste and finery.

He did not seem to understand that simply getting near to other people made it a grand occasion, one to celebrate in frills and scent and laughter. And where so many were, a physician could not be far away. Neither could creature comforts. That wavering fabric of voices ahead was a banner saluting the drive and toil by which they had won through all those miles of rain and mud and desolation. The beauty of this success, here on these incomparably graceful waters, brought a mist of gratitude to Camilla's eyes.

As the raft floated around a final curve, she saw in the distance a wretched scatter of people near conveyances queued up west from the river—buckboards, ox sleds, buggies, carts, and pioneer wagons covered with high-looping canvas. All were waiting for a turn to board a ferry big enough for only one family at a time. The teams of most had been unhitched and turned loose to graze. Some people were fishing, some washing clothes, some rummaging in heaps of effects piled high on every vehicle, some changing babies or chopping wood or yelling after stray children or herding livestock. Many had fires going, and pots over them. One group was butchering a calf, another dressing poultry. Several people floundered after a runaway pig.

But what shocked Camilla into a motionless stare and muted everyone else on the raft was the debasing filth and misery everywhere. A wide area of wet prairie was more black than green, churned up by wading feet, and surely not alone by the creatures now there, but by score on score of refugees during previous days. How many there had been, and how long they had been crossing by this ferry, was indicated by maimed wheels, boxes, furniture, harness, utensils, and papers abandoned to the mud; and the air was tainted by careless deposits of excrement, offal, garbage, and rotted fish.

Two women with five little girls in tow were approaching Indian file along the riverbank toward the first grove. All had been maintaining the downward concentration characteristic of rural females on their way to a privy; but, at sight of the raft, they halted to gape as it glided near. Though it was not thirty feet from shore, Camilla rocked up tiptoe to wave.

"Hadado, ladies," she sang out.

The heavier and older of the two women said, "Lo, miss." Both women were solid and homely and durable, both of coarse ore seemingly molded at the same foundry—sisters, no doubt. Their bonnets, wilted shapeless, let oily strands of hair droop along their cheeks. Their hands were grimy, feet bare except for a coating of gumbo, which also weighted their skirts from knee level downward.

Camilla knew enough about such women to realize, however, that what they wore or failed to wash off was a poor index of what should be thought about them. Moreover she would have been an ingrate to think hard of them, for the lips of the older muttered something sideward which looked and sounded like, "Real peach, aint she!"

While the raft drifted before them Camilla called again as cheerfully as before, "What place is this, please?"

"Ferry," said the older woman. "Ferry crossun for the Liberty Road, and on east."

"How far is Lynchburg, mam?"

"Lynchburg?" The woman wiped a hand across her mouth as if to cleanse it for exceptional performance. "Why, Lynchburg's maybe only twenty mile or such a matter as the crow flies, but a hell of a piece by the crooks and turns of this river. Anyhow, nobody aint headun for Lynchburg now—nobody with any sense aint."

"Oh?"

"No, Lynchburg's south, and govumunt run south. Where they're at it aint a healthy place to be."

"Why so?"

"Them's who the hos-tiles is after, the govumunt."

"The government?" She raised her voice because the raft was gliding away. "The Texas Government?"

"Godalmighty yes, the Texas Govumunt," the woman laughingly shouted. "What other govumunt we got here?—when we got any."

The water between them had widened too far to permit finding out what had brought the government so far down in this corner of Texas. Camilla looked to her father; but, instead of venturing any explanation, he jogged his pipe downstream. "Down at that next point, honey, I'll shoal up along the shore. You and Berta ready your poles."

Ahead of them on the point a compact man in a worn seafaring cap and roundabout had a fishpole upright against a shoulder while four silent, soiled little boys watched him thread a worm onto his hook. The major tillered sharply that way. As the shoreward corner of the raft caught in mud, Camilla and Roberta speared their poles upright along the downstream side to counter the secret pull of waters underneath.

The fisherman hauled the raft a foot or so ashore. Black stubble darkened his jaws; his eyes were black too, yet he had about him a look of waking amiability and favoring estimation.

He thumbed his cap at the major. "Gudday, mister."

"Good day to you, sir."

"How's things where you been at?"

In this Camilla recognized an expectation that decent strangers would be prompt to tell where they came from and who they were. He, it developed (after Major Burleigh named himself, Camilla, and Mrs. Tipton as being from the Otter Creek Country), was a carpenter from Allen's Landing on Buffalo Bayou, formerly a ship's carpenter, and so known as "Salty" Latham. During these exchanges the women and girls Camilla had questioned came along the riverbank after the raft, and other people were converging that way. Salty pointed out the younger woman as Mrs. Latham, the older as her sister, Mrs. Maudie Ward.

"The biggest majority of everbody here," he explained and wagged an elbow toward refugees on the prairie, "comes from in and around Allen's Landun and Harrisburg. Day fore yesterday we flapped outa there like gulls in a typhoon: we'd got word a big force of Mexicans was bound for Harrisburg and likely to cut us off. So we run up here."

"Well," the major grunted and surveyed the growing press of spectators, "everybody's taking it mighty cool today."

"Aye, sir. The panic's spent: we don't apprehend no immediate attack. Our boys captured couple Mexican scouts that swore the enemy's after the govumunt, and not a thought about us, but we aim to get the women and chillern across yonner." He waved toward the river's farther shore, where a sizable camp had formed. "Then they'll have this water tween them and the enemy, which aint got the means to cross it quick, and men that don't go back to join our boys, like I am, can make a good stout resistance."

"You're going to join our boys?" Camilla asked. Her heart wabbled like a cork in carried water. "They're coming this way too?"

"We aint heard, miss, but so we calculate."

"What makes you think so?"

"Where's their munitions come from? East. Where's their reinforcements come from? East. With the enemy east of *them* nowadays, they got to shift east theirselves, and fast. That you can take as certain: they got to hustle this way, or be outfoxed, outflanked, cut off. Knowun Sam Houston, I'd say he'd see to it he aint outfoxed."

"*You* know General Houston?"

"Aye, soldiered under him till three weeks ago. And will again, quick as I get these women and chillern far east as Liberty."

She clung tight to her upright barge pole, borrowing upon its strength. "In the army there's a dear friend of ours, Captain Allan. You know him?"

"Saw him ever day, aye. Got him a good troop of boys, and highly regarded himself. *Very* highly regarded."

Again her heart veered off balance, knocked one way by unspeakable pride, the other by dread. "Wa-was he all right?"

"Him? Certainly."

"I mean he wrote how they were straining so to empty all the country westward, and the enemy so close behind, and that hideous weather, and all that long marching, and the food must be dreadful. Was he sick or anything?"

Mrs. Ward disconnected her stare to nudge Mrs. Latham. "Romance!"

Salty, ignoring her, shook his head. "Miss, a natural-born range horse aint troubled much by spring weather. Sick? Not him."

"Congratulations, Dr. Latham," her father interposed. "You have successfully cured a case of imminent heart failure."

During the shout of laughter which followed, Camilla's cheeks went hot. "Oh, a doctor—is there any doctor near here?"

"Doc MacLeod from Allen's Landun, certainly." Latham's elbow wagged toward the queue of vehicles. "Back yonner in one of them wagons."

"Pa, how lucky this is, a doctor right here!"

"No, miss. He's here, but not right. Not today."

"Salty," Mrs. Ward cautioned, "don't you go talkun Doc MacLeod down." She kept her face almost straight as she added, "Us ladies thinks the world of Doc MacLeod."

"Aint it so," said Mrs. Latham.

"There's a man, uh, Bessie?"

Camilla became a little impatient with these innuendoes. "What's the matter with him?"

"Same thing's the matter with a spare bull: needs cuttun, there's what's the matter with him—or so you'd think. Liquor him some, and no bull's his equal, by his own calculation."

Latham turned on her blandly. "Now, Maudie, why don't you hush a minute? People they ask about a doctor they want a straight answer." To Camilla he resumed, "Nothun permanent the matter with him. Dead drunk is all. Somebody need doctorun bad?"

Camilla explained about her father. A long digression resulted, for everyone in earshot wanted to hear more about the assault on Hoping Hill and the rogues responsible for it.

Reverting to MacLeod, she asked, "When the doctor's sober, what's his standing?"

Before anyone could answer, a stubby, neckless man in a bowler hat yelled at the major from the back of a saddled mule. "What kind of logs you got in them two rafts, sir?" He clubbed a heavy cane in the direction of each. "Any hardwood in there?"

The major dipped his head gravely. "All hardwood, sir." He flicked a fractional wink at Camilla before concluding, "Why?"

"What'll you take for the damn things?"

"What'll you give?"

Camilla watched with eyes enlarging; her purse had been lightened by purchase of these logs, and she had plans which cash would promote.

The man tightened his lips like a fist, squinting at each raft, pretending to be unaware of all the upturned, waiting faces on either side. "Well, les see."

In dismounting, he threw his mule's rein to one of three ragged Africans who had been dogging after him afoot, the puny, lightless, hopeless type lately imported through Cuba, all black as beetles. He pushed past Latham to the raft Camilla and her father were riding. He stomped around it, sounding it thoroughly with mud-caked boots. He jabbed his cane under a loose plank for a squint at the logs. "Give you a gold eagle for both. Ten dollars, gold."

"Reckon you would." The major examined the bowl of his pipe. "Knowing full well they're worth five times that, here where so many families want to cross."

Latham grunted out a laugh. *"There* you are, Cass. He seen right through you like a washed window."

"Goddamnit, Salty, you keep clear of this. Hell of a way for a brother-in-law to act."

"Hell of a way for you to act," said Mrs. Ward in a tone allowing no doubt that Cass was her husband. "Here's fine people been through every description of trouble without no damage to *their* manners, and first thing you try is to skinnum."

"Maudie, if there's one thing the Lord God shoulda left offa you it's that mouth. *Shut* it. All I want is—"

"Why, you mizerble skunk, whenso*ever* you think you're *man* enough to shut it, you'll find out mighty damn quick how this here fist feels on *yours.*"

Amidst backslapping hilarity Cass turned to prod the raft a bit more. He edged closer to the major. "I'm just a mind to do people a service is all. Heap of fokes here waitun to ferry over. All I want is to put these things to work and help people out."

Latham spoke up. "At how much a head?"

"Blazes, Salty, *can't* you keep out of this?"

"And after all the crossun's done," Latham went on calmly, "you'll still have some fine sawlogs to mill when the crisis dies away."

"Well," said Major Burleigh, "it's entirely proper to earn all he can."

"Anyhow," Camilla observed, "whether we ought to stop here we still don't know, do we? Reckon Dr. MacLeod will do when he sobers up?"

Latham nodded. "There's lots worse."

"And better too, is that it?"

"Nowheres around here, no, miss. A big-dose, kill-or-cure doctor, that's Doc MacLeod."

"Gracious, doesn't he sound risky though!"

"Reckon he cures moren he kills, which aint a thing all can say. And for bullets—beun a Texas doctor give him a nice hand at diggun out bullets. But no use till tamarra, sure."

"Wuthless till mornun," Mrs. Ward agreed. "Yall might as well raft acrost and make you a camp and wait there where you're safe. He'll be over endurun the night."

"*They* can't raft acrost, two finicky ladies and a wench," her husband snapped. He jogged his cane toward the major. "Not with him all crippled and down. It's too deep out there to pole, and that current's so stout till where they'd soon find theirselves down in the Gulf. They sell me the raft, I'll take my bucks"—his cane speared toward the three Africans, who were now squatting indifferently by the mule, slack as spent hounds—"they'll row, and I'll tiller." He batted toward the opposite shore. "We'll guarantee to cross them safe."

"No need to," Latham declared and roused himself for action. "I know water like nobody here. Just leave me round up two-three real men, and we'll see them acrost." He flourished at Esau's raft carrying the horses and mules. "You'n fetch thatun, Cass."

"We'd be very grateful," Camilla approved.

"But, goddamn it to hell," Ward exploded, far past his limit of patience, "how *much?* All this palaver, and where's it got us?" He thumped his cane on planks in Major Burleigh's direction. "How *much?*"

"Forty dollars, hard money."

"Great Christ, aint *that* cool though! Forty dollars!"

Camilla too thought it was cool, as it was five more than they had paid.

However, her father had a codicil to add. "Ten now," he offered equably, "and the rest tomorrow, when you've earned it."

"Spoken to admiration!" Latham declared. "Better close with him, Cass. You'll have to foot what's right. I'll let no connection of mine skin a fine family like this."

"You mean a fine looker like this," Mrs. Ward amended. She turned to Mrs. Latham. "Bessie, seems like Salty's got a streak like Doc Mac-Leod. Was I his wife, and he set ary foot on that gal's raft, I'd kick his ass off it."

"Was you my wife *long,* Maudie," he came back in flawless humor, "you'd be a better-contented, sweeter-natured woman, and a lot less lippy." With a mariner's roll, he sauntered over to cup his wife's chin on his hand in gentle assurance. "Like Bessie," he added. This brought upon her face such a whole-souled look of love that, homely and soiled and limply bonneted though she was, she developed a fugitive beauty. He winked at her in concluding, "Don't nobody hear no ornery backtalk from Bessie."

To Major Burleigh he called out, "Mister, you mine if I bring Bessie and our younguns? Don't reckon they'll weigh you down too heavy."

"Indeed you may, sir."

"Very happy to have them," Camilla agreed. "And after all, we do have two rafts. Why can't Mrs. Ward and her children come on the other with Mr. Ward?"

"*There* we are, Maudie!"

Mrs. Ward popped her hands together in glee. "Aint that nice!" She lifted her chin at the mule. "Cass, you tie up that damnfool jackass and les cross."

"Who'll bring all our truck, though?"

"You will—next trip."

3

San Jacinto Crossing
Early Monday Morning
April 18, 1836

Camilla next morning learned that the family of Dr. MacLeod was one of those Cass Ward during the night had ferried over (at fifty cents a head for every man, woman, child, and beast) to the east side of the river, where her own camp was. Her search for him took her to a canvas-topped wagon under a matronly magnolia.

A young woman with a toddling boy nearby was hanging out wash on a rope stretched from that tree to another. She had boldly defined good looks, carnal and unkempt. Her brows were blackly empathic, her lips resentfully outthrust. Camilla nevertheless remained as sunny as the day in riding up to her on Swallow.

"Good morning!" As that brought nothing but a stare, she added, "Perfectly lovely morning, isn't it?" Still no answer, and so she became more direct. "Please, are you Mrs. MacLeod?"

Boils on the back of the woman's neck kept her head tipped forward so that she had to study Camilla sideward. The knuckles of one wet hand stroked a dangle of hair off her cheek.

"And if I am?"

By way of celebrating her triumph in having reached a physician, Camilla had on her freshest riding habit, dove gray trimmed with velvet, and guessed that this sullen reception showed nothing but the smart of envy.

"Where *is* the doctor, please? Anywhere near?"

Mrs. MacLeod turned away to seize up her baby, a pretty blond boy a little soiled around the nose. Planting him on her hip, she faced Camilla as if any woman, seeing her so decorated, would have to adopt a higher opinion of her. Camilla did. He transformed her, boils and all, into a pioneer Madonna chronically out of sorts.

Camilla dismounted for a closer look. He had sunny hair, alert brown eyes, and sweetly gathered lips. Bending toward him, she enlarged her eyes, pointed a finger at his ribs, and spoke gruffly low. "Boo!"

Delight electrified his face.

"What a dear baby! How old?"

"Eleven months tamarra. His name's Ulysses, and smart as snake bite, I'n tell you that."

"I *see* he is. There's a little dandy if I ever saw one."

The mother could not entirely prevent a smile of pride, after which Camilla ventured to return to business. "Mrs. MacLeod, my father needs a doctor. Is he, uh—able to see patients?"

"You mean sober. Damn ole buzzard."

"Well?"

"Aroun yonner." Without stirring her head in its pillory of boils, she rolled her eyes to the right, whereupon Camilla noticed a splashing of poured water beyond that side of the wagon. "But I warn you, miss: *watch* him."

"Oh?"

"And, beings I'm his wife, you hear it from a accountable source."

"Wel-ll, if this isn't a good time—"

"No, see him. He's sober. Just keep a little room to jump in is all."

"Gracious land!"

"Nothing real dangerous, mind—just likes to trifle. Some woman takes his fancy and damn fool don't think she'll realize he's giving you manly notice till he's pinched your ass, or give it a pat anyhow. Ladykiller of the worst degree—oh, aint he though! Anyhow, that's his notion, though it's pretty near all in his head. Or his drinkun jug, one."

Mrs. MacLeod had worked herself up too much to stand idle longer. Fidgety with anger, she put her baby aside, snatched up a wet apron from a basket of wash and hung it to dry. "No, go see him. You lookun so fine and all, it may stun him till where he'll keep his hands to hisself for once."

Stepping around the wagon, Camilla found a shirtless man bowed low over a dishpan, scooping handfuls of water over his head. Bald as a bust of Caesar, with a corona of graying hair above the ears, he had long legs and a short, squarish trunk rising from trousers of good black broadcloth. His neck was skinnily corded, his forearms the same, ending in long, bony, mobile hands, which flapped wide to shake off sudsy water. His towel was evidently a pair of unlaundered drawers hanging on a sapling, for he groped in that direction.

"More to your left, doctor."

His arms, out like the wings of a vulture, froze where they were. His face turned her way, blinded by suds. His voice boomed cavernously. "Who's that?"

"Camilla Palmer. My father has a bullet wound and—"

"Ho!"

"Though he's much better lately."

"Ho-ho!"

He burrowed that skull of his into a flurry of drawers and through them boomed again. "Where you located at?"

"Off yonder in that high grove to the left."

Face about dry, he stopped toweling himself while she said this and stood gazing at her.

"It's on that farther knoll." She flourished a hand across the camp. "See that one with trees on top?"

"Ho!"

But his gaze remained on her. He had bulbous bloodshot eyes set prominently beside a nose cross-hatched by tiny veins. With his arms out, shoulders high, head so bald, neck so scrawny, and body stooped, he did look like what his wife called him—an old buzzard. But buzzards are not dangerous, merely repulsive. Moreover, footsteps behind her told her that Mrs. MacLeod had come around the wagon to see that he behaved, and he did act more businesslike.

"How'd he get shot?"

She explained briefly.

"Ho! Seems like the Lord's down on us lately. Tween rascals preying on us from the east and Santa Anna slaughtering in the west, where are we?" He flung the drawers back into the embrace of the sapling. Both his hands began slicking down the frieze of hair around his skull. "Tween the frying pan and the fire, there's where we are. Well, we'll see. I'll come along next hour or two, and we'll see."

She backed away a step. "Sure you'll find us, doctor?"

"Certainly, certainly! Got some other sick to tend, and then we'll see."

As a gesture of peace and sympathy to Mrs. MacLeod, Camilla, in going by toward Swallow, waved to the baby, who now seemed to her a most astounding result of such parentage. That Dr. MacLeod's child should be so pretty and bright restored her belief in the miraculous. "Bye-bye, sweet thing."

The mother surprised her by flapping his hand. "Look sharp, darling: tell the lady bye-bye."

4

Her own camp was set apart from all the rest on a knoll crowned with a grove of post oaks which (as her father said in selecting it) resembled a Grecian temple, each trunk clean as a pillar and all spaced apart with their foliage joining as a roof. Under their shade were three shelters of oilskins. The central one was for her father, whom she and Roberta were preparing for the doctor's visit: they gave him a bucket bath, dressed his wound, changed his soiled clothes, and compelled him to shave. At no stage was he so brisk or co-operative as she thought he ought to be.

"Come, Pa, don't dawdle so. He'll be along here first thing you know."

"I trust he will." Peering into a mirror she held for him, he drew his razor down one cheek in unchanging leisure, eyes darkened by a look of ranging thought. Swift loss of weight had left his face more bony, more ascetic, more notably mental, and she was aware in watching him that his passage near death had carried him a little beyond reach, where he was less easy to manipulate—a strange result, since the manipulation of mesmerism had helped so to keep him alive. "What's he like that he's worth all this?"

"Oh, very odd. But it's not that he's worth it, dear, rather that you are. I want him to see we think enough of you to keep you up."

"Odd, uh?"

"Dreadfully idiosyncratic. Generally, though, that kind of doctor's very good."

"That so?" He stroked lather off his razor onto a leaf. "Can't say I'd noticed it."

"Pa, you *are* a trial. Why should you be so . . . so *doubting* before you've even laid eyes on the man?"

"Back when I soldiered, Camilla, a pitiful lot of boys went under the surgeon's knife who would have come out about as well in a butcher shop. For at least one in three the encounter with a surgeon was fatal—eventually fatal, you understand, what with bleeding, sepsis, lockjaw, and the like." Tilting back his head to shave under his chin, he jogged his razor at the mirror. "Little higher, please. I'll behave when he's here; but, you see, I'm in less of a hurry to die now than I was a week ago, thanks to you."

The pang this speared through her set her to watching for MacLeod with increased misgivings of her own. Actually, when he did come up the knoll, he looked much altered for the better. Astride a staid, bloaty bay, he had the atmosphere and furnishings discriminating families expected of doctors: a stovepipe hat, a ribboned pince-nez to dignify those bulbous eyes of his, a clawhammer coat, a pearl vest (unequally polka-dotted by grease or gravy), a fluffy black stock, and less mud on his trousers than any other man in camp—aside from her father, whose wound kept him out of it. With the day simmering under a brilliant sun, everyone else was in shirtsleeves, so that his coat gave notice of regard for professional standards, and manifestly at no little sacrifice, as sunlight sloping across his face glistened on trickles of sweat.

Reassured, she welcomed him at the edge of the temple of oaks. While Esau took the doctor's horse, she herself led him toward the middle shelter.

To one side of their route a week's wash hung afloat between pairs of trees. He stopped to focus his spectacles at waving pantalettes, newly in style around New Orleans last winter. Next his gaze took in Camilla's conformation.

"Ho! *You* wear them fanciful things?"

"Uh . . ." She flourished forward. "Over here, please."

"No, miss, leave pants to the men, every *breed* of pants. Ladies, with skirts and petticoats and all, don't need pants. Healthy females, rightly cast in the mold of Eve, have too much bottom to crowd into pants. For the good of generations unborn, they ought to leave their bottoms have play."

"Do come, please, doctor." Camilla strained to preserve her air of highborn hospitality. But, recalling the advice from that Madonna-of-the-Boils, she sidled off without turning her back. "The patient is this way."

"Ah, indeed."

And so to the oilskin shelter. Under one side, which had been poled high to admit air and sunlight, her father reclined on a couch of hay and pillows, writing on a sheet of foolscap tied to a length of plank. Near his elbow his crutches waited to serve him, a wordless boast about how much he had improved without a surgeon's help. Those handsome eyes of his, rising over the edge of his writing board, became unwaveringly intent upon Dr. MacLeod, and without mercy.

To sweeten the situation she spiraled her hands through the gestures most approved for introductions. "Doctor, my father, Major Cedric Burleigh. And, Pa—"

"Quite so," MacLeod cut her off and gave her his hat while he applied a veteran handkerchief to his skull, as if wiping off an overturned pot. "Wellsir, it's pleasurable here in the cool of the trees. Shade's mighty gratifying days like this."

"However," the major observed, "I'd prefer to be able to leave it."

"No doubt. Where'd that bullet hit you at, major?"

"Right where you switch a mule."

"Ho-ho! Hell of a place for a major to get shot."

"Hell of a place for anyone to get shot."

"Ho! Yes." The doctor pulled off his spectacles and handkerchiefed them reflectively, then reseated them and smoothed the ribbon afloat from them to his lapel. "It's never reckoned a badge of valor."

"On him it is," Camilla announced with heat. "Someone shot him from ambush, but he had the stamina and force and courage to drive away four men, hit as he was."

The doctor tilted back his head to gaze at her through gleaming lenses. Uncomfortable, she went on telling about her father's feat the last night at Hoping Hill, but he showed much more interest in her than in what she said.

"Hold on here. Let's see." One long hand on her shoulder drew her around for inspection. "Open your mouth."

She did, meanwhile noticing from him a reek of stale grog and hollow teeth.

"Say *ah*."

"Ahhng."

"Health!" He felt her shoulder for quality before letting her draw free. "Miss, the Lord certainly done right by you. Soldiers fall like wheat to the scythe; whole towns burn; people run like rabbits; crops go to ruin; homeless kinfolk stray around lost from one another; but sometimes the Lord compensates. When he gives you *that* much health, you can still crowd through with spirits high enough to show the world a smile."

The major said, "Or the other way around."

"Yes," she agreed. "Aren't high spirits as likely to keep health sound as health is to keep spirits high?"

"Without a doubt," her father stated.

"No-no!" MacLeod boomed. "Health first, I tell you. Best things in life require health; and, wheresoever health deserts you, there's where the best things end."

The major conceded dryly, "Excellent text for a physician at any rate."

"In health like *this* . . ." The doctor paused to readjust his spectacles in Camilla's direction. "Here you see all the best bounty the Lord can bestow. See that?" He reached a talon out the full length of his arm to pull her chin more toward the light. "The glow in that skin—prodigious!"

"However, it's my father you're here to see, doctor."

"Ho, yes. Man with a bullet in him is seldom better'n half a man till it's out." He swerved over to the major's couch, focused his specs upon him, laid one hand across his forehead and with the other felt his pulse. "No fever. Can't be so bad no more. Well, let's see that rump of yours."

Although Camilla had tended the wound daily, the fiction of lady-like sensibility required her to step around behind the oilskin. From there she heard her father's belt buckle click when loose, and a succession of grunts told her of his struggle to expose his damaged flesh.

"Ho!" the doctor exclaimed. "A deep one, major."

"Uhm."

"Ball must of went up behind the pelvic arch, hit the ilium, then deflected off up here in the small of your back. There's what's kept it out of the visceral sac: it hit the top of the ilium. This hurt?"

"Some."

"*Some?* It ought to be sore as fury, major. But dern thing's begun to heal. Mystery how it could heal so."

"Medicine of the spirit healed it, sir."

"Ho! The more it heals, the worse, till that bullet's out. The channel of this wound has a kink in it down here where the ball deflected off the ilium; that's going to give us trouble; and then the whole channel's healed about half shut, and that's going to give us more trouble. Now we have to force a probe in there and bust it all open again all the way to that ball. Ticklish job, but we'll get it out all the same, I guarantee you that."

Camilla could picture her father lying chest down, face sideward; could imagine an appalled look growing in his eyes as MacLeod talked. She herself found her legs trembling and moved over to support her back against a post oak. Her eyes sought a cooling, calming effect from study of its motionless boughs and from the flawless blue of heavens beyond them.

"If it's healing so well," her father ventured, "why not let it heal?"

"Leave it alone just like it is?"

"Uhm."

"And carry that infernal lead around, a torment to you till you're dead? Ho! Most idiotic nonsense I ever heard of. You want that crippling you your whole life long?"

"Fact is, I've begun hobbling a little already, and it's no torment to me any more the way it is."

"Well, it aint reasonable to be on your feet this soon, no matter how you look at it. Till the ilium's healed, you ought to keep offen it. Enough metal in there to hook a shark with, and you want that gouging you whensoever you stoop or sit or lay down?"

"No-o, but—"

"Certainly not. Man on the frontier's got to have a good back."

"That's true, only—"

"Course he does. Why"—he coughed out a laugh—"where that devilish thing's at now, you couldn't even take pleasure with a woman without it hampering you so you'd be little better'n a cadaver. Ho! We're going to worry it out of there without no more delay and make a man out of you, major." He lifted a cavernous shout in Camilla's direction. "You, miss! See here a minute!"

She stepped around the oilskin. "Yessir?"

"Three things I'll need—six things, if you count it right." He stood one bony finger upright. "Gourd of water to wash down a pill or two."

"Very well."

He put up another finger. "Some lard or tallow to grease my probe good."

"Oh?"

"Ho, and"—he raised four fingers to wag them solemnly before her—"four good stout men."

"But why?"

"To hold him still, miss. He's not so weak but what four will have their hands full too, I'n tell you that."

A more quaky sickliness waved through her, wanting a voice. "Doctor, you ever use mesmerism for reducing pain?"

"Mesmerism?" He reared his head back to gaze at her. "Animal magnetism?"

"Yessir."

"Certainly not."

Her father, scowling at her, tapped a forefinger upright against his lips.

She, though, would not let the subject alone, or not yet. "Ever see it used?"

"Tended a yella wench once that a black African mesmerized or spellbound or voodooed, one. She had her a great big ten-pound boy, and no more pains than if she moved her bowels. That spell he put on her was so strong till where she hardly felt a thing."

"That's what I mean."

"But a due portion of suffering wouldn't harm her either. That female acted no more human than a sheep. Travail was decreed for woman by the Lord above. Conceive in pleasure, bring forth in pain: that's the rule laid down in the Good Book, and we taught that black heathen who voodooed her not to trifle with it no more."

"Rubbish!" Camilla let go a detesting snort, and the last of her sickly weakness left her. "Why didn't I see what a fool you are in the first place?"

"It does show quick," her father concurred.

"Ho! What's this?"

Picking up his sweated hat, she carried it to him. "I said I think you're a fool."

"And I admire her judgment," said the major.

"Tell Esau, Berta," she called to her maid, who was cooking for noon at a fire before the Tiptons' shelter over to her left, "to fetch the doctor's horse right away."

"Yessum."

"Well, doctor, what's your fee?"

"Fee, miss? I aint treated him none nor been any benefit yet. Aint my way to charge a man I done no good to."

That did seem decent of him, and she at once regretted having been so blunt.

Pince-nez off, he used it to scratch the network of veins across his nose. "Queer thing, I will say, a comely lass like you turning so sharp."

"It's only—well, I did speak too sharp, and—" She began walking away from the shelter to draw him away. "I hope you'll forgive me."

"Yes-yes!" He strode up beside her and reassuringly gripped her arm. "Certainly I forgive you, miss. It's a ticklish operation, which the thought of it must of worked on you wrong. However, the longer that bullet's let alone, the worse."

His hand loosened from her arm to drift onto her back. The warning about his weakness for pinching bottoms, she concluded, had indeed come from an "accountable source." With her hopes of help from him in rout, and loathing the smell of his breath, she was severely tempted to take a stick to him, but merely checked her stride to twist out of his talon as if suddenly remembering some oversight.

"Oh, Pa . . . !" She returned briskly toward the shelter. Beside it she stopped to say, "No need to wait for me, doctor. Your horse is ready."

"Ho! But mind what I tell you, miss: where he's got that bullet is no place to have it. We got to get it out. You and him talk it through, and I'll be back."

"Dr. MacLeod, don't you *dare* come back!"

5

Though Cedric expected her to begin at once discussing alternative ways of dealing with the bullet, she did not. Muttering, "Imbecile," she fastened down a loosely flapping corner of oilskin on his shelter and left to take down dried laundry. Not until late afternoon, when she came back from a trip to an easterly plantation after supplies and found him toilsomely crutching around his shelter, did she mention their medical problem.

"Well, Pa, what's your view? How soon should we push on?"

"Push on where?"

"Why, to New Orleans, of course."

That left him motionless, blinking at her. If there was any place she ought not to go, and ought not even think of going, it was New Orleans.

"Well, don't look so . . . so horrified, Pa. What that fool said is true: that bullet has to come out, and the sooner the better. We're most unlikely, anywhere this side of New Orleans, to find any doctor superior to him, and no facilities to speak of anywhere else at all."

He toiled onward a few steps. His hip and leg—both legs, in fact—remained quakily reluctant to carry him at all, even though most of his weight was on the crutches. Patience, he told himself, should take care of that, practice and patience.

"Camilla, I understand many folks from around home are camped at Liberty, the people we know best in Texas. I don't see what's our hurry to go anywhere just now, but we might shift over to Liberty."

"The hurry is, as Dr. MacLeod said, to get that bullet out before the wound heals shut."

"Well, in the first place, if it's healing so well, I think it's sensible to assume that the flesh around the lead is accommodating to it—as many an old soldier's has before. In the second place, if Leticia Springfield is at Liberty, then her father in time will come there or—"

"Leticia Springfield!" The flash in her glance tickled his funnybone, but he kept a straight face as she talked on. "Have you a crush on that ninny that you keep thinking of her all this time?"

He considered that too unfair to notice. He resumed exactly in the tone she had interrupted.

"Her father, you can be sure, will come seeking her out as soon as the course of war will let him, and I rank Dr. Springfield's medical judgment high."

"Yes. Yes, he's able, it's true. But where *is* he? Goodness knows where, or just which way the war will take him."

"It'll bring him where it's bringing the army—toward Harrisburg and south. At least it will if Salty Latham's right, as I believe he is."

"All conjecture, Pa." She settled glumly on a chest at the end of his shelter. "And no way to calculate how long before we'd ever meet him. No, I fear what we ought to do is get you back to New Orleans."

"Which is one place I don't dare go."

"*You* don't? Why? It's I who—"

"Because, if I went there, I'd soon be in jail."

"What nonsense is this?" She lifted him a frown. "In jail for what?"

"Homicide."

"Homicide? What *are* you talking about?"

"There's a man in New Orleans I'd soon kill—would have to kill, because legal means do not exist by which to give him his due. And, when he knows what I know, he will try to kill me, or have me killed, unless I kill him first."

"But who, Pa? Such a rigmarole I never heard!"

"The man who burned your barns at Palmer Hall, or *had* them burned. The man who tried to burn you out at Hoping Hill, or *had* it tried."

"Well, gracious land, if you know that, why haven't you told me who before?"

"Because I knew you wouldn't believe me and would be outraged if I told you. It's Edmond Beaufait."

Her legs straightened suddenly, pushing her to her feet. "Pa!"

"Yes, he's the man."

"I *don't* believe it, no! What a dreadful thing to say!"

"Though you know I wouldn't say it unless convinced, and fully."

"But what proof have you?"

"The fact that Cottier is Edmond's agent, for one thing: Perry saw him working in the Benevolent Loan last fall. That's not legal proof, I grant you, but all deductions convince me Beaufait's behind it. In conscience, if I ever got back there in New Orleans, I'd have to face him with those deductions, prepared to shoot him down, because I know he would not stop short of murder to quiet the accusation."

"No proof, and yet you say things like that? And about a person I owe so much to! Pa, are you possessed?"

"You know very well I'm not. And sometime, honey, when you can look at it all without your blinders on, I'll explain what has convinced me. Till then, let's talk of other things—knowing all the while that, if there is any place I ought to avoid, at least until I do find legally tenable proof, it's New Orleans."

From C. B.'s Journal
April 18, 1836

An uncertain evening, brooding yet fragrant. Most of the sky is blackly overcast, but now and then a new moon glides forth, a silver sloop risking shipwreck among headlands of cloud, and the howl of wolves attracted by our camp offal is answered by ecstatic whistling from a "Dixie nightingale" here in our own grove.

Today I told Camilla who humbled her with fire back home and who tried to here in Texas. She called all I said preposterous. Through the afternoon, though, her eyes showed an assembling of recollections which urged her to think as I do.

This evening Salty Latham returned from Liberty, where he has camped his family on the banks of the Trinity River while he returns to the army. He told of seeing neighbors of ours on the Trinity—the Timberlakes, Wallaces, Nuhns, Bauernschmidts, etc., along with Leticia and her brothers, all part of a large camp delaying there to hear what turn the war may take. Jake Timberlake came along to soldier with Salty. They say the refugees are as miserable as penned foxes in that camp, and stink as bad, all mortally impatient for a favoring turn in the war. Jake and Salty, however, were the only ones ready to take up rifles to help win it.

Jake turned mute as stone over our report that his cabin was one of those Cottier burned down. To him and his family that cabin was more than a home: it was pretty nearly everything they have in this world.

Meanwhile Camilla rallied from her grieving about Beaufait's deceit after a statement from Salty that he was carrying letters to the army from Miss Leticia and would be "proud" to do the same for us. Camilla has settled down to write by this candle I myself am writing by. With her spirit turned outward rather than in, she looks altered for the better without her knowledge, glowingly engrossed as she is in that silent articulation which defies distance, shrinks time, and alters circumstance to keep hearts far apart beating in concord.

CHAPTER XXI

I

Opposite Harrisburg
Late Monday
April 18, 1836

Monday was a day of blazing sunlight interrupted by darkly ponderous clouds, a sweaty day thickened by vapors of moist and heated prairies, a depleting day used without rest to propel the volunteers, their vehicles, their cannon, their sick to the northern bank of Buffalo Bayou, across from Harrisburg. The army managed, despite a remora of mud all the way, to traverse fifty-two miles in two days and a half.

Still, the march had not been fast enough. The enemy was gone. So was Harrisburg. Where clapboard stores and dwellings once had stood, mounds of wind-blown ash lay among studdings gnawed off by fire. The Mexicans, after burning everything they could not carry away, had marched toward New Washington on Galveston Bay in an attempt to overtake the fleeing Government of Texas.

Their absence produced more relief than disappointment. The volunteers, in no condition to fight at once, needed to rest a bit and arrange care for upwards of three-score comrades too sick to march. Houston established a hospital camp in a vale concealed by wooded knolls and protected by a light guard. There the healthy also left all supplies which would prevent a swift advance.

Toward the end of the afternoon, while the troops rested, Perry decided that he must not put off looking into the Cottier puzzle any longer, for Cottier must be left behind with the sick and might heal sufficiently to escape before the army returned from its chase after the Mexicans. One way to draw an animal into your trap, he reflected, is to bait it well. After his troop had bivouacked, he packed a saddlebag with cold roast venison, corn pone, and a demijohn of rum, then rode Marquis to the hospital.

That word "hospital" hardly fit the place. Aside from one abandoned cabin, the only shelters were scabrous structures of brush, hides, prairie hay, and rare pieces of oilskin or canvas. Many of the suffering, in fact, were no better off than the well encamped by Buffalo Bayou: many had between them and the open sky nothing more than the shade of a tree.

For an office Dr. Springfield had two sheets of canvas extending backward from a supply wagon, which served as its cupboard and third wall. As Perry rode up, the weathered little physician was sitting on a keg, peering into the throat of a recruit, eyes dignified by an obligatory benevolence as easy and familiar as the coat on his back.

One keen glance at Perry on Marquis, and he spoke out, *"Well,* young man!"

Perry saluted. "Doctor, sir."

Dr. Springfield again gave all attention to the patient.

Perry dismounted and hunkered down to wait near a box on which stood an apothecary's scales, several packets of herbs, a mortar and pestle. The place gave out an acrid, herbaceous fragrance reminiscent of the Allandale drugstore, where a boy sent after something for an ailing parent could count on a bit of horehound or licorice so delicious that thought of it even now set hunger astir beneath Perry's ribs. That sensation, as he watched the physician, irresponsibly converted itself into illegitimate yearning for the man's daughter, the plain, sweet, womanly Leticia. Where was *she* now? And Camilla? It seemed to him grossly disloyal to have let anyone else enter his head before Camilla, and he roused from his reverie about it to find himself again under keen scrutiny from Dr. Springfield.

"Son, you look tired as a lost dog. Derned if you don't." Having given the sick recruit some powders folded into a piece of old newspaper, he dismissed him and resumed talking to Perry. "Anything else the matter with you?"

"Nosir. Puzzled is all."

"About Bancroft?"

"Yessir."

"Myself likewise."

He began pounding herbs in the mortar. Under the brim of an old bent hat, weedy hair, rustily gray, spilled down his collar and around his ears. His countenance, however, wholly redeemed the uncouth effect: he had a fine, sun-baked skin with active crinkles around eyes which reflected habits of critical, ethical sorrowing, and of public care. Like his daughter, he exemplified the truth that the looks which count take their merit from within.

"Thought I'd be seeing you yesterday, Perry."

"Yessir, only there was no time."

"I understand. Lately the simple logistics of keeping alive have taxed most men severely, and when you're also sheep dog to a troop of recruits, some without any more sense than sheep, why then a little mystery about an ailing stranger has to wait. *Has* to."

"Sir, what you think of that bird?"

"Why, I'll tell you." He measured out powders with a finely balancing hand. "Limitless expenditures of care and labor and grief go to waste in this world, and he proves it.

"A mother waddles around swollen and sickly month on month, then shrieks in travail till the rafters shake and, lo, a new baby boy! Each dimpled hand seems a marvelous little engine perfectly designed by the Lord to carry on His Work in this world. Father and mother daily cajole and feed and lesson him; a doctor applies his balms and splints and pills now and then; a preacher prays for his immortal soul; a threadbare schoolmaster brings him fruits from the world's great orchards of learning. Ships laden with goods ply the seven seas, and steamboats the rivers, barges the canals, wagons the roads, bearing their freight unto him and thousand upon thousand more of his generation. Each day a prodigy of concordant effort assists his growth, and what does it all come to? He's clever, enduring, and has perfectly wonderful vitality, but after all what *is* he? A two-legged hyena crunching the marrow out of other people's bones.

"But that's not all he is. He's a reminder that the infinite possibilities in all of us get warped into dern sorry shapes, that none of us ever turns out as well as beings molded in the image of God ought to. Trouble with him is he makes our failure much plainer than most of us do. *There's* what I think of him."

"Quite a thought too," said Perry, amused.

"See here, young fella, you watch that animal. He's got teeth. I *mean* teeth. Keeps a regular arsenal on him: two pocket pistols that I know of, besides a pair of skinnun knives, and never out of reach of a carbine loaded at all times. When he was too far out of his head to know it, I also felt a money belt on him which isn't what anybody would call in a poorly condition. Very likely that's why his weapons look so slick: he's used them to clean out people's pockets."

"Hm! What's his present state?"

"Pitiful! The pity of it is that toughs like him are so eternal hard to kill."

An amused nod, and Perry stood up. "Won't hurt if we quiz him then?"

"Won't hurt enough, that's sure. But why say *we?* I'm a healer, not a constable. That's not my line."

"Yessir, of course. Only I need a witness from our own district, one everybody respects and trusts."

"But it's time I made my rounds, and—"

"Oh, all the better. When would you naturally be paying him a call?"

"Directly. Any time now."

"Well, as you know, two boys from my company came here with the measles—Skate Shackleton and Burton Doty. While you're tending Bancroft, couldn't I just happen by to inquire after Burt and Skate?"

"Yes-yes, Perry. That'll do."

2

Rex, with his head pillowed on a rolled blanket, lay on one side while the doctor, looking kind as Christ, put him through pure hell by stroking hot water over the mattery holes in his leg. A tortured constriction drew his head up to groan for mercy, and then he noticed that rangy young lawyer from New Orleans riding through camp in the same washed-out blue uniform and wide campaign hat he had seen on him back at Donohos'. Flinching and shivering, Rex dropped his head again, squinched his eyes, and bit his blanket as if only to help him stand the pain, not to hide his face.

Above his own moans he heard the bastard call from horseback, "That you there, Dr. Springfield?"

"Hello, Perry."

A restless trample of hooves came toward Rex's feet. The next remark from the lawyer sounded close. "Afternoon, sir. Where's Burton Doty and Skate Shackleton, doctor, my two boys?"

"Round her somers. Why?"

"Brought them a little good honest rum, and wholesome victuals too."

Rum! Rex had to work to keep his eyes shut. Great God, rum!

What a waste of days had gone by, and never an ardent drop. The doctor, though, thought only of the other patients.

"Well, they'll admire both, I'll guarantee."

"Jupiter, that's ticklish-looking flesh you're working on, doctor."

"It is that. Nothing feels much ornerier than buckshot. Worse than stepping in a bear trap, uh, Bancroft?"

Rex groaned in assent. A drawn squeal of saddle leather told him their visitor was dismounting, so he risked a sidelong glance through eyelids ajar only a slit. The fellow seemed taller than last fall, and no youngster any more, but gaunt and tired and brainy, a man who wore captain's stripes because he deserved to.

"Must hurt right fierce," he remarked. "Rum—wouldn't a tilt or two help him through, doctor?"

"Well, let him refresh a little, if you got it to spare."

"Certainly, certainly!"

From a saddlebag hanging on his horse he brought out the demijohn. Rex frankly loosened his face out of the blanket, since there was no hope now of going unrecognized. To act afraid of being seen plain, he knew, leads to the thought that whoever does it has reason to. He boldly hoisted himself up on an elbow in position to drink as free as any man with nothing whatever to hide.

"Rum! Christ, it *can't* be! No such thing in this army as real rum."

"Scarce article," the captain agreed. "This we requisitioned from a cabin up the bayou. Take a good pull."

Rex did. A sweetish, scalding flood of it scoured the fuzz out of his mouth and washed the puky weakness out of him all the way down. As the captain hunkered on one heel, cavalry fashion, to watch the doctor balm his wounds, not keeping an eye on the demijohn, he had himself a couple more pulls, and man-oh-man!

"Dern mischievous infection," the captain remarked.

"And bound to be awful sore awhile," said the doctor. "See this purple flesh here? That aint but mighty little short of gangrene, a consequence of being swollen so bad and him too long in the saddle, which hampers the circulation."

"But getting better now?"

"Oh, not yet! None to brag about. Now that I got the lead out, the only way, the sole and single way, to make it better is to improve the circulation—keep him flat on his back all the time, massage the leg as much as he can stand, and bathe it with hot water three-four times a day. By doing the best we know how—yes, we might save his leg.

"Still, the chances favor septicemia. Great trouble is, of course, that those shot were in there much too long before he overtook us."

"Hm." During the silence that followed Rex could almost hear the captain's thought and so was not in the least surprised when he was asked, "When'd it happen, sir?"

His eyes leveled at Rex's, a cold gray. Of course, answers to all possible questions were lined up in Rex's mind, neat as bottles in a first-class saloon. "Week ago last Monday."

"Where were you then?"

"Upcountry a piece."

"*Just* where?"

Rex angled him a comprehending grin. So here was what lay behind that liberality with his rum! Though back in New Orleans the bastard had the look of a clean, leggy young jake, he here seemed hatefully schooled and calm and realizing, and on him the hateful stamp of lifelong manners. However, Rex had outfoxed more than one lawyer in his day, older and smarter too. One thing this buck didn't know was that he was dealing with a set of wits which, rum or no rum, came to their best when anybody backed him in a corner. In fact, a good drink was just what he needed to prime him right for any such game as this. He cocked a brow at the doctor, who had stopped trifling around with the wound to listen.

"Doc, you asked me that too, and I don't till yet know exackly how to say. Lost my bearuns two-three days before that, and nobody around to set me right: where I was at it was all vacant country."

The captain shifted his hunker to the other heel, frowny and judgmental. "East of the Brazos or west?"

"West a good piece."

"Hm. What took you way off there times like these?"

"Business, captain. My own."

"No, that's just what it wasn't. Nosir. Your business in Texas——"

"Say, doc," Rex cut him off, "who *is* this boy?"

"A responsible officer in the Army of Texas."

"Maybe so, but what's he doubtun and presumun for? This aint a court. It's a sick camp."

"In troubled times," the doctor observed, "especially in a land of lariat law like this one, *any* place where there's any suspicion of wrong can be turned into a court if necessary. The sensible thing is to not evade what you're asked, but account for yourself. You better give thought to everything Captain Allan's got to say."

"Your business in Texas," Allan resumed, "has been pretty much like your business in Louisiana the first time I saw you—thugging for Edmond Beaufait."

"What's that? Who the nation you talkun bout?"

"About the man you were under the orders of last October first time I met you, which was in the Benevolent Loan of Louisiana."

Rex loosened out a wide-mouthed laugh. The young fool might know a lot that it wasn't convenient to have him know; but, in a situation like this, what could he prove? "Boy, you flatter me considerable with talk of such connection, but you got me confused somehow. I come from Memphis. Aint been in New Orleans but once in my life."

"Then that once was when I talked to you in the Benevolent Loan. I could swear to your identity here or anywhere. You're—"

"See here, why you deviln me so? And me in this condition! Doc, how come you let him do me like this?" Other sick not kept down by their ailments had drifted up to hear the talk, and he now appealed to them. "Men, I put it up to you: aint it a sorry way of doon? When any young buck with too little business of his own to mind can intrude on a sick camp and devil a man when he's on his back, aint that a hell of a thing?"

"If you got nothing to hide," the doctor pointed out, "it won't be troublesome to answer what you're asked. A man able to stand a blast of buckshot can stand a few questions easy enough—if his story's straight."

"How's it happen," Perry resumed, "that you gave the name of Bancroft here, whereas back in New Orleans it was Rex Cottier?"

"Cottier? For God sake, boy, I tell you you got me mixed entirely. I never met nobody in my whole life name of Cottier. I'm Buck Bancroft and—"

"Prove it."

"Prove what?"

"Who you are." He thumbed the front of his hat up and gave him one of those clear, hateful stares. "If you're a sound man, you must have something to show who you are and what your business is."

"Well, I—like everbody the panic caught, I lost pretty near everthing, my papers not excepted. Anyhow, what of I ever done to justify all this deviln and insinuation? Answer me that?"

"For one thing, we know the paint you came on used to belong to a man named Blacky Reed, and—"

"See here, youngster, who-all that horse used to belong to I don't have any idea any more than you know who all ever owned yours. All I know is I bought him in Nacogdoches. He's mine, and that's all."

"How long ago?"

"Oh, been a good spell now. Right when I first come into Texas, which was fore part of March."

"Six-seven weeks ago?"

"Some such a matter."

"However, there is in my troop a witness that says as late as three weeks ago that was Blacky Reed's horse."

Damnation! A fidget of hate made Rex feel under his coat for the handle of his knife. "If he says that, it's purely a goddamn lie. Since when can *any*body prove a paint that looks like half a dozen others belonged to some man that aint here? This is the most infernal, troublesome, mixed-up confusion—"

"How do you know he aint here?"

"Who?"

"Blacky Reed. What makes you so sure he's somewhere else?"

"Great merciful Jesus, this is the first I ever even heard of Blacky Reed!"

"That horse you say you owned six or seven weeks back was seen hardly three weeks ago with Blacky Reed on him. That was on the homestead of Mrs. Palmer above Otter Creek, and that's a place where Banker Beaufait might be likely to send a hired thug if he—"

"If, if, if! Might, might, might! If the dog hadn't stopped to sniff the tree he might of caught the rabbit. Why go tanglun yourself in *ifs* and *mights* about people that I never seen, specially when the pinto that your man seen there is obliged to been a altogether different horse?"

"You wouldn't mind answering a few questions in the presence of Mrs. Palmer?"

Great God! Rex's heart kicked so high it made his throat hurt. Could *she* be somewhere around? His stare at Allan told him nothing except that the bastard was watching every change in his face: the question could be intended only to test him, because there had been no civilians anywhere near the army since the refugees left with Wiley Martin yesterday morning. The countryside here was empty.

"Not if there's any purpose in it. Where's she at?"

"Well, we'll undertake to bring you together in due course. Now another question about that pinto: who'd you buy him from?"

"Huh?"

"You say you bought him in Nacogdoches. Who from?"

"Oh, him. Why, Baxter. Mr. Baxter."

"Which Baxter?"

"Sort of disremember his first name. Believe it was Sam Baxter."

"Well, you better put your mind to it and remember it straight. There must be a dozen or more boys here from Nacogdoches, here in the army." The captain leaned forward from his hunker to pick up the demijohn and rose. "Including General Houston."

"That's so." The doctor nodded. "He's from Nacogdoches."

"Among them they can sift any story about buying a pinto there as singularly marked as that one is." Standing tall and easy, wabbling the demijohn to judge how much rum was left, the captain had ceased entirely to look at Rex. "So you'd better make it a story such men can support. Out here a horse you can't convincingly account for is dangerous property." He reached for his stallion's rein, letting his glance range around the camp. "Now, doctor, where'll I find Skate and Burton?"

3

The sun, when Perry finally left the hospital, was just under the horizon, painting flamboyant red and gold across the west. Soft, cool twilight lay upon new crops of corn and cotton growing each way from the wagon ruts he followed, and the air was sweetened by gathering dew.

Beyond one wide square of corn, on a trail at right angles to his, four horsemen were approaching two and two, the first pair being General Houston and Colonel Thomas Rusk, Secretary of War, the second Houston's aide, Major George Hockley, with Lieutenant Colonel Sidney Sherman, in command of cavalry. They were advancing at a trot, Perry also, but he reined Marquis down to a walk to let them cross well ahead of him as he was in no mood for the saluting and bright readiness to serve which senior officers traditionally expect of juniors.

The general, however, bent a prolonged frown Perry's way and stopped at the conjunction of trails to await him. A sideward nod at

Rusk and Sherman sent them onward, but his inseparable friend Hockley stayed by. Perry let one relinquished breath silently say, "Oh, hell," and at the same time loosened Marq into a canter.

At closer range Old Sam's face looked dead as clay, a reminder that no one else in the army had slept so little, helped so many, or outfaced a fraction so much defamation and abuse. Throughout the long retreat from Gonzales he never passed a family in trouble without some arrangement to aid them, never passed a mired wagon without putting a hand to the wheel unless it already had sufficient men behind it to push it free. At first such behavior created astonishment, but became so familiar, so much a part of Old Sam's way, that people ceased to think it unique in a general. Other officers lately had been doing the same—without acknowledging the instruction of his example. Perry's recognition that this man, after all, was the most man anywhere around, much the most, made him snap off a salute energized by respect.

Returning it, Houston regarded him gravely. "Captain, I hear favoring report about your powers on the stump."

"Sir?"

"Your campfire speech the night before last was roundly admired."

A paining, pleasant heat flooded Perry's face. How in creation had he heard about that? On second thought, he wondered if the old fox might not be twitting him while seeming to praise him. Houston himself rarely bothered to take any notice of camp quarrels: his habit was to remain as aloof to argument as toward the barking of feists. Officers who talked of impeaching or hanging him could not say that he ever had treated their threats as worth his objection. Yesterday morning, before the army reached the fork where trouble was supposed to occur, he pressed the core from the boil of their mutiny by ordering the noisiest, Captain Wiley Martin, to detach his company and escort a train of civilian refugees (which had been tagging after and encumbering the troops) northeastward toward greater safety, thus quietly solving two problems at once. Without any instruction beyond what was implied by that act, he allowed his main column of itself, without orders of any kind, to march down the southeast fork toward Harrisburg in recognition that the necessity for such a move was obvious. The festering mood of the army had been relieved, reduced. And now, with that so well attended to, could he actually be complimenting tactics so different from his own?

"Well," Perry conceded, "we got boys that need persuading now and again."

"Deed they do."

"But, sir, we could all do better by you if only you'd let us know oftener what you expect, what you *want* us to do."

This rushed out as something badly needing to be said, no matter how brash, but Houston did not appear to notice: his frown shifted massively to Marquis. His own horse, a white charger much heavier in the legs and rump, looked about as tired as he had a right to, whereas Marquis, despite carrying all Perry's belongings and two sick recruits during the long march from Donohos', retained an alert flexibility, lungs hungry for each scent the evening brought him, head lofty too, ears active, and eyes darkly aglow.

"George," Houston commented across a shoulder to Hockley, "there's a stud's got more substance to him than any other horse in this army—more wear *and* looks."

"Fine animal," Hockley agreed.

"Like to sell him?"

"Nosir." The subject was not one Perry cared to pursue with anyone so difficult to resist as the commander-in-chief: he hastily changed it. "Speaking of horses, sir, did you ever hear of anybody in or around Nacogdoches named Sam Baxter?"

The general's brows dented. "How's that?"

"I mean, sir, that a man here from New Orleans, giving an assumed name, has a paint we know belonged to somebody else three weeks ago, but he contends he bought him early in March from a man named Sam Baxter in Nacogdoches. So I wondered—"

"No such person there that I ever heard of."

"As we suspected, sir."

"He in your troop?"

"Nosir, a civilian Dr. Springfield's treating."

"If it's a civilian affair, captain, why concern yourself? We have all we can do here in the army. We must leave civil considerations to civilian authorities."

"Wellsir—"

"We have to assume that those authorities, in their own good time, will discharge their duty as competently as we do ours."

"Yessir, but—"

His case against Cottier, so convincing to himself when the scent of hidden evil was close by, now seemed flimsy when he tried to think how to explain it. The look of this devoted and weary general warned him that he would need more time to tell it all than circumstances would allow.

"Yessir, it is a civilian affair, that's true. Only they aren't here, those authorities, and—"

"And you're trained in law and can't let a new case pass."

"Oh, there's more to it than that, sir."

"Proving," Houston said to Hockley with an amused nod, "that if you take rabbit dogs out to hunt a cougar, some will turn off on rabbit trails." The judicious scowl again came upon him. "Captain, we're after bigger game now, and I think we're closing for the kill. That's why I'd like to buy that stud of yours. I want the best mount I can straddle."

"Really, sir, I can't sell him." Perry stroked a hand along Marq's neck, feeling the invaluable silk of his coat and the muscular guarantees underneath. "Need him bad myself."

"You don't use him much," Hockley pointed out. "Generally I see others on him."

"They're from my troop, sir, sick boys, and when they're on him I'm using him."

"True enough," Houston concurred.

"However, when good horses are needed for critical service," Hockley persisted, "they can be requisitioned."

"Not so, sir. Only civilians' horses." Perry, with his future in jeopardy, boldly glared at him. "This horse is already *in* the army, the possession of a troop commander. It can *not* be requisitioned."

One of his most sustaining daydreams through all the strenuous weeks of spring had been of himself showing Marquis and Vision to Camilla, letting these two splendid creatures convince her that his scheme to develop a hundred-mile strain could be realized. Marquis was to be his means of getting to Camilla in a hurry, and back to his land, and deep in a serviceable enterprise: the nurture of animals bred to release people from the prison of empty distance. His failure to respect the wishes of their general put a pained look on Hockley's face, but to hell with them both.

"That is accepted practice, sir: an officer serving in the army cannot be deprived of his horse on behalf of the army. You'll have to look outside it."

"Careful, George." Houston shifted heavily in his saddle, his grin amiably sarcastic. "This is a lawyer from way back East we're dealing with."

"Forgive it, pleasesir, but I can't let him go and still do what I'm here in Texas to do."

"On your homestead?"

"Yessir."

"Won't be practicing law?"

"Some, yessir, but no doubt the handles of a plow will hold me pretty tight to the land a good while."

"You'd better invest a sober thought or two in politics, captain. Once the freedom of this territory is accomplished, we're going to have considerable need for legislators who know how to 'persuade men to do even that which is for their own good,' as Jefferson put it."

"Yessir. Still, thought of things that far off seems a little airy just now."

"Maybe not so far off as most fancy." Houston gathered up his reins, about to go. "We picked up some remarkable intelligence this afternoon."

"Sir?"

"You'll learn more of that tomorrow. Meanwhile, captain, put aside any worry about mere horse thieves and keep your mind on disposing of the *big* enemy."

"Yessir."

Houston adjusted his long weight in both stirrups, saddle leathers creaking as his mount began a dignified advance.

Hockley reined around to follow, bending sideward for one last murmur. "Best not forget what he said about politics, Allan."

"Nosir."

"A word to the wise: General Houston never forgets a loyal friend."

"Thank you, major."

But Perry's itch to unravel Cottier's secret revived during the night. At the first light of dawn he sent Evett Tipton and Hugh Llewelyn up to the meadows around the sick camp to make that pinto gelding stray away so that Rex himself could not.

They arrived too late. The pinto was gone. Rex was too. And such was the business of the day that to send trackers after him was out of the question.

4

Somehow, when a brightening of campfires began saluting the changes from night to dawn, Houston's "remarkable intelligence" already was at large—as Perry thought the general very likely intended it to be. It reached and refreshed troop after troop as they woke. On Perry it had the effect of a good cold dip, flushing the night's torpor off him in one breathtaking splash.

President-General Antonio López de Santa Anna in person, the report stated, was leading the Mexican advance they had been closing upon.

Deaf Smith had brought in proof of a high order. The previous afternoon that indefatigable scout, with certain others, had rafted across the floods of Buffalo Bayou to the Harrisburg side, where they captured a Mexican courier, Captain Miguel Bachiller, carrying official messages addressed to the President-General, who (as Captain Bachiller testified) was at New Washington on Galveston Bay hardly twenty miles southeast, and with him a strength little larger than the Texans' —only some eight hundred men.

From these facts flowed an elating possibility: if the Texans moved fast and struck hard they might be able, in the next few days, to overpower the "Master of Mexico." Who would dispute Texan claims to independence after such a victory? The end of the war, instead of being depressingly distant, as it had seemed only yesterday, now visibly beckoned to them from below Buffalo Bayou.

But how was it possible for a general as clever as Santa Anna to let himself become so dangerously detached from his main forces? Overconfidence may have misled him; perhaps ignorance of geography too. Houston's repeated withdrawals also must have convinced him that he was dealing with cowards, and no doubt the demands of ruling over vast territories had made him impatient to end this trivial war quickly so that he could get back to his capital. What he was doing might well end it, yes, but not in the way he planned.

For, by shifting southeast into the narrowing peninsula where New Washington stood, he had entered a water-locked corner, a web of rivers, creeks, bays and bayous, an area which springtime floods had converted into a natural trap so large that he must not have perceived how it enclosed him. Buffalo Bayou would prevent any quick escape here along the north. Vince's Bayou and then the Brazos would check him on the west, the San Jacinto and Galveston Bay eastward, and the Gulf of Mexico along the south. The rains had crisscrossed the area more intricately than usual with streamlets, lakes, and marshes, and there were roads to only two exits: one to the west over Vince's Bayou by way of Vince's Bridge, which one man with an ax could destroy in an hour; the other eastward over the San Jacinto River (below its confluence with Buffalo Bayou) by way of Lynch's Ferry, which a good hard march could bring under the authority of Texas cannon. Manifestly a swift race toward the region of that ferry impended.

To block that outlet as well as Vince's Bridge, the volunteers would need to enter the same trap: they would have to float the whole army (except the sick) over Buffalo Bayou, cross Vince's Bridge, march on eastward as far as Lynch's Ferry, and risk destruction themselves in the same corner. A fight there would be as final as between two beasts in a pit from which neither could withdraw till the other had been torn to pieces.

Talk about it inflamed the army. For the first time this tedious campaign took on the drama which young hotbloods had expected in letting themselves be enchanted away to war. For the first time the war acquired the sporting quality of a hunt.

And that morning, for the first time since the flight from Gonzales began, General Houston chose to talk about the outlook. After parading all effectives on a meadow near Buffalo Bayou, he ordered a stand-to before a reviewing platform consisting of a supply wagon occupied by himself, Secretary of War Rusk, and Colonel James Neill. From that elevation he made his speech.

As a congressman in Washington, again as governor of Tennessee, he had earned celebrity for sonorous and compelling oratory. Here this morning he declared in his most exalted language that they at last had an opportunity to transmute all their many sufferings into greatness. Perry, hearing him amid silent armed companions, hearing him amid scents of sweated clothes and horse and dew and trampled grass, found his own chest growing more and more tightly crowded with emotion as Houston's eloquence ascended.

The general outlined the risks before them. He enumerated the brutal outrages which they were now in position to avenge. He held before them the beautiful fact that, if they did thrust the blade of their vengeance home, all Texas would be set free. He then concluded with a peroration which was to remain fresh in Perry's memory throughout his life:

"The army will cross the Bayou, and we will meet the enemy. Some of us may be killed and must be killed. But, soldiers, remember Goliad! And remember the Alamo! The Alamo! The Alamo!"

In throat-wrenching yells the army howled back, "Remember the Alamo! Remember Goliad!"

From C. B.'s Journal
April 19, 1836

Two groups as unlike as could be arrived from opposite ways today —Leticia Springfield and her cheerful family from the east this morning, and from the west this afternoon a flotsam of settlers in muddy rags, all too exhausted to be civil.

The latter came directly from the army, in whose shadow they had been crossing Texas until the day before yesterday, when our troops bent southeast after the Mexicans who ravaged Harrisburg. The Mexicans number less than one thousand; therefore no one intimate with the Frontier considers them a match for our boys, who can lick twice their number wherever they have sufficient ammunition and opportunity to maneuver. Much excitement flows from these facts: often now we look southward along the lovely River of Saint Hyacinth to listen for the guttural dispute of cannon far off, and with such confidence that few who are here think any longer of continuing east toward any safer refuge.

A Negro over near the Brazos told the settlers that he had been captured by a Mexican advance numbering about eight hundred, that he had been questioned by their general before his release, and that the general was Antonio López de Santa Anna. No one believes him. Surely the Dictator would not be such a fool as to sally this far across enemy country with less than a thousand men. We all consider the report nothing more than the invention of a poor darky who wanted to be wondered at awhile and fussed over.

But no fresh panic would be justified even though Santa Anna should indeed be in command of the advance our boys are closing upon. There are people who call him more ruthless than Sennacherib, more vengeful than Caligula, more bloody than Timour, but his horrors are puny compared with these, and for sure he is not the Napoleon he fancies himself. At the Alamo, 182 militia were able to cut down 1600 of his best regulars. A commander who lets a garrison so tiny delay him for two weeks, take nine of his men for each one of themselves, dismember his organization, spoil his surprise, and give their countrymen time to muster fresh opposition is no military genius. What they convincingly proved as they died was that Santa Anna's passports to honor and glory in Texas are forged, and that he can be thrown out.

Our new acquaintances do report one cause for apprehension: an attempted mutiny against General Houston a few days ago. Houston ordered the noisiest Hotspurs to escort refugees to safety in the direction of Nacogdoches, a tactic still producing amused admiration among those who deserted the mutineers to come our way.

Before they reached us, and while Camilla, Roberta, and Esau were away after supplies, a lively jingle of harness bells developed from the east: a double span of mules came trotting through the trees, drawing a white-topped pioneer wagon. In it was Leticia looking fresh as dawn under a blue gingham bonnet. With her rode her twin brothers, of course, and both Bauernschmidts too, but she allowed no doubt that their trip back was her doing, inspired by reports from the Lathams and Wards that I wanted no one but her father to treat my wound. Having learned much from assisting him, she supposed she might be of use to me until I can be brought under his care.

Her clothes all show hard wear. She herself does not. She is the sort of lass who, like a spring newly opened, becomes sweeter, livelier, more sparkling, and more wholesome the more she gives of herself to others. She is infinitely more attentive to me, hurt, than when I was whole—to me as a man, or so I choose to believe, so that I cannot help pretending to feel worse than I do. For need and suffering in men are magnets to such as she when the man they truly want evades them, as Perry has her.

Fortunately Camilla failed to return until I had got the Springfields and Bauernschmidts installed up here on the knoll we hitherto reserved for ourselves. When she did come back, their camp was established, I comfortably on my couch and Leticia beside me reading the Book of Matthew, a service so irreproachable that my darling daughter could give her nothing but welcome, though with one of those compelled smiles which reflect manners rather than affection.

What ails Camilla is that she senses what I do—that Leticia's chastity is the ingenuous and vulnerable kind not likely to endure forever. After all, to be chaste and to be generous implies a contradiction in which chastity someday will lose. As the dewy bud of the bluebonnet awaits the bee, and the interplay of pollen, and the fall of petals around ripening seed, so there is in her a secret, swelling impatience for marriage or ruin or both. Or so the Adam in me argues.

Even so, once Camilla had adjusted herself to having company with us, she took it all handsomely. Tonight after "dishes," with a finely drawn moon again afloat above the west like a golden gondola in a dream of Venice, we all spent a quietly delightful evening. Every act and utterance became as subdued and cordial and civilized as if there were no wolves whatever howling beyond the next hill, no voracious bull alligator bellowing along the San Jacinto, no armies converging toward mortal combat some twenty miles south. We behaved exactly as if the only noteworthy voice, other than our own, belonged to that tireless minstrel, the mockingbird, whistling his lays on a moonlit branch above us.

Now and again, though, upon noticing Camilla's glance blaze, I am reminded of those fine old lines:

> *Love is strong as Death;*
> *Jealousy is cruel as the Grave:*
> *   the coals thereof are coals of fire,*
> *   which hath a most vehement flame.*

CHAPTER XXII

I

Below Buffalo Bayou
2:00 A.M. Wednesday
April 20, 1836

Exhaustion overtook the recruits about two hours after midnight, when some began to fall in the dark, asleep before they were down. A hushed command to halt dropped most of the rest on the grass, coldly dewed though it was. They slept without campfires, being then in an area which a general as keen as Santa Anna would likely patrol.

To reach that point had taxed them continuously since yesterday morning. First they had spent all day floating battle gear across Buffalo Bayou on one leaky flatboat and a raft put together from the timbers of a log cabin; then Houston had ordered a quick advance across Vince's Bridge and into the savanna beyond it without any light except that of a young moon quick to set, determined to place Lynch's Ferry under the authority of his cannon before the Mexicans could discover how near he was.

As Perry groped around in the dark among collapsed men to account for all his company, the air smelled of fish and dank lowlands reminiscent of autumn winds back home in Maryland. In his weariness, and with that fish-stained scent around him, this night agreeably sleeved into another twelve years ago when he was a boy en route to the Chesapeake to shoot duck. The sense of adventure which sustained him through that night came back to him now, refreshing him briefly like a cup of strong tea. Unlike most in his troop, he took time to spread a blanket on the grass as a bed, also to convert his saddle into a pillow. He slept the minute his head sank upon it.

Three laconic beats on a drum at 4:00 A.M. summoned all up and away. With hubs under the cannon and wagons freshly tallowed to silence their squeals, the army continued eastward, still carrying no torch or lantern. At daybreak they were marching over a high swell of prairie from which they could see water far ahead. That would be San Jacinto Bay, and all the beautiful land in that direction looked empty of any human being: they had beaten the enemy in gaining this ground. Several head of cattle, however, were grazing nearby. General Houston took notice of them by retiring his column into a strip of dense timber to build concealed breakfast fires while energetic youngsters rounded up the livestock and butchers whetted their knives.

Appetite for beefsteak prevented all but a few from noticing a brief, faint popping of muskets and barking of rifles beyond a rise to the south. Shortly afterward Deaf Smith and his scouts galloped up to report a brush with an enemy patrol which had fled southeast, a sign that the Mexican advance was still at New Washington, but doubtless preparing to move north, since its scouts had been probing in the direction of Lynch's Ferry.

At once all fires were pulled apart and their smoke drowned. Slaughtered beeves were left hanging by the hocks to cool while the recruits, still without breakfast, resumed their thrust toward the ferry. There they ascertained that the enemy anticipated crossing about noon, having in wait a large flatboat laden with meal and other provender, all easily and gratefully captured.

Thus strengthened, the volunteers drew back a furlong or so along a low, densely wooded ridge between Buffalo Bayou and the road to the ferry, parallel to both. From its crest the bluff sloped down to the bayou behind them steeply enough to serve as a breastwork. Along it the infantry companies deployed under cover of laurel, bay, and rhododendron overshadowed by magnolias and live oaks from which long drapes of Spanish moss hung down to perfect the concealment. Patches of marsh beyond the road in front would bring marching men en route to the ferry within one hundred yards of their hidden rifles, and the artillery under Colonel Neill established a battery directly before the screen of trees where their twin cannon, a gift from the city of Cincinnati, could command all the vale curving down to the river.

It was then possible to put together a breakfast at last, to watch where they could not be seen, to await whatever the enemy might undertake.

New Washington
Sunrise, Wednesday
April 20, 1836

Meanwhile nine miles southward along Galveston Bay, Captain Sangrepalo and his lieutenant, Joaquín de Torquemada, had been sitting their horses knee to knee in a field of young corn near a cluster of ratty sheds and shanties called New Washington in the superstition that the magic of a great name might bring this village eventual greatness. Their company of musketeers, now being scolded into shape by their sergeants, stood beside other companies preparing to march north toward Lynch's Ferry.

The day before yesterday the pretending "Government" of Texas had escaped from New Washington by boat. Today His Excellency, President-General Santa Anna, meant to thrust east of the San Jacinto to bring the remainder of Texas to its knees. No known military organization was in position to oppose a swift despoiling of the area ahead, and none westward except a regiment of filibusters mired in mud far up the Brazos, a band of untrained peons commanded by a notorious dissolute named Houston, also known among the Indians as "Big Drunk." The separate forces of General Sesma, General Gaona, and Colonel Urrea were all now advancing toward different points above and below Houston's position, making ready to encircle the filibusters, and the President-General would order their obliteration shortly. At any rate that was the official talk.

Here by Galveston Bay, though streaks of misty gold projected above the east, promising a bright day, spasmodic shivers shook through Sangrepalo. His men, of course, must feel colder still, being in uniforms of sleazy blue cotton, limp, thin, and frayed. How much misery ordinary mortals somehow live through seemed to him a wonder, and he was surprised to discover a look of delight on his lieutenant.

"Before God, captain-sir," Torquemada remarked, "a handsome sight, no?"

"You think that, *amigito?*"

Torquemada's brows arched in surprise. "You not, captain-sir?"

"These poor worn lost-ones"—Sangrepalo opened a hand toward their company—"you think them handsome?"

"This man or that man, no. But the company together, yes. And all the armed foot, yes. And the dragoons over there, yes. This army as one veteran force, yes-yes. Already their victories are admired throughout the world. Now here they stand as one, prepared, at the command of our President-General, to ennoble still another day. It was that which I thought handsome, captain-sir."

Sangrepalo adjusted his weight in his saddle to disguise a sharp internal squirm. True, Torquemada was only lately back from Spain, where the romantic fashion was to be as innocent of common sense as clever people can manage. Still, out here at the end of nowhere, how could such a bright, engaging young fellow persist in being such an ass? Nine out of every ten men under their command were worn out, penniless, hungry, gullible, moody, superstitious, unreliable, careless, homesick, and stale. Most were enslaved to at least one vice, usually several. They were fed too little, paid too little, taught too little, and itchily infested with lice, bedbugs, and fleas. How could a troop of such men deserve very much more admiration than the individuals in it? Was *this* whole somehow greater than the sum of its parts?

As for ennobling another day, the victories scored thus far might have seemed noble to a newly uniformed youngster like Torquemada, learning about them only through inflated official reports, but the raw fact was that the butcheries at the Alamo, Goliad, and San Patricio would unhinge a hangman. Sangrepalo, a survivor of the Alamo, was convinced that, once known, the total slaughter Santa Anna had required in such battles would horrify all civilized nations.

His own men were largely the remnants of three companies shattered at the Alamo. Before they could recover from that nightmare, they had been assigned to his command and sent on this long march across Texas, much of it over prairies which filibusters had scoured, emptied, and fired. Often they had received half-rations or less, often had marched until exhaustion stunned them blind, often shivered bone cold in sudden northers, and nowhere east of San Antonio had they found any frantically compliant women to comfort them, as conquerors had a right to expect—only empty shacks or defiant ashes. How could they consider this campaign anything better than one long cheat?

"My good Joaquín, it is not that I do not admire our men. No, I love them, but I would not call them a handsome sight."

"However, captain-sir, the morning itself!" Torquemada gazed in aesthetic gratification across Galveston Bay. "That brooding sea, that poetic sky, that delicately colored sunrise! And, above everything else, this miraculous change from the chaos of breaking camp to the order and precision and capability of an army ready for fresh adventure—this, sir, I do find beautiful to see."

Torquemada was a dandy. Day in, day out, he kept himself spruce from the plume on his shako to the gleaming patent leather on his boots—with the help of an expert black valet plus five portmanteaus of effects. But he was amiable too: he respected his captain and undertook to please him. So why resent his riches? The darling heir to a hacienda larger than a dukedom, he was yet too good-natured, too considerate, too much the product of sports and hunts and Jesuit instruction to be spoiled. Only twenty-one last week, he was robust and gay, a fine rider, a dreaded swordsman, a successful but discriminating gallant, a poet too—or at any rate a versifier. Indeed, he was so full of becoming thoughts that he kept a diary over his heart, handy for notations all day long.

Beside Torquemada, who was splendidly mounted on a palomino stallion, Sangrepalo on his tired old bay could not help feeling limitlessly unlucky. The President-General not quite one year ago had personally ordered him reduced from lieutenant-colonel to captain because he had visited Liberal friends in jail prior to their execution. Despite his experience as vice-consul in Liverpool, despite long service with honor under arms, the most he could look forward to after this campaign would be a furlough to decent, predictable living back home in Durango. That was not much, but something. Durango! Thought of it brought to mind the drowsily melodious stroke of cathedral bells, and easy conversation over pulque at dusk, and the seductive twanging of guitars, and daily triumphs over familiar forms of cheating which gave sauce to life. More than likely, however, he would be left behind here in Texas with a garrison of reprieved convicts in one of these worthless outposts which the present war was bringing back under the flag of Mexico.

The very distant future, on the other hand, had taken on a somewhat improved appearance since the fifth day after the Alamo, when Joaquín de Torquemada, newly arrived, had been detailed as his lieutenant. Joaquín was in the army for the same reason as were sons of other ambitious and powerful hidalgos: to gain a creditable early record of service under arms. Even without it, promising and pleasing and rich as he was, he would be welcomed at the iron gates and secret tunnels and private stairways leading to elevated office. When he did arrive there (as he very surely would), how could a youth so honorable forget an indulgent superior whom circumstances had left without his due? Thus every temptation to hate him was annulled by any far look ahead. What a shrewd investment is to some men, fatherly companionship with Torquemada was to Porfirio Martínez de Sangrepalo.

And, now that he thought of it, watching the army convert itself from confusion as raucous as a bazaar into an orderly force did please the eye, in some ways the ear as well. Shivering individuals in the band were warming up snatches of melody; sergeants were bawling, mules braying, chilled horses nickering, smiths hammering, cart wheels squealing, and quartermaster's men loading up supplies. All this communicated energy to Sangrepalo himself in proportion as he took in the particulars. Teams pulled their carts into position for the day's march, and tangles of hurrying men unsnarled, forming into parallel ranks as orderly as chessmen newly arranged for the mover's hand. To an old soldier, it was all as familiar as coffee at breakfast and, when savored, about as stimulating.

An alert from the bugles, supported by the drums, proclaimed that two famed officers were riding out of the village to start the army forward: General Manuel F. Castrillon, iron-willed hero of the assault upon the Alamo, and Colonel Juan K. Almonte of the engineers, an affable, polished Spaniard, often irreverent toward Santa Anna but too valuable in too many ways to dismiss or degrade. Both were superbly dressed and deservedly medaled, both familiar with adulation. At the edge of the cornfield, taking position before a squad of horsemen bearing the army's battle flags, they pulled up to consider the assembled units. Foot and horse alike hastily undertook to perfect the geometry of their formations, after which all stood rigid, waiting.

Castrillon stated moderately that each unit should march according to its assigned order. Lesser officers then issued commands which reverberated down the military hierarchy, ever louder in their descent until, in the mouths of sergeants, they became stentorian yells. Hooves and feet together rhythmically struck the ground.

Castrillon and Almonte proceeded first, their glossy chargers springy in the pasterns, and behind them the color guard, with regimental banners afloat beside the Mexican tricolor, on which the talons of the eagle of freedom perpetually shook the serpent of tyranny. Next marched the band. All bugles, horns, cymbals, and trumpets must remain mute until His Excellency should come galloping forward to take his place between Castrillon and Almonte, but the drums rapped out a beat to pace the march.

After the band rode the dragoons, two and two, their lances perpendicular from the right stirrup, a high polish on all their leather and steel, their eyes with ridiculous hauteur overlooking infantry who were to follow them. From the other side of the cornfield a battalion of musketeers marched onto the road next in ranks of four, while the artillery, lords of one fine brass twelve-pounder and two ammunition carts, moved into position to proceed ahead of Sangrepalo's battalion, which would be followed by the baggage and supplies.

A flurry of shouts within the town called Sangrepalo's attention to torch bearers running from store to store, home to home, shed to shed, applying their fire everywhere. Already charging masses of smoke were assaulting the bluff from warehouses down along Galveston Bay.

"Bravo!" Torquemada exclaimed. "His Excellency burns these kennels also."

"True, yes."

The alert Joaquín did not miss the disapproval in that agreement. "Fire is among the oldest weapons of war, captain-sir."

"Yes, but there was no war here, no resistance, no reason to burn them."

"But why leave them? Captain-sir, where have you seen more beastly kennels than these?"

"They are not kennels, Joaquín: they are homes. And what does this mean? It means that certain poor families fleeing somewhere consider New Washington the center of the universe."

"However, sir, as the President-General intends to drive all the goddamns out of Texas, why not let fire restore that beauty which the Artist of Heaven painted here before they came?"

Sangrepalo winced. He spoke very patiently. "Because that same Artist sanctions family life, which would expire without homes. Divine wrath may pursue those who destroy homes for no better purpose than to please themselves."

Torquemada, he discovered, had ceased to listen. Instead he was admiring the President-General's emergence from town. Wonderfully mounted on a raven-black Andalusian, and with those leaping flames behind him to certify his power, His Excellency this morning emanated that courtly ruthlessness, that theatrical and magnetic brutality, that look of confident and implacable will by which he so often frightened and inspired simple men to attain a capability they never displayed under anyone else. Behind him rode his aides, finely uniformed and deferential, not to say fawning, in recognition that this man's writ ran with the force of a Caesar's across an empire wider than the first Caesar ever ruled, one extending from here to the Pacific Ocean and from the border of Oregon to the jungles of the Isthmus.

Once he had ridden beyond reach of the smoke he kneed his stallion around to contemplate the fire, whereupon his aides all did the same, their attitudes graceful and decorations glinting. One of them, Lieutenant Colonel Ramón Gálvez d'Espinosa, a slenderly tall and fastidious hidalgo whom Sangrepalo had learned to detest, spurred over beside His Excellency to exclaim like a dilettante before a masterwork, his gestures more rapturous as the bay breeze stroked each flame larger, larger, larger, until all the homes their arrival had emptied were crimson skeletons filled with roaring fire.

"Magnificent, no?" Torquemada, aping D'Espinosa, tilted his head sideward. "The flames charge up from the sea like conquistadores bringing a continent under their sword."

Grimacing, Sangrepalo itched to kick him. Instead, he kicked his own horse: the time had come to lead their company out upon the road north. His command to march was echoed through Torquemada to their sergeants and loudly down to the ranks, which tramped the earth to the beat of now-distant drums.

The road passed through a gap in a rail fence, then over a meadow toward a belt of woods into which the foremost troops were disappearing. Out of those woods burst a single horseman, Captain Borrima, who had ridden forward long before dawn with a patrol of dragoons to reconnoiter the area in the direction of Lynch's Ferry. He shouted irritably at the infantry choking the road, jostled through them, then crossed the meadow at a dead run. Because the gate was filled by Sangrepalo's marching musketeers, he put his gelding at a section of rail fence beside them. His horse refused to jump, whereupon Sangrepalo hastily signaled his troops aside to let him through.

"Man, what makes?"

"The enemy is upon us, the Army of Revolt."

He spurred onward at a gallop to the President-General. A look of pained amusement passed from Sangrepalo to Torquemada. Everybody knew very well that the sole surviving Army of Revolt still at large was at least sixty-five miles northeast. The only people left in Harrisburg when it was captured were two printers at work composing an issue of a frontier newspaper, the *Texas Telegraph,* which confirmed that on the 14th the filibusters had not left the Brazos. In the time since then, even allowing extra days for delay of news, it would have been impossible to move any army on foot across such a width of soft prairie, certainly not mere militia. Moreover, there was the overflowing Buffalo Bayou to cross as well. At worst Borrima may have come upon a troop of armed settlers, nothing more.

Therefore Sangrepalo and Torquemada sat with their mounts in check, gazing in amusement after the frantic Borrima, while their company resumed the march through the gate into the meadow beyond. They heard him shout to the President-General that the filibusters, in strength, were attacking with two cannon (though everyone knew the only cannon east of the Brazos was their own). They expected His Excellency to snort at him in scorn. After all, whatever any lover of liberty might say against Santa Anna, he had scored more victories than any other general since the days of the Mongol conquerors. His record proved him invincible, and not even madmen, if acquainted with that record, would deliberately seek him out to attack him.

However, the look of masterful containment which His Excellency usually wore like a uniform fell away. He burst into a tirade at those fool officers (Castrillon and Almonte) who had drawn the army out in such a loose column, letting it straggle through fences and woods where it could not possibly form to crush any surprise. He whirled his stallion, his aides all in consternation behind him, and galloped toward the gate northward. Panic convulsed the musketeers still before it. He charged in among them, rode some down, whipped more aside with his saber, kicked at others, and screamed at Sangrepalo and Torquemada as he approached.

"Forward, you fools! Take battle positions beyond the woods! The enemy is upon us! Idiots, quickly!"

Sangrepalo, who had seen this genius throw tantrums before, knew the best policy at such times was to avoid him. But Torquemada, eager to serve, continued trying to move aside the milling, yelling men who blocked Santa Anna's path. Sangrepalo slid off his nag to seize the boy's bridle and jerk his mount back with all his strength. This twisted Torquemada away in time so that the Great Man's flailing saber, instead of hitting him across the head, merely swished past his ear.

"*Qué tal, capitán?*" yelled Colonel d'Espinosa, riding up to help the President-General and turning his own wrath upon Sangrepalo. "You are not soldier enough to control these men? Mount, stupid, and *move* them."

After he and His Excellency had blundered through the crowd choking the gate, they galloped onward along the ranks. Santa Anna reined up once to rear his horse while he screamed orders to rush beyond the woods, then galloped off again, knocking his way through troops where the road narrowed among the trees.

The woodland was about two hundred yards deep. Sangrepalo and Torquemada took their men through at double time. On the far side they discovered not one sign of any enemy northward, only vacant prairie dotted with parklike groves. Profoundly shaken all the same, they shifted their company in haste to battle formation beside others already doing the same.

While the army waited, ready to fight, a reconnoitering party went forward to seek out other dragoons who had been scouting with Borrima. One hour passed and then another before the dragoons returned to report that their assailants had seen no large military organization, only a band of mounted settlers out to learn what had become of His Excellency's advance. The President-General, furious and ashamed, ordered all northward in battle column.

For a time Torquemada rode beside his captain in silence. He looked depressed. At last he coughed into one gloved hand. "Captain-sir, a thousand thanks."

"But for what?"

"Always you try to improve my brains." He reset his shako in droll disquiet. "Today you saved them."

"*De nada, amigito.*" Sangrepalo flipped one hand. "Had I let that saber cut you down, with whom could I dispute?"

3

Buffalo Bayou
Wednesday
April 20, 1836

In midmorning Deaf Smith's scouts sent word to the Texan ambush that the Mexicans were on the march northward but still far away. Riflemen at rest under murmurous oaks, where curtains of moss drowsily waved to the sigh of April breezes, yawned with temptation to sleep. They watched the horizon southward until their vision blurred, and some, dozing despite the crisis, had to be cuffed awake.

Noon came. They ate again. As yet no enemy southward.

At one o'clock they were still waiting. They smoked and chewed. They greased their rifles. They molded bullets. They patched clothes. Some backed down to the bayou to wash. A few scribbled letters to relatives far away.

Shortly before two, though the savanna before them remained as empty as before, all froze in unmoving silence, for a wind out of the south bore the jaunty, foot-teasing strains of Mexican field music. Soon afterward, where the road curved down between two islands of oak, varicolored battle banners showed above a rise, and presently a group of mounted officers abreast. They were then less than half a mile away. Next to appear was that gay band, and after that a troop of dragoons, their polished steel lance tips agleam in the sunlight. A battalion of infantry followed, their bayonets glinting also, then a squadron of artillery with one large brass cannon. A sequel of more infantry in column gave the force a curving, snaky length, and at the end a rattling tail of supply wagons.

For a few long moments it looked as if the whole column might continue down the road, all unaware. Suddenly, however, a saber flourished and bugles sounded a halt. The leading officers, near enough to make their commands faintly audible, took turns focusing a telescope at the two Cincinnati cannon waiting before the woods and at a mist of campfire smoke blowing from the trees concealing the Texans.

Though the best of telescopes could not have shown them much, an abrupt bawling and bugling followed, a peremptory rattling of drums. Segments of the column shifted rapidly to right and left along high ground, where, as smartly as if on parade, they re-formed in line of battle, ready to attack across a wide, graceful vale between themselves and the wooded ridge. But attack what? The battle line remained motionless under their banners, awaiting the issue of more consultation among the officers, more application of the telescope.

The hidden volunteers watched each move as chaparral cocks do a serpent—heads down, hackles up. General Houston, riding his white stallion along the shaded ranks, insisted that they lie low, be silent, fire no gun.

"Steady, men. Steady," he repeated. "Officers, keep your men steady and concealed."

The enemy's first move was to shift a battalion of musketeers down to the groin of the vale between the main force and the woods, where it could enfilade any Texan charge across the vale. Then units of skirmishers advanced to fire upon pickets stationed along the fringe of the woods. A few shots were returned until Houston, unbeguiled by tactics so obviously designed to draw his ranks out into the vale, ordered the pickets to withdraw into the woods and hold their fire. Eventually the skirmishers themselves retired without having entered sure range for rifles.

Next the Mexicans wheeled their long brass cannon forward onto a knoll about three hundred yards from the woods. As it spouted smoky flame, treetops along the Texan ridge convulsed. Each ricocheting roundshot tore leafy limbs loose above the troops, and bull-throated explosions butted in behind. One shot crashed through oaks directly above Perry's company, showering leaves, twigs, moss, and shattered branches down upon them. Another, in bumping from trunk to trunk, knocked a chip against the bridle bit on General Houston's horse.

Even then only the artillerymen under Colonel Neill were permitted to respond. They ran out to their seemingly deserted six-pounders, affectionately known as "the Twin Sisters," and adjusted them so that their lines of fire would converge upon the twelve-pounder. At their first ear-crushing roar a Mexican artillery captain and his horse floundered down in a sinking struggle, and a flight of shattered wood spun off the limber on the twelve-pounder's caisson. The next shot added to the chaos by tearing open two fine mules.

But the Mexicans preserved their discipline and maintained their fire. They changed to grapeshot, after which Colonel Neill, in command of the Twin Sisters, had to be carried back into the woods, badly wounded in the thigh. In time, however, the Texan gunnery damaged the twelve-pounder's carriage too severely to permit accurate fire, whereupon it was withdrawn from the duel. With a flourish of bugles and a beautiful harmony of banners, schooled horses, marching musicians, and well-drilled ranks of foot, the whole Mexican force turned away.

At that stage the afternoon was half spent, the Texan strength and disposition still concealed. The Mexicans marched off to high ground above San Jacinto Bay. There, about three-quarters of a mile distant, most of their column took up a good defensive position. The remainder began preparing a camp.

And still the rebels offered no strong challenge. . . .

Chaparral cocks, though capable of destroying a rattlesnake, prefer to avoid him when he has coiled to strike, waiting instead until he basks. They then dart from behind brush or rocks or trees to sting him, bewilder him, lacerate him, until he is carrion and their nests again safe.

4

Buffalo Bayou
Wednesday Night
April 20, 1836

"Aye, Capun Allan!"

The call rose cheerfully through the moonlight across Buffalo Bayou. Though Perry recognized the voice of Hugh Llewelyn, much too sensible to bother him without cause, he indulged himself in resenting and ignoring it. He and half a dozen others were there for a bedtime swim, briefly free spirits, briefly something more than soldiers controlled by orders from above, and he suspected that Hugh had come to snatch him back.

The whole day's effort had come to nothing, or very little. An hour or so after Santa Anna had withdrawn his forces, Lieutenant Colonel Sherman had led a harebrained cavalry charge to capture the Mexicans' disabled twelve-pounder. Instead he had brought on a counter-charge from adept and courageous dragoons, supported by a battalion of musketeers, who had been getting the better of his horsemen until another deafening storm of grapeshot from the Twin Sisters had driven the enemy back. As twilight had gathered, both sides had cleared the field in tacit agreement to delay their showdown until another day.

Now, refreshed by water presumably too cold to swim in, Perry rolled to his back, ears deaf under the surface, and let each arm in turn pull him like an oar. Coldly laving currents flowed through the thickets of his hair and down his chest, down his flanks, down between his thighs, creating (after all those days of duty, duty, duty) a renascence of pleasure in being young. Westward along the length of the bayou, the arms of a young moon upheld the ghost of the old, the two indivisible as life and death, the old a weakly gray, the new assertive, bright and growing, an inducement to the delusion that youth is the only consequential part of life. Someday, Perry decided, he would discuss this delusion with Camilla under just such a moon, and look forward with her to fruitful days and nights in the fullness of life.

A two-fingered whistle darted across the bayou. He bobbed up to listen. Above splashes and laughs from companions nearer shore, there was still a wide stir of campfire activity high in the woods. A fife dwelt upon a dreamy old tune not in the military repertory; emptied cooking pots clinked together; a smith's hammer knocked out differing notes on a musical anvil; and a laugh rollicked through the trees like a colt showing off. Over to his left something metallic clattered into a box.

"Ay, capun!"

"That you, Hugh?"

"Yessir. Men just come here say they seen Miz Pawmer night fore last."

"Who?" In doubting joy he flung his head both ways to shake the water from his ears. "Miss Camilla?"

"Yessir. Two men come afoot, and so tired they can't sit awake long."

"Be there directly." Head up to talk, Perry stroked toward shore like a frog. "Please say so."

"All right."

"Keep them awake."

"I will, capun."

Hugh, no more than a blur in the dark, disappeared up the wooded ridge. Camilla! Perry exultantly drew himself out on the bank. Shuddering in the night chill of April, he threw a towel over himself, heart jumping around loose inside his chest like a mustang trapped in a pit. Camilla! He snatched on his clothes. To think of it—Camilla! Still busy at his buttons, he scrambled uphill toward firelight aglow among trees crowning the ridge.

5

Most men in his company were down for the night, dead asleep. Hugh and Molineau sat in conversation with two others who were eating leftovers from supper. One he recognized as Jake Timberlake, an Otter Creek settler like himself. The second was Salty Latham, who had left the army west of the Brazos to move his family.

Latham had brought two letters, one from Camilla, the other from Leticia. Manners required Perry to postpone feasting upon them until he could ask the newcomers about their journey and what he could do for them. Invited to sign on with his company, both agreed. While Molineau laboriously printed information about them in the company record, Perry opened the letter from Camilla and read it in total engrossment, not even entertained as yet by her ladylike atrocities in spelling. One passage about fires in the Otter Creek neighborhood stopped him for a swift restudy:

Pa says you know one of the Rascals who brought this Distruction amongst us, a slicked-up Ruffiun named Rex Cotyer, who looks Exactly like what is meant by the axiom, "Wash a dog, comb a dog, Still a Dog." There was another you May have chanced across somewher in Texas—Blacky Reed. He is the man who actually struck the fire at Hoping Hill, though only a creature of Rex Cotyer's. During all the Tumult that night a branch of a tree snatched loose a watch chain bearing an earspoon and a little pearl-handled Pennife we saw Cotyer use during earlier visits, so we know he was there. We fetched these with us as Evidence which may someday produce a Reckoning. . . ."

Perry looked up, wide-eyed over the relevance to problems previously so mystifying. "Jake, you either of you see anything of a lamed-up man on a paint horse? He may have been heading up the Liberty Road."

Both Jake and Salty had begun kicking together beds of leaves while Molineau went off to enter them on the regimental rolls. Jake paused limply. "No such a man, no. Seen a paint grazun though."

"White clover on his face?"

"Didn't notice that, no."

"I seen that, aye," Salty volunteered.

"Look a little like a white ace of clubs?"

"Right like that, aye. But no man close around. There was the paint, grazun on a line, but who staked him out we couldn't see. It was long about dusk, and we thought maybe the rider was huntun a bit of grub nearby. We both hollered right loud, but nobody come."

"No reply," said Jake. "Not a sound."

"So it bean no time to tarry, we hustled on."

Perry sighed. "Godalmighty!"

"Why?"

"Salty, that's the sonofabitch burned Jake's cabin, also Nuhns', and tried to burn Mrs. Palmer's too. Just where was it you saw the paint?"

"A good piece off the road in a wood we short-cutted through yestiddy about dusk. Never would of seen him then, he was so sheltered, only he whickered once."

Jake stood expressionless and straight, absent-mindedly digging at lice in his crotch. "You say *he's* who burnt my place?"

"Mrs. Palmer says so in this letter."

"What in hell's name for?"

"Seems he did it to signify what he'd do to her place too if she didn't sell."

"Oh."

Jake went on clawing himself, eyes stunned, face vacant. Perry returned to Camilla's letter, finished a second reading of that, and tore open Leticia's. Surprisingly it gave less space to her own flight from home than to Major Burleigh and Camilla:

He looks more wasted than you would believe, Perry—so thin and lame it wrenches the heart to see him struggle about on his sticks, yet he forces himself to be cheerful and keep at it, as if a man must not allow a bit of lead to rule him. I like to stay by him and talk with him or read to him because that keeps him down, where he ought to be.

Also it helps me: so often he says something that wakens thought from its slumber. He opens a cage where one's spirit has been drooping on its perch and sends it flying above the treetops. What a fine mind he has, truly exceptional! All the more credit to you that he thinks so well of you, Perry.

Camilla too I daily admire more. Her camp is managed better than any other, and she keeps herself looking so cheerful and lovely and well employed that everyone takes heart at sight of her. I don't wonder at all that you esteem her as you do.

As one act of friendship, please look after Papa some, won't you? When ailing people call for him at all hours, he forgets to eat right and neglects his sleep. Please gently spread among them some notice of his need, and caution him often, as I do at home, because he is unlikely to replenish his strength unless someone insists.

We all hope you will also take good care of you. Texas would be a poorer place without you, and the world too.

Your obt. servant,
Leticia

He recognized in her praise of Camilla a deliberate renunciation of himself, final as could be. While admiring the clarity with which it was done, he could not help regretting it too, for her image evoked that stirring of lust mingled with sad and protective tenderness which always beset him whenever she was around. To feel that stud-horse impulse of his revive at such a time seemed to him brutish. Camilla was avowedly in Texas to be his wife, and desire for any other female was too perverse to allow. He again read *her* letter to help him disallow it.

This time he dwelt longer upon other paragraphs:

If you can merely Write, and not come soon Yourself, please most Particklerly describe the circumstances of your acquaintance with that Cotyer. Behind what he has done, Pa suspecks a greater Wickedness than I thought the world contained, and I grow uneasy upon reflecting how often he is Right.

But if you are so near as we imagine, do find some apt occasion Soon to join us, however briefly. Apart from longing to see thee, I badly need to look at the Future with Thee, to decide how we shall use it. The greatest Wickedness imaginable will seem less to me then, for I venture We Two Together (as you have declaired more than once before) can construct a larger portion of Blessedness than most mortals ever approxomate.

Meanwhile, I do not blush at all to say that I think of Thee every hour, and wonder after Thee, though I relize the need of this suffering Land must not give way, in your dayly acts, to any lesser need. All that looks best for Ourselves, as well as for Texas, depends First upon defeat of the Tyrant.

We believe you will compass that defeat, perhaps Soon. And, oh, dear Perry, as you go into battle to Free us, may God hold His Hand above thee!

> *Yours without end,*
> *Camilla*

His absorption in these lines gave way to observation of Jake Timberlake. Salty was down and quiet, but not Jake, who had rolled his blanket into a bundle—Jake, a bony, narrow, humorless man with a sun-inflamed face and reddish-brown bristle thick on his jaws. His belches were explosive and frequent, a result of gluttony half an hour before, yet he shifted over to jacknife slices off a roasted shoulder of beef. These he laid one above another upon a rag spread flat before him.

"What you doing, Jake?"

"Packun victuals. I got me a man to hunt. Caint nobody do me like that Cotcher done without I pop some hot lead inta him—or lay cold steel on him, one."

"Tomorrow we'll have a battle to win. Do that right and afterwards we can take thought of private quarrels, not before."

"Do that, and afterwerz nobody'll know where he's at. I go hunt him now, and *keep* huntun him, I'm lible to hunt him down."

"Don't you understand though, Jake? You're a soldier now."

"Oh, I understand fine. A man burnt me out of house and home that I never done no harm to. Times like these, nobody'll take the trouble to learn him less I do." In his eye sockets, hollowed and darkened by lack of sleep, a weak fanaticism had begun to glitter.

Perry went over to grip him on both shoulders, reaching at his reason through the laying on of hands. "I'm your neighbor, Jake, your friend too. Because I am, I can't let you go. You're a good shot. You can be a credit to your country here in the next day or two. If you do stay, you'll get a large bounty in land, all clear."

"Only that don't build up my burnt cabin. I got to leave so's I—"

"In the first place we'll all help you build it when we get home. In the second you'd be a deserter if you left. General Houston's sworn he'll shoot any man who deserts, and *I* swear to bring any deserter from *this* company in for trial."

"But I aint but just got here! I wouldn't never of joined if—"

"Now hold on, please." Perry gave him a shake, and out of him came a breath polluted by exhaustion. *"Any* Texian near here is duty-bound to help in this fight. Men who won't are tories or deserters, if not cowards. Cottier has harmed you something terrible, and no justification whatsoever—that's true. He's harmed Major Burleigh worse, and others too. But Santa Anna's harmed thousands, not just a few. Cottier's burned two-three cabins; Santa Anna's burned whole towns. Cottier's shot the major down; Santa Anna's shot down every Texian his troops could take and hold. *There's* the bastard we have to teach a lesson to first." He shook another wag through Jake. "Now aint that so?"

"Ye-es, only—"

"But right now, Jake, you're in no state to fight anybody. Without sleep, you'll be sick. You're *half* sick already. Anyhow, we need you too much to let you go anywhere, except to sleep." After a final bruising grip, he released him. "So let's be sensible and both do that: let's both go to sleep."

Perry turned his back to prepare a pallet for himself.

Salty, who had roused from a doze to listen, growled out at Jake, "Come on, sojer. Lay down thern rest, uh?"

Though doubtfully, Jake did so.

From C. B.'s Journal
April 20, 1836

A far, guttural murmur from the south began a little past two this afternoon. As no thunderheads showed anywhere, we thought it artillery fire. It was faint, less a noise than a shudder of the atmosphere, and yet whoever has heard cannon dueling at a distance could not believe it anything else. Spells of silence intervened, then again that ominous shudder, and what wild images it evoked of desperate effort and torn flesh!

Most families here are keeping their campfires up tonight on the chance that a messenger might pass this way before dawn. Actually, we should not expect to hear before tomorrow night, if then. Though the area we guess to be the battlefield lies little more than twenty miles south, the distance around by the roads must be three or four times that, and no good way to short-cut without mishap because the rains have put so much ground under water down here near the Gulph.

We cannot quiet our impatience, however, until we do get word. Today our volunteers may well have decided whether or not Texas is to fall back under dominations which demean not less than eighty-five in every hundred souls throughout Mexico. The issue is big. The cause is one to revere. The consequences will outlive all our generations across an area wider than Western Europe. Those endeavors whose echoes we heard today dwarf to triviality whatever we inactives may do or think or fear: the mold of the future is the volunteers' to shape.

I do not in the least believe, however, that the shaping can cease when their cannon do. Here we have already discerned sufficiently well

(as we did back in Louisiana) that the Mexicans have no monopoly
on ruthless men.

> *Daily as long as we live*
> *We must unremittingly seek*
> *To baffle those men who contrive*
> *That the earth shall inherit the meek.*

CHAPTER XXIII

I

Liberty Road
1:30 A.M. *Thursday*
April 21, 1836

Not until Rex saw two big wolves on his trail a third time that night did he understand that what he had most reason to fear was inside himself, and no way to shake it.

Riding only by night and avoiding the Liberty Road had turned out to be a tedious, baffling way to cross unfamiliar ground after so much wet weather. Rarely did he find any wide stretch of country without marshes spread upon it here and there, or a lake swollen by rain, or a bayou out of its banks. To make any considerable progress he was forced at last to risk using the road during late hours of darkness when no one else was liable to be on it.

Even so, here he was, with the third night since he left the sick camp better than half gone, and not yet at the San Jacinto. The pains from his leg pierced him everywhere, all through. To the jog of his horse, aches jolted around inside his head like stones in a pot, and never did entirely stop even when he reined up to rest.

Still, he did not intend to baby the damn leg any till he had the river behind him. What the doctor said about needing to lie quiet—he had brains enough to realize it was intended to scare him into staying put, where that young lawyer could worry the truth out of him. Tomorrow, however, he meant to find some hideout over on yonder side of the river, rest the leg good, bathe it with hot water like the doctor said, and massage it good till it got better. After that he could steal on back to Louisiana, where the chief would make sure he got the best doctoring money could buy—and would equally make sure that the law stayed on his side.

Seeing those wolves so often told him, however, that all such calculations might be maybe only dreaming.

The first time was a while beyond midnight, after he had taken to the Liberty Road and chanced to look back. No more than a pistol shot behind him, there they were in the dark, keeping the same pace

442

as his pinto: no howls, no noise at all, simply there, and peaceable as family dogs except for their spooky, silent way of lurking and skulking just so far behind.

After a thought or two he determined not to let them trouble him any. He had seen big lobos like these often in Texas. Game was so plenty that they kept too well fed to jump a horse carrying a man, but they were curious animals and watchful of whatever passed through their territory. The only thing he didn't like was the bothersome way they persevered about sniffing after him.

Once earlier tonight he had had a real scare, the genuine article, and also once yesterday along about dusky-dark. By comparison a pair of wolves should never stir a hair on his head.

Yesterday evening a couple of nosy men carrying rifles strayed through a woods where he had hid for the day. They stopped to investigate his camp and his horse, but it just so happened he had seen them soon enough to hop off one-footed and hide good before a nicker from his pinto drew them his way. Though he got both pistols cocked, and his carbine too, ready to blow their brains out if they poked around behind the bushes were he was hiding, he was as unlike the cool customer he usually was as a man could be. Such a wild case of shakes came over him that he'd have done well to hit the broad side of a barn, much less a man, so sure was he at first that they must be a party sent by that smart-aleck lawyer to hunt him down. From their talk, though, he made out that they too were just curious, like the wolves. With dark coming on and their hollers around his camp bringing back nothing but spooky echoes, they went on in a southwesterly direction, no doubt *to* the army, rather than from it.

Then a little after moonset tonight, when he was risking the road to get through a canebrake running along both sides of a twisty little creek, he heard three horsemen coming from the east at a trot. Fortunately they were talking at the top of their lungs, uneasy themselves. That gave him warning soon enough to ride off on the downwind side, where their horses would not smell his. Again he got the shakes something terrible; but, by sliding off and holding his paint's nose shut, he prevented any nickering, though they passed less than two dozen yards away.

So after two close calls like that, why be uneasy over a couple of sniffy wolves? He made himself think ahead to that tarnal river and how to get across it in this awful condition. After a bit, when he did look back, the wolves were gone.

The second time they showed he knew from the lift of his pinto's head that he was close to where horses and people had been. He himself could smell fishy damps which told him the river was not far off. Mostly he could only smell the sweat on his horse, and the thick, boary stink of his own armpits, but when the wind brushed these aside he could smell the river plain.

There was another smell too. It made his horse snort often, and kept him carrying his muzzle to the left, shunning it. Whenever Rex bent forward to the right, he could smell it himself, a foul gas seeping from the rags around his wound.

More than anything else it brought to mind a possum he had seen in a timber once when he was small. With the thought that it was pretending to be dead, he had called his father over to kill it. His father, eying it, sniffed the air and said, "Son, that thing aint playn possum. It's mortipude." And for years, to bring him down a notch or two, and make company laugh, his father would tell the story about that possum. If his father wanted to gouge him good for any reason at all he would call *him* Mortipude, or Mort for short.

Now here the infernal thing was, back to plague him again, or the smell of it anyway. As the least recollection of it always worked on him wrong, he kept forcing his thought ahead to the river, holding his horse to a cautious walk, watching the dark ahead.

He had reached a patch of trees and passed nearly through when he made out a wide flat beyond it. On the far side stood a parade of sentinel trees which must be cypress, and therefore would mark the near bank of the San Jacinto. There were more mosquitoes here, and a shrill chorus of frogs ahead. The breeze was more fishy too. From far down to the left came the hideous, rumbling bellow of a bull alligator, which he thought the wildest, most savage sound in all nature, but mostly the noise was that singing of frogs by the thousand.

Edging his pinto forward, he saw a weak light, a small blaze in a gap through the row of cypresses. That must be the ferryman's watch-fire, and *there* was really something to think about.

The easy way to cross might be to rouse the ferryman, if he was alone, and let him get the ferry well out over deep water, which would be the place to slip him about eight inches of steel from the handiest bowie knife he ever felt the edge of, then tie an anchor on him and dump him overboard to feed the gators, turtles, and catfish. Him out of the way, he could pull the ferry on to the other side and leave it there just as it should be. No one would ever guess but what the man had gone off somewhere, unmindful of who might want to cross or when, as ferry handlers in these parts so often did.

But Rex knew he could not try that tonight. First, he was too weak and shaky, too uncertain of his footing. Second, he could not risk finding out if the ferryman was alone or even whether the ferry was in fact on this side instead of the other. Third, how could he tell what might be over there on the other side? Far beyond the cypresses he made out what appeared to be faint lights, perhaps dying campfires, and it was his understanding from talk in the sick camp that runaway settlers lingered by these river crossings, hopeful of good news from their own boys in the army. While he weighed it all, a mule far, far over there on a knoll let go a string of silly heartbroken brays, telling pretty plain that there was indeed a camp on that side.

No, he could not cross by the ferry or anywhere near it. He would have to go up the river a ways, or down, swim his horse across, then circle wide around the camp and hole up for the day in a good snug woods three-four miles beyond it. All this must be done well before daylight, though the time was not less than two in the morning already.

While he was thinking so, a faint stir over on his right brought a jerky snort from his pinto and threw prickly gooseflesh over himself. A huge lobo had jumped out into the clear, showing under the starlight as only a ghostly shape in motion. It stopped in the open to lift its muzzle sideward at Rex. A second wolf followed at a deliberate, skulking trot. It too paused to sniff the air adrift from him toward them.

Sick as he was, aching, hurting, burning as he was, this set off a powder keg inside him. A yell was almost out of his mouth before he could choke it off, and he hit his carbine at low-hanging leaves on a tree to drive them away. They did shift a little farther off, but there one lay down and the other sat, watching him as if nobody had to tell them how weak he had become.

Well, to hell with them: he had no time to trifle away on them. The thing to do was get across the river, then treat his leg the way the doctor said, and after a bit he wouldn't be smelling mortipude any more.

To cross some distance south, he decided, had better promise to it than crossing upstream, because the flood would carry a swimming horse down, and he couldn't risk coming ashore anywhere near that camp. His first move was simply to rein back deep into the screen of trees. The wolves, he was pleased to see, trotted off north. He then headed his pinto south.

After a good third of a mile his horse reached softening ground. The near singing of peeper frogs, the humming of gnats and mosquitoes too, told him a branch or bayou lay ahead, too swollen to stay where it should.

A bold turn to the left took him straight over toward that parade of cypresses marking the river. Here and there his pinto was almost thrown down by the depth of the mud, but always showed heart, a good tough horse. Nowhere did Rex see anything more of the two lobos, and this increased a feverish conviction that his escape was almost complete.

The river had scarcely any bank to it: the San Jacinto was swimming all the way up to the cypresses. It did look dangerous, gliding by in the dark, a deep, greasy sort of black, its slicks broken by patches of drift which moved in total silence the way those damn wolves did. Still, the worse it looked the better, because any search party would be less apt to think he had gone beyond it if there was no word of him at the ferry.

First, of course, he had to take heed of his powder and weapons. A bandanna around his neck to keep the mosquitoes off he converted into a bag for both pistols, his powder flask and percussion caps too, then tied it around the barrel of his carbine so that he could carry all high with one hand. His blanket, the food in his saddlebags, all his personals, and that precious substance in the moneybelt around him would get soaked of course. Let them. His firearms were the sole things a driven man had to keep dry.

As he was about to spur into the river, that alligator boomed like a battery of cannon, far downstream. A jerk of terror jarred through his horse; but, himself knowing gators pretty well, he was sure they would steer wide of anything that thrashed the water as strongly as a swimming horse—or even a grown man. Besides, though its bellow sounded tremendous, vibrating along the water, it must actually be too far south to have any place in his reckoning.

However, it did leave behind a startled silence, a closer listening. Everywhere he heard mosquitoes tuning their tiny fiddles, peepers their fifes, and bullfrogs their drums—sort of agreeable music. As he was thinking what a long, long time they had been playing the self-same tunes, a stealthy lapping upstream on his left threw another sheet of gooseflesh over him. His scalp contracted, making his hair whisper inside his hat. Those infernal wolves again! He gouged the spur on his good side into his pinto's flank, knocking out a pained grunt, and started the tedious business of forcing him into the river.

As the water reached over his stirrups and came on up his legs, it felt mortally cold on the good side, but on the other not there at all except above the knee. This, of course, was just what the persevering of those lobos meant: something dead, or awful near it, was hanging to his horse. His death, they knew, was not outside him, waiting to overtake him, but already fastened to him, waiting to have its way. Only the smell of live man kept them from trying to pull the dead part off the saddle.

Therefore, to be carried away in the rising, tugging grip of the river, black and cold as it was, brought a peculiar, shuddery relief. When his pinto was down to his withers, swimming with only his neck and head above water, Rex, lying along his mane, buoyed up by the flood, sighed with a sense of accomplished escape. Uncertainty and the pull of the current turned his horse half around, but a couple of good hard wallops on the skull with the weighted barrel of his carbine straightened him out quick enough. There was really nothing much to swimming a horse, once a man got started, not a good stout animal. Here in the middle of the river his pinto did not need much handling. Tired or not, his horse was a good swimmer and maneuvered sensibly to avoid drifting brush here, a log there.

The sight Rex kept on an extra tall cypress ahead indicated that the current was carrying them down a good bit, as anticipated. This confirmation of his judgment seemed to say that everything would turn out fine. He spoke encouragement to his horse with an affection he was not in the habit of.

They were approaching blacker water, shadowed by lofty cypress trees marking the far shore, when another bellow from that gator rolled upstream. Though still in fact a good piece away, it sounded so much nearer down here on the water and echoed so powerfully off the trees ahead that it startled his pinto bad. The fool lashed around in a brainless fright and began paddling back the way he had come. Rex jerked his rein, knocked the carbine against his skull, gouged the drowned spur into his flank, and so began to get him turned east again.

The two of them, in that splashing struggle, failed until too late to see bearing down upon them a huge dead tree, the ends of its fractured limbs pointing downstream. Rex let go the rein to grab for a branch. While his left hand caught it, the other fastened on his bundle, but the carbine slid through its knot into the water. His single grip on the tree was hardly enough to save him, weak as he was. He pulled his good foot up onto the saddle, thrust it down hard to push himself into a low fork, and thus shoved the pinto underneath the tree.

Rex, his heart fluttering like a chicken with its neck wrung, worked himself and his bundle slowly, weakly onto the drifting trunk. Through it he could feel a wild spasmodic bumping as of a head or hooves or both knocking underneath. Once a strangled snort came out just at the surface, choked off, and shortly there was no bumping any more.

2

The morning of April 21 seemed to Captain Sangrepalo, camped above the area where San Jacinto Bay debouched into Galveston Bay, the finest the Lord had produced since the spring campaign began. The air was light and fragrant, the prairies freshly dewed, the sky a deep azure as far as the eye could see. Across that sky wide-winged birds floated at every altitude to join others spiraling above the savanna where yesterday's skirmishes had strewn the carcasses of slain horses and mules. Rarely did any of the birds beat the air; each one planed around, calmly unhurried, and yet the flight of each so crossed others that the entire spiral looked as turbulent as trash above a dust devil in hot weather.

While he stood thinking so, Corporal Chombo ventured near to say, "There are many, captain-sir. This signifies what?"

Chombo, though one of the most reliable men in the army, was all Indian: superstitions darkened his mind. In advance of any crisis he sought omens in nature, above all in the motion of animals or in the flight and cries of birds. Such creatures he regarded as spirits in disguise who watched every circumstance bearing upon his fate, assuring him that, even though men highly placed might ignore him as they would the dung of a horse, numberless beings very much higher treasured his existence and sought to preserve it. Pitiable self-deceptions of that order endeared him to Sangrepalo at times, but at others infuriated him.

"It signifies," he said flatly, "that dead creatures lie there spoiling."

"And that more die today, captain-sir? I believe it signifies a day of death."

"Santa Maria! We have a skirmish and lose a few mules. Behold, birds come to pick their bones. Does that change them into soothsayers?"

He left. The chance of more action today was slight. The filibusters were taking even greater care than yesterday to stay inside their fortress of oaks above Buffalo Bayou. Nothing tempted them out. At about 10:30 in the morning a reinforcement of 540 men under General Cos, whom His Excellency had sent fast horses to hurry forward by all-night march, crossed the prairie in full view of the Texan pickets without drawing one shot.

Already high breastworks had been constructed across the front of the camp, the only direction from which it could be attacked because it stretched along a rise where a curving belt of swamps protected the rear. The augmentation under Cos had strengthened the position so much, and so very obviously, that any danger of attack had vanished: an easy relaxation lightened the mood of the army.

The President-General, after discussions with Cos, said he doubted that anything could be gained by staying here to try accounts with an enemy too timid to accept any challenge for an open fight. There was no sense in blindly forcing those woods. He talked of abandoning his own position after nightfall in order to shift west toward the Brazos River, where he had a crushing reserve of more than three thousand regulars divided into units under the command of five generals—Filisola, Gaona, Sesma, Urrea and Woll. Once all that power was unified with his present force, the complete conquest of Texas would follow at whatever speed he could march across it.

With Cos's troops exhausted, and the prospect of a night march by all ranks, the plan for the remainder of the day was to rest well. After the noonday meal the army settled down for a siesta longer than usual. Sangrepalo, needing to ease himself, first strolled off behind the camp as far toward the San Jacinto as swamps along it would let him go, and afterward he too lay down for a siesta in the tent he shared with Joaquín de Torquemada, already asleep.

In midafternoon he wakened to find Chombo jerking his foot. He roused up, annoyed. *"Hombre, qué te pasa?"*

"They march, the Señor Goddamns."

"Where?"

"Who knows, Captain-Sir?" He stroked the air eastward with four fingers upright. "Thus."

Torquemada, whom their talking had brought half awake, ventured sleepily, "He means they retreat."

Sangrepalo cocked his head to hear what was going on beyond their tent. Someone was whistling. Three or four men quarreled at cards. The hooves of a horse walking by lazily crushed the sod. Not one thing except the expression on Chombo's face gave the least hint of alarm. Besides, after the frenzy which had so upset the army yesterday morning, nothing would be more deplored today than any sign of fear.

Torquemada put all this to Chombo in terms suited to a simple mind. "If chickens run from the eagle, man, must you disturb the captain? Go away."

A moment of hesitation, and Chombo obeyed. Nevertheless Sangrepalo got up: often Chombo's superstitions turned out to be justified. He forced a yawn and scratched his flank and stumbled with indifference in pulling on his boots. While sauntering out past Torquemada, he drowsily wound his watch. "Four minus five," he remarked through another yawn. "It makes late."

"You have right, captain-sir," Torquemada agreed but subsided on his pallet.

Outside, the day was much warmer than before, very like June. The skies remained flawless, a pure, halcyon blue. The new greens of April gleamed under the sun's golden light. Wherever Sangrepalo turned, a calm perfection rebuked his disquiet. Its harmonies dazed the mind, lulled the senses, drugged the will. Above the front of the camp the regimental colors flipped a little to one side, a little to the other, like the tails of horses grazing. Tepees of stacked arms stood everywhere. Most soldiers slept, some in their tents, some in patches of shade. Here and there a few played three-card monte. Others chatted or sewed on buttons, hunted fleas beneath their shirts or sorted through a comrade's hair to pick out lice. From a grove off to the left, where the dragoons were camped, half-dressed men rode bareback to and from a little bayou where they watered their horses.

Such reassurances, however, were not altogether convincing to Sangrepalo: he was old enough to know that circumstances are never more likely to deteriorate than when they appear at their best. Still, what reason was there to worry? Before the camp lay a wide prairie sweeping downward into a swale which any attack would have to cross, and no cover anywhere nearby. To protect the right a battalion of infantry had occupied a riverside woods somewhat forward of the line. The left was protected by the dragoons concealed by another grove. In the center of the breastwork in front was the repaired twelve-pounder, a mighty weapon indeed. Though loosely put together from felled trees, wagons, baggage, boxes, and carts, that barricade was almost five feet high. From behind it any attack would be easy to cut to pieces, and guards paced each way along the front, dreamily crying, *"Sentinele alerte,"* as camp form required.

Above them on a wagon stood Chombo, his shako and chin strap well set, his gaze steadfastly northwest, toward the enemy's ridge. The captain strolled to the wagon. Across the breastwork he could see plainly enough what held Chombo. Well over half a mile away filibusters in every sort of gear were parading across open ground beyond the swale commanded by the Mexican camp, moving parallel to it toward the right. They marched two and two in a long column, which emerged from behind a plump grove on the left and disappeared far behind another much nearer grove on the right. Mounted officers along the column segmented it into companies, and near the center were the two cast-iron cannon which had dueled against the twelve-pounder with such embarrassing success yesterday afternoon.

"They exercise," Sangrepalo commented at once.

He was sure of it. They did not have their packs, as they would if withdrawing. No stealth showed in their movements. Very likely they were trying to produce an exaggerated impression of their strength by plainly showing part of that column but never its front and rear, a transparent sort of trick which provoked his smile.

"Yes, they drill," he said to Chombo. "Well, let them."

No one else in authority took any interest in them, so why should he? He began peeling off his shirt while sauntering toward an olla of cold water, kicking his orderly awake en route. With the orderly, stupefied by dreams, pouring for him sloppily from the olla, he soaped his face and neck and arms, his whole head too, wanting to wake up and be refreshed. Before he could rinse off, Corporal Chombo came to his elbow at a trot.

Chombo kept his voice low. "Captain-sir, they march the other way."

"Donkey! You see I wash, no?"

"But is true, captain-sir. They change now." He gestured crosswise to indicate that their direction, though still parallel to the camp, was now in the opposite direction, toward the left and much closer.

Though Sangrepalo maintained an irritated nonchalance, he did go back with Chombo to the breastwork, toweling himself as he walked. This time he pulled himself up on a felled tree.

The filibusters were much easier to see than before. The head of their column, at some invisible point beyond the nearer grove on the right, had evidently turned sharp right, advancing as far as that nearer grove and there turning right again to march straight along the shoulder of the swale, this time leftward in relation to the camp. They were now less than a third of a mile away, and their amateur wish to appear military had become even more transparent and amusing. Some were not in step. Few wore uniforms. Most were dressed exactly as they would be on a hunt or at work. They marched in complete silence. Their only flag was a white banner bearing the image of their goddess, Liberty, and the only thing about them not deserving laughter or scorn was the alacrity and spirit that showed in every movement.

Heading the column was an unusually big officer on a stalwart white stallion. He held the entire line to one course until the rear end of it emerged from behind that grove on the right. For the first time all were then in view and puzzlingly careless about exposing their flank within easy range of the twelve-pounder. Sangrepalo quickly estimated their number at about seven hundred. With Cos's reinforcements, of course, there were nearly twice as many men here in camp, trained veterans without exception, but that made the cheek of such display the more arresting, since they too knew about those reinforcements.

At a command from the big officer, faintly audible in the lazy air, the column halted. Another command turned it as one, and surprisingly *toward* the Mexican camp. The officer then waved his hat, and the line started forward.

Sangrepalo's stupefaction at this utterly senseless maneuver increased when a fife-and-drum unit near the two cannon at the center, playing in march time, struck up a beguiling love song he had often heard as a prisoner of reveling Texans in San Antonio last December. To the tune of those fifes and drums the words came alive in his mind:

> *Will you come to the bower*
> *I have shaded for you?*
> *Your bed shall be roses*
> *All sparkling with dew.*
>
> *Will you, will you, will you,*
> *Will you come to the bower?*

Will you, will you, will you,
Will you come to the bower?

A lizard of fear skittered inside his undershirt. At San Antonio he had seen Texans dare maneuvers no less foolhardy than this one to-day and turn them to account. The crazy contrast between the gaiety of their band and the wooden muteness of their ranks hinted that they might be attempting here what they had there: an assault which, all military factors well considered, ought really to bring them down like hay before a scythe.

That lizard of fear moved into his belly. He should not act excited, of course, but act he must. Shouts were going up from sentinels along the barricade. A few began firing at the filibusters even though they were still far beyond musket range. To Sangrepalo, however, it seemed much more stupid that he himself did not have his shirt on, or any-thing in hand but a towel.

Throwing that aside, he lowered his weight off the tree to walk toward his tent in a paunchy hustle. Further thought quickened him until he was running. He found Torquemada asleep again.

"Up, sir!" His voice went shrill. "Now is the hour! Now itself!"

"Pardon?" Torquemada, handsomely comfortable, lifted his head an inch or two. He watched the captain snatch on a tunic without a shirt. "What happens, captain-sir?"

"Santa Maria! Up, sir! All men to the breastwork! *Up*, I say!"

Buckling on his sword, his pistol and ammunition pouch, he rushed outside to kick sleeping or idling men. Some he marshaled to the barri-cade with Chombo's help, calling back to Torquemada to assemble the rest.

Other officers, too, were taking up the cry to arms. Scatters of stupefied men bumped against one another in running after muskets, fixing on bayonets, cramming shakos on just anyhow, shifting toward the barricade. There part of the artillery had come alert and brought their twelve-pounder to bear.

During the few minutes of Sangrepalo's scurry through camp the enemy, still at a rapid walk timed to their fifes and drums, had cov-ered at least two hundred yards, being now hardly more than that distance away. A jolting roar from the twelve-pounder exploded black smoke out around a spout of fire. As the filibusters were low in the swale, however, it shot high, causing no damage, not even a pause in that musical question, "Will you come to the bower?" no falter in their advance, except among their artillerymen, who stopped to aim their twin cannon between the advancing lines of foot.

They fired the six-pounders in rapid alternation, not using ball, but scrap iron. Their first blast smashed the breastwork open. Another tilted the twelve-pounder's carriage so that it became almost useless. With each spray of iron they discharged, a cluster of men behind the breastwork sagged in a wailing tumble, and one cannoneer, a hand shorn off, wrestled his redly spouting wrist as if gripping the neck of a serpent.

Everywhere around Sangrepalo were futile tangles of men in lopsided shakos, many with no shot for their muskets, trying to borrow from others who also had left their ammunition belts behind. They set up a continuous bleating, like sheep in a corral. To knock a little order into his own troop he whipped rumps with his saber, kicked others, and knocked some across the head with his pistol. Few but Chombo were truly ready for battle.

He kept expecting the invincible Santa Anna to stride forth and call for some brilliant stratagem to convert this tumult into orderly, tide-turning resistance. Where *was* His Excellency all this time? Sangrepalo, while ramming a fresh paper cartridge into his pistol, flung a glance over toward the presidential marquee. A restive black charger was there, with a groom at his bridle, but evidently the President-General had not yet finished snatching on clothes after his siesta.

One reassuring performance was that of Joaquín de Torquemada. Firmly resisting panic, he had taken several minutes to assemble a laggard portion of their company in military order deep within the camp and equip them properly. Saber in hand, rapping out smart commands, he marched them forward to defend the breastwork.

The yelling and screaming around camp seemed the more insane because the line of filibusters remained mute, close though they now were. The only sound from their ranks, apart from ear-splitting artillery blasts, was their band's idiotic, lilting invitation to a shaded bower. Dimly, too, he began now to hear the officer on the white stallion shout as he galloped before the ranks from end to end, "Hold your fire, men! Hold your fire!" He was wearing a general's epaulettes and gilt braid. When he was less than one hundred yards from the barricade, the stallion he was riding collapsed, dotted by a splatter of wounds. The general seized the nearest horse from the line, vaulted onto it as its owner slid off, and continued his exhortations.

The ranks were composed of shaggy men in skins and patched

homespun, or in ruined store clothes, each carrying a rifle or shotgun. On their belts, jiggling as they hurried forward, were knives, pistols, and tomahawks or hatchets. Over to Sangrepalo's right were some he recognized from the Battle of San Antonio, and with them an officer on a fine steel gray, which danced with desire to gallop. What was the fellow's name? Rangy and lithe, he wore a bleached blue uniform and a wide hat easy to remember. Though like a brother to him during his shameful surrender in Zambrano Row, he had a name the crisis would not let him recall. He himself, having just shouted orders for the nearest men to cock their weapons for a volley, aimed his pistol at that rider, not because the rider was in a convenient position, since he was well off side, but because Sangrepalo wished to make sure that that youth, of all people, did not find him here among the slayers of the garrison in the Alamo. After all, on being paroled after his surrender in San Antonio, he had given his solemn oath, in the hearing of that youth, never again to fight in Texas. He aimed with care.

Through the smoke which leaped from his own hand at his cry to fire, he could not detect the least result. Here and there were men along those oncoming ranks who flinched or sagged or stumbled down, now that they were so near, but amazingly few in proportion to the fire from the whole length of the breastwork. Not only were they immune to fright from volleys which, by noise alone, would have turned back rioting multitudes down in Mexico proper; they seemed equally immune to the bullets, no doubt because there was scarcely a weapon in steady hands.

While Sangrepalo bawled at his men to reload, while he himself reloaded, another rider carrying an ax galloped along the prairie on a foamily sweated mustang, a dark, heavy-chested man in buckskins, another of those he had met in San Antonio last December, a scout known with awe through all Texas as Deaf Smith.

"Vince's Bridge is down, boys," the scout yelled, waving the ax aloft. "They can't escape us!"

In the meantime a troop of filibuster cavalry had been approaching on Sangrepalo's left, aiming toward the grove where unmounted dragoons had been whiling the afternoon away. At first they had held their horses back to a trot. About a quarter-mile from the grove they began to loosen out into a gallop, whereupon the big general waved his hat high and roared an order for the foot to halt. All the foot, at his next command, knelt down to aim in silence, now deep within range for riflemen.

Sangrepalo at that instant found it necessary to bend low, as if he had dropped a percussion cap while reloading his pistol. The explosion of Texan rifles that followed was far sharper and more emphatic than the pop of muskets loaded with dilute, cheating powder from Mexico —a riotous, stuttering crackle along their line, like an immense vat of boiling grease upset in a creek. It melted down astonishing numbers of musketeers behind the breastwork.

The humming wind of one late bullet stroked Sangrepalo's shoulder blade as he was straightening up, ready to fire again. It ended with a soft slap, as by a child punishing a doll, and he turned to see Chombo clutching his throat. Even though blood fountained through his fingers, Chombo's eyes showed a wild wish to disbelieve that this was his own life his heart was pumping out. In a drowning gurgle, red froth bubbling over his lips, he begged his captain to help him, as if a man who knew so much of the world could undo the caprice of that bullet and stop this destroying fountain. All Sangrepalo could do, all he had time to do, was seize Chombo's arm and ease his fall.

For, as the rifle fire died away, those hitherto silent enemy ranks let go the most hating yell he had heard in all his time on earth. It rose in drawn syllables, and as one gigantic voice, so that the attack seemed not by hundreds but by a host.

"Ree-memberr the Alamo! Ree-memberr Goliad!"

A maniacal lust for revenge resounded through that cry, and so chillingly that dozens of musketeers behind the barricade threw their weapons aside and fled. Coming after so protracted a silence, after the mutilations of that rifle fire too, it unnerved Sangrepalo himself. The hand holding the pistol by which he strove to wave his own faltering men back twitched with an impulse to cross himself.

"Ree-memberr the Alamo!" the oncoming enemy insisted. "Ree-memberr Goliad!"

Every horse among them was now at a gallop, every man on foot at a run. They were coming straight at the barricade, and not far to go.

"Your bayonets!" Sangrepalo screamed at the nearest musketeers. "Receive them on your bayonets!"

Other officers were ordering the same, notably General Castrillon, who had mounted an ammunition cart near the twelve-pounder. The only general in sight, and famed for severity, for personal valor too, he had succeeded in rallying two score or so at that point for disciplined defense. Actually, however, Sangrepalo was sure no good would come of it. Those pealing enemy yells gave warning that spirits of all

the dead the massacres westward had consumed were charging with
them, and that no bayonets or sabers could stop them now.

Men near him who were weakening away he caned back with the
flat of his saber, as did Torquemada to his right. Torquemada then
leaped onto the felled tree behind the barricade, flung his shako aside,
and, handsomely bareheaded, set an example by foiling off a catapult
of Texans with lightning swordsmanship. Sangrepalo, though watery
in the knees, though positive it would be suicidal to expose himself
here, saw that he must support his lieutenant to save his reputation,
his conscience too. Wading through a litter of bodies, he jumped onto
the log beside him.

The blood of men felled there had greased it slick. His boot slipped.
His grip on the rampart, as he toppled over, brought down a large
box weighted with stones that trapped his hips between the log and
a fallen chest.

Immediately Torquemada stepped over to help him. As he bent
above him, compassion turned his eyes gentle as a girl's. "Captain-sir,
you are hurt?"

"Careful, little friend!"

Sangrepalo waved for him to duck aside: a long-armed Texan was
leaning over the breastwork to swing a hatchet at the back of the
boy's head. It struck as if into a packed cigar box. Torquemada's
eyes walled; his features loosened. A geyser of blood spilled around
his ears, and the body that had housed him collapsed upon Sangrepalo.

Often Sangrepalo had seen, but never *felt,* men die, as he did now,
with Torquemada's weight upon him. There was no death jerk as in
animals brained or beheaded; only a total slackening of every part,
a gushing of blood, a release of urine, a windy discharge of the bowels.
Hot vile liquids saturated the captain's clothes. Five minutes earlier
he had envied and loved Joaquín as he might a remarkable son, a
better, more idealistic self. But the burden sprawling heavily across
him and emptying itself upon him was more loathsome than garbage.
He pushed it aside as far as the box entrapping his legs would let him.

In a brief lift of the head to look around he could see no promise
of relief anywhere. From the marquee deep among the tents the
President-General emerged, ordered everyone close around him to lie
face down on the ground, leaped onto his charger, and galloped away
among the tents.

But there were simple men whom chains of duty held in the fight.
About one-fifth of Sangrepalo's command remained among them. The

hundreds of hours of drill they had received in using the bayonet helped them little because of their awkwardness in stumbling among dead or writhing friends. Indeed, the dread bayonet turned out to be almost worthless against men with none. For the enemy carried a weapon more terrible, a fury which freed them of caution or fear. Converting their rifles into war clubs by gripping the barrels, they smashed the bayonets aside and brought down looping blows which crushed skulls, broke shoulders, or snapped arms raised to ward them off.

In the meantime a strong penetration of the camp's right had brought frantic musketeers running for their lives from that direction. Simultaneously the cavalry charge at dragoons on the opposite end of the line drove a wild rush of half-dressed men and naked horses through camp from the left. The two opposing currents swirled together among the tents like spring torrents meeting among boulders, and charging cavalrymen thrust sabers into squirming wretches along the fringes as if they were spearing fish.

Shrieks from men dying there unnerved the musketeers holding the center of the barricade under General Castrillon: they tossed their weapons aside to run away. The intrepid Castrillon lowered his saber in despising resignation and, walking after them, exposed his back to the Texan rifles. Heretofore the luck of extraordinary courage had preserved him, but three bullets in succession now stained his tunic. Still gripping his saber, he continued a few more steps, then knelt as if before an altar and, in bowing forward, toppled down. His calm acceptance of death seemed to diminish it, to scorn it, to defeat it.

With the collapse of resistance behind the barricade, masses of the enemy now surged into camp along most of its length, and again the thunderclap of that wrathful cry: "Ree-memberr the Alamo! Ree-memberr Goliad!"

They swooped this way and that to surround and obliterate the few units still trying to make a stand. One of Sangrepalo's musketeers, a dark little Nahuatlan with a flat, pitted nose, dropped to his knees, hands up together in a prayer for mercy. "Me no Goliad! Me no Alamo!"

This was true. Like Torquemada, he was a replacement from reserves never engaged at either place. Two Texans in unison, however, swung their reversed rifles at his head like axes at a chunk of firewood. As he dodged one, the flintlock of the other crushed his shako into his skull. He wilted to one side, eyes jelling in a stare without focus. Sangrepalo held his breath and pretended to be dead, doubtful that even this would preserve him. Some Texan directly above him, tardy in crossing the barricade, knocked loose a set of joined boards, the tailgate from a wagon. In falling, it slid across Sangrepalo's face and chest. Though it clawed his cheek and jaw and let him see no more of the battle, he took care not to move it.

3

Perry and other officers, in the culmination of that charge at the breastwork, had galloped to it ahead of their troop. Instead of trying to jump or breach it, he reined up before it to fire a pair of horse pistols (both crammed with buckshot for that instant) and then the four-barreled pistol Camilla had given him. Most of the Mexicans at that stage were dangerous only as far as their bayonets could reach: the barricade had become more a hindrance than a help to them, for it held them back far enough to give an advantage to marksmen shooting across it. Perry was able to fire all six charges in his three pistols at less than a dozen feet without damage to himself or his horse. Meantime his men ran up to rip the breastwork open and climb through, as did other Texans along the entire front.

They left not one Mexican upright in that sector, and the battle moved away from the fallen like a prairie fire from blackened grass. Perry and Lieutenant Garrick, their sabers naked, galloped beside units fleeing toward a patch of timber, turning them toward open ground, where recruits on foot overtook them with rifles clubbing, knives flashing, and hatchets or tomahawks bright red.

Here Perry came upon a Mexican officer, short in the neck and trunk, an ugly, furious man who ceased ranting at his troop to walk straight toward him. Perry swerved that way at a trot, his saber rising to strike.

Without the least fear the Mexican extended his saber, hilt first, to Perry. "Por favor, señor, entonces applica Usted este."

Brave as the man was, Perry had to accept his surrender courteously, and that of other survivors of the same command. This burden of prisoners could be managed only by checking as many of his own men as his shouts could reach. The effect was to hold them back where they were and to restore their self-control.

But adjacent troops thrust on, the Mexicans before them running beyond the camp and down toward the San Jacinto, where swamplands lay under a spread of reedy grass. Mud bogged many Mexicans within point-blank range. Those falling pulled others down, where they were trampled by still others from behind, until the rest turned back toward the Texans with their hands up, wailing for mercy.

Many others fled around the ridge toward the southwest, then out upon the savannas in the direction of Vince's Bridge eight miles away, not knowing that Deaf Smith had destroyed it. Cavalrymen, mounted scouts, and runners afoot sped after these wherever they were visible, leaving a scatter of silent bodies upon the grass in that direction.

Within twenty minutes after the assault began General Houston, himself badly wounded in the ankle and carrying a boot full of blood, issued an order that no more of the enemy should be killed or injured; all were to be taken prisoner. One entire regiment of four hundred, assembled by the polished Almonte, came forward to surrender in a body. Many Texans were too widely dispersed to hear Houston's order, too deafened by their own wild shouts and by shrieks of the stricken. As late as sundown Perry, riding across the gruesomely littered battleground looking for men missing from his own troop, still occasionally saw recruits in the distance knocking down wretches who offered no defense.

While he was returning through the former Mexican camp, where volunteers were assembling spoils and recording them for disposition later, two infantrymen he recognized as belonging to Colonel Burleson's command hailed him. They had between them a paunchy, limping captain who had no shako, no weapons, and hardly enough spirit to walk.

"Capun," one called, "here's a Mexican's asked after you. Come to us hisself to surrender sayn he knows you and let him see you."

Perry remembered Captain Sangrepalo, remembered also his pledge never to fight in Texas again, his tearful oath that he would be a friend for life to every man in the platoon—including those since burned at the Alamo. A musing sigh, and Perry spoke to him in the qualified amiability he would have shown the hometown drunk, an incurable liar whom no one disliked and no one believed.

"*Tanto gusto de verle, Capitán Sangrepalo.*"

"*No-no, amigito mio. El gusto es mio, verdamente.*" The hand he extended had no discernible wound and yet was caked with blood.

Perry reached down from Marquis to grip it. "*Que tal, señor?*"

"*Soy un perdito,* my friend, a soul in hell."

His cheek was scored, his hair snarled. His tunic hung open, bloodied widely across the front, though obviously not from within, for his undershirt was stained little.

"Hurt, are you?"

"Well, wounds, no."

"You don't need a surgeon?"

"I need a change, captain." He threw a fatigued hand weakly toward the tents. "I have clothes there. If you would give permission —just a fresh uniform. This one a dog would not wear."

"Yes, all right." Perry nodded at the two recruits. "Take him over yonder, boys. And with consideration, please."

4

That night Rex's leg, from the knee down, no longer seemed his. A day upon the San Jacinto under a hot sun had brought swarms of flies over the wrappings. At first he had flapped at them, cussed at them, kicked his good foot at them, but all no use: they always stayed close, always brought more buzzing around him. He in time stopped fighting the infernal things, too sick to bother. By the hundred they settled down, fitting onto him a squirmy black boot dotted with glints of brass.

Most of the time after that he hadn't done much but lie still, or mostly so. His bundle of weapons he tied good and tight onto a branch where he would not lose it while he slept, then let the river carry him toward the Gulf however it would.

A dizzy, sickly, stupefying weakness slackened every sinew in him. Loose as his clothes hung about him, he must have lost thirty-forty pounds, likely more. Merciful God, how long *was* it since he'd been well? True, hardly two weeks had passed since that buckshot hit him, but that time seemed first cousin to eternity: he felt as if something rotten had poisoned his blood for years and years and years, and no cure ever.

Tonight all sorts of recollections and fancies kept carrying him back to boyhood. One impression often with him (no doubt because those sickly aches never stopped pounding through him) was that his mother was beating him again the way she used to, or else his father or schoolmaster, and then his mother some more. Time after time she used to plead with him, heartbroken, to be a good boy; but what his father said was true—that just scolding him did no more good than picking at a wart, which only got worse. When he kept right on doing wrong, Jupiter, the club she took to him!—a laundry stick stout enough to knock down a mule. The old man favored a harness tug, and his schoolmaster a hickory pointer, but that club of his mother's was what hurt the cruelest.

Why did they all get so they hated him so? That used to eat on him considerable. Nowadays, looking back, he could easy cipher it out. He being the first in the family, the quickest, stoutest, scrappiest one in the whole litter, the folks concluded early that he might be a credit to them someday if only they learned him to do right. They did their best to, but it came to nothing. Study, for one thing, got awful tiresome, plain common niggery work too, and seemed like the harder they beat him the wider his ornery streak grew. The whole neighborhood, those days, called him "Hellion" Leahy (the name Rex Cottier being one he'd taken later to put trouble behind him), and him proud of the title too.

Once he got too big for the folks to handle, or any schoolmaster either, they apprenticed him off to a blacksmith he greatly admired, a giant with a grip like a canthook which would fasten on Rex's collar any time he needed the living hell slapped out of him. That kept him pretty straight a few years, and made him good at smithing, but also increased his strength, and took away all previous admiration for his boss. His apprenticeship ended with the smith's head caved in, himself on the run, and the law only a couple of jumps behind.

Curiously, much as he had wanted all along to get away from home, he missed it considerable after going back was out of the question. He even missed having his mother fuss at him about his clothes, about washing good and minding how he talked. His looks always had been a pride to her, that being before he got his nose crushed, and Sundays she would force him to scrub and comb and doll up till he hardly knew himself. He thought he hated it all at the time, and hated her too. Years later an acquaintance from back there told him she had died with a tumefaction on her neck that tortured her something fierce, putting her out of her head so bad she often talked about him as if he was still half grown, still the boy she hoped would do the family proud. First off he was relieved she was gone so he could forget her at last. That night, though, about to drop off to sleep, he took to remembering how she used to be before she wore out, a big handsome woman full of hope and energy and fierce religion, and first thing he knew he was crying like he never had since he was small. Next day was when he had a tattoo pricked on his hand to always remember her by.

One thing he'd learned over and over since then: a mean man spends a lot of his time a lonesome man. Year on year he'd kept pretty short of breath running from some mean trick or other till he finally settled down with the chief at a calling which let him use his ornery streak with profit. He got to be a high-up spender with a world of style to him and plenty of talky acquaintance around saloons and four-five real choice sporting women that never saw him without putting sugar on his name. That was living, that work with the chief, and no country jake of a lawyer was going to keep him from getting back to it.

No, but he did wonder if his wound might not.

About dawn this morning his tree shoaled on a bend in the river, teetered heavily, and began a slow twist in the pull of flowing water, which drew his dead pinto out from underneath to float away alone. A natural thought then was whether to go ashore and crutch around till he found another horse; but the land was all wild, not a place to catch anything a man could ride. Anyhow, the twisting tree soon pulled free again and took him back to deep water.

Gliding on downstream revived a daydream he used to carry around as a boy, wanting to leave home, thinking someday he might follow a creek that rambled off to the Tennessee River and so to the Mississippi and from there to the Gulf. Though the creek was shallow much of the way, he'd dream of floating off in a scow or raft or even a tub, anything to get away in. He'd fancied it would be so easy—just drift away to freedom and no strain at all. Why should he feel so bad off now? Why shouldn't he take it as lucky to be lazing along, letting this pretty river carry him down to the Gulf in its own sweet time? Down there he might catch a ship (unless he got washed out too far first) and ride that back to New Orleans.

The only thing was, the time it would take this river to get him there could itself be the death of him. The stench the noonday sun brought out of his leg told him if he did not get the lower part attended to soon it would take the rest of him where that much already had gone—into a shroud of blowflies two or three deep.

During the afternoon he slackened into a long, miserable, sickly sleep until a rigmarole of dreams brought him around to an impression that Doc Springfield was treating his leg again, changing the bandages. He woke to find a large turtle sitting there on the log, nipping at them, sleepy-eyed in the sun, trying to chew through. Gooseflesh crawled over him as it had last night when he heard those persevering wolves lap the river close by in the dark. A yell at the turtle, a single fling of the arm, and it bobbled off into the river.

Still, his hope kept on finding reason to perk up a bit after it seemed rightly down for good. Distant explosions southward echoed along the river about four in the afternoon. They sounded to him like ship's cannon at sea. More than once yesterday, when waiting for dark in a grove of oaks he had thought he heard the identical sound, very faint. Today it was too plain to doubt, a distinct HOOM-*pa* which repeated itself irregularly: HOOM-*pa*, HOOM-*pa*, HOOM-*pa*. He took this to mean that down at the mouth of the San Jacinto a Texan man-o-war had cornered a vessel under the Mexican tricolor. All accounts of the Texan Navy gave it much handsomer marks for performance this spring than the forces on land: any Mexican ships overtaken while trying to put in where they could supply Santa Anna's men were captured, driven aground, or sunk.

A man-o-war with Americans on her, of course, would carry a surgeon. If the river took him there soon enough, Rex figured, he could settle accounts with that leg *and* get back to New Orleans, since that was where the Texan Navy provisioned. The comfort of that conclusion eased his mind some, and he dozed in spite of intending not to.

A while after sundown, after the river became speckled with stars and reflected a wabbly piece of moon, he wakened from a long nightmare to discover himself sitting up, ranting aloud, both feet over the side of the log and a bumpy, bubbly milling of invisible creatures in the water before him, centering on the bad leg, trying to tear the wrappings off. They so weighed on it as to come near pulling him in. Feeble as that leg was, he had to lift it with both hands to draw it back aboard. A slippery flopping developed around it as it broke the surface—turtles of course, and fish too, no doubt catfish or carp or both. Inspecting his bandages under the moon, he saw that the thieving, hateful devils had got through in one place where a stinky black showed underneath.

Rewrapping it left him realizing that a ship's surgeon would never trifle over such a leg: if he did reach one in time, it would all get sawn off, sure. How much good would the chief think he was after that? How good a "reasoner" could he be one-legged? How many dolled-up women would sweeten his name then?

He knew—and, Christ, how sick he was! He pulled himself forward along the log for a safer place to ride, among branches high enough to keep his feet out of the water if they dangled. The night was the kind most people would call fine—not a cloud anywhere, a piece of pure white moon hanging in the sky, and stars, stars, stars, stars, even in the water thousands of stars, in that velvety black water with those slimy, evil, gluttonous things underneath making all the beauty of it a hateful goddamned deception.

That was how the whole world was, actually. Wherever his wanderings had taken him he had found every handsome show matched by some hidden evil, never the one anywhere without the other, even the best-regarded people partly wicked, helping to keep in this life the same old mixture of heaven and hell, and no real escape for anybody. Long ago everything fine like this river looked now had stopped having any strong call for him because he knew so well about the secret evil. How many more such nights would he live to see? Not many, surely, and yet why did that matter when he knew so well what an eternal cheat they always were?

High as he was above the water, every shift of position teetered the tree some, and that dizzied him worse. Seeing the moon wabble and the heavenly stars tip around, and the reflected stars too, reminded him of his first days at sea when all his guts together tried to crowd out of his mouth. Tonight, because his fever burned so hot, he loosened his coat wide open, his vest the same, but each least exertion made his heart flutter against his chest like a sparrow behind a window. Queerly faint all through, too weak to fight sleep off any more, he looped both arms around one rising limb and laid his head against it.

He was aware of nothing more until cold water seized hold of him all around. When his brain cleared he realized he was under the tree, thrown off as it tripped on a shoal, and black water everywhere—in his eyes, his nose, his throat. As he fought upward his head and back bumped against the trunk. A stub protruding from it gouged down between his shoulder blades, hooking into his collar and holding him the way that dead blacksmith used to do. His wild clawing around to get a grip on something drew the coat tight against his armpits in a twisty way which the pull of the current would not let him loosen.

The one near branch his hands did reach was slippery from long soaking, pliant too, and little body in it. Whichever way he pulled, it yielded, a slippery, strengthless thing hanging in the way to baffle every attempt at finding one more firm.

At first he thought what an awful pity that a man born to all the ability he used to have should blunder off in this weakly, miserable way, and no one to know or regret it. Soon, though, his gulping struggle for breath produced a lightness in the mind, a declining concern. The end proved easier than he ever supposed it could be. After the terror, after the merciless gagging and suffocation, he had the sense to see that this *was* his final moment, not to be avoided, and then it was no longer terrible at all.

His whole life might have been better, he thought dimly, if somebody had convinced him early that he had it in him to take death so easy when it came, however it came. He might have been in less of a hurry to beat or belittle the other fellow before he got beat or belittled himself. Too late for that sort of regret, of course, too late for anything but this discovery of easy and welcome death. He kept his hold on the branch, yes, but without any more of that long, torturesome endeavor to stay alive.

5

Perry's company next morning was one of those assigned to control the Mexican survivors, about seven hundred in all. A new camp had to be established for the unhurt, an odorless distance from the battlefield, and some two hundred of them, being wounded, needed to be moved northward across Buffalo Bayou to the plantation of the vice-president of Texas, Lorenzo de Zavala, which was converted into a field hospital. With that work well along by midafternoon, his company was shifted to guard Mexican burial parties.

Well over six hundred dead still lay where they fell. The disproportion of losses almost passed belief: the Texans, in overwhelming an army nearly twice the size of theirs, had lost only eight killed and thirty-one wounded, whereas virtually the entire Mexican Army had been killed, wounded, or captured. The spoils included a military chest containing twelve thousand dollars in Mexican specie (all to be divided among the victors as the first pay to any) and generous quantities of weapons, ammunition, horses, mules, tents, carts, tools, and military equipage.

Beyond a doubt a victory so startling would attract a rush of volunteers from the U.S.A., assuring an early end to the war and quick recognition of Texan independence. As yet Santa Anna, the one man who might stop any further combat at once, had not been discovered, but the wiliest scouts the Frontier had produced were searching for him and were not likely to miss him in an area so hemmed around by water. Perry intended, as soon as they did find him, to rush a letter to Camilla by the first courier, saying that the war could be considered as good as over, that he was requesting at least a week's leave to help bring her father to Dr. Springfield, and wouldn't she meanwhile please locate some functionary who could hear their marriage vows?

With such prospects before him, he had difficulty keeping his attention on the burial parties. Already the claims of peace seemed to him enormous. First, homes must be re-established, livestock assembled, and more crops planted before the spring expired. Then, as General Houston had implied during their talk three nights ago, Texas would need permanent republican institutions, guaranteeing the liberties the revolt had set out to win. For months to come, no doubt for years, each public act would be formative in the highest degree.

Altogether, any look ahead revealed opportunities enough to dizzy the mind—and in time to weary it. The day's moist heat was stupefying. It had begun to fatten the dead: already a corrupt puffiness was crowding their uniforms, exuding a stench from which, as Perry rode around the battleground, his breath recoiled until he was starved for air. Wherever he looked a crazy strewage of bodies mutely, insistently, reproached him for being exhilarated about the future. Glazed and unmoving eyes posed questions which he had not reflected upon enough to answer and would much rather not notice at all.

Yesterday afternoon during his search for missing comrades he had seen General Manuel F. Castrillon down and at peace a short way behind ruins of the Mexican barricade. So evident was that soldier's fearless acceptance of death, his still dignity as well, his immunity to

hate or pity or prayer, that the end of life looked to Perry less awesome
and appalling than it had before or since, indeed somehow beautiful
—death of the brave in battle. Today, however, stiffened bodies flung
in shallow trenches seemed limitlessly repulsive, the final excrement
of beings who now appeared little more worthy of admiration than so
many rats crushed in sprung traps.

Pollution of the air drifting across them drove most Texans guard-
ing the burial parties toward the outer limits of sure rifle range, and
Perry himself rode over to the windward side near the San Jacinto
River. There was in fact no need to stay close, because the captive
Mexicans were all aware now that the area had been converted
into a prison by destruction of Vince's Bridge, by removal of Lynch's
Ferry, and by sorties of horse in search of the last few runaways not
overtaken yesterday evening.

Those digging graves had less than a dozen shovels among them.
That and their shrinking approach to their task made Perry wonder
whether all the killed ever would be buried, or even devoured. There
were too many for the shovels, too many for the vultures, too many
for the wolves, wildcats, and panthers.

All the burial parties were supervised by Mexican officers, since
disposition of their own comrades was their own concern. One group
near the river worked under Sangrepalo, who came limping over to
join Perry, sitting Marquis on a hump of land above the San Jacinto.

"Ah, Captain," Sangrepalo began, wagging his head, "a frightful
harvest!"

"Uhm. It's that, sure enough."

"And the day otherwise so perfect!"

Sangrepalo flourished toward the river, which reflected its far
shore with a shaky painter's approximate fidelity. Above it soared a
multitude of gulls, some white, some gray, and ever so graceful on
the wing even though, as Perry knew, they had left no eyes in the
dead along the shore.

Sangrepalo added, "Such a day puts a man's faith on trial, eh,
friend? How can one believe that the spirits of such carrion have
attained Eternal Life?"

Before Perry floated an image of Thomas Dunraven undertaking
last December to cheer up Sangrepalo, lately wounded in Zambrano
Row. Dunraven, though agnostic, admired faith in others and sought
to reinvigorate Sangrepalo's. What was the promise of Christ? That
they are blessed who suffer yet retain their faith: to the faithful,

suffering is only a pupa in which the wings of the spirit grow. Misery, Dunraven put it on another occasion, and labor, hunger, injustice too, are but schools in which men of faith prepare for Eternal Life, attainable only through death.

Sangrepalo, after crossing himself, had resisted such argument. He had seen a good bit of the world. According to him, misery demeans men; labor dulls them; injustice sours them; hunger sharpens their greed; suffering shrinks their courage; and death disposes of them when, in most instances, the world would be about as well off without them.

That view resembled what Dunraven in private had revealed as his own. To him, the Christian effort to negate death was quite misguided: death might better be honored as a cleanser, indeed as a savior of the world, ridding it of its rubbish. What man could name so many as ten persons, intimately known to himself, who should be reckoned worth preserving through all eternity, whether in heaven or in hell? He did not know one, not even his own mother, dear thing. Most of us, he argued, are poor approximations with which life makes do for a time, flawed clay vessels easily broken, and certainly unfit to be honored with perpetuity. Nothing could be worse for the world than to have the defectives who infest it preserved very much longer than the normal life span.

Against Sangrepalo's despair, even so, Tom had recommended faith, faith, faith. Only in the absence of faith, he said, could afflictions fail to help the spirit grow. Afflictions teach men of faith how entirely they are at one with the great disappointed generality of mankind which nothing can altogether destroy. What is a better way to eternal life than through sympathetic identity with this persisting mass of humanity? Might *that* not be what Christ was saying in his talk of Love? Dunraven had made it seem a shame for any professed Christian to look upon his own wretchedness without a certain exaltation.

To Perry his argument had sounded altogether wonderful—except that he knew Dunraven needed to be convinced of it himself. It had benefited Sangrepalo all the same, if only because debating the matter had put his mind to work. It also had reminded Perry that he personally would not begin to know anything primary about the meaning of life until he had fathomed the meaning of death.

Here by the San Jacinto four months later, with death so at large and himself one cause, he recognized that the end of his own very serviceable body was prefigured here. At once, however, he rejected this hideously stinking conclusion as the sole truth about what his living self would be converted into. Neither, therefore, could it be the sole truth about these nameless men, if not of him. There was too boundless a distance between man dead and man living, aspiring, sinning, dreaming, creating, failing, hating, fighting, loving. What putrefied here with sightless stares was manifestly the very least part of the lifetimes terminated yesterday afternoon. Once in Baltimore he had heard a biologist lecture on the theme that nothing in nature is ever wholly destroyed, only converted into new forms. If so, how was it possible without belief in the persistence of the soul, or in some unnamed equivalent, to account for what becomes of a human life after death disposes of its odious dross? For an instant he felt he had under his hand the pulsing heart of the case for conviction that men share a little in what is divine.

An interplay of lazy voices drew his glance upstream, where three lads from Lieutenant Garrick's platoon had sauntered out upon a promontory, rifles slack in their hands, while they waited for this awful afternoon to wear away. What drew them, apparently, was a large fallen tree stuck in shoaly water about a pistol shot from shore. Along it roosted several gulls and turtles, above which, queerly enough, hung a bundle made from a bandanna tied to a middle branch. One of the idlers leveled his rifle at the bundle. Though Perry disapproved of wasteful shooting, he dismissed an impulse to yell at him, feeling in himself what he knew they felt—a strong temptation, in the presence of so much that was loathsome, to let every thought and act become wholly irrelevant. The boy's shot merely jolted the bundle and sent up a flap of gulls, whereupon a companion, trying his skill, ripped a ragged hole just below the knot.

Sangrepalo asked, "What could that be?"

"Looks like a tramp's bundle. Odd place to see one though."

"Very odd."

Before it ceased to sway, the third rifle fired. The cloth split open, voiding three or four articles unidentifiable at this distance. They splashed in the river more heavily than stone, leaving the bandanna limp. Perry thought the fools might better have investigated anything so curious. Since they had not, he should have himself: a log on a deserted river carrying any such oddity poses a problem which ought to be solved. While he was thinking so, a loping roan brought Lieutenant Garrick over the ridge.

"You down there! What's all the gunplay, uh?"

"Just shootun, sir."

"Then stop it, damn you! Put another charge in them rifles."

"Yessir."

"And keep it there till you got a proper target, *which*, if you use what brains you were born with, you'll keep it ready for any runaway Mexican, and that's all."

"Yessir."

Sangrepalo, embarrassed, looked back to his burial party. They had ceased scratching open trenches; instead they were carrying a cadaver down to a firm bit of riverbank under an old supplicating willow as bent as Father Time, where they launched it upon the waters. Already five others, afloat in a loose queue, were drifting away with gradual quickening in the direction of the Gulf. Sangrepalo glanced back to see if Perry might disapprove, but Perry was pretending to be aware of nothing but the dead tree, which had begun to twist loose: the important thing was to get rid of the bodies, and he did not intend to be critical about the method.

Perry gathered up his reins. "Wellsir, I must ride around a bit. Seems the boys are getting out of hand."

"I understand, captain." Sangrepalo released a wearied breath. "An officer must look to his responsibilities."

As must every grown man, Perry thought. And who is not responsible for some attempt to solve each mystery he plainly sees? Like the mystery of the bandanna, the far vaster one of death and what lies beyond death had seemed to open briefly before his eyes today, and he not at all the wiser. Surely peace would tell him more about them than war had—or perhaps not peace alone; but daily observation would, daily thought and daily labor would, an incomparable helpmate too.

Riding away, he found his assurance marred by wonder about whether he and Camilla together could in fact so manage their lives that death, when it overtook them, would not seem about as empty and puzzling and futile as it did here, as it had at Billy Bartlett's bedside, as it had when Milam fell, and in his own private experience with it back home. At a point on the ridge where a grove was about to block his view, he checked Marquis to stare one last time at that torn bandanna while the fallen tree twisted little by little in a current drawing it toward the Gulf.

From C. B.'s Journal
Sunday, April 24, 1836

About four this afternoon a courier on a lathered horse, heading east, stopped among us long enough to drink a gourd of coffee and tell us what has followed that wonderful victory on the 21st.

Near the ruin of Vince's Bridge last Friday, he said, one youth among several on horseback who were scouting after fugitives detached himself to ride up behind a tree for a shot at some deer grazing on a slope. When he was about to fire, a start by all the deer together alerted him that someone afoot was crossing the top of the slope toward the bridge, a Mexican wading waist deep through last year's grass. At sight of his horse the Mexican drew down in the grass to hide. Even so, the Texans did find him, a spiritless creature, cringing, exhausted, and soiled. He lay on one side, a blanket over his head and no weapons about him. Ordered to get up, he uncovered his head but lay still with face averted. Two who knew Spanish talked some about whether to shoot him if he did not obey, but that was only a maneuver, every Texian having been warned severely against roughness toward fugitives who offered no resistance. Another order to rise did bring him up, pathetically eager to shake hands, and the Texians obliged.

Mean though his outer clothes were, his shirt was a fine linen richly embroidered. Questioned about it, he let go a great wash of tears, saying that he was an aide of Santa Anna's, that all was lost now, that he hoped they would forgive his crying because he was tired, had pains in his legs and back, etc. The Texians said there was no need to cry so, as they did not intend to harm him. One rode him behind his saddle several miles back toward camp. The last furlong or two, however, he let him walk to avoid criticism for so much consideration toward an enemy who looked so inconsequential.

At their approach a gasp spread among other prisoners grouped together under guard. Those who were sitting rose at once. All either saluted or took off their hats, murmuring, *"El Presidente! El Presidente!"* The captive then admitted that he was President-General Antonio López de Santa Anna and asked to see General Houston.

Old Sam lay under a tree suffering from an ankle shattered

by a musket ball. Nevertheless he received Santa Anna courteously, inviting him to sit on a box nearby. Santa Anna, again overcome by emotion, asked for an opium pill to help him compose himself. This was granted, whereupon he proposed that they negotiate a settlement.

Houston responded with a question: How could any general polluted in reputation by slaughters of men who honorably put down their arms as prisoners of war expect his pledge to be trusted? Santa Anna declared that he had done only what "the government" ordered (as if the Director himself were not the government in Mexico); but Houston, as a precondition to further talk, demanded a written order that all Mexican forces westward withdraw from Texas forthwith. Santa Anna obliged straightaway, for a press of Texians had been growing around him, eyes aglitter with passion to avenge his massacre of their friends. A troop of scouts under Deaf Smith then took his order west at a gallop, and Col. Edw. Burleson (a steady soldier who led the center in the attack at San Jacinto) followed later with a regiment of foot to hold the Brazos River crossing should the Mexicans fail to comply.

There is little doubt, however, that they will draw off. Those captured say that all their comrades are worn out, hungry, threadbare, and sick of the mud. Their habit of obeying whatever the Dictator commands will surely incline them to welcome this order of his to retire. Thus the capture of Santa Anna should effect the first object of all the fighting—to rid Texas of enemy troops and thereby end the war.

The success of our boys at San Jacinto was remarkably thorough: virtually all enemies in contention with them on the 21st are dead now or in their hands; scarcely one dozen remain at large, and most of those may yet be taken. At one stroke they have not only retrieved our claims to all land as far west as the Rio Grande, but breached the barrier to a still vaster domain beyond, for any study of the maps gives assurance that free American movement across Texas should in time take us all the way to the Pacific.

The courier who brought us this latest reason to think so ingratiated himself further by distributing letters. One to Camilla from Perry declared that, with the Tyrant taken and the westerly Mexicans ordered away, he would seek leave presently to help fetch me to Dr. Springfield, and wouldn't she meanwhile inquire after a preacher or justice or alcalde who can marry them? But merely to wait here till he might reach us seems too spineless to her. This evening she had us all assembling our movables so that we can start early tomorrow, when a jubilant flux of other people will be hastening west to reunite with sons and husbands and brothers and friends who have borne the battle.

Joyous though the latter part of this day has been to others, nothing in it outshone the merit in my own eyes of an interval at dawn which sweetened the whole day. During my wash for breakfast, because my wound prevents me from bending forward far, Leticia came over to hold the bucket high so that I could scoop water against my face without strain. We complimented the morning, as healthy people do if the weather allows the least excuse for it, after which we fell silent, she musing wistfully while I toweled myself dry.

"This washing puts me in mind," I remarked, "of certain verses I thought up yesterday, watching you pass down toward the river after we heard about the victory."

"Yes? Let's hear them."

After I recited them she stood mute, eyes so clear and blue and full of trust as to reflect everything I said, and much more besides. She repeated the same words, repeated the same pauses, the same emphasis, the same feeling of a fist gripping the heart. She gave it all back so charged with identical intention that her voice seemed a younger, clearer, purer echo of my own:

> *We have fled through the rain*
> *and felt only the storm.*
> *We have walked in the dark*
> *and seen only the night.*
> *Today let us bathe ourselves*
> *in visions of better things*
> *and go forth refreshed.*

CHAPTER XXIV

I

Liberty Road
Monday
April 25, 1836

Monday morning bulky, broody clouds hung low above the train of families shifting westward from the San Jacinto. About noon Cedric took warning from a wind chilled and scented by distant rain and advised everyone to stop in woods shoring a prairie across which no other haven was visible. Several of the families had canvas-covered wagons to den in, but he, Camilla, and their retinue needed to put together a three-sided shelter of oilskins. Being expert at it by this time, they had it erected beneath a live oak, a fire bright before it, and bubbly fragrances steaming out of three pots when the first drops fell.

The rain, driven by frigid gusts, continued all the time they were eating, and afterward too. Everyone in the shelter settled down when the meal was over to hear Camilla read from the Bible. In addition to the Tiptons, Springfields, and Bauernschmidts, Mrs. Latham and Mrs. Ward came over from their wagons to hear her; likewise Hanford and Martha Van Diemen, whose cabin on Loping Creek had provided the wanderers from Hoping Hill with comfort through a wet night two weeks earlier. Some stitched up torn clothes or greased harness or put equipment in order or cleaned up the noon dishes, letting her verses link them together in reflection and silence.

While Cedric cut Buddy Tipton's hair because Liz wanted her boys "nice" for Camilla's wedding, he heard a stallion whistling toward the west. Oriole and Swallow, feeding near the carriage, arched their necks around, and Esau snatched up an oilskin to see better in that direction.

Across the prairie a soldier under a big hat was approaching the woods on a forcefully trotting gray so wet as to look blue. Camilla stopped reading. Every hand manipulating a needle or knife or awl ceased. The only sounds were the complaint of wind-blown trees and

475

the splat of gathered raindrops falling off the live oak above them onto the oilskins.

Leticia murmured, "Why, it's *him!*"

Camilla, to keep her last precious shoes and slippers from getting wet, had perched barefoot on one of her trunks while she read, both feet under her knees tailor fashion and a blanket cowling her head and back. Dampness had wilted her dress, a veteran of her travels, and the blanket had mussed her hair some too.

She sprang up in panic. "Dear mercy me, and I look such a fright!"

With the blanket tight about her, she fled barefoot through the grove to hide in Mrs. Latham's canvas-topped prairie schooner thirty or forty yards off.

"Get that fool girl back here, Roberta." Cedric jabbed his scissors in that direction. "He don't care a damn if she's mussed a little."

"Lady got to look high, sah, time like this."

Roberta snatched out two of Camilla's portmanteaus, and she and Leticia together rushed off to help Camilla change.

Smokes from dampened fires meanwhile were drawing Perry toward Cass Ward's pioneer wagon, which stood near the open. There he pulled his horse up respectfully, as if outside a dooryard. "Anybody there?" he called.

"Thisaway, Mass Pey." Already Esau was hurrying forth. "Thisaway, pleasah."

"Well, *Esau!*"

"*Jus* who it is, sah!" He took the stallion's bridle as Perry dismounted to walk in under the trees. "Be some happy times, now you come, sah!"

A spirited welcome erupted from the shelter as he approached. Mrs. Tipton clamored to know about Evett, while Mrs. Latham asked about Salty, and two or three boys at once began asking about the war. Perry took off his hat in nodding to them all, rain or no rain, but stooped into the shelter, almost wordless, his gray eyes affable, anxious and seeking. Still wordless, he came directly to Cedric and took his hand, a judgmental glance noting how events had altered him.

"Sir, how *are* you?"

"On my feet anyhow. Damned if you aint the wettest rascal we've come across in days."

Perry had changed, in part because he looked habituated to command and public care, and his face had burned a morocco brown. His uniform had all but worn out. Wet as it was, it stuck to him like another skin, showing him even leaner than before. His hair, now long and uneven, had crowded oddly against his head under the pressure of a wet hat. Cedric had no doubt he had weathered inside as well as out, and yet saw in him still the growing, seeking, unfinished quality of youth.

A twinkle of fun brightened Perry's glance as he considered Cedric's handiwork on Buddy Tipton. "Looks like I happened on the right place to smarten up, major." He shoved outspread fingers through his own hair. "What's a haircut here?"

"The price of your company is all."

"I'll deal, sir." He then gazed at Cedric point-blank. "Well, major, I'm here to get married if you'll let me. Where *is* she, anyway?"

Giggles rose like startled pigeons among the ladies.

"All business, aint he!" Mrs. Ward remarked. "You're some stud, young man, but you got to bridle up awhile."

The rest of that day every responsible person in the caravan undertook to get him and Camilla joined as soon as possible on the happiest terms. Even the storm assisted them by blowing away. With Camilla lovelied up remarkably when she emerged from the Latham schooner, and with Perry changed into another uniform from his saddlebags, all proceeded westward under clearing skies until they reached a big double cabin belonging to a family named Vogelsang, whole-souled folks who had been among them at San Jacinto Crossing and had hastened ahead at dawn to prepare their home for receiving everyone that night.

The festivities were held outside in the Vogelsang dooryard. Some guests hurried off after wild turkeys and other game, some after spring flowers, some after grains and vegetables and beeves and honey. From secret places in their wagons others brought out additional bounty in flour and whisky and rum, and some fetched wood for an enormous outdoor fire.

In its light all gathered for the ceremony after sundown, after the descent of dusk, after the evening star gleamed, after a maturing moon shone boldly above the east. To read the vows they had no pastor, churches being rarer than banks in Texas. They therefore made do with Hanford Van Diemen, a Quaker who possessed three qualifications—literacy, a seemly comportment, and experience with conducting prayer meetings occasionally back in the U.S.A. He followed the familiar service from the Book of Common Prayer. Out there in the open, with the fire ravenously consuming the logs thrown upon it, with everyone hushed while the oft-repeated poetry of that service re-echoed in each heart, Cedric thought Van Diemen's reading astonishingly fine. It brought unashamed tears down Perry's face, down Camilla's too, and there were many others who wept without knowing why.

Cedric, remembering the ceremony which had joined him to his own long-buried love, and being confronted again with hopeful trust in the old, old cycle of marriage, of foreseen births, of fresh efforts to thwart death (which nevertheless does work its will), was flooded with compassion and loneliness and sorrow. A glance at the heavens brought home to him how insectival each person is by their scale, how tirelessly time arranges that it alone shall never perish. Viewed so, this wedding ceremony, this ever-recurring excursion of human-kind along the same old pathway of anticipated happiness toward the same concealed pit-trap which all at last will stumble into, seemed to him pathetic, whatever else it was. Life he thought of as a monstrous equivalent of the Roman epicure who vomited one feast to make room for another.

Of course it was without limit more than that. At least the healthy always believed it was. Further, the preposterousness of such reflections at the wedding of his one dear child presently routed them from his mind, and the subsequent rush to eat, drink, and be merry kept him pretty well diverted.

When supper was done the company gathered in the firelight to dance to the tune of a sniggering fiddle, a sensual flute, and a row of cooking pots, tubs, and cowbells which Esau fetchingly beat upon. Cedric during the service had been able to stand without crutches to give Camilla away, but he was forced to rest while others danced. Since he could not do that sitting down, wounded where he was, Leticia had his pallet spread close to the musicians, where he could watch while lying on his side, nor did she let him feel lonesome long. The bride was most in demand as a partner to be sure, but she herself little less so. Still, she insisted upon resting by him when she did not dance, assuming that "loss" of a daughter was what had saddened him and that his wound made him feel "left out."

Actually, now that Camilla was so fittingly married, he felt relieved. His conscience-stricken effort to attend her as diligently as she might desire could now become a slough to leave behind him: he was at liberty to shape out a new life of his own. He intended to write President Jackson in a day or two that he would be ready for a consular

post as soon as his wound would permit travel abroad—and he dared
to wonder, with Leticia so attentive this evening, if someday she too
might not like to see more of the world.

While the moon climbed aloft and the rollick turned hilarious Perry
and Camilla slipped away. Once it was known that Marquis and Swallow were missing also, Cedric advised everyone to stop looking for
them because two people on such horses could elude others as long
as they chose. The dancing went on till after the moon had set, almost
till dawn, till the last jug was empty, but no one saw anything more
of them that night.

When they did come back next day they would not say where they
had been. Neither looked at all rested, which Cedric thought fitting
at such a time. Both also looked newly astonished by each other, which
seemed to him no less fitting.

2

Texas Army Headquarters
Saturday Morning
April 30, 1836

Saturday the troops paraded under
an unmerciful sun, and Perry with
them. The swollen green on trees
nearby hung motionless, echoing
commands which manipulated the
veterans of San Jacinto through the geometry of drill until all ranks
had a hot stink of sweat around them, and no breeze at all to blow
them cool.

The cause of it all was Provisional President David G. Burnett,
looking on with outspread legs from an ammunition cart. Today's
parade was at his order, and without any detectable justification
other than to establish that neither his own flight to Galveston Island
nor Houston's heroism at San Jacinto had left him any less able to do
with Texan forces as he saw fit.

General Houston, as usual of late, lay propped against an oak by
the headquarters tent half a furlong away, his bandaged ankle before
him while he busied himself over a writing board. Burnett had not
consulted him prior to ordering this parade. His views about Houston
he disclosed in manly conversation to the effect that the glory of San
Jacinto belonged, not to anyone whose pusillanimity disgraced the

nation before that day, but to loyal and brave Texanians who kept demanding a fight until they got it—as he himself had, though only by letter during his run toward safety.

Once his whim to see the army exercise had been satisfied, Burnett ordered a stand-to. After climbing down from his cart by way of its wheel, he conferred briefly with three colonels (Rusk, Sherman, and Lamar) and brought them along in stride with himself to inspect the troops afoot.

No one could deny that the President had solidity, if nothing else— a natural chestiness accentuated by a Bible in one upper coat pocket and a pistol in the other, plus a stuffing of maps, state papers, homilies, maxims, and mail. His suit must have become familiar with dust, gravy, and ruptured seams long before the Runaway Scrape began, and neither the haste of his flight nor the gumbo of rutted trails had improved it any. His stride, however, so embodied the arrogance of office that watching him made Perry want to spit.

Still, Burnett did have a name as a thoroughly seasoned pioneer, a man who neither drank nor swore, who defended the side of decency and had passably good sense. In fact, there was nothing really wrong with him except for an appearance of wanting all his opinions received like the Tablets of Moses. The necessity of keeping the government out of Santa Anna's reach had made him seem a coward, which was certainly untrue, whereas many now considered Houston a military genius without any living peer, which was at least equally untrue. Here on ground close by the scene of victory, the want of esteem for the President was so marked that he could hardly be blamed for acting damned nasty.

But what could justify his giving out that Houston was nothing but a fraud? Dimly Perry recalled having thought that himself once, and yet his dislike of Burnett bloated him like an undigested dinner. He sat his horse straight, fixed his gaze on a far, sunlit tree, and resolved to watch Burnett no more.

His immobility took him back to a surprising feat of Camilla's last night, when Dr. Springfield had examined Major Burleigh at Vice-President Zavala's plantation on the other side of Buffalo Bayou. The doctor had pleaded with her to show him how she rid her father of pain; and, because her father urged it as well, she had done so.

The major lay on his side, a solitary candle before him. Having told him to look only at the candle, to think only of rest, she began stroking his brow. In scarcely one minute he seemed without any will of his own, in three minutes profoundly mesmerized. Dr. Springfield could press anywhere around the wound without disturbing the motion of his breath or the beat of his pulse, which Perry timed for him throughout the examination.

Dr. Springfield's conclusion was that the ball should be let alone. It lay in a toughening nest of scars in the small of the back like a pearl in an oyster, and no more dangerous to its host. It might trouble him some as time passed, but not enough to justify risking tetanus or blood-poisoning to knife it out. Another month or so under Camilla's treatment ought to make him a well man. There was no reason, certainly, why he could not travel back to Hoping Hill whenever she was ready to go.

So she was ready now. Perry wished he himself could say the same.

When the President came before his company, with the three colonels close by, Perry saluted indifferently, whereas Lieutenant Garrick yelled for the ranks to present arms and himself stood his saber quiveringly upright before his nose, the first officer this morning to honor their chief in that way. Burnett's lips pursed in restrained gratification, after which he shifted his frown upon Perry. Sweat oozed from his whole face at once, and so did an air of offended self-importance. He tilted his head sideward toward Rusk.

"Colonel, who *is* this man?"

"Captain Allan, sir, from the Otter Creek Country."

"Well!"

"And this here's Lieutenant Garrick from the Trinity River."

"Yes, I know him. But pretty near all these newcomers are strange to me."

Perry could feel Burnett looking him over in reciprocal dislike, but gazed steadily at the lone tree ahead. A trickle of sweat crawled down his cheek like a wet ant, and yet he would not stir a hand to brush it away—did not move at all except when Marquis snatched up a hoof to drive flies off his legs or dipped his nose at others on his chest.

"Allan was cited for valor in the assault on San Antonio last fall, sir," Rusk added. "On the twenty-first, too, he showed exemplary calm under fire. He had trained his company well—a highly regarded officer."

Halfway through this Burnett became interested in excavating something from one nostril with his little finger.

"That horse you're on, Allan . . ."

"Yessir?"

"Prize of war, aint he? Mexican spoils, aint he?"

"Nosir."

"Where'd you get him?"

Perry cleansed all expression off his face. The President had taken one popular step in ruling that all men under arms were to share in every prize of war: whatever was saleable had to be auctioned to the highest bidder. A beautiful Andalusian charger, formerly Almonte's, had been apportioned to Houston the day after the battle, but Burnett ordered it sold and had the money placed in the common treasury for division in due course.

"Bought him, sir," Perry answered.

"Where?"

"Mr. President," Rusk inserted hastily, "he's had him all the time I've known him."

"And," Perry added, "I mean to keep him."

"Oh, cheeky, aint you!"

The President screwed his frown tighter. Another trickle of sweat crawled past Perry's eye and down the side of his nose. Still he did not let a muscle stir.

"This afternoon, young man, you come to see me." Burnett squirted tobacco juice sideward. "I want a little talk with you."

Perry did not intend to be in the army after noon, and no nearer to it than he could help. Though ever so tempted to say so, he neither spoke nor moved an eyelash until Burnett strode on, the three colonels hastily adjusting their step to his.

3

Once the review was over, Perry gave his resolution no time to cool: he rode to the oak at headquarters. Old Sam lifted one ponderous brow his way and spoke out as if he had sent for him. "Captain Allan . . ."

"Yessir?"

While Perry dismounted, the general paused to gather his thoughts. Pain, loss of blood, and loss of sleep had shriveled his face, deepening all the hieroglyphs time and dissipation had traced there. He could pass for sixty today, though in fact just forty-three.

"A democratical man, captain, ought not to resist elected authority."

Surprise prevented Perry from answering at once. How could any-one this sick so accurately make out what had transpired half a furlong away? Very likely because he knew Burnett so well, and understood his effect.

"We in the army must always subordinate ourselves to government," Houston added, "never the other way around. Government rules; we only protect. Toward what is civic we need to be civil, and politic to-ward what is political."

"True enough, sir. *Some* politicians, though—haven't you noticed, sir, how many more north ends of horses than horses there are in this world?"

A snort of laughter jolted Houston's chest. His writing board dropped against his wounded leg, and evidently too hard: a grimace bared his teeth while one hand pressed against his thigh, the thumb constricting underneath the palm as if pain had come up into the hand itself. Watching him reminded Perry of a Mexican pulled down by a leg wound near San Jacinto and still lying there two days later with his hand placed much the same, an officer Perry had seen once in New Orleans in the choicest evening clothes.

Houston denied his own suffering to ask, "Major Burleigh—how's he this morning?"

"Doing fine, thank you."

"And Mrs. Allan?"

"About worn out from tending wounded day and night—her and Miss Springfield too."

"Yes, I'm told they're worshiped up there at Zavalas' by men of both nations."

"Frankly, though, knowing how fast ruin overtakes a farm with no one around this time of the year, they pine to get back home and tend the crops—as you yourself advised."

His last phrase referred to a request from the general that all refu-gees return to their homes to raise food.

"Entirely right too," said Houston. "After the destructions of this war, raising corn's a patriotic duty."

"And that's why I'm here troubling you now, sir: to ask your per-mission to resign and get back home."

General Houston's expression altered little more than if Perry had asked for a chew of tobacco. That pain-conscious hand still lay on his thigh, but without any other resemblance to the dead Mexican's.

Whereas Houston's looked massive, able, and unwashed, the Mexican's had been the long, slender, fastidious sort which people persist in calling "artistic" even though real art never comes from such hands. Last October that Mexican, a curled and scented dandy named D'Espinosa, had barely deigned to notice Perry when Camilla had introduced them outside a theater in New Orleans. At San Jacinto a single gunshot must have hit him behind the knee: a severed artery had let his blood spout away, staining the grass behind him. Two days later Perry found him robbed of medals, boots, watch, belt and money, robbed of his buttons too, a colonel his own countrymen had not cared to bury. Pity for the poor devil augmented Perry's revulsion against San Jacinto's sequel of robbed corpses and hideous odors, a revulsion matched by impatience to get away, to live well while he could, to live in ways which would count for many people.

But Houston remained silent about his resignation. A sidelong approach to the subject might be better, Perry thought, than assaulting it head on.

"General, we hear hundreds of volunteers from the States are hurrying this way."

Houston's eyes responded with one long blink accompanied by a nod. "True, sir. Upwards of two thousand ought to be here in three-four weeks."

"But don't the scouts report the Mexicans westward already withdrawing?"

"They do indeed."

"Then, sir, is there really any great need for me here?"

"What's the hurry, captain?"

"Why, Mrs. Allan, Major Burleigh, and the whole Tipton family are all waiting on me, and a world of work to do back home."

"Just farm work?"

"Plenty of that, but also every sort of neighborhood work. We know two cabins, a shed, and a barn were burned down that we'll all have to help rebuild, and much else to do as soon as we can. Not a school exists any nearer than Springfields', twenty-two miles from my place, and not a mill or a store or a church in that whole region, not a constable or court of law either, not one instrument of government nearer than San Felipe, where the burning in March left nothing but ashes."

"Hm, yes." Houston's scowl did not altogether conceal his humor. "Shows you keep the public weal in mind." His arm came up at right angles to the elbow and his index finger straight up from his hand.

"Make very sure it's still there, sir, at election time. You're to stand for the legislature: remember that."

"Yessir, but first I'll have to—"

"*Nothing* else comes first, sir. We'll never have enough men consistently on the side of good sense. We'll never have enough willing to give the common good the care they give their own. I believe you will, and if you stood in my district I'd vote for you."

"But, sir, nobody in *my* district has said they would."

"They will. They will. You've a damned fine countenance; you're well spoken; you know law; you performed admirably for Texas under arms; you've got brains too; and people can trust you. Such traits are what we *ought* to vote for, and I reckon your neighbors will know it. Anyhow, they'll know you have a singularly enchanting wife and elect you because of her."

"Thank you, general."

"Then that's understood. I'll speak with Colonel Rusk, and we'll arrange a suitable change of command in your company. I've no doubt you can in fact serve Texas better out of uniform, just now, than in it."

"Thank you again, sir." A pause, and he cleared his throat for a difficult and delicate matter, but remembered the advantage in a sidelong approach. "Most of the volunteers coming this way are southrons, I'm told."

"The large majority."

"What I'm wondering, sir—isn't there some way we can prevent that from jeopardizing any nigras we manumit?"

Houston lifted a quick, keen, apprehensive stare. "Captain, why should you trouble yourself about such a matter today?"

"Because I've heard talk, sir, of making manumission illegal in Texas, as it is in certain other states."

Houston mulled that over, a twist of distaste on his mouth. Though never much of a slavery man, his glare deplored the new inclination in America to question an institution so firmly established.

"Captain, you're not a slaveholder?"

"I am, sir, and wish to arrange otherwise. Mrs. Allan too."

"You must be very well fixed," Houston observed sourly. "Not many could afford it."

"Nosir, and we can't afford it either, so we don't want to see it brought to nothing by laws the fanatics may pass."

An unequal grin from the general reminded Perry that only people

opposed to slavery were considered fanatics, not those supporting it.
"Look here, captain: don't concern yourself about laws that don't
exist. Get yourself elected on immediate issues. After that a little
idealism will hurt you less—and find you more able to support it."
"I see the point, yessir."
"Excellent." He extended one big hand. "Well, captain, my esteem
and good wishes to Mrs. Allan, please. Likewise to Major Burleigh."
Perry, in riding away, took with him a suspicion that the general
now thought him less qualified for office than he previously supposed.

4

Hoping Hill
Sunday Afternoon
May 8, 1836

Among those who followed Perry
and Camilla to Hoping Hill (which
they reached about noon on Sunday, May 8) were four other veterans from his company—Evett
Tipton, Hugh Llewelyn, Elias Jones, and Mountain Bentley, the latter
three to work for wages payable after harvest. Camilla was aware that
Perry intended to use two of them in developing Highhorse Valley, but
she wanted every part of their home cleaned and repaired right
away. The yard was badly overgrown. It was littered with branches
which storms had blown down, likewise by one fallen tree, the senile
oak beside which her father had been shot when firing at Blacky Reed
to save the house.

Even so, there was much to justify good cheer about the outlook.
Corn planted before she left was a lusty green nearly as high as her
knees. Potatoes and yams were doing well, beans thriving too, and
pumpkin vines about ready to spread. Radishes, onions, and lettuce
in her garden would soon be ready to eat; beets were beginning to
swell, carrots up five or six inches, and cabbage seedlings almost too
big to transplant where they could mature.

Only her gardens, however, had been kept clean—no doubt by Hector during occasional visits from Highhorse Valley. Everywhere else,
amid regiments of eatables growing in disciplined rows, licentious
little weeds without number were debauching each field's potential.

If turned under promptly, of course, they could improve the yield by providing green manure, and Camilla fidgeted with impatience to have all hands begin.

But a decline in Perry's enthusiasm cautioned her that his thought was drifting elsewhere. Two weeks of marriage had convinced her that any stress or strain between them was likely to grow more often from their similarities than from their differences. Service in the army had embedded in him the habit of command, of authority, of responsibility beyond his years, just as superintending a big plantation had in her. Moreover he had a feeling for usable land as strong as hers, if not stronger, and at least equal zeal for creative management. Repeatedly as the afternoon progressed she saw him glance over his shoulder at the sun, and love for him told her why.

It also suggested how to blend her purpose with his. She put on a big pot of coffee, washed afresh, brushed out her hair, changed into a riding habit, and then sought him out in the yard. He was chopping up the fallen oak and had the Tipton boys carrying chunks of it around to the woodbox behind the house.

"Perry-dear . . ."

"Hm?"

"Everyone's worked so hard since noon; wouldn't they like a sip of coffee now?"

His smiling notice of the way she had prettied every sign of work off herself indicated recognition that something more was on her mind than coffee.

"Without a doubt."

"And while they have it, let's ride to the Valley, just you and me. Want to?"

"Wel-ll, that *could* wait."

"No, I know you'd like to see it before sundown, and so would I. Besides, the news you have for Hector won't improve any if he hears it first from somebody else."

For answer he swung his ax one-handed so that it stood angularly upright in the oak, then looped an arm around her shoulders for one quick hug.

Rested as Marquis and Swallow were by that time, they easily loped the two and a quarter miles to the wooded precipice above the Valley in less than ten minutes. From up there the white-washed cabin, which Perry and Hector, with help from the neighbors, had built soon after they arrived, seemed about the size of a tool shed, and scarcely more habitable, though a crumpled skein of smoke above it declared otherwise. Each tree near it, outlined in late sunlight, looked at once distinct and Lilliputian. Crops were growing in thrifty rectangles before it, and emphatic shadows along each row accentuated the impression that thought, diligence, and prosperity had come there to stay.

Close to the nearer end of the valley seven mares were grazing, all captured from the wild herd once at home there. Four had foals beside them. One of the others was the filly Vision, no less daintily trim at this altitude than if molded in bronze for a mantelpiece.

Just where was Hector? All the serene order near the cabin proclaimed his care, but perhaps he was spending this delectable Sunday afternoon asleep, as he had a right to do. Perry suggested riding up under cover of woods near the creek to surprise him.

The cabin, a one-room structure with only one door, was made of upright poles mudded smoothly inside and out, then whitewashed Mexican fashion. Rain had warped the roof beams a bit, letting the eaves relax like the brim of a hat, yet the structure as a whole remained sound.

Opening the door released a scent of lime, dry wood, and quiescent fire. Everything inside was as neatly arranged as the gears of a clock. Four bunks built into the corners were made up and ready to use. Perry's desk, as he remarked in a whisper, was tidier than he himself had left it. His books stood erect on shelves beside it, the lawbooks uppermost. Above them a chart of morning, noon, and evening temperatures which he had begun the hour he unpacked his thermometer contained entries in Hector's squarish figures day by day until this noon, and another chart recorded the date when each foal was born. Every dish in the place waited clean on a shelf by the hearth, and the packed earth of the floor had been decorated by the scratches of a recent sweeping.

So Hector could not be far away, but where? Outside again to listen, Camilla could hear very little except Marquis rubbing his bridle against the sycamore he was tied to, no doubt restless over his earlier look at the mares. Perry took Camilla's arm to lead her farther back through the woods behind the cabin.

They came upon a riot of logs jumbled together, at least two score. Camilla turned alarmed eyes upon Perry, wondering if he planned to build a new house back here in preference to hers. He winked to calm her.

"For a dam," he whispered. "A milldam." He pointed out two large outcroppings of limestone spaced far apart. "He aims to anchor it on those. Behind them he can back up considerable water."

A short way upstream stood two harnessed mules, hitched to a rock sled hewn from the fork of a tree. Hector was partly visible beyond them, digging around a stone, and so intent that Camilla and Perry were able to stroll up beside the mules unnoticed. Hector's head was bare, his back bent round, his shirt wet through. The cuff on his handless arm, in the crook of which he gripped the handle of a mattock, flopped emphatically at each blow. Second on second he remained wholly engrossed, his wedge-shaped face marred by lines between the eyes, his mattock gouging into a groove along the base of the stone.

What finally brought him alert was a nicker from Marquis, left with Swallow before the cabin, a bugled appeal to the other mares. Upon discovering himself observed from such close range, Hector thrust his loose cuff at his eyes as if to clear them.

"Master!" He came forward, tapping his mattock beside him like a cane, face tortured by attempts to control himself. "Lordy-lord, back home safe! *Aint* you a sight to see!" As an afterthought he dipped a bow to Camilla. "You the same, Miz Milla." Belated realization then widened his eyes. "Oh-oh! I reckon there been happy times and a big wedding somewhere, aint that so?"

"That's so," Perry agreed. "And orderly as everything is here, I reckon you been expecting us."

"That's so too, master. Fore day this morning I was lain there asleep, and I seen you plain saddling up Marq in the dark, telling somebody you soon be home."

"As a matter of fact I did saddle up before day." Perry turned upon Camilla a dwelling look charged with other recollections which only she could guess at. "Also, I did say that we'd soon be home, re-member?"

Yes, she did, and his expression in saying so aroused a yawning, stretching sensuality in her even now, catlike and private. Something falling onto their oilskin shelter had startled her awake about four o'clock, perhaps only a swollen drop of dew sliding off a tree, but noisy enough when it struck to bring her head up. Still though that hour was, she could hear nothing further, not even Perry's breath. So soundless and invisible did he lie beside her that, in alarm, she groped for the beat of his heart. His chest reminded her of those on carvings of the crucifixion—ribby, wide, and dropping away to an ascetic hollow below. Though solid as carved wood too, it did communicate to her hand a heartbeat moving at the deliberate and purposeful rate of a long-legged horse walking toward home. Feeling that rhythm persist moment on moment, she wondered wide-eyed at the secretive efficiency of life within us, at the mystery known as sleep, and at the blend of constancy, idiosyncrasy, and fragility in each beating heart. Her own seemed likely to endure the longer because her husband's was so strong and sure.

As she lay sipping the nectar of that thought, his hand came up to close upon hers. His felt rougher than unplaned oak, yet ever so tender too, drawing hers up to press it against his lips, and repeatedly, gently, urgently, as if it were her entire self in miniature.

A timeless while later one of her forearms, subsiding across his chest, found his heart going at an ecstatic gallop, racing beside her own. Little by little both slowed down again; little by little his resumed its deliberate and enduring habit.

"Well," she conceded, "near as we were by then, it was only natural to observe how soon we'd be home."

"Yessum," Hector carried on, "and then some voice said to me plain, 'Rouse up there, Hector, and ready everything good. Capun Perry be here dereckly.' So I got up right quick and done it."

That he had in fact heard such voices Camilla did not doubt. Perry had described his "sixth sense" at work at other times; but, knowing of no way to explain it, he was disposed to act above being taken in by it.

"Hector, you humbug, you know very well you've had the place ready to admiration *every* day I've been gone, not just today. How under the canopy could you also accomplish all this work you've done back here?"

"Oh, it goes slow, master. Dreadful slow. But you said if I built a mill you'd let it pay for Hanna and little Byrd too, so I—"

"That's perfectly true."

"So every Sunday I'm at it. After chores of an evening too, and on pretty moonlight nights, when a lonesome man can't sleep good anyhow, I get in right many good licks till I *can* sleep. It goes slow, sir, but one of these days we'll have us a mill that folks will bring grain to from right many miles away."

"No doubt. And that?" Perry jogged his chin at the flat stone Hector had been digging around. "That your millstone?"

It was. Hector showed how he meant to shape it, then went on to explain each project which would lead at last to a usable mill.

"We'll move it along faster after a bit," Perry assured him. That led to talk of the deterioration at Hoping Hill. "We'll have to keep all hands there awhile except you, Hector. Weeds are about to suffocate everything, and there's a world of things we'll need an ample harvest to buy."

"Yessir, including two-three things to build a mill. Reckon you can spare enough, sir, for iron gears and a circle saw?"

"Two more necessaries to write down, sweetheart," Perry said to Camilla, "if there's any room left on your list."

She drew a sigh: each new "necessary" would require a matching self-denial of something else. Ever since they married they had been thinking of things to buy in that golden time known as "after harvest," adding at least a dozen more in the few hours since returning home.

The biggest item was land, though they were already "land poor." A strip half a mile wide by three long divided the farther edge of the league around Highhorse Valley from the nearer boundary of her own two leagues. Somehow they must secure at least part of that to make their places one. The longer they delayed the worse, because every improvement wrought hereabout would send the value up, and so would the flood of migrants from the States which the freeing of Texas would bring this way.

Nor could Perry proceed far with his plan to develop a strain of hundred-mile horses unless he had his racing stallion Mazeppa shipped out from Maryland. Both places too, as more acreage was tilled, would require new implements of every kind.

In addition there were scores of household items which Camilla knew very well she would pine for ever more achingly until she had them—a cookstove certainly, a piano someday, a good churn right away. New medicines were high on her list, and new glass for broken windows, new dishes, new tableware, new linens, new bedding, new pots and pans. Hoping Hill had in it scarcely one article which she would not want to replace when she could.

The longer she thought about it all, the higher the heap of wants appeared, until a doleful look at Perry set off enough internal laughter in both to shake the whole structure down. The simple truth was that, needy as they were, they had about all the felicity they could stand at present without being spoiled. Of one thing both were passionately sure: blighted as their lives had been by debt heretofore, they must let no longings now trick them into buying more than they could get the cash to pay for.

Perry grunted a muffled explosion of agreement with Hector. "Lumber! We've trees enough here, God knows; but if there's any such thing as a lumber famine, there's one in Texas. A sawmill would bless this whole section."

"Yessir, and I could put a circle blade to work pretty near as quick as we get it—quick as the pond is full and the water wheel in. It'll cut the timbers to build us a grist mill, pay the cost of iron gears, and earn us cash money all the time."

"Hm, yes. And retire the cost of Hanna that much sooner."

"Oh, master, there's the thought I hold tight to day and night, sir! Aint one thing I wouldn't do to get my Hanna, sir."

"Well, you'll get her. And yourself too."

"Myself, sir?"

Perry's way of answering was to turn back toward the cabin, adjusting his motion to draw Camilla along beside him. Hector had the intelligence to make out that he was expected to follow. Perry never stopped until he reached Marquis, whose near saddlebag he now unbuckled.

"I'll say this," he remarked to Hector, "whenever that mill earns enough to pay for Byrd and Hanna, they'll be free. Like yourself. On the same terms as you."

A struggle between doubt and hope tortured Hector's long face. "Free, master?"

"Yes, free. From now on you're your own master."

He handed him three documents similar to others he had prepared for Camilla so that she could manumit Roberta and Esau by means she could make herself afford. One she knew to be a bill of sale for "a slender medium-brown nigra called Hector, about six feet tall, with left arm off above the wrist"; it transferred ownership to Hector himself "for a consideration of $900." A second paper recorded a loan to him of that amount without interest on the understanding that it be repaid at seven dollars per month. The third was a contract for Hector to work for P. K. Allan for eight dollars per month and found, the same wage promised to Hugh, Mountain, and Eli.

"If these papers suit you, Hector, we'll sign them and get them witnessed. You better sit down there." He dipped his head sideward at a stump before the cabin. "Study them through, and Mrs. Allan and I will be back shortly."

Camilla did not need to be told that Perry would want next to look at the mares. She and he together set off that way on Swallow and Marquis. At the corner of the nearest planted field, where Perry glanced backward, she saw his expression change as if a stone had hit his forehead. Turning herself, she discovered Hector hunched forward on the stump, his lame arm clutching the precious instruments of freedom against his chest, his good hand tight across his eyes, and sobs of anguished joy shaking him like violent hiccups. She and Perry thereafter fixed their attention on the mares.

Summer and frequent brushing had slicked them all. Under the glow of late sunlight they looked well fleshed, sound and shapely. Every superlative, however, belonged to Vision, the strongest, cleanest creature there, the most vital, the most alert, the first to lift her head and consider who was coming. Not until Marquis bugled at them did the mares with sucklings stop grazing long enough for a look his way, after which they again dropped their muzzles deep in new grass. Vision, however, kept both ears sharply forward and her large eyes watchful of all that the new arrivals might do. Her effort to circle to windward where she could smell the visitors brought a critical snort from Perry.

"Those damn fetters!" He obviously referred to hobbles on her forelegs to prevent her from jumping fences—so long there that she had accommodated to them with steps as choice as a coquette's when crossing a brook from stone to stone. "That's my doing, and me such a devotee of freedom too!"

"But, Perry, it's only to gentle her. Gentling wild creatures for human use—aren't we *obliged* to do that if we can?"

"Uhm." He thought it over in silence. "I suppose that's what civilization *ought* to do really. Yes, turn things of the earth to human account. That, and liberate men."

Once Vision caught the scent of stallion, and the human smell with it, she went no farther. Though Marquis whickered at her appealingly she resumed grazing where she was in female certainty that he would come to her when he could. Perry, during her first heat this spring, had penned her up so that he could train her and mature her a bit more before letting her get with foal. Now his way of smoothing down Marq's mane while considering her seemed to Camilla an amusing sort of promise to rescind the prohibition in due course.

On their return to the cabin they found Hector coming back from the creek freshly washed, toweling his face on a flour sack. He looked both drained and refreshed by his spell of weeping, as travelers do in fair weather after being seasick.

"Well, Hector," Perry began, "what do you think?"

"Wellsir, I'll tell you, master. Back there in Nor Leans, when they took Byrd and Hanna off to Texas, I thought it was Satan's work, first to last. Instead it was most surely the Lord's: there wasn't but just one way to free us, and He picked it."

"How soon'll you go see them?"

"Oh, can't go no time soon, sir. Them crops got to be tended and the mares cared for and new fences built and the mill brought along. And anyhow I owe you nine hundred dollars."

"You might find work near where Hanna is and pay from there."

"Oh, not likely, sir. Aint nobody there liable pay me eight dollars a month like you."

"Well, six or so."

"And nobody there'll let me build a mill to buy my family with either."

"You'd find someone. You're right convincing when you talk up a mill."

"But thissun's coming fine."

"Still, it's not too late to start over somewhere else."

"Don't you want me here no more, master?"

"There's not any other hand I want as much. A man with a family, though, should never be kept alone against his will. Being free gives you the right to decide whether you go or stay."

"Off there where Hanna's at, sir, nobody knows me, and some mean weasel's liable come along and call me a runaway, say I'm his. Nosir, the sole place I'll surely stay free, and get Hanna free, is right here. That I know." Hector ran his handless cuff around his neck. Wistful longing shadowed his eyes. "Still, sir . . ."

"Yes, Hector?"

"Brazer's River's where you'll haul the harvest to?"

"Yes, and steamboat it on from there."

"That Mr. Gerard who owns them lives over there. So maybe would you let me . . . ?"

"Certainly! Of course. Going, I'll need your help; then you can stay there awhile, and we'll talk with Mr. Gerard about his terms for Hanna."

"That, sir . . . wellsir, the Lord sure put His Arm around us the day you bought me."

5

At the head of the gorge leading to the uplands Perry dismounted to open and close bars in a stretch of pole-and-brush fence sufficient to keep livestock back in the Valley. Camilla rode out upon open ground above to wait for him.

As he walked up that way beside Marquis, having the big purposes of the day accomplished, a sensation of well-being, a growing exhilaration such as used to make him suddenly run and jump in boyhood for no reason he could explain, took shape inside his ribs. It surged through him faster than blood can move. It flowed electrically through his knees, prickled in his fingers, stirred the roots of his hair, and all his senses together became abnormally acute.

The air had begun acquiring the moist smell of dusk, yet long horizontals of light still lanced through the woods shadowing the gorge. The sun rested on the farthest rim of prairies beyond the Valley like a pumpkin on a shelf. Each bush and flower stood motionless in the wait for evening, each blade of grass as well. Aside from the click of a stirrup rocking against Marq's girth and the crush of grass underfoot, the only sounds were flat, stark signals from a crow on a derelict tree leftward along the ridge.

For Perry every visible, audible fact, and even the warmth of active flesh beneath the hand at rest against Marq's neck, seemed charged anew with implications which he did not yet have the wisdom to decipher.

And there before him his incomparable wife waited on Swallow, her self-discipline evident in her easy straightness, her profile both exquisite and emphatic, cupped by her bonnet. Sitting that way, she could be in rags, he thought, and still seem a wonder because what she wore had so little to do with how he felt about her.

She let him bring Marquis up beside Swallow and start the ride back toward Hoping Hill before saying, "Perry . . ."

"Hm?"

"Why that smile?"

"Oh-h, a few years ago I read about an ancient caliph who wrote something queer. After a lifetime laden with honors, with pleasures, with powers rivaling the greatest kings of his time, he concluded that he had felt blessed on only fourteen days that he could remember. For me, though, several during the last fourteen have been such days."

"For me too, dearest. In fact nearly all."

"Yes, not excepting this one. Home again! And already we've started a thing or two we wanted to do."

"Hasn't it been good though!"

"We'd better keep it in mind, sweetheart, to recollect in evil times."

"Yes." Her glance strayed toward the woods darkening under the cliff along which they were riding. Sobriety depressed her voice. "Let's never forget."

That bad times would surely come she plainly did not doubt: she must have observed, just as he had, that even the most enviable life, followed far enough, turns out to be a tragedy. Theirs could be no exception. Death, if nothing else, would permit no exception.

The sun was gone now, and twilight established. As they neared the northern edge of his property three crows from below the bluff flapped toward a grove on his right. He counted eleven trees in that grove, each straight below and full above, a temptation to any sawyer. All stood entranced in the windless air, all spectral in the day's expiring light. Together they composed a unique geometrical form gratifying to contemplate. Cutting any of them would be a desecration. The three crows sank among their boughs with a mute finality which increased the impression of otherworldliness there, and then he saw how to preserve that spot indefinitely as a final bower for his family and friends: he would consecrate it as God's acre for this neighborhood.

He decided, however, not to mention this to Camilla at present. Already their ride was carrying them beyond it toward Hoping Hill, and surely, surely, surely many good years lay before them. The end of those years would seem more bearable, he believed, in proportion as they together, in manifold ways, promoted what their first efforts at pioneering had initiated around them: the process of liberating people and turning things of the earth to human account.